THE MODERN FAERIE TALES

ALSO BY HOLLY BLACK:

THE MODERN FAERIE TALES

HOLLY BLACK

SIMON & SCHUSTER

New York   London   Toronto   Sydney   New Delhi

First published in Great Britain in 2019 by Simon & Schuster UK Ltd
A CBS COMPANY

First published in the USA in 2019 by Margaret K. McElderry Books,
an imprint of Simon & Schuster Children's Publishing Division

Interior designs by Kathleen Jennings

1 3 5 7 9 10 8 6 4 2

Simon & Schuster UK Ltd
1st Floor
222 Gray's Inn Road
London WC1X 8HB

www.simonandschuster.co.uk

Simon & Schuster Australia, Sydney
Simon & Schuster India, New Delhi

A CIP catalogue record for this book
is available from the British Library.

PB ISBN 978-1-4711-8236-5
eBook ISBN 978-1-4711-8237-2

Printed and bound by CPI Group (UK) Ltd, Croydon, CR0 4YY

MIX
Paper from
responsible sources
FSC® C020471

THE MODERN FAERIE TALES

CONTENTS

TITHE

For my little sister Heidi

And pleasant is the faerie land
But an eerie tale to tell,
Ay at the end of seven years
We pay a tithe to Hell;
I am sae fair and fu o flesh,
I'm feard it be mysel.

—"Young Tam Lin"

PROLOGUE

And malt does more than Milton can
To justify God's ways to man.
—A. E. HOUSMAN, "TERENCE, THIS IS STUPID STUFF"

Kaye took another drag on her cigarette and dropped it into her mother's beer bottle. She figured that would be a good test for how drunk Ellen was—see if she would swallow a butt whole.

They were up on stage still, Ellen and Lloyd and the rest of Stepping Razor. It had been a bad set and watching them break down the equipment, she could see that they knew it. It didn't really matter, the sound system was loud and scratchy and everyone had kept drinking and smoking and shouting so she doubted the manager minded. There had even been a little dancing.

The bartender leered at her again and offered her a drink "on the house."

"Milk," Kaye smirked, brushing back her ragged, blond hair and pocketing a couple of matchbooks when his back was turned.

Then her mother was next to her, taking a deep swallow of the beer before spitting it all over the counter.

Kaye couldn't help the wicked laughter that escaped her lips. Her mother looked at her in disbelief.

"Go help load up the car," Ellen said, voice hoarse from singing. She was smoothing damp hair back from her face. Her lipstick was rubbed off the inside of her lips but still clung to the edges of her mouth, smudged a little. She looked tired.

Kaye slid off the counter and leapt up onto the stage in one easy move. Lloyd glared at her as she started to pick up the stuff randomly, so she stuck to what was her mother's. His eyes were glazed. "Hey kid, got any money on you?"

Kaye shrugged and took out a ten-dollar bill. She had more, and he probably knew it—she'd come straight from Chow Fat's. Delivering might pay crap, but it still paid better than being in a band.

He took the money and ambled off to the bar, probably to get some beer to go.

Kaye hauled an amplifier through the crowd. People mostly got out of her way. The cool autumn air outside the bar was a welcome relief, even stinking as it was with iron and exhaust fumes and the subways. The city always smelled like metal to Kaye.

Once the equipment was loaded up, she went back inside, intent on getting her mother in the car before someone smashed the window and stole the equipment. You couldn't leave anything in a car in Philly. The last time Ellen's car had been broken into, they'd done it for a secondhand coat and a bag of towels.

The girl checking IDs at the door frowned at Kaye now that she was solo, but let her in all the same. It was late anyway, almost last call. Ellen was still at the bar, smoking a cigarette and drinking something stronger than beer. Lloyd was talking to a guy with long, dark hair. The man looked too well dressed for the bar. He must have bought a round or something, because Lloyd had his arm over his shoulder and Lloyd wasn't usually a friendly guy. She caught a flash of the man's eyes. Cat-yellow, reflecting in the dim light. Kaye shivered.

But then, Kaye saw odd things sometimes. She'd learned to ignore them.

"Car's loaded," Kaye told her mother.

Ellen nodded, barely listening. "Can I have a cigarette, honey?"

Kaye fished the pack out of her army-surplus satchel and took out two, handing one to her mother and lighting the other.

Her mother bent close, the smell of whiskey and beer and sweat as familiar as any perfume. "Cigarette kiss," her mother said in that goofy way that was embarrassing and sweet at the same time, touching the tip of her cigarette to the red tip of Kaye's and breathing in deeply. Two sucks of smoke and it flared to life.

"Ready to go home?" Lloyd asked. His voice sounded velvety, a shade off of sleazy. Not normal asshole Lloyd voice. Not at all.

Ellen didn't seem to notice anything. She swallowed what was left of her drink. "Sure."

A moment later, Lloyd lunged toward Ellen with a

suddenness that spoke of violence. Kaye reacted without think-ing, throwing herself against him. It was probably only his drunkenness that allowed her slight weight to be enough to throw him off balance. But it worked. He nearly fell, and in an effort to catch himself, dropped what he'd been holding. She only saw the knife when it clattered to the floor.

Lloyd's face was completely blank, empty of any emotion at all. His eyes were wide and his pupils dilated.

Frank, Stepping Razor's drummer, grabbed Lloyd's arm. Lloyd had just enough time to punch Frank in the face before other patrons tackled him and somebody called the police.

By the time the cops got there, Lloyd couldn't remember anything. He was mad as hell, though, cursing Ellen at the top of his lungs. The police drove Kaye and her mother to Lloyd's apartment and waited while Kaye packed their clothes and stuff into plastic garbage bags. Ellen was on the phone, trying to find a place for them to crash.

"Honey," Ellen said finally, "we're going to have to go to Grandma's."

"Did she say it was okay?" Kaye asked, stacking her Grace Slick vinyl albums into an empty orange crate. They hadn't so much as visited once in the six years that they'd been gone from New Jersey. Ellen barely even spoke to her mother on the hol-idays before passing the phone to Kaye.

"More or less." Ellen sounded so tired. "It'll just be a little while. You can visit that friend of yours."

"Janet," Kaye said. She hoped that was who Ellen meant. She hoped her mother wasn't teasing her. If she had to hear another story about Kaye and her cute imaginary friends . . .

"The one you email from the library. Get me another

cigarette, okay, hon?" Ellen tossed a bunch of CDs into the crate.

Kaye picked up a leather jacket of Lloyd's she'd always liked and lit a cigarette for her mother off the stove burner. No sense in wasting matches.

Coercive as coma, frail as bloom
innuendoes of your inverse dawn
suffuse the self;
our every corpuscle become an elf.
—MINA LOY, "MOREOVER, THE MOON," *THE LOST LUNAR
        BAEDEKER*

Kaye spun down the worn, gray planks of the boardwalk. The air was heavy and stank of drying mussels and the crust of salt on the jetties. Waves tossed themselves against the shore, dragging grit and sand between their nails as they were slowly pulled back out to sea.

The moon was high and pale in the sky, but the sun was just going down.

It was so good to be able to *breathe*, Kaye thought. She loved the serene brutality of the ocean, loved the electric power she felt with each breath of wet, briny air. She spun again, dizzily, not caring that her skirt was flying up over the tops of her black thigh-high stockings.

"Come on," Janet called. She stepped over the overflowing,

leaf-choked gutter, wobbling slightly on fat-heeled platform shoes. Her glitter makeup sparkled under the street lamps. Janet exhaled ghosts of blue smoke and took another drag on her cigarette. "You're going to fall."

Kaye and her mother had been staying at her grandmother's a week already, and even though Ellen kept saying they'd be leaving soon, Kaye knew they really had nowhere to go. Kaye was glad. She loved the big old house caked with dust and mothballs. She liked the sea being so close and the air not stinging her throat.

The cheap hotels they passed were long closed and boarded up, their pools drained and cracked. Even the arcades were shut down, prizes in the claw machines still visible through the cloudy glass windows. Rust marks above an abandoned storefront outlined the words SALT WATER TAFFY.

Janet dug through her tiny purse and pulled out a wand of strawberry lipgloss. Kaye spun up to her, fake leopard coat flying open, a run already in her stocking. Her boots had sand stuck to the tops of them.

"Let's go swimming," Kaye said. She was giddy with night air, burning like the white-hot moon. Everything smelled wet and feral like it did before a thunderstorm, and she wanted to run, swift and eager, beyond the edge of what she could see.

"The water's freezing," Janet said, sighing, "and your hair is fucked up. Kaye, when we get there, you have to be cool. Don't seem so weird. Guys don't like weird."

Kaye paused and seemed to be listening intently, her upturned, kohl-rimmed eyes watching Janet as warily as a cat's. "What should I be like?"

"It's not that I want you to be a certain way—don't you want a boyfriend?"

"Why bother with that? Let's find incubi."

"Incubi?"

"Demons. Plural. Like octopi. And we're much more likely to find them"—her voice dropped conspiratorially—"while swimming naked in the Atlantic a week before Halloween than practically anywhere else I can think of."

Janet rolled her eyes.

"You know what the sun looks like?" Kaye asked. There was only a little more than a slice of red where the sea met the sky.

"No, what?" Janet said, holding the lipgloss out to Kaye.

"Like he slit his wrists in a bathtub and the blood is all over the water."

"That's gross, Kaye."

"And the moon is just watching. She's just watching him die. She must have driven him to it."

"Kaye . . ."

Kaye spun again, laughing.

"Why are you always making shit up? That's what I mean by weird." Janet was speaking loudly, but Kaye could barely hear her over the wind and the sound of her own laughter.

"C'mon, Kaye. Remember the faeries you used to tell stories about? What was his name?"

"Which one? Spike or Gristle?"

"Exactly. You made them up!" Janet said. "You always make things up."

Kaye stopped spinning, cocking her head to one side, fingers sliding into her pockets. "I didn't say I didn't."

The old merry-go-round building had been semi-abandoned for years. Angelic lead faces, surrounded by rays of hair, divided the broken panes. The entire front of it was win-dowed, revealing the dirt floor, glass glittering against the refuse. Inside, a crude plywood skateboarding ramp was the only remains of an attempt to use the building commercially in the last decade.

Kaye could hear voices echoing in the still air all the way to the street. Janet dropped her cigarette into the gutter. It hissed and was quickly carried away, sitting on the water like a spider.

Kaye hoisted herself up onto the outside ledge and swung her legs over. The window was long gone, but her leg scraped against glass residue as she slid in, fraying her stockings further.

Layers of paint muted the once-intricate moldings inside the carousel building. The ramp in the center of the room was tagged by local spray-paint artists and covered with band stickers and ballpoint pen scrawlings. And then there were the boys.

"Kaye Fierch, you remember me, right?" Doughboy chuckled. He was short and thin, despite his name.

"I think you threw a bottle at my head in sixth grade."

He laughed again. "Right. Right. I forgot that. You're not still mad?"

"No," she said, but her merry mood drained out of her. Janet climbed on top of the skateboard ramp to where Kenny was sitting, a king in his silver flight jacket, watching the proceedings. Handsome, with dark hair and darker eyes. He held up a nearly full bottle of tequila in greeting.

Marcus introduced himself by handing over the bottle he'd been drinking from, making a mock throwing motion before letting her take it. A little splashed on the sleeve of his flannel shirt. "Bourbon. Expensive shit."

She forced a smile. Marcus resumed gutting a cigar. Even hunched over, he was a big guy. The brown skin on his head gleamed, and she could see where he must have nicked himself shaving.

"I brought you some candy," Janet said to Kenny. She had candy corn and peanut chews.

"*I brought you some candy,*" Doughboy mocked in a high, squeaky voice, jumping up on the ramp. "Give it here," he said.

Kaye walked around the room. It was magnificent, old and decayed and fine. The slow burn of bourbon in her throat was perfect for this place, the sort of thing a man in a summer suit who always wore a hat might drink.

"What flavor of Asian are you?" Marcus asked. He had filled the cigar with weed and was chomping down on one end. The thick, sweet smell almost choked her.

She took another swallow from the bottle and tried to ignore him.

"Kaye! You hear me?"

"I'm half Japanese." Kaye touched her hair, blond as her mother's. It was the hair that baffled people.

"Man, you ever see the cartoons there? They have them little, little girls with these pigtails and shit in these short school uniforms. We should have uniforms like that here, man. You ever wear one of those, huh?"

"Shut up, dickhead," Janet said, laughing. "She went to grade school with Doughboy and me."

Kenny looped one finger through the belt rings of Janet's jeans and pulled her over to kiss her.

"Yeah, well, damn." Marcus laughed. "Won't you hold up your hair in those pigtails for a second or something? Come on."

Kaye shook her head. No, she wouldn't.

Marcus and Doughboy started to play Hacky Sack with an empty beer bottle. It didn't break as they kicked it boot to boot, but it made a hollow sound. She took another long swallow of bourbon. Her head was already buzzing pleasantly, humming in time with imagined merry-go-round music. She moved farther into the dim room, to where old placards announced popcorn and peanuts for five cents apiece.

Against the far wall was a black, weathered door. It opened jerkily when she pushed it. Moonlight from the windows in the main room revealed only an office with an old desk and a corkboard, yellowed menus still pinned to it. She stepped inside, even though the light switch didn't work. In a shadowed corner, she found a knob. This door led to a stairwell with only a little light drifting down from the top. She felt her way up the stairs. Dust covered the palms of her hands as she slid them along the railings. She sneezed loudly, then sneezed again.

At the top was a small window lit by the murderess moon, ripe and huge in the sky. Interesting boxes were stacked in the corners. Then her eyes fell on the horse, and she forgot all the rest. He was magnificent—gleaming pearl white and covered with tiny pieces of glued-down mirror. His face was painted with red and purple and gold, and he even had a bar of white teeth and a painted pink tongue with enough space to tuck a sugar cube. It was obvious why he'd been left behind—his legs on all four sides and part of his tail had been shattered. Splinters hung down from where they used to be.

Gristle would have loved this. She had thought that many times since she had left the Shore, six years past. *My imaginary friends would have loved this.* She'd thought it the first time that she'd seen the city, lit up like never-ending Christmas. But they never came when she was in Philadelphia. And now she was sixteen and felt like she had no imagination left.

Kaye set the bourbon on the dusty floor and dropped her coat next to it. Then she tried to set the horse up as if he were standing on his ruined stumps. It wobbled unsteadily but didn't fall. She swung one leg over the beast and dropped onto its saddle, using her feet to keep it steady. She ran her hands down its mane, which was carved in golden ringlets. She touched the painted black eyes and the chipped ears.

The white horse rose on unsteady legs in her mind. The great bulk of the animal was real and warm beneath her. She wove her hands in the mane and gripped hard, slightly aware of a prickling feeling all through her limbs. The horse whinnied softly beneath her, ready to leap out into the cold, black water. She threw back her head.

"Kaye?" A soft voice snapped her out of her daydream. Kenny was standing near the stairs, regarding her blankly. For a moment, though, she was still fierce. Then she felt her cheeks burning.

Caught in the half-light, she could see him better than she had downstairs. Two heavy silver hoops shone in the lobes of his ears. His short, cinnamon hair was mussed and had a slight wave to it, matching the beginnings of a goatee on his chin. Under the flight jacket, his too-tight white T-shirt showed off his body.

He moved toward her, reaching his hand out and then looking at it oddly, as though he didn't remember deciding to do that. Instead he petted the head of the horse, slowly, almost hypnotically.

"I saw you," he said. "I saw what you did."

"Where's Janet?" Kaye wasn't sure what he meant. She would have thought he was teasing her except for his serious face, his slow way of speaking.

He was stroking the animal's mane now. "She was worried about you." His hand fascinated her despite herself. It seemed like he was tangling it in imaginary hair. "How did you make it do that?"

"Do what?" She was afraid now, afraid and flattered both. There was no mocking or teasing in his face.

"I saw it stand up." His voice was so low she could almost pretend that she didn't hear him right. His hand dropped to her thigh and slid upward to the cotton crotch of her panties.

Even though she had seen the slow progression of his hand, the touch startled her. She was paralyzed for a moment before she sprang up, letting the horse fall as she did. It crashed down, knocking the bottle of bourbon over, dark liquor pouring over her coat and soaking the bottoms of the dusty boxes like the tide coming in at night.

He grabbed for her before she could think, his hand catching hold of the neck of her shirt. She stepped back, off-balance, and fell, her shirt ripping open over her bra even as he let go of it.

Shoes pounded up the stairs.

"What the fuck?" Marcus was at the top of the stairwell with Doughboy, trying to shove his way in for a look.

Kenny shook his head and looked around numbly while Kaye scrambled for her bourbon-soaked coat.

The boys moved out of the way, and Janet was there, too, staring.

"What happened?" Janet asked, looking between them in confusion. Kaye pushed past her, shoving her hand through an armhole of the coat as she threw it over her back.

"Kaye!" Janet called.

Kaye ignored her, taking the stairs two at a time in the dark. There was nothing she could say that would explain what had happened.

She could hear Janet shouting. "What did you do to her? What the fuck did you do?"

Kaye ran across the carousel hall and swung her leg over the sill. The bits of glass she'd mostly avoided earlier slashed a thin line on the outside of her thigh as she dropped into the sandy soil and weeds.

The cold wind felt good against her hot face.

Cornelius Stone picked up the new box of computer crap and hauled it into his bedroom to drop next to the others. Each time his mother came home from the flea market with a cracked monitor, sticky keyboard, or just loads of wires, she had that hopeful look that made Corny want to scream. She just couldn't comprehend the difference between a 286 and a quantum computer. She couldn't understand that the age of guerilla engineering was at a close, that being a motherfucking genius wasn't enough. You needed to be a rich motherfucking genius.

He dropped the box, kicked it hard three times, picked up his denim jacket with the devil's head on the back, and made for the door.

"Can you use that stuff, honey?" His mother was in Janet's room, folding a new pair of secondhand jeans. She held up a T-shirt with rhinestone cats on it. "Think your sister will like it?"

"Thanks, Ma," he said through gritted teeth. "I got to get to work." He walked past The Husband, who was stooped over, getting a beer from the case under the kitchen table. The white cat was waddling along the countertop, its belly dragging with another pregnancy, screaming for canned food or pickles and ice cream or something. He petted its head grudgingly, but before it began rubbing against his hand in earnest, he opened the screen door and went out into the lot.

The cool October air was a relief from the recirculated cigarette smoke.

Corny loved his car. It was a primer-colored Chevy blooming with rust spots and an inner lining that hung like baggy skin from the roof. He knew what he looked like. Beaky. Skinny and tall with bad hair and worse skin. He lived down to his name. Cornelius. Corny. Corn-dog. But not in his car. Inside, he was anonymous.

Every day for the last three weeks he had left a little earlier for work. He would go to the convenience store and buy some food. Then he would drive around, wondering what it would be like to just get on the highway and go, go, go until the gas ran out.

Tonight, he bought a cup of coffee and a package of black licorice. He lingered over a paperback with an embossed metallic dragon on the cover, reading the first few sentences, hoping something would interest him. The game was becoming boring. Worse than boring, it made him feel more pathetic than before. Nearly a week before Halloween and all, he'd been doing this long enough that it was clear he would never really go. He sipped at the coffee and almost spat it out. Too sweet. He sipped at it some more, steeling himself to the taste. Disgusting.

Corny got out of his car and chucked the full coffee into the parking lot. It splashed satisfactorily on the asphalt. He went inside and poured himself another cup. From behind the counter, a matronly woman with frizzy red hair looked him over and pointed to his jacket. "Who are you supposed to be, the devil?"

"I wish," Corny said, dropping a dollar twenty-five on the counter. "I wish."

2

The wind whipped tiny pebbles of rain across Kaye's face. The droplets froze her hands, making her shiver as they slid down her wet hair and under the collar of her coat. She walked, head down, kicking the scattered trash that had eddied up on the grassy shores along the highway. A flattened soda can skittered into a sodden chrysanthemum-covered foam heart, staked there to mark the site of a car crash. There were no houses on this side of the road, just a long stretch of wet woods leading up to a gas station. She was over halfway home.

Cars hissed over the asphalt. The sound was comforting, like a long sigh.

I saw you. I saw what you did.

Awfulness twisted in her gut, awfulness and anger. She wanted to smash something, hit someone.

How could she have done anything? When she tried to make a magazine page turn on its own or a penny land on heads, it never worked. How could she have made Kenny see a broken-legged carousel horse move?

Never mind that she might as well assume that Spike and Lutie and Gristle *had* been imaginary. She'd been home for two weeks, and there was no sign of them, no matter how many times she had called them, no matter how many bowls of milk she left out, no matter how many times she went down to the old creek.

She took a deep breath, snorting rain up her nose. It reminded her of crying.

The trees seemed like lines of lead grille missing the stained glass to fit between their branches. She knew what her grandmother was going to say when she got back, stinking of liquor with a torn shirt. True things.

His hand on her leg was what Janet would really care about—that, and that she had let it rest there, even if only for a moment. And she could imagine what he was telling Janet now—flushed, angry, and drunk—but even a badly managed lie would sound better than the truth.

I saw it stand up.

Kaye couldn't contradict them either. Who would believe that he touched her crotch on purpose, but ripped her shirt by accident? So what was Kaye supposed to say when Janet asked what happened? Janet thought she was a liar already.

She could still feel the heat of Kenny's hand, a stroke of fire along her thigh in contrast to her otherwise rain-soaked skin. She had plenty to feel guilty about.

Another gust of rain stung her cheeks, this one bringing a shout with it from the direction of the woods. The noise was brief, but eloquent with pain. Kaye stopped abruptly. There was no sound except the rain, hissing like radio static.

Then, just as a truck sped past, kicking up a cloud of drizzle, she heard another sound. Softer, this one, maybe a moan bitten off at the end. It was just inside the copse of trees.

Kaye moved down the slight slope, off the short grass and into the woods. She ducked under the dripping branches of an elm, stepping on tufts of short ferns and looping briars. Weeds brushed across her calves, leaving strokes of rain. The storm-bright sky lit the woods with silver. An earthy, sweet odor of rot bloomed where she disturbed the carpet of leaves.

There was no one there.

She half turned toward the highway. She could still see the road from where she was standing. What was she doing? The sound must have carried over from the houses beyond the thin river that ran along the back of the woods. No one else would be dumb enough to go trooping through wet, dripping woods in the middle of the night.

Kaye walked back up to the road, picking her way through spots that looked somewhat drier than others. Burrs had collected along her stockings, and she bent down to pull them off.

"Stay where you are." She jumped at the voice. The accent was rich and strange, though the words were pronounced precisely.

A man was sprawled in the mud only a few steps from her, clutching a curved sword in one hand. It shone like a sliver of moonlight in the hazy dark. Long pewter hair, plastered wetly to his neck, framed a face that was long and full of sharp angles.

Rivulets of rain ran over the jointed black armor he wore. His other hand was at his heart, clutching a branch that jutted from his chest. The rain there was tinted pink with blood.

"Was it you, girl?" He was breathing raggedly.

Kaye wasn't sure what he meant, but she shook her head. He didn't look much older than she was. Certainly not old enough to call her "girl."

"So you haven't come to finish me off?"

She shook her head again. He was long-limbed—he would be tall if he were standing. Taller than most people, taller than any faerie she had ever seen—still, she had no doubt that was what he was, if for no other reason than the pointed tops of his ears knifing through his wet hair—and that he was beautiful in a way that made her breath catch.

He licked his lips. There was blood on them. "Pity," he said quietly.

She took a step toward him, and he twisted into a defensive crouch. Wounded as he was, he still moved swiftly. Hair fell forward across his face, but his eyes, shining like mercury, studied her intently.

"You're a faerie, aren't you?" she said soothingly, holding her hands where he could see them. She had heard stories of the court fey—the Gentry—from Lutie-loo, but she had never seen one. Maybe that was what he was.

He stayed still, and she took another half step toward him, holding out one hand to coax him as if he were some fascinating, dangerous animal. "Let me help you."

His body was trembling with concentration. His gaze never moved from her face. He held the hilt of his sword in a white-knuckled grip.

She did not dare take another step. "You're going to bleed to death."

They stayed like that a few more minutes before he slumped down to one knee in the mud. He bent forward, fingers clutching the leaves, and spat red. The wet lashes over his half-closed eyes were as silver as a safety pin.

She took two steps and knelt down next to him, bracing herself with shaking hands. This close, she could see that his armor was stiff leather sculpted to look like feathers.

"I cannot draw the arrow myself," he said softly. "They are waiting for me to bleed a little more before they come against my blade."

"Who is waiting?" It was hard to comprehend that someone had shot him with a tree branch, but that seemed to be what he was saying.

"If you would help me, draw this arrow." His eyes narrowed, and he shook his head. "If not, then push it in as deep as you can and hope that it kills me."

"It will bleed more," Kaye said.

He laughed at that, a bitter sound. "Either way, no doubt."

She could see the despair in his face. He obviously suspected her to be part of some plan to kill him. Still, he slid his body back until he could lean against the trunk of an oak. He was braced, waiting to see what she would do.

She thought of the faeries she had known when she was a child—impish, quick things—no mention of wars or magical arrows or enemies, certainly no deception. The man bleeding in the dirt beside her told her how wrong her perceptions of *Faerie* had been.

Her fingers flinched away from the wound in his chest. Her

lungs turned to ice as she looked at the grisly wound. "I can't do it."

His voice stayed soft. "What do they call you?"

"Kaye," she said. There was silence for a moment as she noticed the cold cloud of her breath rise up with the word.

"I'm Roiben." Faeries didn't give their names easily, even part of their names, although she had no idea why. He was trying to show her that he trusted her, maybe trying to make up for the assumptions he had made. "Give me your hand."

She let him take it and guide it to the branch. His skin was chilled and wet, his fingers inhumanly long and rough with calluses as they closed over hers. "Just close your hand on it and let me pull," he said. "You don't even have to look. As long as I'm not touching it, I might be able to draw it out."

That shamed her. She had told him that she wanted to help him, he was in a whole lot of pain, and it was no time for her to be squeamish. "I'll do it," she said.

Roiben let go, and she gave a sharp tug. Although his face constricted with pain, the branch only pulled out a short way.

He moaned low.

Were there really other faerie Folk in the trees, waiting for him to be weak enough to defeat? Kaye thought that if so, now would be a great time for them to come down and have a go at it.

"Again, Kaye."

She took note of the angle of the armor, changing her position so that the branch couldn't catch on one of the plates. She raised herself to one knee, braced, and then stood, pulling upward as hard as she could.

Roiben gave a harsh cry as the branch slid free of his chest, its iron tip black with blood. His fingers touched the wound and he raised them, slick with blood, as if suddenly disbelieving that he had been shot.

"Very brave," he said, touching his wet fingers to her leg.

Kaye tossed the stick away from her. She was shuddering, and she could taste the ghost of blood in her mouth. "We have to stop the bleeding. How does your armor come off?"

He seemed not to understand her at first. When he did, he looked at her with a kind of incredulity. Then he leaned forward with a groan. "Straps," he managed.

She came and sat behind him, feeling over the leather for buckles.

A sudden wind shook the branches above, raining an extra shower of heavy droplets down on them, and Kaye wondered again about faeries in the trees. Her fingers fumbled in her haste. If those faeries were still afraid of Roiben, they might not have to worry much longer—he looked as though he might pass out at any minute.

To get off his breastplate, she not only had to detach it from the backplate at his shoulders and sides—there were also straps that connected it to the shoulderplates and to his legplates. Finally, she managed to peel it off his chest. Underneath, the bare skin was mottled with blood.

He tipped back his head and closed his eyes. "Let the rain clean it."

She pulled off her coat and hung it on one of the branches of the tree. Her shirt was ripped already, she reminded herself as she took it off. She tore it into long strips and began winding them around Roiben's chest and arms. He opened his eyes when she touched him. His eyes narrowed, then widened. Their color was mesmerizing.

He straightened up, horrified. "You don't have to do that."

"You have to try to stay awake," Kaye said. "Is there somewhere you can go?"

He shook his head. Fumbling near him, he picked up a leaf and wiped it against the underside of the leather breastplate. It came away shining red. "Drop this in the stream. I—there is a kelpie there—it is no sure thing that I will be able to control it in this weather, but it is something."

Kaye nodded quickly, although she had no idea what a kelpie was, and made to take the leaf.

He did not let it go immediately. "I am in your debt. I mislike not knowing how I must repay it."

"I have questions . . ."

He let her take the leaf. "I will answer three, as full and well as is within my power."

Like a faerie tale, which was what she supposed she'd stumbled into.

"When you drop the leaf in the water, say 'Roiben of the Unseelie Court asks for your aid.'"

"Who do I tell?"

"Just say it aloud."

She nodded again and ran in the direction of the water. The steep bank of the stream was choked with vegetation and broken glass. Roots, swept bare of the mud that should have surrounded them, ran along the ground like the pale arms of half-buried corpses. She forbade herself to think of that again.

She squatted down and set the leaf, blood side down, into the water. It floated there, spinning a little. She worried it would get stuck in the shallows, and tried to blow it farther out.

"Roiben of the Unseelie Court asks for your help," she said, hoping that she had gotten it right. Nothing happened. She said it again, louder, feeling foolish and frightened at the same time. "Roiben of the Unseelie Court needs your help."

A frog surfaced and began to swim in her direction. Would that have something to do with a kelpie? What kind of help were they supposed to get from a shallow, polluted stream?

But then she saw that she had been mistaken. What she had taken for the eyes of a frog were actually hollow pits that quavered as something large swam through the water toward her. She wanted to run, but fascination combined with obligation rooted her to the spot. Hollow pits formed into flaring nostrils on the snout of a black horse that rose up from the black water as if created from it. Moss and mud slid from its dripping flanks as the thing turned its head to regard Kaye with luminous white eyes.

She could not move. How many minutes passed as she stared at those mottled gray flanks, smooth as sealskin, and stared into the impossible glow of those eyes? The creature inclined its neck.

Kaye took a half step backward and tried to speak. No words came.

The horse-thing snuffled closer to her, its hooves sinking in the mud, snapping twigs. It smelled of brackish water. She took another step backward and stumbled.

She had to say something. "This way," she managed finally, pointing through the trees. "He's this way."

The horse moved in the direction she pointed, speeding to

a trot. She was left to follow, shaking with relief. When she got to the clearing, Roiben was already straddling the creature's back. His breastplate had been haphazardly strapped on.

He saw her emerge from under the canopy of branches and smiled. His eyes seemed darker in the moonlight. "Were I you, I would stay clear of the Folk in the future. We are a capricious people, with little regard for mortals."

She looked at him again. There were scratches on his armor that she didn't remember. Could he have been attacked? He could barely lift his head before—it was impossible to believe that he could have fought with something and won. "Did something happen?"

His smile deepened, wiping the weariness from his face. His eyes glittered. "Don't waste your questions." Then the horse rode, moving like no living thing, darting between trees with unearthly speed and grace. Leaves flurried from kicks of its hooves. Moonlight glowed along its flanks.

Before she could think, she was alone in the wood. Alone and shivering and proud of herself. She moved to retrieve her coat, and a glimmer of light caught her eye. The arrow.

She knelt and picked up the branch with its iron tip. Her finger ran up the rough bark and touched the too-warm metal. A shudder went through her, and she dropped it back in the mud. The woods were suddenly menacing, and she walked as quickly as she could back toward the road. If she started running, she didn't think she'd be able to stop.

Kaye dug her feet into the muddy slope that marked the edge of her grandmother's lawn and heaved herself up. She slid past the overflowing trash can, the broken-down Pinto, the rusted coffee cans wired together as a fence for a wilted herb garden.

All the lights in the house seemed to be on, highlighting the grubby curtains. The television flickered in the living room.

She opened the back door and walked into the kitchen. Pots and pans, crusted with food, were piled in the sink. She was supposed to wash them. Instead, she went to the cupboard and took out a bowl, filled it with milk, then put a piece of stale white bread on top of it. It would have to do, she thought as she carefully opened the door and set it on the step—after all, the only things likely to come for it anymore were neighborhood cats.

Kaye crept into the living room.

On the other side of the staircase, Ellen was sitting in front of the television, eating one of the miniature Snickers Grandma had bought for the trick-or-treaters. "Leave me the fuck alone," she muttered to the drink in front of her.

"You think I don't know anything. Okay, you're the smart one, right?" Kaye's grandmother said in that too-sweet voice that pissed off Kaye so much. "If you're so smart, then how come you're all alone? How come the only one to take you in is your old, stupid mother?"

"I heard you the first million fucking times you said it."

"Well, you're going to hear it again," Kaye's grandmother said. "Where is your daughter tonight? It's almost one in the morning! Do you even care that she's out gallivanting around who knows where, trying her damnedest to turn out just like—"

"Don't you start in on my daughter!" Kaye's mother said with surprising vehemence. "She's just fine. You leave her out of your bitching."

Kaye bent her head down and tried to walk up the stairs as quickly and quietly as she could.

She caught her own reflection in the hallway mirror, mascara and glitter eyeshadow smeared across her cheeks and under her eyes, running in crusted and glittering streaks that looked like they were made by tears. Her lipstick was smudged and dull, arching across her left cheek where she must have wiped it.

Kaye turned to take a furtive look into the living room. Her mother caught her glance, rolled her eyes, and motioned her up the stairs with a furtive hand movement.

"While she's in this house she's going to live by the same rules that you lived by. I don't care that she's spent the last six years in a rat-infested apartment with whatever hoodlums you took up with. From now on that girl's going to be raised decent."

Kaye crept the rest of the way up and into her room. She closed the door as quietly as she could.

The tiny white dresser and too-short bed seemed to belong to someone else. Her rats, Isaac and Armageddon, rustled in their fish tank on top of the old toy box.

Kaye stripped off her clothes and, not caring about the wet or the mud or anything, climbed into bed and wrapped a blanket around herself. Kaye knew what obsession was like—she saw how her mother craved fame. She didn't want what she would never have.

But just for tonight, she allowed herself to think of him,

to think of the solemn, formal way he had spoken to her, so unlike anyone else. She let herself think of his flashing eyes and crooked smile.

Kaye slid down into sleep like it was water closing over her head.

3

Kaye was standing in a little stream clutching a Barbie doll
by its blond hair, the cool water tickling her toes. Heat
beat down on her back, and she could smell green things and
the rich mud of summer. She was nine.

It made perfect dream sense, even though she knew that it
hadn't happened quite this way. The warm green memory was
younger than nine. But in this patchwork dream, Spike sat on
the carpet of moss that ran along the bank. He was sewing a
doll's dress and purse out of leaves. Lutie straddled the waist
of a sitting Ken doll, her iridescent butterfly wings fluttering
slightly while she sang bawdy songs that made nine-year-old
Kaye giggle and blush at the same time.

"I could pretend that he could bend,
But I'm bound to be sad when he is unclad.
A smooth plastic chest doesn't make up for the rest;
Even a boy-doll has to try to make a girl-doll sigh."

Gristle stood silently beside Kaye. Laughing, she turned to him, and he made to speak, but the only thing that dropped from his mouth was a single white stone. It splashed into the stream, settling along the bottom along with the other rocks, shining with a strange light.

"A shiny plastic boy's not a proper toy.
Each and every girl's got a pearl."

A squawk made Kaye look up suddenly. A crow had settled in the tree, black feathers shimmering with color, like gasoline floating on the surface of water. When the crow cocked its head down at her, its eyes were as pale as the stone.

"Never mind that you can't find
The thing—he can't even find his ding-a-ling!"

The crow shifted its claws along the branch, then dropped into the air. A moment later she felt the scrape of claws along her wrist and the bite of its beak on her hand as her doll was pulled into the air.

Kaye screamed and reached down to throw something at the bird. Her hand closed on something hard, and she hurled it without thinking.

The crow spiraled into the cushion of trees, and Kaye ran

toward it. The forest around her blurred, and she was suddenly looking down at the black shape. It was still, feathers ruffling slightly in the breeze. Her doll was there too, lying apart from the dead bird, and between them was a smooth white stone. The stone that Gristle had spoken.

And then she woke up.

Kaye's mother was standing in the doorway of the bedroom holding a cordless phone. "I've been calling and calling you from downstairs. Janet's on the phone."

"Uh-oh." Kaye blinked through eyes crusty with day-old makeup. She stretched.

The sun was alive again, glowing with fury at the night's trickery at the hands of Mistress Moon. Flares of lemony light threatened her with a headache if she opened her eyes.

"Rough night?" Kaye's mother leaned against the door-frame and took a drag on her cigarette.

Kaye rubbed her eyes. Her knuckles came away black and glittery.

"Janet's on the phone." Kaye's mother sounded both annoyed and amused at having to repeat herself. "You want me to tell her you'll call her back?"

Kaye shook her head and took the phone. "Hullo?" Her voice was rough.

Ellen left the doorway, and Kaye heard her thump down the stairs.

"What happened last night?" It took Kaye a few moments to understand what Janet was asking.

"Oh. Nothing. Kenny tried to catch me, and my shirt ripped."

"Kaye! How come you ran out like that? I thought he'd done something terrible to you! We were fighting all night about it."

"I didn't think you'd believe me," Kaye said flatly.

That must have sounded enough like best-friend contrition, because Janet's tone softened. "Come on, Kaye. Of course I believe you."

Kaye struggled for what to say to the unexpected reprieve.

"Are you okay?" Janet asked.

"I met someone on the way home last night." Kaye sat up in bed, realizing that she'd gone to bed with her bra, skirt, and muddy stockings still on. No wonder she felt uncomfortable.

"You did?" Janet sounded surprised and skeptical. "A boy?"

"Yeah," Kaye said. She wanted to say it aloud, to hold on to it. Already her recollection of Roiben was blanched by the sun, the way a dream fades when you don't write it down. "He had gray eyes and long hair."

"Like a metal head?"

"Longer," Kaye said. She wrapped the puke-pink comforter more tightly around her. Like everything else in her bedroom, it was slightly too small.

"Weird. What's his name?"

"Robin," Kaye said, a little smile on her face. She was glad Janet couldn't see her right now—she was sure she looked idiotically happy.

"Like Robin Hood? Are you for real? Did he hit on you?"

"We just talked," Kaye said.

Janet sighed. "You didn't meet anyone, did you? You're making this up."

"He's real," Kaye said. He was real, the most real person she had met in a long time. Hyper real.

"The party sucked anyway," Janet said. "I almost kicked this girl's ass. Dough kept telling me to chill, but I was too wasted and upset. Well, come over and I'll tell you the rest."

"Sure, okay. I've got to get dressed."

"Okay, 'bye." The phone clicked as Janet hung up. Kaye turned it off and dropped it on the comforter.

Getting up, she looked around her bedroom. Her clothes lay in drifts on the floor, most still in the black garbage bags. All the furniture was the same as it had been when she was four, child-size white furniture, pink walls, and a reproachful, glass-eyed army of dolls arranged in the bookshelves.

I have to find Gristle and Spike. She hadn't ever needed to call them before. They'd always been around when she had needed them. But that was when she had been little, when she had believed in everything, before her legs stuck out over the end of the bed and she had to bend over to see her face in the dresser mirror. Kaye sighed. She guessed that she wasn't really unicorn-pure anymore. Maybe that kind of thing mattered.

Kaye stripped out of her clothes and found a worn pair of jeans and a blue G-Force T-shirt. In the bathroom, as she splashed cold water on her face and rubbed off last night's makeup, she inspected herself. The purple dye she'd combed into her hair was already faded.

She sighed again and pulled her hair up into ragged pigtails. Hey, if she looked ten again, maybe kid-loving faeries would come to talk to her.

Her leopard coat was too soggy to wear. Kaye pulled on

Lloyd's leather jacket and checked the pockets. A couple of crumpled receipts, a faux-tortoiseshell guitar pick, loose change. Kaye pulled her hand out as though she'd been stung.

There, sticking out of the pad of her finger, was a slim, brown thorn. It just figured that Lloyd would have something awful in his pocket. She pulled it out and sucked the tiny red dot on her finger. Then, dropping the thorn on her dresser, she went downstairs.

Kaye's mother was sitting at the kitchen table, flipping through a magazine. A fifth of gin was sitting uncapped on the table, and a cigarette had almost burned itself to ash on a plate beside her.

"You going to Janet's?" Ellen asked.

"Yeah."

"You want some coffee before you go, honey? You don't look so awake."

"I'm okay. Grandma's gonna freak when she sees that plate." Kaye didn't even bother to mention the gin.

Kaye's mother leaned back in the wooden chair. "Don't try to mommy your mommy," she said. Still, Kaye worried. It wasn't that Ellen didn't drink sometimes, but she didn't usually go straight from tying one on the night before to pouring booze into her coffee.

"Heard from Lloyd?"

Ellen shook her head. "Nah. I called a couple of old friends from Sweet Pussy, but they've all gone respectable."

Kaye laughed. She remembered Liz jumping around the stage in her amazing purple plastic catsuit like a glam-rock Julie Newmar. It was hard to picture what respectable would look like on her. "You going to get together?"

"Maybe," Ellen said airily. "Sue and Liz have some little hole-in-the-wall music store in Red Bank."

"That's great."

Ellen sighed. "Whatever. I wonder when was the last time either one of them picked up a fucking instrument."

Kaye shook her head. It was kind of stupid to think that her mother would just give up on going back to the city, but she couldn't help hoping. "Tell Grandma I won't be home late."

"You come home when you want. I'm your mother."

"Thanks, Mom," Kaye said, and walked out the door.

The wind was blowing gusts of vivid, lipstick-colored leaves across the lawn. Kaye took a deep breath of cold air.

"Lutie-loo," she whispered into the wind. "Spike, Gristle . . . please come back. I need you."

I'll just walk over to Janet's. I'll just go over to Janet's like I said and then I'll figure out a plan.

Janet lived in a trailer park along the main road in back of the gas station where her older brother worked. She waved to him as she cut through the lot.

Corny smiled grudgingly. His hair was a longish brown mop, cut too short in the front and too long in the back. He was wearing a denim jacket and dirty jeans. His skin was red in patches. He was exactly like she remembered him, only taller.

Kaye headed behind the office of the gas station and jumped over some overgrown shrubs to the trailer park. The trailers were vehicles in name only—none of them had wheels, and most of them had fences and porches anchoring them with steel and cement to the firmament. She walked up a pebble road toward Janet's trailer.

Across the way, a brown-haired girl about Kaye's age was

hanging some wash. Behind her, an opulently fat man lounged in a hammock; skin gridded by the crisscrossed strings. A trio of dachshunds barked madly as they chased each other along a chain-link fence.

Kaye banged on Janet's screen door.

"Come on in," Janet called. Kaye could see her feet through the screen, flung over the edge of the grungy blue couch, toes maroon with polish. Wads of toilet paper were stuffed between them so they couldn't quite touch.

The door squeaked hideously as she opened it. Rust had stiffened the hinges where the white enamel was chipped off. The main room of the trailer was dark, the windows covered in drapes. Light flickered from three sources: the door, the dim amber kitchen light, and the television. On the screen, two women were screaming at one another in front of a studio audience. One of the women had rhinestone eyebrows.

"Want to do your nails?" Janet asked. "I have a cool blue."

Kaye shook her head, although Janet probably didn't see her do it. "Can I make some coffee?"

"Sure, make me some too." Janet stretched, pointing her shiny toes as she arched her back. She was wearing a boy's sleeveless undershirt and daisy-print cotton panties. "I am totally hungover."

"Where's everybody?"

"Ma and The Husband are at the flea market. Corny'll be back from work anytime now. You'll never believe what she got me the last time she was out—a half shirt with rhinestone cats on it! I mean—where would you even find something like that?"

Kaye laughed. Janet's mother collected all kinds of kitschy

stuff, but especially all things Star Trek. The trailer walls were covered with collectable plates, framed fan art, and shadow-boxed phasers and tricorders. A collection of Spock-related needlepoint throw pillows competed with Janet for couch space. "I saw Corny when I walked over. I don't think he recognized me."

"He's an asshole. All he does is sit in his room and jerk off. He's probably gone nearsighted."

Kaye took two mugs down from the shelf and filled them with water from the tap. "Maybe I just don't look the way I used to." Kaye punched the keypad of the microwave and put the cups in. They spun on the greasy glass tray.

"I guess." Janet flipped through the channels and stopped on VH1.

"So what happened last night?" Kaye knew that it would please Janet if she asked.

Janet did, in fact, pull herself into a sitting position and turn down the sound on the TV. "Well, when we got to Fatima's place, Aimee was, like, playing with Kenny's hair, rubbing her hands all over it and saying how soft it was. She must have known we were fighting."

"I'm sorry."

"It's cool." Janet pressed a Live-Long-and-Prosper pillow to her chest. "So anyway I go up to her and start rubbing my hands through her hair and telling her how *nice* it felt, really going to town, and Marcus starts laughing. You know that weird, rumbling Buddha-belly laugh he has. So fucking loud."

"What did Kenny do?" Kaye wondered if Kenny hit on every girl he met. She was embarrassed that she'd let him touch her—sometimes she wondered about the sick part of herself that wanted to be liked, wanted it badly enough to be tempted to compromise herself to get it.

"Nothing; he loves girls to fight over him." Janet shook her head as if she were talking about an incorrigible child. "So she starts calling me psycho and dyke, not backing down at all, saying that she was just talking."

Kaye nodded. "Did you hit her?" The microwave beeped, and Kaye stirred instant-coffee "crystals" into both cups. A thin white foam formed on the surface.

Janet nodded. "I tried, but Dough stopped me and Kenny stopped her and Fatima came over and started saying how it was a big misunderstanding and all that, even though she didn't see what happened. She just didn't want her house to get fucked up."

Looking down into the cup, Kaye recalled the dark, still water of the stream. Her heart was suddenly beating triple-time even though nothing at all was happening.

"Are you listening to me?" Janet asked.

"Here's your coffee," Kaye said, stirring sugar and powdered cream into Janet's before handing it to her. "I'm listening."

"Well, have you ever seen an uncircumcised dick?"

Kaye shook her head.

"Me neither. So I say, 'Sure, we'll give you a dollar apiece if you show us.' And he says, 'That's only ten bucks.'"

Kaye smiled and nodded as Janet spoke, but she still saw Roiben in her mind's eye, drenched with rain and blood, shot nearly through the heart with a gnarled arrow.

The hinges screamed their protest as Corny opened the door and stomped into the trailer. He glared at both of them, stalked to the refrigerator, opened it, and then swigged Mountain Dew out of the bottle.

"What's up your ass?" Janet said.

A white cat, her belly swollen with kittens, had slunk in when Corny opened the door. Kaye dropped her hand to pet the little head.

"I just worked two shifts, so don't fuck with me." Kaye could see that the patch on the back of his jacket was a devil's head. In his back pocket, the outline of his wallet was connected to a chain that ran to his front belt loop.

"Mom hates it when you drink out of the bottle," Janet said.

"So what?" Corny said. He took another deliberate swig. "You going to tell her about that? How about I tell her how you need your own Roman vomitorium."

"Shut up, fuckfist." Janet picked up the phone in the kitchen and started punching in numbers. She walked toward her bedroom as she dialed.

Corny glanced at Kaye. She looked away from him and pulled the heavy, soft cat onto her lap. It purred like a hive of hornets.

"You're that girl that believes in faeries, right?" Corny said.

She shrugged. "I'm Kaye."

"Want some soda? I didn't backwash into it." He wiped the side of his sleeve against his mouth.

Kaye shook her head. Something—like a small stone—bounced off her knee.

The windows were closed. Kaye looked at the ceiling, but the overhead light looked intact. Maybe something from a shelf. When she looked down at the floor near her feet, the only object she saw was an acorn. They were abundant outside this time of year, scattering from the nearby tree all over the lawns of homes with room for trees and grass. She picked it up and looked toward the window again. Maybe it was open after all. The acorn was light in her hand, and she noticed a tiny strip of white sticking out from under the cap.

Corny was dampening a towel and wiping off his face. She didn't think he'd thrown the acorn—she'd been talking to him when she'd felt it hit.

Kaye pulled lightly on the acorn cap, and it came loose. Inside the nutshell, all the meat was gone, leaving an empty space where a slip of paper was coiled. Kaye removed it carefully and read the message written in a pinkish red ink: "Do not talk to the black knight anymore. tell no one your name. everything is danger. Gristle is gone. We need your help. meet you tomorrow night. LL&S"

What did it mean, Gristle is gone? Gone where? And the black knight? Could that be Roiben? She hadn't been talking to anyone else that fit that description. What did it mean, that everything was danger?

"Kaye," Janet said, leaning out of her bedroom, "you want to go to the mall?"

Kaye fumbled to tuck the acorn into the pocket of her leather jacket.

"I suppose that you are expecting me to take you," Corny said. "Y'know, most people that go shopping actually have money."

"Shut up, geek," Janet said, and ushered Kaye into her bedroom.

Kaye sat down on Janet's bed. Janet's room was full of

mismatched furniture: a wooden dresser with glass knobs, a white pressboard vanity, and a dented black metal daybed. The room was as messy as Kaye's, with clothes hanging out of open drawers and littering the floor, but the disarray seemed glamorous here. While Kaye's clothes were all T-shirts and retro attic finds, Janet had red skirts with feather fringe, and shirts that shimmered blue and gold like fish scales. Pots of eyeshadow, glittery barrettes, body sprays, and tubes of hair goo covered her vanity and the top of her dresser. On the walls, posters of bands competed with messages written in multicolor markers on the white walls. JANET & KENNY TLF was written in glitter on the back of Janet's door. She wasn't sure, but she thought she saw traces of some other name underneath Kenny's.

"What should I wear?" Janet held up a pink, fuzzy cropped sweater that came to just under her breasts. "Will I freeze?"

"You need a poodle miniskirt." Kaye sat on the bed and leaned back against the pillows. Her hand went to her pocket, pressing the tiny point of the acorn hard enough to indent her thumb.

"What are you going to wear?"

"This." Kaye indicated her faded T-shirt and jeans with a sweep of her hand.

Janet sighed and made a face. "Boys all think you're exotic. I'd kill for that."

Kaye shook her head morosely. What too many white boys liked about Asian girls was weird. It was all mail-order brides and kung fu at the same time.

"How about you wear this?" Janet held up a shiny black shirt that had no back at all. It tied around the neck and waist like a bikini.

"No way," Kaye said.

This time Janet just laughed.

They walked into the mall through the movie theater entrance. Boys and girls were gathered in packs on the steps, waiting for rides or having a cigarette before their movie started. Janet walked past them like a goddess, not looking at anybody, perfectly curled hair and glistening lipstick appearing effortless. It made Kaye wonder where she'd learned this skill with beauty—as a kid Janet had a perpetually woolly perm and unlaced sneakers.

Kaye caught her own reflection in a window and grimaced. Her T-shirt was a bit of thin, faded cloth that even sported a couple of holes from Laundromat abuse. Her jeans were hand-me-downs from her mother, and they hung low on her hipbones, forcing her to hitch them up occasionally when she felt like they were going to fall all the way off. Maybe she should have taken Janet up on her offer of borrowed clothes after all.

"Okay," Janet said. "Want to show me those skills you bragged about?"

Kaye grinned. One thing that they'd emailed about for a while was the audacity of the things they'd shoplifted. Kaye's all-time greatest heist had been her two rats. They might not have been expensive, but pocketing a squirming animal and then keeping it in your pocket was harder than it sounded.

She nodded. "Here are Kaye's Principles of Thieving, okay?"

Janet folded her arms. "Kidding, right?"

"Listen. No mom-and-pop stores. Just chains or megastores—they can afford it, and the people who work there don't give a shit. Oh, and no places where the employees are actually nice."

"I can't believe you have rules."

Kaye nodded solemnly. "Minimizing my karmic damage."

A few hours later they were sitting on the curb outside the Wiz divvying up their loot. It wasn't, strictly speaking, far enough from the mall to be entirely safe, but they were feeling untouchable. Kaye was trying a new, heavy stick of smoky eyeliner, smearing it thickly under her eyes. Janet was drinking a raspberry smoothie—the only thing she'd actually paid for.

Kaye dug through her jeans for matches and lit a cigarette. Taking a deep breath of smoke, she leaned back and exhaled, letting the smoke whorl up and away. She reached up lazily to change the pattern. It shifted at the touch of her fingers, and she could see figures dancing in it—no, they weren't dancing, they were fighting. Swordsmen dueling in the rising smoke.

"How long are you going to be in town?" Janet asked.

Kaye dropped her hand. She'd forgotten where she was. "I figure at least a couple of months."

"It's weird, you know. Us being friends after all this time and you being so far away. I've been thinking about last night."

"Yeah?" Kaye asked warily.

"He was hitting on you, wasn't he?"

Kaye shrugged. There was no way to explain what really happened. She certainly couldn't have explained why she'd let him run his hand up her thigh, why she hadn't minded in the least until she'd suddenly remembered who they were and realized what was really happening. "A little, I guess. But I honestly fell. I guess I drank too much or something."

"How come you were up there in the first place?"

Kaye grinned easily now. "Just exploring. There was the most outrageously cool old carousel horse. Did you see it? The legs were gone but the rest of it was perfect—the paint wasn't even badly faded." She sighed wistfully. "Even if I had some way to bring that thing home, there is no way I could drag it from apartment to apartment."

Janet sighed. It was obvious this was the sort of reason she could easily believe.

Kaye took another drag on her cigarette, wondering why that made her angry. This time the tendrils of smoke reminded her of Roiben's hair, raw silver silk. Thinking about that made her feel even more restless and frustrated. She wanted to see him again. The more time passed, the more it seemed he had stepped from the pages of a storybook.

"Earth to Kaye," Janet said. "What were you thinking about?"

"Robin," Kaye said. That was something else she imagined Janet would easily believe.

"He's for real? Honest?" Janet sucked hard on her straw, trying to draw out a chunk of frozen raspberry that was clogging it.

"Don't be a bitch," Kaye said without real heat.

"Sor*ry*. It's just that it's so unlikely—meeting a guy in a rainstorm while you're walking home. I mean, what was he doing out there? I wouldn't have talked to him. Didn't he have his own car?"

"Look, I'm only going to be in town for a couple of months, at most. The only thing that matters is that he is cross-my-heart-and-hope-to-die beautiful." Kaye waggled her eyebrows suggestively.

That at least brought a scandalized gasp. "You *slut*," Janet crooned joyfully. "Do you even know if he likes you?"

Kaye ground out the stub of her cigarette on the rough cement, smearing ash in a roughly circular line. She didn't want to go over the list of things to recommend her to a faerie knight; there wasn't a single thing she could think of to put on such a list.

"He'll like me," she said, hoping that the charm of speaking words aloud would make those words come true.

That night Kaye let Isaac and Armageddon run all over the bed while the CD player blasted Grace Slick singing "White Rabbit" over and over again. A grown-up, fucked-up Alice suited her. Then she put on Hole and listened to Courtney Love grate out words about girls and cakes.

She cracked the window and lit a cigarette, careful to blow the smoke out onto the lawn.

The row of dolls watched her impassively from the bookshelf, their tea party propriety almost certainly offended. She caught both rats and put them up there with the dolls, to get to know one another. Then she turned back to the bed.

It was short work to drag the mattress off the box spring and onto the floor, where she was used to sleeping. It took up most of the space in the room, but at least her feet would be able to hang comfortably over the edge. And if she covered the box spring with one of her mother's batik throws and lots of pillows, it could almost be a couch.

Putting out her cigarette and lying back down, she watched the rats crawl over the laps of the dolls—heedless of velvet riding coats or gold lace princess gowns—to snuffle plastic hair, and nibble at delicate, porcelain fingers.

All day and all night
my desire for you
unwinds like a poisonous snake.
—SAMAR SEN, "LOVE"

That Monday morning, Kaye woke up early, got dressed, and pretended to go to school.

She had been pretending for the better part of a week now, ever since her grandma had insisted she was going to march down to the school and find out what was taking them so long to enroll her. There was no way to tell her that the transcripts were never coming, so Kaye packed a peanut-butter-and-honey sandwich and an orange and went out to kill time.

When they had first moved to Philadelphia, she had transferred easily to a new school. But then they'd started moving around, living for six months in University City and another four in South Philly and then a couple of weeks in the Museum District. Each time, she either had to find a way to get to her old school or transfer to the new one. About a year back, the

confusion had gotten the better of her, and she'd started working full-time at Chow Fat's instead. Ellen and Lloyd needed the
extra money and, aside from that, they needed the free food.

Kaye kicked a flattened soda can down the street ahead of
her. Even she could see that she was going in no good direction,
and not just literally. Her grandmother was right about her—she
was turning into her mother. No, worse, because she didn't even
have an ambition. Her only talents were shoplifting and a couple
of cigarette-lighting tricks you needed a Zippo to perform.

She considered going to Red Bank and trying to find Sue
and Liz's store. She had some money and could use some new
music, plus she might be able to sneak on the train for the
couple of stops. Her biggest problem was that Ellen hadn't said
what they'd called the place.

It occurred to her that maybe Corny would know. He
probably had another hour before the graveyard shift ended
and the morning guy came in. If she bought him coffee, she
might not mind her hanging around too much.

The Quick Check was mostly empty when she went in and
filled two large paper cups with hazelnut coffee. She fixed hers
with cinnamon and half-and-half, but she didn't know how he
liked his, so she pocketed little packets of sugar and several
creamers. The yawning woman didn't even look at Kaye as she
rang her up.

At the gas station, Kay found Corny sitting on the hood of
his car, playing chess on a small, magnetic board.

"Hey," Kaye called. He looked up with a not-so-friendly
expression on his face. She held out the coffee, and he just
looked confused.

"Aren't you supposed to be in school?" he asked finally.

"Dropped out," she said. "I'm going to get my GED."

He raised his eyebrows.

"Do you want the coffee or not?"

A car pulled up in front of one of the pumps. He sighed, sliding to his feet. "Put it by the board."

She pulled herself onto his car and carefully set down his cup, searching her pockets for the fixings. Then she uncapped hers and took a deep sip. The warmth of the liquid braced her against the cold, wet autumn morning.

Corny came back a few minutes later. After a considering look, he started pouring sugar into his coffee, stirring it with a pen from his pocket.

"Which you are you playing against?" Kaye asked, drawing up her knees.

He looked up at her with a snort. "Did you come here to fuck with me? Coffee is cheap."

"Geez, I'm just talking. Who's winning?"

Corny smirked. "He is, for now. Come on, what are you really doing here? People do not visit me. Being social to me is, like, tempting the Apocalypse or something."

"How come?"

Corny hopped down again with a groan as another car pulled up in front of the gas pump. She watched him sell a carton of cigarettes and fill the tank. She wondered if the owner would hire a sixteen-year-old girl—her last paycheck wasn't going to stretch much further. Corny had worked here when he was younger than she was now.

"Corny," she said when he came back, "do you know of any small CD stores in Red Bank?"

"Trying to bribe me for a ride?"

She sighed. "Paranoid. I just want to know what it's called."

He shrugged, playing out a couple more moves without editorial comment. "My comic book store is next to some CD store, but I don't know the name."

"What comics do you read?"

"Are you saying that you read comics?" Corny looked defensive, like maybe she was leading him into some verbal trap.

"Sure. Batman. Lenore. Too Much Coffee Man. Used to read Sandman, of course."

Corny regarded her speculatively for a moment, then finally relented. "I used to read X-everything, but I read a lot of Japanese stuff now."

"Like Akira?"

He shook his head. "Nah. Girl comics—the ones with the pretty boys and girls. Hey, do you know what *shonen-ai* is?" His expression was dubious.

Kaye shook her head.

Corny frowned. "I thought you *were* Japanese."

She shrugged. "My dad was part of some glam-goth band my mother worshipped in high school. I never met him. It was a groupie thing."

"Wild."

"I guess."

A car pulled into the station, but instead of parking in front of the pumps, it stopped next to Corny's car. A dark-skinned kid in a college letter jacket got out.

"Nice of you to show up today," Corny said, tossing him a set of the keys.

"I said I was sorry, man," the kid said.

Turning to Kaye, Corny said, "Where you going now?"

Kaye shrugged.

"You want to come with? You could hang out and wait for Janet to get home."

She nodded. "Sure."

They walked over to the trailer together.

He switched on the TV and walked back to his room. "I'm going to check my mail."

Kaye nodded and sat down on the couch, only then feeling a little awkward. It was weird to be in Janet's house without Janet. She flipped through the channels, settling on Cartoon Network.

After a few minutes, when he didn't return, she went back to his room. Corny's room was as unlike Janet's as a room could be. There were bookshelves on all the walls, filled to overflowing with paperbacks and comics. Corny was sitting at a desk that looked like it could barely hold up the equipment piled on it. Another box of wires and what looked like computer innards was next to his feet.

He was tapping on his keyboard as she came in. "Almost done."

Kaye sat down on the edge of his bed the way she would have if she was in Janet's room and picked up the nearest comic. It was all in Japanese. Blond hero and bad guy with really, really long black hair and a cool headpiece. A cute, fat ball with bat wings fluttering around as a sidekick. She flipped a little further. Hero naked and lashed in the bad guy's bed. She stopped flipping and stared at the picture. The blond's head was thrown back in either ecstasy or terror as the villain licked one of his nipples.

She looked up at Corny and held out the book. "Let me guess . . . this is *shonen-ai*?"

He shot a glance at her from the computer, but she couldn't miss his expression. "Yeah."

Kaye wasn't sure what to say, which was probably the point. "You like boys?"

"Those are some mighty pretty boys," Corny said.

"Does Janet know?" She couldn't understand why he would tell her if Janet didn't know, but Janet's emails were summaries of her whole day, boring and full of gossip about people Kaye had never met.

"Yeah, the whole family knows. It's no big deal. One night at dinner I said, 'Mom, you know the forbidden love that Spock has for Kirk? Well, then you should understand me liking guys. I'm gay.'" He sounded like he was daring Kaye to say something.

"I hope you aren't expecting a big reaction," Kaye said finally. "Because the only thing that I can think of is that is the weirdest coming-out story I have ever heard."

His face relaxed. Then she started to laugh and both of them were laughing and looking at the comic and laughing some more.

By the time Janet got back from school, Corny was sleeping and Kaye was reading a huge pile of kinky comics.

"Hey," Janet said, looking surprised to see her sofa occupied.

Kaye yawned and took a sip from a half-full glass of cherry cola. "Oh, hi. I was hanging out with your brother and then I figured I'd just wait for you to come home."

Janet made a face, dumping her armful of books onto the chair. "You make school look fun. If you're going to drop out, you might as well . . . I don't know."

"Do something seedy?"

"Totally. Look, I'm gonna go out . . . I gotta meet the guys. You want to come?"

Kaye stretched and got up. "Sure."

The Blue Snapper diner was open twenty-four hours, and they didn't care how long you sat in the mirror-lined booths or how little you ordered. Kenny and Doughboy sat at a table with a girl Kaye didn't know. She had short black hair, red nails, and thin, drawn-on eyebrows. Doughboy was wearing a short-sleeved team shirt over a long-sleeved black undershirt; the laces of his hiking boots spilled out from under the table. He'd cut his hair since she'd seen him last, and it was shaved along the back and sides. Kenny was wearing his silver jacket over a black T-shirt and looked exactly the same: scruffy, cute, and totally off-limits.

"Sorry I freaked the other night," Kaye said, shoving her hands in the pockets of her jeans and hoping no one wanted to talk about it too much.

"What happened?" the girl asked. Something made a clicking sound as she spoke, and Kaye realized that it was the girl's tongue-stud tapping against her teeth.

Doughboy opened his mouth to make some comment, and Kenny cut him off. "'S cool," he said with a jerk of his chin, "C'mon and slide in, ladies."

"Kaye," Janet said, sliding into the booth next to the girl, "this is Fatima—I emailed you about her. Kaye's my friend from Philly."

"Right. Sure. Hi." It was Fatima's party she'd missed two nights ago, and she had no idea what had been said after she left. Kenny was barely glancing in her direction, but Doughboy was watching her like she might do something weird or funny. Kaye wished she'd stayed in the trailer. This was too awkward.

"You're the girl with the mom who's in a band," Fatima said.

"Not anymore," Kaye said.

"Is it true that she fucked Lou Zampolis? Janet said she sang backup for Chainsuck."

Kaye grimaced. She wondered if all her emails had been relayed like this. "Unfortunately."

"Does that freak you out—I mean does she, like, screw your boyfriends and shit?"

Kaye raised her eyebrows. "I don't date guys in bands." She didn't point out that although Lou Zampolis was rumored to date high school girls, he was closer in age to her mother than to them.

"I have this friend, right," Fatima said, "and her mother and her sister both slept with the guy that got her knocked up."

"Erin, right?" Janet said. "She's in rehab."

The waitress stopped by their table. She was wearing a brown uniform, and her name tag read RITA. "Can I get you guys anything?"

"Diet whatever," Janet said.

"Coffee," Kaye chimed in.

"I want . . . Can I have some Disco Fries, Rita?" Doughboy said.

"I'll be back with refills in a minute," the waitress said, smiling at Dough for using her name.

Kenny turned to get his cigarettes and lighter out of the pocket of his coat, and Kaye saw a tattoo on the back of his neck. It was a tribal design of what looked like a scarab. It made her wonder what other tattoos he might have snaking down areas covered by his shirt. Janet would know.

"Anyone want?" he asked, offering up the pack.

"I do," Kaye said.

"Whatever you want, you get," he tossed back, giving her a cigarette with a smirk that made the heat rise to her face.

Janet was talking to Fatima about Erin's baby, not paying attention to either of them at the moment. Doughboy was picking at the cheese-and-gravy-covered fries the waitress plunked down in front of him.

"Want to see a trick?" Kaye asked, even though it was a bad idea to encourage Kenny. "Let me see your lighter."

It was silver with an enamel eight-ball medallion soldered to the front of it. He handed it over.

Kaye had learned this trick from Liz back in her mother's Sweet Pussy days. Liz had offered to teach it to her, claiming that was a sure way to impress the boys, or the girls. Kaye had had no idea why Liz would want to impress anyone since she already had Sue, but she'd learned the trick and it had impressed bartenders, at least.

Kaye held the metal body of the lighter between the first two fingers of her left hand; then she flipped it first over and then under each finger so that the metal shimmered like a minnow. Faster and faster, she made the lighter hurdle her fingers. Then she stopped, flicked the lid open, and lit it, all with her right hand resting on the table. She leaned over and generously offered the flame to Kenny's cigarette.

Once Kaye found the record store, she would have to tell Liz that she had been right. Both the boys looked impressed. Dough wasn't even looking at his fries.

Kenny's lopsided grin was an invitation to mischief.

"Cool," Doughboy said. "Want to show me how to do that?"

"Sure," Kaye said, lighting her own cigarette and taking a deep breath of bitter smoke. She showed him, doing the trick in slow motion so that he could see how it was done, then letting him try it.

"I gotta get out of the booth for a minute," Kenny said, and she and Doughboy scooted out.

Before she could get back in, Kenny nudged her arm and jerked his head toward the bathrooms.

"Be right back," Kaye told Janet, dropping her cigarette into the ashtray.

Janet must not have noticed anything since she just nodded.

Kaye walked behind Kenny to the small hallway. Even though she had no idea what he wanted, her cheeks were already warm, and a strange thrill was coiling in her belly.

Once they were in the hallway, Kenny turned to her and draped his lean body against the wall.

"What did you do to me?" Kenny asked, taking a quick drag from his cigarette and rubbing the stubble along his cheekbone with the back of one hand.

Kaye shook her head. "Nothing. What do you mean?"

He lowered his voice, speaking with a quiet intensity. "The other night. The horse. What did you do?" He paused and looked the other way before continuing. "I can't stop thinking about you."

Kaye was stunned. "I . . . honestly . . . I didn't *do* anything."

"Well, undo it," he said, scowling.

She struggled for an explanation. "Sometimes when I daydream . . . things happen. I was just thinking about riding the horse. I didn't even hear you come in." Her cheeks felt even hotter when she remembered a theory Sue had once explained about why all young girls want their own ponies.

He looked at her as intensely as he had in the attic of the carousel building, bringing his cigarette to his lips again. "This is fucked," he said a little desperately. "I mean it; I can't get you out of my head. You're all I think about, all day long."

Kaye had no idea what to say to that.

He took a step closer to her without seeming to notice. "You have to do something."

She took a step back, but the wall halted her. She could feel the cool tile against her spine. The pay phone to her right blocked her view of the register. "I'm sorry," she said.

He took another step, until his chest was against hers. "I want you," he said urgently. His knee moved between her legs.

"We're in a diner," Kaye said, grabbing him by the shoulders so that he had to look at her face. He was pale except for a touch of hectic pink in the cheeks. His eyes looked glazed.

"I want to stop wanting you," he said and moved to kiss her. Kaye turned her head so that he got a mouthful of hair, but it didn't seem to bother him. He kissed his way down her throat, biting the skin punishingly, licking the bites with his tongue. One of his hands ran up from her waist to cup her breast while the other threaded through her hair.

Her hands were still clenched on his shoulders. She could shove him off. She had to shove him off. But her traitorous body urged her to wait another moment, to glory in the feeling of being wanted. And her traitorous heart was tempted by chaos.

"Guys, I was . . . what the hell?"

Kenny pushed back from Kaye at the sound of Janet's voice. Several strands of long blond hair were still caught on his hand, shimmering like spiderwebs.

He drew himself up. "Don't give me more of your insecure girlfriend bullshit."

Janet had tears in her eyes. "You were kissing her!"

"Calm the fuck down!"

Kaye fled to the bathroom, locking herself in a stall and sliding into a sitting position on the dirty floor.

Her heart was beating so fast, she thought it might beat its way out of her chest. The space was too small for pacing, but she wanted to pace, wanted to do something that would work answers out of her tangled mind. Magic, if there was such a thing, should not work like this. She should not be able to enchant someone she barely knew without even deciding to do it.

The delight was the worst part, the part of her that could overlook the guilt and see the poetic justice in making Kenny unable to stop thinking about her freaky self. It would be easy to like him, she thought, cute and cool and wanting her. And unlike an unattainable faerie knight, he was someone she could really have. Except it would make her a terrible friend and a bad person.

Taking a deep breath, she left the stall. She went to the

sinks and splashed her face with water from the tap. Looking up, she saw her own reflection in the mirror, faded red Chow Fat T-shirt spattered with dark droplets of water, eye makeup smudgy and indistinct, blond hair hanging in tangled strands.

Something caught her eye as she turned away, though. Approaching the mirror, she looked at her face again, closely. She looked the same as ever. Kaye shook her head and walked to the door. For a moment, she had thought that the face she saw in the mirror was pale green with ink-drop black eyes.

More coffees were on the table when she got back, and she sipped at the one in front of where she had been sitting. Her cigarette had burned down to ash in the glass tray. Dough-boy was telling Kenny about the new car he was restoring, and Janet was glaring at Kaye.

"Your pardon," said a voice that was both familiar and strange.

Kaye froze. Her mind was screaming that this was impossible. It was against the rules. They never did this. It was one thing to believe in faeries; it was totally another thing if you weren't allowed to even have a choice about it. If they could just walk into your normal life, then they were a part of normal life, and she could no longer separate the unreal world from the real one.

But Roiben was indeed standing beside their booth. His hair was white as salt under the fluorescent lights and was pulled back from his face. He was wearing a long black wool coat that hid whatever he was wearing underneath all the way down to his thoroughly modern leather boots. There was so little color in his face that he seemed to be entirely monochromatic, a picture shot in black-and-white film.

"Who's the goth?" Kaye heard Doughboy say.

"Robin, I think his name is," Janet replied glumly.

Roiben raised an eyebrow when he heard that, but he went on. "May I speak with you a moment?"

She felt incapable of doing more than nodding her head. Getting up from the booth, she walked with him to an empty table. Neither one sat down.

"I came to give you this." Roiben reached into his coat and took out a lump of black cloth from some well-hidden pocket. And smiled, the same smile she remembered from the forest, the one that was just for her. "It's your shirt, back from the dead."

"Like you," she said.

He nodded slightly. "Indeed."

"My friends told me not to talk to you." She hadn't known she was going to say that till it came out of her mouth. The words felt like thorns falling from her tongue.

He looked down and took a breath. "Your friends? Not, I assume, those friends." His gaze flickered toward the booth, and she shook her head.

"Lutie and Spike," she said.

His eyes were dark when he looked at her again, and the smile was gone. "I killed a friend of theirs. Perhaps a friend of yours."

Around her, people were eating and laughing and talking, but those normal sounds felt as far away and out of place as a laugh track. "You killed Gristle."

He nodded.

She stared at him, as though things might somehow reshuffle to make sense. "How? Why? Why are you telling me this?"

Roiben didn't meet her gaze as he spoke. "Is there some excuse that I could give you that would make it better? Some explanation that you would find acceptable?"

"That's your answer? Don't you even care?"

"You have the shirt. I have done what I came here to do."

She grabbed his arm and moved around to face him. "You owe me three questions."

He stiffened, but his face remained blank. "Very well."

Anger surged up in her, a bitter helpless feeling. "Why did you kill Gristle?"

"My mistress bade me do so. I have little choice in my obedience." Roiben tucked his long fingers into the pockets of the coat. He spoke matter-of-factly, as though he was bored by his own answers.

"Right," Kaye said. "So if she told you to jump off a bridge . . . ?"

"Exactly." There was no irony in his tone. "Shall I consider that your second question?"

Kaye stopped and took a breath, her face filling with heat. She was so angry that she was shaking.

"Why don't you . . . ," she began, and stopped herself. She had to think. Anger was making her careless and stupid. She had one more question, and she was determined that she would use it to piss him off, if nothing else. She thought about the note she'd gotten in the acorn and the warning she'd been given. "What's your full name?"

He looked like he would choke on the air he breathed. "What?"

"That's my third question: What is your full name?" She didn't know what she had done, not really. She only knew that she was forcing him to do something he didn't want to do, and that suited her fine.

Roiben's eyes darkened with fury. "Rath Roiben Rye, much may the knowledge please you."

Her eyes narrowed. "It's a nice name."

"You are too clever by half. Too clever for your own good, I think."

"Kiss my ass, Rath Roiben Rye."

He grabbed her by the arm before she even saw him move. She raised her hand to ward off the coming blow. He threw her forward. She shrieked. Her hand and knee connected hard with the linoleum floor. She looked up, half expecting to see the gleam of a sword, but instead he pulled her jeans hard at the waistband and pressed his mouth against the exposed swell of her hip.

Time seemed to slow as she slipped on the slick floor, as he rose easily to his feet, as diner patrons stared, as Kenny struggled out from the booth.

Roiben stood over her. He spoke tonelessly. "That is the nature of servitude, Kaye. It is literal-minded and not at all clever. Be careful with your barbs."

"Who the fuck do you think you are?" Kenny said, finally there, bending down to help Kaye up.

"Ask her," Roiben said, indicating Kaye with his chin. "Now she knows exactly who I am." He turned and walked out of the diner.

Tears welled up in Kaye's eyes.

"Come on," Fatima was saying, although Kaye was barely paying attention. "Let's take her outside. Just us girls."

Fatima and Janet led her outside and sat down on the hood

of one of the parked cars. Kaye dimly hoped it belonged to one
of them as she sat down, wiping tears from her cheeks. Already
she'd stopped crying; the tears were more from shock than anything else.

Fatima lit a cigarette and handed it to Kaye. She took a
deep drag, but her throat felt thick and the smoke just made
her cough.

"I had a boyfriend like that once. Used to beat the shit out
of me." Fatima sat next to Kaye and patted her back.

"Maybe he saw you with Kenny," Janet said without looking at her. She was leaning against a headlight, staring out
across the highway at the military base opposite the diner.

"I'm sorry," Kaye said miserably.

"Give her a break," Fatima said. "It's not like you didn't do
the same thing to me."

Janet turned to look at Kaye then. "You're not going to get
him, you know. He might want to fuck you, but he'd never go
out with you."

Kaye just nodded, bringing the cigarette to her mouth with
trembling hands. It would have been a better idea, she decided,
if she had sworn off boys entirely.

"Is that Robin guy going to come after you?" Fatima asked.
Kaye almost wanted to laugh at her concern. If he did, no one
could do anything to stop him. He'd moved faster than Kaye
could even see. She'd been very stupid not to be afraid of him.

"I don't think so," she said finally.

Kenny and Doughboy walked out of the diner, swaggering
in tandem toward the girls.

"Everything okay?" Kenny asked.

"Just a couple of bruises," Kaye said. "No big deal."

"Damn," Doughboy said. "Between the other night and tonight, you're going to be too paranoid to hang out with us."

Kaye tried to smile, but she couldn't help wondering how double-edged those words were.

"Want me to drive you home?" Kenny asked.

Kaye looked up, about to thank him, when Fatima interrupted. "Why don't you take Janet home, and I'll drop off Dough and Kaye."

Kenny looked down at the scuffed tops of his Doc Martens and sighed. "Right."

Fatima drove Kaye home in relative silence, and she was grateful. The radio was on, and she just sat in the passenger seat and pretended to listen. When Fatima pulled up in front of Kaye's grandmother's house, she cut the lights.

"I don't know what happened with you and Kenny," Fatima began.

"Me neither," Kaye said with a short laugh.

The other girl smiled and bit one of her manicured nails. "If you were just looking for some way to piss off your boyfriend, don't do it. Janet really loves Kenny, y'know? She's devoted."

Kaye opened the door and got out of the car. "Thanks for the ride."

"No problem." Fatima flicked the car lights back on.

Kaye slammed the door of the blue Honda and went inside.

In the kitchen, Ellen sat at the table with a spiral notebook in front of her, phone to her ear. When she saw Kaye come in, she gestured toward the stove. There was a pot of cold spaghetti and sausages. Kaye took a fork and picked at some of the spaghetti.

"So you think you can get Charlotte?" her mother said into the phone as she doodled on the pad.

"All right, call me when you know. Absolutely. 'Bye, chickadee."

Ellen hung up the phone, and Kaye looked over at her expectantly.

Her mother smiled and took a sip from a mug on the table. "We're going to New York!"

Kaye just stared. "What?"

"Well, it's not totally definite, but Rhonda wants me to front her new all-girl group, Meow Factory, and she thinks she can get Charlotte Charlie. I said that if they can get her, I'm in. There are so many more clubs in New York."

"I don't want to move," Kaye said.

"We can crash with Rhonda until we can find another place to live. You'll love New York."

"I love it here."

"We can't impose on my mother forever," Ellen said. "Besides, she's a pain in your ass as much as mine."

"I applied for a job today. Grandma will be a lot happier once I'm bringing home money. You could join a band around here."

"Nothing's set in stone," Ellen said, "but I think you should really get used to the idea of New York, honey. If I'd wanted to stay in Jersey, I would have done it years ago."

A hundred matchbooks, from a hundred bars that her mother played one gig in, or from restaurants that they got a meal in, or from men that they lived with. A hundred matchbooks, all on fire.

She was on fire too, aflame in a way she was not sure she understood. Adrenaline turned her fingers to ice, drawing her heat inward to dance in her head, anger and a strange sense of possibility thrumming through her veins.

Kaye looked around her dark bedroom, lit only by the flickering orange light. The glassy eyes of the dolls danced with flames. The rats curled up on one another in the far corner of the cage. Kaye breathed in the sharp smell of sulfur as she struck another matchbook, watching the flame catch across the rows of white match heads, the cardboard covering exploding into fire. She turned the paper in her hands, watching it burn.

I ate the mythology & dreamt.
—Yusef Komunyakaa, "Blackberries"

Kaye awoke to a scratching at the window. The room was dark and the house was silent.

Something peered in at her. Tiny black eyes blinked beneath heavy eyebrows, and long ears rose up from either side of a bare head.

"Spike?" Kaye whispered, crawling up off the mattress on the floor where she had been sleeping. The covers tangled with her legs.

He tapped again, eyebrows furrowing. He was smaller than she remembered and clad only in a thin bark that ran over his waist and down part of his legs. At his elbows, points extended into the shape of thorns.

Behind him, she could make out Lutie-loo's thin form, incandescent against the dark tiles of the roof. Her wings were so translucent as to be nearly invisible.

Kaye pushed on the window, but it took several tries to

get it unstuck from the old, swollen sill. Two white moths fluttered in.

"Spike!" Kaye said. "Lutie! Where have you been? I've been back for days and days. I left milk out for you, but I think one of the cats got it."

The little man cocked one eye toward her, like a sparrow. "The Thistlewitch is waiting," Spike said. "Hurry."

His tone of voice was odd, urgent and strangely unfriendly. He had never talked to her that way before. Still, she obeyed out of familiarity: same old room, same little friends coming in the middle of the night to take her to catch fireflies or pick sour cherries. She pulled a black sweater on over the white old-lady nightgown her grandmother had loaned her to sleep in and kicked on her boots. Then she scanned the room for her coat, but it was just another black, soft pile in the dark, and she left it. The sweater was warm enough.

Kaye climbed out onto the roof. "Why does she want to see me?" Kaye had always thought of the Thistlewitch as a crotchety aunt, someone who didn't like to play and who you could get in trouble with.

"There's something she needs to tell you."

"Can't you tell me?" Kaye said. She swung her legs off the edge of the roof while Spike scuttled down over the bark and Lutie glided down on iridescent wings.

"Come on," Spike said.

Kaye pushed herself off the edge and dropped. The dry branches of a rhododendron bush scratched her legs as she landed, spry as a cat, on her two feet.

They ran toward the street, Lutie-loo dancing half in the air around Kaye whispering, "I missed you, I missed you."

"This way," Spike said impatiently.

"I missed you too," Kaye said to Lutie, reaching out her hand to brush the light body. Lutie felt slick as water, smooth as smoke.

The Glass Swamp, so called because of the abundance of broken bottles choking the little stream, ran beneath the road a half a mile along the street. They climbed down the steep bank, Kaye's boots slipping in the mud. The thin rivulets of water shimmered with multicolor hues under the street lights, broken glass turned to panes of a church window.

"What's happening? What's the matter?" she called as quietly as she could and still have Spike hear her. Something was definitely wrong—he was hurrying along like he couldn't look her in the face. But then, maybe she was too old to be fun anymore.

He didn't answer.

Lutie darted up to her, hair whipping the air like a banner of cream. "We have to hurry. Don't worry. It's good news—good news."

"Hush," Spike said.

The heavy growth close to the stream forced her to pick her way near the water's edge. Kaye stepped carefully along the bank, illuminated only by the dim light of Lutie's glow. They walked in silence. She wasn't sure whether the next step would plunge her boot into cold water.

A flash of white caught her eye—cracked eggshells bobbed in the narrow stream. Kaye stopped to watch the armada of shells, some small and spotted, others gleaming supermarket white. In the center of one, a spider scuttled from side to side, an unwilling captain. In another, a black pin anchored the center as the shell spun dizzily.

Kaye heard a chuckle.

"Much can be divined from an eggshell," the Thistlewitch said. Large black eyes peered out from the braided weeds and briars that covered her head like hair. She was sitting on the opposite side of the riverbank, her squat body covered in layers of drab cloth.

"They have even caught us," the Thistlewitch went on, "with the brewing of eggshells. Pride makes braggarts of even the wisest of the Folk, so it is said."

Kaye had sometimes been a little afraid of her, but this time she felt nothing but relief. The Thistlewitch had kind eyes, and her scratchy voice was sweetly familiar. She was as unlike Roiben and his demon-horse as anything could be.

"Hullo," Kaye said, not sure how to address her. When she was a child, most of the times she had spoken to the faerie had involved a splinter or a skinned knee or an apology for dragging one of her friends Ironside for a prank. "Spike said you had something to tell me."

The Thistlewitch regarded her for a long moment, as if taking her measure.

"So much focus on the egg—it is life, it is food, it is answer to a hundred riddles—but look at its shell. Secrets are writ on its walls. Secrets lie in the entrails, in the dregs, at the edges." The Thistlewitch poked a pin into either side of a tiny blue egg and put it to her lips. Her cheeks puffed out with air, and a trickle of clear, thick snotlike liquid drizzled into a copper bowl in her lap.

Kaye looked at the eggshells, still bobbing down the stream. She didn't understand. What secrets did they hold, except a spider and a pin?

The Thistlewitch tapped the damp earth beside her. "Would you see what I see, Kaye? Sit beside me."

Kaye looked for a dry patch and crossed the stream with an easy leap.

A tiny being wearing a moleskin coat slithered onto the Thistlewitch's lap and poked its head inquisitively into the bowl.

"Once, there were two nearby low courts, the bright and the dark, the Seelie and the Unseelie, the Folk of the air and the Folk of the earth. They fought like a serpent devouring its own tail, but we kept from their affairs, kept to our hidden groves and underground streams, and they forgot us. Then they made truce and remembered that rulers must have subjects, especially if they wish to avoid the reach of the High Court of Elfhame. There is such a habit of service among us." The Thistlewitch stroked the gleaming fur of the little faerie's coat absently as she spoke. "They brought back the Tithe, the sacrifice of a beautiful and talented mortal. In the Seelie Court they may steal away a poet to join their company, but the Unseelie Court requires blood. In exchange, those who dwell in Unseelie lands must bind themselves into service. Their service is hard, Kaye, and their amusements are cruel. And now you have drawn their notice."

"Because of Roiben?"

"Oh, do speak his name again," Spike hissed. "Shall we invite the whole Unseelie Court to afternoon tea while we're being daft?"

"Hush," the Thistlewitch soothed. Spike stomped his foot and looked away.

"You mustn't even use their speaking names aloud," the

Thistlewitch told Kaye. "The Unseelie Court is terrible, terrible and dangerous. And of the Unseelie Court, no knight is as feared as . . . the one you spoke with. When the truce was made, each of the Queens exchanged their best knights—he was the offering from the Seelie Court. The Queen sends him on the worst of her errands."

"He is so unpredictable that even his Queen cannot trust him. He's as likely to be kind as to kill you," Spike put in. "He killed Gristle."

"I know," Kaye said. "He told me."

Spike looked at the Thistlewitch in surprise. "That's exactly what I mean! What perverse ovation of friendship is that?"

"How . . . how did he do it?" Kaye asked, half of her dreading the answer, but needing to know nonetheless. "How did Gristle die?"

Lutie flitted to hover in front of her, tiny face mournful. "He was with me. We went to the knowe—the faerie hill. There was cowslip wine, and Gristle wanted me to help him filch a bottle. He was going to trade it for a pair of pretty boots from one of his hob friends.

"It was easy to find the way inside. There's a patch of grass that's all brown and that's the door. We got the bottle, easy-peasy, and were on our way out when we saw the cakes."

"Cakes?" Kaye was baffled.

"Beautiful white honey cakes, heaped on a plate for the taking. Eat 'em and you get wiser, you know."

"I don't think it works that way," Kaye said.

"Of course it does," Lutie-loo scolded. "How else would it work?"

Continuing, the tiny faerie gripped onto a thin twig and

hung from a low bush as she spoke. "He swallowed five before they caught him."

Kaye didn't point out that if these cakes were supposed to make him wiser, it should have occurred to him to stop after one. It didn't make his death any less horrifying.

"They probably would have let him go, but she needed a fox for her hunt. Since he stole the cakes, she said he was the perfect fox. Oh, Kaye it was awful. They had these dogs and horses, and they just rode him down. Roiben was the one that got him."

"What is it with you fools and saying his name?" Spike growled.

Kaye shook her head. Roiben had killed Gristle for fun? Because he stole some food? And she'd helped the bastard. It made her skin crawl to think of the easy way she'd spoken with Roiben, the ways she had thought of him. She wondered what exactly could be done with a name, what sort of revenge she could really have.

The Thistlewitch held out the little egg. "Come, Kaye, blow out the insides and then break it open. There is a secret for you."

Kaye took the little blue egg. It was so light that she was afraid it would break from the slight pressure of her fingers.

She knelt over the Thistlewitch's bowl and blew lightly into the pinhole of the egg. A viscous stream of albumen and yolk slithered from the other side, dropping into the bowl.

"Now break it."

Kaye pressed her thumb against the egg and the whole side of it collapsed, still held together by a thin membrane.

Spike and Lutie looked surprised, but the Thistlewitch just nodded.

"I did it wrong," Kaye said, and brushed the eggshells into the stream. Unlike the little boats, this egg was a shower of confetti on the water.

"Let me just speak another secret then, child, since this one eludes you. If you think on it, I'm sure that you'll admit there's something passing strange about you. A strangeness, not just of manner, but of something else. The scent of it, the spoor of it, warns Ironsiders off, makes them wary and draws them in all the same."

Kaye shook her head, not sure where this was going.

"Tell her a different secret," Spike warned. "This one will only make things harder."

"You are one of us," the Thistlewitch said to Kaye, black eyes glittering like jewels.

"What?" She'd heard what was said, she understood, she was just stalling for time for her brain to start working again. She could not seem to get a breath of air into her lungs. There were grades to impossible, levels, at least, of unreality. And each time Kaye thought things were at their weirdest, the ground seemed to open up beneath her.

"Mortal girls are stupid and slow," Lutie said. "You don't have to pretend anymore."

She was shaking her head, but even as she did it, she knew it was true. It felt true, unbalancing and rebalancing her world so neatly that she wondered how she didn't think of it before now. After all, why would only she be visited by faeries? Why would only she have magic she couldn't control?

"Why didn't you tell me?" Kaye demanded.

"Too chancy," Spike said.

"So why are you telling me now?"

"Because it is you who will be chosen for the Tithe." The Thistlewitch crossed her lanky arms serenely. "And because it is your right to know."

Spike snorted.

"What? But you said I'm not . . ." She stopped herself. Not one single intelligent comment had come out of her mouth all night, and she doubted that was likely to change.

"They figure you're human," Spike said. "And that's a good thing."

"Some crazy faeries want to kill me and you think it's a good thing? Hey, I thought we were friends."

Spike didn't even have the grace to smile at the weak joke. He was entirely wrapped up in his planning. "There is a knight from the Seelie Court. He can pull the glamour off you. It will look like the Unseelie Queen wanted to sacrifice one of our own—the sort of jest many would well believe of her. It will cost her the legitimacy of her rule. And since she will have forfeited the bargain, it will mean the Folk like us will remain unsworn." Spike took a breath. "We need your help."

Kaye bit her upper lip, running her teeth over it in deep concentration. "I'm really confused right now—you guys know that, right?"

"If you help us, we'll be freeeeee," Lutie said. "Seven years of free!"

"So what's the difference between the Seelie Court and the Unseelie Court?"

"There are many, many courts, Seelie and Unseelie alike. But it is nearly always true that the Unseelie Courts are worse and that the gentry of either court enjoy their rule over the commoners and still more over the solitary fey. We, without ties to any courts, are at the mercy of whoever rules the lands to which we are tied."

"So why don't you just leave?"

"Some of us cannot, the tree people, for instance. But for the others, where would we go? Another court might be harder than this one."

"Why do the solitary fey trade their freedom for a human sacrifice?"

"The human sacrifice is a show of power. But it's also a gift to their subjects. Killing mortals—at least those who haven't been tricked into agreeing with it—is forbidden to most of us," said Spike. "They offer us a small delight in exchange for our will, in part to please us and in part because it's a reminder that they could force us into obedience."

"But won't they just take you back by force, then?"

"No. They must obey the agreement as we do. They are bound by its constraints. If the sacrifice is voided, then we are free for seven years. None may command us."

"Look, you guys, you know I'll help you. I'd help you do anything."

The huge smile on Spike's face chased away all her former concern over his gruffness. He must have just been worried she'd say no. Lutie flew around her happily, lifting up strands of her hair and either tangling or braiding them; Kaye couldn't be sure.

She took a deep breath and, ignoring Lutie's ministrations, turned to the Thistlewitch. "How did this happen? If I'm like you, how come I live with my . . . with Ellen? *Is* she my mother?"

The Thistlewitch looked into the river, her gaze following the wobbling egg-boats. "Do you know what a changeling is?

In ancient times, we usually left stock—bits of wood or dying fey—enchanted to look like a stolen babe and left in the cradle. It is rarely that we leave one of our own behind, but when we do, the child's fey nature becomes harder and harder to conceal as it grows. In the end, they all return to Faerie."

"But why—not why do they return, but why me? Why leave me?"

Spike shook his head. "We don't know the answer to that any more than we know why we were told to watch you."

It was staggering to Kaye to realize that there might be another Kaye Fierch, the real Kaye Fierch, off somewhere in Faerie. "You said . . . *glamoured*. Does that mean I don't look like this?"

"It's a very powerful glamour. Someone put it on to stay." Spike nodded sagely.

"What do I really look like?"

"Well, you're a pixie, if that helps." Spike scratched his head. "Usually means green."

Kaye closed her eyes tightly, shaking her head. "How can I see me?"

"I don't advise it," Spike said. "Once you pull the magic off, no one we know can put it back on so well. Just let it be until Samhain—that's when the Tithe is. Someone might figure out what you are if you go messing with your face."

"Soon it'll be off for good and you won't have to pretend to be mortal anymore if you don't want," Lutie chirped.

"If the glamour on me is so good, how did you know what I was?"

The Thistlewitch smiled. "Glamour is the stuff of illusion, but sometimes, if deftly woven, it can be more than a mere disguise. Fantastical pockets can actually hold baubles, an illusionary umbrella can protect one from the rain, and magical gold can remain gold, at least until the warmth of the magician's hand fades from the coins. The magic on you is the strongest I have seen, Kaye. It protects you even from the touch of iron, which burns faerie flesh. I know you to be a pixie because I saw you when you were very small and we lived in Seelie lands. The Queen herself asked us to look after you."

"But why?" Something about the Thistlewitch's story bothered Kaye. It made her wonder just whose plan they were executing.

"Who can tell the whims of Queens?"

"What if I did want to remove the glamour?" Kaye insisted.

The Thistlewitch took a step toward her. "The ways of removing faerie magic are many. A four-leaf clover, rowan berries, looking at yourself through a rock with a natural hole. It is your decision to make."

Kaye took a deep breath. She needed to think. "I'm going to go back to bed."

"One more thing," the Thistlewitch said as Kaye rose from the bank and dusted off the backs of her thighs. "Heed the warning of your shattered eggshell. You have sought chaos and now chaos seeks you."

"What does that mean?"

The Thistlewitch smiled. "Time will tell. It always does."

Kaye stood on the lawn of her grandmother's house. It was dark except for the silvery moon, the moon that didn't seem part of a story right now, just a cold rock glowing with reflected light.

It was the bare trees that looked alive, their twisted branches sharp arrows that might pierce her heart.

Still, she could not go inside the house. She sat in the dew-damp grass and ripped up clumps of it, tossing them in the air and feeling vaguely guilty about it. Some gnome ought to pop out of the tree and scold her for torturing the lawn.

A pixie. The word sounded so . . . so *frolicky*. It made her smile, though, to think of being magical, of having wings like Lutie, of having quick fingers like poor Gristle.

Her stomach clenched when she thought about her mother, though. Her mother, whose head she'd fished out of toilets, who dragged them from apartment to apartment and from bar to bar following some distant dream. Her mother, who once broke one of Kaye's favorite LPs because she was "sick of listening to that talentless bitch." Her mother, who had never told her she was weird, had always encouraged her to think for herself, stood up for her, and never, ever told her that she was a liar.

What would her mother think if she realized that her daughter wasn't the girl she'd lived with for sixteen years? No, Ellen's baby had been boosted by quick-fingered elves.

It was just too fucked-up to dwell on.

And if she wasn't Kaye Fierch, freaky human girl, then what was she? She knew that they didn't want her to mess up the plan for Halloween, but right now, she just wanted to see what she looked like.

There were patches of clover on the lawn.

Leaning into the patch of brown, half-dead clover, she spread her fingers out and searched. There were so many, even in autumn, there had to be one with four leaves.

It was slow going in the dark, and yet none of the clover she dug through had more or less than three leaves. She was getting desperate enough to tear one of the heart-shaped leaves down the middle and find out whether this magic stuff was more symbolic or literal. Still, it wasn't like she had to find it, she only had to touch it. . . .

Oh, that was too stupid. That could never work. Even if it did work it was still stupid.

Kaye spread herself out on the ground, hoping no cars were driving by at this hour. Then she rolled over the patch of clover. The ground was cold, the dew dusted with frost. She rolled dizzily, holding her arms above her head. She had to laugh as she did it—the whole thing was absurd and it was making her damp and really, really cold, but there was something in the smell of the earth and the touch of the grass that enervated her. Her laughter spun up out of her mouth in warm gusts of breath.

She didn't feel changed, but she did feel better. She was grinning like a fool, anxiety put to rest by silliness.

Lying back, Kaye tried to imagine herself as a faerie, all sparkly with hair that was always blowing in the breeze. The only image she could summon up, however, was that of a pale green face she had thought she'd seen as she was leaving the diner bathroom.

Kaye rolled over to get up and go inside when she noticed that a piece of skin on her hand was loose. When she touched it with a tentative finger, it sloughed off like a sunburn, revealing tender green skin. Kaye licked her finger and tried to rub off the pigment. It didn't come off; the area only spread wider. Her hand tasted like dirt.

Kaye stopped moving. She was scared, scared, sick with scared, but calm too, calm as nothing. *Get a grip*, she told herself, *you wanted to see this*.

Her eyes itched, and she rubbed her knucklebones over them. Something came off against her fingers. It felt like a contact lens, but when she looked down, she saw that with the rubbing, even more skin had come off her hands.

As she looked up, it seemed that the whole world had grown brighter, shimmering with light. Colors danced along the grass. The brown of the trees was many-hued, the wrinkles of shadows deep as newly turned secrets, and beautiful.

She spread her arms as wide as they would go. She could smell the pungent green of the grass she stamped as she rose. She could smell the sharp chill of the air as she spun, full of car exhaust, of crumpled leaves, of smoke from some distant leaf pile burning. She could smell the rot of desiccated wood, the spoilage of the hoards that ants piled away for winter. She could hear the churning of termites, the whine of electricity in the house, the wind rustling a thousand paper-dry leaves.

She could taste chemicals in the air—iron, smoke, other things she had no names for. They played over her tongue in dark harmony.

It was too much. It was overwhelming. There were so many sensations buffeting her, too many for her to filter out. She couldn't go inside the house like this, but right now she wanted to; she wanted to burrow under her blankets and wait for all-forgiving dawn. She wasn't ready for this—it had been a whim, her curiosity.

Spike had warned her. Why did she never listen? Why had she never met a bad idea she didn't like?

She should go back now, back to the swamp, confess all, and let the Thistlewitch explain what she'd just done to herself. Kaye forced herself to take a few quick breaths without thinking what they tasted like. She was fine, better than fine, she was fucking supernatural. All she had to do was walk back to the swamp and not touch any of her skin on the way.

But once she started, she knew she couldn't walk. She was running. Running through the backyards of houses, hearing dogs barking, her legs wet from unmowed grass. Running, through a parking lot, mostly empty, where a boy pushing carts stopped to look at her, and into the lot behind, and the sweet reek of trash, where she stopped, panting, and held her sides. There it was, the thin disguise of trees and the small river that flowed through it.

"Spike! Lutie!" Kaye called, frightened by the breathless gasp of her own voice. "Please . . ."

Nothing answered her but silence.

Kaye staggered down the hill, her boots sinking in the mud. The eggshells were gone. There was only the stink of stagnant water. The shattered bottles shimmered like jagged jewels through her new eyes. She stopped, awed by the beauty.

"Please, Lutie, someone . . ."

No one answered.

Kaye sat down in the cold mud. She could wait. She would have to wait.

The leaves over her shifted and blew with the morning wind as she woke from a sleep she didn't recall falling into. Drops of cold water tapped her cheek, then her arm, then the lid of her one eye. Kaye sat up. Her eyes felt hard and her lips were sore and swollen.

The rain must have woken her.

There was a green sheen to Kaye's skin when she turned her arm against the light. Her fingers seemed too long and curled fluidly with a new fourth joint, coiling like snails when she made a fist. She brought up her other hand, where the skin had come loose last night. Beneath it, her skin was emerald.

No one had come. Another droplet spattered her bare leg, and she jerked upright. Her nightgown was filthy, and she was shivering, even under her sweater.

Biting back tears, Kaye folded her arms around herself and started walking. She couldn't go home—not yet, not when she knew she wasn't the girl who belonged there, not when her skin was flaking off so her true self was impossible to hide—but she had to get out of the rain. At least Janet couldn't call her a liar this time.

She stopped in a parking lot and twisted the side mirror of a car toward her so that she could see her profile. Her hair was matted in a nimbus of twigs, wet with dew, and she saw that her skin was shadowed with the lush dark green of moss. Not a stain, but a tint, as though a veil of green lay over her. Her ear was longer, sticking up through her hair to the top of her head. Her cheek, sunken and sharp, and her eye, black, all shiny black, with a pinpoint of white pupil. Like a bird eye or a single bead.

She reached up and touched her face. The skin tore easily, revealing a strip of grass-green skin.

Her hand hit the mirror, spiderwebbing the glass, and surprising her. Ignoring the pain in her wrist and the damp burn of blood on her knuckles, she started to run.

Corny squinted. A girl in green makeup ran across the street and under the awning of the gas station. She looked up, and he thought he recognized her, but when she got closer, he wasn't so sure.

"I was going to Janet's," she said, sounding just like Kaye. "But I just remembered she's at school."

Up close the girl didn't look anything like Kaye. She didn't look anything like anybody. Her eyes were black as oil spills. She was too thin. Tall ears parted her tangled hair on either side of her head. Her skin seemed to be flaking, showing patches of green underneath.

"Kaye?" Corny asked.

The girl smiled at him, but her smile was too fierce. The skin tore on her lower lip.

He was frozen, staring at her.

She scooted past him into the office, stretching her twiglike fingers. He stifled a whimper, trying to keep his eyes focused on the credit-card unit, the dirty papers, the air freshener, all familiar things. He could smell her, a weird combination of pine needles, moss, and leaf piles. It was making him dizzy.

She sat down on the floor on top of papers and cardboard pizza boxes.

"What the hell happened to you?"

Kaye held out her hand and tilted it slightly in the light. "I'm sick," she said. "I'm really sick."

He crouched down beside her. There was a luminescence to her skin, a kind of brightness about her that made her eyes glitter feverishly. There was something about her shape itself that was strange, a hunching of the shoulders, a slight bulge of the back.

He picked up a block of wood with a dangling key. "Let's go in the bathroom. The light's better and you can wash more of this crap off."

She got up off the floor.

"I could take you over to the hospital," he said. She didn't reply, and he didn't pursue it. He knew this wasn't a hospital-type thing—he just felt like he ought to say it.

The bathroom was grimy. Corny certainly couldn't recall anyone doing more than changing the toilet paper in all the time he had worked there. The once-white tiles were cracked and grayed. There was barely enough room for two people, but Kaye squeezed in obediently next to the toilet and stripped off her sweater.

"Take off the rest of it. There's something on your back."

She threw a considering look at him and seemed to decide either he didn't care or she didn't. She kicked off her boots, pulled off the sweater and then the nightgown until she was only in her panties.

Bunching up her nightgown under the faucet, he got it sopping wet. He used the cloth to scrub off what was left of her skin and the pigment of her hair. Her skin was thin as crepe on her back. As he rubbed the cloth over the bump between her shoulders, it cracked.

A thin whitish fluid leaked out between her shoulder blades.

"Uuughh!" Corny moved back from her.

Kaye looked back at him, and her face said that she just couldn't take any more weirdness. Of course it was hard to know whether he was reading her strange eyes right.

"It's okay," he said in as soothing a voice as he could. Outside he heard a car pull into the gas station. He ignored it.

"What happened?" There was something moving under the surface of her back, something slick and iridescent.

"Hold on." He wiped the thick fluid off, showing white-veined iridescence all the way down her back. Suddenly something flicked loose, rising so that it almost slapped Corny before it fell wetly against Kaye's back.

"Oh, God," Corny said. "You have wings."

The damp things moved feebly.

The sight of it sent a thrill through him, despite the fear. This was the real thing.

"C'mon," he said. "My house."

6

Down the hill I went, and then,
I forgot the ways of men
For night-scents, heady, and damp and cool
Wakened ecstasy in me.

—Sara Teasdale, "August Moonrise," *Flame and Shadow*

Kaye sat down gingerly at the edge of the couch, so that her new wings hung off the edge and wouldn't get crushed if she moved suddenly or leaned back.

She was wearing one of Janet's tube skirts and a black, hooded sweatshirt. Corny had taken a pair of scissors and split it up the back. Her skin was so sensitive that she imagined she could feel particles as they drifted through the air.

Corny poured himself a glass of Mountain Dew. "Can you drink soda?"

"I think so," Kaye said. "I could before."

He poured some in a mug and handed it over to her. She didn't sip it—it was the same color as her skin.

She could *smell* the green dyes and the chemical carbonation.

She could smell Corny, the acid of his sweat and sourness of his breath. The air she breathed tasted of cigarettes and cats and plastic and iron in a way she had never noticed before—it nearly made her gag with each breath.

"It's starting to sink in," Corny said. "I can almost look at you without wanting to bang my head against the wall."

"I'm not sure how to explain. It started a long time ago. I'm not sure I remember important things."

"Recently, then." Corny sat down on the couch. He was staring at her with what looked like a combination of fascination and repulsion.

"I rolled in some clover." She gave a short laugh at the absurdity of it.

"Why?" Corny didn't laugh at all. He was totally serious.

"Because the Thistlewitch told me that it was one of the ways I could see myself the way I really am. See—I told you that it gets ridiculous."

"This is the way you really are, then?"

Kaye nodded carefully. "I guess so."

"And this thimble witch? Who is she?"

"Thistlewitch," Kaye corrected. And she told him. Told him how she'd known faeries for as long as she could remember, how Spike would perch on the footboard of her bed when she was small and tell her stories about goblins and giants while Lutie darted around the room like a manic night-light. She told him how Gristle taught her how to make a piercing whistle with a blade of grass and described the Thistlewitch divining with eggshells. How she saw them when she got older, when they came home for the holidays or during periods where they had nowhere else to go.

All the while, Corny stared with greedy eyes.

"Who knew about these friends?"

Kaye shrugged. "My mom, my grandmother—I guess I'm not really related to them at all. . . ." She stopped suddenly. Her voice sounded unsteady, even to herself, and she took a deep breath. "Everyone in my first-grade class. You. Janet."

"Did any of these people see the faeries? Ever?"

Kaye shook her head.

Corny turned his gaze toward the wall, frowning in concentration. "And you can't call them?"

Kaye shook her head again. "They find me when they want to—that's the way it always was. Right now, that's the *problem*. I can't stay like this, and I don't know how to get reglamoured."

"There isn't anywhere you can look?"

"No," Kaye said vehemently. "The swamp was the only place, and I was there all night."

"But you're a faerie too. Don't you have any abilities?"

"I don't know," Kaye said, thinking of Kenny. That was definitely not something she really wanted to discuss right now. Her head hurt enough already.

"Can you cast any spells?"

"I don't know, I don't know, I don't know! Can't you understand that I don't know anything at all?"

"Come on in the back. Let's go online."

They went into Corny's room, and he flicked on his computer. The screen went blue, and then his background picture loaded. It was a wizard hunched over a chess table while the two queen pieces battled, one all black and the other all white.

Kaye flopped onto the tangled sheets of his bed, stomach down, wings up.

Corny tapped a few keys, and his modem groaned.

"Okay. F-A-E-R-I-E. Let's see. Hmmm. Gay stuff—obviously." He still had that challenge in his voice. "Here we go. German changelings. Pictures. Yeats poetry."

"Apparently, I'm a pixie," Kaye supplied. "Click on the changeling thing, though."

"Interesting."

He scrolled through it, and she tried to read it from her slightly-too-distant vantage point. "What?"

"Says you throw 'em in the fire to get your own kid back . . . That or stick a hot poker down their throats."

"Great. Next."

"Here we go. Pixie. Can detect good and evil, hates orcs, and is about one to two feet tall. . . ." He started to laugh. "Makes pixie dust."

"Orcs?" Kaye inquired. She shifted her position, suddenly aware that it was hard to separate which muscles caused her wings to twitch. They seemed to move independently of her will and of each other, like two soft insects alighting on her back.

Corny couldn't stop laughing. "Pixie dust. Like angels make angel dust. International drug cartels grab seraphim and shake 'em. Priests who sweep up churches put that stuff in Ziploc baggies."

She snorted. "You're an idiot, you know that?"

"I try," he said, still laughing.

"Well, try 'Unseelie Court.'"

A few clicks of his mouse and he said, "Looks like that's

where all the bad guys hang out in Faerieland. What does this have to do with you?"

"There's this knight there who may or may not be wanting to kill me. My friends want me to pretend to be human because there's this thing called the Tithe . . . it's complicated."

Corny sat up again. "Why didn't you tell me?"

"I just told you the part that made sense."

"Okay." Corny nodded. "Now tell me the part that doesn't make sense."

"I don't understand it all exactly, but basically there are solitary faeries and court faeries. Roiben is one of the court faeries, and I met him in the woods after he got shot. He's from the Unseelie Court."

"Okay. I'm still with you, if barely."

"Spike and Lutie-loo sent me an acorn message to tell me that he was dangerous. He killed my other friend, Gristle."

"An acorn message?"

"The top came off. It was hollow."

"Right. Of course."

"Ha-ha. Look for 'Tithe' next, okay? As far as I know, it's this sacrifice that makes the faeries that aren't part of any court still do what the court people say. I have to pretend to be human so they can pretend to sacrifice me."

He typed in the keyword. "I'm just getting Jesus Crispy shit. Give-me-ten-percent-of-your-cash-so-I-can-buy-an-air-conditioned-doghouse kind of thing. This sacrifice—how safe is that? I mean, how well do you know these people?"

"I trust them absolutely. . . ."

"But," Corny prompted.

She smiled ruefully. "But they never *told* me. They knew all

this time, and nothing—not one hint." Kaye looked pensively at the joints of her fingers. Why should one extra joint make them horrifying? It did, though—flexing them bothered her.

Corny steepled his palms, cracking his knuckles like a villain. "Tell me the whole story one more time, slowly, and from the beginning."

Kaye woke up muzzily, not sure where she was. She shifted until she felt a solid shape that groaned and pushed at her. Corny. She squinted at him and rubbed at her eyes. It was dark in the room, the only streaks of light sneaking around the edges of the heavy brown curtains. She heard voices from somewhere in the trailer over the distant sound of canned television laughter.

She turned over again, trying to go back to sleep. The bedside table was in front of her line of vision. A book, *Vintage*, a bottle of ibuprofen, an alarm clock with flames on the clockface, and a black plastic chess knight.

"Corny," she said, shaking what she thought was the shoulder of the lump. "Wake up. I know what to do. I know what we can do."

He pushed the covers back from over his head. "This better be good," he groaned from underneath the comforter.

"The kelpie. I know how to call the kelpie."

He pushed back the covers and sat up, suddenly awake. "Right. That's right." He slid out of bed, scratching his balls through his briefs, and sat down in front of the computer. The screensaver dispersed as he shook the mouse.

In the hallway, Kaye could hear Janet's voice distinctly,

complaining to her mother about the fact that she wasn't going to get her license if Corny wouldn't let her borrow his car.

"What time is it?" Kaye asked.

Corny looked at the clock on the screen. "After five."

"Can I use your phone?"

He nodded. "Do it now. You can't use it while I'm signed on. We only have the one line."

Corny's bedroom phone was a copy of the emergency Bat-phone, bright red and sitting under a plastic dome on the floor. It even had a little bulb in it that she imagined might blink when a call came in. Kaye sat cross-legged on the floor, took off the dome, and dialed her house.

"Hello?" Kaye's grandmother answered.

"Grandma?" She dragged her fingers over the synthetic loops of the rug she was sitting on. Her eyes fell on her long green toes with chipped red nail polish on the jagged, untrimmed toenails.

"Where are you?"

"I'm at Janet's," Kaye said, wiggling the toes, willing herself to realize they belonged to her. It was hard talking to her grandmother now. The only reason she put up with Kaye and Ellen was because they were family and you always took care of family. "I just wanted to tell you where I am."

"Where were you this morning?"

"I got up early," Kaye said. "I had to meet some friends before school started." That was true enough, in a way.

"Well, when are you coming home then? Oh, and I have two messages for you. Joe from the Amoco called about some job—I hope you're not thinking of working at a gas station—and some boy named Kenny called twice."

"Twice?" Kaye couldn't help feeling flattered before she remembered to feel afraid.

"Yes. Are you coming home for dinner?"

"No, I'll eat here," Kaye said. "'Bye, Gram, I love you."

"I think your mother would like it if you came home for dinner. She wants to talk to you about New York."

"I've got to go. 'Bye, Gram."

Kaye hung up the phone before her grandmother could start another sentence. "You can sign on now," she said.

A few minutes later, Corny made a noise.

She looked up.

"Your plan has one little problem."

"Don't they all . . . No, tell me, what is it?"

"Kelpies basically like to drown people and then eat most of them—all but their guts. You're not supposed to get on their backs, yadda, yadda, yadda, they're fucking evil as hell, yadda, yadda, yadda, not to mention they shapeshift. Oh, yeah, you can tame them if you happen to manage to get a bridle on them. Fat chance of that."

"Oh."

"Did you ever wonder if some of these sites were designed by faeries? I wonder if I kept looking if I could find a newsgroup or a hub page or something."

"So, if we don't sit on its back, are we safe?"

"Huh? Oh . . . I don't know."

"Well, are there instances there where it drowns people without them getting on its back?"

"No, but then the stuff I'm finding isn't all that comprehensive."

"I'm going to try it. I'm going to talk to the kelpie."

He looked up from the computer desk. "You're not going without me."

"Okay," Kaye said. "I just thought that it might be dangerous."

"This is the real thing," he said, voice dropping low, "and I don't want to miss even one little bit of it. Don't even think of running off."

She held up both hands in mock surrender. "I want you to go with me. Really, okay?"

"I don't want to wake up someplace with a screwed-up memory and nobody ever believing me. Do you understand?" Corny's face was flushed.

"C'mon, Corny, either your mom or Janet is going to hear you and come in here. I'm not leaving you."

Kaye watched as he calmed somewhat, thinking that she should stop trying to anticipate what was going to happen next. After all, when you were already in a slippery place, reality-wise, you couldn't afford to assume that things would be straightforward from here on in.

The metal of the car made her feel heavy and drowsy and sick, the way that carbon monoxide poisoning was supposed to make you feel before it killed you. Kaye rested her cheek against the cool glass of the window. Her throat was dry and her head was pounding. It had something to do with the air in the car, which seemed to scald her lungs as she breathed. It was a short drive, and she was glad of it, practically tumbling out the door when Corny opened it for her.

In the daylight, it was easy to see rows of houses beyond

the trees, and Kaye wondered how it could have seemed like a great woods when she had stumbled through here the night she discovered Roiben. The stream, when they found it, was thick with garbage. Corny leaned down and smeared dirt off a brown bottle that didn't look like it was for beer. It looked like it should be holding some snake-oil salesman's hair tonic or something.

"Vaseline glass," he said. "Some of this stuff is really old. I bet you could sell some of these." He pushed another bottle with his toe. "So, how do we call this thing?"

Kaye picked up a brown leaf. "Do you have anything sharp?"

He reached into his back pocket and pulled out a pocket-knife, flicking it open with a deft movement of his thumb. "Just remember what the site said—no getting on its back, no way, no day, no matter what."

"I saw the page, okay? You don't have to keep reminding me. Kelpie equals evil water horse that drowns people for fun. I get it."

"Well, just so you're sure."

He let her take the knife. She slid the tip of it into the pad of her thumb. A bright dot of blood welled up, and she smeared it on the leaf.

"Now what?" he asked, sounding as though he could barely get the breath to speak.

She dropped the leaf into the stream, blood side down, as she had done for Roiben. "I'm Kaye," she said, trying to remember the words. "I'm not from any court but I need your help. Please hear me."

There was a long moment of silence after that. She could

see Corny start to convince himself that nothing was going to happen, and she was torn between the desire for her idea to work and her fear it might.

A moment later, there was no more doubt as a black horse rose from the water.

With Kaye's new sight, the creature looked different. Its color was not so much black, but a deep emerald. And the nacreous eyes were gleaming like pearls. Still, when it regarded Kaye, she was forced to think of the research Corny had done. That was chilling enough.

The kelpie strode onto the shore and shook its great mane, spraying her and Corny with glittering droplets of swamp water. Kaye held up her hands, but it hardly helped.

"What do you seek?" the horse spoke, its voice soft but deep.

Kaye sucked in her breath, letting it out slowly. "I need to know how to glamour myself and I need to know how to control my magic. Can you teach me?"

"What will you give me, girl-child?"

"What do you want?"

"Perhaps that one would like to ride on my back. I would teach you if you let him ride with me."

Corny gave her a speaking look.

"So that you can kill him? No way."

"I wonder about death, I who may never know it. It looks much like ecstasy, the way they open their mouths as they drown, the way their fingers dig into your skin. Their eyes are wide and startled and they thrash in your hands as though with an excess of passion."

Kaye shook her head, horrified.

"You can hardly blame me. It is my nature. And it has been a very long time."

"I'm not going to help you kill people."

"There might be something else that would tempt me, but I can't think what. I'll give you the opportunity to dream up something."

Kaye sighed.

"You know where to find me."

With that, the kelpie waded back into the water.

Corny was sitting stunned on the bank. "Well, that was terrifying."

Kaye nodded.

"Are you going to try to find something it wants?"

Kaye nodded again. "Yeah."

"I don't know how I feel about that."

"You read the site. You knew it would be like this. *You* warned *me*."

"I guess. It's different to see it . . . to hear it."

"Do you want us to leave?"

"Hell, no."

"Any ideas what it might want that doesn't walk on two feet and bleed?"

"Well," he said, after a moment's consideration, "actually there are a whole lot of people I wouldn't mind feeding to that thing."

She laughed.

"No, really," he said.

"What do you mean?"

"I mean that there are a whole lot of people that I wouldn't mind seeing drowned. Really. I think that we should go for it."

Kaye looked up at him. He didn't look particularly fazed by what he had just proposed.

"No way," she said.

Corny shrugged. "Janet's boyfriend, for example. What a prick."

"Kenny?" Kaye squeaked. "Think of something other than people we can give it."

"Oats?" he said vaguely. "A huge box of instant oatmeal? A subscription to *Equestrian's Digest*? Hay and lots of it?"

"We're not getting people killed, so just give it up, okay?"

She bet that Roiben's name would be a fair price. After all, this thing was probably not part of any court, being tied to the stream here. She bet that he would be counted as a fair price indeed. And it wouldn't change the fact that she knew the name too.

It would be a fine revenge on him for killing Gristle.

But then, she imagined that the kelpie would just order him to bring people for it to drown. And, of course, he would do it.

What else was there to bargain with that a kelpie might like?

She thought about the dolls in her room, but all she could picture was a little girl following a trail of them to the shore of the stream. Ditto with any musical instrument. She had to think about something that the kelpie could enjoy alone. . . . Clothing? Food?

Then she thought of it . . . a companion. A companion that it could never drown. Something that it could talk to and admire. The merry-go-round horse.

"Oh, Corny," Kaye said, "I know just the thing."

Getting back in the car was the last thing that Kaye wanted to do, but she did, sliding into the backseat, pressing her shirt over her mouth as though the fabric could filter the iron out of the air.

"You know where you're going, right?" she asked, wondering if he could understand the words, muffled as they were by the cloth.

"Yeah."

She let her head slide down to the plastic seat. One wing twitched just out of her vision, sending scattered luminescent rainbows through the thin membrane to dance on her leg. Everything narrowed to those rainbows. There was no Corny in the front seat, no scratchy radio song, no passing cars, no houses, no malls, no real things to protect her from the glittering patterns on her grass-green thighs.

There were no words for what she felt, no sounds, nothing. There was no word for what she was, no explanation that would keep back the numb, dumb dark. She felt the dizziness threaten to overwhelm her.

"Can you please open your window?" she asked. "I can't breathe."

"What's wrong with yours?"

She crouched on the edge of the seat and reached her hands into the front of the car, palms up like a supplicant. "Every time I touch the handle, it burns. Look." She held her hand out to him, so he could see that part of it was flushed. Her fingers wiggled. "That's from the door handle."

"Shit." Corny sucked in a breath. Then he rolled down his window.

The salt in the air cleaned her throat with each lungful from the open window, but it wasn't enough to battle the rising nausea. "I have to get out of this car."

"We're almost there." Corny stopped at a red light.

Corny parked the car outside the big building. The overcast sky made the outside of the building look even dingier.

"Are you okay?" Corny asked, and turned his head to see her in the backseat.

Kaye shook her head. She was going to vomit, right there, right on top of the empty soda cans and mashed fast-food boxes. She put her hand in the pocket of the sweatshirt and opened the door.

"Kaye!"

She half fell, half crawled onto the asphalt of the parking lot and dragged herself to the edge of the grass before throwing up. There was little in her stomach, and most of what she coughed up was stomach acid and spit.

"Jesus!" Corny crouched down next to her.

"I'm okay," Kaye said, rising dizzily to her feet. "It's all the metal."

He nodded, glancing back at the car and then looking around skeptically. "Maybe we should forget about this."

Kaye took a deep breath. "No. Come on."

She ran around the back, following the path she had walked with Janet. "Give me your jacket," she said. "There's glass."

Everything was different in daylight.

Up the stairs and there it was, dingier now that she got a good look at it, but still beautiful. The cream of its flanks was closer to brown, and the gilt trim was mostly rubbed off. Its lips were carved in what she thought was a slight sneer, and Kaye grinned to see it.

Together, they dragged the horse over the floor toward the stairs. Corny went first, taking the weight of it as they eased it down step after step. It barely fit.

Downstairs, Kaye climbed out through the window as Corny pushed the carousel horse through.

Outside, Corny started to panic. There was no way it was going to fit in the back of the car. Worse, the trunk was filled with boxes of used books and oddball tools.

"Someone is going to see us!" he said.

"We've got to find a way to tie it to the roof."

"Fuck! Fuck! Fuck!" Corny dug around in the trunk of the car and came up with a single bungee cord, two plastic bags, and some twine.

"That string is very thin," Kaye said skeptically.

Corny twisted it around the wooden creature's neck and body and then through the inside of the car. "Get on the other side. Hurry."

He tossed her the twine, and she looped it over the horse and threw it back to him. Corny knotted it.

"Okay. Good enough. We gotta go."

Corny hopped in on his side, and Kaye walked around and got in, wrapping Corny's jacket around her hand to close the door. He took off, stepping on the pedal so hard that the tires screeched as they pulled out.

Kaye was sure that a cop was going to pull up behind them or that the horse was going to fly off onto the road and hit another car. But they got back in one piece.

Pulling over, they hauled the merry-go-round horse down into the forest and to the stream.

"That thing better like this. I'm going to have splinters for a week," Corny complained.

"It will."

"And I'm going to have to pop the hood of the car back up in the center."

"I know."

"I'm just saying. That thing better like it."

"It will," Kaye repeated

They set the legless horse down on the muddy bank, angling it so that it sat relatively upright without their holding it. Kaye looked around for another leaf, and Corny took the knife out of his pocket without being asked.

"'S okay. I'm just going to pick the scab."

He made a face but didn't say anything.

"Kelpie," Kaye said, dropping the leaf into the water, "I have something I think you might like."

The horse rose up from the deep and stared at the broken merry-go-round horse with its luminescent, inhuman eyes.

Whinnying, it clopped up onto the shore. "It has no legs," the kelpie said.

"It's beautiful anyway," Kaye said.

The kelpie circled the wooden thing, snuffling appraisingly. "More, I think. Crippled things are always more beautiful. It's the flaw that brings out beauty."

Kaye grinned. She'd done it. She'd actually done it. "So you'll teach me?"

The creature looked at Kaye and *shifted*, and where it had been now stood a young man, nude and still dripping, hair tangled with rushes. It looked from Kaye to Corny. "She, I will teach, but you must make it worth my while if you want me to teach you too. Come and sit near me."

"Nothing's worth that," Kaye said.

The kelpie-man smiled, but his eyes were on Corny as he traced a pattern on his chest. Corny's breathing went shallow.

"No," Corny said, so softly that it was hard to hear his voice.

Then the creature transformed again, sinuous energy coiling until Kaye was looking at herself.

"Are you ready to begin then?" the kelpie said in Kaye's voice with Kaye's mouth. And then the smile, not at all Kaye's, curled slyly. "I have much to teach you. And the boy would do well to listen. Magic is not the sole province of the fey."

"I thought you said he had to make it worth your while."

"His fear is worth something, for now. I am allowed so little." The kelpie looked at her with her own black eyes, and she watched those lips, so like her own, whisper, "So long since I have known what it was to hunt."

"How come?" Kaye asked, despite herself.

"We, who are not the rulers, we must obey those that are. Mortals are a treat for the Gentry, and not for the likes of you and me. Unless, of course, they are willing."

Kaye nodded, pondering that.

"Do you know how it feels to build magical energy?" the kelpie asked. "It is a prickling feeling. Cup your hand and concentrate on building the energy in it. What does it feel like?"

Kaye cupped her hand and imagined the air in her hand thickening and shimmering with energy. After a moment, she looked up in surprise. "It feels like when your hand falls asleep and then you move it. Prickly, like you said, like little shocks of energy shooting through it. It hurts a little."

"Move it back and forth between your hands. There you feel magic in its raw state, ready to become whatever you want it to be."

Kaye nodded, cradling the energy that was like a handful of nettles, letting some of it trickle through her open fingers. It was a feeling she remembered, sometimes coiling in her gut or pricking over her lips before some strange thing happened.

"Now, how did you accomplish raising the energy? What did you do?"

Kaye shook her head slightly. "I don't know . . . I just pictured it and stared at my hand."

"You pictured it. That is the easiest of the senses. Now you must learn to hear it, to smell it, to taste it. Only then will your magic become real. And be careful; sometimes a simple glamour can be seen through out of the corner of another's eye." The creature winked.

Kaye nodded.

"When you do magic, there are two stages: focus and surrender. Surrender is the part that so many do not understand.

"To do magic, you must focus on what it is you want to do, then let go of the energy and trust it to do your bidding.

"Close your eyes. Now picture the energy surrounding you. Imagine, for example, a ring on one of your fingers. Add detail to it. Imagine the gold of the band, then imagine the gem, its color, its clarity, how it will reflect the light . . . that's right. Exactly like that."

Her eyes fluttered open as Corny gasped. "Kaye! There really is a ring. A real, imaginary ring. I can see it."

Kaye opened her eyes, and there it was, on her index finger, just as she had imagined it, the silver carved into the shape of a girl and the glittering emerald set in her open mouth. She turned it against the light, but even knowing that she had magicked it into being, the ring was as solid as a stone.

"What about undoing . . . things?" Kaye asked.

The kelpie threw back its head and laughed, white teeth shining even in the gloom. "What have you done?"

"Enchanted someone to . . . like me," Kaye said, in a low voice. Corny looked at her, surprised and a little annoyed. He couldn't be happy that there was another part of the story she'd left out.

The kelpie grinned and clucked its tongue. "You must remove the enchantment on him in the same way that you would take off a glamour. Feel the web of your magic, reach out and tear it. Practice with the ring."

Kaye concentrated, letting the energy swirl around her, feeling it run through her. It seemed to ebb and flow with each beat of her heart.

They were driving back when Kaye pointed to the hill. "Look at those lights. Wonder who's up there."

"I don't see anything." He looked at her sharply in the rearview mirror. "You're seeing magical lights?"

Cemetery Hill had a steep incline on the side that faced the highway. That side had neither graves nor tombs, and in the winter kids would blithely go sledding, piling spare mittens and scarves on the monuments. An abandoned, half-built mausoleum stood on the other side. With two levels but no roof, the top was overgrown with smallish trees and vines. There were dozens upon dozens of monuments, tombs, and gravestones erected around it. Small glowing lights seemed to dart through the air.

"Think that's where the Unseelie Court is?" she asked softly, thinking of the way Lutie-loo had described it.

"Let's check it out."

He drove into the graveyard.

They parked along the tumbled-stone path. She stared through the rear windshield at the darting lights as she waited for Corny to walk around and open her door.

"Those are definitely faeries," Kaye said.

"I can't see anything." There was an edge of panic in Corny's voice.

Kaye followed the lights, saw them dazzle and turn, keeping just enough ahead of her that she could not see them clearly. She sped up her pace. They were so close she could just snatch one out of the air. . . .

"Kaye!" Corny called, and she turned. "Don't fucking leave me behind."

"I'm not leaving you! I'm trying to catch one of these things."

Suddenly there was an impossible explosion of fireflies, darting in and out of the trees. It must be well past midnight and too late in the season for fireflies anyway, the chill of autumn and recent rain stiffening the grass beneath their feet with frost. But the insects darted around them, each blinking for a long moment, then gone, then blinking again. Then she looked at them carefully. They were little winged creatures, even smaller than those she had snatched at. One flitted close to her and showed its teeth.

Kaye made a shrill sound.

"What?" Corny said.

"Not bugs . . . they're tiny, nasty faeries."

He dropped Kaye's hand and snatched out blindly. It darted away. "I can't see anything. Are those the things . . . what you saw from the road?"

She shook her head. "No. Those lights were bigger."

He squatted down, his breath rising from his lips in puffs of white vapor. "Can you see them now?"

She shook her head. "Lutie said something about the opening to the Unseelie Court being in a brown patch of grass, but practically the whole hill is covered with brown grass."

"Maybe the patch is bare by now."

Kaye knelt down next to Corny and cupped her ear to the ground. There was faint music. "Listen. You can hear it."

He moved to her side and pressed his ear to the ground as well. "Music," he said. "Sounds like pipes."

"It's beautiful," she said, the smile on her face before she remembered that this was not a good place they were trying to enter.

"Let's walk a circuit around the hill. We'll both look for any patch that seems weird." Corny stretched from his squat and waited for her to start walking.

The graveyard was unnaturally quiet. The moon was, if anything, fuller and fatter than it had been when she last saw it. It seemed unnatural; the thing looked bloated in the sky, and she thought again about the sun bleeding to death while the moon grew tumescent with devoured light.

The newer, granite gravestones were all polished to an unnatural mirror shine that reflected her and Corny as they passed. The older markers were a pale, milky marble, grass stains and dirt washed out by the moonlight. Pale as Roiben's hair.

"Hey, what about that?" Corny pointed to a patch of grass that did seem a different shade of brown.

Kneeling down beside it, Corny pulled back a corner as though it were the flap of a sod tent. Corny leaned in.

"I should go in there alone."

"You said you wouldn't leave me behind," Corny reminded her.

"It's probably not safe for *me* to go. I'll be back as soon as I can." Kaye shimmied into the entrance. "I promise."

The music seemed louder now, pipes and laughter swelling in the quiet night. Kaye heard Corny say "You said you wouldn't leave me" as she followed the song inside.

7

She slipped inside the hollow hill.

The air itself seemed thick with sweetness, and breathing was disorienting.

Long, low tables were heaped with golden pears, chestnuts, bowls of bread soaking in buttery milk, pomegranates ripped in half and half again, violet petals on crystal plates, and all manner of strange delicacies. Wide silver goblets sat like toads on the tables, upright and overturned in equal proportion. Scarlet-clad faerie ladies brushed past men in torn rags, and courtiers danced with crones.

Revelers cavorted and sang, drank and swooned. The costumes were varied and completely unlike medieval clothes. They were more like some demented, organic couture. Collars rose like great fins. Outfits were composed entirely of petals or leaves. Ragged edges finished off lovely dresses. Ugly, strange, or lovely as the moon, none were plain.

"The Unseelie Court," she said aloud. She had expected something else, a cave, maybe, filled with gnawed human bones and faerie prisoners. Something simple. Looking out into the throng of revelers, she didn't know what to think.

The room itself was massive, so large that she wasn't sure what was on the other side. What looked like a giant slouched near a dais. Each step seemed to push her in a new direction, full of splendors. A fiddler was playing an improbable instrument, with several necks and so many strings that he sawed his bow at them wildly. A long-nosed woman with freckles and ears like a jackal's juggled pinecones. Three men with red hair and double rows of shark teeth dipped their caps in a pile of carnage, soaking up the blood. A huge creature with bat wings and limbs like stilts sat atop a table and lapped at a beaten copper bowl of cream. It hissed at Kaye as she passed it.

Above them all, the domed ceiling was frescoed with dangling roots.

Kaye picked up a goblet off a table. It was ornate and very heavy, but it seemed clean. She poured a thin, reddish liquid from the silver carafe in the center of the table. Small seeds floated at the top, but the drink smelled pleasant and not entirely strange, so she took a swallow. It was both sweet and bitter and went to her head so that, for a moment, she was obliged to hold the table for support.

She took a silvery apple from a pile of strange, thorny fruit, turned it over in her hand, and gingerly bit into it. It was crimson on the inside and tasted like watery honey. It was so good that she ate it core and all, till she was licking her hand for juice.

The next was brown and rotten-looking as she bit into it, but the meat, though gritty, tasted of a fiery and sweet liquor.

She felt an infectious giddiness come over her. Here, nothing she did was strange. She could twirl and dance and sing.

All at once she was aware of how far into the crowd she had gone. She had been turned around so many times she no longer even knew which direction was the way back.

She deliberately tried to retrace her steps. Three woman walked past her, silver gowns trailing like fine mist. The low cut of the identical dresses showed off the women's hollow backs. She looked again, but their concave backs were as smooth and empty as bowls. She forced herself to keep moving. A short man—a dwarf?—with intricate silver bracelets and shoulder-length black curls leered at her as he bit into an apricot.

Every moment became more unreal.

A winged boy skipped up to her, grinning. "You smell like iron," he said, and reached out a finger to poke her side.

Kaye scuttled away from his hand to a chorus of laughter. Her eyes focused on the pale grasshopper green of the insect wings attached to the boy's back.

She pushed through the crowd, weaving past dancers leaping in complex intertwining circles, past a clawed hand that snatched at her ankle from beneath the heavy scarlet cloth on one of the tables, past what looked like a debauched living chess game.

A satyr with a curly beard and ivory horns was hunched over, carefully ripping the wing off a small faerie trapped in his meaty fist. The thing screeched, beating its other wing hummingbird-swift against the fingers that held it. Pale green blood dribbled over the goat-man's hand. Kaye stopped, stunned and sickened to watch as the satyr tossed the little creature in the air. It flew in desperate circles, spiraling to the earthen floor.

Before Kaye could step close and snatch it, the man's boot stamped down, smearing the faerie into the dust.

Kaye reeled back, pushing Folk aside in her haste to get away. Angling through the multitudes, she thought of her own foolishness in coming here. This was the Unseelie Court. This was the worst of Faerieland come to drink themselves sick.

Three men in shimmering green coattails, their arms and legs long and skinny as broomsticks, were pushing a doe-eyed boy with grasshopper legs between them. He crouched warily as if to spring, but each time was unprepared for a sudden grab or push.

"Let him alone," Kaye said, stepping up to them. The boy reminded her too much of Gristle for her to just watch.

The men turned to look at her, all of them identical. The boy tried to slip between them, but one of the skinny men locked his arm around the boy's neck.

"What's this?" a skinny man asked.

"I'll trade you something for him," Kaye said impulsively.

One of the men snickered, and the other drew a little knife with an ivory handle and a metal blade that stank of pure iron. The third threaded his hand through the boy's hair, tipping his head back.

"No!" Kaye yelled as the iron dagger stabbed into the boy's left eye. The orb popped like a grape, clear liquid and blood running down his face as he screamed. The flesh hissed where the iron touched it.

"So much better with an audience," one of the skinny men said.

Kaye stumbled back, reaching around on a nearby table, finding only a goblet. She hefted it like a small club.

One skinny man drew the iron blade over the skin of the boy's cheek, down his neck as the boy trembled and squealed, his one good eye rolling weakly in his head. The iron left a thin red line where it passed, the skin bubbling to white welts.

"Going to save him, poppet?" another of the skinny men called to Kaye.

Kaye's hands were shaking, and the cup seemed nothing more than a heavy thing she held; certainly, it was no weapon.

"We're not going to kill him," the man who was holding the boy's hair said.

"Just softening him up a bit," the one with the knife put in.

Fury surged up in her. The cup flew from her hand, hitting the shoulder of the man with the knife, spotting his coat with droplets of the wine before falling ineffectually to the dirt floor, where it rolled in helpless circles.

One of the men laughed and another lunged for her. She ducked into the crowd, pushing aside a dainty woman and sidling through.

Then she came to a sudden halt. Half hidden by three toad-skinned creatures hunched over a game of dice, there was Corny.

He was sitting with his back against an overturned table, a goblet tipped in his hand. He was rocking back and forth with his eyes shut. A puddle of wine was soaking his pants, but he didn't seem to care.

Revelers were packed in tightly around her, so she scuttled under the table.

"Corny?" Kaye said, breathing hard.

Corny was right in front of her, but didn't seem to see her. She shook him.

He noticed that and finally glanced up. He looked drunk, or worse than drunk. Like he'd been drunk for years.

"I know you," Corny said thickly.

"It's me, Kaye."

"Kaye?"

"What are you doing here?"

"They said it wasn't for me."

"What wasn't for you?"

The hand with the goblet in it stirred slightly.

"The wine?"

"Not for me. So I drank it. I want everything that's not for me."

"What happened to you?"

"This," he said, and twitched his mouth into something that might have been a smile. "I saw him."

She looked quickly back into the throng. "Who?"

Corny pointed toward a raised dais where tall, pale faeries spoke together and drank from silver cups. "Your boy. Robin of the white hair. At least I think it was."

"What was he doing?"

Corny shook his head. It hung limply from his neck.

"Are you going to be sick?" she said.

He looked up into her face and smiled. "I am sick."

He began singing "King of Pain," softly and off-key. His eyes focused on nothing, and he was smiling a little, one of his hands toying idly with a button on his shirt. It seemed as though he was trying to rebutton it.

"I'm going to find him," Kaye said.

She looked at Corny, who was muttering, wiping the inside of his goblet with a finger that he brought to his lips.

"Wait for me here, okay? Don't go anywhere."

He didn't make any reply, but she doubted that he could stand anyway. He looked well and truly wasted.

Kaye reentered the throng, weaving toward where Corny had pointed.

A woman with thick braids of crimson hair sat on a tall wooden throne with edges that came to worn peaks and spires. It was wormed through with termite holes, giving it the appearance of a lattice. At her feet, goblins gamboled.

Roiben walked up to the throne and went down to one knee.

Kaye had to get closer. She couldn't see. Then she noticed there was a small indentation in the wall where she could hide herself, close enough to observe what was going to happen. She would watch and she would find a way to make him sorry for what he had done to Gristle.

Rath Roiben Rye walked through the crowd, past a table where a sprite was squirming in an ogre's embrace, perhaps with pleasure, perhaps in dread. His old self would have stopped, surely. His silver blade was at his hip, but his Lady awaited him and he had learned to be a good little thrall and so he passed on.

Lady Nicnevin, Queen of the Unseelie Court, stood with her courtiers gathered around her. Claret hair blew around a white face inset with sapphire eyes, and he found himself halted once again by her cold beauty. Four goblins frolicked before her. One tugged at her skirts like a toddler. Rath Roiben Rye dropped to his knees and bent his head so that his pewter hair puddled on the ground. He kissed the earth in front of her.

He didn't want to be here tonight. His chest still ached, and he wanted nothing more than to lie down and close his eyes. But when he did close them, all he saw was the human girl's face, full of shock and horror as he threw her down on the dirty floor of a diner.

"You may rise," the Lady said. "Approach me. I have a task to set you to."

"I am yours," Rath Roiben Rye said, brushing the soil from his lips.

She smiled a little smile. "Are you? And do you serve me as well as you served my sister?"

He hesitated before answering. "Better, perhaps, for you try me harder."

The smile curled off her mouth. "You would jest with me?"

"Your pardon, Lady. It is seldom merry work you set me to."

She laughed at that, silvery cold laughter that rose up out of her throat like crows going to wing. "You have no tongue for courtliness, knight. Yet I find you still please me. Why is that?"

"Sport, Lady?" he ventured.

Her eyes were hard and wet as blue beach glass, but her smile was beyond loveliness. "Certainly not wisdom. Rise. I understand that I have a mortal girl to thank for your presence here tonight."

His face was grave as he stood; he made sure of that. It would not do to let his surprise show. "I was careless."

"What a fine girl she must be. Do tell us about her." A few of the Unseelie Gentry watched this game as eagerly as they would a duel.

He was careful, so careful to keep the flinch from his face. His voice had to be easy; his words could not seem to be carefully measured. "She said that she was known to solitary fey. She had the Sight. A clever girl, and a kind one."

The Lady smiled at that. "Was it not the solitary fey that shot you, knight?"

He nodded and could not keep the ghost of a smile off his face. "I suppose they are not all so closely allied, my Lady. As implied in what we call them."

Oh, she didn't like that. He could tell. "I have an idea, then," his Lady said, raising one delicate finger to her smiling lips. "Get us this girl. A young girl gifted with the second sight would be an excellent candidate for the Tithe."

"No," he said. It was a sharp bark, a command, and courtiers' heads turned at the sound. He felt the bile rise in the back of his throat. Not clever, that. He was not being clever. "They will not like it, you choosing a favorite of theirs."

The Lady Nicnevin's smile bent her lips in triumph. "I might point out that if they do know her it will be just the thing to remind them not to break my toys," the Lady said. She did not mention his outburst.

Perhaps he was meant to feel something about being called her toy, but he hardly heard it. He was already watching the girl die. Her lips were already cursing him with his true name.

"Let me find you another," he heard himself say. Once his Lady might have found it amusing for him to struggle with that, finding an innocent to take the place of another innocent.

"I think not. Bring me the girl two days hence. Perhaps after I see her, I will reconsider. Nephamael has just come from my sister's court with a message. Serve me well and perhaps I will allow you to send one back with him."

His gaze flickered to the other knight, who appeared to be speaking to a goat-footed poetess and ignoring their conversation. It made Roiben queasy just to look at the iron circlet burning on his brow. It was said that even when he removed it, the searing scar ran deep and black in his flesh. He wore a cloak lined with thorns. What little revenge there was to be had on the Seelie Court, Roiben had it in the form of Nephamael. He had noticed how often the Seelie Queen sent her new knight back down to the Unseelie Court on some easy task or another.

Roiben bowed low enough for his knee and brow to touch the earth, but her attention was already elsewhere.

He walked through the crowd, passing the table where he had seen the ogre. Nothing remained of the couple save three drops of cherry blood and the shimmery powder of the sprite's wings.

His oaths cut him like fine wire.

Kaye watched Roiben sweep off the dais, fighting down the feelings that seemed to be clawing their way up her throat. *A clever girl and a kind one.* Those simple words had sped her heart in a way she didn't like at all.

Did he know that his voice had softened when he'd spoken of her?

He is so unpredictable that even his Queen cannot trust him. He's as likely to be kind as to kill you.

But the memory of his lips on her skin would not fade. Even if she rubbed the spot. Even if she scratched at it.

Kaye rose as another knight approached the Queen and bowed low to press his lips to the hem of her dress.

"Rise, Nephamael," the Queen said. "I understand that you are here with a message for me." His slim figure rose with the same graceful, measured formality that Roiben had. This knight was wearing a band of metal on his brow; the skin around it was darkened, as though burned. There was something about his yellow eyes that Kaye thought was familiar.

"This is the message my Lady would have you hear." His smile emphasized his implication of disloyalty. "My Lady said that although there has been a truce in the matter of war, she wonders at the matter of mortal influence. She has some favorites that cross your borders and seeks a means of giving them safe passage through your lands. I am told to await your reply. She did not seem to think I need hurry back. I must confess that it is good to be home in time for the Tithe."

"Is that all she said?"

"Indeed, although one of the Queen's courtiers begged me to ask after her brother. It seems that she hasn't had any news from him since he joined your court. A sweet thing, that girl. Very long white hair—one could almost wind a leash of it if one was so inclined." Another mischievous smile. "She wanted to know why you never use Roiben as a messenger."

The Queen smiled too. "It is good to have you home, Nephamael. Perhaps you can help my knight acquire our sacrifice."

"It would be my honor."

Kaye was suddenly caught by the arm and turned. She yelped.

"You shouldn't be here." Roiben's tone was icy, and his hand was tight on her arm.

Taking a breath, she met his eyes. "I just wanted to hear the Queen."

"If one of her other knights had noticed you spying here, they would have undoubtedly enjoyed making an example out of you. This is no game, pixie. It is too dangerous for you to be here."

Pixie? Then she remembered. He was seeing green skin, black eyes, folded wings. He didn't know her, or at least he didn't know that he knew her. She let go a breath she didn't even know she'd been holding.

"I'm no concern of yours," she said, twisting in his grip. Surely he would let her go, she told herself, but Spike's words echoed in her head. She saw Roiben on a black horse with glowing white eyes, face flecked with blood and dirt, riding down poor Gristle as he hurtled through the brush.

"Indeed?" He did not release his hold on her and was, in fact, pulling her through the crowd. From this vantage point it was easy to see that people didn't just make way for him, they practically tripped over themselves to do so. "I am Nicnevin's sworn knight. Perhaps you should be more concerned about what I am going to do to you than what I might do for you."

She shuddered. "So what will you do?"

The knight sighed. "Nothing. Providing that you leave the brugh immediately."

Nothing? She was not sure what she expected to see in his face when she looked at him then, but it was not the weariness she saw there. No madness glittered in the depths of those pale eyes.

But she couldn't leave, and she couldn't tell him that her very human friend was sleeping it off on the other side of the hill. She had to play this out. "I'm not allowed here? It doesn't seem like there's a guest list."

Roiben's eyes darkened at that, and his voice dropped very low. "The Unseelie Court delights in guesting spies for the solitary fey. We so seldom have volunteers for our amusements."

Dangerous ground, now. The sadness was gone, and his features were carefully blank. Her stomach twisted. *Delights . . . our amusements.* The implication of his participation was not lost on her.

"Leave through here," he said, showing her an earthen tunnel that was not the one she had come through. This one was hidden by a chair and closer to the giant. "But you must do it quickly. Now. Before someone sees me speaking with you."

"Why?" Kaye asked.

"Because they might assume that I had taken a liking to you. Then they might assume that it would be amusing to see my face while I hurt you very badly." Roiben's tone was cold and flat. His words seemed to fall from his lips as though they meant nothing, just words dropping into darkness.

Her hands felt very cold as she remembered the diner. What would it be like to be a puppet? What would it be like to watch your own hands disobey you?

Fury rose up in her like a dark cloud. She didn't want to understand how he could have killed Gristle. She didn't want to forgive him. And most of all, she didn't want to want him.

"Now, pixie," he said, "go!"

It made her angry that she couldn't stop thinking about his lips. Maybe tasting them would get it out of her system. After all, if curiosity killed the cat, it was satisfaction that brought it back. "I don't know if I should believe you," she said. "Give me a kiss."

"There is no time for your snatched pixie pranks," he said.

"If you want me to leave quickly, you'd best be quick." She was surprised at her own words, wondering at the daring of them.

She was more amazed when his lips brushed across hers. A sudden shock of feeling lanced through her before he pulled away.

"Go," he said, but he said it in a whisper, as though she had drained the breath from him. His eyes were shadowed.

Kaye ducked through the tunnel before she was forced to think about just what she had done. And certainly before she had time to wonder what it had to do with revenge.

Outside, it was cold and bright. It didn't seem possible, but the night was past. A breeze made the remaining leaves shudder on their branches, and Kaye crossed her arms to seal in whatever warmth she could as she jogged across the hill. She knew where the brown patch of grass had been. It was simply a matter of getting inside again. If she just stuck to the wall, she thought, probably no one would notice her. Corny would be there, and this time, she would pay better attention, mark the exit in some way.

The grass was no browner in one place than another. She remembered the location well enough. Next to the elm tree and by a grave marker that read ADELAIDE. She dropped to her knees and dug, frantically clawing at the half-frozen topsoil. It was dirt and more dirt, hard-packed, as though there had never been a passageway to an underground palace.

"Corny," she shouted, well aware that he would not be able to hear her deep beneath the earth. But that didn't keep her from doing it, over and over, again and again.

8

For beauty is nothing
but the beginning of terror we can just
*   barely endure,*
and we admire it so because it calmly disdains
to destroy us.
—RAINER MARIA RILKE, "THE FIRST ELEGY," *DUINO ELEGIES*

Corny woke on the hillside to the sound of bells. He was shaking with cold. His teeth were chattering, his head felt thick and heavy, and just shifting his weight made his stomach lurch. His jacket was gone.

He was lying alone in a graveyard, and he had no idea how he had come to be there. He saw his car, hazard lights still dimly flashing where he had pulled off alongside the road. A wave of dizziness hit him. He rolled weakly to one side and retched.

The taste of the wine he vomited brought back a memory of a man's mouth on his, a man's hands stroking him. Shocked, he tried to form a face to go along with that mouth and those hands, but his head hurt too much to remember any more.

He pulled himself to his feet, trying to keep his queasiness under control as he stumbled down the hill toward his car. Despite the lights being on all night, when he turned the key, the engine turned over and roared to life. Corny flicked the heater on full blast and sat there, basking in the gush of hot air. His body shuddered with pleasure.

He knew that there was a bottle of aspirin under all the fast-food wrappers and discarded novels. But he couldn't make himself move. He leaned his head back and waited for the warmth that was creeping through his limbs to relax him and chase away the nausea. Then he remembered Kaye in the backseat, and the beginning of the evening flooded back with disturbing intensity.

Kaye's skin cracked and peeling, the first flutter of wet wings, her strange new self stretched out in the car, the music . . . then alone on the hillside, tangled memories tripping over one another. He had read stories like this—men and women waking on a hill that never opened for them again. Angrily, he wondered if Kaye was there still, dancing to distant flutes, forgetting that he'd ever tagged along.

His stomach clenched as he thought of another explanation for being alone on the hill. It was a memory, really, Kaye hunched over him whispering, *I'm going to find him. Wait for me here.*

Because the more that he thought about it, the more he remembered the brutal parts. The distant scream he couldn't place, the sight of some of the revelers, teeth red with blood, and the man, the man with the cloak of thorns who had found him sitting drunk in the dirt and . . .

He shook his head. It was hard to remember the specifics,

only that soft mouth and the scraping of those thorns. His hands fluttered to the sleeves of his shirt, rolling them back. Angry red wounds running up and down his arms were incontrovertible proof of how he'd spent the night.

Just touching them filled him with a longing so intense it made him sick.

Kaye stumbled in the back door. A quick look at the red digital numbers on the microwave told her that it was late morning. Hours and hours before she could return to the hill and get Corny out.

Exhaustion settled over her as she strained to sense the wend and weft of magic in her fingers. She felt like a too-taut piece of string, fraying as it was pulled.

Her senses were overacute; the flimsy glamour she was wearing now was nothing like the one she had before. She could still feel the slight rustle of wings against her back, still smell the trash under the sink, even separate out smells—coffee grounds, eggshells, a bit of moldy cheese, detergents, some thick syrupy poison used to bait roach traps. The air thrummed with energy she had previously ignored. If she opened up to it, she might be able to leave her fatigue behind.

But she didn't want to—she wanted to cling to the facade of humanity with both fists.

"Kaye? Is that you?" Kaye's grandmother came in from the other room. She was wearing a robe and slippers, her thin gray hair pinned up in curlers. "Did you just get in?"

"Hi, Gram," Kaye said, yawning. She went over to the kitchen table, shifted a pile of newspapers and circulars out of her way, and put her head down in her hands. It was almost a relief to just let her grandmother yell at her, as if everything could be normal again.

"I called the school this morning."

Kaye forced herself not to groan.

"Did you know that you are not allowed to drop out of school without a parent's written permission? According to your transcripts you haven't been in school since you were fourteen!"

Kaye shook her head.

"What does that mean? Was that a no?"

"I *know* I haven't been in school," Kaye said, disgusted at how childish her own voice sounded.

"Well, it's a good thing that you know, missy, but *I* want to know what it is you have been doing. Where are you sneaking off to?"

"Nowhere," Kaye said in a small voice. "I just didn't want you to know. I knew you'd be mad."

"Well, why didn't you hightail it back to school then? Do you want to be nothing your whole life?"

"I'll get my GED," Kaye said.

"Your GED? Like a drug dealer? Like a pregnant teenager? Do you want to wind up trailer trash like your little friend?"

"Shut up!" Kaye yelled, holding her head. "You think you know everything about everything, don't you? You think that the world is so easy to understand. You don't know me at all—you don't know one single thing about me! How can you possibly know anything about Janet when you don't know anything about me?"

"I will not have you shouting at me in my own house. You

and your mother are just the same. You think that it's enough to want things. You think that if you just want and want then you're just going to magically get them."

Magically. Kaye felt her face twist with an expression somewhere between a wince and a smirk.

"Nothing but hard work gets anyone anywhere. Even then, people don't get what they want. People just suffer, and no one knows why they suffer. Talented people—like your mother—they don't make it, despite the talent, and what are you going to do then? You can't rely on luck. How do you know you're lucky?"

Kaye was surprised to hear that her grandmother thought that her mother had talent. "I'm not relying on luck," Kaye said numbly.

"Oh really? What are you doing then?"

"I don't know," Kaye said. She was tired, and she could feel a whine creep into her voice. She was afraid that she was going to cry, and if she started crying right now, she wasn't sure she could stop. Worse, she knew she sounded petulant, upset only that she was caught. It wasn't far from the truth. "We needed the money."

Her grandmother looked at her in horror. "What money?"

"Is that what you think? Don't even talk to me," Kaye said, burrowing her face in her folded arms. She mumbled into her own skin, "I was working at a fucking Chinese restaurant, okay? In the city. Full-time. We needed the money."

Her grandmother looked at her in confusion.

"I don't have a job yet here," she confessed, "but I thought I might go work over at the gas station where Janet's brother works. I put in an application there."

"You are going to high school, young lady, and even if you weren't, a gas station is no place for a girl to work."

"That's so old-fashioned," Kaye said. "Look, Mom will sign any form I need to get my GED."

"No, she will not!" Kaye's grandmother said. "Ellen!"

"What?" the annoyed shout came from above.

"Come down here and listen to your daughter! Do you know what she's planning to do? Do you know?"

A couple of minutes later, Kaye's mother was there too, hair pulled back with a red leather kerchief. She was wearing a black T-shirt and sweatpants. "What were you doing?"

"I wasn't doing anything," Kaye said. She should have known this fight was coming, but now she felt distant from it, as though she were watching from far, far away. "I *wasn't* going to school and I *wasn't* telling Grandma about it."

"Don't be smart," Kaye's grandmother said.

Ellen leaned against the doorway to the kitchen. "Look, it doesn't matter what she's been doing because we're going to be in New York the beginning of next week. I'm fronting Meow Factory."

Both Kaye and her grandmother graced Ellen with almost identical looks of horror. Ellen shrugged, moving past them to fill the coffeepot with water. "I was going to tell you last night, but you never showed up for dinner."

"I'm not going to New York," Kaye said, disgusted at how childish she sounded. This was the same girl who had insulted the Unseelie Queen's favorite knight? Who had talked down a kelpie?

"Ellen, you can't seriously mean that you don't care that your only daughter has not been attending high school?"

Kaye's grandmother's lips were pressed in a thin line.

Ellen shrugged. "Kaye's a smart girl, mom. She can make those decisions for herself."

"You're her mother. It's your job to make sure that she makes the right decisions."

"Did that ever work with me? You tried to make all my decisions for me, and see where it got us both. I'm not going to make the same mistake with Kaye. So what if she doesn't want to go to high school? High school sucked when I had to go, and I can't imagine it's any better now. Kaye can read and write—that's more than plenty of high school seniors can say—she's probably read more books than most girls her age."

"Ellen, don't be stupid. What's she going to do for a living? What's in her future? Don't you want something better for Kaye than what you have?"

"I want her to have the future she wants."

Kaye slid out of the room. They would be arguing for long enough that they wouldn't notice or care that she'd gone missing. She just wanted to sleep.

The phone rang close to her head, where she'd dropped it. Kaye groaned and pressed the on button.

"Hello," she said groggily. She hadn't managed more than a fitful sleep, tossing and turning. The blankets were too warm, but kicking them off had made her feel unsafe, exposed. Her dreams were too full of slit-eyed things poking her with clawed fingers.

"Fuck. You're there." She recognized the voice as belonging to Corny. He sounded astonished and very relieved.

"Corny! I got thrown out. I couldn't find a way back to you." She looked at the clock. It was one o'clock in the afternoon. "I thought maybe the hill was only open at night."

"I'm coming over."

She nodded and then, realizing he couldn't see her, spoke the thought aloud. "Yeah. Definitely. Come over. Are you okay?"

The phone clicked off, and she scrubbed a hand restlessly through her hair before letting her head fall back onto the pillow.

"The glamour looks good," was the first thing that Corny said as he walked into her bedroom. Then he looked around. "Hey, you've got rats."

She blinked up at him. "How did you get out? I was going crazy looking for you. If the cops had seen me they would have thought I was some nutjob grave robber trying to dig up bodies with my bare hands."

He grinned. "I woke up outside the hill this morning. I figured that you'd ditched me and I was going to do a Rip Van Winkle and find out that it was the year 2112 and no one had ever even heard of me."

"Roiben threw me out. I'm sorry. I didn't want to leave you, but I was afraid of what he'd do if he found out a mortal was there. He didn't recognize me."

Corny smiled. "He didn't?"

She shook her head and shuddered. "So, what did you think of the Unseelie Court?"

A slow, wicked smile spread on his face. "Oh, Kaye," he breathed. "It was marvelous. It was perfect."

She narrowed her gaze. "I was joking. They were killing things, Corny. For fun. Things like us."

He didn't seem to hear her, his eyes looking past her to the bright window. "There was this knight, not yours. He . . ." Corny shivered and seemed to abruptly change the direction of his sentence. "He had a cloak all lined with thorns."

"I saw him talking to the Queen," Kaye said.

Corny shrugged off his jacket. There were long scratches along his arms.

"What happened to you?"

Corny's smile widened, but his gaze was locked in some memory. He shifted it back to her. "Well, obviously I got inside the cloak."

She snorted. "What a euphemism. Did he hurt you?"

"No more than I wanted him to," Corny said.

She didn't like it, neither what he was saying nor the way he looked when he talked about it.

"How about you, Kaye? Did you revenge yourself on Robin of the White Hair?"

She couldn't help the blush that crept across her cheeks.

"What?" he demanded. And she told him, the blush growing hot as she did. It sounded even more pathetic out loud.

"So what you're telling me is that you got him to kiss you once on the lips and once on the ass."

Kaye glared at him, but she couldn't help giggling.

"I don't know if I should call that slick or be really afraid of what you are going to use that name of his for in the future. Can you just keep ordering him around indefinitely?"

Kaye aimed a mock-kick in his direction. "What about you and your knight? I mean, look at your arms; is that normal?"

"Makes me shiver when I touch them," Corny said reverently.

"At least we're scaring each other."

"Yeah, well, I better get back home. What's next on the faerie agenda?"

Kaye shrugged. "I get sacrificed, I guess."

"Great. When is that?"

Kaye shook her head. "Samhain, that's Halloween, right? Probably at night."

Corny looked at her incredulously. "Halloween is in two days."

"I know," Kaye said. "But it's not like I have to do anything. I just have to yell and scream and pretend to be human for a while."

"What if they get pissed that they were tricked?"

Kaye shrugged. "I don't know. I'm not in charge of the plan. All I have to do is be a good victim."

"Yeah, hopefully not too good a victim."

"Spike and Lutie wouldn't ever put me in any real danger."

"Yeah, okay. Well, that's good."

"You think they would?"

"I think it sounds dangerous. I think we haven't seen too much so far that is part of Faerie and isn't dangerous."

"True," Kaye said.

"Oh," Corny said. "Jimmy saw me when I went by the house. He said that if you want that job, you can start tonight at six. It's the shift before mine, so I guess I'm not fired after all."

She smiled. "So I guess I'll see you tonight. I'm glad you're okay."

"I would be even better if I was still there," Corny said, and all her worry returned in a flood.

"Corny . . ."

He smiled, that weird distant smile that he'd gotten under the hill, and she wanted to shake him by the shoulders. Something had to snap him out of it.

"See you tonight," he said, slipping on his jacket. He flinched as the lining brushed his arms, and, uncharitable as it was, she hoped that it was because the scratches hurt.

As Corny left, she looked at the pink sticky notes posted on the back of her door. They were the phone messages that her mother had taken for her. One was from Jimmy—probably about the job—and the others were all from Kenny.

Kaye settled on the mattress on the floor, picked up the phone, and dialed the number on Kenny's first note. She could leave a message for him about where she was working tonight. It was a public place. If he came to visit her there, she could take off the enchantment, and then everything with Janet could go back to normal.

"Hey," a male voice answered. There was a vaguely metallic whirring and grating in the background.

"Oh. Hi," she stammered. "I thought you'd be at school."

"You called my cell phone," Kenny said. "I'm in shop."

"This is Kaye." She felt stupid again, as though a few words from him were some kind of benediction of which she was unworthy.

"I know. Teacher is about to have a hernia, so we got to talk fast. I want to see you. Today."

"I have to work. You could come by—"

"What time?" he said, interrupting her. She felt awkward,

hyperaware of each word she spoke, waiting for him to start teasing her and absurdly grateful when he did not.

"Six."

"Meet me after school. By my car."

"Why don't you just come by my job?" She tried to wrest back control of the conversation.

"I need to see you sooner. By the entrance, then. The big one. I have to see you."

She hesitated, but she had no real reason not to meet him there. After all, removing the enchantment would only take a moment. What happened after, well, maybe it would be better if she was somewhere she could leave. "Okay."

"Good." With that, the phone hung up, leaving her feeling as though she had drunk two-day-old coffee on an empty stomach. Her nerves were fried. When she lifted a hand, she was unsurprised to find it vibrating slightly, like a struck guitar string. She closed her eyes and took a deep breath, then shucked off Corny's clothes and put on some of her own. They fit over the illusion of a smooth back easily, but her dual senses could feel the soft cotton of the T-shirt against her wings.

It was weird to be standing outside a school that she should have been attending. Some of the kids were familiar, people she had known from grade school. Mostly they were strangers.

Human, her mind whispered. *They're all human and you're not.*

She shook her head. She didn't like where those thoughts took her. It was alien enough that she hadn't been in a high school in years. Sometimes, like now, she missed it. She'd hated elementary school. She and Janet had been friends by default. Kids teased Janet for her secondhand clothes and Kaye for her stories. But in the city no one had known Kaye, and besides, there were lots of weird kids. But just when things in school had gotten better, they'd moved again.

"Hey," Kenny said. He was wearing sunglasses and a gray T-shirt under a heavy navy flannel. He took off the glasses when he got close to her. Dark circles ringed his eyes. "Why didn't you call me yesterday? I left a million messages at your house. Your mother said that you were at Janet's, but I checked. You weren't there."

"I'm sorry," she said. "I was out." He looked so serious that there was something suddenly funny about it. The magic came easily now, rushing to her fingers and spiking along her tongue, but she made no move to lift the enchantment.

"Kaye, I . . . ," he started, then seemed to think better of whatever it was he was going to say. "I can't sleep. I can't eat. All I can do is think about you."

"I know," she said sweetly. Kids passing by them gave Kenny sidelong glances. She suddenly understood why she had let him kiss her in the diner, why she had wanted him at all.

She wanted to control him.

He was every arrogant boyfriend that had treated her mother badly. He was every boy that told her she was too freaky, who had laughed at her, or just wanted her to shut up and make out. He was a thousand times less real than Roiben.

Her face split in a wide grin. She had no desire to play pretend anymore, no need to prove her worth by Kenny's regard, no desire to know how different the lips of a boy everybody liked were from any other boy.

"Please, Kaye," he said, reaching for her wrist, holding it tightly, pulling her to him.

This time she pulled away abruptly, not letting him crush her to him, his lips nowhere near close enough to take another kiss. Instead, she twisted her hand out of his grip and sprung up onto the cement edge of the steps.

"Something you want?" Kaye taunted. Kids had stopped along the path, watching.

"You," Kenny said, reaching for her again, but she was far too quick. Dancing out of his grasp, she laughed.

"You can't have what you can't catch," she goaded, cocking her head to one side. Madness made the blood dance in her veins. How dare any of them make her feel awkward? How dare they make her measure her words?

He snatched for her hand, but she pulled it away easily, spinning along the cement wall.

"Kaye!" he said.

She squatted down, legs wide, chin thrust toward him. "Do you adore me, Kenny?"

"Yes," he said frantically.

"Are you besotted with me? Would you die to have me?"

"Yes!" Kenny's eyes were dark with desire and fury. Behind him, students were laughing and whispering to one another.

Kaye laughed too. She didn't care in the least.

"Tell me again what you would do to have me."

"Anything," he said, without hesitation. "Give me a chance. Make me do something."

The laughter died in her throat. She tossed the magic off him, dispersing the threads of it with a sweep of her hand, as one would brush aside cobwebs.

"Never mind," she said, angry without being sure of why. Angry and ashamed. She was the one being cruel.

Kenny looked around him, the school apparently coming into focus for the first time. She could see the blush creep up his tattooed neck. He looked at her with something like horror in his eyes.

"What the fuck did you do?"

"Tell Janet to call me," she said, not caring that that made no sense, not caring about anything except that she needed to get out of there, needed to get away before she careened totally out of control. She didn't even spare him a glance as she crossed the student parking lot, heading home.

Jimmy was waiting for her in the office of the gas station. He handed her a blue jacket with an Amoco logo in the corner that Kaye had never seen Corny wear. She put it on dutifully while he explained what she had to do.

A few cars had come through, and she had handled the pump gingerly, careful of the metal.

Her head swam with the noxious fumes of the gasoline and the terrible thoughts of what she had done. It had felt so good, so absolutely right to taunt Kenny as she had. And now, knowing what she could do, was it possible to unlearn it, or just a matter of time before she used it again?

There was a rustling sound nearby, and Kaye looked toward the woods warily. It was Mischief Night, and Jimmy had already warned her that kids might try to toilet-paper the place.

But the figure that emerged had hair as black as oil, and the cloak on his shoulders blew back to reveal thorns on the inside, set like a bed of nails. Other than the white of his skin, the only pale thing he wore was a single white stone swinging on a long chain.

"You?" she said. "The knight from the Seelie Court. I should have guessed." She'd seen him talking to Nicnevin at the ball. He had seemed loyal to her, not the Seelie Queen. Kaye hoped Spike knew what he was doing.

"You're in good hands now," Nephamael said.

"You made the marks on Corny's arms."

"Indeed I did. He is exquisite."

Up close his eyes were yellow. Looking into those eyes, she suddenly knew why they seemed familiar. She'd seen them in the bar the night that Lloyd had lost it.

"You," Kaye said. "You did something to Lloyd, didn't you?"

"We needed you to come home, Kaye."

The knight touched the stone around his neck, and Kaye felt magic sweep around her, settling on her body with an oppressive weight. She felt smothered for a moment as scents became vague and her vision dulled.

"Remember, we have to make it look real," he said as she choked.

"What are you doing to me?" Kaye managed to say. Everything felt numb and strange.

"That glamour you were wearing would fool no one. I am simply restoring the one you should have been wearing."

"But Halloween isn't till tomorrow," Kaye protested. There was a strange prickling all along her arms. This time it didn't seem as though it came from inside her. Something was happening. Her heart sped, and she could feel . . . something, a strangeness. And then a dark shape hurtled out of the clouds.

Something roared over them.

Kaye threw her arms up over her face. She tried to scream, but when she opened her mouth, it was filled with wind.

Hands clutched her shirt and legs and hair, lifting her and passing her up into a mass of creatures. She kicked and bit, tearing their long cornsilk hair and ripping their powdery wings. Pointed, catlike faces hissed, and fingers pinched her, but they flew on in a long train of monsters and she was with them.

9

You whom I could not save
Listen to me.
—CZESLAW MILOSZ, "DEDICATION"

Kaye's throat was raw with screaming. Sharp claws bit into her wrists while bat and bird and insect wings moved with less noise than sheets drying on a line. They flew through the streets invisibly. She screamed, but it seemed that they moved between this world and the next because no one looked up and no one spoke and no one did more than shiver, maybe, or twitch a little as a horde of monsters vaulted through the skies above them. Kaye bit and scratched and squirmed and tore, till the feathery dander of her captors' wings shimmered all over her. Not once did they loosen their hold. They were one sinuous being of which she was only a tiny, unwilling part, and all she could do was scream.

Then they swooped down, dropping through the sky so fast it stopped her breath. Cemetery Hill vaulted up to meet her. The air forced her shouts back down her throat, and she swallowed them.

Her ankle twisted as she fell forward onto her hands and knees. For a moment she couldn't breathe. The monsters dropped easily around her, skittering and jumping on the ground. Every cut and bruise seemed to come alive, throbbing with vigor. Her bones felt loose in their sockets.

Black, shiny eyes like her own stared back from the dozen or so creatures that glanced at her. Something grabbed hold of Kaye's hair and pulled her head back so that she was staring up into gold-flecked owl eyes.

"Tasty mousie." The creature's thick, dark lips moved slowly over the words. Its voice was like dried leaves being crushed.

Others were crowding in, their faces pressing too close. Their hungry heat dizzied her. She flailed her hands to keep them away. Little winged creatures flitted around and showed their teeth.

"Grab-snatch great fun," the owl-eyed woman said, jerking Kaye's hair hard enough to pull her whole body with it, "such a fine, fine treat." The creature let go of her, and she fell on already raw knees.

"Let her be," Nephamael said, jerking her to her feet.

It was as if something had sawed the hill off at the base and raised it on fat pillars. Mushrooms, corpse-pale and each the size of her fist, ringed the grounds. Beneath that earthen ceiling, marvelous Folk feasted as though it were a tent.

Nephamael's fingers pressed into her shoulder as though determined to bruise. The thorns that capped each gloved finger scraped across her skin with each stumbling step.

He brought her to the raised earthen dais, and she had to take several deep breaths to keep back the terror that was threatening to overwhelm her. The Queen sat on her throne; twin boys with goat feet knelt on either side of her, one absently playing a flute. Roiben stood on her left side, his clothes all of a dark silver fabric that managed to look like cloth and metal at the same time. Jagged freshwater pearls circled his collar and cuffs, reminding her of teeth. He looked magnificent, shining like the moon herself.

He was as distant as the moon too, expressionless and grim.

On the Queen's right side, there were two more knights, one dressed in a red so dark it was almost brown and the other in smoky blue. Farther back on the dais, mostly hidden by the throne itself, a fox-faced creature wearing an oddly shaped skullcap paused, one claw holding a brush over a long curling sheet of white birch bark that it was using as parchment.

Kaye was pushed roughly to her knees. She could feel Nephamael sinking down behind her.

The Queen of the Unseelie Court looked down on her, lips quirking into a smile. Her blood-red hair was pulled back into thick, jeweled braids, and the dusky gray of her dress made her skin all the more pale and creamy by comparison. She was inhumanly beautiful, but her smile held no fondness. Kaye was disturbed to find herself smiling back into those cruel blue eyes nonetheless, longing for them to light with approval.

The air was thick with a sweet-smelling pollen that made Kaye feel giddy and unfocused. It was hard to get a real breath. The Queen's eyes were too clear, too blue, Kaye thought. They looked fake. Then the vertigo hit.

"Kaye Fierch, the Unseelie Court would bestow a great honor on you." The Queen's words dropped into her mind, each one echoing separately, the words making no sense when put together. "Will you submit to it?"

Kaye knew she had been asked a question and that it was very important she answer it. She tried to gather her scattered thoughts. Blue eyes held hers. She wanted to close her eyes. She wanted to stop the chill that was unfolding inside her, spreading from her chest, filling her with trembling longing. The most she could do was blink slowly.

"Perhaps her silence is answer enough." Kaye heard Roiben's voice as from a great distance. There was some laughter after he spoke.

"Come closer, little mortal." The Queen leaned forward, stretching out one lily-white hand, and before Kaye had time to consider it further, she was crawling forward to touch it. The Queen ran her fingers through Kaye's hair, mussing and then smoothing it down again.

"You want to please us, do you not, little one?"

"Yes." She did. She had never wanted anything more.

Nicnevin smiled at that, a smile that curled up at the ends.

"In fact, your only desire is to please us, is it not?"

"Yes." She shivered with delight as the Queen's hand stroked her cheek.

"You will please us greatly, child, if you are obedient and merry and do not question those things that you find strange. Do you understand?"

"Yes."

"We ask that you honor us with your participation in the Tithe. Will you accept the burden of this honor?"

Something in the phrasing of the question seemed strange, but Kaye knew what answer to give. "Yes."

The Queen's smile was dazzling. Out of the corner of her eye she saw Roiben scowl, and she wondered at that. Wasn't he pleased that his Lady was pleased?

"My knight will have you groomed and properly attired. You mustn't try too hard to please him. It's a hopeless task." The Queen gave an almost imperceptible nod.

Roiben was beside Kaye then, drawing her to her feet. He smelled of burning cloves.

Rath Roiben Rye stood on his Lady's left-hand side, in his place of honor, his fists clenched so tightly he could feel the half-moon incisions his nails made in his palms. The girl was answering fatally in her soft-as-ash voice. She had made no move to say his name, and now it was far too late for that.

He willed his hands to relax. He did not want his Queen to guess at the increasingly dangerous chances he took. Letting the girl ask his name—have absolute power over him— was unintended, but hardly an isolated case of foolishness. At first he had told himself that he was testing himself, but his reasons seemed more complex. He was becoming less clear to himself—a string of actions held together by nothing, with no sequence he could understand.

He let his gaze skim out over the crowd. He knew the Unseelie Court, knew the factions and their plans, their squabbles with one another, their desires and their habits. He knew them as only an outsider could, and his Lady valued that. That value was balanced against her amusement at his pain.

Everything is balance. Everything is ritual. Everything is pain.

The solitary fey had gathered warily at the edges of the brugh. He knew that many among them had no wish to be tied to the Unseelie Court, and for a moment he wondered if they could somehow refuse the sacrifice. But he could see from where he stood that they were drinking the traditional wine pressed from nettles. They had come to accept their servitude. Indeed, servitude might offer them some protection that independence had not.

A soft sound brought his eyes back to Kaye. He noted the bruises and faint raised marks that looked like scratches. She was gazing at the Queen with an adoration that sickened him. Was that how he had once looked at the Seelie Queen when he had vowed himself to her? He remembered that when his Bright Lady had but glanced at one of her knights, it was as if the sun shone for that knight alone. His own oath to her had been so easy to say, all the promises he had wanted to make wrapped into those formalized phrases. And he was still doing her bidding now, wasn't he? He wondered again as he stared into Kaye's face, as she waited happily for him to squire her into the sunless caverns of the Unseelie palace and pretty her up for her murder, just what was worth the pain of this.

"Come," he said.

Roiben walked from the brugh down hallways that shone with mica, their ceilings tangled with roots. Lights were dim and infrequent, candles oozing wax down the side of the wall from the niches they were set into. He heard the dull thud of her heavy boots as she followed him and he wanted to look back, to give her the comfort of a smile at least as she tried to keep pace through these winding passageways, but a smile would be a lie, and how would that serve her?

They passed by orchards of trees, white as bone and heavy with purple fruit. They passed through caverns of quartz and opal. They passed through rows of doors, each with a different face carved on it. Above it all, the ceiling shimmered with a distant light.

"You may ask me what you will. The Queen's strictures are not my own." Roiben hoped that whatever enchantment the Queen had put on her was not irresistible.

"I'm sorry, you know," she said softly. Her eyes were drugged with enchantment, the lids half closed. One of her hands was running across the sparkling mica wall, stroking it as though it were the belly of some great animal.

"Sorry?" he echoed stupidly.

"The diner," she said, swaying slightly, the hand on the wall now holding her upright, "I didn't know what I was asking."

He flinched at that. Her power over him was greater than any oath—he was literally hers to command—and here she was apologizing for her cleverness. But maybe that was the magic too, forcing her mind away from survival.

Her hand had stilled on the wall, and her eyes found the floor.

He took a deep breath. "It was well tricked. Perhaps you will find a way to make it serve you yet." Not wise, that advice. He didn't know why he had put her through all the trouble of drawing the arrow from his chest when he was apparently at such pains to get himself run through again.

Fey as one of his own Folk, she suddenly laughed. "Are we really going to get me a dress?"

He nodded. "There is a seamstress who can weave spiders back from silk. She will make sure you have a dress. . . ." He bit off the end of the phrase, not knowing how to finish it. This wasn't a ball gown—it was a shroud. "A fine dress," he finished badly, but there it was.

Kaye grinned with delight, turning delicately on one foot, improvising a staggering dance as she followed him down the shimmering hallway, repeating his words. "Spiders back from silk . . ."

Skillywidden's quarters were deep in the cavernous depths of the palace where Roiben seldom had reason to go. Bolts of satins glowing summer-warm and golden, silks that would easily pass through the eye of a needle, heavy brocades rich with strange moving animals were all scattered along the floor in the dim room. A long wooden table was covered with silver bowls of varying sizes holding pins, spools of thread, and trims—skins of mice, drops of shimmering dew, leaves that would never fade and other, less pleasant things.

The most fantastical things in the room were those that appeared the most ordinary, Roiben knew. The loom that could weave Folk into tapestries, binding them there till this or that term was met, looked like an old and much abused loom, nothing more. The spindle was much the same, rough wood and plain, but he knew that the long black thread it was wound with was human hair.

The seamstress herself was a small creature with spindly limbs, long and awkward. She was draped in sheer black cloth that hid half of her face and hunched so far over that her long arms almost touched the floor. Roiben bowed shallowly as shining black eyes regarded him. Skillywidden hissed her greetings and shuffled over to lift Kaye's thin arms, measuring their width by squeezing them between her thumb and first finger. When Kaye's brown eyes caught his, he could see the glint of fear in them, although her body remained limp.

"Toothsome," Skillywidden rasped speculatively, "smooth skin. What shall I trade for her? I could make you a tunic with the scent of apple blossoms. That would remind you of home, no?"

Kaye shuddered.

"I am here for a gown, not to trade," Roiben said, repressing a shudder himself. "The Queen would like her better dressed for the revels seeing as she"—again, it was hard to find the right words, so as not to alarm the girl—"is a guest of honor."

Skillywidden chittered and began digging through her bolts of cloth. Kaye's drugged haze seemed to keep her from remembering that the seamstress scared her, and she was now stroking a fabric that shifted color as she touched it.

"Stretch out your arms," the seamstress croaked, "wide as a bird. There."

Kaye held up her arms while Skillywidden draped her with fabrics and whispered incoherently. The little crone grasped Kaye's chin suddenly and jerked it downward, then shuffled over to her bowls, digging around in them. There was nothing for Roiben to do but wait.

Apple blossoms no longer reminded Roiben of home, although the Seelie Court had reeked of them. No, now the scent of apple blossoms reminded him of a treewoman, whose brown face had been tranquil as dirt despite how far she was from her tree. She had been a prophet, but she would not prophesy for the Unseelie Queen. He had been ordered to persuade her.

What he remembered most now, however, were the tree-woman's last words to him, spoken as mossy fingers scraped his cheek and thick sap ran from the many cuts in her body. "Don't envy the dying," she had said.

You can break a thing, but you cannot always guide it afterward into the shape you want.

"Knight?" Skillywidden said, holding up a skein of thin, white silk. "Is it meet?"

"Send the dress to my rooms," Roiben said, pulling himself from his thoughts. "The Queen desires her to be clad and back in the brugh tonight."

Skillywidden looked up from the collection she was assembling, blinked owlishly, and grunted. That was enough of a response for him; he had no need to urge further swiftness on the seamstress. Kaye was likely to benefit from any delays.

"Come," Roiben said, and Kaye followed him tractably. She looked drunken with magic.

Retracing their steps through the Palace of Termites, he at last brought them to a wooden door carved with a crude unicorn. He opened it with a silver key and let her go inside before him. He watched her stop to look at the books that covered a low table, running her hands over slim paperback volumes of Yeats and Milton, lingering as she touched a leather volume with silver clasps. It was a book of old songs, but there was no title on the dusty cover, and she did not unclasp it to look at the pages. On the wall, there was a tapestry, the one he had slashed into shreds one night long ago. He wondered whether his room looked like a cell to her. It couldn't have been what she had expected after the marvelous things she had seen elsewhere.

Kaye was looking at the tapestry, studying what was left of it. "She's pretty. Who is she?"

"My Queen," he said. He wanted to correct himself, but he couldn't.

"Not the Unseelie Queen? The other one?" Kaye sat down on the drab coverlet of his bed, tilting her head, still looking at the figure. He didn't need to look to see the depiction, dark hair falling like a cape over the back of her emerald dress—beautiful, but only stitcheries. A mortal had woven it, a man who, having caught sight of the Seelie Queen, had spent the remainder of his short life weaving depictions of her. He had died of starvation, raw, red fingers staining the final tapestry. It was a long time that Roiben had envied him such perfect devotion.

"The other one," he agreed.

"I read that"—Kaye pointed to *Paradise Lost*—"Well, part of it."

"Horror and doubt distract his troubled thoughts and from the bottom stir the Hell within him, for within him Hell he brings, and round about him, nor from Hell one step more than from himself can fly by change of place," he quoted.

"It was in one of those huge anthology books, but we didn't actually talk about it in class. I kept the book after I dropped out—do you know what high school is?" Her voice sounded drowsy, he thought, but the conversation was relatively normal. While the enchantment lingered, it no longer seemed to overwhelm her. He allowed himself to see that as a positive sign.

"We know about your world, at least superficially. The solitary fey know more. They are the ones huddled around windows, watching television through the blinds. I've seen a stick of lipstick traded for an unseemly amount among dryads."

"Too bad they didn't let me bring my bag. I could have bribed my way out of here." Kaye snickered, pulling herself all the way onto his bed.

She was drawn up against the headboard, black jeans frayed at the ankles where they touched the scuffed boots. Just a girl. A girl who shouldn't have to be this brave. Around her wrist, a rubber band encircled the flesh, faded patterns drawn in blue ink still visible. No rings on those fingers. Nails bitten to the quick. Details. Things he should have noticed.

She looked tired, he realized. He knew little of what her life was like before he had made a mess of it. With a grimace he remembered the ripped shirt that she had ripped further to bind his wound. "At least we think we know something of your world. I do not, however, know near as much as I ought about you."

"I don't know much about the world," Kaye said. "I only know about the crappy town I grew up in and the even crappier city we moved to after that. I've never even been out of the country. My mom wants to be this singer, but mostly she just winds up getting drunk and screaming how other vocalists suck. God, that sounds depressing."

Roiben thought of what would happen if the sacrifice was not made, if by guile or chance or something else, Kaye escaped. The solitary fey would be free for seven years. He imagined the chaos that would ensue.

It very nearly pleased him.

"I don't think I've exactly been cheery myself, fair Kaye."

She sighed, smiling, and let her head fall back, her ragged blond hair spreading out in a halo over his pillows. He thought absently that he would like to braid that hair the way he had once braided his sister's.

"I went to high school for a while," she continued absently, "and then I got out of the habit. People usually think that I'm pretty weird, which is funny at the moment. Maybe funny is the wrong word."

He sat on the end of the bed, just listening.

"I thought weirdness was a good thing. I don't mean that defensively, either. I thought it was something to be cultivated. I spent a lot of time hanging around bars, setting up equipment, breaking it down, loading up vans, fishing my mom's head out of toilets—things other kids didn't do. And sometimes things just happened, magical things that I couldn't control. But still, all this—you—it's so hard to accept that you're really real." She said the last with a hushed reverence that was completely undeserved.

Still, she sounded so normal. Conversational. She even looked normal, if a touch too comfortable on a stranger's bed. "Do you still want to please me?"

Her smile was surprised, a little baffled. "Of course I do."

"It would be better if you did not," he said, hesitating, trying to find a way to reason her out of enchantment. He could do nothing for her if she was like this when the actual ceremony took place. "It would be better if you acted according to your own desires."

She sat up and looked at him intently. "Do *you*? Don't you want to go home?"

"To the Seelie Court?" He allowed himself to say it. For a long moment, he considered what she asked and then he shook his head. "Once, I wanted nothing more. Now, I think I would not be welcome among them and, even were I, it is unlikely we would suit."

"You're not the way everyone says you are," Kaye said, looking at him so fiercely that he couldn't meet her gaze. "I know you're not."

"You know nothing of me," he said. He wanted to punish her for the trust he saw on her face, to raze it from her now so that he would be spared the sight of her when that trust was betrayed.

He wanted to tell her he found her impossibly alluring, at least half enchanted, body bruised and scratched, utterly unaware she would not live past dawn. He wondered what she would say in the face of that.

Instead, he forced a little laugh. "Let me explain again. Of the Host of the Unseelie Court are many unconcerned by blood and death, save as amusement. But the Host is more than a scourge. Nicnevin rules over ancient secrets, buried in the bowels of warrens and fens. The twilight holds as many truths as the dawn, perhaps more, since they are less easily perceived. No, I do not think that I would be welcomed back, now that I can see that."

"But they—" Kaye began, and he held up a hand to forestall her objection.

"Smallish sects of beings, of which Faerie is certainly one, require enemies to give them purpose. Think on Milton's angels. Was not his God wise in giving them a devil to fight?"

Kaye was quiet a moment. "Okay, you're saying that the Seelie Court needs to hate the Unseelie Court. But does that mean that you think that they're not all bad?"

"I can think of no insult too rich for the Unseelie Queen, but I have seen kindness in some of her court. More kindness and wisdom, surely, than I would have ever been given leave to expect."

"So what adversary does the Unseelie Court have?"

"Again, the parallels to your devils are amazing. They struggle with their own boredom. It is a struggle that often requires increasingly cruel diversions."

Kaye shuddered. "And you?"

Roiben shrugged. He had nearly forgotten what it felt like to just sit and talk with someone. "I am some other thing, not of any court, nor truly solitary. There are too many possessors of my soul."

She moved to her knees, and reached for both his hands. "Just so you know, I trust you."

"You shouldn't," he said automatically. Nevertheless, he found himself no longer wanting to punish her for her faith in him. Instead, he found himself wanting to be worthy of it. He wanted to be the knight he had once been. Just for a moment.

He watched her take a breath, steeling herself, perhaps, for the next turn of the conversation. He found that he could not bear it.

Roiben leaned forward before he might think to do otherwise and pressed a kiss to her dry lips. Her mouth opened with a rush of warm breath, and her arms ran over his shoulders to rest lightly, almost hesitantly, at the nape of his neck.

His tongue swept her mouth, searching for some escape from the chill inside him. It felt so good it made his teeth hurt.

Nor from hell one step more than from himself can fly. Charmed. He was kissing a charmed girl. He jerked his mouth back from hers. She looked a little dazed and ran her tongue over her lower lip, but said nothing.

He wondered what exactly she might think of it when her mind was better disposed toward the contemplation of such things. But then, his mind whispered, tomorrow would never come to her, would it? There was only now and if he wanted to kiss her, well, it was only kissing.

Kaye moved slightly back from him, folding her knees against her chest. "Would that piss her off?" Again, he didn't need to ask to whom she referred.

"No," he said, rubbing a hand over his face, giving a short laugh. "Hardly. It would doubtless amuse her."

"What about the other one—the other Lady?"

He closed his eyes reflexively, as if something had been thrown at him. He wondered why he was enamored of a girl that could dissect him with the odd comment, throw him off balance with the idle, earnest question.

"You can kiss me, if you want," she said softly, roughly, before he found an answer. It seemed that the magic had burned out of her, because her eyes were as clear as they were bright. He could not tell whether the Queen's spell held her or what compulsions it put on her. "I should just stop asking you stupid questions."

He leaned forward, but there was a rapping on the door then, soft but insistent. For a moment, he didn't move. He wanted to say something about her eyes, to ask her perhaps a better question about her enchantment, or at least one that might produce a better answer. Tell her that she could ask him anything she wanted. And he wanted to kiss her, wanted it so badly that he could barely pull himself to his feet, march to the door, and heave it open.

Skillywidden had somehow gotten a redcap to do her

delivering for her. It stood in the doorway, stinking of congealed blood and rot. Pointed teeth showed as it smiled, looking beyond him to the girl on his bed.

Roiben snatched the white cloth out of its hands. "This better be clean."

"Lady wants to know if you're done with her yet." The leer on its face made it obvious how the Redcap interpreted those words.

Fury rose in him, choked him so unexpectedly that he feared he was trembling with it. He took a breath, then another. He trusted that the messenger would not notice. Redcaps were not much for details.

"You may tell her that I have not yet finished," he said, meeting that gaze with what he hoped was a small smile and a bow of his head as he shut the door, "but I expect to in short order."

When he turned back to her, Kaye's face was blank.

He swallowed the emotion he felt without even bothering to identify it.

"Put it on," he said harshly, not even trying to keep the anger out of his voice, letting her think it was directed at her. He tossed the gown toward Kaye, watched her flinch as the slippery silk slid over the edge of the bed, watched her lean down mutely to pick it up again.

She didn't trust him after all. Good.

"It is time," he said.

10

Corny sank lower in the warm, silty water as Nephamael swept into the room. The faerie women who had cut his hair and oiled his skin finished and left without being told to do so.

"They have made you quite lovely," Nephamael said, yellow eyes reflecting in the flickering candlelight.

Corny shifted self-consciously. The oil made his skin feel weird, even under the water. His neck itched where stray strands of cut hair stuck to it. "Making me look good is about as likely as turning lead into gold," he murmured, hoping he sounded witty.

"Are you hungry?" Nephamael asked in his rich-as-butter

voice. Corny wanted to ask about Kaye, but it was so hard when the knight was walking toward him with slow, even strides.

Corny nodded. He didn't trust his voice. He still could only half believe that Nephamael had brought him from his ratty, ridiculous life, to this.

"In this country there are fruits that taste better than all the meat of your land." His wide lips twisted into a grin.

"And I'm allowed?"

"Very like, very like." Nephamael gestured to a pile of clothing. "Dress and I will show you."

Corny was both grateful and disappointed when Nephamael left him to dress on his own. Hurriedly pulling on the blue velvet tunic and tight pants, Corny ignored the dampness of his skin.

Nephamael was waiting in the hall. He ran his fingers through Corny's hair, smoothing it back into place. "A compliment would go amiss, I'm sure."

With those hands on him, he could hardly manage a reply.

"Come," Nephamael said, and Corny followed.

Candlewax dripped down the walls in an imitation of the stalactites above them. He could hear music and laughter as from far away. They walked through open doors of silver ivy to a garden where silver apples weighed the boughs of trees nearly to the ground. A slender path of white stones wound around the trees and back over itself throughout the garden. Above the orchard, the curved ceiling glowed as though it were day and they were no longer under the hill. Corny could smell fresh-turned earth, cut grass, and rotting fruit.

"Go ahead," Nephamael said, nodding toward the trees. "Eat whatever you desire."

Corny was no longer sure whether he was hungry. Still, to

avoid displeasing the knight, he went over and plucked an apple from one of the trees. It tumbled easily into his hand. The silver skin was warm to the touch, as though blood ran beneath the surface.

Corny looked up at Nephamael, who appeared to be studying a white bird perched in one of the trees. Corny took a cautious bite of the fruit.

It tasted of fullness, of longing and wishful thinking and want, so that one bite left him empty. Nephamael smirked as he watched Corny lick the broken fruit, devour the pulp, sink to his knees, sucking the pale center pit.

Several of the Host gathered to watch him gorge, beautiful faces with upswept features and teardrop eyes turned toward him like flowers. They were laughing. All Corny could do was eat. He barely noticed Nephamael laughing uproariously. A woman with thin, curving horns tossed him a bruised plum. It burst in the dirt, and he hastened to lap up the pulp, soil and all. He licked the dirt after the fruit was gone, hoping for a darkened drop.

Black ants crawled over the sticky, fallen fruits and he ate those as well, blindly questing for any morsel.

After a time, Nephamael came forward, pressing a cracker to Corny's lips. He took it in his mouth thoughtlessly. It tasted like sawdust, but he swallowed it down.

It felt solid in his stomach, and the overwhelming empty hunger abated. It left him squatting under one of the trees, awake and aware. He looked at his filthy hands, the stained clothes, the laughing Folk, and he choked to keep from crying like a child for sheer helplessness.

"There, there," Nephamael said, patting Corny's shoulder.

Corny stood, fists clenched.

"Poor Cornelius. You look so fragile, I'm afraid your heart will break." There was amusement in the knight's tone.

Corny could feel himself reacting to that rich, smooth voice, could feel the shame and embarrassment receding until they seemed of only distant importance.

"Come here, my pet. You've made a mess of yourself." Nephamael raised his hand, beckoning.

One look into those yellow eyes and he broke like a wishbone. Corny stepped into the circle of Nephamael's arms, basking in the feel of thorns.

Tonight the revels were quieter. No dueling fiddlers or raucous daisy-chain dances. There were no piles of fruit or honey cakes. Instead there were whispers and smothered laughter. The only light came from braziers throughout the brugh and the small faeries that flitted over the congregation.

It was hard to think. Kaye's feet were cold as they padded along the earthen floor. The haze of magic had lifted slowly, but the less she was enchanted, the more she was terrified.

She was going to die. It didn't matter if her feet were cold.

Roiben's back was to her, his pewter hair sliding like mercury over the shoulders of his coat as he led her through the crowd.

She wasn't going to die, she reminded herself. This was a game. Only a game. Her friends would save her.

One finger rose unconsciously to touch her mouth, which felt oddly soft and swollen. She remembered too well the pressure of his lips, their softness, and she remembered the expression on his face when he had pulled back from her—horror, perhaps, or disgust. She shook her head to clear it, but nothing would come clear.

Some of the eyes she passed sparkled with greed, and she wondered how the solitary fey planned on dividing what was left of her.

Kaye took a deep breath of cold, autumn air, then another. Not funny.

Roiben's hand tightened on her upper arm, guiding her past beings both beautiful and grotesque. The dirt was damp under her bare feet, and she concentrated on that, steadying herself.

The Queen was standing at the center of what looked to be a large, silver dance floor. It was composed of several pieces—each engraved with representations of bound humans and fey—fitted together like a puzzle. In the center, Kaye could easily see ornate manacles attached to short, heavy chains. Unlike the base, the manacles and chains were unmistakably iron. She could smell it.

The layers of Nicnevin's diaphanous black robes blew in the breeze. The longest layer, the train, was held up at three points by goblin attendants. Her collar was stiff, rising like a translucent black fin behind her neck. Kaye trained her eyes on the collar, let her gaze stray to the looping mound of red braids piled on the Queen's head, let her gaze fall anywhere but into those deadly blue eyes.

Roiben dropped to one knee, and she did not need any prompting to follow.

"Do rise," the Queen said. Kaye and Roiben rose.

The Queen waved a dismissal at Roiben, an impatient

gesture of her hand. He hesitated a moment, then approached the Queen, lowering himself to his knee again.

"I would give anything for her release," Roiben said in a voice so low Kaye was sure that only those very close could hear it. He stared downward, whether at the earthen floor, or the Queen's slippered foot, Kaye could not say.

The sincerity in his voice frightened her. This was no safe thing, the way he was talking. Did he think he had to do this to repay some debt he thought he owed her? Did he think he had to do this because he'd kissed her?

Nicnevin's hand brushed over the crown of Roiben's head. Her voice was as soft as his, but her eyes sparkled with feral delight. She was looking beyond him and out into the blackness beyond the brugh. "Are you not already my servant in all things? Is there something of yours I do not already possess?"

He raised his head, then, looking up into the Unseelie Queen's blue eyes, and Kaye wanted to yell a warning, something, but the moment was frozen and she did not move.

"Perhaps I could offer my enthusiasm," he said. "You have oft complained of its lack."

The Queen's lips quirked at the edges, an almost smile, but she did not seem amused. "I think not. I find that I like you willful."

"There must be something," Roiben insisted.

Nicnevin put her first finger against her carmine lips and tapped lightly. When she spoke, her voice was loud enough to carry in the natural amphitheater of the hollow hill. "Tragedy is so compelling. I find myself moved to offer to play a game with you. Would you like that?"

"I am grateful, my Lady," Roiben said, his head still bowed.

She turned her gaze on Kaye. "Well, child, it seems that you pleased my knight after all. Answer a riddle, and the Unseelie Court will gift you to him."

There was a murmur in the crowd.

Kaye nodded her head, unsure of what constituted propriety in a faerie court.

There was true amusement in the Queen's voice as she spoke. "Cut me and I weep tears as red as my flesh, yet my heart is made of stone. Pray tell, mortal girl, what am I?"

You are yourself. Kaye bit her lip to keep back the hysterical laughter threatening to bubble up her throat again. Okay—red skin, stone center—what matched that description? She thought she dimly remembered an old story about someone having their heart turned to stone and then restored by tears, but she wasn't sure where the memory came from. No, riddles usually had simple, commonsense, one-word answers. They always seemed obvious once you knew the answer.

Flesh. Maybe some kind of fruit? And the stone could be a pit? Oh—*a cherry.*

Kaye bit her lip. If she answered the riddle correctly, she could walk out of here, something she desperately wanted to do. She cast her eyes to both sides of the Queen, looking for Spike or Lutie, but if they were in the crowd, her surreptitious glances did not find them. Walking out of here was not part of the plan. Right now she wasn't sure she cared much for what was or was not part of the plan.

She bit her lip harder when she realized how far Roiben had already gone for her. Had Lutie and Spike realized that she might need protection while she was a prisoner in the Unseelie Court? If the various comments she had heard tonight were any indication, a knight of the Host could do whatever he wanted with a human prisoner. Now, knowing all this, if Spike thought Roiben was such a scumbag, why convince her to go along with a plan that left her in his hands for the better part of a night?

No, she was going to answer the question before things got out of control. She was going to answer the question, tell Roiben everything—above all how sorry she was—and hope he understood. Then she was going to find Spike and get some real answers.

"A cherry," Kaye said as firmly as she could.

Roiben exhaled with a sharp hiss although he remained on his knees. She wondered how long he had been holding his breath.

"My Lady, you cannot . . . ," the fox-faced scribe began, but the Unseelie Queen quelled him with a gesture of her hand.

"Rise, my knight. You have chosen well. She is yours."

Roiben rose and turned slightly toward Kaye, an expression of unguarded relief on his face. Kaye reached out her hand toward him. She would explain everything as soon as they were dismissed. She would make him understand.

"Now, I order you to offer up your prize to be sacrificed for the Tithe," the Queen said.

There was laughter in the crowd.

She saw fury and shame coalesce into something horrible. She saw Roiben's hand drop, twitching over the hilt of his sword.

Then he seemed to regain control of himself, and he bowed to his Queen with a smile. Turning to Kaye, he pressed his lips against her neck, his hand holding her hip, speaking against the skin so that only she could hear him. "What belongs to you, yet others use it more than you do?"

His mouth moving against the skin of her neck made Kaye shiver. She opened her mouth to speak, but he shook his head, raising his hand to run his thumb over her jawline. "Think on it."

He let go of her and joined the other knights.

Three white-robed figures strapped Kaye down, their heavily gloved hands careful when handling the iron. First they shackled her ankles, then her wrists. The iron cuffs burned softly against her skin.

Four knights of the Unseelie Court stepped to the north, south, east, and west points. Roiben stepped to the south, below her feet. His eyes did not meet hers.

What belongs to you, yet others use it more than you do?

Four short, squat men carried braziers blazing with green fire to the four points around the circle where the knights stood. The little men went down on their knees, balancing the braziers on their backs like living stools.

The Queen's fox-faced scribe raised both his hands, and the brugh was entirely quiet. Eerily quiet. Kaye searched the crowd for some familiar face. For a moment she thought she saw Spike, but then she couldn't be sure. There were so many creatures.

More green flames flared around the edge of the brugh, casting strange shadows.

Somewhere, far outside the circle, a single drum began to beat.

The Unseelie Queen began speaking, her voice echoing in the near silence. "We gather on this sacred night to fulfill our sacred debt. Tonight, we who rule must kneel."

As one being, the Unseelie Court moved to their knees. Only the solitary fey remained standing. Even the Queen knelt, her gown puddling around her.

"We, the Unseelie Court, keepers of the earth's secrets, rulers of blood and bone, offer a willing sacrifice in return for the willing obedience of those who dwell in our lands."

Obviously, it didn't bother anyone that their willing sacrifice was in chains, Kaye thought. The slow beat of the drum was maddening. A calm contrast to her heart, which was beating itself to death against the cage of her ribs.

The Unseelie Queen went on speaking. "What is the sacrifice we offer?"

The Court spoke as one. "Mortal blood. Mortal spirit. Mortal passion."

Off to one side of the Queen, Kaye's eye finally settled on Corny, blankfaced beside Nephamael. His pale brown hair had been cut much shorter and combed toward his face. That and the absence of his glasses made his face look thin and vulnerable. He was dressed all in blue velvet, tricked out as though he was expected to perform Jacobean drama once the sacrifice was over. Kaye was horrified to see him there and even more horrified at his lack of expression.

Nephamael was watching her with his implacable yellow eyes. She hoped he was going to do something very soon.

Experimentally, she reached out her own magic to tug at the glamour that was over her. It did not budge, clinging like a wet sheet. She couldn't even feel her wings.

"What do we ask in return?" The Unseelie Queen's voice rang out, beautiful and terrible.

Again the Host spoke. "Obedience. Restraint. Submission."

Kaye's gaze shifted, and she met Roiben's eyes. On his knees, speaking the words of the ritual, his eyes blazed as he tried to communicate with her through the improbable channel of expression.

What belongs to you, yet others use it more that you do?

It was another riddle, obviously. What belongs to you? In the world of riddles, it's the basics—body, brain, spirit. She was pretty sure that she used all of those more than she let the next person use them.

"We ask: Do you understand the compact we offer?"

This time it was the solitary fey who spoke, their voices not as well timed, creating the effect of echoes. "We do understand."

She was looking at it backward, she decided. He wanted her to do something. The riddle was about something she already knew.

She looked into his drawn face and understood so completely that it knocked the breath out of her.

What belongs to you, yet others use it more than you do?

Your name.

The Unseelie Queen's voice broke her concentration. She seemed to be speaking in time with the distant drum. "Do you accept this mortal as your sacrifice?"

"We do accept."

Kaye looked around, in a panic now. What the hell did he want her to use his name *for*? The brugh was huge and it was full. Did he really think he could somehow get her out of here?

"Do you so bind yourselves to us?"

The solitary fey spoke as one. "We do bind ourselves."

Kaye couldn't help the frantic pulling on her chain. Panic

was spreading through Kaye, turning her blood to ice.

"What is the term of your service?"

Dawn was coming. Kaye saw the red glow out beyond the burning green flames.

"Seven years is the length of our binding."

The Queen raised her dagger. "Let the compact be sealed in blood."

No one was coming to save her. Kaye pulled hard on her chains, throwing her whole weight against them, but they were tight, and the heel of her palm could not slip through them. They burned even more as she shifted. The Unseelie Queen looked surprised. Dimly Kaye realized that her calm and silence must have made her seem as though she was still enchanted.

She struggled to damp down her panic long enough to think.

She had to use his name. She had no idea what to command him to do.

A specific command . . . save me . . . stop this . . . get me out of here?

Roiben was glaring at her.

How could he want her to do this? It made no damn sense, but there was no more time to think.

"Rath Roiben Rye." Her voice was soft, the words running together in her panic. She realized what she was doing, and her throat almost closed up. "Cut my bonds."

Roiben drew his finger-slim sword, and the Unseelie Court seethed with noise. A moment of hesitation, and then he smiled. It was a dark, horrible smile, the most terrible expression she had ever seen.

Three knights were on him before he was even inside the

circle. The green knight's heavy sword crashed against Roiben's at the same moment that a red-clad knight slashed at Roiben's back. He twisted, faster than she would have believed, and his blade sliced the red knight across the face. The faerie clutched at his eyes, staggering, his sword clattering into the circle.

Roiben tried to parry a blow from the third knight, a female wielding an axe, but he was too late. The blade bit into his right shoulder so hard that it probably hit bone.

Roiben staggered back, gasping with pain, sword drooping in his right hand, the tip dragging along the metal circle. It came up just in time to stab through the green knight's chest as he rushed forward. The knight fell on his side, completely still. There was only a small hole in his armor, but it was already welling with blood.

Roiben and the female knight circled each other, exchanging tentative blows. Their weapons were not suited for this kind of combat, his sword too slight and her axe too slow, but both combatants were dangerous enough to compensate. She lunged forward, swinging the axe toward his arm rather than his torso, hoping to catch him off guard. He sidestepped, dodging her blow but missing her with a wide sweep of his own blade.

Other Unseelie troops were surging forward, too many and varied for Kaye to count—trolls and hobmen and redcaps. The Queen was still, her lips pressed together in a thin line.

Kaye pulled at her chains, arching her body up hard. Nothing gave.

Blood had darkened the cloth at Roiben's shoulder in a disturbingly wide stain. Even as she saw him slash the other knight's side hard enough to throw the woman to her knees, there were ten more opponents surrounding him. There was a blurry of parry and lunge, his body spinning to slice at a clawed hand, to gut an exposed belly.

And still more came.

Kaye turned her head as far as it would go and spat at her hands, vainly trying to lubricate them enough to work them out of the manacles, muttering, "No, no, no."

The Queen was shouting now, but Kaye could not make out her words over the ring of blades and the shouts of onlookers.

A small form slid beside Kaye on the metal. Spike was scrabbling at her wrist cuffs with a small knife.

"It's all very bad," the little man said. "Oh, Kaye, it's all gone bad."

"He's going to die!" she yelled. Then it occurred to her, what she could do. As loud as she could, she shouted, "Rath Roiben Rye—run!"

The Unseelie Queen whirled at that, her face savage, advancing on Kaye. Her lips twitched over words, but Kaye still could not hear them.

Roiben slashed at another opponent, keeping his back toward Kaye. She wasn't sure whether he had even heard her command. Perhaps he had run as far as he could.

"Hurry, Spike," Kaye said, struggling to keep her body from the wild, trapped animal thrashing that would prevent Spike from having any chance at popping the lock.

The little man's brows were narrowed in furious concentration, fingers burning where they touched the iron. Suddenly he was knocked aside as if by invisible hands.

"While you have been most diverting, I find this tiresome." The Queen of the Unseelie Court placed a slippered foot on

Kaye's throat. Kaye rasped, the pressure cutting off her air, threatening to crack her neck.

Then the pressure was gone, and the Lady was falling. Droplets of blood spattered across Kaye's cheek before the body fell across her. There was a sickening hiss where the Queen's cheek hit the iron. She was dead.

Roiben looked down at her, but his eyes were unfocused and wild. There was a smear of blood across his mouth, but she didn't think it was his own. He raised his sword, and she only had a moment to scream before it came crashing down on the chains binding her ankles, hitting the metal so hard that it rang.

Spike was crawling close again, poking at the motionless body of the Unseelie Queen and muttering to himself. A hush had fallen over the court.

There was a sudden rippling in the air around Kaye. She could feel the magic swirling over her, making the iron cuffs that still clutched her wrists and ankles burn unbearably. Her skin was suddenly too tight, too hot, peeling back as it had done on her lawn, but this time it was not gentle. Her wings ripped free from the thin flesh that bound them just as Roiben slammed his sword against the chain binding her right hand.

His eyes went wide, and he stumbled back. He was so stunned he missed the parry as another redcap rushed him. He turned, almost too late, and the redcap's small curved blade cut his thigh.

Without the protection of the strange, strong glamour, the iron burned Kaye's wrists and ankles like hot brands. She howled in pain, struggling to get the things off, struggling to get out from under the weight of the Queen's body.

Spike seemed to recover himself enough to get to work on the cuffs again, and this time he managed to pick the lock of the only cuff still attached to the chain. Her flesh was blistered where the iron had touched it.

"We have to go! Move!" Spike was pulling at her hand, his face blank with fear.

The court had erupted in chaos around them. Kay looked around for Corny, but didn't see him in the throng. He seemed to have disappeared with Nephamael. She could not tell which of the creatures battling or running or hiding was a foe, or whether in fact she had any friends here except the hob who was urging her to her feet. And Roiben, whose sword was spinning in an arc, crashing against a spear held by a spotted creature with shining golden eyes.

Blood was running over his right hand; blood had soaked the left leg of his trousers. His movements were stiffening; she could see that.

Kaye tried not to concentrate on the pain of the iron, tried to focus on standing up. "We can't leave him here."

A volley of pinecones flew around them, bursting into flame where they fell.

"Oh, yes we can," Spike said, pulling her with renewed determination. "Better he not get a hold of you after you used his name like that."

"No, you don't understand," she said, but she knew it was she who had not understood. She, who had tried to pretend. Roiben had known all along that he was offering her his life.

You *idiot*, she wanted to scream.

"Rath Roiben Rye, I command you to get the fuck out of here with Spike and me, right now!" She screamed it, as loud as she could, sure that he was close enough to hear her this time.

Roiben turned, his eyes flashing fury. He seemed to channel that anger into his sword, because his next blow cut open the golden-eyed faerie's throat.

Kaye wobbled on her feet, trying to shore up her knees, trying not to fall into blackness. Her ankles and wrist burned, and all she could taste or smell was iron.

Then Roiben was pulling her through the crowd with a blood-soaked hand. He tugged her into a run, and Spike was beside them, running too.

As they stepped outside the brugh, a figure stepped in front of them, but was cut down before she caught more than an impression of something awkwardly tall and pale gray in color.

Then they were in the graveyard, running down the tumbled quartz path, past plastic flower grave markers, and flattened soda cans, stepping on cigarette butts, and all those human things seemed like talismans that might actually keep the monsters at bay.

Until she realized that she was one of the monsters.

*"But lest you are my enemy,
I must enquire."
"O no, my dear, let all that be;
What matter, so there is but fire
In you, in me?"*
—YEATS, "THE MASK"

Kaye trod up the driveway, her mother's Pinto looking both familiar and strange, as though it was part of a painting that might suddenly be turned on its side and revealed as flat. The door to the back porch seemed like a portal between worlds, and, even close as she was, she wasn't sure she would be allowed to step through to the kitchen beyond.

More than tired, she felt numb.

Roiben leaned against an elm tree and closed his eyes, unsheathed sword dangling limply from one hand. His body was trembling lightly, and next to familiar things, the blood soaking his arm and thigh looked ghastly.

Right then, Lutie swooped down from one of the trees, circling Kaye twice before landing on her shoulder and scrabbling to press a kiss against the damp skin of her neck. It surprised Kaye, and she flinched back from the sudden touch.

"Scared, silly-scared, scared, scared, scared," Lutie chanted against her neck.

"Me too," Kaye said, pressing her hand against the buzz of the tiny body.

"There'll be a score of songs about you by nightfall," Spike said, eyes gleaming with pride.

"There would have been twice as many if I had died like you planned, wouldn't there?"

Spike's eyes widened. "We never . . ."

Kaye bit her lip, forcing herself to swallow the hysteria that threatened to bubble up her throat. "If Nephamael was going to take the glamour off me, he was going to take it off my corpse."

"Dismiss me, pixie," Roiben said. His eyes had a hollow look to them that made her stomach clench. "I was careless. I will hold no grudge against you or yours, but this foolishness ends *now*."

"I didn't plan this—your name. I never meant to use it for anything." Kaye reached out her hand to stroke the edge of his sleeve.

The effect was instantaneous. He circled her wrist with his hand, twisting it hard. Lutie squealed, springing from Kaye's shoulder into the air.

There was no anger in his voice, no sarcasm, no heat. It was as strangely hollow as his eyes. "If you wish me to endure your touch, you must order me to do so."

Then he dropped her hand so quickly it might have been made of iron. She was shaking, too scared to cry, too miserable to speak.

Spike looked at her wide-eyed, as though he was reasoning with a lunatic. "Well then, Kaye, tell him he can go. He says he won't hold a grudge—that's a generous offer."

"No," she said, louder than she intended. They all looked at her in surprise, although Roiben's gaze darkened.

She had to explain. She turned to him, careful not to touch him. "Come inside. You can clean up your cuts there. I just want to explain. You can leave tonight."

His eyes were dull no longer; they blazed with rage. For a moment, she thought he was going to kill her before she could manage to stammer out his name. Then she thought he might just walk away, daring her to stop him. But he did neither of these things.

"As you say, my mistress." The words curled off his tongue, cutting deeper than she had thought words could. "I would prefer no one else learned the calling of me."

Spike blinked up at the Unseelie knight, apparently unable to control a shudder. Lutie watched them from the crook of the elm tree.

"The Thistlewitch will need to know what has happened tonight," Spike said slowly.

"Go ahead," she said. "We can talk about it later." Taking the spare key out from underneath a dusty bottle of bleach, she opened the door as quietly as she could. The house was silent.

Roiben followed Kaye into the kitchen, and the sight of him carefully closing the back door and filling what was probably a dirty glass with water from the tap was so incongruous, she had to stop and watch. He drank, tipping back his head so that the column of his neck was thrown into profile. He must have seen her staring; as he finished the last of the water, he looked in her direction.

"Your pardon," he said.

"No, go ahead. I'm just going to make some coffee. Uh, the bathroom is there." She pointed.

"Do you have any salt?" he asked.

"Salt?"

"For my leg. I'm not sure what can be done about the arm."

"Oh." She rummaged around in her grandmother's spice drawer and came up with a canister of Morton's salt. "Wouldn't iodine or something be better?"

He just shook his head grimly and walked in the direction of the bathroom.

A few minutes later he returned in his more human glamour. As before, his hair was more white than silver, the bones of his face were slightly less jagged, and his ears were less prominent. He had discarded his shirt, and she was disconcerted to see the pattern of scars on his chest. He must have found some gauze; one thigh looked padded under the leg of his pants.

She poured the coffee into two mugs, alarmed to see that her hands were shaking. Spooning sugar into one of the cups, she looked a query at Roiben. He nodded and nodded again when she offered milk.

"When I first met you, I didn't know I was a faerie," she said.

He raised an eyebrow. "I presume that you knew you were not human when you blackmailed a kiss from me since you looked as green as you do now."

Kaye felt her face flood with heat. She just nodded.

"The question, of course, is whether you aided me in the forest for the reward of my name."

She stammered, the queasy feeling in the pit of her stomach intensifying. If that was what he thought, no wonder he was furious.

"There was no way I could have known what you were going to offer me. I just wanted to piss you off in the diner . . . and . . . I knew faeries don't like to give out their real names."

"One day, someone is going to cut that clever tongue of yours right out of your head," he said.

She bit her lower lip, worrying it against her teeth as he spoke. What had she expected—a declaration of love because of one half-hearted kiss?

Kaye looked at the steaming cup in front of her. She was sure that if she took a sip of that coffee, she would throw it up.

She needed a cigarette. Ellen's jacket was draped over the back of the chair, and she fumbled through it for a cigarette and a lighter. Lighting it despite Roiben's look of surprise, she took a deep drag.

The smoke burned her lungs like fire. She found herself on her knees on the linoleum floor, choking, the cigarette burning the plastic tile where it had fallen.

Roiben put the cigarette out with a twist of his boot and leaned forward. "What were you doing?"

"I smoke," she said, sitting on the floor. Eyes already watery from coughing could no longer hold back tears. It seemed stupid that this was the thing that would set her off, but she sobbed, feeling more like puking with nothing in her stomach than any crying she'd done.

"They're poison," he said incredulously. "Even Ironsiders die from those."

"I know." She pressed her face against her knees, wiping her cheeks against the faerie gown, wishing she'd let him leave when he'd wanted to.

"You're tired," he said with a long sigh that might have been annoyance. "Where do you sleep? You might consider glamouring yourself as well." His face was impassive, emotionless.

She smeared the tears on her cheeks and nodded. "Are you tired?"

"Exhausted." He didn't exactly smile, but his face relaxed a little.

They went up the stairs quietly. Her new senses were distracting. She could hear the whistling snore of her mother and the lighter, muffled breaths of her grandmother. Up the stairs, she could smell the woodchips and excrement of her rats, smell the chemical soaps and sprays in the bathroom, could even smell the heavy coating of oily dust that covered most surfaces. Somehow, each odor was more vivid and distinct than she could remember it being.

Ignore it, she told herself; things had been the same way the last time she had the heavy glamour removed. Just a perk to make up for the fact she couldn't touch half the metal things in the house and one drag on a cigarette could make her almost pass out.

They went into her bedroom and she turned the old-fashioned key to lock the door. There was no way she was going to be able to explain Roiben to her grandmother, glamour or no.

"Well, I saw your room," she said. "Now you get to see mine."

He waded through the mess to sit on the mattress on the

floor. She dug through the garbage bags and found a musty green comforter riddled with cigarette burns for herself. The pink one she usually slept with was already piled on the mattress, and she hoped that it didn't smell too much like her sweat.

Roiben pulled off his boots, looking around the room. She watched his eyes settle first on the rat cage, then on the drifts of clothing, books, and magazines lining the floor.

"Kind of a dump, I guess." She sat down on the boxspring that still graced the frame of the white bed.

She watched him, stretching out on her mattress, fascinated by the way the compact muscles moved beneath his skin. He looked dangerous, even tired and bandaged and wrapped in her pink comforter.

"What did you do with her?" He looked up through silver lashes of heavy-lidded eyes.

"What?"

"The girl this room really belongs to—what did you do with her?"

"Fuck you," she said, so angry that for a minute she didn't even care that she was supposed to be convincing him how sorry she was.

"Did you think I would credit the tears of a pixie?" he asked, turning so that his face was hidden from her.

Unspoken insults hung on her tongue like thistles, hurting her throat with the effort of swallowing them. They were both tired. She was lucky—he was still talking to her.

As tired as she was, she couldn't sleep. She watched him instead, watched as he tossed and turned, tangling the blankets around him. Watched as his face relaxed into exhaustion, one hand curling tightly around the edge of the pillow.

He never had looked as real to her as he did in that moment, hair loose and messy, one bare foot hanging over the edge of the mattress, resting on a library book she'd always meant to return.

But she didn't want to think of him as real. She didn't want to think of him at all.

And then she was being shaken awake. She blinked in the unnatural darkness of drawn shades. Roiben was sitting next to her on the hard boxspring, hands gripping her shoulders so hard she was sure they would bruise.

"Tell me what you meant to tell me, Kaye," he said, eyes bright.

She struggled to be more fully awake. Nothing about this scene made sense, certainly not the anguish so plain on his face.

"You were going to tell me that you were a faerie," he insisted. "There was no time."

She nodded, still stunned by sleep. He seemed huge; the whole room was swallowed up by his presence so that it was impossible to look anywhere but into his eyes.

"Tell me," he said, letting go of her shoulders, his hands moving to smooth the hair back from her face in a rough caress. "Say it."

"I never meant . . . I wanted to," she stammered drowsily, the words hard to fit together.

His hands stilled. His voice was low this time. "Make me believe it."

"I can't," she said. She had to focus, to find the answer that would make everything right again. "You know I can't."

"Go back to sleep, Kaye," he said softly, no longer touching her, his hands fisted on his knees.

She levered herself up to her elbows, blearily realizing that she had to stop him before he got up from the bed.

"Let me show you," she said, leaning forward to press her mouth to his. His lips parted with no resistance at all, letting her kiss him as though he could taste the truth on her tongue.

After a moment, he pulled back from her gently. "That wasn't what I meant," he said with a small rueful smile.

She flopped back, cheeks reddening, fully awake now and appalled at herself.

Roiben slid off the boxspring and onto the floor. He was looking away from her, at the sliver of light showing under the dirty plastic window shade.

Rolling onto her side, she looked down at what she could see of his face. Her fingers chipped nervously at a drop of wax on the comforter. "I answered the riddle. I thought she would let me go and I answered it anyway."

He looked up at her abruptly, amazed. "You did at that. Why?"

Kaye wanted to explain it as best as she could. He was listening to her, at least for the moment. She made sure to keep her voice completely level, completely sincere. "Because it wasn't supposed to go like it did. I never even thought of using you like that . . . You were never supposed to—"

"Be glad I did," he said, but he said it gently. He reached up and ran three fingers down the side of her jaw. "It's strange to see you this way."

She shivered. "What way?"

"Green," he said, his eyes like mist, like smoke, like all insubstantial things.

She lost her nerve, looking into those eyes. He was too beautiful. He was a spell she was going to break by sheer accident.

His voice was very soft when he spoke again. "I have had a surfeit of killing, Kaye."

And whether that was meant as a prayer for the past or a plea for the future, she could not say.

This time, when he lay down on the mattress and drew the comforter over his shoulders, she watched the cobwebs swing with each gust of air that crept through gaps in the old windows. Words echoed on the edges of her thoughts, phrases she had heard but not heard. She'd seen the scars that ran up and down his chest, dozens of marks, pale white stripes of skin edged in pink.

She imagined the Unseelie Court as she had seen it the night she'd snuck in with Corny, except that now they were all looking at their new toy, a Seelie knight with silver hair and such pretty eyes.

"Roiben?" she whispered into the quiet of the room. "Are you still awake?"

But if he was, he didn't answer her.

The next time she woke, it was because someone was pounding on the door.

"Kaye, time for you to get up." Her mother's voice sounded strained.

Kaye groaned. She unfolded herself stiffly from her uncomfortable position, feeling the impression of every metal coil along her back.

The banging didn't stop. "Your grandmother is going to kill me if I let you miss another day of school. Open this door."

Kaye lurched out of bed, stumbling over Roiben, and turned the key in the lock.

Roiben sat up, eyes slitted with sleep. "Glamour," he said rustily.

"Shit." She had almost opened the door with massive wings attached to her back, and green.

She focused for a moment, drawing energy through her hands, feeling the thrum of it in her fingers. She concentrated on her features, her eyes, her skin, her hair, her wings. Her wrists and ankles were still sore, and she made sure to use the glamour to compensate for the discoloration of the skin where they'd been burned by the iron.

Then she opened the door.

Ellen looked at her and then looked beyond her at Roiben. "Kaye—"

"It's Halloween, mom," Kaye said, pitching her voice in a low whine.

"Who's he?"

"Robin. We got too fucked up to drive anywhere. Don't look at me like that—we didn't even sleep in the same bed."

"Pleasure to make your acquaintance," Roiben said muzzily. In this context, his formality sounded like drunkenness, and Kaye felt an overwhelming urge to snicker.

Ellen raised her eyebrows. "Fine, sleep it off. Just don't make it a habit," she said finally. "And if either of you puke, you clean it up."

"Okay," Kaye yawned, closing the door. Considering the sheer volume of vomit she'd cleaned up over the last sixteen years—most of it belonging to her mother—she thought that was a pretty uncharitable comment, but she was too tired to dwell on it.

A few moments later, Kaye was curled up on the boxspring again, dropping easily back into sleep.

The third time that Kaye woke, it was dark outside the window. She stretched lazily, and her stomach tightened in knots. She reached out to the lamp on the end table and switched it on, bathing the room in dim yellow light.

Roiben was gone.

The pink comforter was crumpled at the foot of the mattress, two pillows beside it. The sheet covering the mattress was pulled off the corner, as though he had slept restlessly. Nothing to suggest where he'd gone; nothing to say good-bye.

She had only asked him to stay for the day. When darkness had come, he had been free to go.

Frantically, she pulled the faerie dress over her head, tossing it on the floor with all the other laundry, tugging on the first clothes she found—a plain white T-shirt and plaid pants with zippers all down the sides. She unbraided her hair and hand-combed it roughly. She had to find him . . . She would find him. . . .

Kaye stopped with one hand still dragging through tangled hair. He didn't want her to follow him. If he'd wanted anything more to do with her, he would have at least said good-bye. She'd apologized and he'd listened. He'd even forgiven her, sort of. That was that. There was no reason to go after him, unless you could count the odd, soft touch of his hand on her cheek or the gentle acceptance of yet another kiss. And what did those things mean anyway? Less than nothing.

But when she went down the stairs, Roiben was there, *right there*, sitting on her grandmother's flowery couch, with Ellen beside him. Kaye's mother was wearing a red dress and had two sequin devil horns sticking out of her hair.

Kaye stopped on the stairwell, stunned as the utter impossibility of the scene crashed up against the utter normalcy of it. The television was on, and its flickering blue light sharpened Roiben's features until she couldn't tell whether he still wore his glamour.

He was drizzling pieces of plain, white bread with honey from the jar, thick amber puddles of it that he as much poured into his mouth as ate.

"I am grateful," he said. "It's very good."

Kaye's mother snorted at his politeness. "I don't know how you can eat that. Ugh." Ellen made a face. "Too sweet."

"It's perfect." He grinned and licked his fingers. His smile was so honest and unguarded that it looked out of place on his face. She wondered if that was what he had looked like before he'd come to the Unseelie Court.

"You're one twisted young man," Ellen said, and that only made his grin widen.

Kaye walked down a few more steps, and Ellen looked up. Roiben turned to her as well, but she could read nothing in those ashen eyes.

"Morning," Roiben said, and his voice was as warm and slow as the honey he'd been eating.

"You still look like shit, kiddo," her mother said. "Drink some water and take an aspirin. Liquor makes you dehydrated."

Kaye nodded and walked down the rest of the stairs.

On the television, a cartoon Batman chased the Joker through a spooky old warehouse. It reminded her of the old merry-go-round building.

"You guys are watching cartoons?" Kaye asked.

"The news is on in ten minutes. I want to see the weather. I'm going up to New York for the parade. Oh, honey, when I saw Liz the other day, I told her how you were doing and everything. She said she had something for you."

"You saw Liz? I thought you were mad at her."

"Nah. Water under the bridge." Ellen was always happier when she was in a band.

"So she sent me an album?"

"No. It's a bag of old clothes. She was going to get rid of them. She can't fit in any of that stuff anymore. It's in the dining room. The gray bag."

Kaye went and opened the plastic bag. It was full of glittering fabrics, leather and shiny vinyl. And yes, there it was, as shimmeringly purple as in her memories, the catsuit. She pulled it out reverently.

"How come you didn't tell me the real reason you didn't want to move to New York?" Ellen glanced meaningfully in Roiben's direction.

Roiben's face was carefully expressionless.

Kaye could not seem to marshal her thoughts well enough to find a reply. "Do you guys want some coffee or something?"

Her mother shrugged. "There's some in the kitchen. I think it's left over from the morning—I could make some new."

"No, I'll get it," Kaye said.

She went out into the kitchen and poured some of the

black stuff into a cup. Adding milk only turned it a dark, sickly gray. She added several liberal spoonfuls of sugar and drank it like penitence.

Roiben hadn't looked angry at all; to the contrary, he looked absurdly comfortable sprawled on the couch. She should have felt better, but instead it seemed as though the knots in her stomach were tightening.

It was evening already, and soon he would be gone. She wanted him, wanted him to want her more than she had any right or reason to expect from him, and that knowledge was as bitter as the day-old coffee.

"Kaye?" It was Roiben, a nearly empty jar of honey in one hand, leaning against the doorframe.

"Oh, hi," she said, stupidly, holding up the cup. "This is really bad. I'll make some new."

"I've been . . . I wanted to thank you."

"For what?"

"For explaining what happened. For making me stay here last night."

She took the old coffee and dumped it in the sink, hiding the embarrassed smile that was playing over her lips. She filled the pot with hot water and swirled a few times before dumping that too.

His voice was very quiet when he spoke again. "For not being afraid of me."

She snorted. "You've got to be kidding. I'm terrified of you."

He smiled at Kaye, one of his quicksilver smiles, dazzling and brief. "Thank you for hiding it, then. Quite realistic."

She grinned back at him. "No problem. I mean, if I'd known you liked it this much and all . . ."

He rolled his eyes, and it was so good to stand there smiling shyly at each other. All the silly words she had wanted to say to him suddenly began clawing up her throat, desperate to be spoken.

"I'm just glad it's over," she said, breaking the spell while she turned to spoon coffee grounds into a filter.

He looked at her incredulously. "Over?"

She stopped in midmotion. "Yeah, over. We're here and safe and it's over."

"Not to distress you," he said, "but I very much doubt—"

"Kaye!" Ellen called from the other room. "Come see this. There's a bear loose."

"Just a minute, Mom," Kaye called back. She turned to Roiben. "What do you mean not over?"

"Kaye, Faerie is a place governed by a set of customs both severe and binding. What you have done has consequences."

"Everything has consequences," she said, "and the consequence of this is that the solitary fey are free again, you're free, and the bad Queen is dead. That seems pretty over to me."

"Kaye, it's going to be off by the time you get here," Ellen called.

Kaye took a deep breath and walked out into the other room.

Ellen was pointing to the screen "Will you look at this?"

On the screen, a newsman was standing in the middle of Allaire State Park announcing that a man had been murdered and partially devoured. The announcer reported that, judging by the claw marks, authorities were speculating that it was a bear.

"Now I'm hungry," Kaye said.

The announcer went on, his salt-and-pepper hair slicked back so that it did not move, his voice overly dramatic. "The man's dog was found attached to the body by a wrist leash and was apparently unharmed. The dog has been taken into custody by the West Long Branch chapter of the SPCA, which is awaiting relatives to come and claim it."

"I wonder what kind of dog it was," Kaye said as Roiben came back into the living room.

Ellen made a face. "I'm going to finish my makeup. Can you just find out for me if it's going to rain? The weather should be on soon."

"Sure," Kaye said, sprawling on the couch.

On the television, the same announcer came back on, with another warning about the animal, reporting that there were several unconfirmed reports about missing infants and children. In some of the more unlikely reports, children were stolen from their beds, out of strollers, off swings in playgrounds. No one had seen anything, however, let alone a bear.

A Popcorn Park Zoo representative was speaking at a press conference. The white-haired man was polishing his glasses methodically, nearly in tears as he explained how it was difficult to tell what animal had escaped, since this morning all the animals had been found in the wrong cages. The tigers had eaten several of the llamas before they could be separated. The deer had been in a bird enclosure, panicking in the small space. He suspected PETA. He didn't understand how this could have happened in such a well-run, tidy zoo.

"In other news, a young girl on her way back from classes at Monmouth University was kidnapped this morning by an unidentified assailant. She was released tonight after a harrowing day in which she was forced to answer riddles to avoid torture. She is currently being held at Monmouth Medical Center and is in stable condition."

Kaye sat bolt upright. "Riddles?!"

Roiben looked at Kaye across the dim living room. "What do you think of the first day of the next seven years?"

Kaye shook her head, not understanding.

The screen showed men and women being strapped to stretchers in Thompson Park. They had been found naked, dancing in a circle, and had to be forcibly restrained by police to make them stop. Their clothes were found nearby, and the available identification showed no common link. They were being treated for dehydration and blistered feet.

Behind the cameras, Kaye could easily see the fat toadstools growing in a thick circle.

Kaye rubbed a hand over her face. "But why? I don't understand."

Roiben spoke as he began to pace the room. "Everything is always easier when considered black and white, isn't it? Your friends are, after all, good and wise, so all solitary fey must be good and wise. Your friends have some respect and fear and knowledge of humans, so all the solitary fey will follow in that example."

The phone rang, startling her. She got up and answered it. "Hello?"

It was Janet. She sounded subdued. "Hi, Kaye."

"Um, hi." Janet was the last person she expected to call.

"I was wondering if you wanted to hang out."

"What?" Kaye said.

"No, seriously. All of us guys are going to a rave tonight. You want to come?"

"Have you seen the news?"

"No, why?"

Kaye fumbled for an explanation. "There's supposed to be a bear on the loose."

"We're going to the Pier. Don't be weird. So are you coming?"

"No one should go. Janet, it really isn't safe."

"So don't go," Janet said. "By the way, have you seen my brother?"

Kaye's insides suddenly turned to ice. "Corny's gone?"

"Yeah," Janet answered. "Since yesterday."

Kaye shouldn't have assumed that Nephamael would only keep him for the night, the way he had the last time. Corny was still under the damn hill. She knew it. She looked desperately at Roiben, but he regarded her blankly. He couldn't hear Janet. He'd never even met Corny.

"I'll see you, okay?" Kaye said.

"Sure. Whatever. 'Bye."

She hung up.

"Who was that?" Roiben asked.

"Janet's brother is still under the hill . . . with Nephamael."

Nephamael's name made Roiben stop in his place. "More secrets?"

She winced. "Corny. He was with me that night . . . when I was a pixie."

"You *are* a pixie."

"He was there that night—the one when you didn't know it was me—and when I left, he . . . met . . . Nephamael."

Roiben's eyebrows shot up at that.

"Corny was totally out of his head. Nephamael hurt him, and he . . . liked it. He wanted to go back."

"You left a friend—a mortal—under the hill . . . alone?" He sounded incredulous. "Are you completely heartless? You saw what you were leaving him to."

"You made me leave! I couldn't get back in. I tried. And he got out on his own that time."

"I thought we were going to be honest with each other. What manner of honesty is this?"

She felt completely miserable.

"Do you know who Nephamael is?"

She shook her head, dread creeping over limbs, making her feel heavy, making her want to sink to the floor. "He . . . he's the one that put the enchantment on me and who took it off."

"He was once the best knight in the Unseelie Court—that is, before he was sent to the Seelie Court as part of the price for a truce. He was sent there, and I was sent to Nicnevin."

Kaye just stood, stunned, thinking about the conversation she had overheard between Nicnevin and Nephamael. Why hadn't she deduced that? What other meaning could there have been? "So Nephamael still serves Nicnevin?"

"Perhaps. It seems more likely that he serves only himself. Kaye, do you know who concocted the plan to sabotage the Tithe?"

"You think it was Nephamael?"

"I don't know. Tell me, how did your friends become aware you were a pixie when not even the Queen of the Unseelie Court could see through your glamour?"

"The Thistlewitch said she remembered when I got switched. She was at the Seelie Court then."

"Now, how is it that they know Nephamael?"

"I don't know."

"We lack some piece of information, Kaye."

"Why would Nephamael want to make trouble for Nicnevin?"

"Perhaps he sought revenge for being sent away. I doubt he found the Seelie Court to his taste."

She shook her head. "I don't know. I have to get Corny."

"Kaye, if what you say is true, you know that he may well no longer be alive."

She took a sharp, shallow breath. "He's fine," she said.

And for those masks who linger on
To feast at night upon the pure sea!
—ARTHUR RIMBAUD, "DOES SHE DANCE"

She'd only ever brought one other person to the Glass Swamp. The summer when she was nine and Janet had taken to constantly teasing her about her imaginary friends, Kaye had decided that she was going to prove they were real once and for all. Janet had stepped on a half moon of bottle glass, cutting through her sneaker and jabbing into her foot on the way to the swamp. They'd never even made it down the ridge.

It had not occurred to her until now to suspect that Lutie or Spike or even poor, dead Gristle had something to do with that.

Darting lights were easily visible from the street, and shouts carried through the still air. She couldn't hear the voices well enough to discern whether they were about to stumble down into a bunch of kids drinking beer or into something else.

Roiben was all in black—jeans and T-shirt and long coat that all must have been conjured up from moonbeams and cobwebs because she was sure they didn't come from any of the closets in her grandmother's house. He had pulled the top part of his hair back, but the shock of white somehow made him seem even more inhuman when he was dressed in modern clothes.

She wondered if she looked inhuman too. Was there something about her that warned people off? Kaye had always assumed that she was just weird, no more explanation necessary. Looking at him, she wondered.

He glanced toward her without turning his head and raised his eyebrows in a silent query.

"Just looking at you," she said.

"Looking at me?"

"I . . . I was wondering how you did that—the clothes."

"Oh." He looked down, as though he'd only then given a thought to what he was wearing. "It's glamour."

"So what are you really wearing?" The words left her mouth before she could consider them. She winced.

He didn't seem to mind; in fact, he flashed her one of his brief smiles. "And if I said nothing at all?"

"Then I would point out that sometimes, if you look at something out of the corner of your eye, you can see right through glamour," she returned.

That brought surprised laughter. "What a relief to us both then that I am actually wearing exactly what you saw me in this afternoon. Although one might point out that in that outfit, your last concern should be my modesty."

"You don't like it?" She looked down at the purple vinyl

catsuit. There had been no reason for her not to put it on immediately. After all, it was still Halloween.

"Now, that's the sort of question I begin to expect from you. One to which there is no good answer."

Kaye grinned, and she could tell that the grin was likely to stay on her face for a long time. They could do this. They could figure this out. Everything was going to be fine.

"Down here?" he asked, and she nodded.

"Indiscreet," was all he said before he hooked his boots in the muddy ledge and carefully walked down the ridge.

Kaye followed him, stumbling along at more or less her own pace.

Green women and men were half immersed in the deeper parts of the stream, androgynous forms rough with bark and shimmery lights.

A few of the creatures saw Roiben and slithered into the pool or back up the bank. There was some whispering.

"Kaye," a voice rasped, and she spun around.

It was the Thistlewitch, sitting on a log. She patted the place beside her. "Things did not go well under the hill."

"No," Kaye said, sitting down. She wanted to put more anger in her voice, but she couldn't. "I almost died."

"Nicnevin's knight saved you, did he not?"

Kaye nodded, looking up to see him, half in shadows, his hands in the pockets of his coat, glowering impressively. It made her want to grin at him, although she was afraid he might grin back and ruin his furious demeanor.

"Why have you brought him among us?"

"If it wasn't for him, I'd be dead."

The Thistlewitch looked in the direction of the knight

and then back at Kaye. "Do you know of the things he has done?"

"Don't you understand? She made him do them!"

"I have no desire to be welcome among you, old mother," Roiben said, kneeling down on one knee in the soft earth. "I only wanted to know whether you were aware of the price of your freedom. There are trolls and worse that are delighted to be without any master but their own desires."

"And if there are, what of it?" Spike asked, coming up behind them. "Let the mortals suffer as we have suffered."

Kaye was astonished. She thought back to Lutie's disdain for mortal girls. If she'd been the mortal she thought she was, they would never have been her friends. Her fingers brushed over the purple plastic covering her legs, letting her nails cut little lines in the vinyl. She had wanted them to be better than people, but they weren't, and she didn't know what they were anymore. She'd been flung back and forth through too many emotions over the past few days, she was hungover from adrenaline, she was worried about Corny and worried about Janet.

"So it's us against them now? I'm not talking about the Unseelie Court, here. Since when are mortals the enemies of the solitary fey?" Kaye said, anger bleeding into her voice, making it rough. She looked at Roiben again, drawing confidence from his proximity, and that worried her too. How had he gone from being someone she half despised to being the one person she was relying on, in the space of mere hours?

Roiben's hand touched her shoulder lightly, a comforting gesture. It amused her how wide Spike's eyes got.

"You think like a mortal," Spike said.

"Well, gosh, I did spend every week of my life except the last thinking I was one."

Spike's thick brows furrowed, and he tilted his head to the side, black eyes glittering. "You don't know anything about Faerie. You don't know where your loyalties should be."

"If I don't understand, it's because you didn't tell me. You kept me in the dark, and you used me."

"You agreed to help us. You saw the importance of what we were doing."

"We have to tell the solitary fey that Nicnevin was innocent of the sacrifice. This has to stop, Spike."

"I won't go back to being bound. Not for any mortal. Not for anything."

"But the Unseelie Queen is dead."

"It doesn't matter. There's always another, worse than the last. Don't you dare try to undo this. Don't you dare go around telling tales."

"Or you'll what?" Roiben said softly.

"It's not her place," Spike protested, twisting the long hairs of one eyebrow nervously between his fingers.

"The Tithe was not completed. The reason matters little. The result is the same. For seven years the solitary fey in Nicnevin's lands are free."

"Unless they enter into a new compact."

"Why would they do that?" Spike demanded. "Rumor has it that the Seelie Queen is coming down from the north, bringing practically the whole court, from what I hear."

Roiben froze at that. "Why is she coming?" he breathed.

Spike shrugged. "Probably to see what she can claim before

the Unseelie Court gets on its feet again. Bad time to be making deals with anyone."

"Do you think Nephamael'll bring Corny to the Seelie Court?" Kaye asked Roiben.

He nodded once. "He'll have to if he intends to keep him." The assumption that if Nephamael didn't intend to keep Corny, he was already dead, went unspoken.

"Do you know where they're going to camp?" Kaye asked Spike.

"It's an orchard," Spike said. "A place where people pick their own apples. They should be there by tomorrow's dawn."

Kaye knew where that was. She'd gone there on a school trip and a couple of times with her grandmother. Delicious Orchards.

"Wait, I want to come with you," Lutie said, flying to Kaye's shoulder. Kaye felt a sharp tug on her hair as Lutie caught a strand.

"I can help," the little faerie said contritely.

"Roiben, this is Lutie-loo. Lutie-loo, Roiben."

Kaye loved it when he grinned. She really did.

"It is my distinct pleasure to make your acquaintance," Roiben said, touching the tiny hand with two fingers.

Kaye walked down the boardwalk, as she had done not even a week before. Tonight, the moon was on the wane, distorted-looking, and the brine off the sea clung to her skin and hair in a fine mist. The tiny specks of silver glittered in the stretchy purple vinyl of Liz's catsuit as she moved.

Helplessness in the face of not knowing where Corny was

had made her restless. She wanted to go everywhere, anywhere Nephamael might have taken him, but she didn't know where any of those places might be. Finally, she decided go to the rave after all. If she couldn't help Corny immediately, maybe she could help Janet. Kaye was so worried that she needed to *do* something, no matter whether it needed doing.

The pounding of music inside the abandoned building was loud enough that she could feel the bass beating through the wooden slats of the boardwalk. Once called Galaxia, the club sat half on the street and half on what remained of the pier. Several years ago part of the pier had burned down, wrecking game booths, a water slide, and a haunted house. The remaining blackened shell was used only to set off the city's annual fireworks. Galaxia had once been a typical Jersey Shore bar and dance club—the airbrushed sign still hung over the doorway, although it was grayed and the edges were abraded from wind-tossed sand.

Tonight she could see glow sticks and bright clothes pulsing with each flash of a strobe light through the window. Kaye wasn't sure if the place had been rented or just broken into. A large crowd was gathered around the door, some costumed for Halloween in masks and face paint, others wearing their normal baggy jeans and T-shirts. A girl with her hair in hundreds of bright braids bounced in place, a teddy bear tethered to her belt loop with a fluorescent yellow cord.

Before they got too close, Roiben picked up two leaves from the gutter. In his hands they became crisp bills that he folded quickly into the pockets of his coat. Lutie peeked her head out and ducked back down.

"I have to work on this glamour thing, don't I?" Kaye said, but he only smiled.

At the entrance, a girl with a blue beehive wig, blue lipstick, and a blue lip ring made change for him.

"Nice outfit," the girl said to Kaye, her gaze flicking enviously over the catsuit. Kaye smiled her thanks, and then they were inside.

Bodies were pressed against one another, undulating like a great wave, dancers having room only to hop in place. A clown was dancing on the bar, his makeup done with neon paint that glowed under the black light. Two girls dressed as cats, both in white leotards with pin-on tails, danced beside him. The music was so loud that Kaye didn't even try to talk to Roiben; she just slipped her hand inside his and pulled him along through the crowd. He let her lead him toward the back where double doors opened onto the blackened boardwalk that was being used as an impromptu dance floor for those that couldn't fit inside the club.

It was as packed as inside, bodies jammed together so that even those that were sitting along the walls were touching.

"See anything?" she yelled.

He shook his head.

Two ends of a horse shouldered by them, holding water bottles. She thought she saw Doughboy in the crowd, not dressed as anything, but she wasn't sure.

"Kaye," Roiben yelled into her ear. "There. Look."

She followed the quick flick of his hand with her gaze, but she didn't see anything. She shrugged, knowing that would be easier to understand than speech.

"Look for your friends," he yelled. She nodded as he set off in the direction of a tall woman with thick lips and maroon hair. The woman stopped dancing and began shouting at him, arms waving wildly when he got close. Then the woman turned, as if to run, and he grabbed her arm.

Kaye left them still arguing and waded through the crowd. If there was just the one faerie and Roiben had already found her, then maybe there was nothing to be nervous about here. In the crush of bouncing dancers, it seemed impossible that there would be anything dangerous and unworldly. Kaye found herself relaxing.

Kenny was on the pier dancing with Fatima and Janet. Fatima had on three different layers of long skirts and a scarf over her head with big hoops in her ears, looking like a pirate. Janet was wearing all black with whiskers drawn on her face in eyeliner. The whiskers reminded Kaye more of a mouse than a cat.

Kaye took a deep breath. "Hey."

Fatima raised her eyebrows, and Kenny stared at her as though she didn't have the glamour on at all.

"Hi," Janet said. Not for the first time, Kaye wondered why Janet had invited her. Had Kenny passed on Kaye's message? Had Janet heard what happened at school? Was it to teach Kenny a lesson? From the way he'd paled when she came up to them, Kaye decided that it was probably working.

Kaye bounced with the music. There was little room to wave her arms unless they were directly above her head.

"Getting some water," Kenny shouted.

He walked off toward the inside of the building.

"Are you going to go after him?" Janet asked.

Kaye looked at her, surprised. Then she shook her head. "I came here to see you. I should have made things more clear, I guess, but there's nothing between me and Kenny. There never was. There never will be."

Janet wore a skeptical expression. "So how come he kept grabbing you and then looked like a kicked puppy when you weren't around?"

"He doesn't look like that anymore," Kaye said. "And, come on, I am a weirdo. What was he going to do with me?"

Janet gave her a reluctant smile. "You're not that weird."

Kaye raised her eyebrows exaggeratedly and got an actual smile.

"Buy me a drink and we'll call it even," Janet said. "No, two drinks."

"Gladly," Kaye said, and went gratefully to the bar.

She ran into Kenny in line for the men's bathroom.

"I'm sorry."

His eyes narrowed. He didn't answer.

She took a breath. Her mind was spinning from all the worry, and she found that she had nothing else to say to him and nothing she needed to hear from him. It was enough that she knew he was all right, eyes clear and free of any enchantment.

"See you back over there." Kaye felt foolish having tried to talk to him. She began to dance her way back to the bar.

Then the music changed.

It was still the spacey, disjointed sound of trance music, but there were unusual instruments in the background, strange reedy sounds and whispers. *Dance.* Kaye's body complied unthinkingly, spinning her into the thick crush of bodies.

Everyone was dancing. People bobbed against one another, arms waving in the air, heads nodding with the music. No one sat against the wall. No one stood in line or smoked a cigarette along the water's edge. Everyone danced—sweaty bodies packed tight, drunk with sound.

At first, it was a gentle compulsion, slipping into Kaye's mind easily. Then she began to notice the fey.

A freckle-faced faerie with flame-red hair that rose up into a Dr. Seuss curl was the first one that she saw. He was dancing like the others, but when he saw her stare, he winked. Looking quickly around, she noticed more, winged sprites with tiny silver hoops piercing the points of their ears, goblins the size of dogs drinking bottled water off the top of the bar, a green-skinned pixie boy with a blue glow stick lighting up the inside of his mouth. And other fey, dim shadows at the edges of the club, flashes of glittering scales, luring dancers into the empty bathrooms and out onto the pier.

Beside Janet danced a disturbingly familiar gray-skinned boy. Kaye pushed brutally through the crowd, knocking people aside with her elbows just in time to see Janet smile up at the kelpie and let him lead her off the edge of the pier.

"Janet!" Kaye screamed, pushing her way to the water.

But when she got there, there were only ribbons of red curls sinking below the waves. She stared for a moment, until desperation rose up in her and she jumped. Bone-cold black water closed over her head.

Her muscles clenched with shock as she went under once and then bobbed up, teeth chattering, spitting out briny water. Her flailing hands caught strands of hair and she pulled, cruelly, desperately. Her legs kicked automatically, treading water.

Her hand came up empty save for a clump of tangled red hair.

"Janet!" she cried as a wave broke almost on top of her, pushing her into the pilings beneath the pier. Taking a deep breath, she dove down, opening her eyes as she went, desperately hoping, casting her hands like claws.

She bobbed up from the water again, out of breath and coughing. It had been too dark to see anything, and the reach of her arms had found nothing.

"Janet!" Kaye screamed, one hand slapping the top of the water, sending a spray of it showering down around her. She was treading water violently, raging at Janet, at herself, and especially at the frigid, black, unfeeling sea that had swallowed Janet up.

Then, rising above the waves like a magnificent statue, there was the kelpie itself, nostrils flaring and clouds of hot breath rising from them.

"Where is Janet?" Kaye shouted.

"Oh no, now you are in my element. No demands."

"A deal then, please. Just let her go." It was hard to speak through chattering teeth. Her body was slowly adjusting, numbing to the temperature of the ocean.

Kaye looked into the softly glowing eyes, their whiteness reflecting in the black sea like distant moons. "Please."

"No need for deals and bargains. I am done. You may have the rest of it if you like."

A body bobbed to the surface beside the black horse, red hair tangled with seaweed, face down, arms floating beneath the surface.

Kaye swam to her and tipped back her head, pushing aside hair to see the sightless eyes, smears of drawn whiskers still staining her cheeks, blue lips and open mouth, full to the teeth with water.

"She thrashed beautifully," the kelpie said.

"No, no, no, no." Kaye hugged the body to her, trying desperately to tip up the head. Water spilled out of Janet's mouth as though it were a decanter.

"Why so sad? She was only going to die anyway."

"Not tonight!" Kaye yelled, swallowing most of a wave she tried to bob above. "She wouldn't have died tonight."

"One day is much like another."

"Tell that to Nicnevin. Someday you're going to know how Janet felt. Everything dies, kelpie, and that includes me and you, faeries or not."

The kelpie looked strangely subdued. It let out a huff of warm air. Then it sank down, leaving her alone in the sea, treading water, holding Janet's body. Another swell came, pushing Janet's body toward the beach. Kaye took one of Janet's hands, no more chill than her own but frighteningly pliant, and scissored her legs toward the shore. As she swam closer, the waves grew larger and more violent, breaking over her. Janet's body was pulled from her grip and tossed up on the beach.

She saw Roiben running toward the edge of the waves. He bent to look at Janet while Kaye struggled to her feet in the shallow water, the pull of receding waves still strong enough to nearly knock her off her feet. She coughed and spat out a mixture of saliva and sand.

"Do you seek out peril? One would think that years of being a mortal would have made you more aware of mortality." He was shouting.

And that had too much of the echo of her previous conversation in it.

He opened his coat and closed it around her, heedless of the wet clothes that dampened his own. Sirens wailed, and she could see flashing lights.

"No." His hand cupped the back of her head before she could turn. "Don't look. We have to go."

Kaye pulled away. "I need to see her. To say good-bye."

Ten steps across the wet sand and she dropped to her knees beside the body, ignoring the edges of waves that sucked at the sand around her knees. Janet had washed up like a piece of rubbish, and her limbs were thrown at odd angles. Kaye smoothed them out so that Janet was lying on her back, arms at her side.

Kaye stroked back red hair, touching Janet's cold face with cold fingers. And in that moment it seemed that the whole world had gone cold and that she would never be warm again.

Kaye woke on the mattress in her bedroom, tangled in the covers, wearing only her underpants and the T-shirt that Roiben had borrowed the day before. Her head was pillowed on his bare chest, and for a moment she could not remember why her hair was stiff and her eyelashes were crusted together with a thin layer of salt. When she did remember, she pulled herself out of bed with a groan.

Janet was dead, drowned. Lungs filled with water. *Dead*. The word echoed in her head as though its repetition held some clue to its reversal.

Vague memories of the night before, of Roiben bringing her home, of him enchanting her grandmother to stop yelling as he led Kaye up the stairs. She'd screamed at him for doing that, screamed and cried and finally fell asleep.

Kaye padded to the mirror. She looked haggard. Her head

felt heavy from crying, and her eyes were swollen with sleep. There were dark smudges the color of bruises under her eyes, and even her lips looked pale and chapped. She licked them. They tasted like salt.

Janet was dead. All Kaye's fault. If only Kaye hadn't gone to the bar. If only she'd told Janet more. If only she'd *made* her believe in faeries, she would have known not to go off with the kelpie.

And Corny was still gone.

Closing her eyes, she tore the glamour she was wearing and let it disperse into the air. What she saw was worse. Her hair was still stiff with salt, her lips were still chapped, and, if anything, the severe faerie features exaggerated how tired she looked.

In the mirror, she saw the reflection of the shirt she was wearing and blearily remembered being stripped down a few blocks from the boardwalk, when no amount of huddling under Roiben's coat could make her teeth stop chattering. The catsuit apparently hadn't been enough like a second skin, trapping water inside it. He'd helped her out of the outfit and then wrapped her in both his shirt and his coat.

Summoning magic to her fingers, she tried to lessen the darkness around her eyes and to shift her hair into magazine-smooth locks. It was easy, and a small, amazed smile tugged at the corner of her mouth when she applied eyeliner with a pass of her nail and dabbed her eyes to be a bright blue. She touched them again and they became a deep violet.

Looking down, she glamoured herself to be dressed in a ball gown and it appeared, ruby silk and puffy crinolines, the whole thing encrusted with gemstones. It looked oddly familiar, and then she realized where the image had come from—it was an illustration from "The Frog Prince" in an old storybook she had. Then, with a pass of her hand, she was wearing an emerald Renaissance frock coat over green fishnet stockings, a modified version of the prince in the same story.

Roiben shifted on the mattress, blinking up at her. He was unglamoured, his hair bright as a dime where the light hit it. Lutie was lying on the same pillow, wrapped in a silver tress as if it were a coverlet.

"I can't go downstairs," Kaye said. She couldn't face her grandmother, not after last night, and Kaye very much doubted that her mother had come home yet. Kaye's memories of the last time she'd gone to the New York Halloween parade were a mass of feathers and glitter and men on stilts. That time, Ellen had drunk so much three-dollar champagne that she'd completely forgotten how to get where they were staying, and they had wound up sleeping the night in the subway.

"We could go out the window," Roiben said easily, and she wondered whether he was teasing her or whether he really had accepted her odd stricture so easily. She couldn't remember much of what she'd said the night before—maybe it had been so awful and irrational that more of the same didn't surprise him.

"How are we going to get to the orchard? It's in Colt's Neck."

He ran fingers through his hair, hand-combing it, and then turned toward Lutie. "You tied knots in my hair."

Lutie giggled in a way that sounded a little like panic.

Sighing, he looked back at Kaye. "There are ways," he said, "but you would mislike most of them."

Somehow, she didn't doubt that.

"Let's take Corny's car," she said.

Roiben raised both eyebrows.

"I know where it is and I know where his keys are."

Roiben got up off the mattress and sat on the boxspring as though it was the couch she had once hoped to make it into. "Cars are made entirely of steel. In case you'd forgotten."

Kaye stood a moment and began rummaging through the drifts of black garbage bags. After a little searching, she held up a pair of orange mittens triumphantly, ignoring his look of disbelief.

"There's steel in my boots," she said, pushing her feet into them as she spoke, "but the leather keeps it from touching me . . . I can barely feel it."

"Would you like a cigarette to go with that?" Roiben asked dryly.

"I think I liked you better before you acquired a sense of humor."

His voice was guarded. "And I thought you liked me not at all."

Kaye brushed back her now-silky hair and rubbed her temples. She should say something, do something, but she was sure that if she stopped to sort out the swirling thoughts in her head, she would fall apart. Was this about the night before? She could barely remember what she had yelled at him now; it was all a blur of grief and rage.

She reached her hand out, touching him lightly just below his collarbone, opening her mouth to speak . . . then closing it again. She shook her head, hoping that somehow he'd understand that she was sorry, that she was grateful, that she liked him too much.

She shook her head again, harder, stepping back.

Corny first. All other things afterward.

They went out the window, Roiben climbing down the tree easily, Lutie flying, and Kaye managing an ungainly cross between jumping and gliding. She stumbled when she landed.

"Flying!" Lutie said.

Kaye glared at her and put on the mittens. Looking down, she realized she was still glamoured in the frock coat. Roiben was wearing all black, head to foot, and mostly leather. Lutie's wings shimmered iridescent rainbows over them both as she looped in the air like a demented dragonfly.

"This way." Kaye directed them to the trailer park. The door to the car was locked, and Kaye didn't hesitate before she pounded one mittened hand against the glass. It spiderwebbed, and she battered at it again and again, until her knuckles were bleeding.

"Stop it," Roiben said, catching her hand when she drew back for another punch.

She stopped, dazed, looking at the window.

He took a knife from inside a boot. Had it always been there, or had he conjured it into existence?

"Use the handle," he said. His voice sounded very tired. "Or use a rock."

She managed to hack open the glass well enough to stick her hand inside and force up the lock. Looking around at the trailer park, she was amazed that no one had even come out to object to her breaking into a car in broad daylight.

Replacing the mitten, she opened the door and got in, wincing as she took a breath of the stale, metallic air. She leaned over and popped the lock on the other side and winched down her window before getting the key down from where it was tucked in the sun visor. Roiben got in the passenger side warily, and Lutie flew in with him, wrinkling her nose at Kaye as she flittered around the backseat and then finally perched on the dusty dashboard.

Kaye put the key in the ignition and turned it, feeling the heat of the iron even through her gloves. It didn't feel unpleasant, not exactly, but there was a buzzing in her head that she knew would get worse.

Kaye pushed down on the gas pedal. The engine wheezed, but the car did not move. Cursing under her breath, she slapped the parking brake down, threw the knob to drive, and pushed on the gas pedal. The car roared forward so fast that she had to slam on the brake to stop. Lutie tumbled into Kaye's lap.

Roiben looked over from where he was braced against the dash. "How many times have you driven?"

"Never," Kaye growled.

"Never?"

"I'm not old enough yet." She giggled at that, but it came out a little high-pitched, almost hysterical. She put her foot on the gas more gently, and the car responded better. Turning the wheel, she began to steer toward the street.

Lutie gave a tiny squeal and clawed her way up Kaye's frock coat.

The smell of iron was overwhelming.

Kaye took the ramp onto the highway, relieved that there would be no more turns, no more merging and stop signs. All she had to do was stay in one lane until they were nearly there. She reminded herself that they had to get there before anything else happened to Corny. She pushed her foot down harder on the gas pedal, willing the car to stay in the middle of the lane as she sped down the highway.

Kaye could feel her vision grow hazy as the iron made her head spin. Even the drafts of air blowing through the window were not enough. She shook her head, trying to throw off the feeling of weight that seemed to settle like a band across the temples of her skull.

"Kaye!" Lutie squeaked, just in time for Kaye to swerve violently to the right and clear of the car she had almost drifted into. The car hit the edge of the grass on the right side of the highway with one wheel before she got it back under control. Lutie's yelp was like the chirp of a sparrow. Roiben had made no sound at all, but she didn't want to take her eyes off the road long enough to see the expression on his face.

Finally, their exit was next and Kaye turned onto the off-ramp, navigating the turn at a dangerous speed. She kept the car on the shoulder of the road since she couldn't find a way to gracefully merge into the regular lanes. It was only two traffic lights, and then she was able to pull into the orchard and park the car, one side hanging far over the yellow line in the parking space. She turned the key with a sigh and the engine died.

Roiben was out of the car nearly before it was fully stopped. Lutie clung to Kaye's coat, still trembling.

"Corny can drive back," Kaye said in a small voice.

"I have a new enthusiasm for our quest." Roiben spoke with great sincerity.

The orchard was acres and acres of fruit trees and had a farmer's-market-type store that sold jam and milk and cinnamon cider that she remembered from her school trip. Today there were piles of pumpkins and gourds, marked down to dirt cheap, some of them looking bruised.

The parking lot was full of minivans spilling out children, their mothers chasing and herding them. Kaye followed Roiben as he wove through the crowd and around a massive monument of hay and pumpkins. One of the mothers pulled her child abruptly to one side, out of their path. Kaye immediately checked her glamour, holding up a hand for inspection and turning it in the light to make sure it was still pink all over. Then she glanced at Roiben and realized that they looked freaky enough for that to be a normal mom-reaction.

The air changed as they stepped into the grove of trees, and the sound of car engines and laughter faded away. She could no longer smell iron, and she took a deep breath, exhaling every exhaust fume. Like when she had stepped into the hill, she felt the odd frisson that she was growing to associate with stepping over into Faerie.

White horses grazed in the meadow, the silver bells on their collars tinkling when they raised their heads. Knotted apple trees still hung heavy with a late-fall harvest of fruit. The air was warm and sweet with the promise of spring and new growth. Denizens of the Seelie Court were spread over the field, silken blankets spread out with Folk sitting or lying on them. As Kaye walked across the grass, she could smell fresh lavender and heather.

The Folk were as varied as in the Unseelie Court, although they were dressed in brighter colors. They passed a fox-faced man in a tattercoat of many fabrics, trailing ribbons. Another fey wore a golden sheath dress, bright as the sun. She whispered in the ear of a boy wearing a dress as well, his all in robin's-egg blue. A group of faeries were crouched over what looked like a game, one tossing shining stones into the center of a circle cut into the earth. She could not see what the object was, but the group would either sigh or cheer, depending, she guessed, on some pattern of how the stones fell.

Nearby, at the edges of the gathering, a treewoman with skin like bark and fingers that turned to leaves at the nails was whispering to a mute apple tree, every so often turning her head slowly to glare at seven little men who were standing on one another's shoulders. They formed a faerie ladder that wove back and forth from base to top, where one little man was grasping desperately for a fat apple.

A winged girl ran by with a very little boy toddling after her, his hair braided with flowers. A human boy. Kaye shuddered.

Looking around again, she noticed more human children, none older than perhaps six. They were being brushed and petted, their eyes half-lidded and dreamy. One sat with a blue-skinned woman, head on the faerie's knees. A group of three children, all crowned with daisies, clumsily danced with three little men in mushroom caps. Faerie ladies and gentlemen clapped.

Kaye sped up her pace, meaning to stop Roiben and ask him about the children. But then she saw where he was looking, and she forgot all her questions.

Next to trees thick with spring blossoms even in fall, there was an auburn-haired faerie dressed in a deep emerald-green coat that flared like a gown. Kaye stopped walking when she saw the woman; she could scarcely remember to breathe. She was the most beautiful thing Kaye had ever seen. Her skin was flawless, her hair shone bright as copper in the sun under a woven circlet of ivy and dogwood blossoms, her eyes were as bright as the green apples that hung near them. Kaye could not just glance at the faerie woman; her eyes were drawn to look until the faerie took up the totality of her vision, rendering all else dull and faded.

Roiben did not need to tell her that this was the Queen of the Seelie Court.

Her women wore dresses in light fabrics of storm grays and morning roses. As they approached, one of the women inhaled so sharply it was almost a scream and covered her mouth with her hand. Roiben turned his head to regard her, and he smiled.

Kaye tensed. The smile seemed to sit incongruously on his lips, more like a twitch of the mouth than any expression of pleasure.

A knight suddenly interposed himself between them and the Queen. He was dressed in jointed green armor, and his hair was as the fine, pale gold of cornsilk. He held an interesting spear, so ornate with decoration that Kaye wondered if it could be used.

"Talathain," Roiben said, inclining his head for a brief nod.

"You are unwelcome here," the knight said.

Lutie clamored out of Kaye's hip pocket and peered at the new knight with unfeigned fascination.

"Announce me to the Queen," Roiben said. "If she does not wish to see me, then I will quit the grove immediately."

Kaye started to object, but Roiben laid a hand on her arm.

"My companions will, of course, be free to stay or go as they please," he continued.

Talathain's glance flickered to the Queen and then back to Roiben with something like jealousy writ in his expression.

A motion of his gauntleted hand signaled several additional knights. A page came, listened to Talathain, then darted off to speak with the Queen.

After bending gracefully to listen to the little page, the Queen stepped away from her ladies and across the grass, toward them. She did not look at Kaye. Her eyes rested only on Roiben.

Kaye could see Roiben's face change as he looked at his Lady. There was a longing there that overwhelmed Kaye. It was the steady look of a dog, gone feral, but still hoping for the kind touch of his master's hand.

She thought of the tapestry on his wall and all the things he had said and not said. And she knew then why he'd drawn back from her kisses—he must have cherished this love all that time, hoping for a chance to see his Queen again. Kaye had been blind, too full of her own wishful thinking to see what should have been apparent.

Kaye was grateful when Roiben knelt, so that she too could go to one knee and shield the pain on her face beneath a bowed head.

"So formal, my knight," the Queen said. Kaye stole a glance upward at the Queen's eyes. They were soft and wet and green as jewels. Kaye sighed. She felt very tired, suddenly, and very plain. Kaye wished Roiben would just ask about Corny so she could go home.

"Yours no longer," he said as though he regretted it.

"If not mine, then whose?" The conversation had too many undertones for Kaye to be sure that she was following it. Had they been lovers?

"No one's, Silarial," he said deferentially, a small smile on his face and wonder in his eyes. He spoke as one who was afraid to speak too loudly, lest some fragile thing—too dear to pay for—shatter. "Perhaps, at last, my own."

Her smile did not fade, did not change. It was a perfect smile—perfect curve of lips, perfect balance between joy and affection—it was so perfect that Kaye couldn't help getting lost in it, losing the thread of the conversation so that she was baffled when the Queen spoke again.

"And why do you come among us then, if not to come home?"

"I seek Nephamael. There is a young man with him that my companion would restore to Ironside."

Silarial shook her head. "He is not among my people any longer. When the Unseelie Queen died and the solitary fey went free . . ." Here she paused, looking at Roiben. Something about her face was unsettled. "He seized her throne and has set himself up as King upon it."

Kaye's neck snapped up. Wide-eyed, without thinking, she spoke. "Nephamael's the King of the Unseelie Court?" She bit her lip, but the Queen turned her gaze on her indulgently.

"Who have you brought to us?"

"Her name is Kaye. She is a changeling." He looked distracted.

The queen's auburn eyebrows rose. "You are aiding her in the recovery of the mortal boy Nephamael has spirited off?"

"I am," Roiben said.

"And what is the price of your service, Roiben who belongs only to himself?" Her hand came up and idly toyed with an amulet around her neck.

Kaye could not bear to look at the perfection of her face.

Instead she looked at the Queen's necklace. The stone was milky-pale and strung on a long chain. It seemed very familiar.

A rosy stain tinted Roiben's cheeks. Could he really be blushing? "Friendship."

Kaye *did* remember that necklace—Nephamael had worn one just like it. He'd had it around his neck the night he'd come to take her for the Tithe.

The Queen leaned forward, almost conspiratorially, as though Kaye was long forgotten. "Once you told me that you would do anything to prove your love for me. Would you still?"

His blush grew deeper, if anything, but when he spoke, his voice was steely. "I would not."

What did that mean, Kaye wondered. It meant something, surely, something that had nothing to do with love and everything to do with the dead Queen. That was what this conversation was about, she realized. His Queen had treated him like a toy she had grown tired of and traded him, not caring whether his new owner would be careless with him, not even caring that his new owner might break him. Clearly, she had plans that included needing her toy back.

"And what if I told you that you had already proven it to my satisfaction? Come, tarry a time with us. There is honey wine and crisp, red apples. Sit by my side again."

Kaye bit her own lip, hard. The pain helped her accept that he was not hers, would never be hers. And if it was much too late to pretend that didn't hurt, she could at least shove it down so deeply inside her that he would never know.

Roiben stared at Silarial with a mixture of longing and scorn. "You must forgive me," Roiben said, "but the smell of apples makes me want to retch. And I have much left to do."

The Queen looked shocked, then angry. Roiben seemed to watch those emotions flit across her face impassively.

"Then you had best make haste," the Queen said.

Roiben nodded and bowed. Kaye almost forgot to.

When they were a few paces away, the white-haired woman caught Roiben's arm, pulling him to face her, laughing.

"Roiben!" It was the woman who had gasped before. Her hair was to her knees, some of it swept up into heavy braids on her head. She wore the costume of one of the Queen's handmaidens.

"I was worried about you," she said, again, the smile wobbling on her face. "The things I had heard—"

"All true, no doubt," Roiben said, a touch lightly. He ran his fingers through the girl's tresses, and Kaye shivered sympathetically, knowing how those fingers felt. "Your hair is so long."

"I haven't cut it since you left." The woman turned to Kaye. "I heard my brother barely introduce you to the Queen. My question is—is Roiben trying to protect us from you or you from us?"

Kaye laughed, surprised.

"Ethine," Roiben said, nodding to one and then the other, "Kaye."

The woman's tinkling laughter was like breaking glass. "You've discarded your courtly airs."

"So I have been told," Roiben said.

Ethine reached up among the branches of the apple tree and broke off a single flower.

"All that matters is that you are now home," she said, tucking the flower behind his ear. Kaye noticed the slight flinch when Ethine touched him and wondered whether his reaction had hurt her.

"This is no longer my home," Roiben said.

"Of course it is. Where else would you go?" Her eyes traveled to Kaye, questioning for the first time. "She hurt you, I know that, but you will forgive her in time. You always forgive her."

"Not this time," he said.

"What did they do to you?" Ethine looked horrified.

"Whatever has been done to me, whatever I have done . . . as surely as blood soaks my hands, and it does, the stain of it touches even the hems of the Queen of Elfland."

"Don't speak so. You loved her once."

"I love her still, more's the pity."

Kaye turned away. She didn't want to hear any more. It had nothing to do with her.

She stalked off toward the car. One of the human children was on his toes, reaching for an apple just out of his grasp. He was wearing a green tunic, tied at his hips with a silk cord.

"Hello," Kaye said.

"Hi." The boy grinned up at her imploringly, and she plucked the fruit. It came free from the branch with a snap.

"Where's your mother?" Kaye asked, shining the apple on her coat.

He scowled at her, one lock of dark brown hair covering his eye. "Gimme."

"Did you always live with faeries?"

"Uh-huh," he said, eyes on the apple.

"For how long?" she asked.

He reached out one chubby hand, and she gave him the

apple. He took a bite immediately. She waited while he chewed, but as soon as he had gulped down one bite, he started gnawing on it again. Then, as if he just remembered her, he looked up guiltily. He shrugged and mumbled through a full mouth. "Always."

"Thanks." Kaye ruffled the chestnut hair. There was no point in asking him anything. He knew about as much as she did. Then, she turned back to him. "Hey, do you know a little girl called Kaye?"

He wrinkled up his face in an exaggeration of thinking, then he pointed toward one of the blankets. "Uh-huh. Prolly over there."

She felt as dizzy as if she'd been hanging upside down. Her fingers were like ice.

Leaving the boy to his apple, she walked among the cloth blankets, stopping each little girl she passed, no matter what they looked like. "Is your name Kaye, sweetie?"

But when she saw herself, she knew. Kaye could manage nothing more than staring as the girl—far, far too young to be Kaye in any reasonable world—picked a weed and, wrapping the stem carefully, flung the head in the direction of a pretty faerie lady who laughed.

All the questions Kaye wanted to ask choked her. She turned on her heel and stomped back to Roiben and Ethine, grabbing his arm hard.

"We have to go *now*," she shouted, furious and trembling. "Corny could be *dead*."

Ethine was wide-eyed as Roiben swallowed whatever he might have said and nodded. Kaye turned on her heel, stalking back to the car, leaving Roiben to follow her.

14

In the hills giant oaks
fall upon their knees
You can touch parts
You have no right to—
—KAY RYAN, "CROWN"

She didn't make it to the car.

"Kaye, stop. Just stop." Roiben's voice came from close behind her.

She paused, looking through the trees at the minivans and the highway beyond. Anything to not look backward at the Seelie Court and the ageless children and Roiben.

"You're shaking."

"I'm angry. You're screwing around while we have stuff to do." His calm was only making her angrier.

"Well, that's finished." He didn't sound sorry exactly, his voice hovering on the edge of sarcasm.

Her face was hot. "Why are you here?"

There was a pause. "Apparently to be scolded by everyone."

"No . . . why are you still here? With me?"

His voice was quiet. She could not see his face unless she turned and she would not turn. "Shall I go, then?"

Her eyes burned with unshed tears. She simply felt overloaded.

"Everything I do . . . ," she started and her voice hitched. "Shit, we don't have time for this."

"Kaye—"

"No." She started pacing. "We have to go. Right now."

"If you cannot calm yourself, you'll do Cornelius little good."

She stopped pacing and held up her hands, fingers splayed wide. "I'm the reason his sister is dead."

He stopped her, placing his hand on her shoulder. She refused to meet his eyes, and abruptly he jerked her forward, pulling her body against his. Her muscles stiffened, but he tightened his hold wordlessly. After a moment, she subsided, her breath rushing from her in a long, shuddering sigh. Long fingers stroked her hair. He smelled of honey and sweat and the detergent her grandmother used.

She rubbed her cheek against his chest, closing her eyes against the thoughts that were gibbering in her head, whispering bids for attention.

"I'm here because you are kind and lovely and terribly, terribly brave," he said, voice pitched low. "And because I want to be."

She looked up at him through her lashes. He smiled and rested his chin on the top of her head, sliding his hand over her back.

"You do?"

He laughed. "Verily. Do you doubt it?"

"Oh," she said, mind unable to catch up with the stunning joy that she felt. Joy, that was, for the moment, enough to push the other sorrows aside. Because it was true, somehow, he was here with her, and not with the Seelie Queen. He was helping her, even though she was a mess and made an even bigger mess. "Oh."

His hands made long even strokes, from beneath the wings at her shoulder blades to the small of her back. "And that pleases you?"

"What?" She tilted her head up again, scowling. "Of course it does. Are you kidding?"

He drew back to look at her for a moment, searching her face. "Good," he sighed, and pressed her head once more to his chest, stroking her hair as he closed his eyes. "Good."

They stood like that for a long moment. Finally he pulled back from the embrace. "Thankfully," he said, "we don't need the car to get into the Unseelie Court. Walk with me."

The tree was gnarled and huge, its knobbed and gored trunk giving it the impression of sagging under its own weight. The bark was thin and chipped, flaking off like dry skin. At its base, there was a gaping hole where the roots split.

Lutie buzzed up from the hole. "No guards," she said, settling her small self in the tangle of Kaye's hair.

"And this leads where?" Kaye was trying to control her trembling, trying not to let on just how not ready for this she was.

"Through to the kitchens," Roiben replied, inching his body, feet first, through the gaps in the tree. Finally, his head disappeared into the dark, strands of silver catching on the splintered bark. She heard a clatter as he dropped down to the floor.

Kaye kicked her boots against the entrance, feeling wood give way. It chipped off as she pushed in further, burying her legs to the knees. Then, on her back, wriggling forward like a snake, she pushed herself through. It was a long drop, and she bit back a yelp as she landed.

The tunnel was hot and cloudy with steam. Beads of moisture dotted Roiben's face, and his hair looked damp and heavy when he combed it back with one hand. He cocked his head to the left, and she moved ahead of him through the billowing steam.

The kitchen was a huge room with a firepit in the center of it and no visible ventilation system. Faeries scuttled around in the smoke with large pots, piles of skinned rats, little cakes, baskets of silver apples, and rolled casks of wine. The reek of blood assailed her. It stained the walls and the floor, boiled in the pots and dripped over the plates of raw meat. Roiben walked behind Kaye, his hand on the small of her back, pushing when he wanted them to move and clutching her coat to signal her to stop.

They crept into the room, staying close to the wall. A withered old faerie sat on a nearby stool, skinny legs dangling off the side, tongue sticking out of his mouth in concentration as he painted black apples a shiny, nail-lacquer red. His white hair stuck up in wild tufts, and he periodically adjusted his small spectacles as they slipped down his nose.

Next to the apple-painter, a huge green man with small horns on his bald head and fangs protruding over a fat upper lip wielded a cleaver over a collection of oddly shaped animal corpses, hacking them into stew-size chunks. Tattoos of roses and thorns ran up both of the man's beefy arms.

Kaye crept as quietly as any time she had snuck in late to the house, as any time she'd left a store with full pockets. She concentrated on her feet, bowing her head slightly and walking slowly and quietly through the doorway.

Soon the narrow hallway sloped down and opened into a larger passageway, this one floored with grayish marble and studded with huge, carved pillars. The ceiling dripped with stalactites. Kaye could hear people up ahead, shoes clicking like beetles on the stone floor.

Roiben pushed them both against the back of the pillar. He drew his sword from the sheath and held it against his chest. She found the dagger he'd given her earlier and clenched the handle desperately.

But the footfalls turned down another corridor.

They crept along like that until they came to a set of black double doors.

"What's in there?" Kaye asked.

"Wine and the aging thereof," he whispered back.

The room was all stone, stinking of yeast, casks lining the walls and glass bottles filled with infusions of various flowers. There were rose petals, violet petals, whole heads of marigolds, nettles floating like organic spaceships, and other herbs she could not identify.

"What are those?" she whispered. There was no one in the room.

"Wormwood, yarrow, cowslip, gillyflowers, agrimony, fennel—"

"I bet you drink a lot of herbal tea," she said.

He did not smile as he directed her toward the smaller of the two doors in the room. She wondered if he even realized it was a joke.

"Laundry," he said.

The next room was filled with as much or more steam than the kitchens. It wafted in through small vents in the ceiling. In the room were several large tubs filled with soapy water. One pale woman with dark eyes was wringing out a white cloth while another was stirring the contents of a tub with a crooked stick. A man with long arms and a hunched back was adding some granules to the mix, making the water hiss.

It was a small space, and Kaye cast a glance at Roiben. There was no way they could get through the room without anyone seeing them.

"Maigret," Roiben said, grinning as he opened his arms wide.

One of the laundry women looked up, her grin showing she was missing a tooth. "Our knight!" She limped over and gave him a highly ordinary hug. Across the room, the man and woman looked up from their duties and smiled too. "You're one I thought sure never to see again."

"I'm looking for a boy," Roiben said. "Human. With your new King."

The woman made a disgusted sound. "That one . . . King indeed! Yes, there's a boy about, but I can't tell you more than that. I've learned better than to draw the eye of Gentry."

Roiben smiled wryly. "And I as well."

"They're looking for you, you know."

He nodded. "I made a rather spectacular end to my service here."

The old laundress cackled and bid them farewell. Roiben opened a small door and they emerged into a hallway of shimmering mica.

"How do you know they won't tell anyone they saw us?"

"Maigret thinks she owes me a debt." He shrugged.

"Is something wrong with her feet?"

"She disappointed one of the Unseelie Gentry. He had iron shoes heated red-hot before he made her dance in them."

Kaye shuddered. "Does that have something to do with the debt she thinks she owes you?"

"Perhaps," he allowed.

"What about through there?"

"There's the library, the music room, the conservatory, and the chess room."

"Chess room?"

"Yes, chess was well loved by the Queen. They gamble with it like mortals gamble with cards. She once used it to win a consort, as I recall."

"Corny loves chess—he was on the chess team in high school."

"We must go through the library to get there." He hesitated.

"What's the matter?"

"We've seen no guards. Not at the entrance and not even here."

"What if that means we're just doing really, really well?"

"Of a surety, it means something."

The door to the library was mammoth and elegant, clearly different from the plainer doors in the lower chambers. It was dark wood, banded with copper, carved with a language she could not read. Roiben pushed the door, and it opened.

Bookshelves were arranged in a maze, so tall that it was impossible to see across the room to whatever exit there was. The shelves themselves were intricately carved with faces of gargoyles and other strange beasts, and there was the overwhelming scent of turned earth. Whenever Kaye looked in one direction, something seemed to shift in the corner of her eye. The books themselves were in such varied sizes that she wondered who read them all. As they walked, she tried to scan the titles, but they were all in strange languages.

As they turned a corner, she saw a shape slide between the shadows. It was slender and vaguely human.

"Roiben," she whispered.

"The keepers of secrets," he said, not looking back. "They will tell no one of our passing."

Kaye shuddered. She wondered what was written in the tomes that lined the shelves of the library if the idea was to keep secrets. Were the shapes custodians or guardians or scribes?

As they came to a crossroads in the bookshelves, she saw another dark shape, this one with long, pale hair that started too high on its forehead and large, glittering black eyes. It slipped into the shadows as easily and soundlessly as the first one.

Kaye was very glad when they came to a small, oval door that opened easily to Roiben's touch.

Heavy draperies hung on the wall of the chess room. The entire floor was inlaid with black-and-white tiles, and five-foot pieces loomed on the edges of the room. Corny was sleeping on the floor, his body overlapping two chess squares.

"Cornelius?" Roiben knelt down and shook Corny by his shoulder.

He looked up. His eyes were vague and unfocused and he was a mass of bruises, but even worse was the satiated smile he turned up at them. His face looked aged somehow, and there was a tuft of white in his hair.

"Hello," he slurred, "you're Kaye's Robin."

Kaye dropped to her knees. "You're okay now," she said, more to herself than to him, reverently smoothing back damp strands of hair. "You're going to be okay."

"Kaye," Roiben said tonelessly.

She turned. Nephamael was stepping into the room, from behind the draperies on the far wall. His hand stroked the marble mane of the black knight chessman.

"Greetings," Nephamael said. "You will pardon my humor if I say that you have been the proverbial thorn in my side."

"I rather think you owe me," Roiben said. "It was I that got you the crown."

"From that point of view, it's a shame that life is so often unfair, Rath Roiben Rye."

"No!" Kaye gasped. It couldn't be. Roiben had been so far away from the others when she'd used his name. She had barely been able to hear herself. He'd killed all the knights close by, all the ones that could have heard.

"No one else knows it," Nephamael said as though reading her thoughts. "I killed the hob after I got it from him."

"Spike," Kaye breathed. It wasn't a question.

"Rath Roiben Rye, by the power of your true name, I order you to never harm me, and to obey me both immediately and implicitly."

Roiben drew in a sharp breath as though to scream, but he was silent.

Nephamael threw back his head and laughed, hand still stroking the chess piece. "I further order that you shall not do yourself any harm, unless I specifically ask you to. And now, my newly made knight, seize the pixie."

Roiben turned to Kaye as Lutie screamed from her pocket. Kaye sprinted for the door, but he was far too quick. He grabbed her hair in a clump, jerking her head back, then just as suddenly let her go. After an amazed moment, Kaye dashed through the door.

"You may be well versed in following orders, but you are a novice at giving them," she heard Roiben say as she ran back into the maze of the library.

Before, she had simply followed Roiben through the winding bookshelves—now, she had no idea where she was going. She turned and turned and turned again, relieved that she didn't see any of the strange secret-keepers. Then, careening past a podium with a small stack of books piled on it, she turned into a dead end.

Lutie crawled out of her pocket and was buzzing around her. "What's to do, Kaye? What's to do?"

"Shhh," Kaye said. "Try to listen."

Kaye could hear her own breathing, could hear pages fluttering somewhere in the room, could hear what sounded like cloth dragging across the floor. No sounds of footsteps. No pursuit.

She tried to draw glamour around her, to color her skin to be like the wall behind her. She felt the ripple of magic roll through her and looked down at her wood-colored hand.

What were they going to do? Guilt and misery threatened to overwhelm her. She put her head between her legs and took a couple of deep breaths.

She had to get them free.

Which was absurd. She was only one pixie girl. She barely knew how to use glamour, barely knew how to use her own wings.

Clever. The word taunted her, the sum of all the things she ought to be and was not.

Think, Kaye. Think.

She took a deep breath. She'd solved the riddles. She'd gotten Roiben out of the court. She'd even more or less figured out how to use her glamour. She could do this.

"Let's go. Please—let's go," Lutie said, settling on Kaye's knee.

Kaye shook her head. "Lutie, there has to be something. If I just think."

They were all faeries. Okay, then she had to think like a human girl. She had to consider things she knew how to do. Lighter tricks. Shoplifting. And she especially had to think about the things that faeries didn't like.

Iron.

Kaye looked back at Lutie. "What would happen if I swallowed iron?"

Lutie shrugged. "You'd burn your mouth. You might die."

"What if I *poisoned* someone with iron?"

Lutie shifted uncomfortably on Kaye's knee, looking incredulous. "But there's no iron here!"

Kaye took a deep breath and let it out slowly. Her mind was

racing ahead too fast, she had to slow down, calm down. There might be iron in the Unseelie Court, part of weapons, certainly, although she had no idea where any of that would be kept. It was all over outside here, everywhere.

She looked down at her body. What did she have that was from Ironside? Her T-shirt, panties, boots . . . the green frock coat was only glamour, after all.

Kaye unlaced her boots quickly. There was definitely iron in them, obscured from directly touching her skin, but there nonetheless. She pulled them off her feet and looked them over. There was iron in the steel grommets, she could feel the warmth, buried under the black plastic coating. There were steel plates buried in the toes of the boots too, although they would be much too big to use unless she could somehow file them down. Kaye took the knife Roiben had handed her out of her frock-coat pocket and began to pry the soles off the boots. There, as the soles were ripped up and off, were exposed shoe tacks, shiny steel nails so small that that they could be swallowed without anyone the wiser.

Kaye took the knife in one hand, a boot in the other, and began digging them out.

Corny was awash in new emotions. He sat on the dirt floor of a massive palace beneath the earth. Courtiers played instruments, and Nephamael fed him fat globes of cloak-dark grapes. Around Corny were creatures, small and large, slaking their thirst, gambling with riddles and a game that involved hurling somewhat round stones.

The world shrank to those grapes. Nothing was better than brushing his mouth over those fingers, nothing sweeter than the burst of each black jewel in his mouth.

"I think you have entirely too much dignity. I command that you dance," Nephamael said to his new prisoner.

Below the dais, a small crowd gathered apart from their regular activities to watch Roiben dance.

The knight's body was a bow string loosed. His silvery hair streamed like a pennant, but his eyes seemed apart from his body, darting like those of an animal that would tear off its leg to be free of a trap. He did not falter, but his movements were sudden, his spirals desperate. Corny did not want to pity him, so he looked away. A grape fell from the King's hand, but Corny was no longer careful.

The knight danced on as the Unseelie Gentry laughed and japed.

"Too easy. It will take too long to tire him. Whip him as he dances."

Three goblins stepped forward to do as he asked. Red lines opened along his chest and back.

Corny was very glad that Kaye wasn't here now.

"What task shall I set him to for his redemption in my court? I want to keep him. He's been a lucky talisman so far."

"Let him find us a wingless bird that can still fly."

"Find us a goat whose teats are filled with wine instead of milk."

"Yes, bring us a sweet goat like that."

"Boring, boring, boring," Nephamael said and leaned back in the throne. Looking down at Corny, he smiled a smile that was like sinking your teeth into cake.

"You missed a few baubles," he said teasingly. "Pick them up . . . with your tongue."

Corny looked away from Roiben, not having realized that his eyes had strayed. He did as he was told.

It was hardly a plan, really. Kaye had glamoured herself to look like Skillywidden, the only person she remembered well from the Unseelie Court that she could guess wouldn't be beside the throne. She did impersonations of the crone quietly in the hall, but Lutie was no help at all, laughing so hard that the little faerie was barely able to control her flying.

Then with the thin iron nails burning the inside of her cupped palm, she went in search of the main hall. It wasn't hard to find. Past the chess room, there were other doors, but only one stairway that led up.

The hall of the Unseelie Court was much as she remembered it and nearly as full tonight as when she'd been there last. This time, coming in as she had from the center of the palace, she entered directly behind the raised dais. Roiben was dancing there, raw red lines open on his back. Nephamael sat on the ornate, wooden throne, iron circlet burning on his brow. She saw him drop a hand to caress Corny's hair.

She took a deep breath and stepped onto the dais, walking straight up to the redcap who was acting as wine steward, holding a silver-and-lizard-skin carafe of wine ready for refilling the new King's goblet.

"Eh, seamstress?" the man queried, giving her a grin that revealed sharp, yellow, overlapping teeth.

And then Lutie did exactly what she was supposed to do,

buzzing past the man's face so that he snatched for her with one hand and didn't notice Kaye dropping iron nails into the wine. Reverse shoplifting. Easy. Much easier than slipping rats into her pockets.

"Skillywidden." Kaye turned to see Nephamael was speaking to her. "Come here, seamstress."

Kaye looked around; Lutie had managed to flutter off, but Kaye couldn't see her. Even though Kaye knew that was the better thing, the safer thing, she couldn't keep from being worried. There were already so many people hurt because of her. Kaye took a deep breath and walked to Nephamael, curtsying in what she hoped was a fair approximation of the seamstress.

"Ah," he said, gesturing in the direction of Roiben. "My new plaything. Strong, as you can see. Lovely, even. I need a costume for him. I think that I would like something in green. Perhaps the livery of a Seelie page? I think I would like that."

Kaye nodded, and when he looked toward Roiben again, she began to back away.

"A moment more," Nephamael said. Her heart beat wildly in her chest. "Come closer."

She stepped obediently forward.

Grinning wickedly, Nephamael sprang from his chair and grabbed her by one spindly shoulder. His expression was near enough to glee to make Kaye's stomach twist in fear. Magic surrounded her, ripping at her glamour. She felt like she was being clawed apart. She knew she was shrieking but she couldn't help it, couldn't do anything as her glamour was rent. She fell to her knees, now in the shirt and underwear she had woken in, hair still stiff with brine.

There were loud gasps and shouts.

"Gag her," he said, "then tie her hands behind her back and give me the leash." One of his people came forward to do so.

Settling back on his throne, he gestured for more wine. Kaye held her breath, but he merely took the goblet and did not drink.

"Now this is an unexpected treat. A prop for my little games. Come here, Roiben."

Roiben paused, his body trembling with the aftershocks of exertion and violence. The red welts across his chest and back, some still bleeding, were horrible to see. He came forward to stand in front of Nephamael.

"Kneel."

Roiben sank to his knees with a small gasp of pain.

Nephamael reached into the folds of his cloak and brought out a dagger. It had a golden blade, the handle made of horn. He tossed it in front of Roiben, where it landed with a clatter.

"My command is this: When I say 'begin,' take the knife and cut the pixie until she dies. The game is whether you will kill her slowly, making her suffer prettily for my amusement as you stall for time . . . or cut her throat in one easy swipe. That would be the considerate thing to do. Ah," he sighed dramatically, lifting the goblet high above his head, "if only you could stop hoping."

Roiben's face went blank with shock.

She shivered. It was hard to take breaths with the gag in her mouth, and there was no way she could speak.

"Begin," Nephamael said, saluting with the goblet.

Roiben turned, his eyes wet, his jaw trembling. He took a

breath, looking at the knife in his hands and then at Kaye. He closed his eyes, and she saw him making some terrible peace with himself, coming to some terrible decision.

She wanted to close her eyes, but she couldn't. Instead, she tried to meet Roiben's eyes, tried to plead with her expression, but he wouldn't look at her.

As she waited for the knife to decide its angle, she saw Nephamael lift the goblet to his mouth, tipping it back for a deep draught. For a moment, there was no reaction; he only wiped the edge of his lips with two fingers. Then he coughed, looking startled, looking wildly around the brugh. His eyes met hers. Nephamael dropped to his knees, scratching at his throat. He opened his mouth, perhaps to speak, perhaps to scream, but there was no sound.

Then her vision was blocked by Roiben, taking a trembling breath, the golden knife still in his hand. She remembered that no counterorder had been given. Roiben was still bound to the command.

She thrashed, side to side.

And she felt tiny fingers working at the loops of the gag.

Roiben's face was a mask of shock and horror as he watched his own hand lower the golden blade toward her skin.

Kaye took a series of deep breaths, preparing herself. When she felt the gag loosen, she spat out the cloth and stepped into the knife, whispering, "Rath Roiben Rye, stop. . . . I command you to stop. . . . I command you to . . ." She felt the knife bite into her arm as she spoke, heard his sob, before the thing dropped from his hand.

Then she sprang up, beating her wings hard. She rose easily toward the overturned bowl of the ceiling, hovering for a moment. Lutie rose up beside her, fumbling with the rope tying Kaye's hands.

Then from one of the entrances, there was the stomping of knights, the sound of armor, and of bells. The Seelie Court had arrived.

15

Better to reign in Hell, then to serve in Heav'n.
—JOHN MILTON, *PARADISE LOST (BOOK I)*

The knights stepped into the room first, all of them costumed in deep green armor that resembled the carapaces of insects. Next came a dozen ladies, each one dressed in a different-color gown. Kaye noted Ethine was in soft gold. After the courtiers came the Queen, resplendent in a moon-pale gown, very like the one in Roiben's tapestry. Over it she wore a peacock-blue cape that swept the floor as she walked calmly toward the dais.

"Roiben," the Queen said. A hissing came from the Unseelie Court. A large creature stumbled forward, only to be quelled by an iron look from one of the knights.

Nephamael writhed still, his fingers scrabbling at his neck and chest. He seemed completely unaware of the arrival of his mistress.

Roiben looked at the Seelie Queen, and his eyes closed with an exhalation of breath that was so evocative of relief, Kaye felt herself fill with dread. There was something wrong with all this.

Around the neck of the Seelie Queen, a white pendant swung on a silver chain. Kaye stared at it as though it could hypnotize her. The Queen's eyes were on the dais, watching the self-made King of the Unseelie Court squirm.

"Nephamael was serving you!" The revelation was so shocking that she spoke it aloud before she had thought it all through. She dropped down to stand beside Roiben.

It seemed as though everything stopped with those words. Even the Queen froze.

Kaye stumbled on, looking at Roiben, willing him to believe. "Roiben, you had to serve Nicnevin and Nephamael had to serve the Seelie Queen. You had to. He couldn't disobey any more than you could."

The Queen made a gentle smile. "The pixie is correct after a fashion. If I had commanded him to stay by my side for all time, he could not have left it. But I had given no such command. Once gone, he could no longer hear my commands and so, did not heed them. I come here today to put things to rights."

The words seemed so reasonable, spoken by those lips. Kaye wanted to be mistaken, but the amulet still swung heavily around the Queen's neck.

"But I saw the amulet. Nephamael was holding it when he glamoured me to look human. He seemed to be drawing his power from it."

"You are mistaken, pixie, and you will be silent. There are more pressing matters at hand." The Seelie Queen's voice was firm, and several of her knights moved toward Kaye.

"Kaye . . . ," Roiben said, shaking his head. "The amulet is hers. It has always been so."

Kaye turned to him, eyes flashing. "I'm not wrong!"

The crowd murmured at that. Kaye was not sure what outcome the Unseelie Court would be most pleased with; probably the one with the greatest bloodshed. She could not doubt that they were at least glad someone was insulting the Seelie Queen.

Roiben held up his hand. "I will hear her." His pronouncement brought some measure of silence to the court. Kaye marveled at that. He was leaning against the throne with blood streaking his clothes, unarmed, and yet he still commanded enough respect that the crowd quieted for him.

He nodded to Kaye. "Speak."

She took a deep breath and when she spoke, she made sure that it was loud enough for everyone to hear. "I guess it's pretty obvious now that I'm a pixie, but I've been disguised as a human for . . . well . . . for sixteen years. I managed to find the human girl that I was switched with. She was still in Silarial's court." Roiben gave Kaye a sharp look, but she hurried on.

"So that means someone in the Seelie Court switched me, even though I was living in Unseelie territory very close to Nicnevin's court. When I was a little girl, I had three faeries that watched over me. They were also from the Seelie Court.

"I moved to Philadelphia where I lived for a couple of years until he"—Kaye pointed to Nephamael—"showed up at one of my mother's shows. He took the guy we were living with aside, and a couple of minutes later, the guy tried to kill my mom. The next day we moved back here. A couple of days after that, my old faerie friends contacted me and said they needed me to play along with their plan.

"But they weren't powerful enough to suggest me to Nicnevin for the Tithe. Nephamael was. He was the one in charge. So how did Nephamael wind up in the middle of a Seelie plot? Because she ordered him. It's the only thing that makes any sense. The only reason he benefited was because Roiben stepped in. If Nicnevin hadn't died, Nephamael wouldn't have benefited at all, only Silarial. Even as things stood with him being King, she would have ruled the Unseelie Court through him."

"I will hear no more!" the Seelie Queen announced.

"You will," Roiben said, his voice rising with impatience and then falling once more. "You are ageless, Silarial, so bide with us a time. I would hear the rest of her tale."

Kaye spoke quickly, words rushing together as she tried to get it all out. "The amulet around her neck. That's what made me realize what was going on. Nephamael had it the night he brought me to be sacrificed. He used it to put a heavy glamour on me. It was her necklace, her glamour. They were going to let me be sacrificed, then reveal the trick and blame Nicnevin. And today, when we got here, Nephamael was waiting for us, but no one knew we were coming to find Corny but Silarial and her court." At the mention of Corny's name, Kaye couldn't keep her gaze from flickering toward Corny. What she saw froze her tongue.

He had crept forward to where Nephamael's body writhed. A lock of hair had fallen across his face. There was a bruise on his cheek the color of his grape-stained mouth. That reminded Kaye entirely too much of Janet's cold lips.

As though he could feel the heat of her stare, Corny looked up. His eyes were anguished.

"Corny," Kaye said, taking a half step forward.

Still looking at her, Corny picked up the golden knife Roiben had dropped. The beginnings of a smile were on his lips as he lifted it.

"No!" Kaye screamed, running toward Corny, frantic to stop him from stabbing himself.

The blade plunged into Nephamael's chest. Again and again, Corny stuck the body of the faerie knight, the knife making a sickeningly liquid sound with each thrust. Blood soaked Corny's pants. A keening sound came from deep in his throat.

The courtiers, Seelie and Unseelie alike, watched in rapt fascination. None made a move to help as Kaye grabbed Corny's wrists and tried to wrestle him away from the body.

He was shaking, but when Kaye pulled him forward to embrace him, she realized it was because he was laughing.

"Look what you've done," the Seelie Queen said. It took Kaye a moment to realize she was talking to Corny and not about him.

A Seelie knight stepped forward and reached beneath his cloak. Kaye watched in horror as he brought out a long branch and smoothed it into a sickeningly familiar arrow. It was pointed right at her.

"Roiben, end this or I will end it for you," the Seelie Queen said. "I have been patient enough. It is long past time for you to return home."

Roiben's voice was not loud but it carried through the brugh as he walked to where Kaye was standing. "I am home, Lady. Now tell your man to put down his weapon, and I will allow you to leave the Unseelie Court unharmed."

A hush settled over the Gentry.

Kaye stood in stunned silence. Nicnevin had used Roiben well, far better perhaps than she realized. She had kept him close to her. She had used him against the rest of the Unseelie Court. Kaye remembered how they had drawn back from him when he escorted her through the crowd. He was not one of them, it was true, but he was remote as a king.

No one challenged him.

The Queen's slim, perfect eyebrows lifted. "You dare?"

Roiben's sister took a step forward, but said nothing. Her eyes were pleading.

He looked around the court, and Kaye could see him take a breath. Then he spoke. "Hear me and know the compact I offer. The solitary fey have gained seven years of freedom, but seven years will pass in the blink of an eye. Bind yourselves to me now, Unseelie and Solitary alike, and I will give you all of Samhain. Freedom from dusk until dawn forevermore."

Kaye saw several Unseelie creatures haul themselves up onto the dais. They did not advance on the Seelie party, but their toothy grins were all malice.

The Queen stiffened. "I think, my knight, that you will find claiming a kingdom far easier than keeping one." With that she turned, her long peacock cloak sweeping a circular pattern in the dust of the floor. Her knights and courtiers turned as well. Only Ethine hesitated.

Roiben shook his head.

Silarial looked back and, spotting Ethine, opened her cloak. Roiben's sister let herself be embraced and drawn away with the rest of the Seelie Court. She never saw the cruel smile that played on the lips of the Seelie Queen nor the way her eyes met Roiben's over his sister's bent head.

As the last Seelie left the hall, Roiben, self-declared King of the Unseelie Court, nearly fell into his throne. Kaye tried to smile at him, but he was not looking at her. He was staring out across the brugh with eyes the color of falling ash.

Corny had not stopped laughing.

The funeral parlor itself was small and Victorian. The furniture was ornate and dark wood. Even the wallpaper was somber, maroon fleurs-de-lis in a raised fuzzy velvet. There were people from school there, people Kaye only vaguely remembered. Kenny, Doughboy, Marcus, and Fatima were all sitting in a huddle, whispering to one another constantly, even when the preacher was speaking.

Corny held Kaye's hand through the whole funeral service, his fingers cold and sweaty and clasping hers hard enough to hurt. He didn't cry, even when she did, but he looked pale and washed out in the black suit he wore. Each time she saw the bluish bruise on his cheek, it looked more obscene.

Kaye's mother had been terrified, thinking that Kaye had died too . . . so terrified that she'd resolved to commute into the city instead of moving there. Even Kaye's grandmother was being nice. Ellen had dropped Kaye off at the funeral parlor that night and promised to pick her up again when she called. It was strange and kind of nice, everyone getting along, but Kaye didn't want to get used to it.

Janet was laid out like a painting, all red curls and red lips. She looked beautiful—Ophelia surrounded by bouquets of flowers that only Roiben could name. But Kaye could smell the chemicals they'd injected into her, could smell the rotting meat of what was left, and she almost gagged when they went close. She couldn't, however, keep her hand from straying to the cold, oddly firm flesh of Janet's arm. Kaye dropped the gift she'd brought—a tube of blue, glittery nail polish—into the coffin.

Corny kept his death grip on her hand as he stared at the body of his sister.

Afterward, Kaye and Corny stood outside, waiting for his mother to finish saying good night to the relatives.

"Oh, I almost forgot," Corny said, his voice very quiet, "my mom stopped by the store before we got here. I had to go in for cigarettes." He reached into the inner pocket of his leather jacket and pulled out several straws with different-color stripes circling down their packaging. "A bouquet of Pixy Stix."

Kaye smiled. "I should be trying to cheer you up."

"You already did your white charger bit," he said. "Check it out . . . rip this sucker open and you get genuine pixie dust. Tastes like sour sugar."

She laughed and so did he, a weird, desperate sound that spiraled up into the night sky.

"What are you going to do now?" Kaye asked.

"I don't know. Shit, I still have to digest what I've already done."

"I know what you mean . . . but, you know none of it's your fault, right?"

"Except the part at the end with the knife?"

"Even that part. Maybe especially that part."

"Next time . . . ," Corny said, eyes alight in a way that

Kaye was relieved to see until she heard the soft words that followed. "Kaye, I will never be powerless again. Whatever it takes. Whatever."

"What do you mean?"

He just squeezed her hand tighter. After a few moments, he said, "So how about you?"

She shrugged. "Did I ever mention that I know how to make leaves into money?"

"Yeah?" he said, eyebrows raised. His mother came over with a few relatives, and Corny finally let go of Kaye to get in the car. Her hand was damp and hot, and when the breeze hit it, it felt like she was wearing her insides on the outside.

The last people had left the funeral parlor and they were locking up, so Kaye crossed the street to use the pay phone in front of the supermarket. She called her mother and then sat down on the curb in front of a plastic horse that rocked back and forth if you fed quarters into it. The fluorescent lights and the organic smell of rotting vegetables and the tumble of plastic bags across the parking lot seemed so utterly normal to her that she felt disconnected from the events of two days before.

She hadn't seen Roiben. It wasn't like anything happened badly between them, it was just that she'd needed to take Corny home and he'd needed to stay and do whatever it was that new monarchs did. She didn't even really feel bad that she hadn't seen him. It was more the feeling of relief that you have when you know that something painful is coming, but you can avoid it for the moment. If she saw him, then she'd have to listen to whatever he really thought about the two of them being together now that he was King.

Looking at the plastic horse, she summoned her magic. A

moment later it shook out its mane and leaped down from the metal suspension it was held in. As she watched, it galloped away into the night, plastic hooves clattering over the asphalt.

"There is something of yours I would like to return to you." Roiben's voice made her jump. How had he managed to get so close without her hearing? Still, she couldn't help hoping any more than she could help scolding herself for doing so.

"What?"

He leaned across the distance between them and caught her mouth with his own. Her eyes fluttered closed and her lips parted easily as she felt the kiss sizzling through her nerves, rendering her thoughts to smoke.

"Um . . ." Kaye stepped back, a little unsteadily. "Why does that belong to me?"

"That was the kiss I stole from you when you were enchanted," he said patiently.

"Oh . . . well, what if I didn't want it?"

"You don't?"

"No," she said, letting a grin spread across her face, hoping her mother would take her time on the drive over. "I'd like you to take it back again, please."

"I am your servant," the King of the Unseelie Court said, his lips a moment from her own. "Consider it done."

VALIANT

For my husband, Theo,
because he likes angsty, angry girls

PROLOGUE

For I shall learn from flower and leaf
That color every drop they hold,
To change the lifeless wine of grief
To living gold.
—SARA TEASDALE, "ALCHEMY"

The tree woman choked on poison, the slow sap of her blood burning. Most of her leaves had already fallen, but those remaining blackened and shriveled along her back. She pulled her roots up from the deep soil, long hairy tendrils that flinched in the chill late autumn air.

An iron fence had surrounded her trunk for years, the stink of the metal as familiar as any small ache. The iron scorched her as she dragged her roots over it. She tumbled onto the concrete sidewalk, her slow tree thoughts filling with pain.

A human walking two little dogs stumbled against the brick wall of a building. A taxi screeched to a halt and blared its horn.

Long branches tipped over a bottle as the tree woman scrambled to pull away from the metal. She stared at the dark glass as it rolled into the street, watching the dregs of bitter poison drip out of the neck, seeing the familiar scrawl on the little strip of paper secured with wax. The contents of that bottle should have been a tonic, not the instrument of her death. She tried to lift herself up again.

One of the dogs started barking.

The tree woman felt the poison working inside of her, choking her breath and befuddling her. She had been crawling somewhere, but she could no longer remember where. Dark green patches, like bruises, bloomed along her trunk.

"Ravus," the tree woman whispered, the bark of her lips cracking. "Ravus."

Valerie Russell felt something cold touch the small of her
back and spun around, striking without thinking. Her
slap connected with flesh. A can of soda hit the concrete floor
of the locker room and rolled, sticky brown liquid fizzing as it
pooled. Other girls looked up from changing into sweats and
started to giggle.

Hands raised in mock surrender, Ruth laughed. "Just a
joke, Princess Badass of Badassia."

"Sorry," Val forced herself to say, but the sudden surprise
of anger hadn't entirely dissipated and she felt like an idiot.
"What are you doing down here? I thought being near sweat
gave you hives."

Ruth sat down on a green bench, looking glamorous in

a vintage smoking jacket and long velvet skirt. Ruth's brows were thin pencil lines, her eyes outlined with black kohl and red shadow. Her hair was glossy black, paler at the roots and threaded with purple braids. She took a deep drag on her clove cigarette and blew smoke in the direction of one of Val's teammates. "Only my own sweat."

Val rolled her eyes, smiling. Val and Ruth had been friends forever, for so long that Val was used to being the overshadowed one, the "normal" one, the one who set up the witty one-liners, not the one who delivered them. She liked that role; it made her feel safe. Robin to Ruth's Batman. Chewbacca to her Han Solo.

Val leaned down to kick off her sneakers and saw herself in the small mirror on her locker door, strands of orangey hair peeking out from a green bandanna.

Ruth had been dyeing her own hair since the fifth grade, first in colors you could buy in boxes at the supermarket, then in crazy, beautiful colors like mermaid green and poodle pink, but Val had only dyed her hair once. It had been a store-bought auburn; darker and richer than her own pale color, but it had gotten her grounded anyway. Back then, her mother punished her every time she did anything to show that she was growing up. Mom didn't want her to get a bra, didn't want her to wear short skirts, and didn't want her dating until high school. Now that she was in high school, all of a sudden her mother was pushing makeup and dating advice. Val had gotten used to pulling her hair back in bandannas, wearing jeans and T-shirts though, and didn't want to change.

"I've got some statistics for the flour-baby project and I picked out some potential names for him." Ruth unshouldered her giant messenger bag. The front flap was smeared with paint and studded with buttons and stickers—a pink triangle peeling at the edges, a button hand-lettered to say "Still Not King," a smaller one that read "Some things exist whether you believe in them or not," and a dozen more. "I was thinking maybe you could come over tonight and we could work on it."

"I can't," Val said. "Tom and I are going to see a hockey game in the city after practice."

"Wow. Something you want to do for a change," Ruth said, twirling one of her purple braids around her finger.

Val frowned. She couldn't help noticing the edge in Ruth's voice when she talked about Tom. "Do you think he doesn't want to go?" Val asked. "Did he say something?"

Ruth shook her head and took another quick draw on her cigarette. "No. No. Nothing like that."

"I was thinking that we could go to the Village after the game if there's time. Walk around St. Mark's." Only a couple of months earlier, at the town fair, Tom had applied a press-on tattoo to the small of her back by kneeling down and licking the spot wet before pressing it to her skin. Now she could barely get him to kiss her.

"The city at night. Romantic."

The way Ruth said it, Val thought she meant the opposite. "What? What's going on with you?"

"Nothing," Ruth said. "I'm just distracted or something." She fanned herself with one hand. "So many nearly naked girls in one place."

Val nodded, half-convinced.

"Did you look at those chat logs like I told you? Find that

one where I sent you statistics about all-female households for the project?"

"I didn't get a chance. I'll find it tomorrow, okay?" Val rolled her eyes. "My mother is online twenty-four, seven. She has some new Internet boyfriend."

Ruth made a gagging sound.

"What?" Val said. "I thought you supported online love. Weren't you the one who said it was love of the mind? Truly spiritual without flesh to encumber it?"

"I hope I didn't say that." Ruth pressed the back of her hand to her forehead, letting her body tip backward in a mock faint. She caught herself suddenly, jerking upright. "Hey, is that a rubber band around your ponytail? That's going to rip out your hair. Get over here; I think I have a scrunchie and a brush."

Val straddled the bench in front of Ruth and let her work out the band. "Ouch. You're making it worse."

"Okay, wuss." Ruth brushed Val's hair out and threaded it through the cloth tie, pulling it tight enough so that Val thought she could feel the tiny hairs on the back of her neck snapping.

Jennifer walked up and leaned on her lacrosse stick. She was a plain, large-boned girl who'd been in Val's school since kindergarten. She always looked unnaturally clean, from her shiny hair to the sparkling white of her kneesocks and her unwrinkled shorts. She was also the captain of their team. "Hey you two, take it elsewhere."

"You afraid it's catching?" Ruth asked sweetly.

"Fuck off, Jen," Val said, less witty and a moment too late.

"You're not supposed to smoke here," said Jen, but she

didn't look at Ruth. She stared at Val's sweats. Tom had decorated one side of them: drawing a gargoyle with permanent marker up a whole leg. The other side was mostly slogans or just random stuff Val had written with a bunch of different pens. They probably weren't what Jen thought of as regulation practice wear.

"Never mind. I got to go anyway." Ruth put out her cigarette on the bench, burning a crater in the wood. "Later, Val. Later, loser."

"What is with you?" Jennifer asked softly, as though she really wanted Val to be her friend. "Why do you hang out with her? Can't you see what a freak she is?"

Val looked at the floor, hearing the things that Jen wasn't saying: *Don't you know that people who hang out with the weird kids are supposed to be bad at sports? Are you hot for me? Why don't you just quit the team before we have to throw you off it?*

If life were like a video game, she would have used her power move to whip Jen in the air and knock her against the wall with two strikes of a lacrosse stick. Of course, if life really were like a video game, Val would probably have to do that in a bikini and with giant breasts, each one made of separately animated polygons.

In real real life, Val chewed on her lip and shrugged, but her hands curled into fists. She'd been in two fights already since she joined the team and she couldn't afford to be in a third one.

"What? You need your girlfriend to speak for you?"

Val punched Jen in the face.

Knuckles burning, Valerie dropped her backpack and lacrosse stick onto the already cluttered floor of her bedroom. Rummaging through her clothes, she snatched up underpants and a sports bra that made her even flatter than she already was. Then, grabbing a pair of black pants she thought were probably clean and her green hooded sweatshirt from the laundry pile, she padded out into the hall, cleated shoes scrunching fairy-tale books free from their bindings and tracking dirt over an array of scattered video-game jewel cases. She heard the plastic crack under her heels and tried to kick a few to safety.

In the hall bathroom, she stripped off her uniform. After rubbing a washcloth under her arms and reapplying deodorant, she then started pulling on her clothes, stopping only to inspect the raw skin on her hands.

"This was your last shot," the coach had said. She'd waited three quarters of an hour in his office while everyone else practiced, and when he finally came in, she saw what he was going to say before he even opened his mouth. "We can't afford to keep you on the team. You are affecting everyone's sense of camaraderie. We have to be a single unit with one goal—winning. You understand, don't you?"

There was a single knock before her door opened. Her mother stood in the doorway, perfectly manicured hand still on the knob. "What did you do to your face?"

Val sucked her cut lip into her mouth, inspected it in the mirror. She'd forgotten about that. "Nothing. It was just an accident at practice."

"You look terrible." Her mother squeezed in, shaking out her recently highlighted blond bob so that they were both reflected in the same mirror. Every time she went to the hairdresser, he seemed to just add more and brighter high-lights, so that the original brown seemed to be drowning in a rising tide of yellow.

"Thanks so much." Val snorted, only slightly annoyed. "I'm late. Late. Late. Late. Like the white rabbit."

"Hold on." Val's mom turned and walked out of the room. Val's gaze followed her down the hallway to the striped wallpaper and the family photographs. Her mother as a runner-up beauty queen. Valerie with braces sitting next to her mother on the couch. Grandma and Grandpa in front of their restaurant. Valerie again, this time holding her baby half sister at her dad's house. The smiles on their frozen faces looked cartoonish and their bared teeth were too white.

A few minutes later, Val's mother returned with a zebra-striped makeup bag. "Stay still."

Valerie scowled, looking up from lacing her favorite green Chucks. "I don't have time. Tom is going to be here any minute." She hadn't remembered to put on her own watch, so she pushed up the sleeve of her mother's blouse and looked at hers. He was already later than late.

"Tom knows how to let himself in." Valerie's mother smeared her finger in some thick, tan cream and started tapping it gently under Val's eyes.

"The cut is on my *lip*," Val said. She didn't like makeup. Whenever she laughed, her eyes teared and the makeup ran as if she'd been crying.

"You could use a little color in your face. People in New York dress up."

"It's just a hockey game, Mom, not the opera."

Her mother gave that sigh, the one that seemed to imply

that someday Val would find out just how wrong she was. She brushed Val's face with tinted powder and then with nontinted powder. Then there was more powder dusted on her eyes. Val recalled her junior prom last summer and hoped her mother wasn't going to try and re-create that goopy, shimmery look. Finally, she actually painted some lipstick over Val's mouth. It made the wound sting.

"Are you done?" Val asked as her mom started on the mascara. A sideways look at her mother's watch showed that the train would leave in about fifteen minutes. "Shit! I have to go. Where the hell is he?"

"You know how Tom can be," her mother said.

"What do you *mean*?" She didn't know why her mother always had to act as if she knew Val's friends better than Val did.

"He's a boy." Val's mother shook her head. "Irresponsible."

Valerie fished out her cell from her backpack and scrolled to his name. It went right to voice mail. She clicked off. Walking back to her bedroom, she looked out the window, past the kids skateboarding off a plywood ramp in the neighbor's driveway. She didn't see Tom's lumbering Caprice Classic.

She phoned again. Voice mail.

"This is Tom. Bela Lugosi's dead but I'm not. Leave me a message."

"You shouldn't keep calling like that," her mother said, following her into the room. "When he turns his phone back on, he'll see how many calls he missed and who made them."

"I don't care what he sees," Val said, thumbing the buttons. "Anyway, this is the last time."

Val's mother stretched out on her daughter's bed and started to outline her own lips in brown pencil. She knew the shape of her own mouth so well that she didn't bother with a mirror.

"Tom," Valerie said into the phone once his voice mail picked up. "I'm walking over to the train station now. Don't bother picking me up. Meet me on the platform. If I don't see you, I'll take the train and find you at the Garden."

Her mother scowled. "I don't know that it's safe for you to go into the city by yourself."

"If we don't make this train, we're going to be late for the game."

"Well, at least take this lipstick." Val's mother rummaged in the bag and handed it over.

"How is that going to help?" Val muttered and slung her backpack over her shoulder. Her phone was still clutched in her hand, plastic heating in her grip.

Val's mother smiled. "I have to show a house tonight. Do you have your keys?"

"Sure," Val said. She kissed her mother's cheek, inhaling perfume and hairspray. A burgundy lip print remained. "If Tom comes by, tell him I'm already gone. And tell him he's an asshole."

Her mother smiled, but there was something awkward about her expression. "Wait," she said. "You should wait for him."

"I can't," Val said. "I already told him I was going."

With that, she darted down the stairs, out the front door, and across the small patch of yard. It was a short walk to the station and the cold air felt good. Doing something other than waiting felt good.

The asphalt parking lot of the train station was still wet with yesterday's rain and the overcast sky swollen with the promise of more. As she crossed the lot, the signals started to flash and clang in warning. She made it to the platform just as the train ground to a stop, sending up a billow of hot, stinking air.

Valerie hesitated. What if Tom had forgotten his cell and waited for her at the house? If she left now and he took the next train, they might not find each other. She had both tickets. She might be able to leave his at the ticket booth, but he might not think to check there. And even if all that worked out, Tom would still sulk. When or if he finally showed up, he wouldn't be in the mood to do anything but fight. She didn't know where they could go, but she'd hoped that they could find someplace to be alone for a little while.

She chewed the skin around her thumb, neatly biting off a hangnail and then pulling so a tiny strip of skin came loose. It was oddly satisfying, despite the tiny bit of blood that welled to the surface, but when she licked it away her skin tasted bitter.

The doors to the train finally shut, ending her indecision. Valerie watched as it rolled out of the station and then started walking slowly home. She was relieved and annoyed to spot Tom's car parked next to her mother's Miata in the driveway. Where had he been? She sped up and yanked open the door.

And froze. The screen slipped from her fingers, crashing closed. Through the mesh, she could see her mother bent forward on the white couch, crisp blue shirt unbuttoned past the top of her bra. Tom knelt on the floor, mohawked head leaning up to kiss her. His chipped black polished fingernails fumbled with the remaining buttons on her shirt. Both of them started at the sound of the door slamming and turned toward her, faces expressionless, Tom's mouth messy with lipstick.

Somehow, Val's eyes drifted past them, to the dried-up daisies Tom had given her for their four-month anniversary. They sat on top of the television cabinet, where she'd left them weeks ago. Her mother had wanted Val to throw them out, but she'd forgotten. She could see the stems through the glass vase, the lower portion of them immersed in brackish water and blooming with mold.

Valerie's mother made a choking sound and fumbled to stand, tugging her shirt closed.

"Oh fuck," Tom said, half-falling onto the beige carpet.

Val wanted to say something scathing, something that would burn them both to ashes where they were, but no words came. She turned and walked away.

"Valerie!" her mother called, sounding more desperate than commanding. Looking back, she saw her mother in the doorway, Tom a shadow behind her. Valerie started to run, backpack banging against her hip. She only slowed when she was back at the train station. There, she squatted above the concrete sidewalk, ripping up wilted weeds as she dialed Ruth's number.

Ruth picked up the phone. She sounded as if she'd been laughing. "Hello?"

"It's me," Val said. She expected her voice to shake, but it came out flat, emotionless.

"Hey," Ruth said. "Where are you?"

Val could feel tears start to burn at the edges of her eyes, but the words still came out steady. "I found out something about Tom and my mother—"

"Shit!" Ruth interrupted.

Valerie went silent for a moment, dread making her limbs

heavy. "Do you know something? Do you know what I'm talking about?"

"I'm so glad you found out," Ruth said, speaking fast, her words almost tripping over each other. "I wanted to tell you, but your mom begged me not to. She made me swear I wouldn't."

"She told you?" Val felt particularly stupid, but she just couldn't quite accept that she understood what was being said. "You knew?"

"She wouldn't talk about anything else once she found out that Tom let it slip." Ruth laughed and then stopped awkwardly. "Not like it's been going on for that long or anything. Honestly. I would have said something, but your mom promised she would do it. I even told her I was going to tell—but she said she'd deny it. And I did try to drop hints."

"What hints?" Val felt suddenly dizzy. She closed her eyes.

"Well, I said you should check the chat logs, remember? Look, never mind. I'm just glad she finally told you."

"She didn't tell me," Valerie said.

There was a long silence. She could hear Ruth breathing. "Please don't be mad," she said finally. "I just couldn't tell you. I couldn't be the one to tell you."

Val clicked off her phone. She kicked a stray chunk of asphalt into a puddle, and then kicked the puddle itself. Her reflection blurred; the only thing clearly visible was her mouth, a slash of red on a pale face. She smeared it, but the color only spread.

When the next train came, she got on it, sliding into a cracked orange seat and pressing her forehead against the cool plastiglass window. Her phone buzzed and she turned it off without looking at the screen. But as Val turned back toward the window, it was her mother's reflection she saw. It took her a moment to realize she was looking at herself in makeup. Furious, she walked quickly to the train bathroom.

The room was grubby and large, with a sticky rubber floor and hard plastic walls. The odor of urine mingled with the scent of chemical flowers. Small blobs of discarded gum decorated the walls.

Val sat down on the toilet lid and forced herself to relax, to take deep breaths of putrid air. Her fingernails dug into the flesh of her arms and somehow that made her feel a little better, a little more in control.

She was surprised by the force of her own anger. It overwhelmed her, making her afraid she might start screaming at the conductor, at every passenger on the train. She couldn't imagine lasting the whole trip. Already she was exhausted from the effort of keeping it together.

She rubbed her face and looked down at her palm, streaked with burgundy lipstick and shaking slightly. Val unzipped her backpack and poured its contents onto the filthy floor as the train lurched forward.

Her camera clattered on the rubber tile, along with a couple of rolls of film, a book from school—*Hamlet*—that she was supposed to have already read, a couple of hair ties, a crumpled package of gum, and a travel grooming case her mother had given her for her last birthday. She fumbled to open it—tweezers, manicuring scissors, and a razor, all glimmering in the dim light. Valerie took out the scissors, felt the small, sharp edges. She stood up and looked into the mirror. Grabbing a chunk of her hair, she started to chop.

Stray locks curved around her sneakers like copper snakes when she was done. Val ran a hand over her bald head. It was slick with pink squirt-soap and felt rough as a cat's tongue. She stared at her own reflection, rendered strange and plain, at unflinching eyes and a mouth pressed into a thin line. Specks of hair stuck to her cheeks like fine metal filings. For a moment, she couldn't be sure what that mirror face was thinking.

The razor and manicuring scissors clattered into the sink as the train came to another stop. Water sloshed in the toilet bowl.

"Hello?" someone called from outside the door. "What's going on in there?"

"Just a minute," Val called back. She rinsed off the razor under the tap and shoved it into her backpack. Slinging it over one shoulder, she got a wad of toilet paper, dampened it, and squatted down to mop up her hair.

The mirror caught her eye again as she straightened. For a moment, it seemed like a young man looked back at her, his features so delicate that she didn't think he could defend himself. Val blinked, opened the door, and stepped out into the corridor of the train.

She walked back to her seat, feeling the glances of the other passengers flinch from her as she passed. Staring out the window, she watched the suburban lawns slip by until they went under a tunnel and she saw only her new, alien reflection in the window.

The train pulled into an underground station and Val got off, walking through the stink of exhaust. She climbed up a narrow, unmoving escalator, crushed between people. Penn Station was thick with commuters, heads down as they passed one another, and stands that sold pendants, scarves, and fiber-optic flowers that glowed with changing colors. Valerie stuck to one of the walls, passing a filthy man sleeping under a newspaper and a group of backpack-wearing girls screaming at one another in German.

The anger she had felt on the train had drained away and Val moved through the station like a sleepwalker.

Madison Square Garden was up another escalator, past a line of taxis and stands selling sugared peanuts and sausages. A man handed her a flyer and she tried to give it back, but he was already past her and she was left holding a sheet of paper promising LIVE GIRLS. She crunched it up and stuffed it in her pocket.

She pushed through a narrow corridor jammed with people, and waited at the ticket counter. The young guy behind the glass looked up when she pushed Tom's ticket through. He seemed startled. She thought it might be her lack of hair.

"Can you give me my money back for that?" Val asked.

"You already have a ticket?" he asked, squinting at her as though trying to figure out exactly what her scam was.

"Yeah," she said. "My asshole ex-boyfriend couldn't make it."

Understanding spread across his features and he nodded. "Gotcha. Look, I can't give you your money back because the game's already started, but if you give me both I could upgrade you."

"Sure," Val said, and smiled for the first time that whole trip. Tom had already given her the money for his ticket and she was pleased that she could have the small revenge of getting a better seat from it.

He passed her the new ticket and she slid through the turn-stile, wading her way through the crowd. People argued, faces flushed. The air stank of beer.

She'd been looking forward to seeing this game. The Rangers were having a great season. But even if they weren't, she loved the way the men moved on the ice, as though they were weightless, all the while balanced on knife blades. It made lacrosse look graceless, just a bunch of people lumbering over some grass. But as she looked for the doorway to her seat, she felt dread roiling in her stomach. The game mattered to all the other people the way it had once mattered to her, but now she was just killing time before she had to go home.

She found the doorway and stepped through. Most of the seats were already occupied and she had to sidle past a group of ruddy-faced guys. They craned their necks to look around her, past the glass divider, to where the game had already started. The stadium *smelled* cold, the way the air did after a snow-storm. But even as her team skated toward a goal, her thoughts flickered back to her mother and Tom. She shouldn't have left the way she had. She wished she could do it over. She wouldn't even have bothered with her mother. She would have punched Tom in the face. And then, looking just at him, she would have said, "I expected as much from her, but I would have thought better of you." That would have been perfect.

Or maybe she could have smashed the windows of his car. But the car was really a piece of junk, so maybe not.

She could have gone over to Tom's house though, and told his parents about the dime bag of weed he kept between his mattress and box spring. Between that and this thing with Val's mother, maybe his family would have sent him off to some rehabilitation facility for mom-fucking stoners.

As for her mother, the best revenge Val could ever have would be to call her dad, get her stepmother, Linda, on speakerphone, and tell them the whole thing. Val's dad and Linda had a perfect marriage, the kind that came with two adorable, drooling kids and wall-to-wall carpeting and mostly made Val sick. Unfortunately, telling them would make the story theirs. They would tell it whenever they wanted, shout it at Val's mother when they fought, report it to shock their golfing buddies. It was Val's story and she was going to control it.

There was a roar from the audience. All around her, people jumped to their feet. One of the Rangers had thrown some guy from the other team down and was ripping off his own gloves. The referee grabbed hold of the Ranger, and his skate slid, slicing a line across the other player's cheek. As they were cleared away, Val stared at the blood on the ice. A man in white came and scraped up most of it and the Zamboni smoothed the ice during halftime, but a patch of red remained, as though the stain had soaked so deep it couldn't be drawn out. Even as her team made the final winning goal and everyone near her surged to their feet again, Val couldn't seem to look away from the blood.

After the game, Val followed the crowd out onto the street. The train station was only a few steps away, but she couldn't face going home. She wanted to delay a little longer, until she could figure things out, dissect what had happened a little more. The very idea of getting back on the train filled her with a sick panic that made her pulse race and her stomach churn.

She started to walk and, after a while, noticed that the street numbers got smaller and the buildings got older, lanes narrowed and the traffic thinned out. Turning left, toward what she thought might be the edge of the West Village, she passed closed clothing stores and rows of parked cars. She wasn't quite sure of the time, but it had to be nearly midnight.

Her mind kept unraveling the looks between Tom and her mother, glances that now had meaning, hints she should have picked up on. She saw her mother's face, some weird combination of guilt and honesty, when she'd told Val to wait for Tom. The memory made Val flinch, as though her body were trying to throw off a physical weight.

She stopped and got a slice of pizza at a sleepy shop where a woman with a shopping cart full of bottles sat in the back, drinking Sprite through a straw and singing to herself. The hot cheese burned the roof of Val's mouth, and when she looked up at the clock, she realized she'd already missed the last train home.

2

Trying their wings once more in hopeless flight:
Blind moths against the wires of window screens.
Anything. Anything for a fix of light.
— X. J. KENNEDY, "STREET MOTHS," *THE LORDS OF MISRULE*

Val dozed off again, her head pillowed on an almost-empty backpack, the rest of her spread across the cold floor tiles under the subway map. She'd picked out a place to nap near the token booth, figuring no one would try to rob her or stab her right in front of people.

She had spent most of the night in the hazy state between sleep and wakefulness, nodding off for a moment, then jolting awake. Sometimes she'd woken from a dream and not known where she was. The station stank of rancid trash and mold, even without the heat to make scents bloom. Above the cracked paint and mildew, a sculptural border of curling tulips was a remnant of another Spring Street station, one that must have been old and grand. She tried to imagine that station as she slipped back to sleep.

Strangly, she wasn't scared. She felt removed from everything, a sleepwalker who had stepped off the path of normal life
and into the forest where anything could happen. Her anger
and hurt had cooled into a lethargy that left her limbs heavy
as lead.

The next time she blearily opened her eyes, people stood
over her. She sat up, the fingers on one hand digging into her
backpack, the other hand coming up as if to ward off a blow.
Two cops stared down at her.

"Morning," one of them said. He had short gray hair and a
ruddy face, as if he'd been standing too long in the wind.

"Yeah." Val wiped jagged bits of sleep from the corners of
her eyes with the heel of her hand. Her head hurt.

"This is a pretty shitty crash spot," he said. Commuters
passed them, but only a few bothered to look her way.

Val narrowed her eyes. "So?"

"How old are you?" asked his partner. He was younger,
slim, with dark eyes and breath that smelled like cigarettes.

"Nineteen," Val lied.

"Got any ID?"

"No," Val said, hoping that they wouldn't search her backpack. She had a permit, no license since she had failed her
driving test, but the card was enough to prove she was only
seventeen.

He sighed. "You can't sleep here. You want us to bring you
someplace you can get a little rest?"

Val stood up, slinging her pack over one shoulder. "I'm
fine. I was just waiting for morning."

"Where are you going?" the older cop asked, blocking her
way with his body.

"Home," Val said because she thought that would sound good. She ducked under his arm and darted up the steps. Her heart hammered as she raced up Crosby Street, through the crowds of people, past the groggy early-morning workers dragging around their backpacks and briefcases, past the bike messengers and taxis, stepping through the gusts of steam that billowed up from the grates. She slowed and looked back, but no one seemed to be following her. As she crossed to Bleecker, she saw a couple of punks drawing on the sidewalk with chalk. One had a rainbow mohawk, slightly dented at the top. Val stepped around their art carefully and kept going.

For Val, New York was always the place that made Val's mother hold her hand tight, the glittering grid of glass-paned skyscrapers, the steaming Cup O' Noodles threatening to pour boiling broth on kids waiting in line for *TRL* just blocks away from where *Les Misérables* played to matinees of high school French students bused in from the suburbs. But now, crossing onto Macdougal, New York seemed so much more and less than her idea of it. She passed restaurants sleepily stirring with activity, their doors still shut; a chain-link fence decorated with more than a dozen locks, each one decoupaged with a baby's face; and a shop that sold only robot toys. Small, interesting places that suggested the vastness of the city and the strangeness of its inhabitants.

She ducked into a dimly lit coffeehouse called Café Diablo. The inside was wallpapered in red velvet. A wooden devil stood by the counter, holding out a silver tray nailed to his hand. Val bought a large coffee, nearly choking it with cinnamon, sugar, and cream. The heat of the cup felt good against her cold fingers, but it made her aware of the stiffness of her limbs, the knots in her back. She stretched, arching up and twisting her neck until she heard something pop.

She headed for a spot in the back, picking a threadbare armchair near a table where a boy with tiny locs and a girl with tangles of faded blue hair and knee-high white boots whispered together. The boy ripped and poured sugar packet after sugar packet into his cup.

The girl moved slightly and Val could see that she had a butterscotch kitten on her lap. It stretched one paw to bat at the zipper on the girl's patchy rabbit-fur coat.

Val smiled reflexively. The girl saw her looking, grinned back, and put the cat on the table. It mewed pitifully, sniffed the air, stumbled.

"Hold on," Val said. Popping off the lid of her coffee, she went up to the front, filled it with cream, and set it down in front of the cat.

"Brilliant," the blue-haired girl said. Val could see that her nose stud was infected, the skin around the glittering stone swollen tight and red.

"What's its name?" Val asked.

"No name yet. We've been discussing it. If you have any ideas let me know. Dave doesn't think we should keep her."

Val took a swig of coffee. She couldn't think of anything. Her brain felt swollen, pressing against her skull, and she was so tired that her eyes didn't focus right away when she blinked. "Where'd she come from? Is she a stray?"

The girl opened her mouth, but the boy put his hand on her arm. "Lolli." He squeezed warningly, and the two shared an intense glance.

"I stole her," Lolli said.

"Why do you tell people things like that?" Dave asked.

"I tell people everything. People only believe what they can handle. That's how I know who to trust."

"You shoplifted her?" Val asked, looking at the kitten's tiny body, the curling pink tongue.

Lolli shook her head, clearly delighted with herself. "I threw a rock through the window. At night."

"Why?" Val slipped easily into the role of appreciative audience, making the right noises, like she did with Ruth or Tom or her mother, asking the questions the speaker wanted asked, but under that familiar habit was real fascination. Lolli was that exact sort of dangerous that Ruth seemed like she might be, but wasn't.

"The woman who owned the pet store smoked. Right in the store. Can you believe that? She didn't deserve to take care of animals."

"You smoke." Dave shook his head.

"I don't own a pet shop." Lolli turned to Val. "Your head looks cool. Can I touch it?"

Val shrugged and bent her head forward. It felt strange to be touched there—not uncomfortable, just weird, as though someone were stroking the soles of her feet.

"I'm Lollipop," the girl said. She turned to the boy with the locs. He was thin and pretty looking. "This is Sketchy Dave."

"Just Dave," Dave said.

"I'm just Val." Val sat up. It was a relief to talk to people after so many hours of silence. It was even more of a relief to talk to people that didn't know anything about her, Tom, her mother, or any of her past.

"Not short for Valentine?" Lollipop asked, still smiling. Val wasn't sure if the girl was making fun of her or not, but since her name was *Lollipop*, how funny could Val's name be? She just shook her head.

Dave snorted and ripped open another sugar packet, pouring the grains onto the table and cutting them into long lines that he ate with a coffee-wetted finger.

"Do you go to school around here?" Val asked.

"We don't go to school anymore, but we live here. We live wherever we want to."

Val took another sip of coffee. "What do you mean?"

"She doesn't mean anything," Dave interrupted. "How about you?"

"Jersey." Val looked at the milky gray liquid in her cup. Sugar crunched between her teeth. "I guess. If I go back." She got up, feeling stupid, wondering if they were making fun of her. "'Scuse me."

Val went to the bathroom and washed up, which made her feel less disgusting. She gargled tap water, but when she spat, she saw herself in the mirror too clearly: splotches of freckles across her cheeks and mouth, including one just below her left eye, all of them looking like ground-in dirt against the patchy tan she had from outdoor sports. Her newly shaved head looked weirdly pale and the skin around her blue eyes was bloodshot and puffy. She scrubbed her hand over her face, but it didn't help. When she came back out, Lolli and Dave were gone.

Val finished her coffee. She thought about napping in the armchair, but the café had grown crowded and loud, making her headache worse. She walked out to the street.

A drag queen with a beehive wig hanging at a lopsided

angle chased a cab, one Lucite shoe in her hand. As the cabbie sped away, she threw it hard enough that it banged into his rear window. "Fucking fucker!" she screamed as she limped toward her shoe.

Val darted out into the street, picked it up, and returned it to its owner.

"Thanks, lamb chop."

Up close, Val could see her fake eyelashes were threaded with silver, and glitter sparkled along her cheekbone.

"You make a darling prince. Nice hair. Why don't we pretend I'm Cinderella and you can put that shoe right on my foot?"

"Um, okay," Val said, squatting down and buckling the plastic strap, while the drag queen tried not to hop as she swayed to keep her balance.

"Perfect, doll." She righted her wig.

As Val stood up, she saw Sketchy Dave laughing as he sat on the metal railing on the other side of the narrow street. Lolli was stretched out on a batiked blue sheet that contained books, candleholders, and clothing. In the sunlight, the blue of Lolli's hair glowed brighter than the sky. The kitten was stretched out beside her, one paw batting a cigarette over the ground.

"Hey, *Prince Valiant*," Dave called, grinning like they were old friends. Lolli waved. Val shoved her hands in her pockets and walked over to them.

"Pop a squat," Lolli said. "I thought we scared you off."

"Headed somewhere?" Dave asked.

"Not really." Val sat down on the cold concrete. The coffee had finally started racing through her veins and she felt almost awake. "What about you?"

"Selling off some stuff Dave scrounged. Hang out with us. We'll make some money and then we'll party."

"Okay." Val wasn't sure she wanted to party, but she didn't mind sitting on the sidewalk for a while. She picked up the sleeve of a red velvet jacket. "Where did all this stuff come from?"

"Dumpster-diving mostly," Dave said, unsmiling. Val wondered if she looked surprised. She wanted to seem cool and unfazed. "You'd be amazed what people will pay for what they throw out in the first place."

"I believe it," Val said. "I was thinking how nice that jacket is."

That must have been the right response, because Dave grinned widely, showing a chipped front tooth. "You're okay," he said. "So, what, you said '*if* you go back'? What's that about? You on the street?"

Val patted the concrete. "I am right now."

They both laughed at that. As Val sat beside them, people passed by her, but they only saw a girl with dirty jeans and a shaved head. She felt as though anyone from school could go by her, Tom could have stopped to buy a necktie, her mother could have tripped on a crack in the sidewalk, and none of them would have recognized her.

Looking back, Val knew she had a habit of trusting too much, being too passive, too willing to believe the best of others and the worst of herself. And yet, here she was, falling in with more people, getting swept along with them.

But there was something different about what she was feeling now, something that filled her with a strange pleasure. It was like looking down from a high building, the way the adrenaline hit you as you swayed forward. It was powerful and terrible and utterly new.

Val spent the day there with Lolli and Dave, sitting on the sidewalk, talking about nothing. Dave told them a story about a guy he knew who got so drunk that he ate a cockroach on a dare. "One of those New York cockroaches, ones that are the size of goldfish. The thing was halfway out of his mouth and still squirming as he bit down on it. Finally, after chewing and chewing he actually swallows. And my brother is there—Luis is some kind of crazy smart, like he read the encyclopedia when he was home with chicken pox smart—and he says, 'You know that roaches lay eggs even after they're dead.' Well, this guy can't believe it, but then he starts yelling how we are trying to kill him and holding his stomach, saying he can already feel them eating him from the inside."

"That is nasty," Val said, but she was laughing so hard she had tears in her eyes. "So deeply nasty."

"No, but it gets better," said Lolli.

"Yeah," Sketchy Dave said. "Because he pukes on his shoes. And the roach is right there, all chopped up, but clearly pieces of a big black bug. And here's the thing—one of the legs moves."

Val shrieked with disgust and told them about the time that she and Ruth smoked catnip thinking it would get them high.

When they had sold a faux crocodile-skin clutch, two T-shirts, and a sequined jacket from the blanket, Dave bought them all hot dogs off a street cart, fished out of the dirty water and slathered with sauerkraut, relish, and mustard.

"Come on. We need to celebrate finding you," Lolli said, jumping to her feet. "You and the cat."

Still eating, Lolli jogged down the street. They crossed over several blocks, Lolli in the lead, until they came to an old guy rolling his own cigarettes on the steps of an apartment building. A filthy bag filled with other bags sat beside him. His arms were as thin as sticks and his face was as wrinkled as a raisin, but he kissed Lolli on the cheek and said hello to Val very politely. Lolli gave him a couple of cigarettes and a crumpled wad of bills, and he stood up and crossed the street.

"What's wrong with him?" Val whispered to Dave. "Why's he so skinny?"

"Just cracked out," Dave said.

A few minutes later, he came back with a bottle of cherry brandy wrapped in brown paper.

Dave rummaged up an almost-empty cola bottle from his messenger bag and filled that with the liquor. "So the cops don't stop us," he said. "I hate cops."

Val took a swig from the bottle and felt the alcohol burn all the way down her throat. The three of them passed it back and forth as they walked down West Third. Lolli stopped in front of a table covered in beaded earrings hanging from plastic trees that jangled whenever a car went past. She fingered a bracelet made with tiny silver bells. Val walked to the next table, where incense was stacked in bundles and samples burned on an abalone tray.

"What have we here?" asked the man behind the counter. He had skin the color of polished mahogany and smelled of sandalwood.

Val smiled mildly and turned back toward Lolli.

"Tell your friends to take more care whom they serve." The incense man's eyes were dark and glittered like a lizard's. "It's always the messengers who are the first to know the customer's displeasure."

"Right," Val said, stepping away from the table. Lolli skipped up, bells jangling around her wrist. Dave was trying to make the cat lick brandy out of the soda cap.

"That guy was really weird," Val said. When she looked back, out of the corner of her eye, for just a moment, the incense man seemed to have long spines jutting up from his back like a hedgehog.

Val reached for the bottle.

They walked aimlessly until they came to a triangle-shaped median of asphalt, lined on both sides with park benches, presumably for suits to eat their lunch in warmer weather and suck in the humid air and car exhaust. They sat, letting the cat down to investigate the flattened remains of a pigeon. There, they passed the brandy back and forth until Val's tongue felt numb and her teeth tingled and her head swam.

"Do you believe in ghosts?" Lolli asked.

Val thought about that for a moment. "I guess I'd like to."

"What about other things?" Lolli mewed, rubbing her fingers together to call the cat over. It paid no attention.

Val laughed. "What things? I mean, I don't believe in vampires or werewolves or zombies or anything like that."

"What about faeries?"

"Faeries like . . . ?"

Dave chuckled. "Like monsters."

"No," Val said, shaking her head. "I don't think so."

"Want to know a secret?" Lolli asked.

Val leaned in close and nodded. Of course she did.

"We know where there's a tunnel with a monster in it," Lolli half-whispered. "A faerie. We know where the faeries live."

"What?" Val wasn't sure she'd heard Lolli right.

"Lolli," Dave warned, but his voice sounded a little slurred, "shut up. Luis would be raging if he heard you."

"You can't tell me what to say." Lolli wrapped her arms around herself, digging her nails into her skin. She tossed back her hair. "Who would believe her anyway? I bet she doesn't even believe me."

"Are you guys serious?" Val asked. Drunk as she was, it almost seemed possible. Val tried to think back to the fairy tales she liked to reread, the ones she'd collected since she was a little kid. There weren't very many faeries in them. At least not what she thought of as faeries. There were godmothers, ogres, trolls, and little men that bargained their services for children, then railed at the discovery of their true names. She thought of faeries in video games, but they were elves, and she wasn't sure if elves were faeries at all.

"Tell her," Lolli said to Dave.

"So how come you get to order me around?" Dave asked, but Lolli just punched him in the arm and laughed.

"Fine. Fine." Dave nodded. "My brother and I used to do some urban exploring. You know what that is?"

"Breaking into places you're not supposed to be," Val said. She had a cousin who went out to Weird NJ sites and posted photos of them on his website. "Mostly old places, right? Like abandoned buildings?"

"Yeah. There're all kinds of things in this city that most people can't see," Dave said.

"Right," said Val. "White alligators. Mole people. Anacondas."

Lolli got up and retrieved the cat from where it was

scratching at the dead bird. She held it on her lap and petted it hard. "I thought that you could handle it."

"How come you know about this stuff that no one else does?" Val was trying to be polite.

"Because Luis has the second sight," Lolli said. "He can see them."

"Can *you* see them?" Val asked Dave.

"Only when they let me." He looked at Lolli for a long moment. "I'm freezing."

"Come back with us," Lolli said, turning to Val.

"Luis won't like it." Dave turned his boot as if he were squashing a bug.

"We like her. That's all that matters."

"Where are we going back to?" Val asked. She shivered. Even though she was warm from the liquor drowsing through her veins, her breath gusted in the air and her hands alternated between icy and hot when she pressed them under her shirt and against her skin.

"You'll see," said Lolli.

They walked for a while and then ducked down into a subway station. Lollipop stepped through the turnstile with a swipe of her card, then passed it back through the bars to Dave. She looked at Val. "Coming?"

Val nodded.

"Stand in front of me," Dave said, waiting.

She walked up to the turnstile. He swiped, then pressed himself against her, pushing them both through at once. His body was corded muscle against her back, and she smelled smoke and unwashed clothes. Val laughed and staggered a little.

"I'll tell you something else you don't know," Lolli said,

holding up several cards. "These are toothpick MetroCards. You break off toothpicks real little and then you jam them in the machine. People pay, but they don't get their cards. It's like a lobster trap. You come back later and see what you caught."

"Oh," Val said, her head swimming with brandy and confusion. She wasn't sure what was true and what wasn't.

Lollipop and Sketchy Dave walked to the far end of the subway platform, but instead of stopping at the end and waiting for the train, Dave jumped down into the well where the tracks ran. A few people waiting for the train glanced over and then quickly looked away, but most of them didn't even seem to notice. Lolli followed Dave awkwardly, moving so that she was sitting on the edge and then letting him half lift her down. She held on to the now-squirming kitten.

"Where are you going?" Val asked, but they were already disappearing into the dark. As Val jumped down onto the litter-strewn concrete after them, she thought how insane it was to follow two people she didn't know into the bowels of the subway, but instead of being afraid, she felt glad. She would make all her own decisions now, even if they were ruinous ones. It was the same pleasurable feeling as tearing a piece of paper into tiny, tiny pieces.

"Be careful not to touch the third rail or you'll fry," Dave's voice called from somewhere ahead.

Third rail? She looked down nervously. The middle one. It had to be the middle one. "What if a train comes?" Val asked.

"See those niches?" Lolli called. "Just flatten yourself into one of those."

Val looked back at the concrete of the subway platform, much too high to climb. Ahead, there was darkness, studded only with tiny lamps that seemed to give off little real light. Rustling noises seemed too close, and she thought she felt tiny paws run over one sneaker. She felt the panic she had been waiting for this whole time. It swallowed her up. She stopped, so gripped by fear that she couldn't move.

"Let's go." Lolli's voice came from the gloom. "Keep up."

Val heard the distant rattle of a train but couldn't tell how far away it was or even what track it was on. She ran to reach Lolli and Dave. She had never been afraid of the dark, but this was different. The darkness here was devouring, thick. It seemed like a living thing, breathing through its own pipes, heaving gusts of stench into the tunnel around her.

The smell of filth and wetness was oppressive. Her ears strained for the steps of the other two. She kept her eyes on the lights, as though they were a breadcrumb trail, leading her out of danger.

A train rushed by on the other side of the tracks, the sudden brightness and furious noise stunning her. She felt the pull of the air, as though everything in the tunnels was being drawn toward it. If it had been on her side, she would have never had time to jump for the niche.

"Here." The voice was close, surprisingly close. She couldn't be sure whether it belonged to Lolli or to Dave.

Val realized she was standing next to a platform. It looked like the station they'd left, except here the tiled walls were covered in graffiti. Mattresses were piled on the concrete shelf, heaped with blankets, throw pillows, and couch cushions—most of them in some variation of mustard yellow. Candle stubs flickered dimly, some jammed in the sharp mouths of beer cans, others in tall glass jars decorated with the Virgin Mary's face on the label. A boy with his hair braided thickly back from his face sat near a hibachi grill in the back corner of the station. One of his eyes was clouded over, whitish and strange, and steel piercings puckered his dark skin. His ears were bright with rings, some thick as worms, and a bar stuck out from either cheek, as though to highlight his cheekbones. His nose was pierced through one nostril and a hoop threaded his lower lip. As he stood, Val saw that he wore a puffy black jacket over baggy and ripped jeans. Sketchy Dave started up a makeshift ladder of wood planking.

Val turned all the way around. One of the walls was decorated with spray paint that read "for never and ever."

"She's impressed," Lolli said. Her voice echoed in the tunnel.

Dave snorted and walked over to the fire. He took out flattened cigarette butts from his messenger bag and dropped them into one of the chipped mugs, then stacked cans of peaches and coffee.

The boy with the piercings lit up one of the butts and took a deep drag. "Who the fuck is that?"

"Val," Val said before Lolli could answer. Val shifted her weight, uncomfortably aware that she didn't know the way back.

"She's my new friend," Lollipop said, settling down in a nest of blankets.

The pierced boy scowled. "What's with her hair?"

"I cut it," Val said. For some reason that made both the pierced boy and Sketchy Dave laugh. Lolli looked pleased with her.

"If you didn't guess, this is Luis," Lolli said.

"Don't enough people find their own way down here without you two playing tour guide?" Luis demanded, but no one answered him, so maybe it wasn't a real question.

Exhaustion was starting to creep over Val. She settled down on a mattress and pulled a blanket over her head. Lolli was saying something, but the combination of brandy, ebbing fear, and exhaustion was overwhelming. She could always go home later, tomorrow, in a few days. Whenever. As long as it wasn't now.

As she dozed off, Lolli's cat climbed over her, jumping at shadows. She reached out her hand to it, sinking her fingers into the short, soft fur. It was a tiny thing, really, but already crazy.

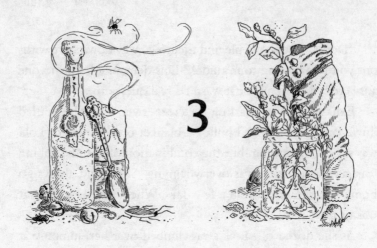

3

Muscles clenching, Val vaulted out of sleep into being fully awake, her heart beating hard against her chest. She nearly cried out before she remembered where she was. She guessed it was afternoon, although it was still dark in the tunnels; the only light came from the guttering candles. On the other mattress, Lollipop was curled up with her back against Luis. He had one arm thrown over her. Sketchy Dave was on her other side, swaddled up in a dirty blanket, head bent toward Lolli the way the branch of a tree grows toward the sun.

Val buried her head deeper in the comforter, even though it smelled vaguely of cat piss. She felt groggy but better rested.

Lying there, she remembered looking through college catalogues a couple of weeks earlier with Tom. He'd been talking about Kansas, which had a good writing program and wasn't crazy expensive. "And look," he'd said, "they have a girls' lacrosse team," as if maybe they'd be together after high school. She'd smiled and kissed him while she was still smiling. She'd liked kissing him; he always seemed to know just how to kiss back. Thinking about it made her feel aching and dumb and betrayed.

She wanted to go back to sleep but she couldn't, so she just stayed still until she had to pee badly enough to go and squat, wide-legged, over the stinking bucket she found in one corner. She tugged down her jeans and underwear, trying to balance on the balls of her feet, while she pulled the crotch of her clothes as far away from her body as she could. She tried to tell herself that it was the same as when you were driving down a highway and there was no rest stop, so you had to go in the woods. There was no toilet paper and no leaves, so she did a little hopping dance that she hoped would shake herself dry.

Making her way back, she saw Sketchy Dave starting to stir and hoped that she hadn't woken him up. She tucked her legs back into the blanket, now noticing that the vivid odors of the platform combined into a smell she couldn't identify. Light streamed down from a grate in the street above, illuminating black, grime-streaked iron beams.

"Hey, you slept for almost fourteen hours," he said, turning on his side and stretching. He was shirtless, and even in the gloom she could see what looked like a bullet wound in the center of his chest. It pulled the rest of his skin toward it, a sinking pool that drew everything to his heart.

Dave moved over to the hibachi and kindled it with matches and balls of newspaper. Then he set a pot on top, shaking grounds out of a tin and pouring water from a plastic gallon milk jug.

She must have stared at him for too long, because he looked up with a grin. "Want some? It's cowboy coffee. No milk, but there's plenty of sugar if you want it."

Nodding, she bundled the blankets around her. He strained her a steaming cup and she held it gratefully, using it first to warm her hands and then her cheeks. She ran her fingers absently over her scalp. She felt thin stubble, like fine sandpaper.

"You might as well come scrounging with me," Sketchy Dave said, looking over at the mattress with something like longing. "Luis and Lolli'll sleep forever if you let 'em."

"How come you're up?" she asked, and took a sip from the mug. The coffee was bitter, but Val found it satisfying to drink, flavored with smoke and nothing else. Grounds floated on the surface, making a black film.

He shrugged. "I'm the junkman. Gotta go see what the suits throw out."

She nodded.

"It's a skill, like those pigs that can smell out truffles. You either got it or you don't. One time I found a Rolex watch in with some junk mail and burned toast. It was like someone tossed everything on the kitchen table right into the garbage without looking at it."

Despite what Dave had said about them sleeping in, Lolli groaned and slid out from under Luis's arm. Her eyes were still mostly closed and she had a dirty kimono-style dressing gown thrown over yesterday's clothes. She looked beautiful in a way that Val never would, lush and hard all at the same time.

Lolli gave Luis a shove. He grunted and rolled over, propping himself up on his elbows. There was a flicker of movement along the wall and the cat strolled out, butting its head against Luis's hand.

"She likes you, see?" Lolli said.

"Aren't you worried about rats getting her?" Val asked. "She's kind of little."

"Not really," Luis said darkly.

"Come on, you just named her last night." Lolli picked the cat up and dumped her on her own lap.

"Yeah," Dave said. "Polly and Lolli."

"Polyhymnia," said Luis.

Val leaned forward. "What does Poly-whatever mean?"

Dave poured another cup for Luis. "Polyhymnia's some kind of Greek Muse. I don't know which one. Ask him."

"Doesn't matter," Luis said, lighting a cigarette stub.

Sketchy Dave shrugged, as if apologizing for knowing as much as he did. "Our mom used to be a librarian."

Val didn't really know what a Muse was, except for a dim recollection of studying the *Odyssey* in ninth grade. "What's your mom now?"

"Dead," said Luis. "Our dad shot her."

Val caught her breath and was about to stammer out an apology, but Sketchy Dave spoke first.

"I thought maybe I'd be a librarian, too." Dave looked at Luis. "The library is a good place to think. Kind of like down here." He turned back to Val. "Did you know I was the first one to find this spot?"

Val shook her head.

"Scrounged it. I'm the prince of refuse, the lord of litter."

Lolli laughed and Dave's smile broadened. He seemed more pleased by his joke now that he knew Lolli liked it.

"You didn't want to be a librarian," Luis said, shaking his head.

"Luis knows all about mythology." Lolli took a sip of coffee. "Like Hermes. Tell her about Hermes."

"He's a psychopomp." Luis gave Val a dark look, as if daring her to ask what that meant. "He travels between the world of the living and the world of the dead. A courier, kind of. That's what Lolli wants me to say. But forget that for a minute; you asked about rats getting Polly. What do you know about rats?"

Val shook her head. "Not much. I think one stepped over my foot on my way in here."

Lolli snorted and even Dave smiled, but Luis's face was intense. His voice had a ritual quality, as though he'd said this many times before. "Rats get poisoned, shot, trapped, beaten, just like street people, just like *people*, just like us. Everybody hates rats. People hate the way they move, the way they hop, they hate the sound of their paws skittering all over the floor. Rats're always the villains."

Val looked into the shadows. Luis seemed to be waiting for her to react, but she didn't know what the right response was. She wasn't even sure she knew what he was really talking about.

He went on. "But they're strong. They got teeth that are tougher than iron. They can gnaw through anything—wood beams, plaster walls, copper pipes—anything but steel." "Or diamond," Lolli said with a smirk. She didn't seem at all unnerved by his speech.

Luis barely paused to acknowledge Lolli had spoken. His eyes stayed on Val. "People used to fight them in pits here in the city. Fight them against ferrets, against dogs, against people. That's how tough they are."

Dave smiled, as if all this made sense to him.

"They're smart, too. You ever see a rat on the subway? Sometimes they get on a car at one platform and detrain at the next stop. They're taking a ride."

"I've never seen that," Lolli scoffed.

"I don't care if you ever saw it or not." Luis looked at Dave, who'd stopped nodding. Then he turned to Val. "I can sing rats' praises morning, noon, and night and it won't change the way you feel about them, will it? But what if I told you that there were things out there that think of you like you think of rats?"

"What things?" Val asked, remembering what Lolli had said the night before. "Do you mean fa—" Lolli sunk her nails into Val's arm.

Luis looked at her for a long time. "Another thing about rats. They're *neophobic*. You know what that means?"

Val shook her head.

"They don't trust new things," said Luis, unsmiling. "And neither should we." Then he stood, chucking his stub of a cigarette out onto the tracks, and walked up the steps and out of the station.

What an asshole. Val picked at a loose thread on her pants, pulling at it, unraveling the fabric. *I should go home,* she thought. But she didn't go anywhere.

"Don't worry about him," Lolli said. "Just because he can see things we can't, he thinks he's better than us." She watched until Luis was out of sight and then picked up a small lunchbox with a pink cat on it. Opening the latch, she took out and unrolled a T-shirt to spread out the contents: a syringe, an antique silver-plated spoon with some of the silver worn off, a pair of flesh-toned pantyhose, several tiny press-and-seal baggies containing an amber powder that glimmered a faint blue in the dim light. Lolli shouldered off one sleeve of her dressing gown and Val could see black marks on the inside of her elbow, like the skin there was charred.

"Chill out, Lolli," Sketchy Dave said. "Not in front of her. Not this."

Lolli reclined against a pile of pillows and bags. "I like needles. I like the feeling of the steel under my skin." She looked at Val. "You can get a little buzz off shooting up water. You can even shoot up vodka. Goes right into your bloodstream. Makes you drunker cheaper."

Val rubbed her arm. "It can't be too much worse than you scratching me." She should have been horrified, but the ritual of it fascinated her, the way all the tools were laid out on the dirty shirt, waiting to be used in turn. It made her think of something, but she wasn't quite sure what.

"I'm sorry about your arm! He was in such a mood, I didn't want him to get started about the faeries." Lolli made a face as she cooked the powder with a little water over the hibachi. It bubbled on the spoon. The sweet smell, like burnt sugar, filled Val's nose. Lolli sucked it up through the needle, then tapped the bubbles to the top, pushing them out with a squirt of liquid. Tying off her upper arm with pantyhose, Lolli inserted the tip slowly into one of the black marks on her arm.

"Now I'm a magician," Lolli said.

It came to Val then that what she was reminded of was her mother putting on makeup—laying out the tools and then using them one by one. First foundation, then powder, eye shadow, eyeliner, blush, all done with the same calm ceremony. The fusion of the images unnerved her.

"You shouldn't do that in front of her," Dave repeated, signaling in Val's direction with a bob of his chin.

"She doesn't mind. Do you, Val?"

Val didn't know what she thought. She'd never seen anyone give themselves a shot like that, professional as a doctor.

"She's not supposed to see," Dave said. Val watched him get up to pace the platform. He stopped under a mosaic of tiles spelling out WORTH. Behind him, she thought she saw the darkness change its shape, spreading like ink dropped into water. Dave seemed to see it, too. His eyes widened. "Don't do this, Lolli."

The gloom seemed to be coalescing into indistinct shapes that made the hair stand up on Val's arms. Blurry horns, mouths crowded with teeth, and claws as long as branches formed and then dissipated.

"What's the matter? You scared?" Lolli sneered at Dave before turning back to Val. "He's afraid of his own shadow. That's why we call him Sketchy."

Val said nothing, still staring at the moving darkness.

"Come on," Dave said to Val, moving unsteadily toward the stairs. "Let's go scrounge."

Lolli pouted exaggeratedly. "No way. I found her. She's my new friend and I want her to stay here and play with me."

Play with her? Val didn't know what Lolli meant, but she didn't like the sound of it. Right then, Val wanted nothing more than to get out of the claustrophobic tunnels and away from the shifting shade. Her heart beat so fast that she feared it would spring out of her chest like the bird in a cuckoo clock. "I have to get some air." She stood up.

"Stay," Lolli said lazily. Her hair seemed bluer than it had a moment ago, shot through with aquamarine highlights, and the air flickered around her the way it did over a street in the hot sun. "You won't believe how much fun you'll have."

"Let's go," Dave said.

"Why do you always have to be so boring?" Lolli rolled her eyes and lit her cigarette off of the fire. A good half of it went up in flames, and she dragged on it anyway. Her voice was slow, slurred, but her gaze, even from drowsy eyes, was severe.

Dave started up the yellow maintenance stairs and Val followed him, filled with an uncertain dread. At the top, Dave pushed up the grating and they stepped out onto the sidewalk. As she emerged into the bright, late-afternoon sunlight, she realized that she'd left her backpack on the platform with her return ticket still inside of it. She half-turned back to the grate and then hesitated. She wanted the bag, but Lolli had been acting so strange . . . Everything had gone so strange. But maybe even the smell of the drug could make shadows move? She ran through a health-class list of substances to avoid— heroin, PCP, angel dust, cocaine, crystal meth, Special K. She didn't know much about any of them. No one she knew did anything more than smoke weed or drink.

"Coming?" Dave called. She noticed the worn-down soles of his boots, the stains covering his jeans, the tightly corded muscles of his thin arms.

"I left my—" she started to say, but then thought better of it. "Never mind."

"It's just the way Lolli is," he said with a sad smile, looking at the sidewalk and not at Val's eyes. "Nothing's going to change her."

Val looked around at the large building across the street and the concrete park they were standing in, with its dried-up and cracked pond, and an abandoned shopping cart. "If it's so easy to get in this way, why did we come through the tunnels?"

Dave looked uncomfortable and he was silent for a moment. "Well, the financial district is pretty packed around five on a Friday, but it's nearly empty on a Saturday. You don't want to be coming up out of the sidewalk with a million people around."

"Is that all?" Val asked.

"And I wasn't sure I trusted you yet," Dave said.

Val tried to smile, because she guessed that he had a little faith in her now, but all she could think of was what would have happened if somewhere, walking through the tunnels, he had decided against her.

Val picked through a dumpster. The food smells still made her gag, but after two previous trash piles, she was getting more used to them. She pushed aside mounds of shredded paper, but found only a few boards studded with nails, empty CD cases, and a broken picture frame.

"Hey, look at this!" Sketchy Dave called from the next bin. He emerged wearing a navy pea coat, one arm of it slightly ripped, and holding up a Styrofoam take-out box that looked like it was mostly filled with linguini in alfredo sauce. "You want some?" he asked, picking up a hunk of noodles and dropping them into his mouth.

She shook her head, disgusted but laughing.

Pedestrians were wending their way home from work, messenger bags and briefcases slung across their shoulders. None of them seemed to see Val or Dave. It was as if the two of them had become invisible, just part of the trash they were sorting through. It was the sort of thing that she'd heard about on television and in books. It was supposed to make you feel small, but she felt liberated. No one was looking at her or judging her based on whether her outfit matched or who her friends were. They didn't see her at all.

"Isn't it too late to find anything good?" Val asked, hopping down.

"Yeah, morning is the best time. Around now on the weekday, businesses are junking office stuff. We'll see what's around, then come back out near midnight, when restaurants toss off the day-old bread and vegetables. And then at dawn you go residential again—we'll have to get there before the trucks pick up."

"You can't do this every day, though, right?" She looked at him incredulously.

"It's always trash day somewhere."

She glanced at a stack of magazines tied together with string. So far, she hadn't found anything she thought was worth taking. "What exactly are we looking for?"

Dave ate the last of the linguini and tossed the box back into a dumpster. "Take any porn. We can always sell that. And anything nice, I guess. If you think it's nice, someone else probably will, too."

"How about that?" She pointed to a rusted iron headboard leaning against an alley wall.

"Well," he said, as if trying to be kind, "we could truck it up to one of those fancy little shops—they paint old stuff like this and resell it for big money—but they wouldn't pay enough for the trouble it'd be." He looked at the dimming light in the sky. "Shit. I have to pick something up before it gets dark. I might have to do a delivery."

Val picked up the headboard. The rust scraped off on her hands, but she managed to balance the cast iron on her shoulder. Dave was right. It was heavy. She put it back down again. "What kind of delivery?"

"Hey, look at this," Dave squatted down and yanked out a box full of romance novels. "These might be something."

"To who?"

"We could probably sell 'em," he said.

"Yeah?" Val's mother had read romances and Val was used to the sight of the covers: a woman tipped back in a man's arms, her hair long and flowing, a beautiful house in the distance. All the fonts curled and some were embossed with gold. She bet none of these books had to do with fucking your daughter's boyfriend. She wanted to see one of the covers show that—a young kid and an old lady with too much makeup and lines around her mouth. "Why would anyone want to read that shit?"

Dave shrugged, carried the box under one arm, and flipped open a book. He didn't read out loud, but his mouth moved as he scanned the page.

They were quiet as they walked for a while and then Val pointed to the book in his hand. "What's it about?"

"I don't know yet," Sketchy Dave said. He sounded annoyed. They walked for a while more in silence, his face buried in the book.

"Look at that," Val pointed to a wooden chair with the seat gone.

Dave regarded it critically. "Nah. We can't sell that. Unless you want it for yourself."

"What would I do with it?" Val asked.

Dave shrugged and turned to walk through a black gate into a mostly empty square, dumping the romance novel back into the box. Val stopped to read the plaque: SEWARD PARK. Tall trees shadowed most of the deserted playground equipment sprawled over the space. The concrete was carpeted with yellow and brown leaves. They passed a dried-up fountain with stone seals that looked as if they might spurt water for kids to run through in the summertime. The statue of a wolf peeked out from a patch of brown grass.

Sketchy Dave walked past all that without pausing and headed for a separate gated area that bordered one of the New York Public Library branches. Dave slid through a gap in the fence. Val followed, climbing into a miniature Japanese garden filled with small piles of smooth, black rocks in stacks of varying heights.

"Wait here," he said.

He pushed over one of the stone piles and lifted up a small, folded note. Moments later he was back out through the fence and unfolding it.

"What does it say?" Val asked.

With a grin, Dave held the paper out. It was blank.

"Watch this," he said. Crumpling it into a ball, he threw it into the air. It flew out and downward, when it suddenly changed direction as though blown by a rebel wind. As Val watched in amazement, the paper ball rolled until it rested beneath the base of a slide.

"How did you do that?" Val asked.

Dave reached underneath the slide and ripped a tape-covered object free. "Just don't tell Luis, okay?"

"Do you say that about everything?" Val looked at the object in Dave's hand. It was a beer bottle, corked with melted wax. Around the neck, a scrap of paper hung from a ragged piece of string. Inside, molasses-brown sand sifted with each tilt of the container, showing a purplish sheen. "What's the big deal?"

"Look, if you don't believe Lolli, I'm not going to argue with you. She told you too much already. But just say that you did believe Lolli for a minute, and say you thought that Luis could see a whole world the rest of us can't, and say that he does some jobs for them."

"Them?" Val couldn't decide if she thought this was a conspiracy to freak her out or not.

Dave squatted down, and with a quick look at the sun's position in the sky, uncorked the bottle, causing the wax around the neck to crumble. He sifted a little of the contents into a tiny baggie like the one she'd seen Lolli pour her drug out of. He shoved the baggie into the front pocket of his jeans.

"Come on, what is it?" Val asked, but her voice was hushed now.

"I can honestly say I have no fucking clue," Sketchy Dave said. "Look. I have to go uptown and drop this off. You can come along with me, but you have to hang back when we get there."

"Is that the stuff Lolli shot in her arm?" Val asked.

Dave hesitated.

"Look," Val said. "I can just ask Lolli."

"You can't believe everything Lolli says."

"What is that supposed to mean?" Val demanded.

"Nothing." Dave shook his head and walked off. Val had no choice but to follow him. She wasn't even sure she could find her way back to the abandoned platform without him to guide her, and she needed her bag to go anywhere else.

They took the F to Thirty-fourth Street then switched to the B, taking that all the way to Ninety-sixth. Sketchy Dave held on to a horizontal metal bar and did pull-ups as the train thundered through the tunnels.

Val looked out the train window, watching the small lights marking distance streak by, but after a while her eyes were drawn to the other passengers. A wiry black man with close-cropped hair swayed unconsciously to the music on his iPod, a load of manuscripts balanced in one arm. A girl seated next to him was carefully drawing a glove of inky swirls up her own hand. Leaning against the doors, a tall man in a striped gray suit clutched his briefcase and stared at Dave in horror. Each person seemed to have a destination, but Val was a piece of driftwood, spinning down a river, not even sure in what direction she was moving. All she knew was how to make herself spin faster.

From the station, they walked a few blocks to the edge of Riverside Park, a sprawling patch of green that sloped down the highway to the water beyond. Across the street, town houses with park views had curling ironwork at the windows and doors. Intricately carved concrete blocks framed doorways and stair railings, forming fantastical dragons and lions and griffons that leered down at her in the reflected glow of street lamps. Val and Dave passed a fountain where a stone eagle with a cracked beak glowered over a murky green pool choked with leaves.

"Just wait here," Sketchy Dave said.

"Why?" Val asked. "What is the big deal? You already told me all kinds of shit you aren't supposed to."

"I told you you're not supposed to be along."

"Fine." Val relented and sat down on the edge of the fountain. "I'll be right here."

"Good," Dave said and jogged across the street to a door without iron grillwork. He walked up the white steps, put down the box of romance novels, and pressed a buzzer near where someone had stenciled a mushroom with spray paint. Val glanced up at the sculpted gargoyles that flanked the roof of the building. As she was looking, one seemed to shudder, like a bird on a perch, stony feathers rustling and then settling. Val froze, staring at it, and after a moment, the gargoyle went still.

Val jumped up and crossed the street, calling Dave's name. But as she got to the steps, the black door opened and a woman stepped into the doorway. She wore a long white slip. Her tangled, brown-and-green hair looked unwashed and the skin under her eyes was dark as a bruise. Hooves peeked out from under the hem of the slip where feet should have been.

Val froze, and the skirt settled, covering them, leaving Val unsure of what she'd seen.

Sketchy Dave turned his head and gave Val a fierce glare before he took out the beer bottle from his bag.

"Come inside?" the hoofed woman asked, her voice rough, as though she'd been shouting. She didn't seem to notice that the seal had been broken.

"Yeah," Sketchy Dave said.

"Who's your friend?"

"Val," Val said, trying not to gape. "I'm new. Dave's show-ing me the ropes."

"She can wait out here," said Dave.

"Do you think me so discourteous? The chill air will cut her to the bone." The woman held open the door and Val followed Dave inside, smirking. There was a marble-lined hall and a staircase railed with old, polished wood. The hooved woman led them through sparsely furnished rooms, past a fountain where silvery koi darted, their bodies so pale that the pink of their insides showed through their scales, past a music room holding only a double-strung lap harp on a table of marble, then into a parlor. She sat down on a cream-colored settee, the brocade fabric worn thin, and beckoned for them to join her. There was a low table near her and on it a glass, a teapot, and a tarnished spoon. The hooved woman used the spoon to measure out some of the amber sand into her cup, then filled it with hot water and drank deeply. She flinched once, and when she looked up, her eyes shone with an eerie, glittering brightness.

Val couldn't stop her gaze from straying to the woman's goat feet. There was something obscene about the glimpses of short, thick fur that covered her slender ankles, the sheen of the black keratin hooves, the two splayed toes.

"Sometimes a remedy can seem another sort of sickness," the goat-footed woman said. "David, be sure to tell Ravus there's been another murder."

Sketchy Dave sat down on the ebonized wood floor. "Murder?"

"Dunnie Berry died last night. Poor thing, she was just coming out of her tree—it's horrible how that iron gate fences her roots. It must have scorched her every time she crossed it. You delivered to her, no?"

Sketchy Dave shifted uncomfortably. "Last week. Wednesday."

"You might well be the last person to have seen her alive," the goat-footed woman said. "Be careful." She lifted her teacup, swigged down a bit more of the solution. "People are saying your master peddles poison."

"He's not my master." Sketchy Dave stood up. "We've got to go."

The goat-footed woman stood, too. "Of course. Come in the back and I'll get what I owe."

"Don't eat or drink anything or you'll be more fucked than you already are," Dave whispered to Val as he followed the woman into another room, leaving his salvaged box of romance novels on the floor. Val scowled and walked over to a display case. Inside the glass door was a large, solid chunk of something like obsidian. Beside it were some other things, equally odd. A bit of bark, a broken stick, a sharp burr in the shape of a pinecone, each fold razor sharp.

A few moments later, Sketchy Dave and the goat-footed woman returned. She was smiling. Val tried to stare at her without catching her eye. If someone had asked Val what she would do if she saw some supernatural creature, she wouldn't have figured she'd do nothing at all. She felt unable to be sure of what she was seeing, unable to decide if there really was a monster right in front of her. As they walked out of the apartment, Val could hear her blood thundering in her head to the speeding beat of her heart.

"I told you to fucking stay over there," Sketchy Dave growled, gesturing across the street, toward the fountain.

Val was too flustered to be angry. "I saw something—a statue—moving." She pointed upward, to the top of the building and the almost-night sky but she was incoherent. "And then I came over and . . . What is she?"

"Fuck!" Dave punched the stone wall, his knuckles coming away raw and scraped. "Fuck! *Fuck!*" He walked away, head hunched as though he were leaning into a strong wind.

Val caught up to him and grabbed him by the arm. "Tell me," she demanded, her grip tightening. He tried to jerk away from her, but he couldn't. She was stronger.

He looked at her strangely, like he was reevaluating them both. "You didn't see anything. There was nothing to see."

Val stared at him. "And what would Lolli say? A faerie, right? Except faeries don't fucking exist!"

He started to laugh. She dropped his arm and shoved him hard. The box of novels fell, scattering paperbacks into the road.

He looked down at them and then back at her. "Fucking bitch," he said and spat on the ground.

All the rage and bewilderment of the last day boiled up in her. Her hands balled into fists. She wanted to hit something.

Dave bent down to pick up the cardboard box and replaced the fallen books. "You're lucky you're a girl," he muttered.

4

We must not look at goblin men,
We must not buy their fruits:
Who knows upon what soil they fed
Their hungry thirsty roots?
—CHRISTINA ROSSETTI, "GOBLIN MARKET"

On the train ride back, Val sat in a plastic seat far from Dave, leaned her head back against a Plexiglas-covered map of the subway, and wondered how a person could have hooves. She'd seen shadows move on their own and bottles of brown sand that had something to do with make-believe gossip about murdered tree people from weird, Upper West Side ladies. What she did know was that she didn't want to be blind and dumb, the kind of girl that didn't notice that her mom and boyfriend were having sex until she saw it with her own eyes. She wanted to know the truth.

When Val got close to the concrete park on Leonard Street she saw Luis sitting on a ledge, drinking something out of a blue glass bottle. A bird-boned girl with mismatched sneakers and a swollen belly sat beside him, trembling fingers holding a cigarette. As Val got closer, she could see sores on the new girl's ankles, leaking pus. The streets were nearly deserted, the only person close by a security guard across the street who walked out to the curb every now and then before she disappeared into the building.

"Why are you still around?" Luis asked, glancing up at her. She was unnerved by the stare from his cloudy eye.

"Just tell me where Lolli is and I won't be," said Val.

Luis gestured with his chin to the grate in the ground as Dave walked up to them both.

The girl dropped her cigarette and then reached for it, her fingers grazing the hot end without her seeming to notice as she fumbled to put it back in her mouth.

"What did you do?" Luis asked Dave, his jaw tightening. "What happened?"

Dave looked at the parked cars that lined the street. "It wasn't my fault."

Luis closed his eyes. "You are such a fucking idiot."

Dave said something else, but Val had already started walking toward the service entrance, the grate that she and Dave had slid out of that afternoon. She got down on her hands and knees, pulled up the unhinged end of the metal bars, and lowered herself onto the steps.

"Lolli?" she called into the darkness.

"Over here," came the drowsy reply.

Val waded across the mattresses and blankets to where she'd slept the night before. Her backpack wasn't where she'd left it. She kicked aside some of the dirty clothes on the platform. Nothing. "Where's my bag?"

"You trust a bunch of bums with your stuff, I guess you get what you get." Lolli laughed and held up the knapsack. "It's here. Chill."

Val unzipped her pack. All her stuff was inside, the razor still choked with her hair, the thirteen dollars still folded up in her wallet right beside her train ticket. Even her gum was still there. "Sorry," Val said and sat down.

"Don't trust us?" Lolli grinned.

"Look, I saw something and I don't know what it was and I'm done getting fucked with."

Lolli sat up, hugging her legs to her chest, eyes wide and smile stretching even wider. "You saw one of them!"

The image of the goat-footed woman moved uneasily behind Val's eyes. "I know what you're going to say, but I don't think it was a faerie."

"So what do you think it was?"

"I don't know. Maybe my eyes were playing tricks on me." Val sat down on an overturned wood tangelo box. It made a cracking sound, but supported her weight. "That doesn't make any sense."

"Believe what you can handle believing."

"But, I mean—faeries? Like 'clap if you believe in faeries'?"

Lolli snorted. "You saw one. You tell me."

"I did tell you. I told you I don't know what I saw. A woman with goat feet? You shooting something weird in your arm? Paper that dances around? Is that supposed to add up?"

Lolli scowled.

"How do you *know* it's real?" Val demanded.

"The troll tunnel," Lolli said. "You won't be able to explain that away."

"Troll?"

"Luis made a deal with him. It was when Dave and their mom got shot. Their mother was dead when the ambulance came, but Dave was in the hospital for a while. Luis promised the troll he would serve him for a year if he saved Dave's life."

"That's who Dave was doing the delivery for?" Val asked.

"He took you on one of those?" Lolli blew out a breath that might have been a laugh. "Wow, he really is the worst spy in the world."

"What is the big deal about telling me? Why does Luis care what I know? Like you said to Dave, no one is going to believe me."

"We weren't supposed to find out, either. Luis tried to hide what he was doing. But since he started doing deliveries for Ravus, some of the other faeries have him doing errands for them. So Dave started doing some of the troll's jobs. He hides just how many."

"My friend Ruth used to make up things. She said she had a boyfriend named Zachary that lived in England. She showed me letters full of angsty poetry. Basically, the truth was that Ruth wrote herself letters, printed them out, and lied about it. I know all about liars," Val said. "It's not like I don't believe what you're saying, but what if Luis is lying to you?"

"What if he is?" asked Lolli.

Val felt a burst of anger, the worse because it was directionless. "Whatever. Where's the troll tunnel? We'll find out for ourselves."

"I know the way," Lolli said. "I followed Luis to the entrance."

"But you didn't go inside?" Val stood up.

"No." Lolli stood, too, dusting off her skirt. "I didn't

want to go alone and Dave wouldn't come with me."

"What do you think a troll is?" Val asked as Lolli scrounged through the cloth and bags on the platform. Val thought of the story of the three goats, thought of the game *WarCraft* and the little green trolls that carried axes and said, "Wanna buy a cigar?" and "Say hello to my little friend" when you clicked on them enough times. None of that seemed real, but the world would certainly be cooler with something so unreal in it.

"Got it," Lolli said, holding up a flashlight that gave off a dim and inconstant glow. "This isn't going to last."

Val jumped off onto the track level. "We'll be quick."

With a sigh, Lolli climbed down after her.

As they walked through the subway tunnel, the failing flashlight washed the black walls amber, highlighting the soot and the miles of electrical cording that threaded through the tunnel. It was like moving through the veins of the city.

They passed a live platform, where people waited for a train. Lolli waved to them as they stared, but Val reached down and picked up the discarded batteries of a dozen CD players. As they moved on, she tried each battery in turn, until she found two that strengthened the beam of the flashlight.

Now it lit piles of garbage, catching the green reflection of rat eyes and the moving walls of roaches that throve in the heat and the dark. Val heard a thin whistle.

"Train," Val yelled, pushing Lolli against the gap in the wall, a shallow crevice thick with grime. Dust gusted through the air a moment before the train barreled past on another track. Lolli cackled and pressed her face close to Val's.

"One fine day in the middle of the night," she intoned. "Two dead boys got up to fight."

"Stop it," Val said, pulling away.

"Back to back they faced each other, pulled out their swords and shot one another. The deaf cop on the beat heard the noise and came and shot the two dead boys." Lolli laughed. "What? It's a rhyme my mother used to tell me. You never heard it before?"

"It's creepy as shit."

Val's knees were shaky as they resumed walking through the endless twisting tunnels. Finally, Lolli pointed to an opening that looked as if it had been bashed through the cement blocks. "Through there," she said.

Val took a step, but Lolli made a noise. "Val," she started, but she didn't continue.

"If you're scared, you can wait here. I'll go in and come right back out."

"I'm not *scared*," Lolli said.

"Okay." Val stepped through the rough concrete doorway.

There was a corridor, murky with water, with calcium deposits hanging down in brittle, chalky stalactites. She took a few more steps, cold water soaking her sneakers and the hem of her jeans. The light from the flashlight illuminated torn, ragged strips of plastic sheeting directly ahead of her. They shifted with the slight wind, like gauzy draperies or ghosts. The movement was unnerving. Splashing along, she ducked through the plastic and into a large chamber choked with roots. They dangled everywhere, long feathery tendrils dragging in the deeper water, thick root trunks cracking through the concrete ceiling to thin and spread. But the strangest part was that fruit hung from them as from branches. Pale globes grew from the hairy coils, warmed by no sun and fed by no soil. Val walked closer.

The skin of each was milky and translucent, showing a rose blush beneath it, as though their centers might be red.

Lolli touched one. "They're warm," she said.

It was then that Val noticed rusted stairs, their railing wrapped with sodden cloth.

She hesitated at the bottom of them. Glancing at the inverted tree again, she tried to tell herself that it was just weird, not supernatural. It didn't matter. It was too late to turn back.

Val started up the steps. Each one echoed and she could see a diffuse light. As trains rumbled above them, a thin, powdery dust fell like rain, catching and streaking the weeping walls. The girls spiraled up, higher and higher until they came to a large casement window shrouded by old blankets hung with nails. Val leaned over the railing and pushed aside the cloth. She was surprised to see a basketball court, apartment buildings, the highway, and the river beyond, sparkling like a necklace of lights. She was inside the Manhattan Bridge.

She kept walking, finally coming to a large open room with pipes and thick cords running along the ceiling and heavy wooden ladders along both sides of the wall. It looked as if it was meant for maintenance workers. Books were piled up on the makeshift shelves and in dusty stacks on the floor. Old volumes, tattered and worn. A sheet of plywood rested atop several dozen cinderblocks near the doorway, creating a makeshift desk. Jam jars lined one edge, and resting against it was a sword that looked as though it was made of glass.

Val took a step closer, reaching out her hand, when something fell on her. It was cold and formless, like a heavy wet blanket, and it stretched to cover her. It blocked out her sight and choked her. She threw up her hands, clawing at the slightly damp stuff, feeling it give under her sharp, short nails. Dimly, she could hear Lolli shrieking as if from very far away. Spots started to form in front of Val's eyes and she reached blindly for the sword. Her hand slid over the blade, cutting her fingers shallowly, but letting her blindly find the hilt.

She braced and swung at her own shoulder. The thing slipped from her, and for a dizzying moment she could breathe again. Hefting the sword of glass as much as she could like a lacrosse stick, she chopped at the white, boneless thing that rippled toward her, its stretched face and flat features making it appear like a pallid, fleshy paper doll. It writhed on the ground and went limp.

Val's hands shook. She tried to still them, but they wouldn't stop trembling, even when she clenched them into fists and dug her fingernails into the heels of her hands.

"What was that thing?" Lolli asked.

Val shook her head. "How the fuck would I know?"

"We should be quick." Lolli walked over to the desk and dumped several jars into her bag.

"What are you doing?" Val asked. "Let's get out of here."

"Okay, okay," Lolli said, rummaging through some bottles. "I'm coming."

Herbs were bound into bundles in one of the jam jars. Another was full of dead wasps, but a third was filled with what looked like knots of red licorice shoelaces. Some had labels on their lids: chokecherry, hyssop, wormwood, poppy. At the center of the plywood was a marble cutting board with spiky green balls waiting to be chopped by the tin half-moon of a knife that rested beside them.

On the wall were a series of pinned objects—a candy

wrapper, a gray wad of chewing gum, the burned-out stub of a cigarette. Hanging in front of each was a magnifying glass, enlarging not only the items but also the handwritten notes surrounding each. "Breath," read one. "Love," read another.

Lolli gasped sharply. Val spun around without thinking, lifting the sword automatically. Someone loomed in the doorway, tall and lean as a basketball player, bending to duck under the doorframe. As he straightened up, lank hair, black as ink, framed the grayish-green skin of his face. Two undershot incisors jutted from his jaw, their tips sinking into the soft flesh of his upper lip. His eyes went wide with something that might have been fear or even fury, but she found herself transfixed by the way the black irises were dusted around the edges with gold, like the eyes of a frog.

"Well." The troll's voice was a deep growl. "What have we here? A pair of filthy street girls." He took two steps toward Val and she stumbled backward, tripping over her own feet, her mind filled only with panic.

With one booted foot, the troll nudged the boneless thing. "I see you've gotten past my guardian. How unlikely." He wore a buttoned black coat that covered him from neck to calf, with black trousers underneath that seemed to emphasize the shock of green at the frayed cuffs and nape where cloth met flesh. His skin was the same horrible color that you might find underneath a band of copper you'd worn for too long. "And you've helped yourself to something else of mine as well."

Fear closed up Val's throat and held her in place. She watched the milky blood run down the sword and felt her hands start to shake again.

"There is only one human who knows this place. So what

did Luis tell you?" The troll took another step toward them, his voice soft and furious. "Did he dare you to go inside? Did he say there was a *monster*?"

Val looked at Lolli, but she was stunned and silent.

The troll ran the point of his tongue over an incisor. "But what did Luis intend, that's the real question. To give you a good scare? To give *me* a good scare? A good *meal*? It is entirely possible Luis might think I would want to eat you." He paused, as if waiting for one of them to deny it. "Do you think I want to eat you?"

Val raised the blade of the sword.

"*Really*? You don't say?" But then his voice deepened to a bellow. "Of course, perhaps you are merely a pair of unlucky *thieves*."

Val's lacrosse instincts took over. She ran toward the exit, toward the troll. As he reached for her, she ducked, passing under his arm and hitting the strips of plastic. She was halfway down the stairs when she heard Lolli scream.

Standing there, trains rattling on the bridge overhead, still holding the glass sword, she hesitated. *She* was the reason Lolli was inside this place. It was Val's own dumb idea to try to prove to herself that faeries were real. She should have gone back when she saw the tree. She shouldn't have come here at all. Taking a deep breath, she ran back up the stairs.

Lolli was sprawled out on the ground, tears running down her face, her body gone weirdly lax. The troll held her by the wrist and seemed to be in the middle of demanding something from her.

"Let her go," Val said. Her voice sounded like someone else's. Someone brave.

"I think not." Leaning down, he ripped Lolli's messenger bag off her shoulder and tipped it upside down. Several coins bounced on the wood floor, rolling next to bottles filled with black sand, needles, a rusted knife, sticks of gum, cigarette butts, and a compact that cracked as it hit the wood, spilling powder across the floor. He reached down for one of the bottles, long fingers nearly touching the neck. "Why would you want—"

"We don't have anything else of yours." Val stepped forward and raised the blade. "Please."

"Really?" He snorted. "Then what have you in your hands?"

Val looked at the sword, gleaming like an icicle under the fluorescent lights, and was surprised. She'd forgotten that it was his. Turning the point toward the floor, she considered dropping it, but was afraid to be wholly unarmed. "Take it. Take it and we'll go."

"You are in no position to command me," said the troll. "Put down the sword. Carefully. It is a thing more precious than you."

Val hesitated, bending as if she was going to set down the glass blade. Not placing it on the ground, she still watched him.

He twisted Lolli's finger abruptly and she shrieked. "May it pain her each time she itches to reach for a thing that isn't hers." He grasped a second finger. "And may it pain you to think you're the cause of her pain."

"Stop!" Val shouted, dropping the sword onto the wood planks of the floor. "I'll stay if you let her go."

"What?" His eyes narrowed, then one black eyebrow rose. "Aren't you the gallant?"

"She's my friend," Val said.

He paused and his face went curiously blank. "Your friend?" he repeated tonelessly. "Very well. You will pay for her foolishness as well as your own. That is the burden of friendship."

Val must have looked relieved, because a small, cruel smile crept onto his face. "How much time is she worth? A month of service? A year?" Lolli's eyes sparkled with tears.

Val nodded. Sure. Anything. Whatever. Just let them leave and then it wouldn't matter what she'd promised.

He sighed. "You will serve me for a month, one week for each item stolen." Pausing for a moment, he added, "In whatever way that I need."

She flinched and he smiled.

"Each dusk you will go to Seward Park. There, you will find a note under the wolf's paw. If you do not do what it says, things will go hard with you. Do you understand?"

Val nodded. He dropped Lolli's hand. She scrambled to shove her things back into her bag.

The troll pointed with one long finger. "Go over to that table. On it, there is a tincture, marked 'Straw.' Bring it to me."

Val fumbled with the jars, reading the looping handwriting: toadflax, knotweed, rue, bloodroot, mugwort. She held up a solution, its contents thick and cloudy.

He nodded. "Yes, that. Bring it here."

She did so, walking close to him, close enough to notice that the cloth of his coat was wool, tattered and full of moth holes. Small, curved horns grew through the top of each ear, making the tips seem like they were hardening to bone.

He took the jar, opened it, and scooped up some of the contents. She flinched away from him; the solution smelled like rotten leaves.

"Stay," he said, as though she were a dog brought to heel.

Angry at her own terror but hopeless against it, she remained motionless. He ran the pads of his fingers over her mouth, slicking them with the stuff. She had braced herself for his skin to feel oily or horrible, but it was merely warm.

Then, when he looked into her face, his gaze was so intent that she shuddered. "Repeat the conditions of your promise."

She did.

People said that video games were bad because they made you numb to death, made you register entrails spattering across a screen as a sign of success. In that moment, Val thought that the real problem with games was that the player was supposed to try everything. If there was a cave, you went in it. If there was a mysterious stranger, you talked to him. If there was a map, you followed it. But in games, you had a hundred million billion lives and Val only had this one.

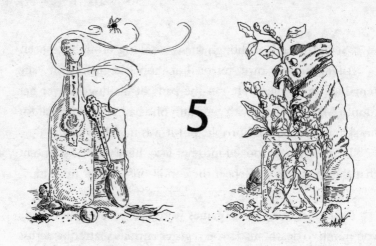

5

Nothing farther then he uttered—not a feather then
he fluttered—
Till I scarcely more than muttered, "Other friends
have flown before—
On the morrow he will leave me, as my Hopes have
flown before."
Then the bird said, "Nevermore."
—Edgar Allan Poe, "The Raven"

The city lights were bright and the streets were clogged with smokers standing outside of bars and restaurants when Val and Lolli staggered out of the bridge and onto the street.

A man sleeping on broken-down cardboard rolled over and wrapped an overcoat tighter around himself. Val started violently at the movement, her muscles clenching so fast that her shoulders hurt. Lolli cradled her messenger bag as if it were a stuffed animal, wrapping her arms around it and herself.

It was strange how when crazy things happened, it was hard to follow the tracery of reasons and impulses and thoughts that got you to the crazy place. Even though Val had wanted to find evidence of faeries, the actual proof was overwhelming. How many faeries were there and what other things might there be? In a world where faeries were real, might there be demons or vampires or sea monsters? How could these things exist and it not be on the front cover of every newspaper everywhere?

Val remembered her father reading *The Three Billy Goats Gruff* when she was a little kid. *Trip trap, trip trap went the littlest Billy Goat Gruff.* This troll was nothing like the illustration in the book—were any of them? *Who's that tripping over my bridge?*

"Look at my finger," Lolli said, holding it in the loose cradle of her other hand. It was puffy and bent at an odd angle from the joint. "He broke my fucking finger."

"It might be dislocated. I've done that before." Val remembered falling on her own hands on the lacrosse field, slipping out of a tree, trips to the doctor with his iodine and cigar-smoke smell. "You have to align it and splint it."

"Hey," Lolli said sharply. "I never asked for you to be my knight in shining armor. I can take care of myself. You didn't have to promise anything to that monster and you don't have to play doctor now."

"You're right." Val kicked a crushed aluminum can, watching it bounce across the street like a stone might skim over water. "You don't need any help. You have everything under control."

Lolli looked intently into the window of an electronics store where televisions showed their faces. "I didn't say that."

Val bit her lip, tasting the remains of the troll's solution.

She remembered his golden eyes and the rich, hot rage in his voice. "I'm sorry. I should have just believed you."

"Yeah, you should have," Lolli said, but she smiled.

"Look, we can get a stick or something for the splint. Tie it off with a shoelace." Val squatted down and started unlacing her sneaker.

"I have a better idea," Lolli said, turning toward the mouth of an alley. "How about I forget about the pain?" She sat down against the filthy bricks and pulled out her soup spoon, needle, lighter, and a glassine bag of whatever-it-was from her pack. "Give me the shoelace anyway."

Val thought of the moving shadows, remembered the amber sand, and had no idea what might happen next. "What is that?"

"Nevermore," Lolli said. "That's what Luis calls it, because there're three rules: Never more than once a day, never more than a pinch at a time, and never more than two days in a row."

"Who made those up?"

"Dave and Luis, I think. After they were living on the street, Luis started couriering for more faeries—I guess they have errands they need someone to run—and Dave took over some of the deliveries. One time he took a little bit of the Never, stirred it into some water like they do, and drank it up. It gives the faeries more glamour or something, to keep the iron from affecting them so much, but it gets us high. Drinking it was okay for a while, but it's so much better when you shoot it in your arm or freebase it like Dave does." Lolli spat into the spoon and lit the lighter. The solution sparkled as though it had just come alive.

"Glamour?"

"The way they make themselves look different, or other things seem different. Magic, I guess."

"What's it like?"

"Never? Like the ocean breaking over your head and sweeping you out to sea," Lolli said. "Nothing else can touch you. Nothing else matters."

Lolli drew up the stuff with the needle. Val wondered if she could ever feel that nothing touched her. It sounded like oblivion. It sounded like peace.

"No," Val said, and Lolli stopped.

Val smiled. "Do me first."

"Really?" Lolli grinned. "You want to?"

Val nodded, unbending her arm and holding it out.

Lolli tied off Val's arm, tapped out the bubbles from the syringe, and slid the needle in as neatly as if Val's skin had been built to sheathe it. The pain was so slight, it was less than the nick of a razor.

"You know," Lolli said, "the thing about drugs is that they make things kind of shift, go leftward and sideways and upside down, but with Never, you can take everyone else upside down with you. What else can do that?"

Val had never thought too much about the inside of her elbow, but now it felt as vulnerable as her wrist, as her throat. She rubbed the bruise left when the needle was gone. There was barely any blood. "I don't know. Nothing, I guess."

Lolli nodded, as though pleased with that answer. As she was cooking up another batch of Never, Val found herself distracted by the sound of the fire, the feel of her own veins squirming like a nest of snakes under her skin.

"I—" Val started, but euphoria melted her bones. The

world turned to honey, thick and slow and sweet. She couldn't think of what she wanted to say, and for a moment she imagined losing her words forever. What if she could never think of what it was she wanted to say?

"Your veins are drinking down the magic," Lolli said, her voice coming from a great distance. "Now you can make anything happen."

Fire flooded Val, washing away the cold, banishing all the small agonies—the blister on her toe, the ache of her stomach, the too-tight muscles across her shoulders. Her fear melted away, replaced with *power*. Power that throbbed inside of her, giddy and eager, opening her up like a puzzle box to find all of her secret hurt and anger and confusion. Power that whispered to her in tongues of fury, with promises of triumph.

"See? It doesn't hurt anymore," Lolli said. She took hold of her finger and twisted. It made a snapping sound, like the crack of a knuckle, and popped back into place.

Everything looked too clear, too bright. Val found herself getting lost in the patterns of grime on the sidewalk, the promise of candy-colored neon signs, the scent of distant pipe smoke, of exhaust pipes, of frying oil. Everything was strange and beautiful and swollen with possibilities.

Lolli grinned like a jackal. "I want to show you something."

The fire was eating away at the inside of her arms, painful, but deliciously so, like being flooded with light. She felt volatile and unstoppable.

"Is this how it always is?" Val asked, even though some distant part of her mind told her that it was impossible for Lolli to know what Val was feeling.

"Yes," Lolli said. "Oh, yes."

Lolli led them down the street, approaching an Asian man with close-cropped graying hair walking in the opposite direction. At first he backed up when they got close, but then something seemed to relax him.

"I'd like some money," Lolli said.

He smiled and reached into the pocket of his coat, pulling out a wallet. He took out several twenties. "Is this enough?" he asked. His voice sounded strange, soft, and dazzled.

She leaned in to kiss his cheek. "Thank you."

Val felt the wind whip off the Hudson, but the scorching cold couldn't touch her now. The fiercest gust seemed like a caress. "How did you make him do that?" she asked, but it was all wonder and no apprehension.

"He wanted to," Lolli said. "They all want us to have whatever we want."

As they walked, each person they passed gave them what they asked for. A woman in a sequined skirt gave them her last cigarette, a young guy in a baseball cap handed over his coat without a word, a woman in a bronze trench pulled a pair of glittering gold hoops right from her ears.

Lolli reached into a trash can and lifted out banana peels, wet paper, slimy bread, and cups filled with sludgy water. "Watch this," she said.

In her hands, the detritus turned into cupcakes so white and fine that Val reached out her hand for one.

"No," Lolli said. "For them." She handed one to an old man as he passed and he gobbled it like an animal, reaching for another and another as though they were the best food in the world.

Val laughed, partially at his delight, partially at their power over him. She picked up a pebble and turned it into a cracker. He ate that too, licking Val's hands for any last trace of it. His tongue tickled and that only made her laugh harder.

They walked a few more blocks; Val couldn't be sure how many. She kept noticing fascinating things she hadn't seen before: the sheen on a roach's wings as it scuttled over a grate, the smirk of a carved face over a lintel, the broken stems of flowers outside of a bodega.

"Here we are," Lolli said, pointing to a dark store. In the window, mannequins posed in pencil skirts printed with scenes from comic books, or lounged on modern, red settees, holding up polka-dotted martini glasses. "I want to go in."

Val walked up to the window and kicked the glass. It spider-webbed but didn't cave. The alarm squawked twice and went silent.

"Try this," Lolli instructed, picking up a plastic straw. In her hand, it changed into a crowbar, heavy and cold.

Val smiled with delight and hit the window with all the built-up aggression of hating Tom and her mother and herself, all the anger at the troll in the tower, and the fury at the entire universe. She beat the glass in until it folded like bent metal.

"Nice." Lolli grinned and crawled through the window. As soon as Val was inside, the glass was back, uncracked, better than new.

Inside the store, lights came on and canned music started to play.

Each new glamour seemed to feed the power inside of Val instead of depleting it. With each enchantment, she felt giddier, wilder. Val wasn't even quite sure which one of them was doing what anymore.

Lolli kicked off her shoes in the middle of the store and tried on a dress of green satin. Val could see her bare feet were red with blisters. "Is this cute?"

"Sure." Val picked out a new pair of underwear and some jeans, tossing her old clothes onto the outstretched arm of a mannequin. "Look at this crap, Lolli. These are a-hundred-and-eighty-dollar jeans and they don't look like anything. They're just jeans."

"They're free," said Lolli.

Val found clothes and then sat down in one of the cartoon-ish armchairs to watch Lolli try on more things. As she danced around with a beaded shawl on her head, Val noticed the display next to the chair.

"See this?" Val said, holding up an avocado-colored wine-glass. "How ugly is this? I mean, who would pay for something this ugly?"

Lolli grinned and reached for a hat with pink feather fringe. "People buy what they're told to buy. They don't know it's ugly, or maybe they do and they think there's something wrong with thinking that."

"Then they need to be protected from themselves," Val said, and hurled the glass at the linoleum tile. It shattered, glass shards spinning out in every direction. "Anyone can see these things are ugly. Ugly, ugly, ugly."

Lolli started to laugh and she kept on laughing as Val broke every last one.

Walking back to Worth Street station with Lolli, Val felt dis-oriented, unsure of what had actually happened. As the Never ebbed from her, she felt more and more faded, as though the fire of the enchantment had eaten away some tangible part of her, had harrowed her.

She remembered a store and people that ate food out of her hands, and walking, but she couldn't quite be sure where she'd gotten what she was wearing. She remembered a blur of faces and gifts and smiles, as hazy as the memory of a monster in a tower before all that.

When she looked down at herself, she saw clothes she couldn't remember picking out—big black ass-kicking boots that were definitely warmer than her sneakers, a T-shirt printed with a heraldic lion, black cargo pants with tons of zippered pockets and a black coat that was much too big for her. It unnerved her to think that her own clothes were just gone, left behind somewhere. The boots pinched her feet as she walked, but she was glad of the coat. It seemed like they'd walked far into SoHo and, without the magic in her body, she felt colder than ever.

As they slipped through the service entrance and down the stairs, Val saw several people in the tunnel. The changing flicker of the candles lit up one of their cheekbones, the curve of a jaw, the paper bag–covered bottle one was lifting to his mouth. The girl with the swollen belly was there, wrapped up in a blanket with another body.

"There you are," Sketchy Dave said. His voice sounded slurred and when the candlelight caught him, she could see that his mouth had the slack look of the very drunk. "Come sit with me, Lolli," he said. "Come sit over here."

"No," she said, picking her way over to Luis instead. "You can't tell me what to do."

"I'm not trying to tell you anything," he said, and now his voice was miserable. "Don't you know I love you, baby? I would do anything for you. Look." He held up his arm. "Lolli" was carved into the skin in sluggishly bleeding letters. "Look what I did."

Val winced. Lolli just laughed.

Luis lit a cigarette and, for a moment, as the match struck, his whole face was illuminated. He looked furious.

"Why don't you believe me?" Dave demanded.

"I believe you," Lolli said, voice gone shrill. "I don't *care*. You're boring. Maybe I would love you if you weren't *boring*!"

Luis jumped to his feet, pointing his cigarette first at Lolli and then at Dave. "Just shut the fuck up, both of you." He turned and glared at Val, as though this all was somehow her fault.

"Who are they?" Val asked, gesturing toward the couple tangled in the blankets. "I thought nobody was supposed to be down here."

"Nobody *is* supposed to be down here," he said, sitting down next to his brother. "Not you, not me, not them."

Val rolled her eyes, but she didn't think he noticed in the candlelight. Scooting close to Lolli, she whispered, "Is he this much of a dick when I'm not around?"

"It's complicated," Lolli whispered back. "They used to squat here before, but Derek got sent upstate for some shit and Tanya moved to some abandoned building out in Queens."

Luis shifted closer to his brother and spoke quietly to him. Sketchy Dave got up, hands fisted. "You get everything," he shouted at Luis, tears on his cheeks, snot running from his nose.

"What do you want from me?" Luis demanded. "I never touched that girl. It's not my fault you're whipped."

"I'm not a thing," Lolli yelled at both of them, a terrible expression on her face. "You can't talk about me like I'm a thing."

"Fuck you," Dave shouted. "I'm boring? I'm a coward? Someday you're going to wish you didn't talk that way."

The girl in the blanket sat up, blinking rapidly. "Wha—"

"Come on," Luis said, taking Dave's arm. "Let's get out of here, Dave. You're just drunk. You need to walk it off."

Dave jerked away from his brother. "Fuck off."

Val stood up, the last lingering threads of Never making the chalky dark of the tunnels swim. Her legs felt rubbery and the soles of her feet burned from all the walking her body was just starting to realize it had done, but the last thing she wanted was to get caught up in claustrophobic bullshit. "Never mind. We're out of here."

Lolli followed her back up the stairs.

"Why do you like him so much?" Val asked.

"I don't like him." Lolli didn't bother to ask who Val meant. "His eye is jacked up. He's too skinny and he acts like an old man."

Val shrugged and threaded her thumb through the belt loop of her new pants, watching her boots step on the cracks in the sidewalk, letting her silence speak for her.

Lolli sighed. "He should be begging me for it."

"He should," Val agreed.

They walked down Bayard Street, past groceries selling bags of rice, piles of pale golden apples, bamboo shoots in bowls of water, and huge spiky fruit that hung down from the ceiling.

They passed little shops selling sunglasses, paper lamps, clumps of bamboo bound with gold ribbons, and bright-green plastic dragons molded to resemble carved jade.

"Let's stop," Lolli said. "I'm hungry."

The mere mention of food made Val's stomach growl. The fear had soured her belly and she realized she hadn't eaten anything since the night before. "Okay."

"I'll show you how to table-score."

Lolli picked a place where several ducks hung, necks bent around a wire, dripping with red glaze, empty pits where their eyes once were. Inside, people lined up to pick out food from an assortment of steaming dishes. Lollie ordered hot teas and egg rolls for both of them. The man behind the counter didn't seem to speak any English, but he dumped the right items onto their tray along with nearly a dozen plastic packets.

They slid into a booth. Lollie looked around, then ripped open a packet of duck sauce and squirted it on her roll, topping that with hot mustard. She nodded her head casually in the direction of an empty booth with a few plates still on it. "See those leftovers?"

"Yeah," Val bit into her egg roll, grease slicking her lip. It was delicious.

"Hold on." Lolli got up, walked over to a half-eaten plate of lo mein, picked it up, and walked back to their table. "Table-score. See?"

Val snorted, slightly scandalized. "I can't believe you just did that."

Lolli smiled, but her smile faded into a weird expression. "Sometimes you wind up doing a lot of crazy stuff that you can't believe you did."

"I guess so," Val said slowly. After all, she couldn't believe that she'd spent the night in an abandoned subway station with a bunch of homeless kids. She couldn't believe that instead of screaming and crying when she'd found out about Tom and her mom, she'd shaved her head and gone to a hockey game. She couldn't believe that she was sitting there calmly eating someone else's dinner when she'd just seen a monster.

"I moved in with my boyfriend when I was thirteen," Lolli said.

"Really?" Val asked. The food going into her mouth was calming her, letting her believe that the world would go on, even if there were faeries and weird faerie drugs. There would still be Chinese food and it would still be hot and greasy and good.

Lolli made a face. "Alex. He was twenty-two. My mom thought he was a pervert and told me not to see him. Eventually, I got sick of sneaking around and just took off."

"Shit," Val said, because she couldn't think of what else to say. When she was thirteen, boys had been as mysterious and unattainable as the stars in the sky. "What happened?"

Lolli took a couple of quick bites of lo mein and washed them down with tea. "Alex and I argued all the time. He was dealing out of the apartment and he didn't want me doing anything, even when he was shooting up right in front of me. He was worse than my parents. Finally, he found some other girl and just told me to get out."

"Did you go back home?" Val asked.

Lolli shook her head. "You can't go back," she said. "You change and you can't go back."

"I can go back," Val said automatically, but the memory of the troll and her bargain haunted her. It seemed unreal now, in the light and heat of the restaurant, but it nagged at the back of her thoughts.

Lolli paused for a moment, as if she were considering that. "You know what I did to Alex?" she asked, wicked smile returning. "I still had the keys. I went back when no one was there and I trashed the place. I threw everything out the window—his clothes, her clothes, the television, his drugs, every fucking thing I could get my hands on got dusted onto the street."

Val cackled with delight. She could just imagine Tom's face if she done that to him. She pictured his new computer cracked open on the driveway, iPod smashed into white pieces, black clothes spread out over the lawn.

"Soooo," Lolli said with a mock innocent look. "You enjoyed that story way too much not to have an asshole-boyfriend story of your own."

Val opened her mouth, not sure what she was going to say. The words stalled on her tongue. "My boyfriend was sleeping with my mom," she finally forced out.

Lolli laughed until she was choking, then stared at Val for a moment, eyes wide and incredulous. "Really?" she asked.

"Really," Val said, strangely satisfied that she'd managed to shock even Lolli. "They thought I got on the train and they were making out on the couch. Her lipstick was all over his face."

"Oh, nasty! *Nasty!*" Lolli's mouth contorted with honest, giggling disgust. Val laughed too, because, suddenly, it *was* funny. Val laughed so hard that her stomach hurt, that she couldn't breathe, that tears leaked out to wet her cheeks. It was exhausting to laugh like that, but she felt like she was waking from a strange dream.

"Are you really going back home to *that*?" Lolli asked.

Val was still half drunk with laughter. "I have to, don't I? I mean, even if I stayed here for a while, I can't live the rest of my life in a tunnel." Realizing what she'd said, she glanced up at Lolli, expecting her to be insulted, but she just leaned her head on her hands and looked thoughtful.

"You should call your mom, then," Lolli said finally. She pointed toward the lobby. "There's a pay phone out there."

Val was shocked. It was the last piece of advice she expected to get from Lolli. "I've got my cell."

"So call your mom already."

Val fished out her cell phone with a feeling of dread and turned it on. The screen flashed, calls missed count climbing. It stopped at sixty-seven. She'd only gotten one text. It was from Ruth and read: "where r u? your moms going crazy."

Val hit reply. "Am still in city," she typed, but then she stopped, not sure what to write next. What was she going to do? Could she really go home?

Bracing, she clicked over to voice mail. The first message was from her mom, her voice soft and strangled sounding: "Valerie, where are you? I just want to know you're safe. It's very late and I called Ruth. I guess you heard a lot from her. I-I-I don't know how to explain what happened or to say how sorry I am." There was a long pause. "I know you're very mad at me. You have every right to be mad at me. Just please let someone know you're all right."

It was weird to hear her mother's voice after all this time. It

made her gut clench with hurt and fury and acute embarrassment. Sharing a boy with her mom stripped her deeper than
bare. She deleted the message and clicked to the next one. It
was from Val's dad: "Valerie? Your mother is very concerned.
She said that you two had a fight and you ran off. I know how
your mother can be, but staying out all night isn't helping
anything. I thought you were smarter than this." In the background, she could hear her half sisters shrieking over the sound
of cartoons.

An unfamiliar man's voice spoke next. He sounded bored.
"Valerie Russell? This is Officer Montgomery. Your mother
reported you as missing after a disagreement the two of you
had. Nobody is going to make you do anything you don't want
to do, but I really need you to give me a call and let me know
that you're not in any trouble." He left a number.

The next message was a silence punctuated by several
wet-sounding sobs. After a few moments, her mother's choked
voice wailed, "Where are you?"

Val clicked off. It was horrible to listen to how upset her
mother was. She should go home. Maybe it would be okay—if
she never brought a boyfriend to the house, if her mom would
just stay out of her way for a while. It would be less than a year
before Val was out of high school. Then she wouldn't ever have
to live there again.

She scrolled to "home" and pressed the call button. The
phone on the other end rang as Val's fingers turned to ice.
Lolli arranged the remaining lo mein noodles into the shape of
something that might have been the sun, a flower, or a really
poorly rendered lion.

"Hello," Val's mother said, her voice low. "Honey?"

Val hung up. The cell rang almost immediately and she turned it off.

"You knew I couldn't do it," she accused Lolli. "Didn't you?"

Lolli shrugged. "Better to find out now. It's a long way to travel just to come right back."

Val nodded, afraid in a new, acute way. For the first time she realized that she might never be ready to go home.

6

Reality is that which, when you stop believing in it,
doesn't go away.
—Philip K. Dick

Val woke to the shriek of a train barreling past. Sweat stuck the wool coat to her clammy skin, despite the cold. Her head throbbed, her mouth burned, and even with all the food she'd eaten the night before, she felt ravenous. Shivering, she wrapped the covering tighter around herself and curled her legs closer to her body.

She tried to think back, past the table-scored food and the phone call home. There had been a monster and a sword made of glass, then a needle in her arm and a rush of power that still filled her with longing. She scrambled into a sitting position, looking down at new clothes that proved her memories were not formed only from bits of half-remembered dreams. Dave's arm had bled and strangers had done whatever she told them and magic was real. She reached for her backpack, relieved that she hadn't left that somewhere along with the rest of her clothes.

Only Lolli was still sleeping, curled up in the fetal position, a new dress layered over a skirt and a new pair of jeans. Dave and Luis weren't there.

"Lolli?" Val crawled over and shook Lolli's shoulder.

Lolli turned, pushed blue hair out of her face, and made a small, irritated noise. Her breath was sour. "Go away," she slurred, pulling the stained blanket over her face.

Val stood up unsteadily. Her vision swam. She picked up her backpack and forced herself to walk through the darkness up onto the night streets of Manhattan. The evening skies were bright with clouds and the air was thick with ozone, as if there was a storm blowing in fast.

She felt dried up and cracked and fragile as one of the few leaves that blew out from the park. It seemed that if you stripped away all the sports and the school and the normal life, what was within her wasn't much at all. Her body felt bruised, as though something else had been riding around in her skin the night before, something so awful and vast that it had charred her insides. There was a feeling of satisfaction, though, in spite of the fear. *I did this,* she thought, *I did this to myself.*

Deep breaths of cold air settled her stomach, but her mouth just got hotter.

The creature's words came back to her unbidden: *You will serve me for a month. Each dusk you will go to Seward Park. There, you will find a note under the wolf's paw. If you do not do what it says, things will go hard with you.* She was already late.

Val thought of the slick solution the troll had spread over her skin and felt a tremor shoot through her, an electric charge that jolted her hand to her lips. They were dry and swollen to the touch, but she found no cut or wound to explain the stinging.

She walked into a deli and bought a cup of ice water with some of the change at the bottom of her bag, hoping that it might cool her mouth. Outside the shop, she sat down on the concrete and sucked a cube of ice, her hand shaking so much that she was afraid to take a sip.

A woman coming out of the liquor store next door glanced down at Val and dropped some change into Val's cup of water. Val looked up, startled and ready to protest, but the woman had already walked on.

By the time Val removed the folded slip from under the wolf's paw, her whole mouth was sore as a wound. She squatted near the dried-up fountain and leaned her head against a chipped bar of metal fencing as her fingers numbly opened the paper.

She half expected a blank page she'd have to crumple and toss, like the one Dave had gotten, but there were words, written in the same looping hand that had addressed the bottle of amber sand:

"Come beneath the support of the Manhattan Bridge and knock thrice on the tree that squats where no tree should."

She jammed the note into her pocket, but as she did, her hand bumped something else. She pulled it out—a silver money clip with a huge, rough piece of turquoise at its center, the clasp stuffed with a twenty, two fives, and at least a dozen singles.

Had she taken the money? Had Lolli? Val couldn't remember. She'd never stolen anything before. One time she'd walked out of a Spencers in the mall with a Rangers poster in her hand, not realizing she hadn't paid for it until she and her friends reached the escalators. Her friends were impressed so she acted as if she'd done it on purpose, but afterward she felt so bad that she never hung it on her wall.

Val tried to think back to the night before, but it was as if she were remembering a story told by someone else. It was all a blur that, despite everything, made her skin itch for Nevermore.

She started walking, in too much pain to do anything else. Dread coiled in her stomach. She started down Market, passing Asian stores and a bubble tea place with a group of teenagers standing in front of it, all talking over one another and laughing. Val felt as disconnected from them as if she were a hundred years old. She reached for her backpack, wanting more than anything to call Ruth, wanting to hear someone who knew her, someone who could remind her of that old self. But her mouth hurt too much.

Cutting across onto Cherry, she walked a little farther, close enough to the East River that no buildings blocked her view. The water shone with the reflected radiance of the bridge and the far shore. A barge nearly became a mass of negative space except for a few lights glittering at the prow.

The bridge loomed directly ahead of her, the supports like the tower of a castle, rough stonework rising high above the street, ruddy with runoff from rust on the metal above. The stretch of rock was interrupted by casement windows high above the street.

Broken glass crunched beneath Val's boots as she passed under the graceful arch of the underpass. The sidewalk stank of stale urine. On one side was a makeshift wire fence, blocking the way into a construction area where a mound of sand waited to be spread. On the other, close to where she walked, was what looked like a bricked-up doorway. Below it, Val saw the stump of a tree, its roots digging deep into the concrete.

"The tree." Val kicked the stump softly. The wood was wet and dark with filth, but the roots sank down into the concrete sidewalk, as though they stretched past the tunnels and pipes, worming their way into some secret, rich soil. She wondered if this was the same tree that bloomed with pale fruit.

It was an eerie thing to see a stump here, nestled up against a building as if they were kin. But perhaps no eerier than the idea that she'd fallen into a fairy tale. In a video game, there would have been some pixilated storm of color and maybe even an on-screen message warning her that she was leaving the real world behind. *Portal to Faerieland. Do you want to go through? Y/N.*

Val knelt down and rapped three times on the stump. The wet wood barely made a sound under her knuckles. A spider scuttled out toward the street.

A sharp noise made Val look up. A fracture appeared in the stone above the stump, as though something had struck it. She stood and reached out to run her finger across the line, but as she touched the wall, patches of stone cracked and fell away, until there was a rough doorframe.

She stepped through onto the stairwell, steps extending up and down from the landing. When she looked back, the wall was solid. A sudden burst of terror nearly overwhelmed her and only pain held her in place.

Trip Trap.

"Hello?" she called up the steps. It hurt to move her mouth.

Trip Trap.

The troll appeared on the landing.

Who's trip trapping over my bridge?

"Most people would have come sooner." His rough, gravelly voice filled the stairway. "How your mouth must hurt to bring you here at last."

"It wasn't so bad," she said, trying not to wince.

"Come up, little liar." Ravus turned and walked back to his rooms. She hurried up the dusty stairs.

The large loftlike space flickered with fat candles set on the floor, their glow making her shadow jump on the walls, huge and terrible. Trains rumbled above them and cold air rushed in through covered windows.

"Here." In the palm of one six-fingered hand, he held a small, white stone. "Suck on it."

She snatched the stone and popped it in her mouth, in enough pain not to question him. It felt cool on her tongue and tasted like salt at first and then like nothing at all. The pain abated slowly and with it, the last of the nausea, but she found exhaustion taking its place. "What do you want me to do?" she asked, pushing the rock into her cheek with her tongue so she could talk.

"For now, you can shelve a few books." Turning, he went to his desk and began to strain the liquid from a small copper pot thick with sticks and leaves. "There may be an order to them, but since I have lost the understanding of it, I don't expect you to find one. Put them where they will fit."

Val lifted one of the volumes off a dusty pile. The book was heavy, the leather on it cracked and worn along the binding. She flipped it open. The pages were hand lettered and there were watercolor and ink drawings of plants on most of the pages. "Amaranth," she read silently. "Weave it into a crown to speed the healing of the wearer. If worn as a wreath, confers invisibility instead." She closed the book and pushed it into the plywood and brick shelves.

Val rolled the stone around in her mouth like a candy as she put away the troll's scattered tomes. She took in the mish-mash of moth-eaten army blankets, stained carpet, and ripped garbage bags that served as curtains not even the outside streetlights could pierce. A dainty flowered teacup, half full of a brackish liquid, rested beside a ripped leather chair. The idea of the troll holding the delicate cup in his claws made her snort with laughter.

"To know your target's weakness, that is the intuitive genius of great liars," said the troll without looking up. His voice was dry. "Though the Folk differ greatly, one from another and from place to place, we are alike in this: We cannot outright speak what is untrue. I find myself fascinated by lies, however, even to the point of wanting to believe them."

She didn't reply.

"Do you consider yourself skilled in lying?" he asked.

"Not really," Val said. "I'm more of an accomplished sucker."

He said nothing to that.

Picking up another book, Val noticed the glass sword hanging on the wall. The blade was newly cleaned and looking through it, she could see the stone, each pit in the rock magnified and distorted as though it was under water.

"Is it made from spun sugar?" His voice was close by and she realized how long she'd been staring at the sword. "Ice?

Crystal? Glass? That's what you're wondering, isn't it? How something that looks so fragile is so hard to break?"

"I was just thinking how beautiful it was," Val said.

"It's a cursed thing."

"Cursed?" Val echoed.

"It failed a dear friend of mine and cost him his life." He ran one hooked nail down the length of it. "A better blade might have stopped his opponent."

"Who . . . who was his opponent?" she asked.

"I was," the troll said.

"Oh." Val could think of no reply. Although he seemed calm now, even kind, she heard the warning in his words. She thought of something her mother had told her when she'd finally broken up with one of her most dysfunctional boy-friends. *When a man tells you he's going to hurt you, believe it. They always warn you and they're always right.* Val pushed the words out of her head; she didn't want any of her mother's advice.

The troll walked back to the table and picked up three waxed and stoppered beer bottles. Through the amber glass she couldn't see the color of the contents, but the idea that it might be that very same amber sand that ran through her veins the night before made her skin thrill with possibility.

"The first delivery will be in Washington Square Park, to a trio of fey there." One hooked nail pointed to a map of the five boroughs and most of New York and New Jersey taped on the wall. She walked closer to it, noticing for the first time that there were thin black pins stuck into various points along the surface. "The second can be left outside of an abandoned building, here. That . . . recipient may not wish to show himself.

I want you to take the third to an abandoned park, here." The troll seemed to be indicating a street in Williamsburg. "There are small grassy hills, close to the rocks and the water. The creature that you seek will wait for you at the river's edge."

"What are the pins for?" Val asked.

He gave the map a quick sideways look and seemed to hesitate before speaking again. "Deaths. It isn't unusual for the Folk to die in cities—most of us here are in exile or in hiding from other fey. Living so close to so much iron is dangerous. One would only do it for the protection it affords. But these deaths are different. I'm trying to puzzle them out."

"What am I delivering?"

"Medicine," he said. "Useless to you, but it eases the pain of the Folk exposed to so much iron."

"Am I suppose to collect anything from them?"

"Don't concern yourself with that," said the troll.

"Look," Val said. "I'm not trying to be difficult, but I never lived in New York before. I mean, I've been up here for things and I've walked around the Village, but I can't find all these places with a glance at a map."

He laughed. "Of course not. Had you hair, I would give you three knots, one for each delivery, but since you don't, give me your hand."

She held it out, palm up, ready to snatch it back if he took out anything sharp.

Reaching into one of the pockets of his coat, the troll drew out a spool of green thread. "Your left hand," he said.

She gave him her other hand and watched as he wound her first, middle, and ring fingers with the string, tying one knot on each digit. "What is this supposed to do?" she asked.

"It will help you make your deliveries."

She nodded, looking at her fingers. How could this be magic? She'd expected something that glittered and glowed, not mundane stuff. String was just string. She wanted to ask about it again, but she thought it might be rude, so she asked something else she'd been wondering about. "Why does iron bother faeries?"

"We don't have it in our blood like you do. More than that, I don't know. There was a king of the Unseelie Court poisoned with but a few shards quite recently. His name was Nephamael and he thought to make an ally of iron—he wore a band of it at his brow, letting the burns scar deep until his flesh was so toughened it could scar no more. But that did not toughen his throat. He died choking on the stuff."

"What are these courts?" Val asked.

"When there are enough faeries in an area they often organize themselves into groups. You might call them gangs, but the Folk usually call them courts. They occupy some territory, often fighting with other nearby courts. There are Seelie Courts, which we call Bright Courts, and the Unseelie Courts, or Night Courts. You might, at first glance, think that the Bright Courts were good and the Night Courts evil, but you would be much, although not entirely, mistaken. And then there's the High Court and the least said about it and the whole Greenbriar line, the better."

Val shuddered. "Am I going to be doing deliveries alone? Are any of the others coming with me?"

His golden eyes glittered in the firelight. "Others? Luis is the only human courier I've ever had. Is there someone else you are thinking of?"

Val shook her head, not sure what she should say.

"I would ask that you do these tasks alone and that you do not speak of them with any of the . . . *others*."

"Okay," Val said.

"You are under my protection," he said, letting her take the bottle. "Still, there are things I would have you know about the fey. Do not tarry with them and take nothing they offer, especially food." She thought of the magicked stone she had fed to an old man and nodded grimly, guiltily. "Put this comfrey in your shoe. It will help you keep safe and speed your travel. Rowan berries. And here's madwort to keep you from fascination. You can tuck that into your pocket."

Val took the plants, toed off her left sneaker, and tucked the comfrey inside. She could feel it there, nestled against her sock, oddly comforting and alarming because it was comforting.

When she emerged on the street again, she felt a tug from the thread twined around her first finger. Magic! It made her smile despite everything else as she started in that direction.

It was still early evening when she made it to Washington Square Park. She'd stopped along the way and spent stolen money on a ham sandwich that she was still too sick to digest, despite her hunger, and had to toss it away half-eaten. She'd even managed to wash her face in an icy fountain, where the water tasted of rust and pennies.

The three bottles of whatever-they-were clanked together in her backpack, heavier than they would have been if she hadn't been so tired. She longed to uncork one and taste the contents, to bring back the power and fearlessness of the night before, but she was wary enough of her exhaustion today that she didn't.

Walking through the park, past NYU students in bright scarves, past people hurrying to dinner or walking their tiny, sweatered dogs, she realized that she had no idea what she was looking for. The thread pulled her toward a pack of middle-schoolers in expensive skater clothes climbing up on one of the interior fences. One floppy-haired boy in low-slung jeans, skull-print knee pads and checkerboard Vans was louder than the rest, standing on the top rung and whooping at three girls leaning against the thick trunk of a tree. They all had bare feet and hair the color of honey.

The thread all but dragged her to the three girls before it unraveled.

"Um, hi," Val said. "I have something of yours, I think."

"I can smell the glamour on you, thick and sweet," said one. Her eyes were gray as lead. "If you're not careful, a girl like you could get carried off under the hill. We'd leave a bit of wood behind and everyone would weep over it, because they'd be too stupid to know the difference."

"Don't be awful to her," said another, twirling a lock of hair around her hand. "She can't help being blind and dumb."

"Here," Val said, pushing the bottle into the hands of the one that hadn't spoken. "Take your medicine like good little girls."

"Ooooh, it has a tongue," said the girl with the gray eyes.

The third girl just smiled and glanced at the boy on the fence.

One of the others followed her look. "He's a pretty one," she said.

Val could barely tell the girls apart. They all had long, wil-lowy limbs and hair that seemed to move with the slightest breeze. With their thin clothes and unshod feet, they should have been cold, but she could see they weren't.

"Do you want to dance with us?" a faerie girl asked Val.

"*He* wants to dance with us." The gray-eyed faerie gave the loud skater boy a wide grin.

"Come dance with us, messenger," said the third, speaking for the first time. Her voice was like a frog croaking and when she spoke, Val saw that her tongue was black.

"No," Val said, thinking of the troll's warnings and the madwort in her pocket. "I have to go."

"That's all right," said the gray-eyed faerie, toeing the earth with one bare foot. "You'll visit us again when you aren't so gaudy with spells. At least I hope you will. You're almost as pretty as he is."

"I'm not pretty at all," said Val.

"Suit yourself," said the girl.

She wasn't sure what she should expect to find as she passed by boarded-up tenement houses and bodegas with broken front windows. The building that the string on her finger tugged her toward was boarded up, too, and Val was sur-prised to see a garden blooming on the roof. Long tendrils of plants hung over the side and what looked like half-grown trees sprouted from what must have been thin soil, all of it trapped by an aluminum cage that capped the building. Val walked up to the entrance, now overgrown with ivy. On the second floor, the windows were completely missing, gaping holes in the brick. She could almost see the rooms inside.

As she stepped onto the cracked front steps, the thread untied itself from her middle finger to drop into the nearby grass.

She took out the bottle from her backpack and set it down, thinking of the troll's directions.

Something rustled in the grass and Val yelped, jumping back, suddenly aware of how strangely quiet things had gotten. The cars still streaked by and the city sounds were still there, but they had faded somehow. A brown rat poked its head out of the grass, beady black eyes like polished pebbles, pink nose twitching. Val laughed with relief.

"Hey there," she said, squatting down. "I hear that you can bite through copper. That's really something."

The rat turned and scurried back through the grass as Val watched. A figure moved out of the shadows to scoop up the rodent and set it on a wide shoulder.

"Who . . . ," Val said and stopped herself.

He stepped into the light, a creature nearly tall as the troll and thicker, with horns that curved back from his head like a ram's and a thick brown beard that ran to green at the tips. He was clad in a patchwork coat and hand-stitched boots.

"Come inside and warm up," he said, picking up the corked beer bottle. "I have some questions for you."

Val nodded, but her gaze slid toward the street, wondering if she could run for it. The faerie's hand came down hard on her shoulder, deciding the question. He steered her around the back of the building and through a door that hung by only the top hinge.

Inside the building were an array of mannequin parts,

stacked unnervingly along the walls, a pyramid of heads in one corner and a wall of arms in multiple skin tones in another. A pile of wigs sat like a large, resting animal in the middle of the floor.

A tiny creature with moth wings buzzed through the air, holding a needle, and settling on a man's torso to sew a vest to the body.

Val looked around, afraid, noting anything that could be a weapon, backing up so her fingers could reach behind her and grab. She didn't like the idea of swinging a plastic leg at the creature, but if she had to, she would, even if she had no hope of it doing much damage. But as her fingers closed on what she thought was a whole arm, the mannequin hand came off in hers. "What is all this?" she asked loudly, hoping the faerie wouldn't notice.

"I make stock," said the horned creature, sitting down on a milk crate that bowed with his weight. "Me and Needlenix, we're the best you're like to find this side of the sea."

The moth-winged faerie buzzed. Val tried to put the hand back on the shelf behind her, but without looking, she couldn't seem to find a place for it. She settled for tucking it into her back pocket, under her coat.

"The Queen of the Seelie Court, Silarial herself, uses our work."

"Wow," Val said, as he clearly wanted her to be impressed. Then, in the silence that followed, she was obliged to ask, "Stock?"

He smiled and she could see that his teeth were yellowed and quite pointed. "It's what we leave behind when we steal someone away. Now, your logs or sticks or whatever, they work all right, but these mannequins are superior in every way. More convincing, even to those rare humans with a little bit of magic or Sight. Of course, I suppose that's cold comfort to you."

"I suppose it is," Val said. She thought of the girls in the park saying *We'd leave a bit of wood behind*. Was that what they'd meant?

"Of course, sometimes we leave one of our own to pretend to be the human child, but that silliness doesn't concern me." He looked at her. "We can be cruel to those that cross us. We blight crops, dry up the milk in a mother's breast, and wither limbs for the merest of slights. But sometimes I've thought that we are worse to those who have won our favor.

"Now, tell me," he said, sitting up and reaching for the potion bottle. In the firelight, she saw that his eyes were completely black, like his rat's. "Is this poison?"

"I don't know what it is," Val said. "I didn't make it."

"There have been quite a few deaths among the Folk."

"I heard something about that."

He grunted. "All of them were using Ravus's solution to stave off the iron sickness. All of them had deliveries from a courier just like yourself near their time of death."

Val thought of the incense man of a few days before. What was it he'd said? *Tell your friends to be careful whom they serve.* "You think Ravus . . ." She let the name sit in her mouth for a moment. "You think Ravus is the poisoner?"

"I don't know what I think," the horned man said. "Well, be on your way, then, courier. I'll find you again if I need to."

Val left quickly.

Passing an old theater, Val was drawn by the smell of popcorn and promise of heat. She could feel the roll of money in the pocket of her coat, more than enough to go inside, and yet the idea of seeing a movie seemed unimaginable, as though she would have to cross some impossible dimensional barrier between this life and the old one to sit in front of a screen.

When she was younger, Val and her mother had gone to movies every Sunday. First they would go to the one that Val wanted to see and then the one her mother chose. It usually wound up being something like a zombie film followed by a tearjerker. They would sit in the darkened theater and whisper to each other: *I bet he's the one that did it. She's going to die next. How can anyone be so stupid?*

She walked closer to the posters, just to be contrary. Most of what was playing were art films she hadn't heard of, but one called "Played" caught her eye. The poster showed an attractive guy posing as the jack of hearts, a tattoo of the card drawn on his bare shoulder. He was holding a page of cups card.

Val thought of Tom, dealing out his tarot deck into patterns on her kitchen counter. "This is what crosses you," he'd said, turning over a card with the image of a blindfolded woman holding swords in both her hands. "Two of swords."

"No one can tell the future," Val had said. "Not with something you can buy at Barnes and Noble."

Her mother had walked over to them and smiled down at Tom. "Will you do my cards?" she'd asked.

Tom had grinned back and they'd started talking about ghosts and crystals and psychic shit. Val should have known right then. But she'd poured a glass of soda, perched on a stool, and watched as Tom read a future for her mother in which he would have a part.

She walked up the steps, bought a ticket for the midnight show and walked into the café area. It was deserted. An array of small, metal tables with marble tops surrounded a pair of brown leather couches. Val flopped down on one sofa and stared up at the single chandelier glittering in the center of the room, hanging from a mural of the sky. She rested there, watching it glitter for a few moments and enjoying the luxury of heat before she forced herself into the bathroom. There was a half hour before the movie started and she wanted to get cleaned up.

Wadding up paper towels, Val gave herself a half-decent sponge bath, scrubbing her underpants with soap before putting them back on damp, and gargling mouthfuls of water. Then, sitting down in one of the stalls, she leaned her head against the painted metal wall and closed her eyes, letting the hot air from the ducts wash over her. *Just a moment,* she told herself. *I'll get up in just a moment.*

A woman with a thin face leaned over her. *"Pardon?"*

Val leaped to her feet and the cleaning woman backed away from her with a yelp, mop held out in front of her.

Embarrassed and stumbling, Val grabbed her backpack and rushed for the exit. She pushed through the metal doors as the suit-clad ushers started toward her.

Disoriented, Val saw that it was still dark. Had she missed the movie? Had she been asleep for only a moment?

"What time is it?" she demanded from a couple trying to flag down a cab.

The woman looked at her watch nervously, as though Val was going to snatch it off her wrist. "Almost three."

"Thanks," Val muttered. Although she'd gotten less than four hours of sleep sitting on a toilet, now that she was walking again, she found that she felt far better. The dizziness was almost gone and the smell of Asian food from an all-night restaurant a few blocks away made her stomach rumble in hunger.

She started walking in the direction of the smell.

A black SUV with tinted windows pulled up next to her, windows down. Two guys were sitting in the front seats.

"Hey," the guy on the passenger side said. "You know where the Bulgarian disco is? I thought it was off Canal, but now we're all turned around." He had blond streaks in his carefully gelled hair.

Val shook her head. "It's probably closed by now anyway."

The driver leaned over. He was dark-haired and dark-skinned, with large, liquid eyes. "We're just looking to party. You like to party?"

"No," Val said. "I'm just going to get some food." She pointed toward the mock-Japanese exterior of the restaurant, glad it wasn't that far off, but painfully aware of the deserted streets between her and it.

"I could go for some fried rice," said the blond. The SUV rolled forward, keeping up with her as she walked. "Come on, we're just regular guys. We're not dangerous or anything."

"Look," Val said. "I don't want to party, okay? Just let me alone."

"Okay, okay." The blond looked at his friend, who shrugged. "Can we at least give you a ride? It's not safe for you to be out here walking around on your own."

"Thanks, but I'm okay." Val wondered if she could outrun them, wondered if she should just take off and get a head start. But she kept walking, as if she weren't scared, as if they were only two nice, concerned guys trying to talk her into their truck.

She had comfrey in her shoe and madwort in her pocket and a plastic hand under the back of her shirt, but she wasn't sure how any of those things could help her.

The doors clicked unlocked as the truck rolled to a stop and she made a decision. Turning toward the open window, she smiled and said, "What makes you think I'm not one of the bad people?"

"I'm sure you're bad," said the driver, all smiles and insinuation.

"What if I told you that I just cut off some chick's hand?" Val said.

"What?" The blond guy looked at her in confusion.

"No, really. See?" Val pitched the mannequin hand through the window. It landed in the driver's lap.

The truck swerved and the blond yelped.

Val took off across the street, sprinting toward the restaurant.

"Fucking freak," the blond shouted as they pulled away from the curb, tires squealing.

Val's heart was beating double time as she walked into the safe heat of Dojo. Sitting down at a table with a sigh of relief, she ordered a huge bowl of steaming miso soup, cold sesame noodles dripping with peanut glaze, and ginger fried chicken that she ate with her fingers. When she was done, she thought she would fall asleep again, right at the table.

But she had one more delivery to do.

The street looked mostly unused and the sides of it were strewn with trash—broken glass, dried condoms, a ripped pair of panty-hose. Still, the smell of dew on the pavement, on the rust of the fence and the sparse grass, along with the empty streets made Williamsburg seem far away from Manhattan.

She ducked under a chain-link fence. The lot was empty, but she could see a ditch between the cracked concrete and the small hills. She stepped into it, using it like a path to walk out to where black rocks marked the space between the beach and the river.

Something was there. At first Val thought it was a lump of drying seaweed, a stray plastic bag, but as she got closer she realized it was a woman with green hair, lying facedown on the rocks, half in and half out of the water. Rushing over, Val saw the flies buzzing around the woman's torso and her tail drifting with the current, scales catching the streetlights to shine like silver.

It was the corpse of a mermaid.

The first time Val saw anything dead up close was at the mall by her dad's house when she was twelve. She'd tossed a penny into the fountain by the food court and wished for a pair of running shoes. A few minutes later, she reconsidered and rushed back to try and find her coin and do the wish over. But what she saw, floating on the still water, was the limp body of a sparrow. She'd reached in and lifted it up and water had poured out of its tiny beak like from a cup. It smelled awful, like meat left in the refrigerator to defrost and forgotten. She had stared at it a moment before she realized it was dead.

As Val ran through the streets and over the Manhattan Bridge, breath gusting into the air, she thought of the little drowned bird. Now she'd seen two dead things.

The magical doorway under the bridge opened the same

way that it had last time, but as she stepped onto the dark landing, she saw she wasn't alone. Someone was heading down the steps, and it was only when the candle he cradled made the silver loops through his lip and nose glitter and the white of his eyes shine that she realized it was Luis. He looked as startled as she was and in that uncertain light, exhausted.

"Luis?" Val asked.

"I hoped that you were long gone." Luis's voice was soft and remorseless. "I hoped that you ran back to Mommy and Daddy in the suburbs. That's all you bridge-and-tunnel girls know—running away when things get tough. Run to the big bad city and then run home."

"Fuck you," Val said. "You know nothing about me."

"Well, you don't know shit about me, either. You think I've been a dick to you, but I've done you nothing but favors."

"What is your problem with me? You hated me the minute I showed up!"

"Any friend of Lolli's is going to stir shit up, and that's just what you did. And here I am, getting interrogated by an angry troll because of you two bitches. What do you *think* my problem is?"

Anger made Val's face hot, even in the cold stairwell. "I think this: The only thing special about you is that you have the Sight. You talk shit about faeries, but you love that you're the one who can see them. That's why you're disgustingly jealous of anyone else that so much as talks to one."

Luis gaped at her as if he'd been slapped.

Words fell from Val's mouth before she even realized what she was about to say. "And I think something else, too. Rats might be able to chew their way through copper or whatever, but the only reason they survive is because there are bazillions of them. That's what's so special about rats—they fuck all the time and have a million rat babies."

"Stop," Luis said, holding up his hand as if to ward off her words. His voice dropped low, the anger seeming to go out of him like a popped balloon. "Fine. Yeah. To Ravus and the rest of the faerie Folk, that's all humans are—pathetic things that breed like crazy and die so fast you can't tell the difference between one and another. Look, I have spent the past I don't know how long answering questions after drinking some kind of noxious crap that made me tell the truth. All because of you and Lolli breaking in here. I'm tired and I'm pissed." He rubbed his face with his hand. "You're not the first straggler that Lolli invited home, you know. You don't understand what you're playing around with."

Val was unnerved by the sudden change in Luis's tone. "What do you mean?"

"There was another girl a couple of months ago—another stray Lolli decided to bring underground. It was when Lolli first got the idea that they could inject the potions. Lolli and the girl, Nancy, wanted to cop some dope, but didn't have any money. Then Lolli started talking about what else they could shoot and they did some of the stuff from one of Dave's deliveries. All of a sudden, they start talking like they can see things that aren't there and, even worse, Dave starts seeing the shit, too. Nancy got hit by a train and she was grinning right up until it hit her."

Val looked away from the flickering candle, into the darkness. "That sounds like an accident."

"Of course it was a fucking accident. But Lolli loved the stuff, even after that. She got Dave to do it."

"Did she know what it was?" Val asked. "Did she know about the faeries? About Ravus?"

"She knew. I told Dave about Ravus because Dave's my brother, even though he's an idiot. He told Lolli because she's a tease and he would do anything to impress her. And Lolli told Nancy, because Lolli can't keep her fucking mouth shut."

Val could hear Lolli's brittle laugh in her mind. "What's the big deal if she tells people?"

Luis sighed. "Look at this." He pointed at the pale pupil of his left eye. "Disgusting, right? One day when I was eight, my mother takes me to the Fulton Fish Market with her. She's buying some soft-shell crabs—bargaining with the fish guy, really getting into it because she loved to haggle—and I see this guy carrying an armful of gory sealskins. He sees me looking and grins real big. His teeth are like a shark's: tiny, sharp, and set too far apart."

Val clutched the banister, paint flaking under her fingernails.

"'You can see me?' he asks, and because I'm a dumb kid, I nod. My mother is right next to me, but she doesn't notice anything. 'Do you see me with both eyes?' he wants to know. I'm nervous now and that's the only thing that keeps me from telling him the truth. I point to my right eye. He drops the skins and they make a horrible, wet sound, falling all together like that."

Wax dripped down the side of the candle and onto Luis's thumb, but he didn't flinch or change the way he held it. More wax followed, forming a steady drip onto the stairs. "The guy grabs me by the arm and pushes his thumb into my eye. His face doesn't change at all while he's doing it. It hurts so bad and I'm screaming and that's when my mother finally turns around, finally sees me. And do you know what she and the soft-shell crab guy decide? That I scratched my own fucking eye somehow. That I ran into something. That I blinded myself."

The hair was standing up along Val's arms and she had that chill running down her spine, the one that told her just how freaked out she really was. She thought about the sealskins in his story, about the mermaid body she'd seen by the river, and came to no conclusions, except that there was no escape from horrible things. "Why are you telling me this?"

"Because it sucks to be me," Luis said. "One wrong step and they decide I don't need my other eye. That's what the big deal is.

"Dave and Lolli don't get it." His voice dropped to a whisper and he leaned close to her. "They're playing around with that drug, stealing from Ravus when I'm supposed to be repaying a debt. Then they bring you in." He stopped, but she saw the panic in his eyes. "You're stirring shit up. Lolli is getting worse instead of better."

The troll appeared at the top of the ledge and looked down at Val. His voice was low and deep as a drum. "I cannot think what it was you came back for. Is there something you require?"

"The last delivery," she said. "It was a . . . mermaid? She's dead."

He went quiet, stared.

Val swallowed. "She looks like she's been dead awhile."

Ravus started down the stairs, frock coat billowing. "Show me." His features changed as he got closer, the green of his skin fading, his features shifting until he looked human, like a gawky boy only a little older than Luis, a boy with odd, golden eyes and shaggy black hair.

"You didn't change your—" Val said.

"That's the way glamour is," said Ravus, cutting her off. "There's always some hint of what you were. Feet turned backward, a tail, a hollow back. Some clue to your true nature."

"I'll just get out of here," Luis said. "I was on my way anyhow."

"Luis and I have had an interesting conversation about you and the manner of our meeting," said the troll. It was disorienting to hear that deep, rich voice come from a young man.

"Yeah," Luis said, with a half smile. "He conversed. I groveled."

That made Ravus smile in turn, but even as a man, his teeth looked a touch too long at the incisors. "I think this death concerns you too, Luis. Put off sleep a little longer and let's see what we might learn."

The only sounds on the waterfront came from waves lapping against the stones at the edge of the shore when Ravus, Val, and Luis arrived. The body was still there, hair flowing like seagrass, necklaces of shell and pearl and sand-dollar doves caught around her neck like strangling ropes, white face looking like a reflection of the moon on the water. Tiny fish darted around her body and swam in and out between her parted lips.

Ravus knelt down, cupped the back of the mermaid's skull in long fingers, and lifted up her head. Her mouth opened farther, showing thin, translucent teeth that looked like they might be made from cartilage. Ravus brought his face so close to the mermaid's that, for a moment, it looked like he might kiss her. Instead he sniffed twice before gently lowering her back into the water.

He looked at Luis with shadowed eyes, then shouldered off his frock coat and spread it on the ground. He turned to Val. "If you take her tail, we can move her onto the cloth. I need to get her back to my workroom."

"Was she poisoned?" Luis asked. "Do you know what killed her?"

"I have a theory," said Ravus. He pushed back his hair with a wet hand, then waded into the East River.

"I'll help," Luis said, starting forward.

Ravus shook his head. "You can't. All that iron you insist on wearing could burn her skin. I don't want the evidence contaminated more than it has to be."

"The iron keeps me safe," Luis said, touching his lip ring. "Safer, anyway."

Ravus smiled. "At the very least, it is going to keep you safe from a repugnant task."

Val waded into the water and lifted the slippery tail, its ends as ragged as torn cloth. The fish scales glittered like liquid silver as they flaked off on Val's hand. There were patches of pale flesh exposed along the mermaid's side, where fish had already started to feed on her.

"What a petty drama to watch play out," said a voice coming from the valley between the mounds.

"Greyan." Ravus looked toward the shadows.

Val recognized the creature that came forward, the mannequin maker with the greening beard. But behind him were other Folk she didn't know, faeries with long arms and blackened hands, with eyes like birds, faces like cats, tattered wings that were as thin as smoke and as bright as the neon lights from a distant bar sign.

"Another death," one of them said, and there was a low murmur.

"What is it that you are delivering this time?" Greyan asked. There was a burst of uncomfortable laughter.

"I came to discover what I could," said Ravus. He nodded to Val. Together, they moved the body onto the coat. Val felt nauseated as she realized that the fishy smell was coming from the flesh in her hands.

Greyan took a step forward, his horns white in the streetlight. "And look what is discovered."

"What are you implying?" Ravus demanded. In his human guise, he looked thin and tall, and beside Greyan's bulk, terribly outmatched.

"Do you deny you are a murderer?"

"Stop," said one of the others, a voice in shadow attached to what appeared to be a long and spindly body. "We know him. He has made harmless potions for us all."

"Do we know him?" Greyan moved closer and from the folds of his cracked leather coat pulled out two short, curved sickles with dark bronze blades. He crossed them over his chest like an entombed pharaoh. "He went into exile because of a murder."

"Have a care," said a tiny creature. "Would you have all of us be judged now by the reason for our exile?"

"You know that I cannot refute the charge of murderer," Ravus said. "Just as I *know* it is cowardly to wave a sword at someone who has sworn not to swing a blade again."

"Fancy words. You think you're still a courtier," Greyan

said. "But your clever tongue won't help you here."

One of the creatures smirked at Val. It had eyes like a parrot and a mouthful of jagged teeth. Val reached around and picked up a length of pipe from the rocks. It felt so cold that it burned her fingers.

Ravus held up his hands to Greyan. "I don't wish to fight you."

"Then that's your ruin." He swung one sickle at Ravus.

The troll dodged the sickle and ripped a sword out of the hand of another faerie, his fist wrapping around the sharp metal. Red blood ran from his palm. His mouth curled with something like pleasure and his glamour slipped away as though it was forgotten.

"You need what I make," Ravus spat. Fury twisted his face, making his features dreadful, forcing his fangs to bite into the flesh of his upper lip. He licked away the blood and his eyes seemed as full of glee as they were of rage. He tightened his grip on the blade of the sword, even as it bit deeper into his skin. "I give it freely, but were I the poisoner, were it my whim to kill one of the hundred I help, you would still have to live at my indulgence."

"I will live at no one's indulgence." Greyan swept his sickles toward Ravus.

Ravus swung the hilt of the sword, blocking the strike. The two circled each other, trading blows. Ravus's weapon was unbalanced by being held backward, and slippery with his own blood. Greyan struck quickly with his short bronze sickles, but each time Ravus parried.

"Enough," shouted Greyan.

A faerie with a long and looping tail rushed forward,

gripping one of Ravus's arms. Another stepped forward holding a silver knife in the shape of a leaf.

Just then Greyan swung at Ravus's wrist and Val moved before she knew she was moving. Instinct took over. All the lacrosse practices and video games came together somehow, and she swung the pipe at Greyan's side. It hit with a soft, fleshy sizzle, throwing him off balance for a moment. Then he wheeled toward her, both bronze blades slamming down. Val barely had time to raise the pipe and brace herself before they hit, making the metal spark. She twisted to the side and Greyan stared at her in amazement before slamming both the bronze blades into her leg.

Val felt cold all over and the background noises faded to a rushing in her ears. Her leg didn't even really hurt that much, although blood was soaking through her already-ripped cargo pants.

In Val's other life, the one where she'd been almost a jock and didn't believe in faeries, she and Tom had played video games and fooled around in the finished basement of his house after school. Her favorite game was *Avenging Souls*. Her character, Akara, had a curved scimitar, a power move that let her chop off the heads of three of her opponents at once, and lots of health points. You could see them at the top of the screen, blue orbs that would turn to red with a popping noise the more wounded Akara got. That's all that happened. Akara didn't slow down when she got hurt, didn't stumble, scream, or faint.

Val did all those things.

Someone gripped Val's arm too tightly. She could feel nails against her skin. It hurt. Everything hurt. Val opened her eyes.

A young man was standing over her and at first she didn't know him. She pulled back, scuttling away from him. Then she saw the inky black hair and the swollen lips and the gold-flecked eyes. Luis stood in the background.

"Val," Luis said. "It's Ravus. Ravus."

"Don't touch me," said Val, wanting the pain to stop.

A bitter smile touched his mouth as his hands left her. "You could have died," Ravus said quietly.

Val took that as an encouraging sign that she wasn't actually dying.

Val woke, warm and sleepy. For a moment, she thought that she was back in her own bed, back at home. She wondered if she'd overslept and was missing school. Then she thought that maybe she'd been sick, but when she opened her eyes, she saw the flickering candlelight and the shadowy roof far above her. She was wrapped in a cocoon of lavender-scented blankets on top of a pile of cushions and rugs. Overhead the steady roar of traffic sounded almost like rain.

Val propped herself up on her elbow. Ravus was standing behind his worktable, chopping a block of some dark substance. She watched him for a moment, watched his long, efficient fingers cradling the knife, then she swung out one leg from under the covers. It was bare and bandaged at the thigh, wrapped with leaves and oddly numb.

He glanced over at her. "You're awake."

She flushed, embarrassed that he must have taken off her

pants and that they'd been filthy. "Where's Luis?"

"He went back to the tunnels. I'm making you a draught. Do you think you can drink it?"

Val nodded. "Is it some kind of potion?"

He snorted. "It's naught but cocoa."

"Oh," Val said, feeling foolish. She looked over at him again. "Your hand isn't bandaged."

Ravus held it up, the palm unscarred. "Trolls heal fast. I'm hard to kill, Val."

She looked at his hand, at the table of ingredients, and shook her head. "How does it work, the magic? How do you take ordinary things and make them magical?"

He looked at her sharply and then resumed chopping at the brown bar. "Is that what you think I do?"

"Isn't it?"

"I don't make things magical," he said. "I could, perhaps, but not in any quantity or potency. It would be beyond me, beyond almost anyone save a high Lord or Lady of Faerie. These things . . ." His hand swept over the worktable, over the hardened nuggets of chewed gum, the various wrappers and cans, the lipstick-stained butts of cigarettes. "Are already magical. People have made them so." He picked up a silvery gum wrapper. "A mirror that never cracks." He picked up a tissue with a blotted lipstick mouth on it. "A kiss that never ends." A cigarette. "The breath of a man."

"But mirrors and kisses aren't magical either."

At that he laughed. "So you don't believe a kiss is efficacious in transforming a beast or waking the dead?"

"And I'm wrong?"

"No," he said, characteristically wry. "You're quite correct.

But, luckily, this potion is intended to do neither of those things."

She smiled at that. She thought about the way she noticed all his glances, his sighs, the subtle changes in his face. She thought about what it might mean and she worried.

"Why do you always look like you do?" she asked. "You could look like anything. Anyone."

Ravus put down his mortar with a scowl and walked around the table. She felt a thrill run through her that was only part terror.

She was very conscious of lying in what must be his bed, but she didn't want to get out without any pants on.

"Ah, you mean with glamour?" He hesitated. "Make myself look less terrifying? Less hideous?"

"You're not—" Val began, but he held up his hand and she stopped.

"My mother was very beautiful. Doubtless, I have a broader idea of beauty than you do."

Val said nothing, nodding. She didn't want to think too closely about whether she had a broad idea of beauty. She'd always thought that she had a fairly narrow one, one that included her mother and other people who tried too hard. She'd always been a little contemptuous of beauty, as though it was something you had to trade away some other vital thing for.

"She had icicles in her hair," he continued. "It got so cold that frost would form, clumping her braids together into crystalline jewels that would clatter together when she moved. You should have seen her in the candlelight. It lit up that ice like it was made of fire. It's a good thing she couldn't stand in the sunlight—she would have lit up the sky."

"Why couldn't she stand in the sunlight?"

"None of my people can. We turn to stone in the sun—and stay that way until nightfall."

"Does it hurt?"

He shook his head, but didn't answer. "Despite all that beauty, my mother never showed her true self to my father. He was mortal, like you, and around him, she always wore a glamour. Oh, she was beautiful glamoured, too, but it was a muted beauty. My brothers and sisters—we had to wear it, too."

"He was mortal?"

"Mortal. Gone in one faerie sigh. That's what my mother used to say."

"So you're . . . ?"

"A troll. Faerie blood breeds true."

"Did he know what she was?"

"He pretended not to know what any of us were, but he must have guessed. At the very least, he must have suspected we weren't human. He had a mill that sawed and dried wood from the several hundred acres of trees that he owned. Ash, aspen, birch, oak, willow. Juniper, pine, yew.

"My father had another family in the city, but my mother pretended to know nothing about that. There was a great deal of pretending. She made sure all my father's timber was fine and flat. It was beautifully planed and would neither warp nor rot.

"Faeries—we do nothing in moderation. When we love, we are all love. So was my mother. But in return she asked that he ring a bell at the top of the hill to let her know he was coming.

"One day my father forgot to ring the bell." The troll got up and walked over to the boiling milk and poured it into a porcelain cup. The smell of cinnamon and chocolate wafted toward her.

"He saw us all as we really were." Ravus sat beside her, long black coat pooling on the floor. "And fled, never to return."

She took the cup from him and took a cautious sip. It was too hot and burned her tongue. "What happened then?"

"Most people would be content for the story to end there. What happened then is that all my mother's love turned to hate. Even her children were nothing to her after that, just reminders of him." Val thought about her own mom and how she'd never questioned that she loved her. Of course she loved her mother—but now Val hated her. It didn't seem right that one could so easily become another.

"Her vengeance was terrible." Ravus looked at his hands and Val remembered the way he'd sliced them open holding a sword by its blade. She wondered if his rage was so great that he hadn't noticed the pain. She wondered if he loved the way his mother did.

"My mother was very beautiful, too," said Val. She wanted to speak again, but the single sip of the hot chocolate had filled her with such a delicious languor that she found herself slipping down into sleep once more.

Val woke to voices. The goat-hooved woman was there, speaking softly to Ravus.

"A stray dog, I might understand," she said. "But this? You are too softhearted."

"No, Mabry," Ravus said. "I am not." He looked in Val's direction. "I think she wants to die."

"Maybe you can help her after all," Mabry said. "You're good at helping people die."

"Have you come here for any purpose other than to smear me with my own filth?" he asked.

"That would be purpose enough, but there's been another death," Mabry said. "One of the merfolk in the East River. A human found her body, but enough of it had been eaten by crabs that I doubt there will be much scandal."

"I know that," Ravus said.

"You know too much. You knew all of them. Every single one that has died," Mabry said. "Are you the murderer?"

"No," he said. "All the dead are exiles from the Seelie Court. Surely someone has noticed that."

"All poisoned," Mabry said. "That's what's being noticed."

Ravus nodded. "The scent of rat poison was on the mermaid's breath."

Val muffled a gasp, smothering her face with the blankets.

"Folk hold you responsible," Mabry said. "It is too like coincidence for all the dead to be your customers and to die within hours of getting a delivery from one of your human couriers."

"After the tithe failed in the Night Court, dozens of Unseelie Solitary fey must have left Nicnevin's lands. I don't see why anyone would think it more likely that I turned poisoner."

"Lord Roiben's lands now." Mabry's voice was full of something Val couldn't identify. "For as long as Silarial lets him keep them."

Ravus sniffed and Val thought she could see something in him that she hadn't before. He was dressed in a frock coat, but one that was too new to be from the period it depicted. It was a costume, she realized, and was suddenly sure that Ravus was much younger than she'd assumed. She didn't know how faeries aged, but she thought that he was trying too hard to be sophisticated in front of Mabry. "I don't care who the Lord or Lady of the Night Court is at the moment," he said. "May they all murder each other so we don't have to contend with them."

Mabry looked at him darkly. "I don't doubt that you wish that."

"I am going to send a message to the Lady Silarial. I know that she ignores the Folk so near the cities, but even she could not be indifferent to the murder of Bright Court exiles. We are still within her lands."

"No," Mabry said quickly, her tone different. "I think that would be unwise. To invoke the gentry might make things worse."

Ravus sighed and looked over at where Val was lying. "I find that difficult to imagine."

"Wait another little while before you send any messages," Mabry said.

He sighed. "It was kind of you to give me a warning, whatever you think of me."

"Warning? I just came to gloat," she said and swept out of the room, hooves clattering down the steps.

Ravus turned to Val. "You can stop pretending to be asleep now."

Val sat up, frowning.

"You think that she's unkind," said Ravus, standing with his back to her. Val wished she could see the expression on his face; his voice was difficult to interpret. "But it is my fault that she's trapped here in this city of stinking iron and she has other, even better reasons to hate me."

"What reasons?"

Ravus waved his hand above a candle and out of the smoke formed a young man's face, too lovely to be human. "Tamson," Ravus said. Pale gold hair dusted the figure's neck, blown back from his face, and as carelessly arranged as his smile.

Val gasped. She had never seen glamour used this way before.

The rest of Tamson formed out of nothingness, wearing armor that looked like it was made from bark, rough and dotted with moss. The glass sword was strapped to his side and, on him, it looked liquid, like water forced to hold an unlikely shape.

"He was my first and best friend in the Bright Court. He didn't care that I couldn't abide the sun. He would visit me in darkness and tell me funny stories about what happened throughout the day." Ravus frowned. "I wonder that I was any good company."

"So the glass sword was his?"

"It is too slender a thing for me," Ravus said. Next to Tamson, another misty figure appeared, this one familiar to Val, although it took a moment to identify her. The faerie woman's brown hair was threaded with green, like the leafy carpet of a wood, and under the sweep of her red gown were goat's feet. She was singing a ballad, her rich, throaty voice thickening the words with promise. The troll gestured toward her. "Mabry, Tamson's lover."

"Was she your friend, too?"

"She tried to be, I think, but I was hard to look at." The

glamoured Tamson put his hand on Mabry's arm and she turned toward him, song interrupted by their embrace. Over her shoulder, the smoky image of Tamson stared at Ravus, eyes burning like coals.

"He talked about her endlessly." Ravus's smile quirked his mouth.

The glamoured Tamson spoke. "Her hair is the color of wheat in high summer, her skin the color of bone, her lips red as pomegranates."

Val wondered if Ravus thought those descriptions were accurate. She bit the inside of her cheek.

"He wanted to impress her," Ravus said. "He asked me to partner him so that he could show off his skill at dueling. I'm tall and I suppose I can look fierce.

"The Queen of the Bright Court likes fighting best of all the sports. She would organize tournaments where the Folk could show off their skill. I was new to the court and I did not much like to compete. My delights came in my work, my alchemy.

"It was a hot night; I remember that. I was thinking of Iceland, of the cool forests of my youth. Mabry and Tamson had been hissing words back and forth. I heard him say 'I saw you with him.'

"I wish I knew what it was Tamson saw, although I can guess." Ravus turned toward the cloaked windows. "The Folk do nothing by halves, we can be capricious. Each emotion is a draught that we must drain to the bottom, but sometimes I think we love the sour as much as the sweet. There is no sense in the Bright Court that because Mabry had dallied with Tamson and he loved her that she ought not dally with another."

"Tamson's armor was formed from bark, magicked to be harder than iron." He stopped speaking, closed his eyes and started up again. "He was a better swordsman than I, but he was distracted and I struck first. The sword, it cut through the bark like it was paper."

She saw the blow fall in the glamoured candle smoke. The armor crumbled around the blade, Tamson's look of surprise, Mabry's scream cutting through the air, high and sharp as though she'd realized what had happened a moment before anyone else had. Even the glamoured sound of it carried through the dusty room.

"When I fight, I fight like a troll—fury overtakes me. Perhaps another could have checked his blow; I could not. I still held the hilt of my sword, as though it was welded to my hand and impossible to let go. The blade looked like it had been painted red.

"Why would he take the magics off his own armor?" Ravus looked at her, and for a moment she thought he might be waiting for an answer. His gaze slid from her to the wall and the glamour dispersed. "And yet he must have. No one else had any reason to wish him ill." Ravus's voice was low and harsh. "I knew he was in distress—I could see it on his face. I thought it would pass as all things passed . . . and selfishly, I was glad that Mabry had disappointed him. I had missed his companionship. I thought he would be mine again. He must have seen that vulgarity in me—why else would he choose me as the vehicle for his death?"

Val didn't know what to say. She composed sentences in her head: *It wasn't your fault. Everyone thinks terrible, selfish things. It had to have been an accident.* None of them seemed to mean anything. They were just words to fill silence. When he began speaking again, she realized how long she must have been quietly debating.

"Death is in poor taste in Faerie." He laughed mirthlessly. "When I said I would come to the city, go into exile here after Tamson's death, it suited them to let me. They didn't so much blame me for the death, as thought me tainted by it.

"Silarial, the Bright Court's Queen, commanded Mabry to accompany me so that we might grieve together. The stench of death clung to her, too, and made the other Folk restive. So, she had to accompany me, the murderer of her lover, and here she must stay until I complete the term of my self-exile or I die."

"That's awful," Val said and at his silence realized how stupid and inadequate her words were. "I mean, obviously it's awful, but what I was thinking of was the part about sending her along with you. That's cruel."

He snorted, almost a laugh. "I would cut my own heart out to have Tamson's beating once more in his chest. Even for a moment. No sentence would have bothered me. But to have punishment and exile heaped on top of grief must have been almost too much for her to bear."

"What's it like here? I mean, to be in exile in the city?"

"I am constantly distracted by the press of smells, the noise. There is poison everywhere, and iron so close that it makes my skin itch and my throat burn. I can only imagine how Mabry feels."

She reached one hand toward him and he took it, running his fingers over her calluses. She looked up into his face, trying to convey her sympathy, but he was looking intently at her hand.

"What are these from?" he demanded.

"What?"

"Your hands are rough," he said. "Calloused."

"Lacrosse," she said.

He nodded, but she could tell from his face that he didn't understand her. She might have said anything and he would have nodded that way.

"You have a knight's hands," he said finally, and let go of her.

Val rubbed her skin, not sure if she was trying to erase the memory of his touch or to recall it.

"It's not safe for you to keep doing deliveries." Ravus went to one of his cabinets and took out a jar where a butterfly fluttered. Then he pulled out a tiny scroll of paper and began to write in miniature script. "I owe you a greater debt than I can easily repay, but at least I can cancel your promise of servitude."

She looked toward the wall where the glass sword hung glimmering in the gloom, nearly as dark as the wall behind it. She remembered the feeling of the pipe in her hand, the adrenaline rush and clarity of purpose that she felt on the lacrosse field or in a fistfight.

"I want to keep doing deliveries for you," Val said. "There is something you could do to repay me, though, but you might not want to do it. Teach me how to use the sword."

He looked up from where he was rolling the scroll and attaching it to the leg of the butterfly. "Knowing it has caused me little joy."

She waited, not speaking. He hadn't said no.

He finished his work and blew, setting the little insect into the air. It flew a little unsteadily, perhaps unbalanced by the slip of paper. "You want to kill someone? Who? Greyan? Perhaps you want to die?"

Val shook her head. "I just want to know how. I want to be able to do it."

He nodded slowly. "As you wish. It is your debt to dismiss and your right to ask."

"So you'll teach me?" Val asked.

Ravus nodded again. "I will make you as terrible as you desire."

"I don't want to be—" she started, but he held up his hand.

"I know you're very brave," he said.

"Or stupid."

"*And* stupid. Brave *and* stupid." Ravus smiled, but then his smile sagged. "But nothing can stop you from being terrible once you've learned how."

8

Black milk of daybreak we drink you at night
we drink you at morning and midday we drink you
*   at evening*
we drink and we drink
—PAUL CELAN, "DEATH FUGUE"

Dave and Lolli and Luis sat on a blanket in the concrete park, some of Dave's finds spread out in front of them. Cardboard stuck out from underneath the cloth where it had been used as a liner between them and the cold that seeped up from the sidewalk. Dave's head was tilted back into Lolli's lap as she rolled his locs in her palms, twisting and rubbing the roots. Lolli paused, picking fluff out of his hair, pinching it between her nails and slicking her fingers with wax from the tin beside her leg. Dave's eyes opened; then he closed them again in something like rapture.

Lolli's flip-flop–covered foot, splotchy and red with cold, stroked one of Luis's thighs. A book was open in front of him, and he squinted at it in the dimming light.

"Hey, guys," Val said, feeling shy as she walked up to them, as though being away for two or three days made her a stranger again.

"Val!" Lolli slid out from under Dave, leaving him to twist onto his elbows to avoid his head hitting the pavement. She ran over to Val, throwing her arms around her.

"Hey, my hair!" Dave yelled.

Val embraced Lolli, smelling unwashed clothes and sweat and cigarettes, and felt relief wash over her.

"Luis told us what happened. You're crazy." Lolli smiled, as though that was great praise.

Val's gaze skated to Luis, who looked up from his book with a grin that made his face seem handsome. He shook his head. "She is crazy. Head to head with a fucking ogre. Loony Lolli, Sketchy Dave, Crazy Val. You're all a bunch of freaks."

Val made a formal bow, dipping her head in their direction, and then sat on the blanket.

"Loony Luis, more likely," Lolli said, kicking her flip-flop in his direction.

"Luis One-Eye," Dave said.

Luis smirked. "Bug-Head Dave."

"Princess Luis," Dave said. "Prince Valiant."

Val laughed, thinking of the first time Dave had called her that. "How about Dreaded Dave."

Luis leaned over, grabbing his brother in a headlock, both of them rolling on the cloth, and said, "How about Baby Brother? Baby Brother Dave?"

"Hey," Lolli said. "What about me? I want to be a princess like Luis."

At that, the boys broke off, laughing. Val leaned back on

the cloth and cardboard, the cold air pricking the hair along her arms, even under the coat. New Jersey seemed far away, and school an odd and nonsensical ritual. She smiled with contentment.

"Luis said that someone thinks we're poisoning faeries?" Lolli asked. She'd draped another blanket over her shoulders.

"Or that Ravus is," Val said. "Ravus said something about stopping the deliveries. He thinks it might be too dangerous for us."

"Like he really cares," Luis said. "I bet he made a big, courtly show of thanks, but you're still a rat to him, Val. Just a rat that did a really good trick."

"I know that," Val lied.

"If he wants us to stop doing deliveries, it's to save his own ass." There was something in Luis's face as he said it, maybe the way he didn't meet her eyes, that made her wonder if he was wholly convinced himself.

"It had to be Ravus doing the poisoning," said Dave. "Getting us to do his dirty work. We don't know what we're carrying."

Val turned to look at him. "I don't think so. While I was staying there, that goat-footed woman—Mabry—came by. He said something to her about writing to the Seelie Queen. I guess if the court's a gang, then the city is still somehow the Queen's turf. Anyway, why would he write to her if he was guilty?"

Dave sat upright, pulling his loc out of Lolli's fingers. "He's going to frame us. Luis just said it—we're all rats to them. When there's some problem, you just poison the rats and call it a day."

Val was uncomfortably reminded that it had been rat poison that killed the mermaid. Poison the rats. Rat poison. A glance at Luis showed him to be indifferent, however, biting a loose thread off his fingerless gloves.

Luis looked up and caught Val's eye, but there was nothing in his face, neither guilt nor innocence. "It is weird," he said. "With the shit you all shove up your noses and in your arms that you never hit any of the poison."

"You think I did it?" Lolli asked.

"You're the one who hates faeries," Dave said, speaking at the same time Lolli did so that their words overlapped. "You're the one who sees shit."

Luis held up his hands. "Wait a fucking minute. I don't think any of us poisoned any faeries. But I have to agree with Val. Ravus asked me a lot of questions the other night. He made me—" He scowled in Lolli's direction. "Some of it was about how you two wound up crawling around his place, but he asked me direct if I was the poisoner, if I knew who it was, if anyone had bribed me to do some sketched-out delivery. Why would he do all that if he took out those fey himself? He doesn't need to look good in front of me."

Val nodded. Although the knowledge that rat poison killed the faeries nagged at her, she remembered Luis's face inside the bridge. She believed that he'd been questioned thoroughly. Of course, maybe they were being set up, if not by Ravus, then by someone else. "What if something glamoured itself to look like one of us?"

"Why would it do that?" Lolli demanded.

"To make it seem like we're behind the deaths."

Luis nodded. "We should stop doing deliveries. Make

whoever it is find some other suckers to frame."

Dave scratched his arm where the razor marks were. "We can't stop the deliveries."

"Don't be such a fucking junkie," said Luis.

"Val can get some Never, can't you, Val?" Lolli said with a sly look up through her pale lashes.

"What do you mean?" Val said, her voice sounding too defensive even to her own ears. She felt guilty, but she couldn't quite say why. She looked at Lolli's finger, as straight as if it had never been twisted out of its socket.

"The troll owes you, doesn't he?" Lolli's voice was pitched low, almost sensual.

"I guess." Val remembered the smell of the Never, Nevermore, burning on the spoon, and it filled her with longing. "But he paid his debt. He's going to show me how to use a sword."

"No shit?" Dave looked at her strangely.

"You should be careful," said Luis. Somehow, those words filled Val with an unease that had little to do with physical peril. She didn't meet Luis's eyes, staring instead at a mirror with a cracked frame on the blanket. Only moments earlier, she had felt great, but now unease had crept into her heart and settled there.

Lolli stood up suddenly. "Done," she pronounced, tousling Dave's locs so that they rustled like fat-bellied snakes. "Forget about all this. Time to play pretend."

"We don't have much left," Dave said, but he was already standing up, already gathering the things from the blanket.

Together, the four of them crept back through the grate and into the tunnel.

Luis frowned as Lolli brought out the amber sand and

her kit. "That isn't for mortals, you know. Not really."

In the near darkness, Dave brought a piece of foil to his nose, lighting beneath it so that the Never smoked. He took a deep sniff and looked solemnly at Lolli. "Just because something is a bad idea doesn't mean you can help doing it." His gaze traveled to Luis, and the look in his eyes made Val wonder what exactly it was he was thinking of.

"Give me some," Val said.

The days passed like a fever dream. During the day, Val did deliveries before going to Ravus's place inside the bridge where he would show her swordplay in his shadowed rooms. Then at night, she shot her arms up with Never, and she and Dave and Lolli did whatever they pleased. They might sleep after or drink a little to ride out the hollowness that followed the high, when the world settled back into less magical patterns.

More and more, it was hard to remember the basic things, like eating. Never made crusts of bread into banquet tables groaning with food, but no matter how much she ate, Val was always hungry.

"Show me how you hold a stick," Ravus said, during the first lesson. Val gripped the half broomstick like it was a lacrosse stick, both hands on it, separated by about a foot.

He slid her hands closer together and lower. "If you held a sword like that, you would cut your hand on the blade."

"Yeah, only an idiot would do that," Val said, just to see what he'd say.

Ravus didn't react with more than a quirk of his lip. "I know the weight feels off, but with a sword, it won't be. Here." He took down the glass sword and put it in her hand. "Feel the weight. See? It's balanced. That's the most important thing, balance."

"Balance," she repeated, letting the sword teeter in the palm of her hand.

"This is a pommel," he said, pointing to each place in turn. "This is the grip, the hilt, the crossguard. When you hold the sword, the edge pointing to your opponent is the true edge. You want to hold the blade so that the point follows your opponent. Now stand like I'm standing."

She tried to copy him, legs apart and slightly bent, one foot in front of the other.

"Almost." He pushed her body into position, careless where he touched her. Her face heated when he pushed her thighs farther apart, but it embarrassed her more that only she seemed to notice his hands on her. To him, her body was a tool and nothing more.

"Now," he said, "show me how you breathe."

Sometimes Val and Dave and Luis and Lolli would talk about the strange things they'd seen or the creatures they'd spoken with. Dave told them about going all the way out to Brooklyn only to get chased through the park by a creature with short antlers growing from his brow. He'd screamed and run, dropping the bottle of whatever-it-was, and not looked back. Luis told them about running around town to find unsprayed flowers for a bogan that lived up near the Cloisters and had some kind of wooing planned. For his trouble, Luis had been given a bottle of wine that would never empty so long as you didn't look down the neck. It must have really been magic, too, not just glamour, because it worked, even for Luis.

"What else do they give you?" Val asked.

"Luck," Luis said. "And the means of breaking faerie spells. My dad never did anything with his power. I'm going to be different."

"How do you break spells?" Val asked.

"Salt. Light. Eggshell soup. Depends on the spell." Luis took another pull from the bottle. He reached up to finger the metal bar that ran through his cheek. "But mostly iron."

There were no sword moves at the next practice, just stance and footwork. Back and forth across the dusty boards, keeping the half broomstick trained on Ravus as Val advanced and retreated. He corrected her when she took too large a step, when her balance was off, when her toe wasn't straight. She bit the inside of her cheek in frustration and continued moving, keeping the same distance between them, as though waiting for a battle that never began.

He turned suddenly to one side, forcing her to follow awkwardly. "Speed, timing, and balance. Those are the things that will make you into a competent fighter."

She gritted her teeth and stepped wrong again.

"Stop thinking," he said.

"I have to think," said Val. "You said I was supposed to concentrate."

"Thinking makes you slow. You need to move as I move. Right now, you're merely following my lead."

"How can I know where you're going to go before you've gone there? That's stupid."

"It's no different from knowing where any opponent might move. How do you know where a ball is likely to go on the lacrosse field?"

"The only things you know about lacrosse are what I told you," Val said.

"I might say the same about you and sword fighting." He stopped. "There. You did it. You were so busy snapping at me that you didn't notice you were doing it."

Val frowned, too annoyed to be pleased, but too pleased to say anything more.

Lolli, Dave, and Val walked through the streets of the West Village, magicking fallen leaves into a slew of jeweled frogs that hopped in chaotic patterns, enchanting strangers to kiss, and otherwise making what trouble the three of them could imagine.

Val glanced across the street, through the gauzy drapes of a ground-floor apartment at a chandelier hung with carved monkeys and glittering with drops of crystal in the shape of tears.

"I want to go in there," Val said.

"Let's," said Lolli.

Dave walked up to the door and pressed on the bell. The intercom by the door buzzed to life and a garbled voice said something indecipherable.

"I'd like a cheeseburger," Dave said with a loud laugh, "a milk shake, and onion rings."

The voice spoke again, louder, but Val still couldn't understand the words.

"Here," she said, pushing Dave aside. She pressed the buzzer and held it until a middle-aged guy came to the door. He was wearing faded cords and a loose T-shirt that covered his slight paunch. Glasses rode low on his nose.

"What's your problem?" he demanded.

Val felt Never fizzing inside her arms, bursting like champagne bubbles. "I want to come in," she said.

The man's face went slack and he opened the door wider. Val smiled at him as she walked past and into his apartment.

The walls were painted yellow and hung with gilt-framed finger paintings. A woman was stretched out on the couch, holding a glass of wine. She started as Val came in, splashing her shirt with the red liquid. A little girl sat on a rug by the woman's feet, watching a program on the television that seemed to be about ninjas kicking each other. The little girl turned and smiled.

"This place is so nice," Lolli said from the doorway. "Who lives like this?"

"No one," said Dave. "They hire cleaners—maybe a decorator—to fake their life."

Val walked into the kitchen and opened the refrigerator. There were boxes of take-out, a few withered apples, and a carton of skim milk. She took a bite of the fruit. It was brown and mealy on the inside but still sweet. She couldn't understand why she'd never eaten a brown apple before.

Lolli picked up the bottle of wine from the coffee table and swigged from it, letting red juice run over her chin and cheeks.

Still eating the apple, Val walked to the couch where the

woman sat numbly. The lovely apartment, with its stylish furniture and happy family, reminded Val of her dad's house. She
didn't fit in here any more than she fit in there. She was too
angry, too troubled, too sloppy.

And how was she supposed to tell her dad what had happened with Tom and her mom? It was like confessing to her
father that she was bad in bed or something. But not telling
him just let his new wife label her as Lifetime movie material,
a troubled teen runaway in need of tough love. "See," Linda
would say. "She's just like her mother."

"You never liked me," she told the woman on the couch.

"Yes," the woman repeated robotically. "I never liked you."

Dave pushed the man into a chair and turned to Lolli. "We
could just make them leave," he said. "It would be so easy. We
could live here."

Lolli sat down next to the little girl and plucked a ringlet of
her dark hair. "What you watching?"

The girl shrugged.

"Would you like to come and play with us?"

"Sure," the little girl said. "This show is boring."

"Let's start with dress-up," Lolli said, leading the little girl
into the back room.

Val turned to the man. He looked docile and happy in his
chair, his attention wandering to the television.

"Where's your other daughter?" Val asked.

"I only have one," he said, with mild bafflement.

"You just want to forget about the other one. But she's still
here."

"I have another daughter?"

Val sat down on the arm of his chair and leaned in close, her voice dropping to a whisper. "She's a symbol of the spectacular fuck-up that was your first marriage. Every time you see how big she is, you are reminded how old you are. She makes you feel vaguely guilty, like maybe you should know what sport she plays or what her best friend's name is. But you don't want to know those things. If you knew those things, you couldn't forget about her."

"Hey," Dave said, holding up a bottle of cognac that was mostly full. "Luis would like some of this."

Lolli walked back into the room wearing a leather jacket the color of burnt butter and a string of pearls. The little girl had a dozen glittering rhinestone pins in her hair.

"Are you happy at least?" Val asked the woman.

"I don't know," said the woman.

"How can you not know?" Val shouted. She picked up a chair and threw it at the television. The screen cracked and everyone jumped. "Are you happy?"

"I don't know," the woman said.

Val tipped over a bookcase, making the little girl scream. There were shouts outside the door.

Dave started laughing.

The light from the chandelier reflected in the crystals, sending shining sparks to glitter along the walls and ceilings. "Let's go," Val said. "They don't know anything."

The kitten wailed and wailed, pawing at Lolli with sharp little nails, jumping on her with its soft little body. "Shut up, Polly," she mumbled, rolling over and pulling the heavy blanket over her head.

"Maybe she's bored," Val said drowsily.

"It's hungry," Luis said. "Fucking feed it already."

Yowling, Polly jumped onto Lolli's shifting back, batting at her hair.

"Get off me," Lolli told the cat. "Go kill some rats. You're old enough to be on your own."

A shriek of metal grinding against metal and a dim light signaled the approach of a train. The rumbling drowned out the sound of the cat's cries.

At the last moment, as the whole platform was flooded with light, Lolli shoved Polly onto the tracks, right in front of the train. Val jumped up, but it was too late. The cat was gone and the metal body of the train thundered past.

"What the fuck did you do that for?" Luis shouted.

"She always pissed on everything anyway," Lolli said, curling up into a ball and closing her eyes.

Val looked over at Luis, but he just looked away.

After Ravus was satisfied with her stance, he taught her one move and made her repeat it until her limbs ached and she was convinced he thought she was stupid, until she was sure that he didn't know how to teach anyone anything. He taught her each move until it was automatic, as much a habit as biting the skin around her fingernails or the needle she shoved in her arm.

"Exhale," he shouted. "Time your exhalation to your strike."

She nodded and tried to remember to do it, tried to do everything.

Val liked dumpster-diving with Sketchy Dave, liked walking through the streets, enjoyed the hunt and the occasional amazing find—like the stack of quilted blankets with silver lining that movers used to pad furniture, found piled up near a dumpster, and that kept the four of them warm as mice even as November wore on or the cool old rotary dial phone that someone paid ten bucks for. Most of the time, though, they were too dazed with Never to manage to make the old rounds. It was easier to take what they wanted anyway. All they had to do was ask.

A watch. A camera. A gold ring.

Those things sold better than a bunch of old crap anyway.

Then, finally, Ravus let her begin to put the moves together and spar. Ravus's longer arms put him at a continual advantage, but he didn't need it. He was pitiless, broomstick knocking her to the ground, driving her back against the walls, knocking over his own table when she tried to put it between them. Instinct and years of sports combined with desperation to let her get an occasional blow in.

When her stick struck his thigh, it was great to see the look on his face, rage that changed to surprise and then to pleasure in the space of a moment.

Backing off, they began again, circling each other. Ravus feigned and Val parried, but as she did, the room began to spin. She slumped against the wall.

His stick slammed into her other side. Pain made her gasp.

"What's wrong with you?" he shouted. "Why didn't you block the blow?"

Val forced herself to stand upright, digging her fingernails into her palm and biting the inside of her cheek. She was still dizzy, but she thought she might be able to pretend she wasn't. "I don't know. . . . My head."

Ravus swung the broomstick against the wall, splintering the wood and scratching the stone. Dropping the remains of his stick, he turned back to her, black eyes hot as steel in a forge. "You should have never asked me to teach you! I can't restrain my blows. You'll be hurt by my hand."

She took an unsteady step back, watching the remains of the stick swim in her vision.

He took a deep, shuddering breath that seemed to calm him. "It might be the magic in the room that unbalanced you. I can often smell it on you, on your skin, in your hair. You're around it too much, perhaps."

Val shook her head and lifted her stick, assuming a starting position. "I'm okay now."

He looked at her, his face intense. "Is it the glamour that is making you weak or is it whatever you're doing out there on the street?"

"It doesn't matter," she said. "I want to fight."

"When I was a child," he said, making no move to change his stance, "my mother taught me how to fight with my hands before she let me use any kind of weapon. She and my brothers and sisters would beat me with brush, would pelt me with snow and ice until I fell into a rage and attacked. Pain was no excuse, nor illness. It was all supposed to feed my fury."

"I'm not making excuses."

"No, no," Ravus said. "That's not what I meant. Sit down. Fury doesn't make you a great sword fighter; it makes you an unstable one. I should have seen that you were sick, but all I saw was a weakness. That is my flaw and I don't want it to be yours."

"I hate not being good at this," Val said as she flopped onto a stool.

"You are good. You hate not being great."

She laughed, but it sounded fake. She was upset that the world still wouldn't settle back into stillness and even more upset by his anger. "Why do you make potions when you had all that training to be a swordsman?"

He smiled. "After I left my mother's lands, I tried to leave the sword behind. I wanted to make something of my own."

She nodded.

"Although some among the Folk would be scandalized, I learned potion making from a human. She brewed cures, potions, and poultices for other mortals. You would suppose that people don't do that anymore, but in certain places, they do. She was always polite to me, a distant politeness as if she thought she was appeasing an uncertain spirit. I think she knew I wasn't mortal."

"But what about the Never?" Val asked.

"The what?"

She could see that he'd never heard it called that. She wondered if he had any idea what it could do for humans. Val shook her head, like she was trying to shake the words away. "The faerie magic. How did you learn what would make the potions magic?"

"Oh that." He grinned in a way that was almost goofy. "I already knew the magic part."

In the tunnels, Val practiced the motion of a cut, the way she had to twist her hands as if she were wringing out a kitchen towel. She practiced the sweeping figure eight and turning the sword in her hands like girls flipped flags at game halftimes. Invisible opponents danced in the moving shadows, always faster and better balanced, with perfect timing.

She thought about lacrosse practice, drills of reverse-stick passes and sword dodges and change-of-hand dodges. She recalled learning to ball off the shaft of the stick, off the side wall, and catch the ball behind her back or between her legs.

She tried those moves with her half broomstick. Just to see if it could be done. Just to see if there was anything she could learn from it. She bounced a soda can off the makeshift hilt of her stick, then kicked it with the side of her foot, sending it off at her shadow opponents.

Val looked at her face in a window as the rush hit. Her skin was like clay, endlessly malleable. She could change it into whatever she wanted, make her eyes big like an anime character, stretch her skin taunt across cheekbones sharp as knives.

Her forehead rippled, her mouth thinned, and her nose became long and looping. It was easy to make herself beautiful— she had gotten bored with that—but making herself grotesque was endlessly interesting. There were just so many ways it could be done.

Val was playing a game she couldn't remember the name of, where you were trapped inside the necromancer's tower, running up endless stairs. Along the way, you picked up potions. Some of them made you smaller and some of them made you very tall so that you could fit through all the different doors. Somewhere there was an alchemist trapped very high up, so high that he couldn't see anything that was going on beneath him. Somewhere there was a monster, too, but sometimes the alchemist was the monster and the monster was the alchemist. She had a sword in her hand, but it didn't change when she did, so it was either a sharp toothpick in her palm or a huge thing she had to drag behind her.

When Val opened her eyes, she saw that she was lying on the sidewalk, her hips and back aching, her cheek patterned with concrete. People passed her in a steady stream. She'd missed practice again.

"What's wrong with that lady?" she heard a child's voice ask.

"She's just tired," a woman answered.

It was true; Val was tired. She closed her eyes and went back to the game. She had to find the monster.

Some afternoons she arrived at the bridge from the night before, glamour riot still licking at her veins, her eyes feeling charred around the edges as though they had been lined with ash, her mouth gone dry with a thirst she could not slake. She tried to hold her hands steady, to keep them from trembling and revealing her weakness. When she missed a blow, she tried to pretend that it was not because she was dizzy or sick.

"Are you unwell?" Ravus asked one morning when she was particularly shaky.

"I'm fine," Val lied. Her veins felt dry. She could feel them pulse along her arms, the black sores on the insides of her elbows hard and hurting.

He perched on the edge of his worktable gesturing toward her face with his practice stick as though it were a wand. Val held up her hand automatically, but if he had been going to strike her she would have been much too late to stop the blow.

"You're observably pale. Your parries are dismal . . ." He let the sentence remain unfinished.

"I guess I'm a little tired."

"Even your lips are pallid," he said, outlining them in the air with the wooden blade. His gaze was intense, unflinching. She wanted to open her mouth and tell him everything, tell him about stealing the drug, about the glamour it gave them, about all the confused feelings that seemed to be canceling themselves out inside of her, but what she found herself doing was taking a step closer so that he had to stop gesturing and move the stick aside to keep from injuring her with it.

"I'm cold," she said softly. She was always cold these days, but it was winter, so maybe that wasn't so strange.

"Cold?" Ravus echoed. He took her arm and rubbed it between his hands, watching them as though they were betraying him. "Better?" he asked warily.

His skin felt hot, even through the cloth of her shirt, and his touch was both soothing and electric. She leaned into him without thinking. His thighs parted, rough black cloth scratching against her jeans as she moved between his long legs.

His eyes were half-lidded as he pushed himself off the desk, their bodies sliding together, his hands still holding hers. Then, suddenly, he froze.

"Is something—" she started, but he pushed away from her abruptly.

"You should go," he said, walking to the window and then just standing there. She knew he dared not part the blinds while it was still day outside. "Come back when you are feeling improved. It does neither of us any good to practice when you're sickly. If you need something, I could—"

"I said I was fine," Val repeated, her voice pitched louder than she'd intended. She thought of her mother. Had she thrown herself at Tom like that? Had he turned away from her at first?

Ravus was still turned toward the window when she lifted an entire bottle of Never and put it in her backpack.

That night Lolli and Dave congratulated her on her score, shouting her name so loudly that people stopped on the grate above. Luis sat in shadows, chewing on his tongue ring and remaining silent.

That morning she collapsed onto her filthy mattress, like she did most mornings, and fell into a deep and dreamless sleep, as though she had never had any other life but this one.

*Those who restrain desire do so because theirs is weak
enough to be restrained.*

—WILLIAM BLAKE, *THE MARRIAGE OF HEAVEN AND HELL*

Val woke up with someone pulling at the fastenings of her
jeans. She could feel fingers at her waist, the twist and
pinch of a button as it came undone.

"Get off me," she said, even before she realized it was
Dave hunched over her. She twisted away from him and sat
up, still flushed with the dregs of Never. Her skin was sweaty,
even though cold air blew down from the grate above, and her
mouth felt dry as sand.

"Come on," he whispered. "Please."

She looked down at her fingers and saw Lolli's chipped
blue nail polish. Lolli's white boots were on her feet and
she could see long faded blue locks of hair falling past her
shoulders.

"I'm not her," she said, her voice thick with sleep and
confusion.

"You could pretend," Sketchy Dave said. "And I could be anyone you wanted. Change me into anyone."

Val shook her head, realizing he'd glamoured her to be Lolli, wondering if he'd done it before with others, wondering if Lolli knew. The idea of playing at being other people was appalling, but with the remnants of Never still swarming inside of her, she was intrigued by the sheer wickedness of it. She felt the same thrill that had propelled her into the tunnels, the giddy pleasure of making a choice that is clearly, obviously a bad one.

Anyone. She looked over at Lolli and Luis, sleeping close together but not touching. Val allowed herself to imagine Luis's face on Dave. It was easy; their faces weren't so different. Dave's expression shifted, taking on a bored and annoyed look that was all Luis.

"I knew you'd pick him," Dave said.

Val tilted her head forward and was surprised when hair fell to cover her face. She'd forgotten how shielded hair made her feel. "I didn't pick anyone."

"But you'll do it. You want to do it."

"Maybe." Val's mind made the figure above her more familiar. Tom's stiff mohawk shone with hairspray and when he smiled, his cheeks dimpled. She could even smell the familiar scent of his patchouli aftershave. She leaned into it, flooded with a sense that she was back home and that none of this had ever happened.

The Tom above her sighed with what she thought might be relief and his hands moved under her shirt. "I knew you were lonely."

"I wasn't lonely," Val said automatically, pulling back. She didn't know if she was lying or not. Had she been lonely? She thought of faeries and their inability to lie and wondered what they did when they didn't know what the truth was.

At her thought of faeries, Tom's skin turned green, his hair blackened and fell around his shoulders until it was Ravus she saw, Ravus's long fingers that touched her skin and his hot eyes staring down at her.

She found herself frozen, repulsed by her own fascination. The tilt of his head was just right, his expression inquiring.

"You don't want me," she said, but whether she was speaking to the image of Ravus in front of her or to Dave, she wasn't sure.

He pressed his mouth against hers and she felt the sting of his teeth against her lip and she shuddered with desire and with dread.

How could she not have known she wanted this, when now she wanted nothing else? She knew it wasn't really Ravus and that it was obscene to pretend it was, but she let him ease her jeans off her hips anyway. Her heart thudded against her chest, as though she'd been running, as though she was in some danger, but she reached up her arms and threaded her fingers through oil-black hair. His long body settled over hers and she gripped the muscles of his back, focusing on the hollow of his throat, the glittering gold of his slitted eyes, as she tried to ignore Dave's grunts. It was almost enough.

The next afternoon, as Ravus put Val through a series of sword moves holding the wooden blade, she watched his closed, remote face and despaired. Before, she had been able to convince herself that she didn't feel any way about him, but now she felt as if she'd had a taste of food that left her starving for a banquet that would never come.

Walking back from the bridge, she passed near where the Dragon Bus let off. Three hookers shivered in their short skirts. One girl in a faux ponyskin coat walked toward Val with a smile, then turned away as though she realized Val wasn't a boy.

At the next block, she crossed the street to avoid a bearded man in a miniskirt and floppy boots with their laces undone. Steam rose from under his skirt as he urinated on the sidewalk.

Val picked her way through the streets to the entrance to the tunnel platform. As she got close to the concrete park, she saw Lolli arguing with a girl wearing a monster-fur coat with a spiky rubber backpack over it. For a moment, Val felt an odd sense of disorientation. The girl was familiar, but so totally out of context that Val couldn't place her.

Lolli looked up. The girl turned and followed Lolli's glance. Her mouth opened in surprise. She started toward Val on platform boots, a sack of flour clutched in her arm. It was only when Val noticed someone had painted a face on the flour that she realized she was looking at Ruth.

"Val?" Ruth's arm twitched up like she was going to reach for Val, but then thought better of it. "Wow. Your hair. You should have told me you were going to cut it off. I would have helped you."

"How did you find me?" Val asked numbly.

"Your friend," Ruth looked back at Lolli skeptically. "She answered your phone."

Val reached automatically for her bag, even knowing that her phone must not be inside of it. "I turned it off."

"I know. I tried to call you a zillion times and your voice mail is full. I've been freaking out."

Val nodded, at a loss as to what to say. She was conscious of the ground-in dirt on her pants, the black half-moons of her fingernails and the stink of her body, the smells that scrubbing in public restrooms with your clothes mostly on didn't really make better.

"Listen," Ruth said. "I brought someone to meet you." She held out the sack of flour. It had eyes outlined with heavy black liner and a tiny, pursed mouth shaded with glittering blue nail polish. "Our baby. You know, it's hard on him with one of his mommies gone and it's hard on me, being a single parent. In Health class, I had to do all the worksheets alone." Ruth gave Val a wobbly smile. "I'm sorry I was such an asshole. I should have told you about Tom. I started to, like a million times. I just never got the words all of the way out."

"It doesn't matter anymore," Val said. "I don't care about Tom."

"Look," said Ruth. "It's freezing. Can we go inside? I saw a bubble tea place not too far from here."

Was it freezing? Val was so used to being cold when she wasn't using Never that it seemed normal for her fingers to be numb and her marrow to feel like it was made from ice. "Okay," she said.

Lolli had a smug expression on her face. She lit a cigarette and blew twin streams of white smoke from her nostrils. "I'll tell Dave you'll be back soon. I don't want him to worry about his new girlfriend."

"What?" For a moment, Val didn't know what she meant. Sleeping with Dave seemed so unreal, something done in the middle of the night, drunk with glamour and sleep.

"He says you two made it last night." Lolli sounded haughty, but Dave obviously hadn't told her that Val had looked like Lolli when she'd done it. It filled Val with a shameful relief.

Now Val understood why Ruth was here, why Lolli had lifted her cell phone and set up this scene. She was punishing Val.

Val guessed it was just about what she deserved. "It's no big deal. It was just something to do." Val paused. "He was just trying to make you jealous."

Lolli looked surprised and then suddenly, awkward. "I just didn't think you liked him like that."

Val shrugged. "Be back in a while."

"Who is she?" Ruth asked as they walked toward the bubble tea place.

"Lolli," Val said. "She's okay, mostly. I'm crashing with her and some of her friends."

Ruth nodded. "You could come home, you know. You could stay with me."

"I don't think that your mom would be down with that." Val opened the wood and glass door and stepped into the smell of sugary milk. They sat at a table in the back, balancing on the small rosewood boxes the place had for seats. Ruth thrummed her fingers on the glass top of the table as though her nerves had settled into her skin.

The waitress came and they ordered black pearl tea, toast with condensed milk and coconut butter, and spring rolls. She stared at Val for a long moment before she left their table, as if evaluating whether or not they could pay.

Val took a deep breath and resisted the urge to bite the

skin around her finger. "It's so weird that you're here."

"You look sick," Ruth said. "You're too skinny and your eyes are one big bruise."

"I—"

The waitress set their things down on the table, forestalling whatever Val had been about to say. Glad for the distraction, Val poked at her drink with the fat, blue straw, and then sucked up a large, sticky tapioca and a mouthful of sweet tea. Everything Val did seemed slow, her limbs so heavy that chewing on the tapioca felt exhausting.

"I know you're going to say that you're fine," Ruth said. "Just tell me that you really don't hate me."

Val felt something inside her waver and then she finally was able to start to explain. "I'm not mad at you anymore. I feel like such a sucker, though, and my mother . . . I just can't go back. At least not yet. Don't try to talk me into it."

"When then?" Ruth asked. "Where are you staying?"

Val just shook her head, putting another piece of toast in her mouth. They seemed to melt on her tongue, gone before she realized she'd eaten them all. At another table, a group of glitter-covered girls exploded in laughter. Two Indonesian men looked over at them, annoyed.

"So what did you name the kid?" Val asked.

"What?"

"Our flour baby. The one I ran off on without even paying child support."

Ruth grinned. "Sebastian. Like it?"

Val nodded.

"Well, here's something that you probably won't like," Ruth said. "I'm not going home unless you come with me."

No matter what Val said, she couldn't talk Ruth into leaving. Finally, thinking that seeing the actual squat might convince her, Val brought her down to the abandoned platform. With someone else there, Val noticed anew the stink of the place, sweat and urine and burnt-sugar Never, the animal bones on the track and the mounds of clothes that never got moved because they were crawling with bugs. Lolli had her kit unrolled and was shaking some Never onto a spoon. Dave was already soaring, the smoke from his cigarette forming the shapes of cartoon characters that chased each other with hammers.

"You've got to be kidding me," Luis said. "Let me guess. Another stray cat for Lolli to shove off onto the tracks."

"V-Val?" Ruth's voice trembled as she looked around.

"This is my best friend, Ruth," Val said before she realized how juvenile that sounded. "She came looking for me."

"I thought we were your best friends." Dave smiled a smile that was half-leer and Val regretted letting him touch her, letting him think he had some power over her.

"We're all best friends," Lolli said, shooting him a glare as she rested one of her leg's on Luis's, her boot nearly touching his crotch. "All the bestest of friends."

Dave's face crumpled.

"If you were any kind of friend to her, you wouldn't drag her into this shit," Luis told Val, twisting away from Lolli.

"How many people are down here? Come out where I can see you," a gruff voice called.

Two policemen walked down the stairs. Lolli froze, the spoon in her hand still over the fire. The drug started to blacken and burn. Dave laughed, a weird crazy laugh that went on and on.

Flashlights cut through the dim station. Lolli dropped her spoon, grown too hot to hold, and the beams converged on her, then moved to blind Val. She shaded her eyes with her hand.

"All of you." One of the cops was a woman, her face stern. "Stand against the wall, hands on your head."

One beam caught Luis and the male cop nudged him with his boot. "Go. Let's go. We heard some reports there were kids down here, but I didn't believe it."

Val stood slowly and walked to the wall, Ruth beside her. She felt so sick with guilt that she wanted to vomit. "I'm sorry," she whispered.

Dave just stood stock still in the middle of the platform. He was shaking.

"Something wrong?" the female cop shouted, making it not at all a question. "Against the wall!" With that, her speech turned to barking. Where she had stood was a black dog, larger than a Rottweiler, with foam running from its mouth.

"What the hell?" The other cop turned, pulled out his gun. "That your dog? Call it off."

"It's not our dog," Dave said with an eerie smile.

The dog turned toward Dave, growling and barking. Dave just laughed.

"Masollino?" the policeman yelled. "Masollino?"

"Stop fucking around," Luis called. "Dave, what are you doing?"

Ruth dropped her arms from her head. "What's going on?"

The dog's teeth were bright as it advanced against the

policeman. He pointed the gun at it and the dog stopped. It whined and he hesitated. "Where's my partner?"

Lolli giggled and the man looked up sharply, then quickly back at the dog.

Val took a step forward, Ruth still holding her arm so tight that it hurt. "Dave," she hissed. "Come on. Let's go."

"Dave!" Luis yelled. "Turn her back!"

The dog moved at that, turning and leaping toward where they stood, lolling tongue a slash of red in the dark.

Two sharp pops were followed by silence. Val opened her eyes, not even aware she had closed them. Ruth screamed.

Lying on the ground was the female cop, bleeding from her neck and side. The other officer stared in horror at his own gun. Val froze, too stunned to move, her feet like lead. Her mind was still groping for a solution, some way to undo what had been done. *This is just an illusion,* she told herself. *Dave is playing a joke on all of us.*

Lolli jumped down into the well of the tracks and took off, gravel crunching under her boots. Luis grabbed Dave's arm and pulled him toward the tunnels. "We have to get out of here," he said.

The police officer looked up as Val leaped off the side of the platform, Ruth behind her. Luis and Dave were already disappearing into the darkness.

A shot rang out behind them. Val didn't look back. She ran along the track, clutching Ruth's hand like they were little kids crossing the road. Ruth squeezed twice, but Val could hear her start to sob.

"Cops never understand anything," Dave said as they moved through the tunnels. "They got all these quotas about arresting people and that's all they care about. They found our place and they were just going to lock it up so nobody could ever use it and where's the sense in that? We're not hurting anyone by being down there. It's our place. We found it."

"What are you talking about?" Luis said. "What were you thinking back there? Are you bug-fuck crazy?"

"It's not my fault," Dave said. "It's not your fault. It's not anybody's fault."

Val wished he would shut up.

"That's right," Luis said, his voice shaking. "It's nobody's fault."

They emerged in the Canal Street station, hopping on the platform and getting on the first train that stopped. The car was mostly empty, but they stood anyway, braced against the door as the train swayed along.

Ruth had stopped crying, but her makeup made dark smudges on her cheeks and her nose was red. Dave seemed emptied of all emotion, his eyes not meeting anyone else's. Val couldn't imagine what he was feeling at that moment. She wasn't even sure how to name what she felt.

"We can crash in the park tonight," Luis said. "Dave and I did that before we found the tunnel."

"I'm going to take Ruth to Penn Station," Val said suddenly. She thought of the policewoman, the memory of her death like a weight that got heavier with each step away from the corpse. She didn't want Ruth dragged down with the rest of them.

Luis nodded. "And you're going with her?"

Val hesitated.

"I'm not getting on that train alone," Ruth said fiercely.

"There's someone I have to say good-bye to," Val said. "I can't just disappear."

They got off at the next stop, transferred to an uptown train and rode to Penn Station, then walked upstairs to check the times. Afterward they settled in the Amtrak waiting area, and Lolli bought coffee and soup that none of them touched.

"Meet me here in an hour," Ruth said. "The train leaves fifteen minutes after that. You can say good-bye to this guy in that time, right?"

"If I'm not back, you have to get on the train," Val said. "Promise me."

Ruth nodded, her face pale. "So long as you promise to be back."

"We're going to be by the weather castle in Central Park," Lolli said. "If you miss your train."

"I'm not going to miss it," Val said, glancing at Ruth.

Lolli swirled a spoon into a tub of soup, but didn't raise it to her mouth. "I know. I'm just saying."

Val stumbled out into the cold, glad to be away from them all.

When she got to the bridge, it was still light enough to see the East River, brown as coffee left too long on the burner. Her head hurt and the muscles in her arms spasmed and she realized that she hadn't had a dose of Never since the evening before.

Never more than two days in a row. She couldn't remember when that rule had been forgotten and the new rule had become every day and sometimes more than that.

Val knocked on the stump and slipped inside the bridge, but despite the threat of daylight, Ravus was gone. She considered finger painting a message on a torn grocery flier, but she was so tired that she decided to wait a little while longer. Sitting down in the club chair, the scents of old paper, leather, and fruit lulled her into leaning back her head and parting the curtain just slightly. She sat for an oblivious hour, watching the sun dip lower, setting the sky aflame, but Ravus didn't return and she only felt worse. Her muscles, which had ached like they did after exercise, now burned like a charley horse that woke you from sleep.

She looked through his bottles and potions and mixtures, careless of what she disturbed and where things were moved, but she found not a single granule of Never to take away the pain.

A family was finishing their picnic on the rocks as Val shuffled into Central Park, the mother packing up leftover sandwiches, a lanky daughter pushing one of her brothers. The two boys were twins, Val noticed. She'd always found twins sort of creepy, as though only one of them could be the real one. The father glanced at Val, but his eyes rested on a cyclist's long, bare legs as he slowly chewed his food.

Val walked on, legs aching, past a lake thick with algae, where a riderless boat floated along in the dimming light. An older couple strolled by the bank, arm in arm, as a jogger in spandex huffed his way around them, MP3 player bobbing against his biceps. Normal people with normal problems.

The path continued over a courtyard whose walls were

carved with berries and birds, vines so intricate they nearly looked alive, blooming roses, and less familiar flowers.

Val stopped to lean against a tree, its roots exposed and tangled like the pattern of veins under her skin, the pewter bark of the trunk, wet and dark with frozen sap. She'd been walking for a while, but there was no castle in sight.

Three boys with low-slung pants passed, one bouncing a basketball off his friend's back.

"Where's the weather castle?" she called.

One boy shook his head. "No such thing."

"She means Belvedere Castle," said the other, pointing his hand at an angle, halfway back in the direction she'd come from. "Over the bridge and through the Ramble."

Val nodded. *Over the bridge and through the woods.* Everything hurt, but she kept going, anticipating the sting of the needle and the sweet relief it would bring. She thought back to Lolli sitting by the fire with the spoon in her hand and her breath stopped at the thought that all the Never was still back there, in the tunnels, with the dead woman, then hated herself that that was what she worried about, that that was what stopped her breath.

The Ramble was a maze of trails, crossing one another, trailing off into dead ends, and doubling back on themselves. Some paths appeared intentional, others seemed created by pedestrians sick of trying to pick their way through the fickle course. Val trudged along, crunching leaves and twigs, her hands in her pockets, gripping her skin through the thin backing of the coat as though digging fingers could punish her body into not hurting.

In the cover of the patchy branches, two men were twined

together, one of them in a suit and overcoat, the other in jeans and denim jacket.

At the top of the hill was a large, gray castle with a spire that reached far above the tree line. It appeared to be a grand and ancient estate, rendered strange by being set against the shining lights of the city at dusk, a thing completely out of place. As Val walked closer, she saw that an array of taxidermied creatures were just inside the window, their black eyes watching her through the glass.

"Hey," a familiar voice called.

Val turned to see Ruth leaning up against a pillar. Before she could think of what to say, she noticed Luis stretched out against the landing that overlooked a lake and a baseball diamond, kissing Lolli with deep, wet, soft kisses.

"I knew you never intended to show up," Ruth said, shaking her head.

"You said that you would get on the train even if I didn't," Val said, trying for self-righteous anger, but the words came out sounding lamely defensive.

Ruth crossed her arms over her chest. "Whatever."

"Where's Dave?" Val asked, looking around. The park was getting darker and she didn't see him anywhere close by.

Ruth shrugged and reached for a cup by her feet. "He went off to do some thinking or something. Luis went after him, but came back alone. I guess he's freaked out. Shit, I'm freaked out—that woman changed into a dog and now she's dead."

Val didn't know how to explain things so that Ruth would understand, especially because it would make everything so much worse. It was better to believe that the cop had turned into a dog than that she had been turned into one. "Dave's not going to be happy about that." Val gestured with her chin toward Lolli and Luis, ignoring the question of magic altogether.

Ruth grimaced. "It's disgusting. Those callous fuckers."

"I don't get it. All this time she's been after him and he picks now to get it on?" Val couldn't understand. Luis was an asshole, but he cared about his brother. It wasn't like him to leave Dave to wander around Central Park while he got it on with a girl.

Ruth frowned and held out the cup she was holding. "They're your friends. Here, have some tea. It's disgustingly sweet, but at least it's hot."

Val took a sip, letting the liquid warm her throat, trying to ignore the way her hand was shaking.

Luis pulled back from Lolli and gave Val a lopsided grin. "Hey, when did you show up?"

"Do either you have any Never?" Val blurted. She didn't think she could stand the pain much longer. Even her jaw felt cramped.

Luis shook his head and looked at Lolli. "No," she said. "I dropped it. Did you get anything from Ravus?"

Val took a deep breath, trying not to panic. "He wasn't there."

"Did you see Dave on your way in?" Lolli asked.

Val shook her head.

"Let's go down to the crash spot," Luis said. "I think it's dark enough to keep us hidden."

"Can Dave find us?" Ruth asked.

"Sure," Luis said. "He'll know where to look. We slept there before."

Val gritted her teeth in frustration, but she followed the others as they jumped the gate on one side of the castle and crept down the rocks beneath it. There was a shadowed plateau overhung enough by another boulder to give them a little shelter. Val noticed that they'd already loaded it up with some cardboard.

Luis sat down and Lolli leaned against him, eyes going half-lidded. "I'll scrounge up some better supplies tomorrow," he said, leaning down to press his mouth to hers.

Ruth put one arm around Val and sighed. "I can't believe this."

"Me either," Val said, because suddenly all of it seemed equally surreal, equally random and unbelievable. It felt less possible that Ruth should be sleeping on cardboard in Central Park than that faeries existed.

Luis slid his hands up under Lolli's skirt and Val took another sip of the cooling tea, ignoring the flash of skin, the glimmer of steel rings, trying not to notice the wet sounds and the giggling. As she turned her head, she saw the leg of Luis's baggy pants, hiked up so high that the scorch marks on the inside of his knee were visible, scorch marks that could only come from Never.

As Ruth's breath evened out into sleep and Lolli and Luis's breath escalated into something else, Val bit the inside of her lip and rode out the pain of withdrawal.

They love not poison that do poison need.
—WILLIAM SHAKESPEARE, *RICHARD II*

As the night wore on, Val got no better. The cramping of the muscles under her skin grew until she stood up and crept away from their crash spot so that she could at least twist and move as her discomfort urged. She walked across the rocks and started back through the Ramble, scattering a flurry of crumpled leaves from their branches. She took another sip of the tea, but it had turned icy cold.

Val had grown up thinking of Central Park as dangerous, even more than the rest of New York, the kind of place where perverts and murderers lurked behind every bush, just waiting for some innocent jogger. She remembered countless news stories about stabbings and muggings. But now the park just seemed tranquil.

She picked up a stick and did lunging drills, thrusting the tip of the wood into the knothole of a thick elm until she figured she'd cowed any squirrels that might have lived there.

The movements made her feel dizzy and slightly nauseated and when she shook her head, she thought she saw moving lights on a nearby path.

The wind picked up just then and the air felt charged, the way it did before a thunderstorm, but when she looked again, she saw nothing. Scowling, she squatted down and waited to see if there was anyone there.

The wind whipped past her, nearly pulling her backpack off her shoulder. This time she was sure she heard laughter. She turned, but there were only the thick bands of ivy crawling up a nearby tree.

The next gust of wind hit her then, knocking the cup out of her hand, spilling the remains of the tea in a puddle and rolling the white cup in the wet dirt.

"Stop it!" Val yelled, but in the silence that followed, her words seemed futile, even dangerous to shout into the still air.

A whistle turned her head. There, sitting on a stump, was a woman made entirely of ivy. "I smell glamour, thin as a dusting of snow. Are you one of us?"

"No," Val said. "I'm not a faerie."

The woman inclined her head in a slight bow.

"Wait. I need—" Val started, but she didn't know how to finish. She needed to score; she needed Never but she had no idea if the faeries had a name for it.

"One of the sweet tooths? Poor creature, you've wandered far from the revels." The ivy woman walked past Val and down toward the bridge. "I'll show you the way."

Val didn't know what the ivy woman meant, but she followed, not only because Lolli and Luis were breaking Dave's heart on some nearby rocks and she didn't want to have to see it, not just because the dead eyes of the policewoman seemed to follow her in the darkness, but because the only thing that seemed important right then was stopping her own pain. And where there were faerie revels, there would be some way to find surcease.

The ivy woman led Val back to the terrace with its carved walls of birds and branches, the fountain at its center, and the lake beyond. The faerie rustled across the tiles, a moving column of greenery. Fog rolled up off the water, a silvery mist that hung in the air for a moment before it roiled forward, too dense and fast to be natural. Val's skin prickled but she was too dazed and full of aches to do more than stumble back as the fog came in like the tide on some dark shore.

It settled around her, warm and heavy, carrying a strange perfume of rot and sweetness. Music ghosted through the air— the tinkling of bells, a moan, the shrill notes of a flute. Val walked unsteadily, engulfed and blinded by swells of mist. She heard a chorus of laughter, close by, and turned. The fog ebbed in places, leaving Val looking at a new landscape.

The terrace was still there, but the vines had grown from the stone into wild looping things, blooming with strange flowers and thorns long and thin as needles. Birds flew from their sculpted nests to pick at the swollen grapes that hung from the stair rails and squabble with fist-size bees over the steely apples that littered the pier.

And, too, there were faeries. More than Val might have imagined could live among the iron and steel of the city, faeries with their strange eyes and knifelike ears, in skirts woven of nettle or meadowsweet, in T-shirts and vests with embroidered roses and in nothing at all, their skin gleaming under the moon.

Val passed a creature with legs that seemed to be branches and a face carved from bark and a little man that peered at her through opera glasses with lenses of blue beach glass. She passed a man with spines that ran along his hunched back. He smelled of sandlewood and she thought she knew him. Each fey creature seemed bright as leaping flame and wild as wind. Their eyes glowed hot and terrible in the moonlight and Val found herself afraid.

Along the edge of the lake were cloths woven with gold and heaped with all manner of delicacies. Dates, quinces, and persimmons lay on platters of cracked and dried leaves, next to decanters of sapphire and peridot wines. Cakes piled with roasted acorns were stacked beside spits of limp pigeons and cups of viscous syrups. Nearby them, in a heap, were Ravus's white apples, their red innards visible through vellum skin, promising Val respite from pain.

She forgot her fear.

She grabbed one, and bit into the warm, sweet flesh. It slid down her throat like a bloody chunk of meat. Fighting back nausea, she bit again and again, juice sluicing over her jaw, the skin of the fruit giving under her sharp teeth. It didn't feel like Never, but it was enough to numb her limbs and still her trembling.

Relieved, Val sank down by the lake as a creature of moss and lichen surfaced for a moment with a flailing pewter fish in her mouth, then dove again. Too tired to move and too relieved to be anything but sated, Val contented herself by watching the crowd. To her surprise, she saw that she was not the only human. A girl, too young to be out of middle school, rested her head in the lap of a blue faerie with black lips that braided tiny bells and beggarsweed into the child's pigtails. A man with graying hair and a tweed coat knelt beside a green girl with mossy, dripping hair. Two young men ate slivers of white apples off the edge of a blade, licking the knife to get all of the juice.

Were they the sweet tooths? Human thralls, willing to do anything for a taste of Never, not even knowing what it was to stick it in your arm or burn it up your nose. *Never*, Val told herself. *Never again Never. Never more. Never Never NeverNeverLand*. She didn't need to make the shadows dance. She didn't need to keep choosing the wrong path, gloating that at least she was picking her disaster. No matter how bad her decisions, they weren't keeping any other troubles at bay.

Another faerie came down the stairs. There was something wrong with his skin; it looked mottled and bubbling in places. One of his ears and part of his neck appeared as though they were sculpted crudely from clay. Some of the others drew back as he strode across the terrace.

"Iron sickness," someone said. Val turned to see one of the honey-haired faerie girls from Washington Square Park. Her feet were still bare, although she wore an anklet of holly berries.

Val shuddered. "Looks like he was burned."

"Some say that's going to happen to all of us if we don't stay in the park or go back where we came from."

"Were you exiled here?"

The faerie girl nodded. "One of my lovers was also the lover of a well-favored Lord. He made it appear as though I had stolen a bolt of cloth. It was magical fabric, the kind that shows you stories—precious stuff—and the punishment from the weaver was likely to be both elegant and severe. My sisters and I went into exile until we could prove my innocence. But what of you?"

Val had leaned forward, imagining the marvelous material, and was caught off guard by the faerie's question. "I guess you could say I was in exile." Then, looking around, she asked. "Is it always like this here? Do all the exiles come here every night?"

The honey-haired faerie laughed. "Oh, yes. If you have to go Ironside, at least you can come here. It's almost like being back at court. And, of course, there's gossip."

Val smiled. "What kind of gossip?" She was back to being a sidekick. It was automatic for her to ask the questions that her companion wanted to answer and a relief to listen. The faerie's words drowned out her own restless thoughts.

The girl grinned. "Well, the best bit of gossip is that the Bright Lady, the Seelie Queen Silarial, is here in the iron city. They say that she's to take care of the poisonings. Apparently Mabry—one of the exiled Gentry—knows something. Everyone's heard they had a meeting."

Val sank her nails into the back of her other hand. Had Mabry accused Ravus? She thought of Ravus's abandoned place inside the bridge an scowled.

"Oh, look," the faerie whispered. "There she is. See how everyone hangs back, pretending they aren't dying to ask her to prove the rumors."

Val stood up. "I'll ask her."

Before the honey-haired faerie could protest or applaud, Val threaded her way through the Folk. Mabry wore a gown of palest cream, her green-and-brown hair piled up on her head with a comb made from the inside of a shell. It looked strangely familiar to Val, but she couldn't place it.

"That's a pretty comb," she said, since she'd been staring at it.

Mabry drew it from her hair, letting the locks tumble down her back, and gave Val a wide, lush smile. "I know you. The servant Ravus has become overfond of. Take this little trinket if you like. Perhaps your hair will grow into it."

Val ran her fingers over the cool surface of the shell, but she was sure that a gift delivered with such a barb didn't deserve any thanks.

Mabry reached out a finger and touched the side of Val's mouth. "I see you've had a taste of what your skin has been drinking."

Val started. "How did you know?"

"It is my habit to know things," Mabry said, turning to walk off before Val got to ask a single thing she wanted to know.

Val tried to follow Mabry, but a faerie with hair of long weeds and a smile full of wicked laughter interposed himself. "My lovely, let me devour your beauty."

"You've got to be joking," Val said, trying to push past him.

"Not in the least," he said, and suddenly, strangely, Val could feel desire twist in her belly. Her face went hot. "I can make even your dreams be of want."

A hand caught her throat and a deep, rough voice spoke low and close to her ear. "And now what is your training good for?"

"Ravus?" Val asked, although she knew his voice.

The other faerie slunk away, but Ravus kept his fingers at

her neck. "It's dangerous here. You should be more careful. Now I'd like you to at least try and break free."

"You never taught me—" she began, but then she stopped, ashamed of the way her voice sounded like whining. He was teaching her now. After all, he was giving her time to think what the possible moves might be. It wasn't as though he was choking her. He was giving her time to win.

Val relaxed, pressing her back to his chest and grinding against him. Startled, he loosed his grasp and she pulled free. He clutched her arm, but she spun around and pressed her mouth to his.

His lips were rough, chapped. She felt the sting of fangs against her bottom lip. He made a sharp sound in the back of his throat and closed his eyes, mouth opening under hers. The smell of him—of cold, damp stone—made her head swim. One kiss slid into another and it was perfect, was exactly right, was real.

He pulled back abruptly, turning his head so that he wasn't looking at her. "Effective," he said.

"I thought maybe you wanted me to kiss you. Sometimes I thought I could see it." Her heart was thundering in her chest and her cheeks were scalding, but she was pleased that she sounded calm.

"I didn't want you . . . ," Ravus said. "I didn't want you to see it."

She almost laughed. "You look so shocked. Hasn't anyone ever kissed you before?" Val wanted to do it again, but she didn't dare.

His voice was cool. "On rare occasions."

"Did you like it?"

"Then or now?"

Val sucked in a breath, let it out with a sigh. "Both. Either."

"I liked it," he said softly. It was then that she remembered he could not lie.

She ran her hand over his cheek. "Kiss me back."

Ravus caught her fingers, clutched them so hard that they hurt. "Enough," he said. "Whatever game you are playing at, end it now."

She pulled her hand out of his grip, sobering abruptly, and took several steps back from him. "I'm sorry—I thought—" In truth, she couldn't recall what she'd thought, what had made this seem like a good idea.

"Come along," he said, not looking at her. "I'll take you back to the tunnels."

"No," Val said.

He stopped. "It would be unwise to remain here, no matter your—"

Val shook her head. "That's not what I mean. Someone found our place. There's nowhere to go back to." It had been a long time since there was something to go back to, anything to go back to anywhere.

He spread his hand as though trying to express something inexpressible. "We both know that I am a monster."

"You're not—"

"It demeans you to cover rotten meat with honey. I know what I am. What would you want with a monster?"

"Everything," Val said solemnly. "I'm sorry I kissed you—it was selfish and it upset you—but you can't ask me to pretend I didn't want to."

He regarded her warily as she took a step closer to him.

"I'm not very good at explaining things," she said. "But I think you have beautiful eyes. I love the gold in them. I love that they're different from my eyes—I see mine all the time and I'm bored with them."

He snorted with amusement, but stayed still.

She reached up and touched the pale green of his cheek. "I like all the things that make you monstrous."

His long fingers threaded through the peach fuzz of her hair, clawed nails resting carefully against her skin. "I'm afraid that whatsoever I touch is spoilt by the contact."

"I'm not scared of being spoiled," Val said.

The side of Ravus's mouth twitched.

A woman's voice pierced through the air, sharp as the clang of a bell. "You sent for Silarial after all."

Val whirled. Mabry stood in the courtyard, tendrils of hair caught by the breeze. All around them, Folk were staring. After all, here was a chance for gossip.

Ravus's hand rested on the small of Val's back and she could feel the curl of nails against her spine. His voice was flat as he addressed Mabry. "Lady Silarial's mercy may be dreadful, but I have little choice but to throw myself on it. I know she came to talk to you—perhaps when she sees how unhappy you have been and how helpful you are, she will take you back to court."

Mabry's mouth bent into a wry smile. "We all must avail ourselves of her mercy. But now I want to give you something for what you have given me."

Val reached into her back pocket to give back Mabry's comb, the tines of it poking her fingers as she drew it out. Seaweed-wrapped pearls and tiny doves from the inside of sand dollars clung to the crest of the comb. Looking at it, Val suddenly saw the mermaid, necklace coiling in ropes of pearls and shell birds, dead eyes staring forever up at Val while her hair floated along the surface of the water, bereft of a matched comb.

Holding the comb in numb fingers, Val realized that it had come from a corpse.

"Mabry gave me this," Val said.

Ravus looked at it mildly, clearly not attaching any significance to it.

"It came from the mermaid," Val said. "She took this from the mermaid."

Mabry snorted. "Then, how is it that it came to be in your hand?"

"She gave it—"

Mabry turned to Ravus, interrupting Val smoothly. "Did you know she's been stealing from you—skimming off the top of your potions like a boggart drinks the head of cream off a bottle of milk?" Mabry snatched Val's arm, pushing up the sleeve so that Ravus could see the black marks inside the crook of her elbow, the marks that looked like someone had put out a cigarette in her flesh. "And look what she's been doing—stuffing her veins with our balm. Now, Ravus, you tell me who's the poisoner. Will you suffer for her mistakes?"

Val reached her hand toward Ravus. He pulled back.

"What have you done?" he asked, tight-lipped.

"Yes, I shot up the potions," Val said. There was no point in denying anything now.

"Why would you do that?" he asked. "I thought it was harmless, just something to keep the Folk from pain."

"Never . . . it gives you . . . it makes humans . . . like faeries." That wasn't it, not exactly, but his face already said, *You didn't mind that I was monstrous because you are a monster.*

"I had thought better of you," Ravus said. "I had thought everything of you."

"I'm sorry," Val said. "Please, let me explain."

"Humans," he said, the word soaked with repugnance. "Liars, all of you. Now I understand my mother's hate."

"I might have lied about that but I'm not lying about the comb. I'm not lying about everything."

He grabbed Val's shoulder, his fingers so heavy she felt as if she was held by stone. "Now I know what you saw in me to love. Potions."

"No!" Val said.

When she looked up at Ravus's face, there was nothing there that was familiar, nothing that was kind. His clawed thumb pressed against the pulse of her throat. "I think it is time that you were gone."

Val hesitated. "Just let me—"

"Go!" he shouted, pushing her away from him and curling his fingers into a fist so tight that his claws cut the pads of his own hand.

Val stumbled back, her throat stinging.

Ravus turned to Mabry. "Say that you feel revenged on me. At least tell me that."

"Not at all," Mabry replied with a sour smile. "I did you a good turn."

Val went, retracing her steps along the path, through the wall of fog, the woods and up to the castle, her eyes blurry and her heart aching. There, watching the distant flicker of the city lights, Val thought suddenly of her mother. Was this how she had felt, after Tom and Val were gone? Had she wanted to go back and change everything, but lacked the power?

Crawling along the rocks, Val saw the red tip of Ruth's clove cigarette before she saw the rest of their makeshift camp. Ruth stood up when Val got close. "I thought you left me again."

Val looked over at Lolli and Luis, curled up together. Luis looked different, his eyes circled darkly and his skin pale. "I just went for a walk."

Ruth took another long drag, the end of her cigarette sparking. "Yeah, well, your friend Dave just went for a walk, too."

Val thought about the revel and wondered if Dave had been there, another sweet tooth, wandering dazed among capricious masters.

"I . . . I . . . ," Val sat down, overwhelmed, and covered her face with her hands. "I fucked up. I really, really fucked up."

"What do you mean?" Ruth sat down next to Val and put her arm over her shoulder.

"It's too hard to explain. There are faeries, like real *Final Fantasy* faeries, and they've been poisoned and this stuff I've been taking—it's kind of a drug, but it's kind of magic, too." Val could feel tears trickle over her face, and swiped at them.

"You know," Ruth said, "people don't cry when they're sad. Everyone thinks that, but it's not true. People cry when they're frustrated or overwhelmed."

"What about grief?" asked Val.

"Grief is frustrating and overwhelming."

The mermaid's comb was still in Val's hand, she realized, but she'd been clutching it so tightly that it had broken into pieces. Just thin sheets of shell, nothing more. No reason to think it proved anything.

"Look, I'll admit you sound a little crazy," Ruth said. "But so what? Even if you are completely delusional, we still have to work out your delusion, right? An imaginary problem needs an imaginary solution."

Val let her head fall onto Ruth's shoulder, relaxing in a way she hadn't relaxed since before she'd seen her mother and Tom and maybe before that. She'd forgotten how much she loved talking to Ruth.

"Okay, so start at the start."

"When I came to the city, I was just operating on autopilot," Val said. "I had tickets to the game, so I went. I know it sounds insane. Even when I was doing it, I thought it was crazy, like I was one of those people who kills their boss and then sits back down at their computer to finish reports.

"When I ran into Lolli and Dave, I just wanted to lose myself, to be nothing, to be nothingness. That sounds all wrong and dumb, I know."

"Very poetic," Ruth smirked. "Kind of goth."

Val rolled her eyes, but smiled. "They introduced me to some faeries and that's the part where everything stops making sense."

"Faeries? Like elves, goblins, trolls? Like the ones on Brian Froud panties at Hot Topic?"

"Look, I—"

Ruth held up her hand. "Just checking. Okay, faeries. I'm going with it."

"They have trouble with the iron, so there's this stuff that Lolli calls Nevermore. Never. It keeps them from getting too sick. Humans can . . . take it . . . and it makes you able to create illusions or to make people feel the way you want them to. We were doing deliveries of it for Ravus—he's the one that makes the Never—and we would take some for ourselves."

Ruth nodded. "Okay. So Ravus is a faerie?"

"Something like that," Val said. She could see a laugh in Ruth's eyes and was grateful when it didn't move to her lips. "Some of the Folk died of poison and they blamed Ravus. I think this comb came from one of the dead faeries and Mabry had it and I just don't know what that means.

"Everything is so crazy. Dave turned that cop into a dog on purpose and Mabry told Ravus we were stealing from him so he thinks I had something to do with the deaths and I haven't had Never in two days and my whole body hurts." It was true, the aches had started up again, the pain dim but growing, the temporary reprieve of faerie fruit not enough to keep her veins from clamoring for more.

Ruth squeezed Val's shoulders in a sideways hug. "Shit. Okay, that's crazy. What can we do?"

"We can figure it out," Val said. "I have all these clues; I just don't know how they fit together."

Val looked at the remains of the comb and thought of the mermaid again. Ravus had said rat poison killed the faerie, but rat poison was a dangerous and unlikely substance for a faerie poisoner to use, especially an alchemist like Ravus. And why would he want to kill a bunch of harmless faeries?

A human could have done it. A human courier was expected, not at all suspicious.

Val remembered the first delivery she'd ever been on and the bottle of Never Dave had unstoppered, breaking the wax. Shouldn't Mabry have been worried? With all the poisonings, wasn't that like taking an aspirin with the safety seal broken? The only way that anyone would do that was if they already know who the poisoner was or if they were the poisoner themselves.

And Mabry had known that Val was using. Someone was telling her.

"But why?" Val said out loud.

"Why what?" asked Ruth.

Val stood up and paced on the rock. "I'm thinking. What's the result of the poisonings? Ravus gets in trouble!"

"So?" Ruth asked.

"So Mabry wants revenge on him," Val said. Of course: Revenge for the death of her lover. Revenge for her exile.

Mabry then. Mabry and a human accomplice. Dave was obvious, since he'd been the one that didn't bother to disguise that he was skimming Never from Mabry, but what reason did he have to kill faeries?

It could have been Luis. He hated faeries for what they'd done to his eye. He wore all that metal to protect himself. And he was using the Never, as the marks under his knee proved, even if he denied it. But for what if he couldn't see glamour? And why didn't he care that Dave had gone missing? Why pick now to hook up with Lolli when she'd wanted him for longer than Val had known her? He was so unworried. It was as though he knew where his brother was.

Val stopped at that thought.

"This is what we have to do," Val said. "We have to go to Mabry's house while she's still at the revel and find proof that she's behind the poisonings." Proof that would convince Ravus that she was innocent and proof that would convince the others he wasn't the poisoner at all. Proof that would save him so that he would forgive her.

"Okay," said Ruth, shouldering her backpack. "Let's go help your imaginary friends."

Strike a glass, and it will not endure an instant;
simply do not strike it, and it will endure a thousand
years.

—G. K. CHESTERTON, *ORTHODOXY*

V al and Ruth made it to Riverside Park in the cold hours
before dawn. The sky was deep dark and the streets were
hushed. Val's heart beat rabbit-fast, adrenaline and muscle
cramping keeping her from noticing the chill air or the late
hour. Ruth shivered and wrapped her monster-fur coat tighter
as the wind blew up off the water. Her cheeks were streaked
with makeup, smudged by tears and careless hands, but when
she smiled at Val, Ruth looked like her old, confident self.

The park itself was mostly empty, with a small group of
people huddled near one of the walls, one of them smoking
what smelled like a joint. Val looked down the row of apartment buildings across from the park, but none of them was
quite right. She picked out the clogged fountain she'd stood
at days earlier, but when she looked across the street, the door

facing her was the wrong color and there was a metal grate over the windows.

"Well?" Ruth asked.

Val shifted her weight. "I'm not sure."

"What are we going to do if you find it?"

Looking up, Val saw a gargoyle in a place slightly different from where she remembered, but the stone monster was enough to convince her that the house she was looking at had to be Mabry's. Perhaps her memory was just off.

"Watch for anyone coming," Val said, starting to cross the road. Her heart thundered in her chest. She had no idea what she was getting them into.

Ruth hurried after her. "Great. Lookout. I'm a lookout. Another thing to put on my college applications. What do I do if I see someone?"

Val looked back. "I'm not sure, actually."

Staring at the building for a long moment, Val grabbed hold of one of the gutter rings on the downspout and hoisted herself up the wall. It was like climbing a tree, like climbing a rope in gym class.

"What are you doing?" Ruth called, her voice shrill.

"What did you think I needed a lookout for? Now shut up."

Val climbed higher, her feet pushing against the brick of the building, her fingers digging into the loops of metal as the gutter groaned and dented under her scrambling weight. As she reached for a windowsill, she found her hand in the mouth of a gargoyle, its chicken-bred-with-terrier face tilted to one side, eyes wide with surprise or excitement. She snatched her fingers back moments before the stone teeth snapped closed. Off balance, she kicked at the air for a moment, her full weight on the gutter and her one hand. The aluminum bent, tearing free of the supports.

Val jammed her foot into the brick and heaved hard, jumping and scrambling to catch the ledge. She heard a high-pitched squeak from below as she grabbed hold of the windowsill. Ruth. For a moment, she just hung on, afraid to move. Then she pulled herself up along the molding and pushed the window. It stuck and for a moment, she was afraid it was locked or painted shut, but she pushed harder and it gave. Climbing inside, past the tangled curtains, Val found herself in Mabry's bedroom. The floor was gleaming marble and the bed was a curving canopy of willow branches, the whole thing piled with rumpled silks and satins. One side of the bed was clean, but the other was dusted with dirt and brambles.

Val went out into the hall. There was a series of doors that opened into empty rooms and a staircase of ebonized wood. She walked down it and into the parlor, the squeak of the floorboards and the splash of the fountain the only sounds she heard.

The parlor was like she remembered, but the furniture seemed differently arranged and one of the doorways appeared larger. Val walked out of the apartment and into the main hallway, careful to brace Mabry's door open. She flipped the lock on the front door and jerked it open. Ruth gaped at her for a moment from the sidewalk, then ran inside.

"You've gone crazy," Ruth said. "We just broke into some posh building."

"It's protected by glamour," Val said. "It has to be." For the first time, Val considered the two doors she'd assumed went to other apartments. One was set opposite the door to Mabry's, the other at the end of the hall. Given the size of the rooms and the staircase in Mabry's apartment and the size of the building from the outside, it didn't seem possible that the doors led to anywhere at all. Val shook her head to clear it. It didn't matter. What mattered was that she found some evidence to implicate Mabry, something that would prove she poisoned the other fey, prove it not just to Ravus, but to Greyan and anyone else who thought Ravus was behind the deaths.

"At least it's warm in here," Ruth said, walking into the apartment and turning around on the gleaming marble floor. Her voice echoed in the nearly empty rooms. "If we have to be cat burglars, I'm going to see what's to steal in the fridge."

"We're trying to find evidence she's a poisoner. Just a thought before you start putting random things in your mouth." Ruth shrugged and walked past Val.

A display cabinet rested in one corner of the sitting room. Val peered through the glass. There was a bit of bark inside, braided with crimson hair; a figurine of a ballerina, her arms on her hips and her shoes red as roses; the broken neck of a bottle; and a faded and browned flower. Val thought she remembered different bizarre treasures from her earlier visit.

It made Val conscious of how impossible her task was. How would she know evidence, even if she saw it? Ravus might recognize these objects—know their uses and perhaps even part of their history, but she could make nothing of them.

It was hard to imagine Mabry as sentimental, but she must have been once, before Tamson's death made her hateful.

"Hey," Ruth said from the next room. "Look at this."

Val followed her voice. She was in the music room, beside the lap harp, sitting on an ottoman covered in an odd, pinkish leather. The body of the instrument looked to be gilded wood, carved with acanthus swirls, and each of the strings was a different shade. Most of them were brown or gold or black, but a few were red and one was leaf green.

Ruth knelt down beside it.

"Don't—" Val said, but Ruth's fingers brushed a brown string. Immediately a wailing flooded the room.

"Once I was a lady in waiting to the Queen Nicnevin," a voice full of tears intoned, accent rich and strange. "I was her favorite, her confidante, and I took my pleasure in harrying the others. Nicnevin had a particular toy, a Knight from the Seelie Court that she was overfond of. His tears of hate gave her more pleasure than another's cries of love. I was called before the Queen—she demanded to know if I was intriguing with him. I was not. Then she held up a pair of his gloves and demanded that I look at the embroidery along the cuffs. It was a careful pattern sewn with my own hair. There was more proof—sightings of us together, a note in his hand swearing devotion, none of it true. I fell down, begging Nicnevin, wild with fear. As they led me to my death, I saw one of the other ladies, Mabryn, smiling, her eyes bright as needles, her fingers reaching out to pluck a single strand of hair from my head. Now I must tell my tale forevermore."

"Nicnevin?" Ruth asked. "Who is that supposed to be?"

"I think she's the old Unseelie Queen," Val said. She dragged her fingers across several cords at once. A cacophony of voices rose up, each one telling its bitter tale, each one mentioning Mabry. "They're all hair. The hair of Mabry's victims."

"This is some spooky-ass shit," Ruth said.

"Shhh," Val said. One of the voices sounded familiar,

but she couldn't quite place where she'd heard it before. She plucked a golden string.

"Once I was a courtier in the service of the Queen Silarial," a male voice said. "I lived for sport, for riddles, and dueling and dance. Then I fell in love and all those things ceased to matter. My only joy was in Mabry. I desired a thing only if it delighted her. I basked in her gladness. Then, one lazy afternoon, as we gathered flowers to weave into garlands, I saw that she'd wandered off. I followed and overheard her speaking with a creature from the Unseelie Court. They seemed well acquainted and her voice was soft as she told him the information she had gathered for the Unseelie Queen. I should have been angry, but I was too afraid for her. If Silarial had found out, the consequences would have been terrible. I told Mabry that I would tell no one, but that she must leave directly. She told me she would and wept bitterly over deceiving me. Two days later I was to duel in a tournament with a friend. When I donned my armor, it felt strange, lighter, but I paid it no mind. Mabry told me she'd stitched her own hair into it as a token. When my friend struck, the armor crumbled and the sword cut me right through. I felt the silk of her hair against my face and knew I was betrayed. Now I must tell my tale forevermore."

Val sat down hard, staring at the harp. Mabry was a spy for the Unseelie Court. She had killed Tamson herself. Ravus had only been her instrument.

"Who was that?" Ruth asked. "Did you know him?"

Val shook her head. "Ravus did, though. He was the one swinging the sword in that story."

Ruth bit her lower lip. "This is so complicated. How are we going to figure out anything?"

"We already figured out something," Val said.

She stood up and walked into the next room. It was the kitchen. There was no stove, however; no refrigerator, only a sink in a long expanse of polished slate. Val opened up one of the cabinets, but it was filled only with empty jars.

Val thought about Ravus's glamoured form, his golden eyes the flaw in his disguise. There was something disquieting about these perfect rooms, dustless and echoing only with footsteps and the splash of water. But if there was a glamour, she had no idea what was beneath it.

Ruth walked into the room and Val noticed the white powder drizzling from her backpack.

"What's that?" Val asked.

"What?" Ruth looked behind her, on the floor, and shouldered off the bag. She laughed. "Looks like I ripped the canvas and popped a hole in our baby."

"Shit. This is worse than a bread-crumb trail. Mabry's going to know we were in here."

Ruth squatted down and started sweeping the powder together with her hands. Instead of forming a pile, it gusted up in white clouds.

As Val looked at the flour, she got an idea. "Wait. Hey, I think I might have to commit infanticide."

Ruth shrugged and pulled out the sack. "I guess we can always have another one."

Val ripped open the paper packaging and started sprinkling flour on the floor. "There has to be something here, something we can't see."

Ruth grabbed a handful of white powder and threw it at the door. Val tossed another fistful. Soon the air was thick with it.

Their hair was covered and when they breathed, flour coated their tongues.

It settled all over the apartment, showing the fish pond as a broken pipe spilling water into buckets and pooling on the floor, revealing the sagging sheetrock of the ceiling, the chipped tiles along the walls and tracks of mouse droppings on the floor.

"Look." Ruth walked over to one of the walls, powder making her ghostly. Flour was stuck to most of the wall, but there was a large bare patch.

Val tossed more powder at the gap, but instead of hitting the wall, it seemed to go through the space.

"We got it." Val grinned and lifted her fist. "Wonder twin powers activate!"

Ruth grinned back, knocking her fist into Val's. "Shape of two fucking lunatics."

"Speak for yourself," Val said, and ducked through the gap.

There, in a shadowed room hung with velvet drapes, was Luis. He lay on a carpet patterned with pomegranates and was wrapped in a woolen blanket, but despite that, he was shivering. There was blood on his scalp and several of his braids had been cut off.

At first Val just gaped at him. "Luis?" she finally managed.

He looked up, squinting, as though against a bright light. "Val?" He scrambled to a sitting position. "Where's Dave? Is he all right?"

"I don't know," she said absently. Her mind was racing. "What are you doing here?"

"Can't you see that I'm chained to the floor?" Luis said. He turned his wrists and she saw that his own braids were wrapped around them, pulled taut.

"The floor?" Val repeated stupidly. "But what about the carpet?"

Luis laughed. "I suppose this place looks beautiful to you."

Val looked at the low couches, the bookshelves overflowing with cloth-covered fairy stories, the faded grandeur of the carpet and painted molding on the walls. "It's one of the most gorgeous rooms I've ever been in."

"The plaster walls are cracked and there's a leak in the ceiling that pretty much means that whole corner is black with mold. There's no furniture here, either, and certainly no rug—just floorboards with some old nails sticking up out of them."

Val looked around at the soft light coming from a pewter lamp with a fringed shade. "Then what is it that I'm seeing?"

"Glamour, what else?"

Ruth ducked her head into the room. "What's goi—Luis?"

"Hold on. How can we be sure it's really you, Luis?" Val asked.

"Who else would I be?"

Ruth came most of the way in, her foot still in the glamoured opening, as though she thought it might close at any moment without a wedge. "We just left you in the park and you were sleeping."

Luis let his head fall back. "Yeah, well, the last time I saw Ruth, I was with Lolli and Dave in the park. We'd picked out a place to sleep near the weather castle. Lolli was leaned up against me, dozing off when Dave just got up and walked off. I knew he was upset. Shit, I was freaking out, too. I thought maybe he wanted to be alone.

"But then he didn't come back and I didn't know what to think. I went out looking. I saw him walking back through the Ramble. He wasn't alone, either. At first I thought it was some guy—I don't know, hitting on him—but then I saw the guy had feathers instead of hair. I started toward them and that's when tiny fingers covered my mouth and my good eye, grabbed hold of my arms and my legs. I could hear them snickering as they lifted me up into the air and my brother saying, 'Don't worry. It's just for a little while.' I didn't know what to think. I sure didn't think I'd wind up here."

"Did you see Mabry?" Val asked. "Did she say anything to you?"

"Not much. She was distracted by something that was going down. Someone visited her and she was pissed about it."

"There's something we have to tell you," Val said.

Luis went quiet, his mouth pressed into a thin line. "What?" he asked, and his voice was so quiet that it made Val's heart ache.

"It was Dave that we thought was missing. He's gone. Someone's pretending to be you."

"So you came here looking for Dave?"

"We came here looking for evidence. I think Mabry's behind all the faerie deaths."

Luis scowled. "Wait, so where's my brother? Is he in trouble?"

Val shook her head. "I don't think so. Whatever's pretending to be you seems to be spending all its time screwing Lolli. I don't think that's exactly on the supernatural agenda, but it's definitely on Dave's."

Luis winced, but he said nothing.

"We should hurry," Ruth said, patting Val's head, her fingers threading through the stubble. "Just because this bitch can't tie you up with your own hair doesn't mean we should hang around."

"Right." Val leaned over Luis, looking at the braids that bound him to the floor. She tried to snap them or pull them loose, but they were as hard as if they were made of steel.

"Mabry cut them with scissors," Luis said. "And cut me, too."

"Do you think scissors would slice through the braids?" Ruth asked.

Val nodded. "She has to have a way to sever her own spells. Where do you think they would be?"

"I don't know," Luis said. "They might not even look like scissors."

Val stood up and walked out into the parlor, stopping at the fountain where the flour had dissolved, then walked over to the display cabinet.

"Do you see anything?" Val called.

Ruth pulled out a drawer and dumped the contents onto the floor. "Nothing."

Val looked in the cabinet, noticing the ballerina again, noticing the loops her arms made and the bloody color of the toe shoes. Reaching in, Val picked her up, sticking her fingers through the arm gaps and pushing. The figurine's legs closed and opened, just like scissors.

"Get the harp," Val said. "I'll get Luis."

It wasn't quite dawn when they picked their way back through the Ramble, up through the branching trails to where they'd left Lolli and what had appeared to be Luis. The chords of the harp jangled as they moved, but Ruth muffled it by hugging it tighter to her chest. As Val, Ruth, and Luis approached, they saw that the other Luis was awake.

Lolli's voice was high and trembling. "It's so cold and you're burning up with fever."

The disguised Luis looked at them. His eyes were blackened around the edges and his mouth was dark. His skin was pale as paper and had a sheen of sweat over it that made it appear like plastic. With trembling fingers, he brought a cigarette to his lips. The smoke didn't leave his body.

"Dave," the real Luis said. His voice was even, calm, just like Val's had been after she'd seen her mother with Tom. It was a voice so full of emotion that it sounded like no emotion at all.

Lolli looked at Luis, and then at his twin. "Wha—what's happening?"

"You couldn't tell the difference, could you?" the disguised Luis said to Lolli. His face changed, features subtly shifting to become Dave's. The blackened mouth and eyes remained, as did the sheen on his skin.

Lolli gasped.

He laughed like a maniac, his voice raspy. "You couldn't even tell the difference, but you would never give me a chance."

"You fucking shit." Lolli slapped Dave. She hit him again, blows raining against the hands he threw up to ward her off.

Luis grabbed her arms, but Dave laughed again. "You think you know me? I'm Sketchy Dave? Dave the Coward? Dave the Idiot? Dave who needs his brother's protection? I don't need nothing." He looked Luis in the face. "You're so smart, right? So smart you didn't see any of this coming.

Who's the moron, huh? You got some fancy fucking word for how stupid you are?"

"What have you done?" Luis asked.

"He made a deal with Mabry," Val said. "Didn't you?"

Dave smiled, but it looked like a rictus grin, the skin of his mouth too tight. When he spoke, Val saw only blackness beyond his teeth, as though she were looking into a dark tunnel. "Yeah, I did a deal. I don't need the Sight to know when I have something somebody wants." He wiped his forehead, eyes increasingly wide. "I wanted—"

He collapsed, his body shaking. Luis sank to his knees next to Dave and reached out to smooth his locs back from his face, then abruptly pulled his hand back. "He's way too hot. It's like his skin is on fire."

"Never," Val said. "He's been using Never much more than once a day. He had to take it this whole time to keep that shape."

"In the movies they put people with crazy fevers in a bathtub with ice," Ruth said.

"What, when they OD on faerie drugs?" Lolli snapped.

"Grab him," Val said. "The lake should be cold enough."

Luis slid his hands under his brother's shoulders. "Be careful. His body is really warm."

"Take my gloves." Ruth pulled a pair out of her coat pocket and handed them to Val.

Pulling them on quickly, she grabbed Dave's ankles. Touching his skin was like grabbing the handle of a pot of boiling water. She lifted. He was so light, he might have been hollow.

Together she and Luis hurried down the steps, down the paths of the Ramble to the edge of the water. The heat of Dave's body scorched her skin through the gloves and he twitched and writhed as if he were fighting some unseen force. Val gritted her teeth and held on.

Luis waded into the water and Val followed, the frigid cold at her calves a terrible contrast to the burn of her hands.

"Okay, down," Luis said.

They lowered Dave into the water, his body steaming as it touched the lake. Val let go and started back to the shore, but Luis held on, keeping his brother's head above water, like a preacher performing a terrible baptism.

"Is it helping?" Ruth called.

Luis nodded, rubbing his brother's floating face. Val could see that Luis's hand was bright pink, but whether he was burned or just cold she wasn't sure. "Better, but we have to get him to a hospital."

Lolli waded in, staring down at Dave. "You fucking moron," she shouted. "How could you be so stupid?" She looked suddenly lost. "Why would he do this for me?"

"You can't feel responsible," Val said. "If I were you, I think I'd want to kill him."

"I don't know what to feel," Lolli said.

"Val," said Luis. "We have to go ask Ravus for help."

"Ravus?" Ruth demanded.

"He saved his life before," Luis said.

Val thought of Ravus's face, closed, his eyes dark with fury. She thought of the things she knew about Mabry and the things she just guessed about the currency Dave had used to pay for her help. "I don't know if he'll be willing to now."

"I'll take Dave to the hospital," Lolli said.

"Go with her, okay?" Val asked Ruth. "Please."

"Me?" Ruth looked disbelieving. "I don't even know him."

Val leaned close to her. "But I know you."

Ruth rolled her eyes. "Fine. But you owe me. You owe me like a month of mute servitude."

"I owe you like a year of mute servitude," Val said and waded into the water to help Luis lift his brother's body once more. Slowly they made their way to the street. The first cab they hailed pulled up and then, seeing Dave's body, drove off before Lolli could grab hold of the door. The next one stopped, seemingly indifferent as the two girls got in and Luis draped his writhing brother across their laps.

"Here," Ruth said, handing over the harp.

"We'll take care of him," Lolli said.

"I'll be there as soon as I can." Luis hesitated shutting the door.

The taxi started to move and Val saw Ruth's pale face staring from the back window, her lips mouthing something Val couldn't make out as the car got farther and farther away.

12

And her sweet red lips on these lips of mine
Burned like the ruby fire set
In the swinging lamp of a crimson shrine,
Or the bleeding wounds of the pomegranate,
Or the heart of the lotus drenched and wet
With the spilt-out blood of the rose-red wine.

—Oscar Wilde, "In the Gold Room: A Harmony"

A horse-drawn carriage had stopped beneath the arch of the bridge support. It was a long way from the park or anywhere else that a carriage should be and the dun horse looked restless in the pale, dawn light. There was no driver.

"Do you think someone took a ride to the supermarket?" Val asked.

"That's no horse," Luis said, pulling Val wide of it. His eyes were bloodshot, his lips cracked with cold. "Be glad you can't see what it really is."

It looked like any other city horse, with its big sagging back and fat hooves. Val squinted at it until the image blurred, but she still didn't know what Luis saw and she decided not to ask. "Come on."

Sticking near the opposite wall, she crept beneath the overpass, Luis right behind her. She knocked on the stump, but as they slipped through the doorway, Val heard someone banging down the bridge stairs.

It was too late for them to do anything but gape at Greyan. His hands were covered in blood, blood that dripped off the tips of his fingers and clotted on the dusty steps, too bright to seem real. He held his bronze knives together in one hand. They, too, glistened with gore.

"It is done," the ogre said. He looked tired. "Little humans, let me lesson you to intrude no more in the dealings of the fey."

"Where's Ravus?" Val demanded. "What happened?"

"Would you fight me again, mortal? Your loyalty is commendable, if misplaced. Save your courage for a more worthy foe." He pushed past her and walked down the remaining steps. "I have no lust for dealing more death today."

Everything narrowed to that moment, that word. Death. *Surely not,* Val told herself, touching the cold stone wall for support. For a moment, she didn't think she could walk the rest of the way up the stairs. She couldn't bear it.

Luis walked slowly up the steps, up to the landing, and then back down. He brought his finger to his lips. "She's in there."

Val started moving, too fast, and Luis's hand clamped down on her arm. "Quiet," he hissed.

Val nodded, not daring to ask about Ravus. Together, they inched up the steps, each footfall causing a little puff of dust, the creak of the iron frame, the jangle of the harp strings, things that Val hoped were hidden by the steady rumble of traffic overhead. As they neared the landing, she heard Mabry's voice, full of anxiety. "Where do you keep it? I know you have to have some poison somewhere. Come now, do me one last service."

Val waited to hear Ravus's answer, but he didn't speak.

Luis looked grim.

"You used to be so eager to please," Mabry went on bitterly. Something fell inside the room and Val thought she heard the sharp sound of shattering glass.

Val crept forward, parting the plastic sheeting. Ravus's desk was turned over, his books and papers scattered across the room. The armchair was sliced cleanly across the back, leaking feathers and foam. A few candles flickered from the floor, some encircled with rivulets of wax. The stone of the walls was grooved with deep cuts. Ravus lay stretched out on his back, one hand over his chest as blood rose between his fingers. Dark, wet streaks painted the floor, as though he had crawled across it. Mabry bent over a cabinet, one hand rummaging through the contents, the other holding a dish that contained the red remains of something.

Val crawled closer, heedless of Luis's warning fingers digging into her skin, fear numbing her to anything but the sight of Ravus's body.

"Do you know how long I've waited for you to die?" Mabry asked, her voice almost frantic now. "Finally, I would be free from exile. Free to return to the Bright Court and my work. But now all the pleasure I thought to have from your death is robbed from me.

"Someone has to appear to have murdered all those faeries, so at least you were good for one thing. No one likes loose ends." Mabry selected a vial from the cabinet and took a breath. "This will have to do—my new Lady is impatient and wants things taken care of before Midwinter. Isn't it ironic that after all this time, after all your loyalty, it is I who was chosen to be her agent in the Unseelie Court? I would not have thought the Queen of the Seelie Court would want a double agent of her own. Perhaps I can come to enjoy working for Silarial. After all, she's proven to be as ruthless a mistress as my own dear Lady."

Val parted the plastic sheeting and crawled into the room. Ravus's head was turned toward the wall where Tamson's sword hung, his golden eyes dull and unfocused. There was a deep pit in his chest that his hand half-covered, as though he were pledging something in death. The room reeked of a weird, heavy sweetness that made Val want to gag.

I cross my heart and hope to die.

Val was shaking as she stood, no longer caring about Mabry, about politics or plans or anything except Ravus.

She couldn't look away from the blood that stained the edges of his lips and pinked his teeth. His skin was far too pale, the green of it the only color left.

Mabry spun, the plate in her hand clearly holding the piece of flesh missing from Ravus's chest. His heart. Val felt dizziness threaten to overwhelm her. She wanted to scream, but her throat closed up on the sound.

"Luis," said Mabry, "your brother will be sorry to hear you tired so quickly of my hospitality."

Val half-turned. Luis was standing behind her, a muscle in his jaw trembling.

"And my harp." Mabry's voice held a certain, teasing

pleasure that was at odds with their surroundings, with the broken furnishings and the blood. "Ravus, look what your servants have brought. A little music."

"Why are you talking to him?" Val shouted. "Can't you see he's dead?"

At the sound of her voice, Ravus shifted his head slightly. "Val?" he groaned.

Val jumped, edging back, away from his body. It wasn't possible for him to speak. Hope warred with horror and she felt the gorge rise in her throat.

"Go ahead, Luis," Mabry said. "Play it. I'm sure he would rest easier knowing."

Luis strummed one string and Tamson's voice echoed through the chamber, recounting his tale. In the moment that Tamson said the word "betrayed," the glass sword fell from the wall, cracking deep under the surface, like ice on a lake.

"Tamson," Ravus said softly. His head came up, eyes hard with hate, but his arm was too slippery with blood to support him. He fell back with a groan.

Mabry's lip curled and she stalked over to Ravus. "Oh, to see your face when you stuck your sword through him. Your hair will be the next string in my harp, wailing your pathetic story for all time."

"Get away from him," Val said, picking up the broken leg of a table.

Mabry held up the plate. "Surprising, isn't it, that trolls can live a time without their hearts? He's got perhaps an hour if I don't hurry him along, but I'll dash his heart to the ground if you don't stay out of my way."

Val went still, dropping the table leg.

"Well and good," Mabry said. "I'll leave him in your capable hands."

Her hooves clattered down the steps, gown sweeping after her.

Val dropped to her knees beside Ravus. A long, clawed finger reached up to touch her face. His lips were smeared a dark crimson. "I wished for you to come. I shouldn't have, but I did."

"Tell me what to bring you," Val said. "What herbs to combine."

He shook his head. "This I cannot heal."

"Then I'll go get your heart." Val said, her voice hard. She jumped up, ducking through the plastic and down the stairs. She hit the wall and pushed through the doorway onto the street. The cold air stung her hot face, but both Mabry and the carriage were gone.

Everything had spun madly, dizzily so far out of control that she couldn't stop it. There was no way. No plan.

The only thing she had any power over was herself. She could walk away from here, run away again and again until she was so cold and numb that she felt nothing at all. At least she would be the one making the decision; she would be *in control*. She wouldn't have to watch Ravus die.

There, squatting on the sidewalk, she choked with dry-eyed sobs. It was like being sick when there was nothing left in her stomach. She ground her nails into the wrist of her hand, the pain focusing her mind until she could force herself to walk back up the stairs and not scream.

Luis was kneeling near Ravus, their hands clasped.

"A cord of amaranth," the troll said hoarsely, a red bubble forming at his lip. "The sleep of a child, the scent of summer.

Weave it into a crown for your brother and set it on his head with your own hands."

"I don't know how to get those things," Luis said, his voice breaking.

Val stared at them both, then at the wall and the dusty blinds. "Forgive me," she said.

Ravus turned to her, but she couldn't wait for his answer. She tugged at the cloth, ripping down the curtains, and the room flooded with light. Dust motes danced through the air.

"What are you doing?" Luis screamed.

Val ignored him, rushing to the next window.

Ravus pushed himself up on one elbow. He opened his lips to speak, but his skin had already gone to gray and his mouth froze, slightly parted, words silenced. He became stone, a statue made by the hand of some twisted sculptor, and the smeared blood turned to rubble.

Luis ran to where she was ripping down more drapes. "Are you crazy?"

"We need time to stop Mabry," Val shouted back. "He won't die while he's stone. He won't die until dusk."

Luis nodded slowly. "I thought I could—I didn't think of the sunlight."

"Ravus can weave the crown for Dave himself when he wakes up. That was what you asked him about, wasn't it?" Val picked up Tamson's sword, shining so brightly in the sunlight that she could not look at it directly. She held the hilt between the palms of her two hands. "We'll find Mabry and then we'll save them both."

Luis took a step back from her. "I thought magic swords weren't supposed to break."

Val sat down cross-legged on the floor, letting the sword rest across her knees. The crack was visible underneath the glass, but when she ran her fingers over the surface, it was smooth.

"Mabry said something about being an agent in the Unseelie Court."

"A double agent." Luis spun the ball on his lip ring with his thumb and index finger as he considered. "And she was looking for poison."

"The faeries in the park said Silarial had come to see Mabry. They thought Mabry had some evidence. Maybe they made some kind of deal?"

"A deal for her to poison someone?"

"Okay," Val said. "If Silarial knew Mabry had been responsible for the poisoning of the Seelie exiles, then she really had Mabry over a barrel. She'd have to do whatever Silarial said to save her skin. Even go back to her own court and kill someone."

"My brother poisoned them, didn't he?" Luis asked.

"What?"

"That's what Dave did for Mabry. He poisoned all those faeries so it would look like Ravus was behind their deaths. What she did for Dave was tie me up in her house. That's what you meant when you said Silarial is responsible. You mean she orchestrated it, but someone else did the poisoning."

"I didn't mean that. We don't know that."

Luis said nothing.

"I'm surprised you care," Val said, frustration and fear making her snap. "I didn't think you would think killing faeries was all that big of a deal."

"You thought I was the killer, didn't you?" Luis turned his face away from her.

"Of course I did." Val knew she was being cruel, but the words poured past her lips like they were living things, like they were spiders and worms and beetles eager to get out of her mouth. "All your talk about faeries being dangerous and then, oh look, they're getting killed with rat poison. If you'd ever guessed Dave was the poisoner, what would you have done? Would you have really stopped him?"

"Of course I would have," Luis spat.

"Oh, come on. You hate faeries."

"I'm afraid of them," Luis shouted, then took a deep breath. "My dad had the Sight and it made him crazy. My mom's dead. My brother is catatonic. I'm a one-eyed fucking bum at seventeen. Faerieland must be a nonstop party."

"Well, then, break out the champagne," Val said, walking so close to him that she could feel the heat of his body. She swept her hand around the room. "Another one of them's dead."

"That's not what I meant." Luis turned away from her, the light washing the color from his face. He walked to Ravus's body, reached out a hand to touch the stone, and then pulled back as though he was about to be burned. "I just don't know what we can do."

"Who do you think Silarial wants Mabry to poison? It has to be someone in the Unseelie Court."

"That's what Ravus called the Night Court."

Val walked to the map on the wall of Ravus's room. There, outside New York City, far from the pins marking each of the poisonings, were two black marks, one in Upstate New York, the other in New Jersey. She touched the one in Jersey. "Here."

"But who? This is way over our heads."

"Isn't there a new king there?" Val asked. "Mabry said

something about Midwinter. Could he be the one she's supposed to make dead?"

"Maybe."

"Even if he isn't—it doesn't matter. All we need to know is where she is."

"But the courts aren't places humans are supposed to be, especially the Unseelie Court. Most *faeries* won't even go there."

"We have to go—we have to get Ravus's heart. He's going to die if we don't."

"What are we going to do? Go down there and ask for it?"

"Pretty much," Val said. As she got up, she saw a tiny vial of Never lying beside asphodel and rose hips. She lifted it up.

"What's that for?" Luis asked, although he must have known perfectly well.

Her thoughts strayed to Dave, but even his pallid skin and blackened mouth didn't make her any less hungry for Never. She might need it. She needed it now. One pinch and all this pain would be gone.

But she stuffed it into her pack and fished out the return train tickets she'd bought weeks before, holding them out to Luis. The paper was so worn from riding around in her bag that it felt as soft as cloth between her fingers, but when Luis took his, the ticket sliced shallowly over her flesh. For a moment, her skin seemed so surprised that it forgot to bleed.

13

Immediately after the monsters, die the heroes.
—Roberto Calasso, *The Marriage of Cadmus*
     and Harmony

Val perched in her seat for a few moments, then paced restlessly in the aisle. Each time the conductor passed her, she asked him what the next stop was, were they running late, could they go faster. He said they couldn't. Glancing over at the sword swaddled in a dirty blanket and tied with shoelaces, he hurried on.

Val had had to show the hilt to prove that it was merely decorative when she boarded. It was only glass, after all. She'd explained that she was making a delivery.

Luis spoke softly into Val's cell, his head turned against the window. He'd called all the hospitals he could think of before he thought to call Ruth's phone and now that he'd gotten her, his body had relaxed, his fingers no longer digging into the canvas of Val's backpack, jaw no longer clenched so tight that the muscles in his face jumped.

He clicked off the phone. "You only have a little power left."

Val nodded. "What did she say?"

"Dave is in critical condition. Lolli fucked off. She couldn't handle the hospital, hates the smell or something. They're giving Ruth a hard time because she won't tell them what Dave took, and, of course, they won't let her in to see him, 'cause she's not family."

Val fingered the torn edge of the plastic seat, nostrils flaring as she breathed hard. It was more fury, heaped on what already felt like too much fury to bear. "Maybe you—"

"Nothing I could do." Luis looked out the window. "He's not going to make it, is he?"

"He will," Val said firmly. She could save Ravus. Ravus could save Dave. Like dominoes, set up in winding rows, and the most important thing was that she didn't tip over.

Looking at her own hands, splintered and smudged with dirt, it was hard to imagine that they would be the hands that saved anyone.

Her thoughts settled on the Never in her bag. It promised to sing down her veins, to make her swifter and stronger and finer than she was. She wouldn't be stupid about it. She wouldn't wind up like Dave. Not more than a pinch. Not more than once today. She just needed it now, to keep herself together, to face Mabry, to let all the rage and sorrow be swallowed up into something larger than herself.

Luis settled on the other side of the seat, lying down as much as he could, eyes closed, arms folded across his chest, head pillowed on her backpack and pushed up against the metal lip of the window. He wouldn't know if she slipped into the bathroom.

Val stood, but something caught her eye. The cloth wrapping

had slipped, revealing a little of the glass sword, ethereal in the sunlight. It made her think of icicles hanging from Ravus's mother's hair.

Balance. Like a well-made sword. Perfect balance.

She couldn't trust herself with Never working inside of her, making her alternately formidable or distracted, dreamy or intense. Off balance. Unbalanced. She didn't know how long she could keep herself from taking it, but she could keep putting it off for another moment. And maybe a moment after that. Val bit her lip and resumed her pacing.

Val and Luis got off at the Long Branch station, pushing onto the concrete platform as soon as the doors opened. A few taxis idled nearby, roofs crowned by yellow caps.

"What do we do now?" Luis asked. "Where the hell are we?"

"We're going to my house," Val said. Holding the sword by its hilt, she leaned the wrapped blade against her shoulder and started walking. "We need to borrow a car."

The brick house looked smaller than Val remembered it. The grass was brown and leaf covered, the trees black and bare. Val's mother's red Miata sat in front, parked on the street even though she should have been at work. Balled-up tissues and empty coffee cups littered the dashboard. Val frowned. It wasn't like her mother to be messy.

Val pulled open the screen door, feeling as if she were walking through a dream landscape. Everything was at once familiar and strange. The front door was unlocked, the television off in the living room. Despite the fact that it was past noon, the house was dark.

It was unnerving to be in the same place where she had seen Tom draped over her mother, but weirder still was how small the room seemed. Somehow it had grown in her mind until it was so vast that she couldn't imagine crossing it to get back to her own bedroom.

Val swung the sword off her shoulder and dropped her backpack onto the couch. "Mom?" she called softly. There was no answer.

"Just find the keys," Luis said. "It's easier to get forgiveness than permission."

Val half-turned her head to snap at him, but movement on the stairs stopped her.

"Val," her mother said, rushing down the steps, only to stop at the lower landing. Her eyes were red-rimmed, her face un–made up, and her hair wild. Val felt everything at once: guilt at making her mother so upset, serves-her-right satisfaction that her mother was suffering, and profound exhaustion. She wanted them both to stop feeling so miserable, but she had no idea how to make that happen.

Val's mother walked the last few steps slowly and hugged her hard. Val leaned against her mother's shoulder, smelling soap and faint perfume. Eyes burning with sudden emotion, she pulled away.

"I was so worried. I kept thinking you would come in, just like this, but you didn't. For days and days you didn't." Her mother's voice shrilled and broke.

"I'm here now," Val said.

"Oh, honey." Val's mother reached out hesitantly to stroke her fingers across Val's head. "You're so thin. And your hair—"

Val twisted out from under her hand. "Leave it, Mom. I like my hair."

Her mother blanched. "That's not what I meant. You always look beautiful, Valerie. You just look so different."

"I am different," Val said.

"Val," Luis warned. "The keys."

She scowled at him, took a breath. "I need to borrow the car."

"You've been gone for weeks." Val's mother looked at Luis for the first time. "You can't be leaving again."

"I'll be back tomorrow."

"No." Val's mother's voice had a note of panic in it. "Valerie, I'm so sorry. I'm sorry about everything. You don't know how worried I've been about you, the things that I've been imagining. I kept waiting for the phone call that would say the police had found you dead in a ditch. You can't put me through that again."

"There's something I have to do," Val said. "And I don't have much time. Look, I don't understand about you and Tom. I don't know what you were thinking or how it happened, but—"

"You must think that I—"

"But *I don't care anymore*."

"Then why—" she started.

"This isn't about you, and I can't come home until it's finished. Please."

Her mother sighed. "You failed your driving test."

"Can you drive?" Luis asked.

"I have my permit," Val said to her mother, then glanced at Luis. "I can drive fine. I just can't parallel park."

Val's mother padded into the kitchen and came back with a key and an alarm hanging from a keychain with a rhinestone "R" on it. "I owe you some trust, Valerie, so here it is. Don't make me regret it."

"I won't," Val said.

Val's mother dropped the keys into Val's hand. "You promise you'll be back tomorrow? Promise me."

Val thought of the way her lips had burned when she hadn't kept her promise to return to Ravus on time. She nodded. Luis opened the front door. Val turned toward it, not looking at her mother. "You're still my mom," Val said.

As Val walked down her front steps, she felt the sun on her face, and it seemed that at least one thing might be okay.

Val drove the car through the familiar roads, reminding herself to signal and watch her speed. She hoped that no one would pull them over.

"You know," Luis said, "the last time I was in a car it was my grandma's Bug and we were going to the store for something on a holiday—Thanksgiving, I think. She lived out on Long Island where you need cars to get around. I remember it because my dad had pulled me aside earlier to tell me that he could see goblins in the garden."

Val said nothing. She was concentrating on the road.

She steered the Miata past the pillars that flanked the entrance of the graveyard, the brick of them covered by looping tendrils of leafless vines. The cemetery itself swelled into a hill, dotted with white stones and burial vaults. Despite the fact that it was late November, the grass there was still green.

"Do you see anything?" Val asked. "It just looks like any other cemetery to me."

Luis didn't answer at first. He stared out the window, one hand unconsciously coming up to touch the clouding glass. "That's because you're blind."

Val stepped on the break, stopping them short. "What do you see?"

"They're everywhere." Luis put his hand on the door handle, his voice little more than breath.

"Luis?" Val turned off the car.

His voice sounded distant, as if he were speaking to himself. "God, look at them. Leathery wings. Black eyes. Long, clawed fingers." Then he looked over at Val, like he'd suddenly remembered her. "Get down!"

She lunged over, throwing her head into his lap, feeling the warmth of his arms coming down on her as air whipped over the top of the car.

"What's happening?" Val shouted over the keening of the wind. Something scratched at the leather roof of the car and the hood shook.

Then the air stilled, dropping away to nothing. As Val slowly lifted her head, it seemed to her that not even a leaf moved with a breeze. The whole graveyard had gone quiet.

"This whole car is fiberglass." Luis looked up. "They could claw right through the roof if they wanted to."

"Why don't they?"

"I'm guessing they're waiting to see if we're here to dump some flowers on a grave."

"They don't need to do that. We're coming out." Leaning into the backseat, Val unwrapped the glass sword. Luis grabbed Val's backpack and slung it over his shoulder.

Val closed her eyes and took a deep breath. Her stomach churned, the way it did before a lacrosse game, but this was different. Her body felt distant, mechanical. Her senses narrowed to notice every sound, each shift in color and shape, but little else. Adrenaline called to her blood, chilling her fingers, speeding her heart.

Looking down at the sword, Val opened the door and stepped out onto the gravel. "I come in peace," she said. "Take me to your leader."

Invisible fingers closed on her skin, pinching the flesh, tearing at her hair, pushing and pulling her into the hill, where clumps of grass rose up and scampered away from the black dirt. She tried to scream as she fell forward, facedown in the earth, breathing the rich mineral smell as she choked on her shriek. Her arms pushed against the soil as she tried to lever herself up, but the dirt and rock and grass gave beneath her and she tumbled down into the root-wrapped darkness.

Val awoke in golden chains in a hall filled with faeries.

On a dais of dirt, a white-haired knight sat on a throne of braided birch, its bark as pale as bone. He leaned forward and beckoned to a green-skinned, winged girl who regarded Val with black, alien eyes. The winged faerie leaned down and spoke softly to the knight on the throne. His lips twisted into what might have been a smile.

Above her was the underside of the hill, hollow as a bowl, and hung with long roots that grasped and turned as though they were fingers that couldn't quite reach what they desired.

All around Val a bevy of creatures whispered and winked and wondered at her. Some were tall and thin as sticks, others tiny creatures that flitted through the air like Needlenix had. Some had horns that twisted back from their brows like vines, some tossed back mottled green manes as thick as thread on a spool, and a few tripped along on strange and unlikely feet. Val flinched back from one girl with powdery wings and fingers that deepened in color from moonstone white to blue at the tips. There was no place she could look and see anything familiar. She was all the way down the rabbit hole now, right at the very bottom.

A shrunken man with long golden hair went down on one knee in front of the creature on the throne and then rose as nimbly as if he were a boy. He looked slyly in Val's direction. "They found the entrance as easily as if they were directed, but who would direct a pair of humans? A conundrum for your pleasure and delight, my Lord Roiben."

"As you say." Roiben nodded to him and the faerie man stepped back.

"I can address this mystery," a familiar voice said.

Val rolled onto her back, banging up against Luis's body, and twisting her head toward the speaker. Luis grunted. Mabry stepped over them, the hem of her ruddy gown brushing Val's cheek. She held out a sculpted silver box and sank into a shallow curtsy. "I have what they seek."

Roiben raised a single white brow. "The Court of Termites is not pleased to have sunlight make merry and dance in our halls, even if it is only for a moment's admission of prisoners."

Luis rolled on his side and Val could see that he was chained like she was, but that his face was bloody. Each of his steel piercings had been cut from his flesh.

Mabry cast her eyes down, but she didn't look very abashed. "Allow me to settle both the light and its bringers."

"You fucking bitch—" Val started, but was interrupted by a cuff on the shoulder.

"He asks you nothing," the golden-haired faerie spat. "Say nothing."

"No," said the Lord of the Night Court. "Let them speak. It is so rare that we guest mortals. I can think of the last time, but then, it was nothing if not memorable." Some of the assembled throng tittered at that, although Val wasn't sure why. "The boy has true Sight, if I'm not mistaken. One of us put out your eye, yes?"

Luis looked around the room, fear etched in his face. He licked blood from his lip and nodded.

"I wonder what you see when you look at me," Roiben said. "But come, tell us what it is you came for. Is it truly in Mabry's possession?"

"She cut out the heart of my—" Val said. "Out of one of the Folk—a troll. I've come to get it back."

Mabry laughed at that, a deep, sensual laugh. Some of the throng laughed, too. "Ravus is long dead by now, rotting in his chambers. Surely you know that. What good is his heart to you?"

"Dead or not," Val said. "I have come for his heart and I will have it."

A wry smile touched Roiben's mouth and Val felt dread creep over her. He looked at Val and Luis with pale eyes. "What you ask is not mine to give, but perhaps my servant will be generous."

"I think not," said Mabry. "If you consume the heart of

the thing, you consume some of its power. I will relish Ravus's heart." She looked down at first Luis and then Val. "And I will savor it all the more knowing you wanted it."

Val shifted up onto her knees and then stood, wrists still bound behind her back. Blood beat in her ears, so loud it nearly drowned out any other sound. "Fight me for it. I'll wager his heart against mine."

"Mortal hearts are weak. What need have I for such a heart?"

Val took a step toward her. "If I'm so weak, then you must be a real fucking coward not to fight me." She turned to the faeries, to the cat-eyed, those with skin of green and gold, those with bodies stretched too long or too squat or all manner of unnatural proportions. "I'm just a human, aren't I? I'm nothing. Gone in one sigh from one of your mouths, that's what Ravus said. So if you are afraid of me, then you are less than that."

Mabry's eyes glittered dangerously, but her face remained placid. "You have great daring to speak so, here, in my own court, at the steps of my new Lord."

"I dare," Val said. "As much as you dare to act all high and mighty when you're just here to murder him like you murdered Ravus."

Mabry laughed, short and sharp, but there was muttering from some of the assembled Folk.

"Let me guess," Roiben said lazily. "I shouldn't listen to the mortal for one more moment."

Mabry opened her mouth and then closed it again.

"Accept her challenge," said Roiben. "I will not have it said that one of my court could not best a human child. Nor shall I have it said my murderer was a coward."

"As you wish," said Mabry, turning to Val abruptly. "After I'm done with you, I will put out Luis's other eye and make a new harp from both your bones."

"String me in your harp," Val hissed. "And I'll curse you every time you pluck it."

Roiben stood. "Do you agree to the terms of her challenge?" he queried, and Val suspected that he was giving her a chance to do something, but she didn't know what.

"No," Val said. "I can't bargain for Luis. He's got nothing to do with my challenge."

"I can bargain for myself," Luis said. "I agree to Mabry's terms provided she put up something for them. She can have me, but if Val wins, then we go free. We get to walk out of here."

Val glanced at Luis, grateful for his perception and amazed by her own stupidity.

Roiben nodded. "Very well. If the mortal wins, I will give her and her companion safe passage through my lands. And since you have not decided the terms of your combat, I will choose them—you will fight until first blood." He sighed. "Do not think there is any pity in that. Living, should Mabry win your hearts and bones, does not seem so preferable to being safely dead. I, however, have some questions for Mabry that I need her alive to answer. Now, Thistledown, unclasp the mortals and give the girl her arms."

The golden-haired man slid a jagged-toothed key in the locks and the manacles sprang open, dropping to the ground with a hollow sound that echoed through the dome.

Luis stood a moment later, rubbing his wrists.

A woman with chin hair so long that it was woven into tiny

braids brought the glass sword to Val and went halfway down on one knee, raising the blade in her palms. Tamson's sword. Val glanced at Mabry, but if she had any reaction to the sight of it, if she even remembered to whom it had once belonged, she gave no sign.

"You can do it," Luis said. "What does she know about fighting? She's no knight. Just don't let her distract you with glamour."

Glamour. Val looked at her backpack, the strap still draped over Luis's shoulder. There was nearly a bottle full of Never there. If glamour was Mabry's weapon, then Val could fight her on those terms. "Give me the bag," Val said.

Luis slid it down his arm and handed it to her.

Val reached in and touched the bottle. Digging down past it, her hand closed on a lighter. It would just take a moment and then Val would be flooded with power.

As she turned, she saw her face reflected in the glass of the blade, saw her own bloodshot eyes and grime-streaked skin before the roving lights under the hill shot the sword through with sudden radiance. Val thought of the girl, Nancy, hit by a train because she was so full of Never that she hadn't seen the gleaming of headlights or heard the scream of brakes. What might Val miss while she was weaving her own illusions? She felt the weight of the knowledge hit her gut like a swallowed stone; she had to do this without any Never singing under her skin.

Val had to fight Mabry with what she knew—years of lacrosse and weeks of the sword, fistfights with neighbor kids, who never said she hit like a girl, the ache of pushing her body past what she thought she could endure. Val couldn't fight fire with fire, but she could fight it with ice.

She dropped the lighter and lifted the glass sword from the girl's hands.

I can't fall, she reminded herself, thinking of Ravus and Dave and dominoes all together in neat little rows. *I can't fall and I can't fail.*

The court gentry had cleared away a square path in the middle of the court and Val stepped into it, shrugging off her coat. It puddled on the floor, the cool air prickled the hairs on her arms. She took a deep breath and smelled her own sweat.

Mabry stepped out of the crowd, clad in mist that congealed into the shape of armor. In her hand she held a whip of smoke. The tip dragged tendrils behind it that reminded Val of the way that sparklers burned.

Val took a step forward, parting her legs slightly and keeping her knees slightly bent. She thought of the lacrosse field, of the tight-but-loose way to hold the stick. She thought of Ravus's hands, pushing her body into the right formation. Val longed for Never, scorching her from the inside, filling her with fire, but she gritted her teeth and prepared to begin.

Mabry stalked toward the center of the square. Val wanted to ask if they should start now, but Mabry sent her whip whirling and there was no more time for questions. Val parried, trying to slice the whip in half, but it became insubstantial as fog and the blade passed right through.

Mabry shot the whip out again. Val blocked, feigned, and thrust, but her reach was too short. She barely staggered out of the way of another blow.

Mabry twirled the whip above her head as if it were a lasso. She smiled at the crowd and the throng of faeries howled. Val wasn't sure if they were showing favor or just crying for blood.

The whip flew out, snaking toward Val. She ducked and rushed in under Mabry's guard, trying one of those fancy moves that looked great if you could manage them. She missed entirely.

Two more parries and Val was tiring fast. She'd been awake for two days and her last meal was a pale faerie apple. Mabry beat her back, so that the court had to part for Val's stumbling retreat.

"Did you think you were a hero?" Mabry asked, her voice full of mock pity, pitched loud enough for the crowd.

"No," Val said. "I think you're a villain."

Val bit her lip and concentrated. Mabry's shoulders and wrists weren't moving with the refined control it would take to make the strikes that lanced out at Val. It was her mind that was doing the work. The whip was an illusion. How could Val win, when Mabry could think the whip into changing direction or snaking farther than its length?

Val swung up her sword to block another strike and the misty cord wrapped around the length of the blade. A hard tug jerked it out of Val's hands. The sword flew across the hall, forcing several courtiers to shriek and fall back. As the blade hit the hard-packed earthen floor, it cracked into three pieces.

The whip reached for Val again, flicking out to strike her face. Val ducked and ran toward the remains of the sword, whip whirring just behind her.

"Don't let it bother you that you're about to die," Mabry said with a laugh that invited the other faeries to laugh with her. "Your life was always destined to be so short as to make no difference."

"Shut up!" Val had to concentrate, but she was disoriented,

panicked. She was fighting all wrong; she was fighting as if she wanted to kill Mabry, but all she had to do to win was hit her once and all she had to do to lose was to get hit.

Mabry was vain; that much was obvious. She looked cool and she fought cool. Even though she was leaning heavily on her glamour, she was doing it in such a way that made her seem like the better combatant. If she could make the whip grab the blade of the sword, couldn't she just have made it strike Val's hand? Couldn't she conjure knives at Val's neck?

She must want a dramatic triumph. A small scar on Val's cheek. A long laceration across her back. The cord wrapping around Val's neck. It was a performance, after all. The performance of a master performer before a court about to pass judgment on her.

Val stopped, standing just a foot from the hilt of the glass sword, the tang unmarred and part of the blade still attached. She turned.

Mabry was striding toward her, lips curling back into a smile.

Val had to do something unexpected, so she did. She continued just to stand there.

Mabry hesitated only a moment before she sent the smoke whip slashing toward Val. Val dropped to the ground, rolled and grabbed the hilt of what was left of the glass sword, thrusting it up, inelegantly, gracelessly, and completely uncoolly into Mabry's knee.

"Hold," cried the golden-haired faerie.

Val dropped the hilt, smeared with just a little blood. It was enough. Her hands started to shake.

Mabry's smoke armor and arms faded away and she was

in her gown again. "It matters little," she said. "Your gory memento will rot as your love rots. You will find a corpse no fit companion."

Val couldn't help the smile that spread on her face, a smile so wide it hurt. "Ravus isn't dead," she said, enjoying the blank look that came over Mabry's features. "I pulled down all the curtains and turned him to stone. He's going to be *fine.*"

"You couldn't—" Mabry reached out her hand and smoke coalesced into a scimitar. She swept it jaggedly forward. Val stumbled back, turning her head away from the strike. The blade grazed her cheek, tracing a burning line across the skin.

"I said hold," the golden-haired faerie shouted, lifting up the silver box.

"Stop," said the King of the Unseelie Court. "Thrice you have displeased me, Mabry, spy or not. Because of your carelessness, mortals have let daylight into the Night Court. Because of your lack of valor, a mortal won a boon from us. And because of your pettiness, my promise that the mortals would not be harmed in my lands is dishonored. Henceforth, you are banished."

Mabry shrieked, an inhuman noise that sounded like rushing wind. "You dare banish me? I, Lady Nicnevin's trusted spy in the Seelie Court? I, who am a true servant of the Unseelie Court and not a pretender to its throne?" Her fingers became knives and her face pulled unnaturally long and monstrous. She lunged at Roiben.

Val's body moved automatically, the moves she had practiced a hundred, hundred times in the dusty bridge as unconscious as a smile. She knocked aside Mabry's strike and stabbed her in the neck.

Blood spilled down her red dress, spattering Val. The knife fingers clutched Val, opening long wounds in her back as Mabry drew her close, pushing them together like lovers. Val screamed, pain throbbing, cold shock creeping up to paralyze her. Then abruptly, Mabry fell, blood blackening the earthen floor, hands slipping down Val's back. She did not move again.

A wave of noise came from the gentry. Luis rushed forward, pushing aside the faeries in his way to grab Val as she swayed forward.

All Val saw was the glass sword, shattered into jagged pieces, and covered with blood. "Don't fall," she reminded herself, but the words didn't seem to be in context any longer. Her vision swam.

"Give me the heart!" Luis shouted, but in the chaos, no one heeded him.

"Enough," someone—probably Roiben—said. Val couldn't concentrate. Luis was speaking and then they were moving, pushing through the blur of bodies. Val stumbled along, Luis holding her up, as they turned through corridors underground. The noise of the court faded away as they made their way out onto the cold hill.

"My coat," Val mumbled, but Luis didn't stop. He steered her into the car and leaned her against it as he pushed back the passenger seat. "Get in and lie down on your stomach. You're going into shock."

There was something about a box. A box with a heart inside, just like in *Snow White*. "Did you get it from the woodsman?" Val asked. "He tricked the evil queen. Maybe he tricked us, too."

Luis took a ragged breath and let it out in a rush. "I'm taking you to the hospital."

That cut through her haze enough to fill her with panic. "No! Ravus and Dave are waiting for us. We have to go play dominoes."

"You're scaring the shit out of me, Val," Luis said. "Come on, lie down and we'll go to the city. But don't you go to sleep on me. You stay the fuck awake."

Val climbed into the car, pressing her face into the leather of the seat. She felt Luis's coat settle over her and she flinched. Her back felt as if it was on fire.

"I did it," she whispered to herself as Luis turned the key in the ignition and pulled out onto the street. "I finished the level."

14

*All human beings should try and learn before they
die what they are running from, and to, and why.*
—James Thurber

They arrived in the city as the sun dropped behind them.
The drive had been slow. Congested traffic and long lines
at the tolls had made the trip stretch longer and Val shifted constantly in the backseat. The icy air from windows Luis refused
to close froze her and the pain when the upholstery touched
her back made it impossible to turn over.

"You still okay back there?" Luis called.

"I'm awake," Val said, kneeling up and holding on to the
passenger side headrest, ignoring how light-headed she felt
once she was upright. The silver box sat in the center of the
front seat, the dim outside lights highlighting the sculptural
wreath of brambles that surrounded a single rose on the surface. "It's already dark."

"We can't go any faster. Traffic is crazy, even in this
direction."

She looked at Luis and it felt as if she were seeing him for the first time. His face was bleeding and his braids were loose, hairs frizzing out in a nimbus around his head, but his expression was calm, even kind.

"We'll get there in time," she said, trying to sound brave and sure.

"I know we will," Luis replied, and Val was glad of the human comfort of lies as they continued to weave through traffic.

They pulled up half on the sidewalk of the underpass. Luis turned off the car and jumped out, pushing down the seat so Val could get out too. She grabbed the box and slid from the car as Luis pounded on the wooden tree stump.

Val ran up the stairs, holding the box to her chest. She was already crying as she walked into the dark room.

Ravus lay in the middle of the floor, no longer stone, his skin as pale as marble. Val sank to her knees beside him, opening the silver box and taking out her gory treasure. It was cold and slippery in her fingers as she placed it into the wet, gaping wound in his chest. The blood on the floor had dried in black streaks that flaked where she'd stepped and her stomach churned at the sight of it.

She looked up at Luis and he must have seen something in her face, because he kicked over a stack of books, setting dust swirling through the air. Neither of them said anything as the moments slid by, each one meaningless now that they were too late.

Her tears dried on her cheeks and no more came. She thought that she should scream or sob, but neither of those things seemed to express the growing emptiness inside of her.

Val leaned down, letting her fingers slide through Ravus's soft hair, pushing stray locks back from his face. He must have woken when he turned back from stone, woken to an empty chamber and terrible pain. Had he called out for her? Cursed her when he realized that she'd left him to die alone?

Bending low and ignoring the smell of blood, she pressed her mouth to his. His lips were soft and not as cold as she feared.

He coughed and she pulled back, falling into a sitting position. Skin was growing over his chest and his heart was beating in a steady staccato.

"Ravus?" Val whispered.

He opened his golden eyes.

"I hurt everywhere." He laughed and then started to choke. "I can only surmise that's good."

Val nodded, the muscles of her face hurting as they tried to smile.

Luis crossed the room to kneel down on Ravus's other side.

Ravus looked up at him and then back to Val. "You both . . . you both saved me?"

"Come on," said Luis. "You make it sound like it was hard for Val to go to the Unseelie Court, strike a deal with Roiben, challenge Mabry to a duel, win back your heart, and then get back here during rush hour."

Val laughed, but her laugh sounded too loud and too brittle, even to her own ears. Ravus's gaze settled on Val and she wondered if he hated that it was she who'd saved him, if he felt that he would now be indebted to someone who disgusted him.

Ravus groaned and started to sit up, but his strength

seemed to fail him and he fell back. "I am a fool," he said.

"Stay where you are." Val scuttled over to a blanket and pushed it under Ravus's head. "Rest."

"I'll be all right," he said.

"Really?" Val asked.

"Really." He reached up to squeeze her shoulder, but she flinched as his fingers grazed over the cuts on her back. His eyes held hers for a long moment, then he pulled a wad of the material of her shirt up. Even out of the corner of her eye, she could see it was stiff with blood. "Turn around."

She did, kneeling up and lifting the back of her T-shirt over her head. She held that pose for a moment, then dropped her shirt back to cover her. "Is it bad?'

"Luis," Ravus said, his voice sharp. "Bring me some things from the table."

Luis collected the ingredients and set them on the floor beside Ravus. First Ravus showed Luis how to salve and treat Val's back, then how to doctor his own ripped piercings, and finally he wove together amaranth, crusts of salt, and long stalks of green grass. He handed them to Luis. "Tie that into the shape of a crown and place it on David's brow. I only hope it will be enough."

"Take the car," Val said. "Come back for me when you can."

"Right," Luis nodded, moving to stand. "I'll bring Ruth."

Ravus touched Luis's arm and he paused. "I was thinking about what was said and unsaid. If rumors from either court implicate your brother, he will be in great danger."

Luis stood up, gazing out the windows at the glittering city. "I'll just have to think of something. I'll make some kind of bargain. I've protected my brother so far; I'll keep protecting him." He looked at Ravus. "Will you tell anyone?"

"You have my silence," Ravus said.

"I'll try to make sure I deserve it." Luis shook his head as he walked through the plastic curtain.

Val watched him go. "What do you think will happen to Dave?" she asked, her voice low.

"I don't know," Ravus said equally quietly. "But I confess that I care much more about what will happen to Luis." He turned to her. "And you. You know, you look terrible."

She smiled, but her smile faded a moment later. "I am terrible."

"I know that I have behaved badly toward you." He looked to one side, at the planks of the floor and his own dried blood, and Val thought how strange it was that sometimes he seemed ages and ages older than she, but at other times, he didn't seem any older at all. "What Mabry told me hurt more than I expected. It was easy for me to believe that your kisses were false."

"You didn't think I really liked you?" Val asked, surprised. "Do you think I really like you now?"

He turned toward her, uncertainty in his face. "You did go to quite a lot of effort to be having this conversation, but . . . I don't want to read too much of what I hope into that."

Val stretched out beside him, resting her head in the crook of his arm. "What do you hope?"

He pulled her close, hands careful not to touch her wounds as they wrapped around her. "I hope that you feel for me as I do for you," he said, his voice like a sigh against her throat.

"And how is that?" she asked, her lips so close to his jaw that she could taste the salt of his skin when she moved them.

"You carried my heart in your hands tonight," he said. "But I have felt as if you carried it long before that."

She smiled and let her eyes drift closed. They lay there together, under the bridge, city lights burning outside the windows like a sky full of falling stars, as they slid off into sleep.

A note arrived in the beak of a black bird with wings that glistened purple and blue, as though it were made of pooling oil. It danced on Val's windowsill, tapping at the glass with its feet, eyes shining like bits of wet onyx in the fading light.

"That's pretty weird," Ruth said. She got up from where she was stretched out on her stomach, library books scattered around her. They had been working on a report they were calling "The Role of Postpartum Depression in Infanticide" for health class extra credit, considering how badly they'd flunked the flour-baby project.

It had been weird to walk through the halls again after being gone for almost a month, the soft fabric of her T-shirt brushing against the scabbed-over cuts along her back, the clean smell of shampoo and detergent in her nose, the promise of pizza and chocolate milk lunches. When Tom passed her, she had barely even noticed him. She'd been too busy rushing around, kissing ass, getting makeup work, and promising never to miss another day of school ever again.

Val went to the window and pushed it open. The bird dropped its scrolled paper onto the rug and flew off, cawing. "Ravus has been sending me notes."

"Noootes?" Ruth asked, her voice threatening to assume

the most obscene thing unless she was given details.

Val rolled her eyes. "About Dave—he's supposed to get out of the hospital next week. And Luis moved into Mabry's old place. He says that even though it's a dump, it's a dump on the Upper West Side."

"Any word on Lolli?"

Val shook her head. "Nothing. No one's seen her."

"Is that all he's writing about?"

Val kicked some loose papers in Ruth's direction. "And that he misses me."

Ruth rolled onto her back, snickering gleefully. "Well, what does this one say? Come on, read it out loud."

"Fine, fine, I'm working on it." Val unrolled the paper. "It says, 'Please meet me tonight at the swing set behind your school. I have something to give you.'"

"How does he know that there's a swing set at school?" Ruth sat up, clearly puzzled.

Val shrugged. "Maybe the crow told him."

"What do you think he's going to give you?" Ruth asked. "A little hot troll action?"

"You are so disgusting. So, so, so vile." Val shrieked, throwing more papers at her, scattering their work completely. Then, she grinned. "Well, no matter what it is, I'm not introducing him to my mom."

It was Ruth's turn to shriek in horror.

That night, on her way out the door, she passed her mom, sitting in front of the television, where a woman's lip was being injected with collagen.

For a moment, the sight of the needle made Val's muscles clench, her nose scent for the familiar burning sugar smell, and her veins twist like worms in her arms, but it was accompanied by a visceral disgust just as strong as the craving.

"I'm going for a walk," she said. "I'll be back later."

Val's mother turned, her face full of panic.

"It's just a walk," Val said, but that didn't settle the unasked and unanswered questions that lay between them. Her mother seemed to want to pretend the last month hadn't happened. She referred to it only vaguely, saying, "When you were away," or "When you weren't here." Behind those words seemed to be vast, black oceans of fear, and Val didn't know how to navigate them.

"Don't be too late," her mother said faintly.

The first snow had fallen, encasing the branches in sleeves of ice and turning the sky bright as day. Val picked her way to the school playground as flurries started up again.

Ravus was there, a black shape sitting on a swing that was too small for him, hunching forward to avoid the chains. He wore a glamour that made his teeth less prominent, his skin less green, but mostly he just looked like himself in a long, black coat, gloved hands holding a gleaming sword across his lap.

Val walked closer, sticking her hands in her pockets, finding herself suddenly shy. "Hey."

"I thought you should have one of your own," Ravus said.

Val reached out and ran a finger down the dull metal. It was thin, the crossguard in the shape of braided ivy and the hilt unwrapped by leather or cloth.

"It's beautiful," Val said.

"It's iron," he said. "Crafted by human hands. No faerie will ever be able to use it against you. Not even me."

Val took the blade and sat in the swing beside his, letting her feet drag through the snow, making it into muddy slush. "That's some present."

He smiled, seemingly pleased.

"I hope you'll keep teaching me how to use it."

His smile widened. "Of course I will. You have only to tell me when."

"I was looking at NYU—Ruth likes their film department and they have a fencing team. I know that's a different thing than the kind of fighting you've been teaching me, but I don't know, I was thinking it might not be completely different. And there's always lacrosse."

"You would come to New York?"

"Sure." Val looked back at her slushy feet. "I have some school to finish. I got all your messages." She could feel that her cheeks were hot and blamed the cold. "I was wondering if there was a way to send something back to you."

"Do you mind birds?"

"No. The crow you sent was beautiful, although I don't think he liked me."

"I will have my next messenger await your response."

Just a short time ago, she might have been that messenger. "Have you heard anything about Mabry? What is everyone saying?"

"Rumors from the courts hold that Mabry was some kind of double agent, but each court denies her. The exiles in the city know she was the poisoner—the Bright Court appears to be claiming that she was killing at the behest of the Night

Court—but so far she has not been linked with Dave. Regrettably, I fear time will reveal his involvement."

"And then?"

"We Folk are a fickle, capricious people. Whim will decide his fate, not some mortal idea of justice."

"So are you going to return to the Bright Court? I mean, now that you know the truth about Tamson there's no reason to stay exiled."

Ravus shook his head. "There is nothing for me there. Silarial counts deaths too lightly." He reached out a gloved hand and stilled her swing. "I would remain nearer you for what time there is."

"Gone in one faerie sigh," she quoted.

Leather-clad fingers brushed over her short hair, rested on her cheek. "I can hold my breath."

IRONSIDE

To my parents, Rick and Judy,
for not sticking a hot poker down my throat
or otherwise attempting to trade me back to the faeries

PROLOGUE

Through the mosses bare,
They have planted thorn-trees
For pleasure here and there.
If any man so daring
As dig them up in spite,
He shall find their sharpest thorns
In his bed at night.

—WILLIAM ALLINGHAM, "THE FAIRIES"

Despite her casting him down to this place, despite the fresh bruises on his skin and the blood under his nails, Roiben still loved Lady Silarial. Despite the hungry eyes of the Unseelie Court and the gruesome tasks its Queen Nicnevin set him. Despite the many ways he'd been humiliated and the things he wouldn't let himself think on while he stood stiffly behind her throne.

If he concentrated hard, he could remember the flame of *his* Queen's copper hair, her unreadable green eyes, the strange smile she'd given him as she'd pronounced his fate just three months past. Choosing him to leave her Bright Court and be a servant among the Unseelie was an honor, he told himself once more. He alone loved her enough to remain loyal. She trusted him above her other subjects. Only his love was true enough to endure.

And he did love her still, he reminded himself.

"Roiben," said the Unseelie Queen. She had been eating her dinner off the back of a wood hob, his green hair long enough to serve as a tablecloth. Now she looked up at Roiben with a dangerous sort of smile.

"Yes, my Lady," he said automatically, neutrally. He tried to hide how much he loathed her, not because it would displease her. Rather, he thought it would please her too well.

"The table trembles too much. I am afraid my wine will spill."

The hollow hill was almost empty; what courtiers remained to amuse themselves beneath garlands of hairy roots did so quietly as the Queen took her supper. Only her servants were close by, all of them grim as ghosts. Her chamberlain cleared his throat.

Roiben stared at her dumbly.

"Fix it," she commanded.

He took a step forward, unsure of what she wanted him to do. The hob's wizened face looked up at him, pale with terror. Roiben tried to smile reassuringly, but that seemed to only make the little man tremble further. He wondered if binding would make the hob steadier, and then was disgusted with himself for the thought.

"Chop his feet so they're even with his hands," a voice called, and Roiben looked up. Another knight, hair dark as his coat, strode toward Nicnevin's throne. A dull circlet sat on his brow. He smirked broadly. Roiben had seen him only once before. He was the knight that the Unseelie Court had sent up to the Seelie as their symbol of peace. Roiben's twin in servitude, although he could only suppose this knight's thralldom was easier than Roiben's own. At the sight of him Roiben's heart leaped with an impossible hope. Could the exchange be done with? Was it possible he would be sent home at last?

"Nephamael," the Queen said, "has Silarial tired of you so quickly?"

He snorted. "She sends me as a messenger, but the message is of little consequence. I rather think she doesn't like me, but you seem better pleased with the trade."

"I could not stand to part with my new knight," Nicnevin said, and Roiben bowed his head. "Will you do what Nephamael suggests?"

Roiben took a deep breath, struggling for a calm he didn't feel. Every time he spoke, he was half afraid he would snap and say what he really thought. "I doubt his plan's efficacy. Let me take the hob's place. I will not spill your wine, Lady."

Her smile widened with delight. She turned to Nephamael. "He asks so prettily, doesn't he?"

Nephamael nodded, although he looked less amused than she had. His yellow eyes seemed to take Roiben's measure for the first time. "And no concern for dignity. You must find that refreshing."

She laughed at that, a laugh that seemed startled from her throat and as cold as ice breaking over a deep lake. Somewhere in the vast, dim cavern, a harp began to play. Roiben shuddered to think what it might be strung with.

"Be my table, then, Roiben. See to it that you do not

tremble. The hob will suffer for any failing on your part."

Roiben took the place of the little faerie easily, barely counting it as a humiliation to get down on his hands and knees, to
bow his head and let the silver plates and warm dishes be set
gingerly on his back. He did not flinch. He remained still, even
as Nephamael seated himself on the floor beside the throne,
resting yet another goblet on the curve of his spine. The man's
hand rested on his ass, and Roiben bit his lip to avoid flinching
in surprise. The stench of iron was overwhelming. He wondered how Nicnevin could bear it.

"I've grown bored," Nephamael said. "Although the Seelie
Court is lovely, certainly."

"And there is nothing to amuse you there? I find that hard
to believe."

"There are things." Roiben thought he could feel the smile
in those words. The hand slid across the hollow of his back. He
stiffened before he could help himself, and heard the goblets
tinkle together with his movement. "But my delight is in finding weakness."

Nicnevin didn't so much as reprimand Roiben. He doubted
it was out of any generosity on her part.

"Somehow," she said, "I wonder if you are speaking to me
at all."

"It is you I am speaking to," Nephamael said. "But not you
I am speaking about. Your weaknesses are not for me to know."

"A charming, ingratiating answer."

"But take your knight here. Roiben. I know his vulnerability."

"Do you? I would think that would be rather obvious. His
love of the solitary fey has him on his knees even now."

Roiben steeled himself not to move. That the Queen of

Filth spoke about him as though he were an animal didn't surprise him, but he found that he was more afraid of what Nephamael might say. There was something hungry in the way that Nephamael spoke, a hunger Roiben wasn't sure what might sate.

"He loves Silarial. He declared himself to her. And the quest she gave him was this—to be your servant in exchange for peace."

The Queen of the Unseelie Court said nothing. He felt a goblet lifted from his back and then replaced.

"It is delightfully cruel, really. Here he is, being loyal and brave for a woman who used him poorly. She never loved him. She's forgotten him already."

"That's not true," Roiben said, turning, so that silver dishes crashed around him. He leaped to his feet, uncaring of the gaping courtiers, the spilled wine, the hob's frightened cry. He didn't care about anything right then but hurting Nephamael, who'd stolen his place—his home—and dared gloat over it.

"Stop!" Nicnevin called. "I command you, Roiben, by the power of your promise to cease moving."

Against his will, he froze like a mannequin, breathing hard. Nephamael had twisted out of his way, but the half smirk Roiben expected to find on his face was missing.

"Kill the hob," the Unseelie Queen commanded. "You, my knight, will drink his blood like wine, and this time you will not spill a drop."

Roiben tried to open his mouth to say something to stay her hand, but the command forbade even that movement. He had been stupid—Nephamael had been goading him in the hope of just such a mistake. Even the Queen's lack of rebuke earlier had probably been planned. Now he had made a spectacular fool of himself and cost an innocent creature its life. Self-loathing gnawed at his belly.

Never again, he told himself. No matter what they said or did or made him do, he would not react. He would become as indifferent as stone.

The grim servants were quick and efficient. Within moments they had prepared a warm goblet and raised it to his unmoving lips. The corpse was already being cleared away, open eyes staring at Roiben from beyond death, damning him for his vanity.

Roiben could not stop himself from opening his mouth and gulping the warm, salty liquid. A moment later, he gagged and retched on the dais.

The flavor of that blood stayed with him through the long years of his service. Even when a pixie accidentally set him free, even when he'd won the Unseelie crown. But by then he could no longer remember whose blood it was, only that he had grown used to the taste.

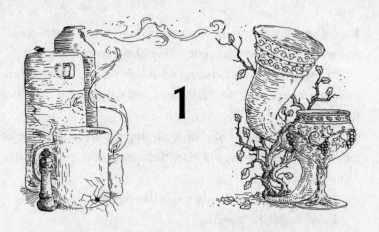

1

I prefer winter and fall, when you feel the bone structure in the landscape—the loneliness of it—the dead feeling of winter. Something waits beneath it— the whole story doesn't show.
—ANDREW WYETH

Human girls cry when they're sad and laugh when they're happy. They have a single fixed shape rather than shifting with their whims like windblown smoke. They have their very own parents, whom they love. They don't go around stealing other girls' mothers. At least that's what Kaye thought human girls were like. She wouldn't really know. After all, she wasn't human.

Fingering the hole on the left side of her fishnets, Kaye poked at the green skin underneath as she considered herself in the mirror.

"Your rat wants to come," Lutie-loo said. Kaye turned toward the lidded fish tank, where the doll-size faerie had her thin, pale fingers pressed against the outside of the glass. Inside,

Kaye's brown rat, Armageddon, sniffed the air. Isaac was curled in a white ball in the far corner. "He likes coronations."

"Can you really understand what he's saying?" Kaye asked, pulling an olive skirt over her head and wriggling it onto her hips.

"He's just a rat," Lutie said, turning toward Kaye. One of her moth wings dusted the side of the cage with pale powder. "Anyone can talk rat."

"Well, I can't. Do I look too monochromatic in this?"

Lutie nodded. "I like it."

Kaye heard her grandmother's voice calling from downstairs. "Where are you? I made you a sandwich!"

"Be there in a second!" Kaye shouted back.

Lutie kissed the glass wall of the cage. "Well, can the rat come or not?"

"I guess. Sure. I mean, if you can get him to not run away." Kaye laced up one thick-soled black boot and limped around the room looking for its mate. Her old bed frame was in pieces in the attic, her old dolls were dressed in punk-rock finery, and above the new mattress on the floor Kaye had painted a mural where a headboard might have been. It was half finished—a tree with deep, intricate roots and gilded bark. Although she'd thought it would, the decorating still hadn't made the room feel like hers.

When he'd seen the mural, Roiben had remarked that she could glamour the room into looking any way she wanted, but a magical veneer—no matter how lovely—still didn't seem real to her. Or maybe it seemed too real, too much a reminder of why she didn't belong in the room at all.

Shoving her foot into the other boot, she tugged on her

jacket. Leaving her hair green, she let magic slide over her skin, coloring and plumping it. There was a slight prickling as the glamour restored her familiar human face.

She looked at herself a moment longer before pocketing Armageddon, scratching behind the ears of Isaac, and walking toward the door. Lutie followed, flying on moth wings, keeping out of sight as Kaye jogged down the stairs.

"Was that your mother on the phone before?" Kaye's grandmother asked. "I heard it ring." She stood at the kitchen counter, pouring hot grease into a tin can. Two peanut butter and bacon sandwiches sat on chipped plates; Kaye could see the brown meat curling past the edges of the white bread.

Kaye bit into her sandwich, glad that the peanut butter glued her mouth shut.

"I left her a message about the holidays, but can she bother to call me back? Oh no, she's much too busy to talk. You'll have to ask her tomorrow night, although why she can't come down here to see you instead of insisting you go visit her at that squalid apartment in the city, I will never know. It must really gall her that you've decided to stay here instead of following her around like a little shadow."

Kaye chewed, nodding along with her grandmother's complaints. In the mirror beside the back door, she could see, beneath the glamour, a girl with leaf green skin, black eyes without a drop of white in them, and wings as thin as plastic wrap. A monster standing beside a nice old lady, eating food intended for another child. A child stolen away by faeries.

Brood parasites. That's what cuckoos were called when they dropped their eggs in other birds' nests. Parasitic bees, too, leaving their spawn in foreign hives; Kaye had read about them in one of the moldering encyclopedias on the landing. Brood parasites didn't bother raising their own babies. They left them to be raised by others—birds that tried not to notice when their offspring grew huge and hungry, bees that ignored that their progeny did not collect pollen, mothers and grandmothers who didn't know the word "changeling."

"I have to go," Kaye said suddenly.

"Have you thought more about school?"

"Gram, I got my GED," Kaye said. "You saw it. I did it. I'm done."

Her grandmother sighed and looked toward the fridge, where the letter was still tacked with a magnet. "There's always community college. Imagine that—starting college before the rest of your class even graduates."

"I'll go see if Corny is outside yet." Kaye started toward the door. "Thanks for the sandwich."

The old woman shook her head. "It's too cold out there. Stand on the porch. He should know better than to ask a young girl to wait outside in the snow. I swear, that boy has no manners at all."

Kaye felt the whoosh of air as Lutie flew past her back. Her grandmother didn't even look up. "Okay, Gram. Bye, Gram."

"Stay warm."

Kaye nodded and used the sleeve of her coat to turn the knob of the door so that she could avoid touching the iron. Even the smell of it burned her nose when she got close. Walking through the porch, she used the same trick on the screen door and stepped out into the snow. The trees on the lawn were encased in ice. Hail from that morning had stuck to whatever it had touched, freezing into solid sparkling skins that covered branches and flashed against the dull gray sky. The slightest breeze sent the limbs jangling against one another.

Corny wasn't coming, but her grandmother didn't need to know that. It wasn't lying. After all, faeries couldn't lie. They only bent the truth so far that it snapped on its own.

Above the doorway, a swag of thorn wrapped in green marked the house as watched over by the Unseelie Court. A gift from Roiben. Each time Kaye looked at the branches, she hoped that being protected by the Unseelie Court included being protected *from* the Unseelie Court.

She turned away, walking past a ranch house with aluminum siding hanging off in patches. The woman who lived there raised Italian ducks that ate all the grass seed anyone in the neighborhood planted. Kaye thought of the ducks and smiled. A trash can rolled in the street, bumping up against plastic bins of beer bottles set out for recycling. Kaye crossed over the parking lot of a boarded-up bowling alley, where a sofa rested near the curb, cushions hard with frost.

Plastic Santas glowed on lawns beside dried grapevine reindeer wrapped with fiber-optic lights. A twenty-four-hour convenience store piped screechy carols that carried through the quiet streets. A robotic elf with rosy cheeks waved endlessly next to several snowman windsocks fluttering like ghosts. Kaye passed a manger missing its baby Jesus. She wondered if kids had stolen him or if the family had just taken him in for the night.

Halfway to the cemetery, she stopped at a pay phone outside a pizza place, put in quarters, and punched in Corny's cell number. He picked it up after the first ring.

"Hey," Kaye said. "Did you decide about the coronation? I'm on my way to see Roiben before it starts."

"I don't think I can go," Corny said. "I'm glad you called, though—I have to tell you something. I was driving past one of those storage places. You know the kind with the billboards that have quotes on them like 'Support Our Troops' or 'What Is Missing in C-H-blank-blank-C-H? U-R.'"

"Yeah," Kaye said, puzzled.

"Well, this one said 'Life Is Like Licking Honey from a Thorn.' What the fuck is that?"

"Weird."

"No shit, it's weird. What is it supposed to mean?"

"Nothing. Just don't dwell on it," Kaye said.

"Oh, right. Don't dwell. That's me. I'm so good at not dwelling. It's my skill set. If I was going to take one of those tests to see what job I was best suited for, I would rate a perfect ten for 'not dwelling on shit.' And what job do you think that would qualify me for exactly?"

"Storage unit manager," Kaye said. "You'd be the one to put up those sayings."

"Ouch. Right between the legs." She could hear the smile in his voice.

"So, you're really not coming tonight? You seemed so sure it was a good idea for you to face your fears and all that."

There was a long silence on the other end of the line. Just as she would have spoken, he said, "The problem with facing my *fears* is that they're my fears. Not to mention that a fear of megalomaniacal, amoral fiends is hard to rationalize away." He laughed, a brittle, strange cackle. "Just once I'd like them to finally give up their secrets—tell me how to really protect myself. How to be safe."

Kaye thought of Nephamael, the last King of the Unseelie

Court, choking on iron, and Corny stabbing him again and again.

"I don't think it's that simple," Kaye said. "I mean, it's almost impossible to protect yourself from people, forget faeries."

"Yeah, I guess. I'll see you tomorrow," Corny said, and ended the call.

"Okay." She heard him hang up the phone.

Kaye walked on, drawing her coat more tightly around her. She stepped into the cemetery and started up the snowy hill, muddy and grooved by the sleds that had gone over it. Her gaze strayed to where she knew Janet was buried, although from where Kaye stood, the polished granite stones looked the same with their plastic garlands and wet red bows. She didn't need to see the grave for her steps to slow, weighed down by the memory like sodden clothes must have weighed down Janet's drowning body.

She wondered what happened when the baby cuckoo realized it wasn't like its brothers and sisters. Maybe it wondered where it had come from or what it was. Maybe it just pretended nothing was wrong and kept on gulping down worms. Whatever that bird felt, though, it wasn't enough to keep it from pushing the other chicks out of the nest.

Cornelius Stone closed his cell phone against his chest and stood still for a moment, waiting for the regret to ebb. He wanted to go to the coronation, wanted to dance with the terrible and beautiful creatures of the Unseelie Court, wanted to gorge on faerie fruit and wake up on a hillside, scourged and sated. He bit his cheek until he tasted blood, but the yearning only rose with the pain.

He sat down in the library aisle on carpeting so new it had a clean, chemical smell that was probably evaporating formaldehyde. Opening the first of the books, he looked at woodcuts and turn-of-the-century line art. He saw pictures of ponies with flippers that looked nothing like the kelpie that had murdered his sister. He leafed to an illustration of a ring of tiny cherubic faeries with red cheeks and pointy ears dancing in a circle. *Pixies,* he read. None of them resembled Kaye in the least.

He tore each page carefully out of the binding. They were bullshit.

The next book was no better.

As he started ripping apart the third, an elderly man looked down the aisle.

"You shouldn't be doing that," he said. He was holding a fat hardback western in one hand and squinted at Corny as though, even with his glasses, he couldn't see him very clearly.

"I work here," Corny lied.

The man looked at Corny's scuffed biker jacket and his shaggy almost-a-mullet hair. "Your job is to rip apart perfectly good books?"

Corny shrugged. "National security."

The guy walked away muttering. Corny shoved the rest of the books into his backpack and walked out the doors. Disinformation was worse than no information at all. Alarms clanged behind him, but he didn't worry. He'd been to other libraries. The alarms didn't do anything but make a pretty sound, like a church bell from the future.

He started in the direction of the coronation hill. No, he

wasn't going to party with Kaye and her prince-of-darkness boyfriend, but that didn't mean he had to stay home. None of those books could help with what he had planned, but he'd expected that. If he wanted answers, he was going to have to go right to the source.

The servants didn't like to let Kaye into the Palace of Termites. She could tell by the way they looked at her, as though she were only the scuff of her shoes, the dirt under her fingernails, the stench of coffee and cigarettes that clung to her clothes. They spoke grudgingly, eyes never meeting hers, and they led her through passageways as though their feet were made of lead.

Here was the place to which she ought to belong, but instead the grim and fabulous court, the cold halls, and the ferocious denizens made her uneasy. It was all very lovely, but she felt self-conscious and awkward against such a backdrop. And if she did not belong here and she didn't belong with Ellen, then she couldn't think of any place left to belong.

It had been nearly two months since Roiben had assumed the title of Unseelie King, but a formal coronation could only occur on the darkest day of winter. After tonight he would be the true Lord of the Night Court, and with the title would come the resumption of the endless war with the Seelie fey. Two evenings past he'd woken Kaye by climbing a tree, tapping against her bedroom window, and drawing her out to sit on the frozen lawn. "Stay Ironside for a time after I'm crowned," he'd told her. "Lest you be dragged into more danger." When she'd tried to ask him for how long or how bad he thought it was going to get, he'd kissed her quiet. He'd seemed restless, but wouldn't say why. Whatever the reason, his restlessness had been infectious.

She followed the shuffling feet of a hunchbacked steward to the doors of Roiben's chambers.

"He will be with you soon," the steward said, pushing open the heavy door and stepping inside. He lit several fat candles along the floor before retreating silently. A tufted tail dragged behind him.

Roiben's rooms were largely unfurnished, the walls an expanse of smooth stone broken up by stacks of books and a bed covered in a brocade throw. There were a few other things, farther inside—a jade bowl of washing water, a wardrobe, a stand with his armor. The chamber was formal, austere, and forbidding.

Kaye dropped her coat onto the end of the bed and sat down beside it. She tried to imagine living here, with him, and failed. The idea of putting a poster on the wall was absurd.

Reaching over, she pulled a bracelet from one of the pockets of her coat, cupping it in her hand. A thin braid of her own green hair, wrapped in silver wire. She'd hoped to surprise him before the ceremony started, hoped that even if she couldn't see him for a while, he'd keep it with him, like storybook knights wore their ladies' tokens when they rode into battle. Lutie and Armageddon had even gone ahead to the hall so that she'd have a moment alone in which to present it.

Next to the grandeur of the room, though, her gift now seemed ugly and homemade. Not worthy of a King.

There was a sound like the clatter of hooves in the hall and Kaye stood, pushing the bracelet back into the pocket of her coat, but it was only another glowering servant, this one bringing a glass of spiced wine as thick and red as blood.

Kaye took the glass and sipped at it politely, then set it down on the floor as the servant left. She flipped through a few books in the flickering candlelight—military strategy, *Peasepod's Ballads,* an Emma Bull paperback she'd loaned him—and waited some more. Taking another sip of wine, she stretched out at the end of the bed, wrapping the brocade cloth around her.

She woke suddenly, a hand on her arm and Roiben's impassive face above her. Silvery hair tickled her cheek.

Embarrassed, she sat up, wiping her mouth with the back of her hand. She had slept restlessly, and the coverlet was half on the floor, soaking up spilled wine and melted candle wax. She didn't even remember closing her eyes.

A scarlet-clad servant bearing a long cloak with black opal clasps stood in the center of the room. Roiben's chamberlain, Ruddles, was near the door, his mouth overfull of teeth in a way that made him seem as though he wore an unpleasant grin.

Roiben frowned. "No one told me you were here."

She wasn't sure if that meant that he wished someone had or that he would have preferred her not to be there at all. Kaye slung her coat over her arm and stood up, her cheeks hot with shame. "I should go."

He stayed seated on the wreckage of his bed. The scabbard on his hip touched the floor. "No." He gestured to the servant and Ruddles. "Leave us."

With shallow bows, they departed.

Kaye remained standing. "It's late. Your thing is going to start soon."

"Kaye, you have no idea what time it is." He stood and reached for her arm. "You've been asleep."

She stepped back, clasping her hands together, pressing her nails into her palm to keep calm.

He sighed. "Stay. Let me beg your forgiveness for whatever it is I've done."

"Stop it." She shook her head, talking faster than she was thinking. "They don't want you to be with me, do they?"

His mouth curved into a bitter smile. "I am forbidden nothing."

"No one wants me here. They don't want me near you. Why?"

He looked startled, ran a hand through silver hair. "Because I'm gentry and you're . . . not," he finished awkwardly.

"I'm low class," she said dully, turning her back to him. "Nothing new there."

Roiben's boots tapped against the stone as he walked behind her and pulled her against his chest. His head rested in the crook of her neck, and she felt his breath as he spoke, his lips moving against her skin. "I have my own thoughts on the subject. I care nothing for the opinions of others."

For a moment, she relaxed into his touch. He was warm and his voice was very soft. It would be easy to crawl back under the coverlet and stay. Just stay.

But Kaye turned in his arms instead. "What's the big deal about you slumming?"

He snorted, one of his hands lingering on her hip. He was no longer looking at her; his stare focused on the cold stone floor, the same gray as his eyes. "It is a weakness. My affection for you."

She opened her mouth to ask another question, and closed it again, realizing he'd answered more than she'd asked. Perhaps that was the reason that the servants didn't like her, perhaps it was the reason that courtiers sneered at her, but it was also what he believed. She could see it in his face.

"I really should go," she said, pulling away. She was relieved to find that her voice didn't catch. "I'll see you out there. Break a leg."

He released her from the cradle of his arms. "You cannot stand on the dais during the ceremony nor walk in the procession. I do not want you to be taken for part of my court. Above all, you must not swear fealty. Promise me, Kaye."

"So, I'm supposed to act like I don't know you?" The door was only a few steps across the floor, but she was conscious of each one. "Like you don't have any *weaknesses?*"

"No, of course not," he said, too quickly. "You are the only thing I have that is neither duty nor obligation, the only thing I chose for myself." He paused. "The only thing I want."

She let a small teasing smile creep onto her face. "Really?"

He snorted, shaking his head. "You think I'm being absurd, don't you?"

"I think you're trying to be nice," said Kaye. "Which is pretty absurd."

He walked to her and kissed her smiling mouth. She forgot about his sullen servants and the coronation and the bracelet she hadn't given him. She forgot about anything but the press of his lips.

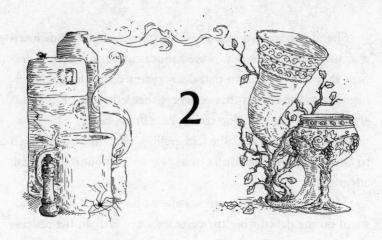

Silarial had not openly moved against Roiben these two long months between Samhain and Midwinter's Eve, and he began to wonder what she intended. The dark, cold months were considered an unlucky time for the Seelie Court to strike, so perhaps she only waited for the ice to melt into spring, when she would have every advantage. Still, he could occasionally believe that she had considered renewing the truce between the Bright and the Night Courts. Even with her greater numbers, war was still costly.

"The envoy from the Seelie Court is here, my Lord," Dulcamara repeated, the silver soles of her boots ringing with each step. Roiben heard "Lord" echo off the walls again and again, like a taunt.

"Send him in," Roiben said, touching his mouth. He wondered if Kaye was already in the hall, if she was alone.

"If I might presume to inform, the messenger is a she."

Roiben looked up with sudden hope. "Send her in, then."

"Yes, my Lord." The envoy stepped out of the way, letting the faerie woman come forward. She was dressed in glacial white cloth, with no armor whatsoever. When she looked up at him, her silver eyes gleamed like mirrors, reflecting his own face.

"Welcome, little sister." The words seemed to steal his breath as he spoke them.

Her hair was cropped close, a white halo around her face. She bowed and did not lift her head.

"Lord Roiben, my Lady sends you her greetings. She is saddened that she must fight against one of her own knights and bids you reconsider your rash position. You could even now renounce all this, surrender, and return to the Bright Court."

"Ethine, what happened to your hair?"

"For my brother," she said, but still did not look at him as she spoke. "I cut it when I lost him."

Roiben just stared at her.

"Have you any message?" Ethine inquired.

"Tell her I will not reconsider." His voice was clipped. "I will not step down and I will not surrender. You may say to your mistress that having tasted freedom, her service no longer tempts me. You may tell her that nothing about her tempts me."

Ethine's jaw clenched as though she were biting back words. "I am instructed to remain for your coronation. With your leave, of course."

"I am always glad of your company," he said.

She left the hall without waiting for his dismissal. As his chamberlain walked into the room wearing a wide and toothy grin, Roiben tried not to see it as an ill omen that of late he was better at pleasing those he hated than those he loved.

Cornelius leaned back against the rough bark of an elm tree just inside the cemetery. He tried to concentrate on something other than the cold, something other than the iron poker clutched in one bare hand or the fishing wire in the other. He had turned his white clothes inside out just in case some of the shit from the books worked, and he'd rubbed himself down with pine needles to disguise his smell. He hoped, in the gray and starless night, it would be enough.

No matter how ready he had told himself he was, hearing faeries shuffling through the snow filled him with panic. He didn't really think the poker was much of a defense against the legions of the Unseelie Court. All he could do now was hold his breath and try not to shiver.

They were gathering for the first coronation in more than a century. Everyone who was anyone in Faerie would be there. Corny wished Kaye were crouched in a snowbank with him tonight, not under the hill at the faerie ball. She always made crazy plans seem like they were going to work, made it seem like you could figure out the un-figure-outable. But to get Kaye to come, he would have had to tell her what he was doing, and there was no way that would have gone well. Sometimes he forgot she wasn't human, and then she would look at him with something alien in her eyes, or smile with a smile far too wide and too hungry. Even though she'd become his best friend, she was still one of *them*. He was better off working alone.

Corny repeated that thought to himself silently as the first of the faerie processional passed. It was a group of trolls, their lichen green limbs as long and gnarled as branches. They kicked up snow as they passed, growling to one another softly, hooked noses scenting the air like hounds'. Tonight they did not bother with disguises.

A trio of women followed, all dressed in white, their hair blowing around them even though there was no wind. They smiled secret smiles at one another. As they passed, oblivious of him, he saw that their curved backs were as hollow and empty as eggshells. Despite the filmy gowns they wore, they appeared to not mind the cold.

Horses wound their way up the hill next, their riders solemn and quiet. Corny's eye caught on the shock of red berries encircling dark hair. He could not stop himself from staring at the rich and strange patterns of the clothes, the shining locks, and the faces, so handsome that just looking made him ache with longing.

Corny bit his lip hard and forced his eyes shut. His hands were trembling at his sides and he was afraid that the clear plastic fishing wire would pull up through the snow. How many times would he be caught off guard like this? How many times could he be made a fool?

Keeping his eyes closed, Corny listened. He listened for the snap of branches, the scrunching of snow, the whispered snatches of conversation, the laughter that was as lilting as any flute. He listened for them to pass, and when they had, he opened his eyes at last. Now he just had to wait. He was betting that no matter what the party was for, there were always latecomers.

It took only a few more minutes for a troop of short gray-clad elves to come up the hill. Hissing impatiently at one another, they waded through the snow. Corny sighed. There were too many for him to be able to do what he'd planned, and they were too large, so he waited till they passed.

A smallish faerie tramped behind them, hopping in the long footfalls of the trolls. Clad in scarlet with a half-pinecone hat, its black eyes glittered like an animal's in the reflected light. Corny clutched the handle of the poker tighter and took a deep breath. He waited for the little faerie to take two hops more, then Corny stepped out of the trees and in one swift movement thrust the poker against the faerie's throat.

It shrieked, falling prone in the snow, hands flying to cover where the iron had touched it.

"Kryptonite," Corny whispered. "I guess that makes me Lex Luthor."

"Please, please," the creature wheedled. "What does it want? A wish? Surely a little thing like myself would have too small wishes for such a mighty being."

Corny jerked hard on the thin fishing wire. An aluminum crab trap snapped together around the faerie.

The little creature screeched again. It scrambled from side to side, breathing hard, clawing at any small gaps, only to fall back with a yowl. Corny finally permitted himself to smile.

Working quickly, he twisted four thin steel wires into place, fixing the trap closed. Then he hefted the cage in the air and ran down the hill, slipping in the ankle-deep snow, careful to take a different path from the one the faeries had come up. He stumbled to where he'd parked his car, the trunk still open, the spare tire within dusted with a fine layer of white.

Dropping the cage there, he slammed the trunk shut and hopped into the front of the car, turning the ignition. The heat came on full blast and he just sat there a moment, letting himself enjoy the warmth, letting himself feel the beat of his heart, letting himself glory in the fact that now, finally, he would be the one making the rules.

Kaye tipped back her goblet, drinking it to the dregs. The first sip of mushroom wine had been foul, but afterward she had found herself touching her tongue to her teeth, searching for more of the earthy, bitter flavor. Her cheeks were hot to the press of her own palms and she felt more than slightly dizzy.

"Don't—that isn't good to eat," Lutie-loo said. The little faerie was perched on Kaye's shoulder, one hand clutching a silver hoop earring and the other holding on to a lock of hair.

"Better than good," Kaye said, drawing her fingers across the bottom of the goblet, sifting the sediment, then licking it from her hand. She took an experimental step, trying to spin, and catching herself moments before she crashed into a table. "Where's my rat?"

"Hiding like we should be. Look," Lutie said, but Kaye couldn't see what she was gesturing at. It could have been anything. Trolls skulked among the tables next to selkies without their skins, while hollow-backed dopplers danced and whirled. There was at least one kelpie—the stench of brine was heavy in the air—but there were also nixies, sprites, brownies, bogies, phookas, a shagfoal in the corner, will-o'-the-wisps zipping among stalagmites, grinning spriggans, and more.

Not just the local denizens either. Folk had traveled from distant courts to witness the coronation. There were envoys from more courts than Kaye had known existed, some Seelie, some Unseelie, and others that claimed those distinctions were meaningless. Even the High Court, to which the Court of Termites was not pledged, sent their own representative, a prince who appeared delighted by the flowing wine. All of them here to watch the Night Court pledge fealty to its new master. They smiled at her, smiles full of thoughts Kaye could not decipher.

The tables were spread with dark blue cloths and set with platters of ice. Branches and holly berries rested beside sculptures composed of frozen blocks of greenish water. A black-tongued monster licked at a chunk containing a motionless minnow. Bitter acorn cakes frosted with a sugary blackberry paste were stacked near pinned and roasted pigeon feet. Slushy black punch floated in an enormous copper bowl, the metal sweating and cloudy with cold. Occasionally someone dipped a long-stemmed icicle cup into it and sipped at the contents.

Kaye looked up as the hall went silent.

Roiben had entered the room with his courtiers. Thistledown, the Unseelie herald, ran in front of the procession, long golden hair streaming from his wizened head. Then came the piper, Bluet, playing her lilting instrument. Next marched Roiben with his two knights, Ellebere and Dulcamara, following him at an exact three paces. Goblins held up the edges of Roiben's cloak. Behind them were others—his chamberlain, Ruddles, a cupbearer holding a winding goblet of horn, and several pages clutching the harnesses of three black dogs.

Roiben mounted a moss-covered dais near a great throne of woven birch branches and turned toward the crowd, going to his knees. He leaned his head forward and his hair, silver as a knife, fell like a curtain over his face.

"Will you take the oath?" Thistledown asked.

"I will," Roiben said.

"The endless night," Thistledown intoned, "of darkness, ice, and death is ours. Let our new Lord be also made from ice. Let our new Lord be born from death. Let our new Lord commit himself to the night." He lifted a crown woven of ash branches, small broken stubs of twigs forming the spires, and set it on Roiben's head.

Roiben rose.

"By the blood of our Queen which I spilled," he said. "By this circlet of ash placed upon my brow I bind myself to the Night Court on this, Midwinter's Eve, the longest night of the year."

Ellebere and Dulcamara knelt on either side of him. The court knelt with them. Kaye crouched awkwardly.

"I present to you," called the herald, "our undoubted Lord, Roiben, King of the Unseelie Court. Will you humble yourselves and call him sovereign?"

A great joyful shrieking and screaming. The hair stood up along Kaye's arms.

"You are my people," Roiben said, his hands extended. "And as I am bound, you are lashed to my bidding. I am naught if not your King."

With those words, he sank into the chair of birch, his face blank. Folk began to stand again, moving to make their obeisance to the throne.

A spriggan chased a tiny winged faerie under the table, making it tremble. The ice bowl sloshed and the tower of cubes collapsed, tumbling into disarray.

"Kaye," Lutie squeaked. "You're not looking."

Kaye turned to the dais. A scribe sat cross-legged next to Roiben, recording each supplicant. Leaning forward from his throne, the Lord addressed a wild-haired woman dressed in scarlet. As she moved to kneel, Kaye glimpsed a cat's tail twitching from a slit in her dress.

"What am I not looking at?" Kaye asked.

"Have you never seen a declaration, pixie?" sneered a woman with a necklace of silver scarabs. "You are the Ironside girl, aren't you?"

Kaye nodded. "I guess so." She wondered if she stank of it, if iron leaked from her pores from long exposure.

A lissome girl in a dress of petals came up behind the woman, resting slim fingers on her arm and making a face at Kaye. "He's not yours, you know."

Kaye's head felt as though it were filled with cotton. "What?"

"A declaration," the woman said. "You haven't declared yourself." It seemed to Kaye that the beetles paced a circle around the woman's throat. Kaye shook her head.

"She doesn't know." The girl snickered, snatching an apple off the table and biting into it.

"To be his consort," the woman spoke slowly, as though to an idiot. An iridescent green beetle dropped from her mouth. "One makes a declaration of love and asks for a quest to prove one's worth."

Kaye shuddered, watching the shimmering beetle scuttle

up the woman's dress to take its place at her neck. "A quest?"

"But if the declarer is not favored, the monarch will hand down an impossible expedition."

"Or a deadly one," the grinning petal girl supplied.

"Not that we think he would send you on a quest like that."

"Not that we think he meant to hide anything from you."

"Leave me alone," Kaye said thickly, her heart twisting. Lurching forward through the crowd, she knew that she'd gotten far drunker than she had intended. Lutie squeaked as Kaye shoved her way past winged ladies and fiddle-playing men, nearly tripping on a long tail that swept the floor.

"Kaye!" Lutie wailed. "Where are we going?"

A woman bit pearl-gray grubs off a stick, smacking her lips in delight as Kaye passed. A faerie with white hair cropped close enough to her head that it stuck up like the clock of a dandelion looked oddly familiar, but Kaye couldn't place her. Nearby, a blue-skinned man cracked chestnuts with his massive fists as small faeries darted to snatch up what he dropped. The colors seemed to blur together.

Kaye felt the impact of the dirt floor before she even realized that she had fallen. For a moment she just lay there, gazing across at the hems of dresses, cloven feet, and pointed-toed shoes. The shapes danced and merged.

Lutie landed close enough to Kaye's face that she could barely focus on the tiny form.

"Stay awake," Lutie said. Her wings were vibrating with anxiety. She tugged on one of Kaye's fingers. "They'll get me if you go to sleep."

Kaye rolled onto her side and got up, carefully, wary of her own legs.

"I'm okay," Kaye said. "I'm not asleep."

Lutie alighted on Kaye's head and began to nervously knot locks of hair.

"I'm perfectly okay," Kaye repeated. With careful steps she approached the side of the dais where Lord Roiben, newly anointed King of the Unseelie Court, sat. She watched his fingers, each one encircled in a metal band, as they tapped the rhythms of an unfamiliar tune on the edge of his throne. He was clad in a stiff black fabric that swallowed him in shadow. As familiar as he should have been, she found herself unable to speak.

It was the worst kind of stupid to be pining after someone who cared for you. Still, it was like watching her mother onstage. Kaye felt proud, but was half afraid that if she went up, it wouldn't turn out to be Roiben at all.

Lutie-loo abandoned her perch and flew to the throne. Roiben looked up, laughed, and cupped his hands to receive her.

"She drank all the mushroom wine," Lutie accused, pointing to Kaye.

"Indeed?" Roiben raised one silver brow. "Will she come and sit beside me?"

"Sure," Kaye said, levering herself up onto the dais, unaccountably shy. "How has it been?"

"Endless." His long fingers threaded through her hair, making her shiver.

Only months ago she'd thought of herself as weird, but human. Now the weight of gauzy wings on her back and the green of her skin were enough to remind her that she wasn't. But she was still just Kaye Fierch and no matter how magical or clever, it was hard to understand why she was allowed to sit beside a King.

Even if she had saved that King's life. Even if he loved her.

She couldn't help but recall the beetle-woman's words. Did the dreadlocked girl with the drum intend to make a declaration? Ask for a quest? Had the girl with the cat tail already done so? Were the fey laughing at her, thinking that because she had grown up with humans, she was ignorant of faerie customs?

She wanted to make things right. She wanted to make a grand gesture. Give him something finer than a ragged bracelet. Swaying forward, Kaye went down on both her knees in front of the new King of the Unseelie Court.

Roiben's eyes widened with something like panic and he opened his mouth to speak, but she was faster.

"I, Kaye Fierch, do declare myself to you. I . . ." Kaye froze, realizing she didn't know what she was supposed to say, but the heady liquor in her veins spurred her tongue on. "I love you. I want you to give me a quest. I want to prove that I love you."

Roiben gripped the arm of his throne, fingers tightening on the wood. His voice sank to a whisper. "To allow this, I would have to have a heart of stone. You will not become a subject of this court."

She knew that something was wrong, but she didn't know what. Shaking her head, she stumbled on. "I want to make a declaration. I don't know the formal words, but that's what I want."

"No," he said. "I will not allow it."

There was a moment's hush around her and then some scattered laughter and whispering.

"I have recorded it. It has been spoken," said Ruddles. "You must not dishonor her request."

Roiben nodded. He stared off into the brugh for a long

moment, then stood and walked to the edge of the platform. "Kaye Fierch, this is the quest that I grant. Bring me a faerie that can tell an untruth and you shall sit beside me as my consort."

Shrieking laughter rose from the throng. She heard the words: *Impossible. An impossible quest.*

Her face heated, and suddenly she felt worse than dizzy. She felt sick. She must have gone white or her expression must have turned alarming, because Roiben jumped off the platform and caught her arm as she fell.

Voices were all around her but none of them made sense.

"I promise that if I find who put this idea in your head, they will pay for it with their own."

Her eyes blinked heavily. She let them close for a moment and slipped down into sleep, passing out cold in Faerieland.

3

I shall have peace, as leafy trees are peaceful
When rain bends down the bough;
And I shall be more silent and cold-hearted
Than you are now.
—SARA TEASDALE, "I SHALL NOT CARE"

The little hob shivered in the corner of the cage as Corny heaved it out of the trunk. Dumping the wire box into the backseat, he got in next to it and slammed the door. Dry heat pumped from vents as the engine idled.

"I'm a powerful being . . . a *wizard*," Corny said. "So don't try anything."

"Yes," said the little faerie, blinking black eyes rapidly. "No. Try nothing."

Corny turned those words over in his head, but the possible interpretations seemed too varied and his mind kept getting tangled. He shook the thoughts out of his head. The creature was caged. He was in control. "I want to keep myself from being charmed, and you're going to tell me how to do it."

"I weave spells. I don't lift spells," it chirped.

"But," Corny said, "there has to be a way. A way to keep from being happily led off the side of a pier or craving the honor of being some faerie's footstool. Not just some herb. Something permanent."

"There is no leaf. No rock. No chant to keep you completely safe from our charms."

"Bullshit. There must be something. Is there any human who is resistant to being enchanted?"

The little faerie hopped to the edge of its cage, and when it spoke, its voice was low. "Someone with True Sight. Someone who can see through glamours. Perhaps a geas."

"How do you get True Sight?"

"Some mortals are born with it. Very few. Not you."

Corny kicked the back of the passenger-side seat. "Tell me something else then, something I'd want to know."

"But such a powerful wizard as yourself—"

Corny shook the crab trap, sending the little faerie sprawling, its pinecone hat falling out through one of the holes in the aluminum cage to land on the floor mat. It yowled, a moan rising to a shriek.

"That's me," Corny said. "Very freaking powerful. Now, if you want out of here, I suggest that you start talking."

"There is a boy with the True Sight. In the great city of exiles and iron to the north. He's been breaking curses on mortals."

"Interesting," Corny said, holding up the poker. "Good. Now tell me something else."

That morning, while the slumbering bodies of faeries still littered the great hall of the Unseelie Court, Roiben met with his councillors in a cavern so cold his breath clouded. Tallow candles burned atop rock formations, the melting fat stinking of clove. *Let our King be made from ice.* He wished it too, wished for the ice that encased the branches out on the hill to freeze his heart.

Dulcamara drummed her fingers against the polished and petrified wood of the table, its surface as hard as stone. Her small wings, the membranes torn so that only the veins remained, hung from her shoulders. She regarded him with pale pink eyes.

Roiben looked at her and he thought of Kaye. Already he could feel the lack of her, like a thirst that is bearable until one thinks of water.

Ruddles paced the chamber. "We are overmatched." His wide, toothy mouth made him look as though he might suddenly take a bite out of any of them. "Many of the fey who were bound to Nicnevin fled when the Tithe no longer tied them to the Unseelie Court. Our troops are thinned."

Roiben watched a flame gutter, flaring brightly before going out. *Take this from me,* he thought. *I do not want to be your King.*

Ruddles looked pointedly at Roiben, closed his eyes, and rubbed just above the bridge of his nose. "We are further weakened as several of our best knights died by your own hand, my Lord. You do recall?"

Roiben nodded.

"It vexes me that you do not seem to expect an imminent attack from Silarial," said Ellebere. A tuft of his hair fell over one eye, and he brushed it back. "Why should she hesitate now that Midwinter's Eve is past?"

"Perhaps she is bored and lazy and sick of fighting," said Roiben. "I am."

"You are too young." Ruddles gnashed those sharp teeth. "And you take the fate of this court too lightly. I wonder if you would have us win at all."

Once, after the Lady Nicnevin had whipped Roiben—he could no longer recall why—she had turned away, distracted by some new amusement, leaving Ruddles—her chamberlain, then—free to indulge in a moment's mercy. He had dribbled a stream of water into Roiben's mouth. He still remembered the sweet taste of it and the way it had hurt his throat to swallow.

"You think that I don't have the stomach to be Lord of the Night Court." Roiben leaned across the petrified wood table, bringing his face so close to Ruddles's that he could have kissed him.

Dulcamara laughed, clapping her hands together as if anticipating a treat.

"You are correct," said Ruddles, shaking his head. "I *don't* think you have the stomach for it. Nor the head. Nor do I think you even truly want the title."

"I have a belly that craves blood," said Dulcamara, tossing her sleek black hair and stepping so that she was behind the chamberlain. Her hands went to his shoulders, her fingers resting lightly at his throat. "He need not hurt anyone himself. *She* never did."

Ruddles went stiff and still, perhaps realizing how far he had overstepped himself.

Ellebere looked between the three of them as if judging

where his best alliance might be made. Roiben had no illusions that any one of them was in the least part loyal beyond the oath that bound them. With one lethal word Roiben could prove he had both the stomach and the head. That might cultivate something like loyalty.

"Perhaps I am no fit King," Roiben said instead, sinking back into the chair and relaxing his clenched hands. "But Silarial was once my Queen, and while there is breath in my body, I will never let her rule over me or mine again."

Dulcamara pouted exaggeratedly. "Your mercy," she said, "is my mischance, my King."

Ruddles's eyes closed with relief too profound to hide.

Long ago, when Roiben was newly come to the Unseelie Court, he had sat in the small cell-like chamber in which he was kept, and he had longed for his own death. His body had been worn with ill-use and struggle, his wounds had dried in long garnet crusts, and he'd been so tired from fighting Nicnevin's commands that remembering he could die had filled him with a sudden and surprising hope.

If he were really merciful, he would have let Dulcamara kill his chamberlain.

Ruddles was right; they had little chance of winning the war. But Roiben could do what he did best, what he had done in Nicnevin's service: *endure*. Endure long enough to kill Silarial. So that she could never again send one of her knights to be tortured as a symbol of peace, nor contrive countless deaths, nor glory in the appearance of innocence. And when he thought of the Lady of the Bright Court, he could almost feel a small sliver of ice burrow its way inside him, numbing him to what would come. He didn't need to win the war, he just needed to die slowly enough to take her with him.

And if all the Unseelie Court died along with them, so be it.

Corny knocked on the back door of Kaye's grandmother's house and smiled through the glass window. He hadn't had much sleep, but he was flushed and giddy with knowledge. The tiny hob he'd captured had talked all night, telling Corny anything that might make him more likely to let it go. He'd uncaged it at dawn, and true knowledge seemed closer to him now than it ever had before.

"Come in," Kaye's grandmother called from inside the kitchen.

He turned the cold metal knob. The kitchen was cluttered with old cooking supplies; dozens of pots were stacked in piles, cast iron with rusted steel. Kaye's grandmother couldn't bear to throw things away.

"What kind of trouble did the two of you get into last night?" The old woman loaded two plates into the dishwasher.

Corny looked blank for a moment, then forced a frown. "Last night. Right. Well, I left early."

"What kind of gentleman leaves a girl alone like that, Cornelius? She's been sick all morning and her door's locked."

The microwave beeped.

"We're supposed to go to New York tonight."

Kaye's grandmother opened the microwave. "Well, I don't think she's going to be up to it. Here, take her this. See if she can keep something down."

Corny took the mug and bounded up the stairs. Tea sloshed

as he went, leaving a trail of steaming droplets behind him. In the hall outside Kaye's door, he stopped and listened for a moment. Hearing nothing, he knocked.

There was no response.

"Kaye, it's me," he said. "Hey, Kaye, come on and open the door." Corny knocked again. "Kaye!"

He heard shuffling and a click, then the door swung open. He took an involuntary step backward.

He'd seen her faerie form before, but he hadn't been prepared to see it here. The grasshopper green of her skin looked especially strange when contrasted with a white T-shirt and faded pink underwear. Her shiny black eyes were rimmed with red, and the room beyond her smelled sour.

She lay back on the mattress, bundling the comforter around her and smothering her face against the pillow. He could see only the tangled green of her hair and the overly long fingers that pulled the fabric against her chest as though it were a stuffed toy. She seemed like a cat resting, more alert than it looked.

Corny came and sat down on the floor near her, leaning back on a satiny tag-sale pillow.

"Must have been a great night," he whispered, experimentally, and her ink black eyes did flicker open for a second. She made a sound like a snort. "Come on. It's the ass crack of noon. Time to get up."

Lutie swooped down from the top of the bookshelves, the suddenness startling Corny. The faerie alighted on his knee, her laughter so high that the sound reminded him of chimes. He resisted the urge to recoil.

"Roiben's chamberlain, Ruddles himself, along with a bogan

and a puck, carried her back. Imagine a bogan gently tucking a pixie into bed!"

Kaye groaned. "I don't think he was that gentle. Now, can everyone be quiet? I'm trying to sleep."

"Your grandma sent up this tea. You want it? If not, I'll drink it."

Kaye flipped over onto her back with a groan. "Give it to me."

He handed over the mug as she shifted into a sitting position. One of her cellophane-like wings rubbed against the wall, sending a shower of powder down onto the sheets.

"Doesn't that hurt?"

She looked over her shoulder and shrugged. Her long fingers turned the tea cup, warming her hands against it.

"I take it we're not going to make it to your mother's show."

She looked up at him and he was surprised to see that her eyes were wet.

"I don't know," she said. "How am I supposed to know? I don't know much about anything."

"Okay, okay. What the hell happened?"

"I told Roiben I loved him. Really loudly. In front of a huge audience."

"So, what did he say?"

"It was this thing called a declaration. They said—I don't know why I even listened—that if I didn't do it someone would beat me to it."

"And they are . . . ?"

"Don't ask," Kaye said, taking a sip of the tea and shaking her head. "I was so drunk, Corny. I don't ever want to be that drunk again."

"Sorry . . . Go on."

"These faeries told me about the declaration thing. They were kind of—I don't know—bragging, I guess. Anyway, Roiben told me I had to stay in the audience for the ceremony, and I kept thinking about how I didn't fit in and how maybe he was disappointed, you know? I thought that maybe he secretly wished I knew more of their customs—maybe he wished I would do something like that before he had to send someone else on a quest."

Corny frowned. "What? A quest?"

"A quest to prove your love."

"So dramatic. And you did this declaration thing? You declared."

Kaye turned her face, so that he couldn't read her expression. "Yeah, but Roiben wasn't happy about it, as in not at all." She put her head in her hands. "I think I really fucked up."

"What's your quest?"

"To find a faerie that lies." Her voice was very low.

"I thought faeries couldn't lie."

Kaye just looked at him.

Suddenly, horribly, Corny understood her meaning. "Okay, hold on. You are saying that he sent you on a quest that you can't possibly complete."

"And I'm not allowed to see him again until I do complete it. So basically, I'm not going to see him ever again."

"No faerie can tell an untruth. That is why it is one of the nice quests given to put off a declarer—no endless labor," said Lutie suddenly. "There are others, like 'Siphon all the salt from all the seas.' That's a nasty one. And then there are the ones that seem impossible, but might not be, like 'Weave a coat of stars.'"

Corny moved onto the bed next to Kaye, dislodging Lutie from his knee. "There has to be a way. There has to be something you can do."

The little faerie fluttered in the air, then settled in the lap of a large porcelain doll. She curled up and yawned.

Kaye shook her head. "But, Corny, he doesn't *want* me to finish the quest."

"That's bullshit."

"You heard what Lutie just said."

"It's still bullshit." Corny kicked at a stray pillow with his toe. "What about seriously stretching the truth?"

"That's not lying," Kaye said, taking a deep swig out of the mug.

"Say that the tea is cold. Just try. Maybe you can lie if you push yourself."

"The tea is . . . ," Kaye said, and stopped. Her mouth was still open, but it was as though her tongue were frozen.

"What's stopping you?" Corny asked.

"I don't know. I feel panicked and my mind starts racing, looking for a safe way to say it. I feel like I'm suffocating. My jaw just locks. I can't make any sound come out."

"God, I don't know what I would do if I couldn't lie."

Kaye flopped back down. "It's not so bad. You mostly can make people believe things without actually lying."

"Like how you made your grandmother believe I was with you last night?"

He noticed that she wore a small smile as she took the next sip from the cup.

"Well, what if you said you were going to *do* something and didn't? Wouldn't that be lying?"

"I don't know," Kaye said. "Isn't that like saying something that you think is true, but turns out not to be? Like something you read in a book, but the book turns out to be wrong."

"Isn't that still lying?"

"If it is, I guess I'm in good shape. I sure have been wrong about things."

"Come on, let's go to the city. You'll feel better when you get out of town. I know I always do."

Kaye smiled, then sat bolt upright. "Where's Armageddon?"

Corny glanced at the cage, but Kaye was already shuffling toward it on her knees.

"He's there. Oh, jeez. They're both there." She sighed deeply, her whole body relaxing. "I thought he might still be under the hill."

"You brought your rat?" Corny asked, incredulous.

"Can we just not talk any more about last night?" Kaye asked, pulling on a pair of faded green camouflage pants.

"Yeah, sure," Corny said, and yawned. "Want to stop for breakfast on the way? I'm feeling like pancakes."

With a queasy look, Kaye began to gather up her things.

On the drive up, Kaye put her head down on the ripped plastic seat, gazing out the window at the sky, trying not to think. The strips of sound-insulating forest cushioning the highway gave way to industrial plants spouting fire and billowing white smoke that blew up until it blended into clouds.

When they got to the part of Brooklyn her mother claimed was still Williamsburg, but was probably actually Bedford-Stuyvesant, the traffic grew less congested. The roads were riddled with potholes, the asphalt cracked and pitted. The streets were deserted and the sidewalks heaped with banks of dirty snow. Only a few cars were parked on the sides of the road, and as soon as Corny pulled up behind one, Kaye opened the door and stepped out. It was strangely lonely.

"You okay?" Corny asked.

Kaye shook her head, leaning over the gutter in case she vomited. Lutie-loo's tiny fingers dug into Kaye's neck as the little faerie tried to keep perched on Kaye's shoulder. "I don't know which part of feeling like shit is from riding for two hours in an iron box and which part is from a wicked hangover," she said, between deep breaths.

Bring me a faerie that can tell an untruth.

Corny shrugged. "No more driving for the whole visit. All you have to do now is put up with riding on the subway."

Kaye groaned, but she was too tired to smack him on the arm. Even the streets stank of iron. Beams of it propped up every building. Iron formed the skeletons of the cars that congested the roads, clogging them like slow-moving blood through the arteries of a heart. Gusts of iron seared her lungs. She concentrated on her own glamour, making it heavier and her senses duller. That managed to push away the worst of the iron sickness.

You're the only thing I want.

"Can you walk?" Corny asked.

"What? Oh, yeah." Kaye sighed, shoving her hands into the pockets of her purple plaid overcoat. "Sure." Everything felt as if it were happening in slow motion. It took effort to concentrate on anything but the memories of Roiben and the taste of iron in her mouth. She pressed her nails into the flesh of her palm.

It is a weakness. My affection for you.

Corny touched her shoulder. "So, which building?"

Kaye checked the number she'd written on the back of her hand and pointed to an apartment complex. Her mother's apartment cost twice as much as one they'd lived in three months ago in Philadelphia. Ellen's promise to Kaye that she'd commute to New York so they could stay in New Jersey had lasted until the first huge fight between Ellen and *her* mother. Typical. But this time Kaye hadn't moved with her.

They walked up the steps to the apartment entrance and leaned on the button. A buzzer droned and Kaye pushed inside, Corny right behind her.

The door to Kaye's mother's apartment was covered in the same dirty maple veneer as the others on the eighteenth floor. A gold plastic nine stuck to the wood just beneath the peephole. When Kaye knocked, the number swung on its single nail.

Ellen opened the door. Her hair was freshly hennaed the same rootless red as her thin eyebrows, and her face looked freshly scrubbed. She was wearing a black spaghetti-strapped tank and dark jeans.

"Baby!" Ellen hugged Kaye hard, swaying back and forth, like the number on the door. "I've missed you so much."

"I missed you, too," Kaye said, leaning against her mother's shoulder heavily. It felt weirdly, guiltily good. She imagined what Ellen would do if she knew that Kaye wasn't human. Scream, of course. It was hard to think beyond the screaming.

After a moment, Ellen looked over Kaye's shoulder. "And Cornelius. Thanks for driving her up. Come on in. Want a beer?"

"No thanks, Ms. Fierch," Corny said. He carried his gym sack and Kaye's garbage bag of overnight things into the room.

The apartment itself was white-walled and small. A queen-size bed filled up most of the room, pushed up against a window and covered in clothing. A man whom Kaye didn't know sat on a stool and strummed a bass.

"This is Trent," Ellen said.

The man stood up and opened his guitar case, settling his instrument delicately inside. He looked like most of the guys Ellen liked: long hair and the stubbly beginnings of a beard, but unlike most, his were streaked with gray. "I got to get going. See you down at the club." He glanced at Corny and Kaye. "Nice to meet you."

Kaye's mother pulled herself onto the counter of the kitchenette, picking up her cigarette from where it scorched a plate. The strap of her tank slid off one shoulder. Kaye stared at Ellen, finding herself looking for some resemblance to the human changeling she'd seen in the thrall of the Seelie Court—the girl whose life Kaye had stolen. But all Kaye saw in her mother's face was a resemblance to her own familiar human glamour.

With a quick wave, Trent and his bass guitar swept out into the hall. Lutie took that moment to dislodge herself from Kaye's neck and fly to the top of the refrigerator. Kaye saw her settle behind an empty vase in what appeared to be a bowl of take-out menus.

"You know what you need?" Ellen asked Corny, picking up the half-empty beer beside her and taking a pull, washing down a mouthful of smoke.

He shrugged, grinning. "Direction in life? Self-esteem? A pony?"

"A haircut. You want me to do it for you? I used to cut Kaye's hair when she was a little girl." She hopped down and headed for the tiny bathroom. "I think I have some scissors around here somewhere."

"Don't let her bully you into it." Kaye raised her voice so she was sure her mother could hear her. "Mom, stop bullying Corny into things."

"Do I look bad?" Corny asked Kaye. "What I'm wearing— do I look bad?" There was something in the way he hesitated as he asked that gave the question weight.

Kaye gave him a sideways look and a grin. "You look like you."

"What does that mean?"

Kaye gestured to the camo pants she'd pulled off the floor that morning and the T-shirt she'd slept in. Her boots were still unlaced. "Look at what I'm wearing. It doesn't matter."

"You're saying I look terrible, aren't you?"

Kaye tilted her head and studied him. His skin had cleared up away from so much exposure to gas station fumes and it wasn't like he'd ever been bad looking. "No one in their right mind would *choose* a mullet as a hairdo unless they were trying to give the world the finger."

Corny's hand traveled self-consciously to his head.

"And you have a collection of wide-wing-collared polyester button-downs in colors like orange and brown."

"My mom buys them at flea markets."

Picking up her mother's makeup case off of a mound of clothes by the bed, Kaye pulled out a stick of glittery black liner. "And you wouldn't look like you without them."

"Okay, okay. I get it—what if I didn't want to look like me anymore?"

Kaye paused for a moment, looking up from smudging her eyelid. She heard a longing in his voice that troubled her. She wondered what he would do with a power like hers, wondered if he wondered about it.

Ellen came out of the bathroom with a comb, scissors, a small set of clippers, and a water-stained paper box. "How about some hair dye? I found a box that Robert was going to use before he decided to bleach. Black. Would look cute on you."

"Who's Robert?" Kaye asked.

Corny glanced at his reflection in the greasy door of the microwave. He turned his face to the side. "I guess I couldn't look any worse."

Ellen blew out a thin stream of blue smoke, tapped off the ash, and set her cigarette firmly on her lip. "Okay, sit on the chair."

Corny sat down awkwardly. Kaye pulled herself up onto the counter and finished off her mother's beer. Ellen handed her the cord for the clippers.

"Plug that in, sweetheart." Draping a bleach-stained towel around Corny's shoulders, Ellen began to buzz off the back of his hair. "Better already."

"Hey, Mom," Kaye said. "Can I ask you something?"

"Must be bad," Ellen said.

"Why do you say that?"

"Well, you don't usually call me 'Mom.'" She abandoned the clippers, took a deep drag on her cigarette, and started chopping at the top of Corny's hair with manicuring scissors. "Go ahead. You can ask me anything, kiddo."

The smoke burned Kaye's eyes. "Have you ever thought

about me not being your daughter? Like if I was switched at birth." As the words came out of her mouth, her hand came up involuntarily, fingers curving as if she could snatch the words out of the air.

"Wow. Weird question."

Kaye said nothing. She just waited. She wasn't sure she could bring herself to say anything else.

"It's funny. There was this one time." Running her fingers through Corny's hair, Ellen found stray pieces and cut them. "God, you were not even two, toddling around. I'd stacked up a bunch of books on a chair so you could sit at the table when we visited your grandmother's house. It wasn't real safe, but I wasn't real smart, either. Anyway, I go out to the kitchen, and when I come back, you're on the floor and the pile of books is all over the place. I mean, clearly you fell and clearly I am a terrible mother. But you're not crying. Instead, you have one of the books open and you're reading out of it—clear as a bell. And I thought: My child is a genius. And then I thought: This is not my child."

"Huh," Kaye said.

"And you were so honest—nothing like me as a kid. You'd bend the truth, sure, but you'd never outright lie."

My life is a lie. It was such a relief not to say it. It was a relief to just let the moments slide by until the subject got changed and the awful galloping of her heart slowed again.

"So did you ever imagine what things would be like if you were secretly adopted?" Ellen asked.

Kaye froze.

Ellen mixed the black dye in a chipped cereal bowl with a round metal spoon. "When I was a kid, I used to pretend I was a baby from a circus, and the fire-swallowers and jugglers and tightrope-walkers would come back for me and I'd have my own caravan and I'd tell people their fortunes."

"If you weren't my mother, who would give my friends fabulous makeovers?" As she said the words, Kaye knew she was a coward. No, not a coward. She was greedy. She was that cuckoo chick unwilling to give up the comforts of a stolen nest.

It was amazing how deceptive she could be without lying outright.

Corny reached up to touch the sudden spiky shortness of his hair. "I used to pretend that I was from another dimension. You know, like the mirror-universe Spock with the goatee. I figured, in that other dimension my mom was really the monarch of a vast empire or a wizard in exile or something. The downside was that she probably had a goatee too."

Kaye snickered. The cigarette smoke combined with the chemical stink of the hair dye turned her laughter to choking.

Ellen spooned a glop of black goop onto Corny's head and smeared it with a comb. Flecks stained the back of her hand, and her bracelets jangled together.

Dizzily, Kaye crossed the tiny room and pushed open the window. She could hear the paint crack as it came unstuck. Gulping in lungfuls of cold air, she looked out at the street. Her eyes stung.

"It's just going to be another minute," Ellen said. "Then I'll plastic-wrap his hair and toss this shit out."

Kaye nodded, although she wasn't sure her mother was looking. Out on the street, small clusters of people stood together in the snowy landscape, their breath spiraling up like smoke.

The streetlight reflected off strands of long pale hair and for a moment, before one of the figures turned, she thought of Roiben. It wasn't him, of course, but she had to stop herself from calling down anyway.

"Honey, I'm done here," Ellen said. "Look around and see if you can find this boy another shirt. I ruined his, and anyway, he's too skinny to be drowning in that thing."

Kaye turned. Corny's neck was red and splotchy. "Mom, you're embarrassing him!"

"If this was a television show, I would be the one doing the makeovers," Corny said darkly.

Ellen put out her cigarette on a plate. "God help us."

Kaye rummaged around in the stacks of clothing until she came up with a dark brown T-shirt with the black silhouette of a man riding a rabbit and holding a lance.

She held it up for Corny's inspection. He laughed nervously. "It looks tight."

Ellen shrugged. "It's from a book signing at a bar. Kelly something. Chain? Kelly Chain? It'll look good on you. Your jeans are okay and so's the jacket, but those sneakers aren't working. Double up your socks and you can wear Trent's Chucks. I think he left a pair over by the closet."

Corny glanced up at Kaye. Black dye ran in rivulets down the back of his neck, staining the collar of his T-shirt. "I'm going to retreat to the bathroom now."

As the water in the shower started, filling the tiny apartment with vapor, Ellen sat down on the bed. "While we're primping, how about you do my eyes? I can't manage that smoky thing you do."

Kaye smiled. "Sure."

Ellen lay back on the bed, while Kaye leaned over, carefully painting her mother's lids in shining silver, shadowing and outlining the edge of her lashes in black. This close, Kaye saw the gentle crow's-feet at the corners of her eyes, the enlarged pores in her nose, the slight purplish discoloration below her lashes. When she brushed her mother's hair out of the way, the shimmer of some strands revealed where the red dye covered gray. Kaye's fingers shook.

Mortal. This is what it means to be mortal.

"I think I'm done," Kaye said.

Ellen pushed herself into a sitting position and kissed Kaye on the cheek. Kaye could smell the cigarettes on her mother's breath, could smell the decay of teeth and the faint traces of sugary gum. "Thank you, baby. You're a real lifesaver."

I'm going to tell her, Kaye assured herself. *I'm going to tell her tonight.*

Corny emerged from the bathroom in a gust of steam. It was odd to see him in the new clothes with the shorter and darker hair. It shouldn't have made as much of a difference as it did, but the hair made his eyes shine and the tight shirt turned his scrawniness into slenderness.

"You look good," Kaye said.

He plucked self-consciously at the fabric and rubbed at his neck as though he could feel the stain of the dye.

"What do you think?" Ellen asked.

Corny looked back toward the bathroom, as though remembering his reflection. "It's like I'm hiding in my own skin."

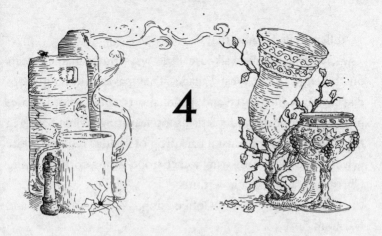

4

Bread does not nourish me, dawn disrupts me, all
    day
I hunt for the liquid measure of your steps.
—Pablo Neruda, "Love Sonnet XI"

The ride on the subway was awful. Kaye felt the iron all around her, felt the weight of it and the stink pressing down, suffocating her. She gripped the aluminum pole and tried not to breathe.

"You look kind of pale," Corny said as they climbed the concrete steps to the street.

She could feel her glamour being eaten away, weakening with each moment.

"Why don't you kids walk around awhile?" Ellen's lips shone with gloss and her hair was sprayed so thickly that it didn't move when the breeze hit it. "It'd be boring watching us set up."

Kaye nodded. "Also, if I would just see how cool New York was, I would move up here instead of wasting my time cooling my heels in Jersey?"

Ellen smiled. "And that."

Kaye and Corny walked a little ways through the streets on the edge of the West Village. They passed clothing shops displaying ruffled hats and plaid shorts, tiny record stores promising imports, and a fetish shop featuring a vinyl ball/gag mask with cat ears against a backdrop of holiday red-and-white velvet. A guy in a torn army jacket stood near a corner playing Christmas carols on a nose flute.

"Hey," Corny said. "Coffee shop. We can sit down and warm up."

They walked up the stairs and through the gold-stenciled door.

Café des Artistes was a series of rooms leading one into another through large passageways. Kaye walked past the counter and through a doorway into a chamber that featured a mantel covered in melted white candles, like a monstrous sandcastle eroded by waves. Dimly lit by black chandeliers that hung from a black tin ceiling and reflected in the glass of the aged prints and gilt mirrors, the rooms felt shadowy and cool. A faint and reassuring smell of tea and coffee in the air made her sigh.

They sat down in ornate gilt armchairs, worn so that white molded plastic showed on the hand rests. Corny picked at a golden swirl, and a small piece chipped off with his fingernail. Kaye idly opened the drawer of the small cream-colored table in front of her. Inside, she was surprised to find a collection of paper—notes, postcards, letters.

A waitress walked over and Kaye pushed the drawer shut. The woman's hair was blond on top and a glossy black underneath. "What can I get you?"

Corny picked up a menu off the middle of the table and read from it, as though he were picking things at random. "An omelet with green peppers, tomatoes, and mushrooms, a cheese plate, and a cup of coffee."

"Coffee for me, too." Kaye grabbed the paper out of his hands and ordered the first thing she saw. "And a piece of lemon pie."

"Real well-balanced diet," Corny said. "Sugar and caffeine."

"There might be meringue," Kaye said. "That's eggs. Protein."

He rolled his eyes.

As the waitress walked away, Kaye opened the drawer again and picked through the cards.

"Look at these." Girlish handwriting described a trip to Italy: *I couldn't stop thinking about Lawrence's prediction that I would meet someone in Rome*. A card with a hastily drawn mug in one corner had words written in blocky print with a pencil: *I spit into my coffee and then switched with Laura's boyfriend so that he would taste me in his mouth*. Kaye read the words out loud and then asked, "Where do you think these came from?"

"Garage sales?" Corny said. "Or maybe these are notes people never mailed anywhere. You know, like if you want to write something down, but don't want to let the person it was intended for read it. You leave it here."

"Let's leave something," Kaye said. She fumbled with her bag and pulled out two scraps of paper and an eyeliner pencil. "Be careful. It's soft and it smears."

"So, what, you want me to write down a secret? Like, how about I always wanted a comic book villain for a boyfriend, and after Nephamael, I'm not sure a nice guy is ever going to do it for me."

A couple at another table looked up as though they had caught a few of the words, but not enough to make any sense of what he'd said.

Kaye rolled her eyes. "Yeah, why would one sadistic lunatic put you off sadistic lunatics in general?"

Smirking, Corny took the piece of paper and wrote on it, pressing hard enough that the letters were fat and smudgy. He spun the slip in her direction. "'Cause I know you're going to read it anyway."

"I won't if you say not to."

"Just read it."

Kaye picked up the paper and saw the words: *I would do anything not to be human*.

She took the eye pencil and wrote hers: *I stole someone else's life*. She turned it toward Corny.

He slid them both into the drawer without comment. The waitress came with silverware, coffee, and cream. Kaye busied herself making her coffee as light and sweet as she could.

"You thinking about the quest?" Corny asked.

She'd been thinking about what he'd written, but she said, "I just wish I could talk to Roiben one more time. Just hear him *say* that he doesn't want me. It feels like I got broken up with in a dream."

"You could send him a letter or something, couldn't you? That's not technically seeing him."

"Sure," Kaye said. "If he got mail that wasn't, like, acorn-based."

"There's stuff you still don't understand about faerie customs. Everything that happened—it might not mean what you think it means."

Kaye shook her head, shaking off Corny's words. "Maybe it's good that we split up. I mean, as boyfriends go, he was always busy working. Running an evil court takes a lot of time."

"And he's too old for you," Corny said.

"And moping around all the time," Kaye said. "Too emo."

"No car, either. What's the point of an older boyfriend with no car?"

"Hair longer than mine," Kaye said.

"I bet he takes longer to get ready, too."

"Hey!" Kaye punched him on the arm. "I get ready fast."

"I'm just saying." Corny grinned. "You know, though, dating supernatural creatures is never easy. Admittedly, being supernatural yourself should make it easier."

Across the room, a group of three men looked up from their cappuccinos. One said something and the other two laughed.

"You're freaking them out," Kaye whispered.

"They just think we're plotting out a really bizarre book," Corny said. "Or roleplaying. We could be LARPing, you know." He crossed his arms over his chest. "Now I'm obfuscating, and you have to pay for my dinner."

Kaye caught the eye of a girl hunched over a table. The tips of her stringy hair trailed in her coffee and she was bundled in a series of coats, one layered over another, until it seemed like her back was hunched. When the girl saw Kaye looking, she held up a slip of paper between two fingers and slipped it into a drawer in front of her. Then, with a wink, she slugged back the last of her coffee and got up to leave.

"Hold on," Kaye said to Corny, rising and crossing to the

table. The girl was gone, but when Kaye opened the cabinet, the paper was still there: "The Queen wants to see you. The Fixer knows the way. Page him: 555-1327."

Corny and Kaye walked over to the club just as it started to snow again. The building had a brick front, papered over with posters in tattered layers worn by rain and dirt. Corny didn't recognize any of the bands.

At the front door, a woman in black jeans and a zebra-print coat took the five-dollar cover charge from a short line of shivering patrons.

"ID," the woman said, tossing back tiny braids.

"My mom's playing," Kaye said. "We're on the list."

"I still need to see ID," said the woman.

Kaye stared, and the air around them seemed to ripple, as if with heat. "Go right in," the woman said dreamily.

Corny stuck out his hand to be stamped with a sticky blue skull and walked toward the door. His heart thundered against his chest.

"What did you do to her?" he asked.

"I love this smell," Kaye said, smiling. He wasn't sure if she hadn't heard his question or if she'd just decided not to answer it.

"You have got to be kidding." The inside of the club was painted flat black. Even the piping high above their heads had been sprayed the same matte tone so that all the light in the room seemed to be absorbed by the walls. A few multicolor lights strobed over the bar and across the stage, where a band wailed.

Kaye shouted over the music. "No, really. I love it. Stale beer and cigarette residue and sweat. It burns my throat, but after the car and the subway ride, I barely care."

"That's great," he shouted back. "Do you want to say hi to your mom?"

"I better not." Kaye rolled her eyes. "She's a bitch when she's getting ready. Stage fright."

"Okay, let's grab a seat," Corny said, weaving his way toward one of the tiny tables lit with a red electric votive that looked like a bug light.

Kaye went to get drinks. Corny sat and observed the crowd. An Asian boy with a shaved head and fringed suede chaps gestured to a girl in a knitted wool dress and tarantula-print cowboy boots. Nearby, a woman in a moiré coat slow danced with another woman up against a black support pole. Corny felt a wild surge of excitement fill him. This was a real New York club, an actual cool place to which he should have been forbidden according to the rules of nerd-dom.

Kaye came back to the table as the other band cleared off the stage and Ellen, Trent, and the other two members of Treacherous Iota strode on.

Moments later, Kaye's mother was bent over, raking the strings of her guitar. Kaye watched in rapt fascination, the pools of her eyes wet as she chewed on a plastic stirrer.

The music was okay—candy punk with some messed-up lyrics. Kaye's mom didn't look like the faded middle-aged woman Corny had seen a couple of hours ago, though. This Ellen looked fierce, like she might lean out and eat up all of the little girls and boys gathered around the stage. Even though they weren't biologically related, as she screeched through the first song, Corny thought he could see a lot of Kaye in her.

Watching her transformation made him uncomfortable, especially because his fingers were still stained with black dye from his own. He looked around the room.

His gaze ran over the beautiful boys and the insect-slender girls, but it stopped on a tall man leaning against the far wall, a messenger bag slung over his shoulders. Just looking at him made gooseflesh bloom on Corny's arms. His features were far too perfect to belong to a human.

Looking at that stiff, arrogant posture, Corny thought it was a glamoured Roiben come to beg Kaye's indulgence. But the hair was the color of butter, not salt, and the tilt of the jaw was not like Roiben's at all.

The man stared at Kaye, so fixedly that when a girl in pigtails stopped in front of him, he moved to the left to continue watching.

Corny stood up without really meaning to. "Be right back," he said to Kaye's questioning look.

Now that he was walking in the man's direction, Corny was no longer sure what to do. His heart beat against his rib cage like a ricocheting rubber ball until he thought he might choke. Still, as he got closer, more details added to Corny's suspicions. The man's jaw and cheekbones were too sharp. His eyes were the color of bluebells. He was the most poorly disguised faerie Corny had ever seen.

Onstage, Ellen bellowed into the mic, and the drummer went into a solo.

"You're doing a crap-ass job of blending in, you know that?" Corny shouted over the rhythmic pounding.

The faerie narrowed his eyes. Corny looked down at his

borrowed sneakers, suddenly remembering that he could be charmed.

"Whatever do you mean?" The man's voice was soft. It showed none of the anger that had been in his face.

Corny ground his teeth together, ignoring his longing to look into those lovely eyes again. "You don't look human. You don't even talk human."

A smooth, warm hand touched Corny's cheek, and Corny jumped. "I feel human," the faerie man said.

Without meaning to, Corny leaned into the touch. Desire flared in him, so sharp it was almost pain. But as his eyes drifted closed, he saw his sister's face disappearing under briny water, saw her screaming great gulps of sea as a beautiful kelpie-turned-boy dragged her down. He saw himself crawling through the dirt to bring a pulpy fruit to drop at a laughing faerie knight's feet.

His eyes snapped open. He was so furious his hands shook. "Don't flirt," Corny said. He wasn't going to be weak again. He could do this.

The faerie watched him with arched eyebrows and a smile filled with mockery.

"I'll bet you want Kaye," Corny said. "I can get her for you."

The faerie frowned. "And you would betray another of your kind so easily?"

"You know she's not my kind." Corny took him by the elbow. "Come on. She might see us. We can talk in the bathroom."

"I beg your pardon."

"Keep begging," Corny said, grabbing the faerie's arm and

leading him through the crowd. A glance back told him that Kaye was preoccupied with the performance onstage. Adrenaline flooded him, narrowing his focus, making rage and desire seem suddenly indistinguishable. He swept into the bathroom. The single stall and two urinals were empty. On a dark purple wall, beside a hand-lettered sign promising decapitation to employees failing to wash their hands, hung a shelf piled with toilet paper and cleaning supplies.

An utterly unpleasant idea occurred to Corny. He had to fight not to smile.

"The thing is," he said, "that's not how human guys dress at all. It's not sloppy enough. Roiben always makes the same mistake."

The fey man's lip curled slightly, and Corny tried to keep his face blank, as though he had missed that rather interesting tell.

"Look at yourself. Fix your glamour so that you look more like you're wearing what I'm wearing, okay?"

The faerie looked Corny over. "Repugnant," he said, but unshouldered his messenger bag, leaning it against the wall.

Corny grabbed a can of Raid off the shelf. If Kaye couldn't even have a cigarette anymore, the effects of a concentrated insect poison should be impressive. He didn't need to speculate long. As the faerie turned, Corny sprayed him full in the face.

The blond choked and fell immediately to his knees, glamour dropping from him, revealing dreadful, inhuman beauty. Corny reveled for a moment in the look of him convulsing on the filthy floor, then he pulled the lace out of his sneaker and used it to tie the creature's hands behind its back.

The faerie squirmed as the knots went tight, trying to twist away as he coughed. Corny scrambled for the can and hit the faerie with it as hard as he could.

"I swear to fucking God, I will spray you again," Corny said. "Enough of this shit will kill you."

The faerie went still. Corny stood up, straddling the faerie's body, fingering the nozzle on the Raid can. He caught his own gaze in the mirror, saw his short dyed dark hair and his borrowed clothes, how pathetic they were. He still looked painfully, disappointingly human.

Thin, strong fingers wound around Corny's calves, but Corny pressed the sole of his sneaker against the faerie's neck and squatted down over him. "Now you're going to tell me a whole bunch of things I've always wanted to know."

The creature swallowed.

"Your name," Corny said.

The blue eyes flashed. "Never."

Corny shrugged and slid his foot off of the faerie, suddenly uncomfortable. "Fine. Something I can call you, then. And not some stupid 'me myself' bullshit. I read."

"Adair."

Corny paused, thinking of the paper in the drawer. "Are you the Fixer? Did you slip Kaye a note?"

The man looked puzzled, then shook his head. "He's a human, like you."

"Okay. Adair, if you're not the Fixer, what do you want with Kaye?"

The faerie was silent for a long moment. Corny slammed the can into the side of the creature's head.

"Who told you to come here?"

Adair shrugged and Corny hit him again. Blood stained his mouth.

"Silarial," he gasped.

Corny nodded with satisfaction. He was breathing hard, but each breath came out like a laugh. "Why?"

"The pixie. I'm to take her to the Seelie Court. Many of my Lady's subjects are seeking her out."

Corny sat down on Adair's stomach and fisted his hand in the golden hair. "Why?"

"Queen wants to talk. Just talk."

A man with a fauxhawk opened the door, blanched, and then shut it with a slam. The faerie twisted himself around, pushing upright.

"Tell me something else," Corny said. His clenched fingers shook. "Tell me how to protect—"

At that moment the bathroom door swung open again. This time it was Kaye. "Corny, they're—" she said, then seemed to focus on the scene in front of her. She blinked her eyes rapidly and coughed. "This is so not what I expected to see when I walked in here."

"Silarial sent him," Corny said. "For you."

"The bartender's calling the cops. We have to get out of here."

"We can't let him go," Corny said.

"Corny, he's *bleeding*." Kaye coughed again. "What did you do? I feel like my lungs are on fire."

Corny started to stand, to explain.

"I curse you." The faerie rolled onto his side and spat a reddish gob of spittle onto Corny's cheek. It ran like a tear. "Let everything that your fingers touch wither."

Corny staggered back, and as he did so, his hand brushed the wall. The paint under his fingers buckled and flaked. Stopping, he looked at his palm, the familiar lines and grooves and calluses seemed, suddenly, to form a new and horrible landscape.

"Come on!" Kaye grabbed him by the sleeve, steering him toward the door.

The metal of the knob tarnished at the stroke of his skin.

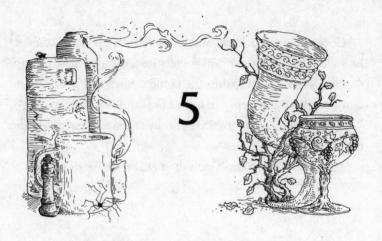

Hell is oneself,
Hell is alone.
—T. S. ELIOT

A faun with bloodstained claws sank into a low bow before Roiben's throne. They had come, each of his vassals, to boast of their usefulness, to tell him of their service to the crown, to win his favor and the promise of better tasks. Roiben looked out at the sea of them and had to fight down panic. He gripped the arms of his throne hard enough that the braided wood groaned.

"In your name," said the creature, "I have killed seven of my brethren and kept their hooves." He emptied out a sack with a clatter.

"Why?" Roiben asked before he thought better of it, his eye drawn to the jagged chopped bone of the ankles, the way the gore had dried black. The mortar that grooved the floor of the audience chamber was already discolored, but this gift freshened the ruddy stains.

The faun shrugged. Brambles snarled the fur of his legs. "It was a token that often pleased Lady Nicnevin. I sought only to ingratiate myself with you."

Roiben closed his eyes tightly for a moment, then opened them again and took a deep breath, schooling himself to indifference. "Right. Excellent." He turned to the next creature.

A delicate fey boy with tar-black wings curtsied. "I am pleased to report," he said in a soft, shivery voice, "I have led nearly a dozen mortal children off of rooftops or to their deaths in marshes."

"I see," Roiben said with exaggerated reasonableness. For a moment, he was afraid what he might do. He thought of Kaye and what she would think of this; he thought of her standing on her own roof in the T-shirt and underwear she wore to bed, swaying forward drowsily. "In my name? I think you amuse only yourself. Perhaps you could find something more vicious than children to torment now that the war has begun."

"As my Lord commands," said the winged faerie, scowling at his feet.

A small hunched hob came forward. With gnarled hands, he unrolled a hideous cloth and spread it over the floor.

"I have killed a thousand mice, keeping only their tails and weaving those together into a rug. I present it now as a tribute to your magnificence."

For the first time he could recall, Roiben had to bite the inside of his cheek to keep from laughing. "Mice?" He looked at his chamberlain. Ruddles raised a single brow.

"Mice," said the hob, puffing out his chest.

"This is quite an effort," said Roiben. His servants rolled up the rug as the hob walked away, looking pleased with himself.

A silky made a bobbing bow, her tiny body clothed only in her pale yellow-green hair. "I have caused fields of grapes to wither on the vine, becoming black and heavy with poison. The wine from their juice will harden the hearts of men."

"Yes, because the hearts of men aren't nearly hardened enough." Roiben frowned. His diction sounded human. He didn't have to guess where he had picked up those phrases.

The silky did not appear to notice the sarcasm. She smiled as though he were offering her great praise.

And so they came, a parade of deeds and gifts, each more grisly than the last, all of them done in the name of Roiben, Lord of the Unseelie Court. Each hideous feat laid before him as a cat drops the bird it has finally killed, once all possible amusement has been wrung from toying with it.

"In your name," each one said.

In his name. The name that no one living knew in full, save for Kaye. His name. Now that it belonged to all these others to conjure and to curse by, he wondered who had the greater claim to it.

Roiben gritted his teeth and nodded and smiled. Only later, in his chambers, sitting on a stool in front of his mouse-tail rug, did he allow himself to be filled with loathing. For all those of the Unseelie Court, who cut and slit and gutted everything they touched. For himself, sitting on a throne in a court of monsters.

He was still staring at the gifts when a terrible, thunderous crash made the walls shake. Dirt rained down on him, stinging his eyes. A second shock reverberated through the hill. He raced out of the room, toward the noise, and passed Bluet in the hallway. Dust covered her, and the long twisted spikes of her hair nearly obscured a fresh cut on her shoulder. Her lips were the color of a bruise.

"My Lord!" she said. "There has been an attack!"

For a moment, he just stared at her, feeling foolish, not quite able to understand. For all his hatred of Silarial, he couldn't quite accept that he was at war with those he had loved, those whom he still considered his people. He couldn't accept that they'd struck first.

"Attend to yourself," he told her dazedly, moving on toward the sound of screams. A handful of faeries darted past him, silent and covered in dirt. One, a goblin, stared at him with wet eyes before rushing on.

The great hall was on fire. The top was cracked open like an egg, and a portion of one side was missing. Gusts of greasy black smoke rose up to the starry sky, devouring the falling snow. At the center of the brugh was a truck—a semi—its iron body burning. The chassis was twisted, the cab crushed under heaps of dirt and rock, as red and gold flames licked upward. A sea of burning oil and diesel fuel spread to scorch everything it touched.

He stared, stunned. There, under the debris, were dozens upon dozens of bodies: his herald, Thistledown; Widdersap, who had once whistled through a blade of grass to make a serving girl dance; Snagill, who'd carefully limned the ceiling of the feasting room in silver. The hob who'd woven the mouse-tail rug screamed, rolling around in fire.

Ellebere pushed Roiben to the side, just as a granite tombstone fell from above, cracking on the floor of the hall. "You must leave, my Lord," he shouted.

"Where is Ruddles?" Roiben demanded. "Dulcamara?"

"They don't matter." Ellebere's grip on Roiben tightened. "You are our King."

Through the smoke, figures appeared, chopping at the fallen and the injured.

"Get the fey in the hallways to safety." Roiben wrenched his arm free. "Take them to the Kinnelon ruins."

Ellebere hesitated.

Two bolts flew through the rancid smoke to embed themselves in what remained of the earthen wall. Thin shafts of glass that Seelie knights used for arrows—so fine that you could barely feel them as they pierced your heart.

"As you said, I *am* your King. Do it now!" Roiben pushed his way through the choking brume, leaving Ellebere behind.

The same faun who had brought Roiben the hooves of his fellows was trying to dig another faerie out from beneath a mound of earth. And nearby lay Cirillan, who loved tears so much that he saved them in tiny vials that cluttered up his room. His aqua skin was smeared with dusty blood and silver burrs that had been shot from Bright Court slings.

As Roiben watched, the faun gasped, his body arched, and he fell.

Roiben drew his curved sword. All his life he had been in service to battle, but he had never seen the like of what was happening all around him. The Bright Court had never fought so *inelegantly*.

He dodged just before the tines of a golden trident caught him in the chest. The Seelie knight swung again, her teeth bared.

He slammed his sword into her thigh and she faltered. Grabbing her trident at the base, he sliced her throat, quick and clean. Blood sprayed his face as she fell to her knees, reaching for her own neck in surprise.

He didn't know her.

Two humans rushed at him from either side. One held up a gun, but he cut off the hand that held it before the mortal had a hope of firing. He stabbed the other through the chest. A human boy—perhaps twenty, with a Brookdale College T-shirt and rumpled hair—slumped over Roiben's hooked sword.

For a moment, the boy reminded him of Kaye.

Kaye. Dead.

There was a shout and Roiben turned to see a shower of silver pinecones burst just short of where he stood. Through the smoke he saw Ruddles, taking a bite out of the side of a Seelie fey's face, Dulcamara dispatching two others with knives. One of Roiben's pages, Clotburr, slammed a burning harp into another faerie.

Here, in his once majestic hill, human corpses still held their iron weapons in stiffening hands as they slumped beside more than a dozen unmoving Unseelie troops in shining armor. The fire lit the bodies, one by one.

"Quickly," Dulcamara said. Choking black smoke was everywhere. Somewhere in the distance, Roiben could hear sirens wailing. Above them, the mortals came to pour water on the burning hill.

Clotburr coughed, slowing, and Roiben lifted him up, settling the boy against his shoulder.

"How did she do this?" asked Dulcamara, her fingers clenched white-knuckled around the hilt of her blade.

Roiben shook his head. There were protocols to faerie battles. He could not imagine Silarial putting decorum aside, especially when every advantage was hers. But too, who of her people would know what she had done this day? Only those few she had sent to command the mortals. Most were dead. One cannot dishonor oneself before the dead. It occurred to him then that he'd misunderstood Dulcamara's question. She didn't want to know how Silarial could be so hideously inventive; she was puzzling out how it had been accomplished.

"Mortals," Roiben said, and now that he considered it, he had to admit a grudging awe for so radical and terrible a stratagem. "Silarial's Folk are charming humans instead of leading them off roofs. She's making troops of them. Now we are more than overmatched. We are lost."

The weight of the soot-smeared faerie in his arms made him think of all of the Folk of the Night Court, all those he had sworn to be sovereign over. All those lives he'd been willing to accept in trade for Silarial's death. And he wondered in that moment what he might have accomplished if he'd done more than just endure. Whom he might have saved.

As though catching his thoughts, Ruddles turned toward him with a frown. "What now, my King?"

Roiben found himself wanting to win the unwinnable war.

He had known only two rulers, both great and neither good. He did not know how to be any kind of King nor how to win, other than to be even more ruthless than they. But in that moment, he wondered what might happen if he bent his will to finding out.

Kaye pushed Corny ahead of her, through the crowd near the door of the club, out past the ID-check woman, who still looked giddy with enchantment. He held his hands above his head, as in surrender, and when people came close, he flinched. They walked like that for several blocks, past people in their heavy coats shuffling through the slush. Kaye watched the heels of a woman's ostrich-leather boots stab through an icy mound of snow. The woman stumbled.

Corny turned toward her, dropping his hands so that they now hung in front of him. He looked like a zombie lurching toward its next victim.

"I know where," Kaye said, taking deep breaths of the acrid iron air.

She crossed several blocks, Corny behind her. The streets were a maze of names and bodegas, similar enough for her to get easily turned around. She found her way back to Café des Artistes, though, and from there to the fetish shop.

Corny looked at her in confusion.

"Gloves," she told him firmly as she steered him inside.

The scent of burning patchouli thickened the air in the Irascible Peacock. Leather corsets and thongs hung from the walls, their metal buckles and zippers gleaming. Behind the desk a bored-looking older man read the paper, not even glancing up at them.

In the back of the store, Kaye could see the restraints, floggers, and whips. The hollow eyes of masks watched her as she threaded her way toward a pair of elbow-length rubber gloves.

She grabbed them, paid the bored clerk with five glamoured leaves, and bit off the plastic tag with her teeth.

Corny stood next to a marble table, fingers pressed to a stack of flyers advertising a fetish ball. The paper yellowed in widening circles, aging beneath his hands. Withering. A slow smile curved on his mouth, as though watching it gave him pleasure.

"Stop that," Kaye said, holding out the gloves.

Corny started, looking at her as though he didn't know her. Even as he slid on the gloves, he did so numbly, and then stared at his rubber-encased arms in puzzlement.

Walking out, the shine of a pair of chromed handcuffs lined in mink caught Kaye's eye and she picked them up, running her thumb over the soft pelt. Years of shoplifting instincts made her slip them into her pocket before she hit the door.

"I can't believe you jumped some guy in a bathroom," Kaye said as soon as they'd crossed the street.

"What?" Corny glowered. "*I* can't believe you just stole a pair of fuzzy handcuffs, klepto. Anyway, he wasn't *some guy*. He was from the Seelie Court. He was one of them."

"One of *them*? A faerie? Like I'm one of them?"

"He was there to get you. He said he was supposed to bring you to Silarial," Corny yelled at her, and the name seemed to carry through the cold night air.

"And for that you almost kill him?" Kaye's voice rose, sounding shrill even to her own ears.

"I hate to break this to you," Corny said nastily, "but Silarial hates you. You're the one who screwed up her plan to take over the Unseelie Court, plus you've been screwing her ex-boyfriend—"

"Will you stop with the—"

"Right, I know. Impossible quest. Look, I'm sure I could list more things about you she hates, but I think you get my point. Whatever she wants, we want the opposite."

"I don't care about her or her messengers!" Kaye shouted. "I care about you, and you're acting crazy."

Corny shrugged and turned away from her, looking through the window of a shop as if he were seeing some other place in the racks of clothing. Then he smiled at himself in the glass. "Whatever, Kaye. I'm right about Adair. They love to hurt people. People like Janet."

Kaye shuddered, guilt over Janet's death too fresh for his words not to feel like an accusation. "I know—"

Corny interrupted her. "Anyway, I got cursed, so I guess I got what I deserved, right? The universe is in balance. I got what I was asking for."

"That's not what I meant," Kaye said. "I don't even know what I mean. I'm just freaked out. Everything's coming apart."

"*You're* freaked out? Everything I touch rots! How am I going to eat food? How am I going to jerk off?"

Kaye laughed despite herself.

"Not to mention I am going to have to dress up in down-market fetish-wear forever." Corny held up a gloved hand.

"Good thing that turns you on," Kaye said.

He rolled his eyes. "Okay, it was dumb. What I did. At least I should have found out what Silarial wanted."

Kaye shook her head. "It doesn't matter. Let's go back to Brooklyn and figure out what to do about your hands."

Corny pointed to a pay phone hanging outside of a bar. "You want me to call your mom's cell? I could tell her we got kicked out of the club for being underage. I can lie like crazy."

Kaye shook her head. "After you beat up someone in the bathroom? I think she knows what we got kicked out for."

"He was hitting on me," Corny said primly. "I had to protect my virtue."

Kaye let herself and Corny into her mother's apartment and threw herself down on the bed. Corny flopped down beside her with a groan.

Looking up at the popcorn of the ceiling, she studied the grooves and fissures, letting her mind drift from Corny's curse and the explanation she didn't have for running out on her mother's show. She thought of Roiben instead, standing in front of the entire assemblage of the Unseelie Court, and of the way they'd bowed their heads. But that made her think of all the children they'd snatched from cradles and strollers and swing sets to replace with changelings, or worse. She imagined Roiben's slender fingers circling flailing, rosy limbs. Looking across the bed, she saw Corny's fingers instead, each one encased in rubber.

"We're going to fix things," Kaye said.

"How are we going to do that, exactly?" Corny asked. "Not that I'm doubting you, mind."

"Maybe I could take the curse off of you. I have magic, right?"

He sat up. "You think you can?"

"I don't know. Let me get rid of my glamour so I can use whatever I've got." She concentrated, imagining her disguise tearing like cobwebs. Her senses flooded. She could smell the crusts of burnt food in the burners of the stove, the exhaust from cars, the mold inside the walls, and even the filthy snow they'd tracked across the floor. And she felt the iron, heavier than ever, eating away at the edges of her power, as clearly as she felt the brush of wings across her shoulders.

"Okay," she said, rolling toward him. "Take off a glove."

He removed one and held out the hand to her. She tried to imagine her magic as she'd been told to, like a ball of energy prickling between her palms. She concentrated on expanding it, despite the iron-soaked air. When it settled over Corny's hands, her skin stung like she clutched nettles. She could change the shape of his fingers, but she couldn't touch the curse.

"I don't know what I'm doing," she said finally, helplessly, letting her concentration lapse and the energy dissipate. Just the attempt had exhausted her.

"That's okay. I heard about a guy who breaks spells. A human."

"Really? How'd you hear about him?" Kaye fumbled with her pocket.

Corny turned his face away from her, toward the window. "I forget."

"Remember the paper that girl gave me? The Fixer? There's a place to start. Fixing sounds like what we're looking for."

Corny yawned and put the glove back on. "Your mom is going to totally make us sleep on the floor, isn't she?"

Kaye turned to him, pressing her face against his shoulder. His shirt smelled like bug spray and she wondered what the faerie who'd cursed him had wanted. She wondered about the other Kaye, still trapped in the Seelie Court. "Do you think I should tell her?" she mumbled into the T-shirt.

"Tell her what? That we want the bed?"

"That I'm a changeling. That she has a daughter who got stolen."

"Why would you want to do that?" He lifted his arm and Kaye ducked under it, pillowing her head on his chest.

"Because none of this is real. I don't belong here."

"Where else would you belong?" Corny asked.

Kaye shrugged. "I don't know. I'm neither fish nor fowl. What's left?"

"Good red herring, I think," he said. "It's a fish."

"At least I'm good and red."

A key rattled in the door.

Kaye jumped up and Corny grabbed her arm. "Okay, tell her."

She shook her head hurriedly. The door opened and Ellen walked into the room, her shoulders dusted with new-fallen snow.

Kaye reached for the shreds of her glamour to make herself human-seeming, but it came to her uneasily. The magic and the iron had eaten up more of her energy than she'd supposed. "It's not working," Kaye whispered. "I can't change back."

Corny looked panicked. "Hide."

"I heard you guys got into some trouble, eh?" Ellen laughed as she dumped her guitar case on top of the paper-covered kitchen table. She tugged off her coat and dropped it on the floor.

Kaye turned her back to her mother, hiding her face beneath her hair. She wasn't sure how much her glamour hid, but at least she could no longer feel her wings.

"He was hitting on me," Corny said.

Ellen raised her eyebrows. "You should learn to take a compliment better."

"Things got out of hand," Kaye said. "The guy was a jerk."

Walking over to the bed, Ellen sat down and started tugging off her boots. "I guess I should be glad you two vigilantes weren't hurt. What happened to you, Kaye? You look like you got a jar of green dye dropped on you. And why are you hiding your face?"

Kaye sucked in her breath so hard that she felt dizzy. Her stomach twisted.

"You know," Corny said. "I think I'm going to walk down to the corner store. I feel a sudden need for cheese curls. Want anything?"

"Some kind of diet drink," Ellen said. "Grab some money out of my coat pocket."

"Kaye?" he called.

She shook her head.

"Okay, I'll be right back," Corny said. Out of the corner of her eye, she saw him give her a look as he unlatched the door.

"I have something to tell you," Kaye said without turning.

She could hear her mother banging in the cabinets. "There's something I want to tell you, too. I know I promised we'd stay in Jersey, but I just couldn't. My mother—she just gets to me, you know that. It hurt me when you stayed behind."

"I—" Kaye started, but Ellen cut her off.

"No," she said. "I'm glad. I guess I always figured that so long as you were happy, then I was an okay mother no matter how strange our lives got. But you weren't happy, were you? So, okay, Jersey didn't work out, but things will be different in New York. This place is mine, not some boyfriend's. And I'm bartending, not just doing gigs. I'm turning things around. I want another chance."

"Mom." Kaye half turned. "I think you should hear what I have to say before you go on."

"About tonight?" Ellen asked. "I knew there was more to

the story. You two would never attack some guy because he—"

Kaye cut her off. "About a long time ago."

Ellen took out a cigarette from a pack on the table. She lit it off of the stove. Turning, she squinted, like she'd just noticed Kaye's skin. "Well? Shoot."

Kaye took a deep breath. She could feel her heartbeat like it was pounding in her brain instead of her chest. "I'm not human."

"What is that supposed to mean?" Ellen frowned.

"Your real daughter has been gone a long time. Since she was really little. Since we were both really little. They switched us."

"What switched you?"

"There are things—supernatural things out in the world. Some people call them faeries, some people call them monsters or demons or whatever, but they exist. When the . . . the faeries took your real daughter, they left me behind."

Ellen stared at her, the ash on her cigarette growing long enough to rain on the back of her hand. "That is complete bullshit. Look at me, Kaye."

"I didn't know until October. Maybe I should have guessed—there were clues." Kaye felt as though her eyes were raw, as though her throat were raw as she spoke. "But I didn't know."

"Stop. This isn't funny and it isn't nice." Ellen's voice sounded torn between being annoyed and being truly frightened.

"I can prove it." Kaye walked toward the kitchen. "Lutie-loo! Come out. Show yourself to her."

The little faerie flew down from the refrigerator to alight on

Kaye's shoulder, tiny hands catching hold of a steadying lock of hair.

"I'm bored and everything stinks," Lutie pouted. "You should have taken me with you to the party. What if you had gotten drunk and fallen down again?"

"Kaye," Ellen said, her voice shaking. "What is that thing?"

Lutie snarled. "Rude! I will tangle your hair and sour all your milk."

"She's my evidence. So that you'll listen to me. *Really* listen."

"Whatever it is," Ellen said, "you're nothing like it."

Kaye took a deep breath and dropped what glamour was left. She couldn't see her own face, but she knew how she looked to Ellen now. Eyes black and glossy as oil, skin green as a grass stain. She could see her hands, folded in front of her, her long fingers, with an extra joint that made them seem curled even when they were at rest.

The cigarette dropped from her mother's fingers. It burned the linoleum floor where it fell, the edges of the melting plastic crater glowing, the center black as ash. Black as Kaye's eyes.

"No," Ellen said, shaking her head and backing away from Kaye.

"It's me," Kaye said. Her limbs felt cold, as though all the blood in her body rushed to her face. "This is what I really look like."

"I don't understand. I don't understand what you are. Where is my daughter?"

Kaye had read about changelings, about how mothers got their own babies back. They heated up iron pokers, threw the faerie infants on the fire.

"She's in Faerieland," Kaye said. "I've seen her. But you *know* me. I'm still me. I don't want to scare you. I can explain everything now that you'll listen. We can get her back."

"You stole my child and now you want to help me?" Ellen demanded.

In pictures Kaye'd been a skinny black-eyed little thing. She thought of that now. Of her bony fingers. Eating. Always eating. Had Ellen ever suspected? Known in that kind of gut-motherly way that no one would have believed?

"Mom . . ." Kaye walked toward her mother, reaching out her hand, but the look on Ellen's face stopped her. What came out of Kaye's mouth was a startled laugh.

"Don't you smile," her mother shouted. "You think this is funny?"

A mother is supposed to know every inch of her baby, her sweet flesh smell, every hangnail on her fingers, the number of cowlicks in her hair. Had Ellen been repulsed and ashamed of her repulsion?

Had she stacked up those books as a seat, hoping that Kaye would fall? Was that why she'd forgotten to stock the fridge? Why she'd left Kaye alone with strangers? Had her mother punished her in little ways for something that was so impossible that it could not be admitted?

"What the fuck did you do with my child?" Ellen shouted.

The nervous giggling wouldn't stop. It was like the absurdity and the horror needed to escape somehow and the only way out was through Kaye's mouth.

Ellen slapped her. For a moment Kaye went completely silent, and then she howled with laughter. It spilled out of her like shrieks, like the last of her human self burning away.

In the glass of the window, she could see her wings, slightly bent, glistening along her back.

With two beats of them, Kaye leaped up onto the counter-top. The fluorescent light buzzed above her head. The blackened wings of a dozen moths dusted its yellowed grill.

Ellen, startled, stepped back again, flattening herself against the cabinets.

Looking down, Kaye could feel her mouth grinning wide and terrible. "I'll bring you back your real daughter," she said, her voice full of bitter elation. It was a relief to finally know what she had to do. To finally admit she wasn't human.

And at the very least, it was a quest she might be able to accomplish.

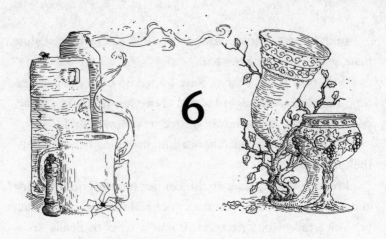

All was taken away from you: white dresses,
wings, even existence.
—CZESLAW MILOSZ, "ON ANGELS"

Corny shivered on the steps of the apartment building. The cold of the cement soaked up through the thin fabric of his jeans as flurries of snow froze in his hair. The hot coffee he had bought at the bodega tasted like ashes, but he grimaced through another sip for the warmth. He tried not to notice that thin hairline cracks had already begun to form at the very tips of his rubber gloves.

He didn't want to think too carefully about the relief he'd felt when Kaye couldn't remove the curse. He'd felt diseased at first, like it was him rotting away and not the things he touched. But it wasn't him withering. Only everything else. He imagined all the things he hated, all the things he could destroy, and found his grip on the cup so tight that the cardboard bent and coffee splashed his leg.

Kaye pushed though the front door with enough force to

nearly send it crashing against the side of the building. Lutie fluttered alongside her, darting out into the safety of the air.

Corny stood up reflexively.

Kaye paced back and forth on the steps. "She pretty much hates me. I guess I should have pretty much expected that."

"Well, then I'm not bringing her a soda," Corny said, popping the tab and taking a swig. He made a face. "Ugh. Diet."

Kaye didn't even smile. She wrapped her purple coat around herself. "I'm going to get back the other Kaye for her. I'm going to switch us back."

"But . . . Kaye." Corny struggled to find the words. "You're her daughter, and that other kid . . . she doesn't even know Ellen. Ellen doesn't know her."

"Sure," Kaye said hollowly. "It might be awkward at first, but they'll work it out."

"It's not that simple—" Corny started.

Kaye cut him off. "It *is* that simple. I'm going to call the number on that piece of paper and go see the Queen. If she wants something from me, then I have a chance of getting the other Kaye back."

"Sure. I bet she'd trade Chibi-Kaye for your head on a platter," Corny said, frowning.

"*Chibi*-Kaye?" Kaye looked as if she didn't know whether to laugh or hit him.

He shrugged. "You know, like in those mangas where they draw the cute, small version of a character."

"I know what a chibi is!" She dug around in her pocket. "Give me your cell phone for a second."

He looked at her evenly. "You know I'm coming with you, right?"

"I don't—" Kaye started.

"I can handle it," Corny said before she could finish. "Just because this is dumb doesn't mean you get to do it alone. And I don't need your protection."

"And I don't want to screw up your life more than I already have!"

"Look," Corny said. "Before, you mentioned that maybe this Fixer guy would know something about my curse. We would have called this person and I would have gone with you anyway."

"Fine, okay, okay. Cell?"

"Let me call," Corny said, holding out his hand.

Kaye sighed, seeming to deflate. She held out the paper. "Fine."

Corny punched in the number, although it took a few tries with the thick gloves. The phone rang once and a computer voice said, *"Hit pound and dial your number."*

"Pager," he said to Kaye's questioning look. "Yeah, your guide to the Seelie Court is totally a dealer."

Lutie settled on Kaye's shoulder and grabbed a clump of green hair, wrapping it around her tiny body like a cloak. "Bitter coldy cold," she said.

"Let's head toward your car. Maybe by the time we get there, he'll call back."

Corny jumped off the steps. "Otherwise, we can sleep in the back covered in fast-food garbage like the brother and sister in 'Babes in the Wood' who got—"

"Lutie," Kaye said, interrupting him. "You can't come. You have to watch over my mom. Please. Just to make sure that she's okay."

"But it smells and I'm bored."

"Lutie, please. Where we're going—it could be dangerous."

The little faerie flew up, wings and clotted cream hair making her seem like a tossed handful of snow. "I'm half sick of iron, but I will stay. For you. For you." She pointed one toothpick-tiny finger down at Kaye as she rose toward the apartment window.

"We'll come for you as soon as we can," Corny called, but he was relieved. Sometimes it was tiring trying not to stare at her delicate hands or her miniature bird-black eyes. There was nothing human about her.

As they crossed the street, Corny's phone rang. He flipped it open. "Hey."

"What you want?" It was a young man's voice, soft and angry. "Who gave you this number?"

"I'm sorry. Maybe I dialed wrong." He made wide eyes at Kaye. "We're looking for a . . . the . . . the Fixer."

The line went quiet, and Corny winced at how stupid he sounded.

"You still haven't told me what you want," the boy said.

"My friend got a note. Said you could help her see the Queen."

"Okay."

"So, wait, you *are* the Fixer?" Corny said. Kaye looked over impatiently.

"Ask him about the curse," she said.

"Yeah, that's me." The boy's tone made it hard for Corny to decide if he was actually offering his services. "And yeah, I'm supposed to take a girl upstate. Tell her to come over here in the morning and we can go. You got paper?"

"Hold on." Corny fumbled for something to write with. Kaye reached into her pockets and came up with a marker. When she held it out, he took it and her arm. "Okay, go."

The boy gave them his address. Riverside Drive on the Upper West Side. Corny wrote it on Kaye's skin.

"I want to leave now," Kaye said. "Tell him. Tonight."

"She wants to leave tonight," Corny repeated into the phone.

"Is that girl crazy?" the boy asked. "It's two in the morning."

Kaye pulled the phone out of Corny's hands. "We just need directions.

"Uh-huh," she said. "Okay." She hung up. "He wants us to head over to the address he gave you."

Corny wondered what it was in Kaye's voice that convinced him.

Corny parked in front of a metered spot, figuring he could move the car later. Out beyond the park, the river glistened, reflecting the lights of the city. Kaye took a deep breath as she stepped out, and he saw human color cover her green cheeks.

They walked back and forth on the street, checking numbers until they came to a short building with a glossy black door.

"This isn't really the place, is it?" Corny asked. "It's kind of really nice. Too nice."

"The address is right." Kaye held up her arm to show him what he'd written.

A woman with red-rimmed eyes and frizzy hair stepped out onto the landing, letting the door swing behind her. Corny stepped out of the way and caught it before it slammed closed.

As she walked down the steps, he thought he saw a swaddled-up bundle of twigs in her arms.

Kaye's gaze followed the bundle.

"Maybe we should think more about this," Corny said.

Kaye pressed the buzzer.

After a few moments, a dark-skinned boy with his hair in thick herringbone cornrows opened the door. One of his eyes was cloudy, the lower part of the pupil obscured by a milky haze. Metal studs threaded through his eyebrow, and a stretch of pale scar tissue on his lower lip seemed to indicate that a ring had once been ripped loose from his mouth, although a new one gleamed next to the scar.

"You're in with the Seelie Court?" Corny asked, incredulous.

The boy shook his head. "I'm as human as you. Now, her, on the other hand." He looked at Kaye. "The Queen never said nothing about a pixie. I don't let Folk in my house."

Corny looked over at Kaye. To him, she seemed glamoured, her wings gone, her skin pink, and her eyes a perfectly average brown. He looked back at the boy in the doorway.

"So what exactly *did* she say?" Kaye asked. "Silarial."

"Her messenger told me that you were a little jumpy around faeries," the boy said, looking at Corny. "That you might feel more comfortable with me."

Kaye poked Corny in the side and he rolled his eyes. Jumpy wasn't exactly how he wanted to be thought of.

"I was supposed to tell you that the Lady Silarial invites you to visit her court." The boy turned his lip ring idly. "She wants you to consider your part in the coming war."

"Okay, that's enough," Corny said. "Let's get out of here."

"No," Kaye said. "Wait."

"She anticipated your hesitation." The boy smiled.

Corny interrupted him. "Let me guess. For a limited time only the Queen offers a free magazine subscription with each forced march to Faerieland. You can choose between *Nearly Naked Nixies* and *Kelpie Quarterly.*"

The boy let out a surprised laugh. "Sure. But not just the magazine. She's also offering both of you her protection for the duration of the trip. There and back again."

Corny wondered if it were possible that this guy had just made a Tolkien reference. He really didn't look like the type.

Kaye squinted. "I've seen you before. In the Night Court."

The smile dropped from the boy's face. "I was only there once."

"With a girl," Kaye said. "She dueled one of Roiben's people. You probably don't remember me."

"You're from the Night Court?" the boy demanded. His glance went to Corny and his eyes narrowed.

Corny reminded himself he didn't care what this guy thought of either one of them.

Kaye shrugged. "More or less."

The boy sucked on his teeth. "Not such a nice place."

"And the Bright Court is full of sugar and spice and everything nice?" Kaye asked him.

"Point." The boy slid his hands into the pockets of his oversize coat. "Look, the Lady wants me to take you to her, and I don't have much choice about being her bitch, but you've still got to come back in the morning. I've got someone coming really early, and I've got to take care of him before I head out."

"We can't," Corny said. "We don't have anywhere to sleep."

The boy looked at Kaye. "I can't let her stay here. I do jobs for people—*human* people. They see some faerie and her boy hanging around and think they can't trust me."

"So I guess they don't know that you're Silarial's boy," Corny said. "Then they'd *know* not to trust you."

"I do what I have to do," he said. "Not like you—a little Night Court lackey. Does it bother you when they torture humans, or do you like to watch?"

Corny shoved him, hard, the force of his rage surprising even him. "You don't know anything about me."

The boy laughed, short and sharp, stumbling back. Corny thought of his own hands, deadly inside thin gloves. He wanted to stop the boy's laughing.

Kaye pushed between them. "So if I were to take off my glamour and sit here on your stoop, that would be a problem?"

"You wouldn't do that. Your glamour protects you a lot more than it does me."

"Does it?" Kaye asked.

A pixie. The boy had known right away, not just that Kaye was a faerie, but the *kind* of faerie she was. Corny thought about the little hob and what he'd said: *There is a boy with the True Sight. In the great city of exiles and iron to the north. He's been breaking curses on mortals.* The boy had True Sight. He couldn't tell if she was wearing glamour or not.

He turned to Kaye and widened his eyes slightly in what he hoped would seem like surprise. Then he turned back to the boy and smiled. "Looks like she meant it. Wow, I can never get used to her wings and green skin—so freaky-looking. I guess we'll just be hanging out on your steps now. It's not like we have anywhere else to go. But don't worry—if anyone comes by looking for you, we'll tell them you'll be right out . . . as soon as you're done helping a phooka find his keys."

The boy frowned. Corny put his gloved hand on Kaye's arm, willing her to play along. With a quick glance in his direction, she shrugged her narrow shoulders.

"At least you'll know where to find us in the morning," she said.

"Fine," said the boy, holding up his hands. "Get in here."

"Thanks," Corny said. "This is Kaye, by the way. Not 'the pixie' or 'my Night Court mistress' or whatever, and I'm . . ." He paused. "Neil. Cornelius. People call me Neil."

Kaye looked over at him, and for a terrible moment he thought she was going to laugh. He just didn't want this boy calling him Corny. *Corny,* like he was King of the Dorks, like his very name announced how uncool he was.

"I'm Luis," the boy said, oblivious, opening the door. "And this is my squat."

"You squat *here*?" Kaye asked. "On the Upper West Side?"

Inside, the plaster walls were cracked, and chunks of debris covered the scuffed wooden floors. Wet brown stains soaked the ceiling in rings, and a tangle of wires inside the framing were visible in one corner.

Corny's breath clouded the air as though they were still outside. "More majestic than a trailer," he said. "But also oddly shittier."

"How did you find this place?" Kaye asked.

Luis looked at Kaye. "Remember that faerie my friend Val dueled with in the Unseelie Court?"

Kaye nodded. "Mabry. She had goat feet. Tried to kill Roiben. Your friend killed her."

"This is Mabry's old place." Luis sighed and turned back to her. "Look, I don't want you talking to my brother. Faeries messed him up pretty bad. You leave him alone."

"Sure," Corny said.

Luis led them into a parlor room furnished with over-turned milk cartons and ripped-up sofas. A very thin black boy with locs that stuck up from his head like spikes sat on the floor, eating jelly beans out of a cellophane bag. His features reminded Corny of Luis's, but there was an eerie hollowness around his eyes, and his mouth looked sunken and strange.

Kaye plopped herself onto the mustard plaid couch, sprawling against the cushions. The back was ripped, and stuffing tufted up from the torn cloth beside a stain that looked a lot like blood. Corny sat down next to her.

"Dave," Luis said. "Some people I'm helping out. They're going to stay the night. That doesn't mean we all need to get friendly—" A buzzing interrupted him. He stuck his hand into the pocket, pulling out his beeper. "Shit."

"You can use my cell," Corny volunteered, and immediately felt like a sucker. What was he doing being nice to this guy?

Luis paused for a moment, and in the dim light his clouded eye looked blue. "There's a pay phone at the bodega on—" He interrupted himself. "Yeah, okay. I'd appreciate it."

Corny stared a moment too long, then looked away, fumbling through his pockets. Dave narrowed his eyes.

Dialing, Luis walked out of the room.

Kaye leaned over to Corny and whispered, "What were you doing out there?"

"He sees through glamour," Corny whispered back. "I heard about him—he's been breaking faerie curses."

She snorted. "No wonder he doesn't want humans knowing he's in bed with the Seelie Court. He's playing both sides. When he comes back, you should ask him about your hands."

"What do you mean 'in bed'?" Dave asked. His voice was dry, like rustling paper. "What's my brother doing?"

"She doesn't mean anything," Corny said.

"How come we're not supposed to talk to you?" Kaye asked.

"Kaye," Corny warned.

"What?" Her voice was low. "Luis isn't here. I want to know."

Dave laughed, hollow and bitter. "Always trying to be the big brother. He's trippin' if he thinks he can stop them from killing me."

"Who wants to kill you?" Corny asked.

"Luis and I used to be delivery boys for a troll." Dave dumped a handful of jelly beans into his mouth and talked around the chewing. "Potions. Keep the iron sickness from getting to them. But if a person takes it—you know what you can do?"

Corny leaned forward, intrigued despite himself. "What?"

"Anything," Dave said. "All the shit they can do. All of it."

There was a distant banging, like someone had come to the door. Kaye turned toward the doorway, wide-eyed.

A half-chewed licorice bean fell from Dave's mouth. "Sounds like my brother's going to be busy awhile. Did you know that drinking urine drives out faerie enchantments?"

"Nasty." Kaye made a face.

Dave wheezed with what might have been laughter. "Bet he's pissing in some cups right now."

Kaye scrunched down in the sofa, kicking off her boots and putting her feet on Corny's lap. They smelled like the crushed stems of dandelions and he thought of dandelion milk covering his fingers, sticky and white, on a summer lawn years ago, while he pulled off flower heads and tossed them at his dozing sister. He was abruptly choked by grief.

"So wait," Kaye said. "Why do they want to kill you?"

"'Cause I poisoned a bunch of them. So I'm a dead man, but what good does it do to stay shut up in here while Luis tries to bargain for an extra week or two of boredom? At least I can have some fun with the time I got left." Dave grinned, but it looked more like a grimace, the skin on his cheeks pulled painfully tight. "Luis can tell me what to do all he wants, but he's going upstate this week. While the cat's away, the mouse'll finally get some play."

Corny blinked hard, like the pressure of his eyelids could push back memories. "Wait," he said. "You murdered a bunch of faeries?"

"You think I didn't?" Dave asked.

"Hey!" Luis stood in the doorway. A Latina girl and an older woman stood behind him. "What are you doing?"

Corny circled one of Kaye's ankles with a gloved hand.

"I'll talk to whoever I want, " Dave said, standing up. "You think you're better than me, giving orders."

"I think I *know* better than you," Luis said.

The girl turned toward Corny, and he saw that her arms and face were shadowed by something that looked like vines growing beneath her skin. Tiny smears of dried blood dotted where the points of thorns stuck up through her flesh.

"You don't know anything." Dave kicked a table, sending

it crashing onto its side, and walked out of the room.

Luis turned toward Kaye. "If I hear—if he tells me you came anywhere near him," he shouted. "If you spoke to him—"

"Please," said the woman. "My daughter!"

"I'm sorry," Luis said, shaking his head, glancing at the door.

"What's wrong with her?" Corny asked.

"She sees these boys all the time hanging around the park," the woman told Corny. "They're pretty but they're trouble. Not human. One day they bother Lala and she insults them. Then this. Nothing in the *botánica* is helping."

"You should both go wait in the other room," Luis said, rolling up the sleeves of his coat. "This is about to get messy."

"I'm good here," Corny said, trying to seem unimpressed. He had several different fantasies of himself that he liked to trot out when he was feeling miserable. In one, he was the scary lunatic—the guy who was going to snap one day and bury the bodies of all the people who'd wronged him in a mass grave in the backyard. Then there was the misunderstood genius, the person whom everyone discounted but who triumphed in the end through his superior competence. And the most pathetic fantasy of all—that he had some secret mutant power he was always on the verge of discovering.

"I need her to lie down on the floor." Luis walked over to the tiny kitchen and came back with a crude knife. The woman's eyes never left the blade. "Cold iron."

Luis actually had a secret power and was competent. That pissed Corny off. All he had was cursed hands.

"What's that for?" Lala asked.

Luis shook his head. "I won't cut you. I promise."

The woman narrowed her eyes, but the girl seemed reassured and sank down onto the floor. The vines squirmed under her skin, rippling as they shifted. Lala winced and cried out.

Kaye looked up at Corny and raised her eyebrows.

Luis crouched over Lala, straddling her slender body.

"He knows what to do, yes?" the woman asked Corny.

Corny nodded. "Sure."

Luis reached into his pocket and scattered a white substance—maybe salt—over the girl's body. She bucked, screaming. The vines crawled like snakes.

"He's hurting her!" Lala's mother gasped.

Luis didn't even glance up. He threw another handful, and Lala shrieked. Her skin stretched and rippled away from the salt, up into her neck, choking her.

Her mouth opened, but instead of a sound, thorn-covered branches burst out, winding toward Luis. He slashed at them with his knife. The iron cut through the vines easily, but more came, splitting and curling like tentacles, grabbing for him.

Corny yelled, pulling his legs up onto the couch. Kaye stared in horror. Lala's mother's cries had become one long teakettle scream.

One branch wrapped around Luis's wrist, while others crawled toward his waist and writhed along the floor. The long thorns sank into his skin. Lala's eyes rolled back in her head, and her body convulsed. Her lips shone with blood.

Luis dropped the knife and wrapped his hands around the stems, ripping the brambles even as they coiled around his hands.

Corny lunged forward, grabbing the knife and cutting at the thorns.

"No, you idiot," Luis yelled. A knot of branches suddenly

ripped free of Lala's mouth, wormlike white roots sliding out of her throat, glistening with saliva. The great vine blackened and shriveled.

Lala started to cough. The woman knelt by her, weeping and smoothing back the girl's hair.

Luis's arms were striped with scratches. He stood up and looked away as if dazed.

Lala's mother helped the girl to her feet and began to lead her toward the door. *"Gracias, gracias,"* she muttered.

"Wait," Luis said. "I need to talk to your daughter for a minute. Without you."

"I don't want to," Lala said.

"Can't she come back once she's rested?" the woman asked.

Luis shook his head and after a moment, the woman relented. "You saved her life, so I am trusting you, but be quick. I want her home and away from all of this." She closed the door separating the hall from the room.

Luis looked at Lala. The girl swayed a little and caught herself by bracing her hand against the wall.

"What you told your mother," he asked, "that's not exactly what happened, is it?"

She hesitated, then shook her head.

"One of those boys gave you something to eat—maybe you just ate a little bit? Maybe just one seed?"

She nodded again, not meeting his eyes.

"But now you know better, right?" Luis asked her.

"Yes," she whispered, then fled to join her mother. Luis watched her go. Corny watched him watch her.

"Your pixie talked to my brother, didn't she?" he demanded, nodding to Kaye.

"What do you think?" Corny replied.

Luis yawned. "I think we're out of here as soon as possible. I'll show you where to sleep."

Corny arranged himself on the floor of mattresses spread out over what might have once been a dining room. Dave had already rolled himself into a shroud of blankets against the far wall, beneath what was left of a chair rail. Kaye staggered in from the parlor, curled herself around a throw pillow, and fell immediately into sleep. Luis lay down nearby.

Flexing his fingers, Corny watched the rubber tighten over his knuckles. Already the sheen had gone off the gloves. They might be brittle by morning. Carefully, he slid out one hand and touched the edge of Luis's duvet. The thin fabric tore, threads fraying, bleeding feathers. He watched them blow in the slight draft from the window, dusting everything like snow.

Luis turned in his sleep and feathers caught in his braids. One settled at the very corner of Luis's mouth, fluttering with each breath. It seemed like it would tickle. Corny wanted to brush it out of the way. His fingers twitched.

Luis's eyes slitted. "What are you looking at?"

"You drooling," Corny lied quickly. "It's disgusting."

Luis grunted and rolled over.

Corny pulled his glove back on, heart beating so hard that he felt light-headed.

I like him, he thought in horror, the unfairness of that on top of everything else filling him with unfocused rage. *Shit. I like him.*

Kaye woke to sunlight streaming through large windows. Corny was sprawled beside her, snoring slightly. Somehow he had stolen all her blankets. Both Dave and Luis were gone.

Her mouth tasted stale, and she was so thirsty that she didn't think about where she was or why she was there until she went into the bathroom and gulped down several handfuls of water. It tasted of iron. Iron seemed to be everywhere, bubbling up from the pipes and sifting down from the ceiling.

Padding across the cold floors to try to find something to eat, Kaye heard a strange noise, like a purse upended. The smells of mildew were more intense now and she could feel her glamour being worn away. She looked down at her hand, green as a leaf. Heading in the direction of the noise, she came to the scavenged-sofa room, where a fire blazed in the grate.

A middle-aged man with short curly hair and an overstuffed messenger bag stood near the windows. As Kaye walked in, the man started to speak. But instead of sounds, copper coins fell from his lips to clatter and roll on the worn wooden floorboards.

Luis put his hand on the man's arm. "Did you do what I told you?" he asked, bending to pick up the pennies. "I know the metal tastes like blood, but you just got to do it."

The man nodded and gestured wildly to his mouth.

"I told you, the cure was to eat your words. That means every single coin that came out of your mouth. You're telling me you did that?"

This time the man hesitated.

"You spent some, didn't you? Please, please tell me that you didn't go to CoinStar or some stupid shit like that."

"Ugh," the man said, and pennies scattered.

"Go find the rest. It's the only way you're going to be cured." Luis crossed his arms over his chest, lean muscles showing through the thin fabric of his T-shirt and along his bare arms. "And no more deals with the Folk."

There were so many things Kaye didn't know about faeries.

The man looked like he wanted to say something, probably that he didn't appreciate being ordered around by some kid, but he merely nodded as he took out his wallet. After counting out a stack of twenties, he gathered the coins on the floor and departed without a sign of thanks.

Luis tapped the bills against the palm of one hand as he turned to Kaye. "I told you to stay out of sight."

"Something's happening to me," Kaye said. "My glamour's not working so good."

Luis groaned. "You're telling me that he was looking at a green girl with wings?"

"No," she said. "It's just that it seems so much harder to keep up."

"The iron in the city sucks up faerie magic quick," he said with a sigh. "That's why faeries don't live here if they have a choice. Only the exiled ones, the ones that can't go back to their own courts for whatever reason."

"So why don't they join another court?" Kaye asked.

"Some do, I guess. But that's dangerous business—the other court's as likely to kill them as take them in. So they live here and let the iron eat away at them." He sighed again. "If you really need it, there's Nevermore—a potion—staves off the iron sickness. I can't get you any right now—"

"Nevermore?" Kaye asked. "Like 'quoth the raven'?"

"That's what my brother calls it." Luis shifted uncomfortably, smoothing back his braids. "In humans it bestows glamour—makes us almost like faeries. Gets us high. You're *never* supposed to use it *more* than once a day or *more* than two days in a row or *more* than a single pinch at a time. *Never. More.* Don't let your friend near it."

"Oh. Okay." Kaye thought of Dave's haunted eyes and blackened mouth.

"Good. You ready to go?" Luis asked.

Kaye nodded. "One more question—have you ever heard of a curse where whatever someone touches withers?"

Luis nodded. "It's a King Midas variation. Whatever you touch turns to—fill in the blank. Gold. Shit. Jelly doughnuts. It's a pretty powerful curse." He frowned. "You'd have to be young and rash and really pissed off to toss all that power at a mortal."

"So the King Midas—you know how to cure it?"

He frowned. "Salt water. King Midas walked out into a brackish river and let it wash away his curse. The ocean would be better, but it's basically the same principle. Anything with salt."

Corny walked into the room, yawning hugely. "What's going on?"

"So, Neil," Luis said, his eyes going to Corny's gloves. "What happen? She curse you by accident?"

Corny looked blank for a moment, like the nickname had thrown him completely. Then his eyes narrowed. "Nope," he said. "I got cursed on purpose."

7

Snow fell lightly around the abandoned Untermeyer estate, dusting the dirt and dead grass with white. The remains of the old fire-blackened mansion showed through the bare branches. A vast fireplace stood like a tower, overgrown with dead vines. Underneath what remained of a slate roof, the gentry of the Unseelie Court had hastily prepared camp. Roiben sat on a low couch and watched as Ethine entered his chambers. She moved gracefully, feet seeming to only lightly touch the ground.

He had composed himself, and when one of his Folk's clawed hands happened to push her, causing her to stumble as she crossed the threshold, he only looked up as though annoyed by her clumsiness. Beside him were bowls of fruit, brought cold from dark caverns; cordials of clover and nettle; and tiny bird hearts still glossy with blood. He bit into a grape, not minding the crack of seeds against his teeth.

"Ethine. Be welcome."

She frowned and opened her mouth, then hesitated. When she spoke, she merely said, "My Lady knows she dealt you a terrible blow."

"I did not realize your Lady liked to brag, even by proxy. Come, have a bite of fruit, take something to cool your hot tongue."

Ethine moved toward him stiffly and perched on the very edge of the lounge. He handed her an agate goblet. She took the shallowest of sips, then set it down.

"It chafes you to be polite to me," he said. "Perhaps Silarial should have taken your feelings into consideration when she chose her ambassador."

Ethine contemplated the earthen ground, and Roiben stood.

"You begged her to let someone else go in your place, didn't you?" He laughed with vindictive certainty. "Perhaps even told her how much it hurt you to see what your brother had become?"

"No," Ethine said softly.

"No? Not in those words, but I'll wager you said it all the same. Now you see how she cares for those who serve her. You are one more thing with which to needle me and nothing more than that. She sent you despite your pleading."

Ethine had closed her eyes tightly. Her hands were clasped in her lap, fingers threaded together.

He took her glass and drank from it. She looked up, annoyed, the way she had once been annoyed when he'd pulled her hair. When they were children.

It hurt him to look at her as an enemy.

"I do not see that you care for my feelings any more than she does," Ethine said.

"But I do." He made his voice grave. "Come, deliver your message."

"My Lady knows she dealt you quite a blow. She further knows that your control of the other faeries in your lands is spotty after the botched Tithe."

Roiben leaned against the wall. "You even sound like her when you say it."

"Don't jest. She wants you to fight her champion. If you win, she will leave your lands unmolested for seven years. If you lose, you will forfeit the Unseelie Court to her." Ethine looked at him with anguished eyes. "And you will *die*."

Roiben barely heard her plea, he was so surprised by the Bright Queen's offer. "I cannot think but that this is either generosity or some cunning beyond my measure. Why should she give me this chance at winning when now I have near none?"

"She wants your lands hale and whole when she takes them, not weakened by a war. Too many great courts have fallen into rabble."

"Do you ever imagine no court at all?" Roiben asked his sister quietly. "No vast responsibilities or ancient grudges or endless wars?"

"We have come to rely on humans too much," said Ethine, frowning. "Once, our kind lived apart from them. Now we rely on them to be everything from farmers to nursemaids. We live in their cast-off spaces and sup off their tables. If the courts fall, we will be parasites with nothing to call our own. This is the last of our old world."

"I hardly think it is as serious as all that." Roiben looked past Ethine. He didn't want her to see his expression. "How about this. Tell Silarial that I will take her insulting and lop-sided bargain with one variation. She must wager something too. She must put up her crown."

"She will never give you—"

Roiben cut her off. "Not to me. To you."

Ethine opened her mouth, but no sound came out.

"Tell her that if she loses, she makes you the Bright Queen of the Seelie Court. If I lose, I will give her both my crown and my life." It felt good to say, even if it were a rash wager.

Ethine rose. "You mock me."

He made a dismissive gesture. "Don't be silly. You know very well that I do not."

"She told me that if you wished to bargain, you must do so with her." She paced the room, gesturing wildly. "Why won't you just come back to us? Pledge yourself to Silarial, ask for her forgiveness. Tell her how hard it was to be Nicnevin's knight. She could not have known."

"Silarial has spies everywhere. I very much doubt that she was ignorant of my suffering."

"There was nothing for her to do! Nothing for any of us to do. She spoke often of her fondness for you. Let her explain. Let her be your friend again. Forgive each other." Her voice dropped low. "You don't belong in a place like this."

"And why is that, dear sister? Why don't I belong here?"

Ethine groaned and slapped one open hand against the wall. "Because you are not a fiend!"

She reminded Roiben so much of his old, innocent self that for a moment he hated her, for a moment he only wanted to shake her and scream at her and hurt her before someone else did. "No? Is it not enough, what I have done? Is it not enough to have cut the throat of a nix that dared laugh too loud or too long before my mistress? Is it not enough to have hunted down a hob that stole a single cake from her table? Is it not enough to have been deaf to their entreaties, their begging?"

"Nicnevin commanded you."

"Of course she did!" he shouted. "Again and again and again she commanded me. And now I am changed, Ethine. This is where I belong if I belong anywhere at all."

"What about Kaye?"

"The pixie?" He gave her a quick look.

"You were kind to her. Why do you want me to think the worst of you?"

"I was not kind to Kaye," he said. "Ask her. I am not kind, Ethine. Moreover, I no longer have any interest in kindness. I mean to win."

"If you were to win," Ethine said, her voice faltering, "I would be the Queen and you would be *my* enemy."

He snorted. "Now don't go casting a pall over my best outcome." He held out the cup to her. "Drink something. Eat. After all, it is natural for siblings to squabble, is it not?"

Ethine took the cup back from him and lifted it to her mouth, but he had left her only a single swallow.

Kaye cradled a large ThunderCats thermos of coffee as she walked to Corny's car. Luis followed, wrapped in a black coat. It hung voluminously from his shoulders, its inner lining torn to pieces. He had taken it out of the back of one of the closets, from a pile strewn with chunks of plaster.

She was glad to keep moving. As long as there was something in front of her, something still to do, things made sense.

"You got a map of Upstate New York?" Luis asked Corny.

"I thought you knew the way," Corny said. "What kind of guide needs a map?"

"Can you two not—" Kaye started, but stopped in front of a newspaper vending machine. There, in a sidebar on the front page of the *Times*, was a picture of the cemetery on the hill by Kaye's house. The hill where Janet was buried. The hollow hill under which Roiben had been crowned. It had collapsed beneath the weight of an overturned truck. The photo showed smoke billowing up from the hill, fallen gravestones scattered like loose teeth.

Corny slid quarters into the machine and pulled out a paper. "A bunch of bodies were found, too burnt to identify. They're looking for dental matches. There was some speculation that maybe people were sledding when the truck hit. Kaye, what the fuck?"

Kaye touched the picture, running her fingers over the ink of the page. "I don't know."

Luis frowned. "All those people. Can't the Folk kill each other and leave us out of it?"

"Shut up. Just shut up," Kaye said, walking to Corny's car and jerking on the handle. Pieces of chrome came off on her singed fingers. She felt sick.

"I've got to unlock it," Corny said, opening the door for her with his keys. "Look, he's okay. I'm sure he's okay."

She threw herself into the backseat, trying not to imagine Roiben dead, trying not to see his eyes dulled with mud. "No, you're not."

"I'm calling my mom," Corny said. He started the car while he dialed, his gloved fingers awkward.

Luis pointed out the turns and Corny drove with the phone cradled against his shoulder. This time Kaye welcomed the iron sickness, welcomed the dizziness that made it hard to think.

"She says Janet's coffin wasn't disturbed, but the stone's gone." Corny pushed his phone closed. "Nobody saw anyone sledding that late, and according to the local paper the truck wasn't even supposed to be making deliveries in the area."

"It's the war," Kaye said, putting her head down on the vinyl seat. "The faerie war."

"What's wrong with her?" she heard Luis ask softly.

Corny's eyes stayed on the road. "She was dating someone from the Unseelie Court."

Luis looked back at her. "Dating?"

"Yeah," Corny said. "He gave her his class ring. It was a whole big thing."

Luis looked incredulous.

"Roiben," Corny said. At the sound of Roiben's name, Kaye closed her eyes, but the dread didn't ebb.

"That's not possible," said Luis.

"Why do you think Silarial wants to see me?" Kaye demanded. "Why do you think it's worth two messengers and a guarantee of protection? If he isn't dead already, she thinks I can help kill him."

"No," said Luis. "You can't *date* the Lord of the Night Court."

"Well, I'm not. He dumped me."

"You can't *get dumped* by the Lord of the Night Court."

"Oh, yes you can. You so completely can."

"We're all on edge." Corny rubbed his face with gloved fingers. "And it's a bad day when I'm the voice of reason. Relax. We're going to be stuck in this traffic for a long time."

They drove upstate while the late afternoon sunlight filtered through the leafless trees and the new-fallen snow melted into slush. They passed strip malls hung with wreaths and garlands, while kicked-up road salt streaked tide lines onto the sides of cars.

Kaye looked out the window, counting silver cars, reading every sign. Trying not to think.

At sunset they finally pulled onto a dirt road and Luis told them to stop.

"Here," he said, and opened the door. In the fading light Kaye could see an ice-covered lake stretching out from a bank just beyond the lip of the road. Mist shrouded the center of the lake from view. Dead trees rose from the water, as though there had once been a forest where the lake now stood. A forest of drowned trees. The fading light turned the trunks to gold.

Wind whipped loose snow into Kaye's face. It stung like chips of glass.

"There's a boat," Luis said. "Come on."

They walked downhill, shoes skidding on the ice.

Corny gasped and Kaye looked up from watching her feet. A young man stood in front of her, half obscured by the branches of a fir tree. She yelped.

He was as still as a statue, in a down jacket and a woolen cap. He stared past the three of them as though they weren't there. His skin was darker than Luis's, but his lips had gone pale with cold.

"Hello?" Luis said, waving his hand in front of the guy's face.

The man didn't move.

"Look," Corny said. He pointed through the evergreen trees to a woman in her fifties standing by herself. Her ginger hair fluttered in the slight breeze. Squinting, Kaye could see other spots of color along the lake. Other humans, waiting at attention for some signal.

Kaye's gaze dropped to the man's chapped fingers. "Frostbite."

"Wake up!" Luis shouted. When that got no response, he slapped the man across one cheek.

The frozen man's gaze shifted suddenly. Without a trace of expression he threw Luis to the ground and stomped on his stomach.

Luis groaned in pain, rolling to his side, his body curling up defensively.

Corny threw himself at the man. They fell backward, cracking through the thin ice of the lake as they splashed into the shallow water.

Kaye rushed forward, trying to pull Corny onto the shore. A hand closed on her arm.

She turned to see a creature, as tall and thin as a scarecrow, shrouded in tattered black fabric that whipped through the air. His eyes were a dead, pupil-less white, and his teeth were clear as glass.

Kaye's scream died in her throat. Her nails scrabbled at the creature's arm and he let her go, pushing past. He moved so nimbly that by the time she'd turned her head, his skeletal hand was on the frozen man's throat.

Corny splashed up onto the bank and collapsed in the snow.

The creature pressed a thumb against the man's forehead and hissed some words that Kaye didn't know. The frozen man moved slowly to resume standing like an indifferent sentry, clothing soaked through and dripping.

"What do you want?" Kaye demanded, taking off her coat and wrapping it around a shivering Corny. "Who are you?"

"Sorrowsap," said the creature, bowing his head. His hair was thin and coiled like the tangle of roots beneath a weed. "At your service."

"Great! That's just fucking great." Luis held his stomach.

Corny shuddered reflexively and pulled the coat tighter.

"*My* service?" Kaye asked. Looking across the forest, she saw the other human figures walk back to their original positions. They had been coming, had been perhaps only moments away from entering the fight.

"The King of the Unseelie Court commands that I guard your steps. I have followed you since you left his court."

"Why would he do that?" Kaye blurted. She thought of Roiben covered in collapsed dirt, his face as pale as a marble tombstone, and she closed her eyes against the image. He should have been protecting himself and been less worried about her.

Sorrowsap tilted his head. "I serve his whims. I need not understand them."

"But how could you stop the frozen people like that?" Luis

asked. "This barrier has to have been created to keep you out more than us."

At the question, Sorrowsap smiled, his clear wet teeth making his mouth look poisonous. He reached into a sack beneath his robes and threw down what at first seemed like green leather lined in red silk. Then Kaye saw the fine hairs dotting the surface and the sticky wetness underneath. Skin. The skin of a faerie.

"She told me," said Sorrowsap.

Luis made a noise in the back of his throat and turned away, like he was going to retch.

"You can't—I don't want—" Kaye said, furious and terrified. "You killed her because of me."

Sorrowsap said nothing.

"Never do that! Never!" She walked up to him, hands fisted. Before she thought better of it, she slapped him. Her hand stung.

He didn't even flinch. "Just because I am to protect you does not give you governance over me."

"Kaye," Luis said stiffly. "It's done."

Kaye looked toward Luis, but he avoided meeting her eyes.

"I'm freezing," Corny said. "As in 'to death.' Let's get where we're going."

"All these people are going to die from the cold," Kaye said, although it seemed that, lately, her trying to make things better had only succeeded in making them worse. "We can't just leave them."

Corny took out his phone. "Let's call the—"

Luis shook his head. "I don't think we should lead more victims out here. That's what you'd be doing if the police came."

"I'm not getting reception anyway," Corny said. "You break curses. Can't you do anything for them?"

Luis shook his head. "This is way beyond what I know how to handle."

"We have to dry this guy off," Kaye said. "Maybe cover his fingers before they get worse. Sorrowsap, can you keep him . . . deactivated?"

"You have no governance over me." Yellow eyes watched her with as little expression as an owl's.

"I didn't think I did," Kaye said. "I'm asking for your help."

"Let them die," said Sorrowsap.

She sighed. "Can't you snap them out of it? Remove whatever enchantment is keeping them like this—remove it permanently? Then they could just go home."

"No," he said, "I cannot."

"I am going to help this guy. If he attacks me, you are going to have to stop him. And if you don't keep him turned off, he's going to attack."

Sorrowsap's face seemed expressionless, but one of his hands curled into a fist. "Very well, pixie-who-has-my-King's-favor." He strode to the frozen man and placed his thumb on the man's forehead once more.

Kaye sat down in the snow and pulled off her own boots as Sorrowsap chanted the unfamiliar words. Taking off her socks, she wrapped them over the man's hands. Luis draped the guy in his coat and ducked out of the way of a swinging arm when the hissing chant faltered.

"It's not going to help," Corny said. "These people are screwed."

Kaye stepped back. The cold felt like razors cutting her

skin. Even wearing her coat, Corny's lips had gone blue. The frozen man would die with all the others.

"The Seelie Court's close," Luis said.

"There I cannot follow," said Sorrowsap. "If you go, you will be without my protection and that would cause my Lord deep displeasure."

"We're going," Kaye said.

"As you say." Sorrowsap bowed his head. "I will wait for you here."

Kaye looked at Corny. "You don't have to come. You'd warm up quickly in the car."

"Don't be an idiot," he told her through chattering teeth.

"The next leg of the journey means getting into that," Luis said, pointing along the shore. For a moment Kaye saw nothing. Then the wind rippled the water, setting something to rock and glisten in the moonlight. A boat, carved entirely from ice, its prow shaped like a swan ready to soar into flight. "The Bright Lady didn't exactly tell me about her frozen zombie sentries, so I'm thinking she's full of surprises."

"Great," Corny said, stumbling over the frozen snow.

Kaye stepped gingerly onto the slippery surface of the boat and sat down. The seat was cold against her thighs. "So, would this water fix Corny's curse?"

Corny got in next to her. "I don't—"

"Corny?" Luis frowned.

"Neil," Kaye said. "I mean fix Neil's curse."

"No," Luis pushed the boat hard and it slid out onto the water. Luis hopped in, making them rock wildly as he sat. He looked over at Corny. "Too still and not salt."

They didn't paddle, but a strange current propelled them

across the lake, past the drowned trees. Beneath the dripping hull of the boat the water was choked with vibrant green duckweed, as though a forest grew underneath the waves.

Green and gold fish darted under the boat, visible through the ice hull. Fish had to keep swimming to breathe, Kaye thought. She knew how they felt. There was nothing safe to think about, not Roiben, not her mother, not all the people slowly dying on the far shore. There was nothing to do but keep going until despair finally froze her.

"Kaye—check it out," Corny said. "It's like from a book."

Through the mist, Kaye saw the outline of an island filled with tall firs. As they got closer, the sky grew lighter and the air became warm. Although there was no sun, the shore was lit bright as day.

Corny glanced at his watch and then held it out to show her. The digital numbers had stopped on December 21 at 6:13:52 p.m. "Bizarre."

"At least it's warmer," Kaye said, rubbing his arms through the coat, hoping she could rub the chill out of him.

"That would be better news if we weren't in a *boat made of ice.*"

"I don't know about you all," Luis said. He smiled slightly, almost like he was embarrassed. "But I can't even feel my ass anymore. Swimming might be better."

Corny laughed, but Kaye couldn't smile. She was putting Corny in danger. Again.

The last of the haze blew off and Kaye saw that each tree on the island was white with cocoon silk in place of snow. She thought she could see masses of caterpillars writhing at the peaks of the trees, and she shuddered.

The boat dug into the soft mud. They climbed out, feet sinking slightly so there was a sucking noise with each step across the shore.

Stupid mud, Kaye thought. *Stupid boat. Stupid faerie island.* She found herself suddenly exhausted. Stupid, stupid me.

There was music, distant and faint, accompanied by the sound of laughter. They followed it into a grove of flowering cherry trees, the blooms blue instead of pink, petals falling like a shower of poison with every slight breeze.

She thought of something the Thistlewitch had told her when she had explained to Kaye that she was a changeling: *The child's fey nature becomes harder and harder to conceal as it grows. In the end, they all return to Faerie.*

That couldn't be true. Kaye didn't want it to be true.

Corny shivered once, hard, like his body was shaking off the cold, and toed off his sodden and mud-covered shoes. It was warm, but not hot, on the island—so perfect a temperature, in fact, that it was as though there were no weather at all.

A few of the Bright Folk strolled on the grass. A boy in a skirt of silver scale mesh held the hand of a pixie with wide azure wings. Clouds of tiny buzzing faeries hovered in the air like gnats. A knight in white painted armor looked in Kaye's direction. A singing voice, heartbreakingly lovely, drifted down to where she stood. From the branches of the trees, pointed faces stared down.

A knight with eyes the color of turquoises walked up to meet them and bowed deeply. "My Lady is pleased by your arrival. She asks that you come and sit with her." He glanced at her companions. "Only you."

Kaye nodded, worrying her lip with her teeth.

"Beneath the tree." He gestured toward a massive willow, its drooping branches covered with struggling cocoons. Every now and again one of the silken purses would rip open and a white bird would flutter loose and take flight.

Kaye made herself lift one of the heavy leathery branches and duck underneath.

Light filtered through the leaves to glimmer on the faces of Silarial and her courtiers. The Lady of the Bright Court did not sit on a throne, but rather on a collection of tapestry cushions heaped upon the ground. Other faeries were strewn about like ornaments, some of them horned, others thin as sticks and sprouting leaves from their heads.

Silarial's hair was parted in two soft waves at her brow, the strands shining like copper, and for a moment Kaye thought of the pennies that had fallen from the man's mouth in Luis's apartment. The Bright Lady smiled, and she was so stunning that Kaye forgot to speak, forgot to bow, forgot to do anything but stare.

It hurt to look at her.

Perhaps like great pain, great loveliness must be forgotten.

"Will you have something?" asked Silarial, gesturing to bowls of fruit and pitchers of juice, their surfaces beading from the chill of the contents. "Unless it is not to your taste."

"I'm sure it is very much to my taste." Kaye bit into a white fruit. Black nectar stained her lips dark and ran over her chin.

The courtiers laughed behind their long-fingered hands and Kaye wondered whom exactly she had been trying to impress. She was letting herself be baited.

"Good. Now take off that silly glamour." The Lady turned to the faeries that lounged beside her. "Leave us."

The assemblage rose lazily, lifting their harps and goblets, pillows and books. They made their way out from beneath the tree as haughtily as offended cats.

Silarial turned on the pillows. Kaye sat at the very edge of the pile of cushions and wiped the black juice from her mouth with her sleeve. She let the glamour fall from her, and when she saw her own green fingers, she was surprised by her relief at not having to hide them.

"You mislike me," Silarial said. "Not without reason."

"You tried to have me killed," Kaye said.

"One of my people—any one of my people—was a small price to pay to trap the Lady of the Night Court."

"I'm not one of your people," Kaye said.

"Of course you are." Silarial smiled. "You were born in these lands. You belong here."

Kaye had no answer. She said nothing. She wished she did know who had birthed her and who had switched her, but she didn't want to hear it from the Lady's lips.

Silarial plucked a plum from one of the plates, looking up at Kaye through her lashes. "This war began before I came into the world. Once, there were little courts, each huddled together near a circle of thorn trees or beside a meadow of clover. But as time passed and our places thinned, we drew together in larger numbers. The High Court was making inroads. My mother won Folk to her with the keen edge of her blade and her tongue.

"But not my father. He and his people dwelt here in the mountains and they had no use for her or her kin, at least at first. In time, however, she fascinated even him, becoming his consort, gaining governance over his lands and even bearing two children by him."

"Nicnevin and Silarial," Kaye said.

The Bright Lady nodded. "Each girl as unlike the other as two of the Folk could be. Nicnevin and our mother were of a kind, with their taste for blood and pain. I was as our father, content with less brutal amusements."

"Like freezing a ring of humans to death around a lake?" Kaye asked her.

"I do not find that particularly diverting, merely necessary," Silarial said. "Nicnevin killed our father when he gave a boon to a piper she preferred to torment. I am told our mother laughed when my sister explained how it had been done, but then, death was my mother's meat and drink. I served her a banquet of my grief." The Bright Queen looked upward, into the wriggling shadows of the willow. "I will not let my father's lands fall to my sister's court."

"But they don't want your lands. Your sister's dead."

Silarial looked surprised for a moment. Her fist tightened around the plum. "Yes, dead. Dead before my plan could break her. I spent all the long years of peace between our people building my strategy and biding my time, and she died before my bereavement could be sated. I will not give her court the chance to plan as I planned. I will take her lands and her people and that will be my vengeance. It will secure the safety of all of the Bright Court.

"This is your home, whether you wish it or no, and your war. You must pick a side. I know of your pledge to Roiben— your declaration—and he was right to rebuff you. He went to the Unseelie Court as a hostage for peace. Do you think he wants you to be tied to them as his consort would be? Do you think he wishes you to suffer as he's suffered?"

"Of course not," Kaye snapped.

"I know what it is to give up something you desire. Before Roiben left for the Unseelie Court, he was my lover—did you know that?" She frowned. "Passion made him occasionally forget his place, but oh, do I regret giving him up."

"You forget his place now."

Silarial laughed suddenly. "Let me tell you a story of Roiben when he was in my court. I think of it often."

"Sure," Kaye said. She felt strangled by the things she could not say. She didn't believe Silarial meant anything but harm, but to let the Queen know that would be foolish. And she did want to hear any story about Roiben. The way that Silarial spoke gave her hope he was still alive.

Some of the tension went out of her, some of the dread.

"Once there was a fox that got tangled in a thornbush near our revels. Tiny sprites darted around, trying to free it. The fox didn't understand the faeries were being helpful. It only understood that it was in pain. It snapped at the sprites, trying to catch them in its teeth, and as it moved, the thorns dug deeper into its fur. Roiben saw the fox and went over to keep it still.

"He could have held its muzzle and let it twist its body deeper into the bush. He could have let go of it when it bit him. He did neither of those things. He let the fox bite his hand, again and again until the sprites freed it from the thorns."

"I don't get the point of the story," Kaye said. "Are you saying that Roiben lets himself get hurt because he thinks he's being helpful? Or are you saying Roiben used to be good and kind, but now he's a prick?"

Silarial tilted her head, brushing back a stray lock of her hair. "I am wondering if you aren't like that fox, Kaye."

"What?" Kaye stood up. "I'm not the one who's hurting him."

"He would have died for you at the Tithe. Died for a pixie he'd met only days before. Then he refused to join me when we might have united the courts and forged a real peace—an enduring peace. Why do you think that is? Maybe because he was too busy disentangling you and yours from thornbushes."

"Maybe he didn't see it that way," Kaye said, but she could feel her cheeks go hot and her wings twitch. "There could still be peace, you know. If *you* would just stop biting his hand. He doesn't want to fight you."

"Oh, come now." Silarial smiled and sank her teeth into the plum. "I know you've seen the tapestry of me he slashed to pieces. He doesn't just want to fight me. He wants to *destroy* me." The way she said "destroy," it sounded pleasurable. "Do you know what happened to the fox?"

Kaye snorted. "I'm pretty sure you're going to tell me."

"It ran off, stopping only to lick its cuts, but the next morning it was caught in the bushes again, thorns buried deep in its flesh. All Roiben's pain for nothing."

"What do you want me to do?" Kaye asked. "What did you bring me here for?"

"To show you that I am no monster. Of course Roiben despises me. I sent him to the Unseelie Court. But he can come back now. He is far too biddable to lead them.

"Join us. Join the Seelie Court. Help me show Roiben. Once he gets past his anger, he will see that it would be best if he ceded control of his court to me."

"I can't—" Kaye hated that she was tempted.

"I think you can. Convince him, that is. He trusts you. He gave you his *name*." Silarial's expression didn't change, but something in her eyes did.

"I'm not using that."

"Not even for his own good? Not even for peace between our courts?"

"You mean make him surrender. That's not the same thing as peace."

"I mean convince him to surrender the terrible burden of the Night Court," Silarial said. "Kaye, I am not so vain that I cannot appreciate that you outwitted me once, nor so foolish that I cannot understand your desire to preserve your own life. Let us be at odds no more."

Kaye sank her nails into her palm, hard. "I don't know," she managed to say. It was a seductive thought that the war might not go on, that everything could be so easily resolved.

"Think on it. Should he no longer be the Lord of the Night Court, your pledge would be void. You would never have to complete the impossible quest. Declarations are only made to Lords or Ladies."

Kaye wanted to say that it didn't matter, but it did. Her shoulders slumped.

"Were you willing to help me, I could arrange for you to see him, even to speak with him, despite the declaration. He is on his way here now." Silarial stood. The soft susurrations of her gown were the only sounds under the canopy of branches as she crossed to where Kaye stood. "There are other ways to persuade you, but I do not like to be cruel."

Kaye took a quick breath. He was alive. Now she just had

to do what she'd come for. "I want the human Kaye. Ellen's daughter. The real me. Switch her back. If you do that, I'll think about what you said. I'll consider it."

After all, it wasn't like Kaye was really agreeing to anything. Not really.

"Done," said Silarial, reaching out to stroke her cheek. Her fingers were cool. "After all, you are one of mine. You had only to ask. And, of course, you will have the hospitality of the Bright Court while you consider."

"Of course," Kaye echoed faintly.

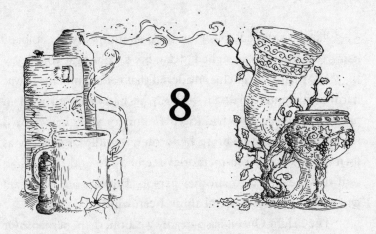

8

Forest, I fear you! in my ruined heart
your roaring wakens the same agony
as in cathedrals when the organ moans
and from the depths I hear that I am damned.
—CHARLES BAUDELAIRE, "OBSESSION"

You're a fool," Ellebere said. He looked out of place in the city, though he'd glamoured himself a red pin-striped black suit and a silk tie the color of dried blood.

"Because it's a trap?" Roiben asked. His long wool coat whipped in the breeze from the river. The stench of iron seared his nose and throat.

"It must be." Ellebere turned, so that he was walking backward, facing Roiben. He gestured wildly, ignoring the people who had to veer out of his way. "Just her offer of peace is suspicious, but if she agrees to your absurd demand, then she must have some sure way of killing you."

"Yes," Roiben said, grabbing his arm. "And you're about to walk into a road."

Ellebere stopped, pushing back strands of wine-colored hair from his eyes. He sighed. "Can her knight beat you?"

"Talathain?" Roiben considered that for a moment. It was hard to imagine Talathain—whom he had wrestled with in patches of clover, who had loved Ethine for years before he'd found the courage to bring her a mere bundle of violets—as formidable. But those memories seemed old and unfamiliar, as if they belonged to another person. Perhaps *this* Talathain was another person too. "I think I can win."

"The Bright Queen has a deadly weapon, then, perhaps? Or armor that cannot be pierced? Some way to use iron weaponry?"

"It could be that. I turn it over again and again in my mind, but I have no more answer than you do." Roiben looked at his hand and saw all the throats he had cut in Nicnevin's service. All the pleading eyes and trembling mouths. All the mercy that he could not bestow, least of all on himself. He let go of Ellebere. "I only hope that I am a better murderer than the Bright Lady imagines me."

"Tell me that there is some plan, at least."

"There is some plan," Roiben said, with a twist of his mouth. "Although without knowing what Silarial intends, I know not what good it is."

"You shouldn't have come Ironside yourself. In the mortal world you are vulnerable," said Ellebere, glowering. They crossed the road next to a too-thin mortal pushing an empty stroller and another furiously punching keys on her cell phone. "Dulcamara could have accompanied me. You could have explained what we were to do and sent us off to do it. That's how a proper Unseelie King behaves."

Roiben veered off the sidewalk, ducking under a torn

chain-link fence that singed his fingers and snagged on the cloth of his coat. Ellebere clambered over the top, jumping down with a flourish.

"I'm not sure it's *proper* for a knight to tell a King how to behave," Roiben said. "But come, indulge me a little longer. As you rightly point out, I am a fool and I am about to make a series of very foolish bargains."

The building behind the fence looked like several of the neighboring boarded-up buildings, but this one had a garden on the roof, long tendrils of winter-dead plants hanging over onto the brick sides. On the second floor, the windows were completely missing. Shadows flickered against the inner walls.

Roiben paused. "I would like to say that my time in the Unseelie Court changed my nature. For a long time it was a comfort for me to think so. Whenever I saw my sister, I would recall how I had once been like her, before I was *corrupted*."

"My Lord . . ." Ellebere blanched.

"I am no longer sure if that's true. I wonder if I found my nature instead, where before it was hidden, even from me."

"So what is your nature?"

"Let's find out." Roiben walked across the cracked front steps and knocked against the wood covering the door.

"Will you at least tell me what we're doing here?" Ellebere asked. "Visiting exiles?"

Roiben put a finger to his lips. One of the boards swung open from a nearby window. An ogre stood, framed in the opening, his horns curving back from his head like a ram's and his long brown beard turning to green at the tip. "If it isn't Your Dark Majesty," he said. "I'm guessing you heard about my changeling stock. The best you're like to find. Not carved from logs or sticks, but lovingly crafted from mannequins—some with real glass eyes. Even mortals with a bit of the Sight in them can't see through my work. The Bright Queen herself uses me—but I bet you knew that. Come around the back. I'm eager to make something for you."

Roiben shook his head. "I'm here to make *you* something. An offer. Tell me, how long have you been in exile?"

Kaye rested beside Corny and Luis in a bower of ivy, the soft earth and sweet breeze lulling her to dozing. Night-blooming flowers perfumed the air, dotting the dark with constellations of white petals.

"It's weird." Kaye leaned back against the grass. "It's dark now, but it was night when we got here and it was bright then. I thought it was going to stay eternal day or something."

"That is odd," said Corny.

Luis ripped open his second protein bar and bit into it with a grimace. "I don't know why she's making me stay. This is bullshit. I did everything she told me. Dave is . . . ." He stopped.

"Dave is what?" Corny asked.

Luis looked at the wrapper in his hands. "Prone to getting into trouble when I'm not around to stop him."

Kaye watched the petals fall. The human changeling was probably returned to Ellen by now, taking up all Kaye's space in the world she knew. With one quest done and the other impossible, she had no idea what would happen next. She very much doubted the Queen would just let her leave. Keeping Luis at court was both encouraging and discouraging—encouraging because maybe Silarial would let him guide them back at some not-too-distant point, but discouraging because the Seelie Court felt like a web that thrashing would only wrap more tightly around them.

Not that she had anywhere else to go.

Silent hobmen brought a tray of hollowed-out acorns filled with a liquid as clear as water and placed them beside plates of little cakes. Kaye had already eaten three. Lifting a fourth, she offered it to Corny.

"Don't," Luis said when Corny reached for it.

"What?" Corny asked.

"Don't eat or drink anything of theirs. It's not safe."

Music started up somewhere in the distance, and Kaye heard a high voice begin to sing the tale of a nightingale who was really a princess and a princess who was really a pack of cards.

Corny took the cake.

She wanted to put a cautioning hand on Corny's arm, but there was something brittle in his manner that made her hold back. His eyes glittered with banked fire.

He laughed and dropped the confection into his mouth. "There is no safe. Not for me. I don't have True Sight. I can't resist their enchantments, and right now I don't see why I should bother trying."

"Because not trying is stupid," Luis said.

Corny licked his fingers. "Stupid tastes pretty good."

A faerie woman approached, her bare feet silent on the soft earth. "For you," she said, and placed three packets of clothing on the grass.

Kaye reached over to touch the first one. Celery green fabric felt silky under her fingertips.

"Let me guess," Corny said to Luis. "We're not supposed to wear anything of theirs either. Maybe you're going to walk around naked?"

Luis frowned, but Kaye could see that he was embarrassed.

"Stop being a dick," she said, tossing Corny his pile of clothes. Corny grinned as if she'd paid him a compliment.

Ducking behind a bush, she pulled off her T-shirt and slid the dress over her head. She'd been wearing the same camo pants and T-shirt since she'd left Jersey, and she couldn't wait to get out of them. The faerie cloth felt as light as spider silk when she pulled it over her head, and it reminded her of the only other faerie gown she'd worn—the one she'd almost been sacrificed in, the one that had come apart in the sink when she'd tried to wash the blood out of it. Her memories of the averted Tithe were still a shuddersome blur of bedazzlement and terror and Roiben's breath tickling her neck as he'd whispered: *What belongs to you, yet others use it more than you do?*

His name. The name she'd tricked out of him without knowing its worth. The name she'd used to command him and could use still. No wonder his court didn't like her; she could make their King do her bidding.

"I look ridiculous, don't I?" Corny said, stepping out from the branches and causing Kaye to start. He wore a brocaded black and scarlet tunic over black pants, and his feet were bare. He looked handsome and not at all ridiculous. He frowned. "My clothes are soaked, though. At least this is dry."

"You seem like a decadent aristocrat." Kaye turned, letting the thin skirt whirl around her. "I like my dress."

"Nice. All that green really brings out the pink of your eye membranes."

"Shut up." Picking up a twig from the ground, she twisted up her hair with it like she'd done with pencils in school. "Where's Luis?"

Corny pointed with his chin. Turning, Kaye spotted him leaning against a tree, chewing on what was probably the last of the protein bar. Luis glowered as he shoved his hands deeper into the pockets of a long brown jacket, clasped with three buckles at his waist. Kaye's damp purple coat hung from the branch of a tree.

"I guess we're supposed to go to the party like this," Kaye called.

Luis sauntered closer. "They call it a revel."

Corny rolled his eyes. "Let's go."

Kaye headed toward the music, letting her fingers run through the heavy green leaves. She plucked a great white flower down from one of the branches and pulled off one bruised petal after another.

"He loves me," Corny said. "He loves me not."

Kaye scowled and stopped. "That's not what I was doing."

Shapes moved through the trees like ghosts. The laughter and music seemed always a little more distant until suddenly she was among a throng of faeries. Crowds of Folk danced in wide and chaotic circles or diced or simply laughed as though the breeze had carried a joke to their ears only. One faerie woman crouched beside a pool, conversing intently with her reflection, while another stroked the bark of a tree as though it were the fur of a pet.

Kaye opened her mouth to tell Corny something but stopped when her eye was caught by white hair and eyes like silver spoons. Someone threaded through the crowd, cloaked and hooded, but not hooded enough.

There was only one person Kaye knew with eyes like that.

"I'll be right back," she said, already weaving between a damp girl in a dress of woven river grass and a hob on crude mossy stilts.

"Roiben?" she whispered, touching his shoulder. She could feel her heart speeding and she hated it, she hated everything about how she felt at that moment, so absurdly grateful she would have liked to slap herself. "You fucker. You could have told me to go on a quest to bring you an apple from the banquet table. You could have sent me on a quest to tie a braid in your hair."

The figure drew back its hood, and Kaye remembered the other person who would have eyes like Roiben's. His sister, Ethine.

"Kaye," Ethine said. "I had hoped I would happen on you."

Mortified, Kaye tried to back away. She couldn't believe she had just blurted things she wasn't sure, in retrospect, that she wanted even Roiben to hear.

"I have only a moment," Ethine said. "I must bring the Queen a message. But there is something I would know. About my brother."

Kaye shrugged. "We're not exactly speaking."

"He was never cruel when we were children. Now he is brutal and cold and terrible. He will make war on us whom he loved—"

It startled Kaye to think of Roiben as a child. "You grew up in Faerie?"

"I don't have time for—"

"Make time. I want to know."

Ethine looked at Kaye for a long moment, then sighed.

"Roiben and I were brought up in Faerie by a human midwife. She'd been stolen away from her own children and would call us by their names. Mary and Robert. I misliked that. Otherwise, she was very kind."

"What about your parents? Do you know them? Love them?"

"Answer my question, if you please," Ethine said. "My Lady wants him to duel instead of lead the Unseelie Court into battle. It would prevent a war—which the Unseelie Court is too depleted to win—but it would mean his death."

"Your Lady is a bitch," Kaye said before she thought better of it.

Ethine wrung her hands, fingers sliding over one another. "No. She would accept him back. I know she would if he were only to ask her. Why won't he ask her?"

"I don't know," Kaye said.

"You must discern something. He has a fondness for you."

Kaye started to protest, but Ethine cut her off.

"I heard the way you spoke to me when you supposed me to be him. You speak to him as to a friend."

That was not how Kaye would have characterized it. "Look, I did this declaration thing. Where you get a quest. He pretty much told me to fuck off. Whatever you think I know about him or can tell you about him, I just don't think I can."

"I saw you, although I didn't hear the words. I was in the hill that night." Ethine smiled, but her brow furrowed slightly, as though she were puzzling through Kaye's human phrasings. "Still, one must assume the quest was not an apple from a banquet table nor tying a braid in his hair."

Kaye blushed.

"If you thought the King of the Unseelie Court would give you so simple a quest, you must think him besotted."

"Why wouldn't he? He said that I . . ." Kaye stopped, realizing that she shouldn't repeat his words. *You are the only thing I want.* It wasn't safe to say that to Ethine, no matter what had happened.

"A declaration is very serious."

"But . . . I thought it was, like, letting everyone know we were together."

"It is far more immutable than that. There is only ever a single consort, and more often there is none. It joins you both to him and to his court. My brother declared himself once, you know."

"To Silarial," Kaye said, although she hadn't known, not really, not before right then. She remembered Silarial standing in the middle of a human orchard and telling Roiben that he'd proved his love to her satisfaction. How angry Silarial had been when he turned away. "He finished his quest, didn't he?"

"Yes," Ethine said. "He was to stay at the Unseelie Court, as Nicnevin's sworn knight, until the end of the truce. Nicnevin's death ended it. He could be the Bright Lady's consort now if he wanted, if he returned to us. A declaration is a compact and he has fulfilled his side of the bargain."

Kaye looked around at the revelers and felt small and stupid. "You think they should be together, don't you? You wonder what he saw in me—some dirty pixie with bad manners."

"You're clever." The faerie woman did not meet Kaye's gaze. "I imagine he saw that."

Kaye looked down at the scuffed tops of her boots. *Not that clever, after all.*

Ethine looked thoughtful. "In my heart I believe that he

loves Silarial. He blames her for his pain, but my Lady . . . she did not intend for him to suffer so—"

"He doesn't believe that. At best he thinks she didn't care. And I think he very much wanted her to care."

"What quest did he send you on?"

Kaye frowned and tried to keep her voice even. "He told me to bring him a faerie that can tell a lie." It hurt to repeat it, the words a reproach for her thinking he liked her enough to put feelings above appearances.

"An impossible task," Ethine said, still considering.

"So you see," Kaye said, "I'm probably not the best person to answer your questions. I very much wanted him to care too. And he didn't."

"If he doesn't care for you, for her, or for me," Ethine said, "then there is no one else I can think of whom he cares for, save himself."

A blond knight strode toward them, his green armor making his body nearly disappear into the leaves.

"I really do have to go," Ethine said, turning away.

"He doesn't care about himself," Kaye called after her. "I don't think he's cared about himself for a long time."

Corny strolled through the woods, trying to ignore how his heart hammered against his chest. He tried not to make eye contact with any faeries, but he was drawn to their cats' faces, their long noses and bright eyes. Luis's scowl was fixed, no matter what they passed. Even a river full of nixes—cabochons of water beading on their bare skin—did not move him, while it was all Corny could do to look away.

"What do you see?" Corny asked finally, when the silence between them had stretched so long that he'd given up on Luis's speaking first. "Are they beautiful? Is it all illusion?"

"They're not exactly beautiful, but they're dazzling." Luis snorted. "It sucks, when you think of it. They have forever, and what do they do—spend all their time eating and fucking and figuring out complicated ways to kill each other."

Corny shrugged. "I probably would too. I can see myself with bag after bag of Cheetos, downloading porn, and playing *Avenging Souls* for weeks straight if I was immortal."

Luis looked at Corny for a long moment. "Bullshit," he said.

Corny snorted. "Shows what you know."

"Remember that cake you ate before?" said Luis. "All I saw was an old mushroom."

For a moment Corny thought he was joking. "But Kaye ate one."

"She ate, like, *three*." Luis said with such glee that Corny started to laugh, and then they were both laughing together, as easy and silly as if they were going to be friends.

Corny stopped laughing when he realized that he wanted them to be friends. "How come you hate the Folk?"

Luis turned so that his cloudy eye was to Corny, making it hard for Corny to read his expression. "I've had the Sight since I was a little kid. My dad had it and I guess it got passed down to me. It made him crazy; or maybe *they* did." Luis shook his head wearily, as though he were already tired of the story. "When they know you can see them, they fuck with you in other ways. Anyway, my dad got the idea in his head that no one was safe. He shot my mother and my brother; I think he was trying to protect them. If I had been there, he would have shot me, too. My brother made it—barely—and I had to put myself in debt to a faerie to get him better. Can you imagine how things would be without the fey? I can. Normal."

"I should tell you—one of them, a kelpie, killed my sister," Corny said. "He drowned her in the ocean about two months ago. And Nephamael, he did stuff to me, but I still wanted . . ." His words trailed off as he realized that maybe it wasn't okay for him to talk about a guy *that way* in front of Luis.

"What did you want?"

In the clearing ahead, Corny spotted a group of faeries tossing what looked like dice into a large bowl. They were lovely or hideous or both at once. One golden-haired head looked uncomfortably familiar. Adair.

"We have to go," he whispered to Luis. "Before he spots us."

Luis took a quick look over his shoulder as they walked faster and faster. "Which one? What did he do?"

"Cursed me." Corny nodded as they ducked under the curtain of a weeping willow. Neither mentioned that Silarial had promised no harm would come to them. Corny guessed that Luis was as cynical about the parameters of that promise as he was.

A tangle of faeries rested near the trunk of the tree: a black-furred phooka leaning against two green-skinned pixie girls with brownish wings; an elfin boy slumped by a drowsy-looking faerie man. Corny stopped short, surprised. One of them was reciting what seemed to be an epic poem on the subject of worms.

"Sorry," Corny said, turning. "We didn't mean to bother anybody."

"Nonsense," said a pixie. "Come, sit here. You will give us a story too."

"I'm not really—" he started, but a faerie with goat feet pulled him down, laughing. The black dirt felt soft and damp under his hands and knees. The air was heavy with the rich smells of soil and leaf.

"The drake rose up with wings like leather," intoned a faerie. "Its breath set afire all the heather." Perhaps the poem was about *wyrms*.

"Mortals are so interestingly shaped," said the elfin boy, running his fingers over the smoothness of Corny's ears.

"Neil," Luis said.

The phooka reached over to touch the roundness of Corny's cheek, as though fascinated. A faerie boy licked the inside of Corny's arm and he shivered. He was a puppet. They pulled his strings and he danced.

"Neil," Luis said, his voice distant and unimportant. "Snap out of it."

Corny leaned into their caresses, butting his head against a phooka's palm. His skin felt hot and oversensitized. He groaned.

Long fingers tugged at his gloves.

"Don't do that," Corny warned, but he wanted them to. He wanted them to caress every part of him, but he hated himself for wanting it. He thought of his sister, following a dripping kelpie boy off a pier, but even that didn't curb his longing.

"Come, come," said a tall faerie with hair as blue as the feathers of a bird. Corny blinked.

"I'll hurt you," Corny said languorously, and the faeries around him laughed. The laughter wasn't particularly mocking or cruel, but it hurt all the same. It was the amusement of watching a cat threaten the tail of a wolf.

They slid off the gloves. Decayed rubber dust flaked from the tips of his fingers.

"I hurt everything I touch," Corny said dully.

He felt hands at his hips, in his mouth. The soil was cool against his back, soothing when the rest of him was prickling with heat. Without meaning to he reached out for one of the faeries, feeling hair flow across his hands like silk, feeling the shocking warmth of muscled flesh.

His eyes opened with the sudden knowledge of what he was doing. He saw, as from a great distance, the tiny pinholes in cloth where his fingers touched, the blackberry stains of bruises blooming on necks, the brown age spots spreading like smeared dirt across ancient skin. They didn't even seem to notice.

A slow smile spread over his lips. He could hurt them even if he couldn't resist them.

He let the pixies stroke him, arching up and biting at the exposed neck of the elfin boy, inhaling their strange mineral-and-earth scents, letting lust overtake him.

"Neil!" Luis shouted, pulling Corny up by the back of his shirt. Corny stumbled, reaching out to right his balance, and Luis pulled back before Corny's hand could catch him. Corny grabbed Luis's shirt instead, the fabric singeing. Corny stumbled and fell.

"Snap out of it," Luis ordered. He was breathing fast, maybe with fear. "Stand up."

Corny pushed himself onto his knees. Desire made speaking difficult. Even the movement of his own lips was disturbingly like pleasure.

A faerie rested long fingers on Corny's calf. The touch felt like a caress and he sagged toward it.

Warm lips were next to his. "Get up, Neil." Luis spoke softly, against Corny's mouth, as if daring Corny to obey. "Time to get up."

Luis kissed him. Luis, who could do everything that he couldn't, who was smart and sarcastic and the last boy in the world likely to want an awkward geek like Corny. It was dizzying to open his mouth against Luis's. Their tongues slid together for a devastating moment, then Luis pulled back.

"Give me your hands," he said, and Corny obediently held out his wrists. Luis bound them with a shoelace.

"What are you—" Corny tried to make some sense of what was happening, but he was still reeling.

"Thread your fingers together," Luis said in his competent, calm voice and pressed his mouth to Corny's again.

Of course. Luis was trying to save him. Like he saved the man with the mouth full of pennies or Lala with the snaking vines. He knew about cures and poultices and the medicinal value of kisses. He knew how to distract Corny long enough to bind his hands, how to use himself as bait to lure Corny away from danger. He saw right through to Corny's carefully hidden desire, and—worse than using it against him—Luis had used it to rescue him. Exhilaration turned to acid in Corny's stomach.

He stumbled back and staggered toward the curtain of branches. They scraped his face as he passed through.

Luis followed. "I'm sorry," he called after Corny. "I'm—I didn't—I thought—"

"I'm? I didn't? I thought?" Corny shouted at him. His face was suddenly too hot. Then his stomach clenched. He barely had time to turn before retching up chunks of old mushrooms.

Predictably, Luis had been right about the cakes.

An owl's yellow eyes caught the moonlight, making Kaye jump. She'd given up on calling Corny's name and was now just trying to find her way back to the revel. Each time she turned toward the music, it seemed to be coming from another direction.

"Lost?" asked a voice, and she jumped. It was a man with greenish-gold hair and white moth wings that folded across his bare back.

"Kind of," Kaye said. "I don't suppose you could show me the way?"

He nodded and pointed one finger to the left and the other to the right.

"Hilarious." Kaye folded her arms across her chest.

"Both ways would bring you to the revel eventually. One would just take quite a bit longer." He smiled. "Tell me your name and I'll tell you which is better."

"Okay," she said. "Kaye."

"That's not your real name." His smile was teasing. "I bet you don't even know it."

"It's probably safer that way." She looked into a dense copse of trees. Nothing seemed familiar.

"But someone must know it, mustn't they? Someone who gave it to you?"

"Maybe no one gave me a name. Maybe I'm supposed to name myself."

"They say that nameless things change constantly—that names fix them in place like pins. But without a name, a thing isn't quite real either. Maybe you're not a real thing."

"I'm real," Kaye said.

"You know a name that isn't yours, though, don't you? A true name. A silver pin that could stick a King in place."

His tone was light, but the muscles in Kaye's shoulders tensed. "I told Silarial that I wouldn't use it. I won't."

"Really?" He cocked his head to the side, looking oddly like a bird. "And you wouldn't trade it for another life? A mortal mother? A feckless friend?"

"Are you threatening me? Is Silarial threatening me?" She stepped back from him.

"Not yet," he said with a laugh.

"I'll find my own way back," she mumbled, and headed off, refusing to be lost.

The trees were heavy with impossible summer leaves, and the earth was warm and fragrant, but the woods were as still as stone. Even the wind seemed dead. Kaye walked on, faster and faster, until she came to a stream pitted with rocks. A squat figure crouched near the water, the brambles and branches of her hair making her look like a barren bush.

"You!" Kaye gasped. "What are you doing here?"

"I am sure," the Thistlewitch said, her black eyes shining, "you have better questions for me than that."

"I don't want any more riddles," Kaye said, and her voice broke. She sat down on the wet bank, not caring about the water soaking her skirt. "Or eggshells or quests."

The Thistlewitch reached out a long, lanky arm to pat Kaye with fingers that felt as rough as wood. "Poor little pixie. Come and rest your head on my shoulder."

"I don't even know which side you're on." Kaye groaned, but she scooted over and leaned against the faerie's familiar bulk. "I'm not sure how many sides there are. I mean, is this like a piece of paper with two sides or like one of those weird dice that Corny has with twenty sides? And if there are really twenty sides, then is *anyone* on my side?"

"Clever girl," the Thistlewitch said approvingly.

"Come on, that made no sense. Isn't there *anything* you can tell me? About anything?"

"You already know what you need and you need what you know."

"But that's a riddle!" Kaye protested.

"Sometimes the riddle is the answer," the Thistlewitch replied, but she patted Kaye's shoulder all the same.

9

Fair as the moon and joyful as the light;
Not wan with waiting, not with sorrow dim;
Not as she is, but was when hope shone bright;
Not as she is, but as she fills his dream.
—Christina Rossetti, "In an Artist's Studio"

In the darkness of early dawn, Corny woke to distant bells and the thunderous pounding of hooves. He rolled over, disoriented, sore, and filled with sudden panic. Somehow he'd gotten his leather jacket back on, but the edges of the sleeves looked tattered. His wrists ached and when he inadvertently pulled against the shoelace that tied them, it made them hurt more. His mouth tasted sour.

Realizing he was still in the Seelie Court explained the dread and the discomfort. But when he saw Luis, wrapped in Kaye's purple coat, cheek pillowed against the burl of a nearby blackthorn tree, he remembered the rest. He remembered what an idiot he'd been.

And the agonizing softness of Luis's lips.

And the way Luis had brushed Corny's hair off his face while he puked in the grass.

And the way that Luis had only been being kind.

Shame made his face hot and his eyes burn. His throat closed up at the thought of actually having to talk about it. He rolled onto his knees and stood awkwardly, physical distance the only thing that calmed him. Maybe Kaye was in the direction of the noise. If he could find her, Luis might not say anything. He might act like it had never happened. Corny threaded his way alone through the trees, until he spotted the procession.

Silver-shod horses raced past, their manes streaming and eyes glittering, the faces of the faeries on their backs covered by helms. The first rider was arrayed in dark red armor that seemed to flake like old paint, the next in white as leathery as a snake's egg. Then a black steed galloped toward Corny, only to rear up, front hooves dancing in the air. This rider's armor was as black and shining as crow feathers.

Corny stepped away. The rough bark of a tree trunk scraped his back.

The black-clad rider drew a curved blade that glittered like rippling water.

Corny stumbled, terror making him stupid. The horse trotted closer, its breath hot on Corny's face. He threw up his tied hands in warding.

The sword cut through the shoelace binding his wrists. Corny cried out, falling in the dirt.

The rider sheathed the sword and pulled off a ridged helm.

"Cornelius Stone," Roiben said.

Corny laughed in hysterical relief. "Roiben! What are you doing here?"

"I came to bargain with Silarial," Roiben said. "I saw Sorrowsap on the other side of the lake. Who bound your hands? Where's Kaye?"

"This is, um, for my own good," Corny said, holding up his wrists.

Roiben frowned, leaning forward in the saddle. "Favor me with the story."

Reaching up, Corny touched one of his fingers to a low green leaf. It curled, turning gray. "Pretty nasty curse, huh? Tying me up with the shoelace was supposed to keep me from touching anyone by accident. At least I think that was what it was for—I don't remember everything about last night."

Roiben shook his head, unsmiling. "Leave this place. As quickly as you can. Sorrowsap will get you safely out of the Bright Court lands. Nothing is as it seems now, apparently, not even you. Kaye—she ought—" He paused. "Tell me she's well."

Corny wanted to tell Roiben that he could shove his bull-shit pretense of caring up his ass, but he was still a little shaken by the sword so recently swung at his head. "What do you care?" he asked instead.

"I care." Roiben closed his eyes, as though willing himself calm. "Whatever you think of me, get her out of here." He leaned back in the saddle and twitched the reins. The horse stepped back.

"Wait," Corny said. "There's something I've been wanting to ask you: What's it like being a king? What's it like finally being so powerful that no one can control you?" It was sort of a taunt, sure, but Corny really wanted the answer.

Roiben laughed hollowly. "I'm sure I wouldn't know."

"Fine. Don't tell me."

Roiben tilted his head. Corny was disconcerted to suddenly have the faerie Lord's full attention. When he spoke, his voice was grave. "The more powerful you become, the more others will find ways to master you. They'll do it through those you love and through those you hate; they will find the bit and the bridle that fits your mouth and makes you yield."

"So there's no way to be safe?"

"Be invisible, perhaps. Be worthless."

Corny shook his head. "Doesn't work."

"Make them yield first," Roiben said, and the half smile on his lips wasn't quite enough to render the suggestion frivolous. "Or be dead. No one can yet master the dead." He replaced his helm. "Now get Kaye and go."

With a flick of the reins Roiben wheeled the horse around and rode down the path, dust clouding behind the shining hooves.

Corny threaded his way back through the woods, only to find Adair leaning against a tree.

"You're an ill fit among such beauty," said the faerie, pushing back butter blond hair. "It's a mistake you humans often make—being so ugly."

Corny thought of Roiben's words. *Make them yield first.*

"This was a pretty cool gift," he said, letting his hand trail across the bark of a nearby oak, blackening the trunk. "The curse. I should thank you."

Adair stepped back.

"You must have been really pissed off. The curse even withers fey flesh." Corny smiled. "Now I just have to decide what's the best way to express my gratitude. Whatever do you think Miss Manners would advise?"

Kaye tried to keep her face expressionless as Roiben ducked under the canopy of branches that formed Silarial's chamber. His silver hair poured over his shoulders like mercury, but it was sweat-darkened at his neck.

Longing twisted in her gut along with a terrible, giddy anticipation she couldn't seem to quash. The human glamour Silarial had covered her with felt tight and heavy. She wanted to call out to him, to touch his sleeve. It was easy to imagine that there had been some misunderstanding, that if she could just speak to him for a moment, everything would be like it had been before. Of course, she was supposed to stand near the trunk of the massive willow and keep her eyes on the floor the way the human attendants did.

The glamour had seemed clever at first, when Silarial had suggested it. Kaye wasn't supposed to approach Roiben until she'd succeeded in her quest. Since she hadn't, the glamour would make like she wasn't there. Kaye was just supposed to wait until he and Silarial were done talking, and then she was supposed to try to convince him to go along with the Seelie Queen's plan. If she agreed with it, of course. Which she was pretty sure she wouldn't, but at least she would get the smug satisfaction of pissing him off.

It had sounded like a better scenario than it felt now as she stood there, watching him through her lashes as if they were strangers.

Silarial looked up lazily from her cushions. "Ethine tells me that you will not agree to my conditions."

"I do not think you expected me to, m—" He stopped suddenly, and Silarial laughed.

"You nearly called me 'my Lady,' didn't you? That's a habit in need of breaking."

He looked down and his mouth twisted. "Indeed. You have caught me being foolish."

"Nonsense. I find it charming." Smiling, she swept her hand toward where Kaye stood among Silarial's attendants. "You must be parched for a taste of the changeless lands of your youth."

A willowy human in a simple blue shift stepped out of the line as if by some signal Kaye could not discern. The servant leaned into a copper bowl on the table as if she were bobbing for apples. Then, kneeling in front of Roiben, she bent backward and opened her mouth. The surface of the wine shimmered between her teeth.

Kaye was reminded suddenly and terribly of Janet drowning, of how her lips had been parted just like that, of how her mouth had looked filled with seawater. Kaye pressed her fingernails into her palms.

"Drink," said the Bright Lady, and her eyes were full of laughter.

Roiben knelt down and kissed the girl's mouth, cupping her head and tilting her so that he might swallow. "Decadent," he said, settling back onto the cushions. He looked amused and far too relaxed, his long limbs spread out as though he were in his own parlor. "Do you know what I really miss, though? Roasted dandelion tea."

Silarial petted the girl's hair before she sent her back to fetch a mouthful from another bowl. Kaye reminded herself not to stare, to look up only through her lashes, to keep her face carefully neutral. She dug her fingernails deeper into her skin.

"So tell me," said Silarial. "What conditions do you propose?"

"You must risk something if you wish me to risk everything."

"The Unseelie Court has no hope of winning a battle. You ought to take whatever I offer and be grateful for it."

"Nonetheless," Roiben said. "If I lose the duel against your champion, you will become sovereign of the Unseelie Court, and I will be dead. Quite a lot for me to wager against your offer of transient peace, but I do not ask for equal stakes. If I win, I only ask that you agree to make Ethine Queen in your place."

For a moment Kaye thought she saw Silarial's eyes shine with triumph. "Only? And if I don't agree?"

Roiben leaned back on the cushions. "Then war, winnable or no."

Silarial narrowed her eyes, but there was a smile at the corners of her mouth. "You have changed from the knight that I knew."

He shook his head. "Do you recall my eagerness to prove myself to you? Pathetically grateful for even the smallest regard. How tedious you must have found me."

"I admit I find you more interesting now, bargaining for the salvation of those whom you despise."

Roiben laughed, and the sound of it—thick with self-loathing—chilled Kaye.

"But perhaps you despise me even more than they?" Silarial asked.

He looked down at the fingers of his left hand, watching them pluck at the onyx clasps of his other cuff. "I think of the way I longed for you, and it makes me sick." He looked up at her. "But that doesn't mean I've stopped longing. I yearn for home."

Silarial shook her head. "You told Ethine you would never step down from being Lord of the Night Court. You would never reconsider your position. You would never serve me. Is that still true?"

"I won't be as I once was." Roiben gestured to Kaye and to the other girls standing against the wall. Mute servants. "No matter what I long for."

"You have said that nothing about me tempts you," Silarial said. "What of it?"

He smiled. "I told Ethine to tell you that. I never said it."

"And is it so?"

He stood, walked the short distance to where Silarial reclined, and knelt before her. He lifted his hand to her cheek, and Kaye could see his hand tremble. "I am tempted," he said.

The Bright Queen leaned closer and pressed her mouth to his. The first kiss was short and careful and chaste, but the second was not. Roiben's hands cupped her skull and bent her back, kissing her like he wanted to break her in half. When he drew back from Silarial, her lip bled and her eyes were dark with desire.

Kaye's face flamed hot and she could feel her heartbeat even in her cheeks. It seemed to her that Roiben's hand's shaking as he reached for Silarial was worse than the kisses, worse than anything he had said or could say. She knew what it felt like to tremble like that before touching someone—desire so acute that it became despair.

Kaye forced herself to look at the dirt, to concentrate on the winding roots next to her slipper. She tried not to think about anything. She didn't know how much she'd been hoping that he still loved her, until she felt how much it hurt to realize he didn't.

A rustle of clothes made Kaye look up automatically, but it was only Silarial rising from her cushions. Roiben's eyes were wary.

"You must want me to agree to your terms very much," the Bright Queen said lightly, but her voice was unsteady. She brushed a strand of hair away from his face.

"Ethine would very probably give you back your crown were she to win it," Roiben replied.

"If you should defeat my champion . . . ," Silarial began, then paused, looking down at him. She brought one white hand to his cheek. "If you should defeat my champion, you will regret it."

He half smiled.

"But I will grant you your boon. Ethine will be Queen if you win. See that you do not win." She walked to the bowls of liquids, and Kaye saw Silarial's face reflected in all their surfaces. "Of course, all this negotiating matters not at all if you will merely join me. Leave the court of those you detest. Together we can end this war today. You would be my consort—"

"No," he said. "I told you that I won't—"

"There is someone here with the means to convince you."

He stood suddenly, whirling toward the wall of servant girls. His gaze shifted across them and stopped on her. "Kaye." His voice sounded anguished.

Kaye looked around, gritting her teeth.

"How did you guess?" Silarial asked.

Roiben walked to Kaye and put his hand on her arm. She jumped, shifting away from his touch. "I should have guessed sooner. Very clever to glamour her so thoroughly."

Kaye felt sick thinking of the way he'd kissed Silarial. She wanted to slap him. She wanted to spit in his face.

"But how did you choose her from among my other maidens?"

He took Kaye's hand and turned it over so that the Queen could see the reddened half-moons where Kaye's nails had dug into her flesh. "It was that, really. I don't know anyone else with that particular nervous habit."

Kaye looked up at him and saw only a strange human face reflected in his eyes.

She snatched her hand away, rubbing it against her skirt as if she could rub off his touch. "You're not supposed to see me until I can solve your stupid riddle."

"Yes, I deserve whatever scorn you heap on me," he said, voice soft. "But what are you doing here? It's not safe. I told Corny—"

His lips were still kiss-reddened and it was hard not to concentrate on them. "This is where I belong, isn't it? This is where I came from. The other Kaye is home now, like she always should have been. With her mother, Ellen."

He looked momentarily furious. "What did Silarial make you promise for that?"

"It must suck to love her, since you don't trust her at all," Kaye said, tasting bile on her tongue.

There was a silence, in which he looked at her with a kind of terrible desperation, as though he wanted very much to speak, but could not find the words.

"It doesn't matter what he thinks of me or of you," Silarial said, coming close to where Kaye stood. Her words were soft, spoken with great care. "Use his name. End the war."

Kaye smiled. "I could, you know. I really, really could."

He looked very grave, but his voice was as soft as the Bright Queen's. "Will you rule over me, Kaye? Shall I bow to a new mistress and fear the lash of her tongue?"

Kaye said nothing. Her anger was a live thing inside of her, twisting in her gut. She wanted to hurt him, to humiliate him, to pay him back for everything she felt.

"What if I promise that I won't use the name, won't even repeat it?" Silarial said. "He would be yours alone to command. Your toy. I would just advise you how to use him."

Kaye still said nothing. She was afraid of what would come out if she opened her mouth.

Roiben paled. "Kaye, I . . ." He closed his eyes. *"Don't,"* he said, but she could hear despair in his voice. It made her even angrier. It made her want to live down to his expectations.

Silarial spoke so close to Kaye's ear that it made her shiver. "You must command him, you know. If not, I would threaten your mother, that human boy of yours, your changeling sister. You would be persuaded. Don't feel badly about giving in now."

"Say you won't repeat it," Kaye said. "Not just 'if I promise,' the real oath."

Silarial's voice was still a whisper. "I will not speak Roiben's true name. I will not bid him with it, nor will I repeat it to any other."

"Rath Roiben," Kaye said. He flinched and his hand went to the hilt at his belt, but it stayed there. His eyes remained shut. *Rye*. The word was poised on her lips. *Rath Roiben Rye*.

"Riven," Kaye finished. "Rath Roiben Riven, do as I command."

He looked up at her, quickly, eyes widening with hope.

She could feel her smile grow cruel. He'd better do what she said, right then. If he didn't, Silarial would know that Kaye had spoken the wrong name.

"Lick the Queen of the Seelie Court's hand, Rath Roiben Riven," she said. "Lick it like the dog you are."

He went down on one knee. He almost rose before he remembered himself and drew his tongue over Silarial's palm. Shame colored his face.

She laughed and wiped her hand against her gown. "Lovely. Now what else shall we make him do?"

Roiben looked up at Kaye.

She smirked.

"I deserve this," he whispered. "But, Kaye, I—"

"Tell him to be silent," said Silarial.

"Silence," Kaye said. She felt giddy with hate.

Roiben lowered his eyes and went quiet.

"Command him to pledge his loyalty to me, to be forever a servant of the Seelie Court."

Kaye sucked in her breath. That she would not do.

Roiben's face was grim.

Kaye shook her head, but her fury was replaced with fear. "I'm not done with him yet."

The Bright Queen frowned.

"Rath Roiben Riven," Kaye said, trying to think of some command she could give to stall for time. Trying to think of a way to twist Silarial's words or make some objection that the Bright Queen might believe. "I want you to—"

A scream tore through the air. Silarial took a few steps from them, distracted by the sound.

"Kaye—" Roiben said.

A group of faeries pushed their way under the canopy, Ethine among them. "My Lady," a boy said, then stopped as if stunned at the sight of the Lord of the Night Court on his knees. "There has been a death. Here."

"What?" The Queen glanced toward Roiben.

"The human—" one of them began.

"Corny!" Kaye yelled, pushing through the curtain of willow branches, forgetting Silarial, the commands, anything but Corny. She raced in the direction that others were going, ran toward where a crowd gathered and Talathain pointed a weird crossbow. At Cornelius.

The ground where he sat had withered in two circles around his hands, tiny violets turning brown and dry, toadstools rotting, the soil itself paling beneath his fingers. Beside Corny the body of Adair rested, a knife still in his hand, his neck and part of his face shriveled and dark. His dead eyes stared into the sunless sky.

Kaye stopped abruptly, so relieved that Corny was alive that she almost collapsed.

Luis stood nearby, his face pale. Her purple coat hung from his shoulders. "Kaye," he said.

"What happened?" she asked, realizing that Corny still wasn't safe. Kneeling by the body, Kaye slipped Adair's knife up her sleeve, the hilt hidden by the loose cradle of her hand.

"Neil killed him," Luis said finally, his voice low. "The Seelie fey don't like to see death—especially not here, in their court. It offends them, makes them remember that even they will eventually—"

Corny laughed suddenly. "I bet he didn't see that coming. Not from me."

"We have to get out of here," Kaye said. "Corny! Get up!"

Corny looked up at her. He sounded strange, distant. "I don't think they're going to let me leave."

Kaye glanced at the gathering crowd of fey. Silarial stood by Talathain. Ethine watched as Roiben spoke with Ellebere and Ruddles. Some of the Folk pointed at the body in disbelief, others ripped at their garments and wailed.

"You promised Corny would be safe," Kaye told the Queen. She was stalling for time.

"He *is* safe," said Silarial. "While one of my people lies dead."

"We're going." Kaye walked away from Corny. Her hands were trembling and she could feel the sharp edge of the knife against her skin. Just a few more steps.

"Let them go," Roiben said to Silarial.

Talathain turned his crossbow toward Roiben. "Do not presume to command her."

Roiben laughed and drew out his sword, slowly, as if daring Talathain to fire. His eyes were full of rage, but he seemed relieved, as though the clarity of his hate pushed back his shame. "Come," he said. "Let us make another corpse between us two."

Talathain dropped the crossbow and reached for his own blade. "Long have I waited for this moment."

They circled each other as the Folk moved back, giving them room.

"Let me fight him," said Dulcamara, dressed all in red, her hair in looping ropes stitched together with black thread.

Roiben smiled and shook his head. Turning toward Kaye, he mouthed, "Go," then swung at Talathain.

"Stop them," Silarial said to Kaye. "Order him to stop."

Advancing and retreating, they seemed partners in a swift and deadly dance. Their swords crashed together.

Ethine took a step toward her brother and then halted. She turned pleading eyes to Kaye.

"Roiben," Kaye yelled. "Stop."

He went still as stone. Talathain lowered his weapon with what appeared to be regret.

Silarial walked up to Roiben. She ran her hand over his cheek and then looked back at Kaye. "If you want to leave here with your friends," Silarial said, "you know what you must order him to do."

Kaye nodded her head, walking toward them, her heart beating so hard that it felt like a weight inside her. She stopped behind Ethine. There had to be a way to get Luis and Corny and herself free before Silarial figured out that Kaye hadn't used Roiben's true name. She needed something she could bargain with, something she would be willing to trade.

Kaye put Adair's knife to Ethine's neck.

She heard her name echo in half a dozen shocked voices.

"Corny! Get up! Luis, help him!" She swallowed hard. "We're leaving right now."

Silarial was no longer smiling. She looked stunned, her lips white. "There are things I could—"

"No!" Kaye shouted. "If you touch my mother, I'll cut Ethine. If you touch Luis's brother, I'll cut Ethine. I am going to walk out of here with Luis and Corny, and if you don't want her hurt, you and all of yours are just going to let me."

"My Lady," Ethine gasped.

Talathain pointed his sword in Kaye's direction, twisting it like a promise.

"Let the pixie and the humans through," Silarial said. "Although I think she will regret it."

With a wave of Silarial's hand, the glamour was gone. Kaye found herself drinking the air deeply, suddenly tasting the green of the plants and smelling the rich dark earth and the worms crawling through it. She had forgotten the dizzying sensations of being a faerie and the terrible weight of such a powerful glamour; it had been like filling her ears with cotton. She nearly stumbled, but she pushed her nails into her hand and stayed still.

"Not with my sister," Roiben said. "Not my sister, Kaye. I won't let you."

"Rath Roiben Riv—" Kaye started.

"That's not my name," he said, and there were gasps from the other fey.

Kaye looked him in the eye and put every bit of fury into her voice. "You can't stop me." She pushed Ethine toward Luis and Cornelius. "Try, and I *will* command you."

A muscle in his jaw twitched. His eyes were as cold as lead.

They marched past, making their way to the edge of the island. As they climbed into the ice boat they had beached among the reeds, Ethine made a soft sound that was not quite a sob.

They paddled to the far, snow-covered shore, past a young man standing as stiffly as a Christmas nutcracker, his gold and red scarf tucked into a toggle coat. His lips and cheeks were blushed with blue, and frost covered his chin like stubble. His pale, sunken eyes still stared at the waves. Even in death, he waited to serve the Seelie Queen.

Kaye could never run far enough or fast enough to escape them all.

10

*To win one hundred victories in one hundred battles
is not the acme of skill. To subdue the enemy without
fighting is the acme of skill.*
— Sun Tzu, The Art of War

The car was still parked in the ditch by the side of the highway, the windows on the passenger side coated with spattered slush that had frozen to ice. The door made a cracking sound when Luis opened it.

"Get in," Kaye told Ethine. Kaye's heart beat like a rattle and her face was as cold as her fingers; all the heat in her body had been eaten up by panic.

Ethine looked at the car dubiously. "The iron," she said.

"Why aren't they following us?" Luis asked, looking back over his shoulder.

"They are," said a voice.

Kaye shrieked, raising the blade automatically.

Sorrowsap stepped out onto the road, black clothes loose and boots crunching on the gravel as he strode toward them.

"My Lord Roiben was displeased with me for letting you go across the water." There was a threat in his voice. "He will be even more displeased if you do not depart immediately. Go. I will hold whatever comes. When you cross the border into the Unseelie Court, you will be safe."

"You must see that it would be madness to keep me against my will," Ethine said, touching Kaye's arm. "You are away from the court. Allow me to return and I will speak on your behalf. I will swear to it."

Luis shook his head. "What is going to keep them from hurting my brother if we let you go? I'm sorry. We can't. We all have people we love that we have to protect."

"Do not let them take me," Ethine said, throwing herself to her knees and taking Sorrowsap's bony hand. "My brother would want me returned to my people. He seeks me, even now. If you are loyal to him, you will give me succor."

"So I guess Roiben's not such a villain anymore?" Kaye asked her. "Now he's your loving brother?"

Ethine pressed her mouth into a thin line.

"I have no orders to help you," Sorrowsap said, pulling his fingers from Ethine's grip. "And little desire to help anyone. I do as I am commanded."

Ethine rose slowly and Luis grabbed her arm. "I know that you are a great lady and all that, but you have to get in the car now."

"My brother will hate you if you hurt me," she told Kaye, her eyes narrowed.

Kaye felt sick, thinking of the last, terrible look he had given her. "Come on, we're just going on a road trip. We can play I Spy."

"In. Now," Luis told her.

Ethine climbed into the backseat and skooched over the cracked vinyl and the crumbling foam. Her face was stiff with fear and fury.

Corny drew a swirl along the hood that turned almost immediately to rust. He didn't seem to notice that he was standing barefoot on snow. "I'm a murderer."

"No, you're not," said Luis.

"If I'm not a murderer," asked Corny, "how come I keep killing people?"

"There's plastic bags here," said Kaye. She reached into the well of the backseat and fished them out from the piles of empty cola cans and fast-food wrappers. "Put these on until we get gloves."

"Oh, very well," Corny said with a lunatic half smile. "Don't want to wither the steering wheel."

"You're not driving," Luis said.

Kaye wrapped Corny's hands in the bags and steered him to the passenger side. She jumped into the back, beside Ethine.

Luis started the car and, finally, they were moving. Kaye looked through the rear window, but no faeries seemed to follow. They did not fly overhead, did not swarm down and stop the vehicle.

The hot, iron-soaked air of the heater dulled Kaye's thoughts, but she forced her eyes open. Each time dizzy slumber threatened to overtake her, terror that the Host were almost upon them startled her awake. She kept her eyes on the windows, but it seemed to her that the clouds were dark with wings and all the woods they passed were full of hungry wet mouths.

"What are we going to do now?" Luis asked.

Kaye thought of Roiben's long fingers knotted in Silarial's red hair, his hands pulling her down to him.

"Where are we even going?" Corny asked. "Where's this safe place that we're in such a rush to get to? I mean, I guess we have a better chance with Roiben than Silarial, but what happens when we give Ethine back? Do you really think Silarial's going to leave us alone? I killed Adair. I *killed* him."

Kaye paused. The enormity of how isolated and helpless they were settled into her bones. They had taken a hostage that both of the courts wanted back, and Silarial needed something that only Kaye knew. There was no secret weapon this time, no mysterious faerie knight to keep her safe. There was only a crappy old car and two humans who hadn't deserved to get dragged into this. "I don't know," she said.

"No such thing as safe," said Corny. "Just like I said. Not for us. Not ever."

"There's no safe for anyone," Luis said. Kaye was surprised at how calm he sounded.

Ethine moaned in the backseat.

Luis glanced at her in the rearview mirror.

"It's the iron," said Corny.

Luis nodded uncomfortably. "I knew it bothered them."

Corny smirked. "Yeah, watch out. She might puke on you."

"Shut up," Kaye said. "She's sick. She's not even as used to it as I am."

"'Last exit in New York,'" Corny read off the sign. "I guess we can pull over at the next rest stop. Get her some air. We should be in Unseelie land by now."

Kaye scanned the skies behind them, but there was still no sign that they were being followed. Were they going to be bargained with? Shot with arrows that would burrow into their hearts? Were Silarial and Roiben working together to get Ethine back? They had left the map of what Kaye knew, and she felt as though they were about to fall off the edge of the world.

A gust of fresh, icy wind woke her from her miserable reverie.

They had pulled into a gas station and Luis was getting out. He headed toward the station while Corny started filling the tank. His bag-covered hands slipped, thin plastic tearing. He staggered back in surprise, gasoline splashing the side of the car.

Kaye stumbled out. The air was heady with vapors.

"What happened back there?" she asked him quietly. "You killed Adair? Why?"

"You don't think I just did it because I could? I killed Nephamael, didn't I?" Corny shoved the nozzle back into the car.

"Nephamael was already dying," Kaye said. Her head hurt. "Because of me, remember?"

He pushed bag-covered fingers through his hair, hard, like he wanted to tear it out. Then he held his hand out in front of him. "It all happened so fast. Adair was talking to me, being scary, and I was trying to be scary back. Then Luis walked up. Adair grabbed him—he was going on about how Silarial made no promise about *Luis* being unharmed. He said he should put out Luis's other eye, and he put his thumb right up against it. And I just—I just grabbed his wrist and shoved him. Then I grabbed his throat. Kaye, when I was in middle school, I got my ass kicked pretty regularly. But the curse—I didn't have to press very hard. I just held on to him and then he was dead."

"I'm so—" Kaye started.

Corny shook his head. "Don't say you're sorry. I'm not sorry."

She leaned her head against his shoulder, breathing in the familiar smell of his sweat. "Then I'm not sorry either," she said.

Luis walked back from the small store with a pair of lemon yellow dishwashing gloves and flip-flops. Kaye looked down and realized that Corny's feet were still bare.

"Put these on," Luis told him, avoiding looking either of them in the face. "There's a diner across the street. We could get something to eat. I called Dave and he's going to hide out with a friend in Jersey. I told him to get out of Seelie territory—even if the city is mostly just full of exiles."

"You should call your mom," said Corny, pulling out his cell. "Battery's dead. I can charge it in the diner."

"We have to get some other clothes at least," said Kaye. "We're all dressed crazy. We're going to stand out."

Luis peered into the car. Ethine watched him with her knife gray eyes.

"Can't you guys use glamour?" he asked.

Kaye shook her head. The world swam a little. "I feel like shit. Maybe a little."

"I don't think some T-shirts are going to make up for the fact that you're green," Luis said, turning around. "Get her out. We'll take our chances with the diner crowd."

"Do not presume that you may give orders." Ethine stepped carefully onto the asphalt and immediately turned to vomit on the wheels. Corny grinned.

"Watch her—she could try to run," Luis said.

"I don't know." Corny frowned. "She looks pretty sick."

"Wait a minute," Kaye said. She leaned over to Luis and reached into the pocket of the purple plaid coat he wore—her coat. She pulled out fuzzy handcuffs lined in fur. After slapping one on Ethine's wrist, she clasped the other one onto her own.

"What is this?" Ethine objected.

Luis laughed out loud. "You do *not*." He looked at Corny. "She does *not* have a pair of handcuffs handy in case she happens to take a prisoner."

"What can I say?" Corny asked.

Ethine shivered. "Everything reeks of filth and iron and rot."

Corny shouldered off his leather jacket and Ethine took it gratefully, sliding it on over her free arm. "Yeah, Jersey pretty much blows," he said.

Kaye concentrated, hiding her wings, changing her eyes and the color of her skin. That was all she had energy for. The car ride and the Queen's ripping off of the human glamour had left her sapped. Ethine had not even bothered to make her own ears less pointed or her features less elegant or inhuman. As they climbed the steps, Kaye considered saying something, but bit her tongue when Ethine shrunk back from the metal on the door. If Kaye felt bad, Ethine probably felt worse.

The outside of the diner was faux stone and beige stucco with a sign on the door proclaiming TRUCKERS WELCOME. Someone had sloppily painted the windows with reindeer, Santas, and large wreaths. Inside, they were seated without a second glance by a stout older woman with carefully groomed white hair. Ethine stared at her lined face with undisguised fascination.

Kaye slid into the booth, letting the familiar smell of brewed coffee wash over her. She didn't care that it stank of iron. This was the world she knew. It almost made her feel safe.

A cute Latino boy handed them their laminated menus and poured their water.

Luis drank it gratefully. "I'm starving. I ate my last protein bar yesterday."

"Do you really have more power over us if we eat your food?" Corny asked Ethine.

"We do," Ethine said.

Luis gave her a dark look.

"So I—" Corny started, but then he opened his menu, hid his face, and didn't finish.

"It fades," Ethine said. "Eat something else. That helps."

"I have to make a call," Kaye told Corny.

Corny leaned down to plug the cord into an outlet sitting underneath a painting of happy trees and a moose. He sat back up and handed the slim phone to Kaye. "As long as you don't jerk it out of the wall, you can use it while it's charging."

She dialed her mother's number, but the phone just rang and rang. No voice mail. No answering machine. Ellen didn't believe in them.

"Mom's not home," Kaye said. "We need a plan."

Corny put his menu down. "How can we make a plan when we don't know what Silarial's scheming?"

"We need to do something," Kaye said. "First. Now."

"Why?" Luis asked.

"The reason that Silarial wanted me to come to the Seelie Court is because I know Roiben's true name."

Ethine looked over at Kaye, eyes wide.

"Oh," Corny said. "Right. Shit."

"I managed to deceive her about what his name is for a while, but now she knows I played her."

"What a typical pixie you are," Ethine said.

She might have said more, but at that moment the waitress walked over, taking her pen and pad out of her apron. "What can I get you kids? We have an eggnog pancake special still going."

"Coffee, coffee, coffee, and coffee," Corny said, pointing around the table.

"A strawberry milkshake," said Luis. "Mozzarella sticks and a deluxe cheeseburger."

"How would you like that cooked?" the waitress asked.

Luis looked at her strangely. "Whatever. Just on a plate in front of me."

"Steak and eggs," Corny said. "Meat, burnt. Eggs, over easy. Dry rye toast."

"Chicken souvlaki on a pita," Kaye said. "Extra tzatziki sauce for my fries, please."

Ethine looked at them all blankly and then looked at the menu in front of her. "Blueberry pie," she said finally.

"You kids been to that Renaissance Faire up in Tuxedo?" the woman asked.

"You guessed it," said Corny.

"Well, you all look real cute." She smiled as she gathered their menus.

"How horrible to be dying all your life," Ethine said with a shudder as the waitress walked away.

"You're closer to death than she is," Luis told her. He poured a line of sugar on the table, licked his finger, and ran it through the powder.

"You're not going to kill me." Ethine lifted her cuffed hand. "You don't know what to do. You're all just frightened children."

Kaye tugged abruptly against the other end of the cuff, pulling Ethine's hand back down to the vinyl-covered booth seat. "I heard something about a duel. Silarial agreed to give you her kingdom if Roiben won. What's up with that?"

Ethine turned to look at Kaye in confusion. "She agreed?"

"Well, maybe she got distracted during all the kissing that preceded it."

"Whoa," Corny said. "What?"

Kaye nodded. "It wasn't like he had her right there in front of me, but there was some definite pitching and catching of woo." Her voice sounded rough.

Ethine smiled down at the table. "He *kissed* her. That pleases me. He does have feelings for her, even still."

Kaye tried to think of an excuse to tug on the cuff again.

"Back to what you know about the duel," prompted Luis.

Ethine shrugged. "It is to take place in neutral territory— Hart Island off of New York—a day from tonight. At best, my brother could win the Unseelie Court a few years of peace, perhaps long enough to build up a larger legion of fey or a better strategy. At worst, he could lose his lands and his life."

"Doesn't sound worth it," Corny said.

"No, wait," said Kaye, shaking her head. "The problem is that it sounds totally worth it. It sounds *possible* for him to win. I bet Roiben thinks he can beat Talathain. Silarial didn't want them to go at it today, but Roiben didn't seem to mind. Why would she give him even a chance to win?"

Luis shrugged. "Maybe it's no fun if it's too easy to take over the Unseelie Court?"

"Maybe she's got some other plan," Kaye said. "Some way to give Talathain an advantage."

"What about cold iron bullets?" Corny said. "Fits in with her use of that big rig. She's on a whole mortal tech kick."

"Is any bullet really more terrible than an arrowhead that burrows through your skin to strike your heart?" Ethine asked. "No mortal weapon will kill him."

Luis nodded. "Then Roiben's name. That's the most obvious, right? Then the whole duel becomes a smoke screen because she can force him to lose."

"Whatever my Queen's plan, I imagine it is beyond your ken," said Ethine.

The waitress came and poured coffee into their cups. Corny raised his in one yellow-gloved hand. "Here's to us." He looked at Ethine. "Brought to this table by friendship or fate—or because you're a prisoner—and here's to the sweet balm of coffee, by the grace of which we shall accomplish the task before us and ken what we need to ken. Okay?"

The three of them lifted their cups of coffee and clinked them together. Kaye clinked her cup against Ethine's.

Corny closed his eyes in bliss as he took his first sip. Then he sighed and looked over at them. "Okay, so what were we talking about?"

"The plan," Kaye said. "The plan we don't have."

"It's hard to come up with a scheme to thwart some other scheme you don't even know about," Luis said.

"This is what I think we should do," said Corny. "Lay low until after the duel. We surround ourselves with iron and keep her for insurance." He gestured toward Ethine with his coffee spoon, and a few drops spattered on the table. One hit the faerie woman's gown, soaking into the strange fabric. "So, Kaye, if you're the linchpin of Silarial's plan, the plan won't happen. The duel will go fairly. May the best monster win."

"I don't know," said Kaye. The waitress set a steaming plate in front of her. Her mouth watered at the smell of the cooked onions. Across the table, Luis picked up a mozzarella stick and dredged it through a dish of red sauce. "I feel like we should be doing something more. Something important."

"Do you know what fairy chess is?" Corny asked.

Kaye shook her head.

"It's what they call it when you change the rules of the game. Usually it's just a single variation."

"They really call it that?" Kaye asked. "Like in chess club?"

He nodded. "I was the president. I should know."

"There were absolutely no blueberries in that pie, were there?" Ethine asked as she climbed into the car beside Kaye, the handcuffs taut.

"Dunno," said Corny. "How was it?"

"Barely edible," said Ethine.

"Right there, that is the great thing about diners. The food is much tastier than you would think. Like those mozzarella sticks."

"*My* mozzarella sticks," Luis said as he started the car.

Corny shrugged, a wicked grin spreading across his features. "Worried about getting my germs?"

Luis looked panicked, then abruptly angry. "Shut it."

Kaye poked Corny in the back of his neck, but when he turned to her, his expression was hard to decipher. She tried to mouth a question. He shook his head and turned back to the road, leaving her more puzzled than before.

She leaned against the cushions of the seat, letting her glamour slip away with relief. She was coming to hate the weight of it.

"Once more, I ask you to release me," said Ethine. "We're well away from the court, and my continued captivity will only draw them to you."

"No one likes being a hostage," said Luis, and there was some satisfaction in his voice. "But I think they're coming whether you're tagging along or not. And we're safer with you here."

Ethine turned to Kaye. "And you are going to let the humans speak for you? Will you side against your people?"

"I would think you'd be glad you're here," Kaye said. "At least you don't have to watch your beloved Queen kill your beloved brother. Who she's probably in love with." As she said it, her stomach clenched. The words echoed in her ears, as if she'd doomed him.

Ethine pressed her mouth into a thin, pale line.

"Not to mention the pie," said Corny.

Exits streamed by as Kaye stared out the window, feeling sick and helpless and guilty.

"Do we need to pick up Dave somewhere?" Corny asked softly, his voice pitched so that Kaye knew she wasn't included in the conversation.

Luis shook his head. "I'll call from your place. My friend Val said she'd pick him up at the station and keep an eye on him. She could probably even drop him off if we need her to." He sighed. "I just hope my brother actually got on the train."

"Why wouldn't he?" Corny asked.

"He doesn't like to do what I say. About a year ago, Dave

and I were living in an abandoned subway station. It was shitty, but the iron kept away the faeries, and this bargain I'd struck with the faeries kept away most everyone else. Then Dave found this junkie girl and brought her down to live with us. Lolli. Things were tense between me and my brother before that, but Lolli just made everything worse."

"You both liked her?" Corny asked.

Luis gave him a quick look. "Not really. Dave followed her around like a puppy dog. He was obsessed. But she . . . Inexplicably, she liked me."

Corny laughed.

"I know," said Luis. He shook his head, clearly embarrassed. "Hilarious, right? I hate this girl's guts and am blind in one eye and . . . Anyway, Dave never really forgave me. He used this drug, Never—it's magic—to make himself look like me. Got really strung out. Killed some faeries to get more."

"And that's why you have to work for Silarial?" Corny asked.

"Yeah. Only her protection really keeps him safe in New York." Luis sighed. "It barely works. The exiles are sworn to nobody and they were the ones he was killing. If he would just straighten himself out . . . I know things could be better. Next year he'll be eighteen. We could get loans from the state on account of both our parents being dead. Go to school."

Kaye thought about what Dave had said when they were in New York, about having some fun before he died. She felt awful. He wasn't thinking about getting an education.

"Go to school for what?" Corny asked.

Luis sighed. "It's going to sound dumb. I thought about being a librarian—like my ma—or a doctor."

"I want to stop at my house," Kaye said loudly, interrupting them. "If you turn here, we're really close."

"What?" Corny turned around in his seat. "You can't. We have to stick together."

"I want to make sure my grandmother's okay and get some clothes."

"That's stupid." Corny turned around farther in his seat to look back at her. "Besides, you're handcuffed to our prisoner."

"I have the key. You can cuff her to yourself. Look, I'll meet you at your house after I get my stuff." She paused, fishing around in her pocket. "I need to feed my rats. They've been alone for days and I bet their water bottle is getting low."

"You'll never feed them again if you get *carried off by faeries*!"

"And I don't wish to be left alone with two mortal boys," Ethine said softly. "If you won't let me free, then you are charged with my comfort."

"Oh, please," Kaye said. "Corny's *gay*. You don't have to worry about—" She stopped as Corny glowered at her, and she sucked in her breath. He liked Luis. And he thought Luis knew, but didn't like him. That was what all the defensiveness about the mozzarella sticks and the germs had been about.

"Sorry," she mouthed, but it only made him glare more. "Turn here," she said finally, and Luis turned.

"You misunderstand my concern," said Ethine, but Kaye ignored her.

"I know you want to check on your grandma and your mother." Corny's voice was low. "But even if your grandmother

knows something about what's going on with your mom—
which is a long shot—I really doubt you are going to like what
you hear."

"Look," Kaye said, and her voice was as soft as his, "I don't
know what happens next. I don't know how we fix things. But
I can't just disappear forever without saying good-bye."

"Fine." He pointed for Luis. "Stop there." He looked at
Kaye. "Be quick."

They pulled up in front of Kaye's grandmother's house.
She uncuffed her wrist, handed the key to Corny, and got out.

Luis cranked down the window. "We'll wait for you."

She shook her head. "I'll meet you guys at the trailer."

All the lights on the second floor were on, glowing like jack-
o'-lantern eyes. No holiday lights trimmed the front steps,
although all the neighboring houses were bright and twinkling.
Kaye climbed up the tree in front of her bedroom, the frozen
bark rough and familiar under her palms. As she stepped onto
the snow-covered asphalt of the shingles, she could see figures
in her bedroom. Crouching, she scooted closer.

Ellen stood in the hallway, talking to someone. For a
moment, Kaye touched her hand to the window, ready to throw
it open and call to her mother, but then she noticed her rat cage
was missing and her clothes had been piled in two garbage bags
on the floor. *Chibi-Kaye*, Corny had said, joking. Chibi-Kaye
came into the room, wearing Kaye's Chow Fat T-shirt. It hung
to her scabby knees.

The little girl did look like Kaye in miniature—dirty blond
hair in tangles over her shoulders, brown eyes and a snubbed

nose. Looking through the window was like seeing a scene out of her own past.

"Mom," Kaye whispered. The word clouded in the air, like a ghost that could not quite manifest. Her heart hammered against her chest.

"You need anything, Kate?" Ellen asked.

"I don't want to sleep," the little girl said. "I don't like to dream."

"Try," said Kaye's mother. "I think—"

Lutie flew down from the branch of a tree, and Kaye was so startled that she fell back, sliding a little ways on the roof. From inside, she heard a high-pitched shriek.

Ellen walked to the window and looked out at the snowy roof, her breath clouding the glass. Kaye scuttled back, out of Ellen's line of sight. Like a monster. Like a monster waiting for a child to fall asleep so she could creep in and eat it up.

"There's nothing," Ellen said. "No one to steal you away again."

"Who's *she*?" Lutie whispered, alighting on Kaye's lap. Lutie's wings brushed Kaye's fingers like fluttering eyelashes. "Why is she sleeping in your bed and wearing your clothes? I waited and waited like you said. You have taken a long time coming back."

"She's the baby who got taken to make room for me. She's who I thought I was."

"The changeling?" Lutie asked.

Kaye nodded. "The girl who belongs here. The real Kaye."

The cold of the snow seeped through her faerie gown. Still, she sat on the roof, peering at the girl inside as Ellen shut off everything but the night-light.

It was a simple thing to wait until the hallway light went dark, climb a little ways, then push open the window to the attic. Kaye ducked inside, swinging her feet over the ledge and slithering through.

Her feet touched grime-covered floorboards, and she pulled the switch to turn on the single bulb.

Her hip hit a box, sending the contents spilling out. In the sudden light, she saw dozens and dozens of photographs. Some of them were stuck together while others were chewed at the edges, but they all featured a little girl. Kaye bent low. Sometimes the girl was a swaddled-up baby sleeping on a patch of grass, sometimes she was a skinny thing dancing around in leg warmers. Kaye didn't know which photos were of her and which ones were of the other girl—she had no memory of how old she'd been when the switch occurred.

Kaye traced her fingers through the dust. *Impostor*, she wrote. *Fake*.

A gust of wind blew through the open window, scattering the photographs. With a sigh, she started gathering them up. She could smell the droppings of squirrels, the termite-eaten wood, the rotted sill. In the eaves something had made a nest of pink insulation, garish against the planks. Looking up at it, she thought again of cuckoos. She shoved the pictures into a shoebox and headed for the stairs.

No one was inside the second-floor bathroom, but another night-light glowed beside the sink. Kaye felt empty in this familiar space, as though her heart had been scraped hollow. But she had guessed right; no one had packed away her dirty clothes.

Picking through the hamper, she pulled out T-shirts,

sweaters, and jeans she'd worn the week before, balled them up, and tossed them out the window onto the snowy lawn. She wanted to take her records and notebooks and novels too, but she didn't want to risk going into her bedroom to get them. What if the changeling screamed? What if Ellen walked in and saw her there, clutching the stupid rubber necklace she'd five-fingered at a street fair?

Carefully, Kaye opened the door and stepped out into the hallway, straining for the sound of her rats. She couldn't just leave them to get dumped out in the snow or given to a pet store like her grandmother threatened whenever their cage was particularly filthy. She felt panicky at the thought of not being able to find them. Maybe someone had put them on the enclosed porch? Kaye crept down the staircase, but as she snuck into the living room, her grandmother looked up from the couch.

"Kaye," she said. "I didn't hear you come in. Where were you? We were very worried."

Kaye could have glamoured herself invisible or run, but her grandmother's voice sounded so normal that it rooted her to the spot. She was still in the shadows, the green of her skin hidden by the darkness.

"Do you know where Isaac and Armageddon are?"

"In your mother's room—upstairs. They were bothering your sister. She's afraid of them—has quite an imagination. She says they're always talking to her."

"Oh," Kaye said. "Right."

A Christmas tree sat near the television, trimmed with angels and a glitter garland. It was real—Kaye could smell the crushed pine needles and wet resin. Underneath sat a few boxes wrapped in gold paper. Kaye couldn't remember the last time they'd put up a tree, never mind bought one.

"Where have you been?" Her grandmother leaned forward, squinting.

"Around," Kaye whispered. "Things didn't go so well in New York."

"Come on, sit down. You're making me nervous, standing there where I can't see you."

Kaye took another step back, into deeper darkness. "I'm fine here."

"She never told me about Kate. Can you imagine that? Nothing! How could she not tell me about my own flesh and blood? The spitting image of you at that age. Such a sweet little girl, growing up robbed of a family to love her. It hurts my heart to think of it."

Kaye nodded again, stupidly, numbly. *Robbed*. And Kaye was the robber, the shoplifter of Kate's childhood. "Did Ellen say why Kate is here now?"

"I'd thought she'd have told you—Kate's dad checked himself into a rehab. He had promised not to bother Ellen, but he did and I'm glad. Kate's a strange child and she's clearly been raised terribly. Do you know that all she'll eat is soybeans and flower petals? What kind of diet is that for a growing girl?"

Kaye wanted to scream. The disconnect between the normalcy of the things her grandmother was saying and what she knew to be true seemed unendurable. Why would her mother tell her grandmother a story like that? Had someone enchanted her to believe that was the truth? Magic choked Kaye, the words that would conjure silence sharp in her mouth. But she swallowed them, because she also wanted her grandmother to keep talking, wanted everything to be normal for one more minute.

"Is Ellen happy?" Kaye asked quietly instead. "To have . . . Kate?"

Her grandmother snorted. "She was never really ready to be a mother. How will she manage in that little apartment? I'm sure she's happy to have Kate—what mother wouldn't be happy to have her child? But she's forgetting how much work it all is. They're going to have to move back here, I'm sure."

With growing dread, Kaye realized that Corny had been right all along. Giving her mother a changeling child had been a terrible plan. Ellen had just been getting ahead with her job and the band, and a kid completely derailed that. Kaye'd screwed up, really screwed up in a way she had no idea how to fix.

"Kate's going to look up to you," her grandmother said. "You can't be running around anymore, missing important family things. We don't need two wild children."

"Stop! Stop!" Kaye said, but there was no magic in her words. She put her hands over her ears. "Just stop. Kate isn't going to look up to me—"

"Kaye?" Ellen called from the top of the stairs.

Panicked, Kaye headed for the kitchen door. She yanked it open, glad for the cold air on her burning face. Right then she hated everyone—hated Corny for being right, Roiben for being gone, her mother and grandmother for having replaced her. Most of all, she hated herself for making all those things happen.

"Kaye Fierch!" Ellen shouted from the doorway in her

seldom-used "mom" voice. "You get back in here right now."

Kaye stopped automatically.

"I'm sorry," Ellen said, and Kaye turned toward her, saw the distress in her face. "I handled things badly, I admit that. Please don't leave. I don't want you to leave."

"Why not?" Kaye asked softly. Her throat felt tight.

Ellen shook her head, walking out into the yard. "I want you to explain. What you were going to tell me last time, at my apartment—tell me now."

"Okay," Kaye said. "When I was little, I got switched with the—the human—and you raised me, instead of the—the human girl. I didn't know until we moved back here and met other faeries."

"Faeries," Ellen echoed. "Are you sure that's what you are? A faerie? How can you tell?"

Kaye held up one green hand, turning it over. "What else would I be? An alien? A green girl from Mars?"

Ellen took a deep breath and let it out all at once. "I don't know. I don't know what to make of any of this."

"I'm not human," Kaye said, those words seeming to cut to the thing that was the most terrible and incomprehensible about the truth.

"But you sound—" Ellen stopped, correcting herself. "Of course you sound like you. You are you."

"I know," Kaye said. "But I'm not who you thought I was, right?"

Ellen shook her head. "When I saw Kate, I was so afraid. I figured you did something dumb to get her back from whatever had her, didn't you? See, I know you. *You.*"

"Her name's not Kate. She's Kaye. The real—"

Ellen held up one hand. "You didn't answer my question."

"Yeah." Kaye sighed. "I did something pretty dumb."

"See, you're exactly who I think you are." Ellen's arms went around Kaye's shoulders and she laughed her deep, cigarette-rough laugh. "You're my girl."

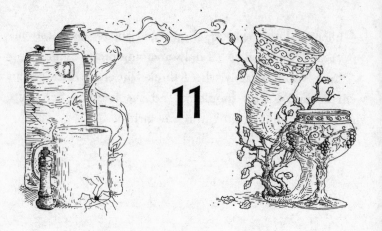

11

The lawn in front of Corny's trailer was decorated with a giant inflated penguin wearing a green scarf and hat and a red *Star Trek* shirt complete with an insignia on the left breast. It sat on the lawn, glowing erratically. As Luis pulled into the gravel drive, multicolored lights strobed from the roof of the trailer next door, turning the whole lot into a disco.

"Aren't you going to tell me what a beautiful home I have?" Corny said, but the joke felt forced, lame.

Ethine leaned forward, her fingers on the plastic seat.

Luis shut off the car. "Is that penguin dressed as—"

"Tip of the iceberg," said Corny.

Leading Ethine by the fur-lined handcuff, Luis waited as Corny unlocked the front door. Inside, the rainbow fiber-optic tree illuminated a pile of dirty dishes. Framed needlepoint samplers hung on the wall next to signed pictures of Captain Kirk and Mr. Spock. A cat jumped down with a thud and started to wail.

"My room's down that hall," Corny whispered. "Home sweet home."

Luis padded over the worn carpet, leading Ethine behind him. There was a musty smell that Corny hadn't noticed before. He wondered if he'd just gotten used to it.

Corny's mother opened the hall door. There was something sad about her thin nightgown, her tangled bed-hair and bare feet. She hugged him before he spoke.

"Mom," Corny said. "This is Luis and . . . Eileen."

"How can you just walk in here like this?" she said, stepping back and looking him over. "You missed Christmas, this year of all years. The first Christmas since your sister's funeral. We thought you were dead too. Your stepfather cried like I've never seen him."

Corny squinted, as though some problem with his vision could explain her words. "I missed Christmas? What day is it?"

"It's the twenty-sixth," she said. "What are you three wearing? And your hair's black. Where have you been?"

Five days gone. Corny groaned. Of course. Time ran differently in Faerieland. It had seemed like two days when it had been twice that. Crossing to that island had been like crossing another time zone, like flying to Australia, except there was no way to gain that time on the way back.

"What is wrong with you? What have you been doing that you don't know how long you've been gone?"

Corny plucked at his tunic with a yellow-gloved hand. "Mom—"

"I don't know if I can ever forgive you." She shook her head. "But it's the middle of the night and I'm too tired to listen to your excuses. I'm exhausted from worrying."

She turned toward Luis and Ethine. "There's some more blankets in the closet if you get cold; remind Corny to turn on the space heater."

Ethine seemed ready to say something, but Luis spoke first. "Thank you for letting us stay." He looked almost shy. "We'll try not to be any trouble."

Corny's mom nodded absently, then squinted her eyes at Ethine. "Her ears are . . ." She turned to Corny. "Where *have* you been?"

"A sci-fi convention. I'm so sorry, Mom." Corny opened the door to his bedroom and switched on the light, letting Luis and Ethine walk past him, inside. "Seriously, I don't know how I lost track of so much time."

"A convention? ChristmasCon? I expect to hear a much more convincing story in the morning," she said, and went back into her own room.

A computer hummed on his desk, the screen fading between a series of screen shots from *Farscape*. A poster of two angels hung above his bed, one with black wings and one with white, their hands twined together by a cord of thorns, their blood the only color on the large glossy paper. Piles of books were stacked where he dropped them right before he fell asleep. Manga volumes sat on top of graphic novels and paperbacks. He kicked a few under the bed, embarrassed.

He had always thought of his room as an extension of his interests. Now, looking around the room, he thought it looked as dorky as the penguin on his lawn.

"You can sleep here," Corny told Ethine, nodding toward his bed. "The sheets are pretty clean."

"Gallant," she said.

"Yeah, I know it is." He walked over to his dresser, where a white King and a black King stood side by side. He liked to signal his moods by which one was in front, but he'd stopped doing that after Janet died; there was no annoying sister to signal to. And besides, it made him think about just how much he missed her. Opening the drawers, he pulled out a T-shirt and boxers and tossed them onto the bed. "You can wear these, if you want. To sleep in."

Luis unlaced his boots. "Can I grab a shower?"

Corny nodded and rummaged for the shirt that had the least pathetic logo. He found a faded navy blue one that said, I CAN DRINK MORE COFFEE THAN YOU CAN. Looking up, ready to hand it to Luis, he froze as Ethine stripped off her dress with complete nonchalance. The blades of her shoulders were covered with what looked like the buds of wings, pink against the handkerchief white of her skin. As she slid his boxers up her thin legs, she looked over at him and her eyes were chilling in their emptiness.

"Thanks," Luis said too loudly, taking the cloth out of his hands. "I'm going to borrow jeans, if you don't mind."

Corny nodded toward a few pairs stacked on a basket of clean clothes. "Take whatever."

Ethine sat on the edge of the bed, the unnaturally long toes of her bare feet scrunching in the rug as Luis left the room.

"I could enchant you," she said.

He stepped back, looking away from her face. "Not for long. Luis or Kaye would come in, and you can't enchant them." But, of course, Kaye was at her grandmother's house and Luis was in the shower. A quick glance told him that he hadn't bothered to lock her other cuff to anything. She'd have plenty of time.

"Even with the sound of my voice, I could make you do my bidding."

"You wouldn't tell me that if you were going to." He thought about the little faerie he'd captured the night of the coronation, and slid his hand behind the dresser, to where the iron poker was leaning. "Just like if I say that I could make your skin wrinkle like the old waitress at that diner, you can be pretty sure I'm not planning on it."

"And your sweet mother, I could enchant her, too."

He turned around, whipping the brand through the air, toward her throat. "Lock the other cuff. Do it right now."

She laughed, high and bright. "I only meant that you should not forget that by bringing me here, you are putting those you love in danger."

"Lock the cuff anyway."

She leaned over and cuffed herself to the support on his headboard, then twisted so that she was lying on her stomach. Her gray eyes flashed as they caught the light of the side table. They were as inhuman as those of a doll.

Crossing to the window, Corny took the key out of his jacket, opened the window, and tossed it out into a leaf pile. "Good luck ordering me around now. Enchanted or not, it's going to take someone a while to find that key."

He watched her, poker in hand, until Luis came back wearing Corny's jeans and a bleached towel wrapped around his braids. The mahogany skin of his chest was still flushed with the heat of the shower.

Corny looked down quickly at his gloved fingers, at the thin layer of rubber that protected him from ruining everything he touched. It was better, looking down, instead of taking the chance that his eyes might stare too long at all that bare skin.

Luis unwrapped the towel from his head and seemed to suddenly notice the poker and the locked cuff. "What happened?"

"Ethine was just messing with me," Corny said. "No big deal." He set down the metal rod and stood, going into the hall and leaning against the wall for a moment, eyes closed, breathing hard. Where was Kaye? Almost half an hour had passed; if she was quick about getting her stuff and if she walked fast, she could show up at any minute. He wished she would. She always came through for him, saving his ass when he'd thought he was beyond saving.

But they had a creepy hostage and no idea what the next attack would be or when it would happen, and he didn't think even Kaye could get them out of this one.

She could be in a lot of danger.

She was too upset to be thinking straight.

And he'd let her get out of the car. He hadn't even thought to give her his phone.

Pushing himself off of the wall, he gathered up a bunch of blankets and old pillows from a shelf over the the water heater in the hall closet. Everything would work out—things would be okay. Kaye would come back here and she'd have a clever plan. They'd trade Ethine for the promise of safety for their families and themselves—something like that, but smarter. Kaye wouldn't give up Roiben's name. Without Silarial knowing his name, he'd win the duel against the Seelie Court champion. Roiben would apologize to Kaye. Things would go back to normal, whatever normal was.

And Corny would wash his hands in the same ocean that had killed his sister, and the curse would be gone.

And Luis would ask him out on a date, because he was so cool and collected.

Walking back into the bedroom, Corny dumped the pile of blankets onto the bed. "Kaye can take the bed with Ethine when she shows. We can just spread out a few of these on the floor. I think it'll be bearable."

Luis had the borrowed T-shirt on and was sitting on the floor, flipping through a dog-eared copy of *Swordspoint*. He looked up. "I've slept on much worse."

Corny unfolded an afghan with a zigzag pattern of yellow and neon green and arranged it, then rolled out another layer of a slightly stained baby blue comforter on top. "Here," he said, and started to prepare his own bed beside that one.

Luis settled himself, pulling a blanket up to his neck and stretching luxuriously. Corny tucked himself into his makeshift pallet. His room looked different from the floor, like an alien landscape full of discarded paper and dropped CDs. Leaning his head back, he stared up at the water stains on the ceiling, spreading from a dark center like the rings of an old tree.

"I'll get the light," Luis said, getting up.

"We're still waiting for Kaye. And your brother, right?"

"I tried to call again, but I couldn't get him. I left your address with Val in case he calls her or shows up. I hope he did what he said he would and got on a train."

Luis stopped. "You know, though, Val said something else. She's got a friend among the exiled fey in the city. He'd been paid a visit from your Lord Roiben a couple of days ago. *Before* Roiben's visit to the Seelie Court."

Corny frowned. His tired brain couldn't make any sense of that. "Huh. Weird. Well, I guess now all we do is wait. Kaye knows her way in. Maybe your brother can tell us more about Roiben's visit. We'd all be better off if we could get some real sleep."

Luis hit the switch, and Corny blinked, letting his eyes adjust to the room. Lights trimming nearby trailers made it bright enough to see Luis kneel back down on the blankets.

"You're gay?" Luis whispered.

Corny nodded, although Luis might not see that in the dim light. "You knew, didn't you? You acted like you knew. You kissed me like you knew."

"I figured it didn't matter."

"Nice," Corny whispered.

"No, I don't mean it like that," Luis said, kicking his feet out from under the afghan. He laughed softly. "I mean, you were bespelled. Girls, boys, you didn't care. If it had a mouth, you were kissing it."

"And you had a mouth," said Corny. He could feel the close proximity of their bodies, noticed every movement of his thighs, the clamminess of his hands inside the gloves. His heart beat so loudly he was afraid that Luis could hear it. "It was smart, though. Quick thinking."

"Thanks." Luis's voice seemed slowed somehow, like he couldn't quite get his breath. "I wasn't sure it would work."

Corny wanted to lean in and taste those words.

He wanted to tell him it would have worked, even if he hadn't been bespelled.

He wanted to tell him that it would work right now.

Instead, Corny flipped over, so that Luis couldn't see his face. "Good night," he said, and shut his eyes against regret.

Corny woke from a dream where he'd been paddling, doggy-style, through an ocean of blood. His legs would tire, and when he missed a kick, he would drop under and glimpse, through the red, a city under the waves, full of friendly beckoning fiends.

He woke as his leg kicked ineffectually at the blankets. He saw a figure near the window and for a moment thought that it was Kaye, sneaking in so as not to disturb his mother and stepfather.

"Brought us right to your hidey spot, he did," a voice hissed. "For just a lick of nectar."

Cold air drifted down to chill Corny.

"I get it," he heard Luis whisper. He was the figure, but Corny couldn't see who he was speaking with. "I'll trade. Ethine for my brother. I'll bring her to the front door."

Corny's whole body tightened with betrayal.

Metal flashed in the moonlight as the creature passed the discarded handcuff key through the open window. Corny felt like an idiot. He'd thrown it right to them.

He stayed very still as Luis walked toward the bed, then grabbed his leg. Luis fell and Corny rolled on top of him. He ripped off the glove with his teeth and brought down his fingers, spread like a net, to inches above Luis's face.

"Traitor," Corny said.

Luis bent his head back, as far from Corny's hands as he could get. He swallowed, his eyes wide. "Oh, shit. Neil, please."

"Please what? With sugar on top? Pretty please, let me fuck you over?"

"They have David. My brother. He didn't get on the train—he went to them instead. They'll kill him."

"Ethine is the only thing keeping us safe," Corny said. "You can't trade away our safety."

"I can't let them have him," Luis said. "He's my *brother*. I thought you'd understand. You said yourself that there was no safe for us."

"Oh, come on. You thought I'd understand? That's why you're sneaking around in the dark. You seem *real sure*." His bare hand clenched in a fist just inches from Luis's throat. "Oh, I understand all right. I understand you'd sell us out."

"That's not it—" Luis started. *"Please."* Corny could feel Luis's body tremble beneath him. "My brother is a fuckup—but I can't stop wanting to save him. He's my brother."

Roiben's words came back to him. *The more powerful you become, the more others will find ways to master you. They'll do it through those you love and through those you hate.*

Corny hesitated, bare hand shaking. He thought of Janet, drowned after following a boy out onto the pier. He thought of being under the hill, kneeling at the feet of a faerie Lord while his sister gulped lungfuls of ocean. He thought of water closing over his head.

Whatever you loved, that was your weakness.

That didn't stop Corny from wishing he'd saved his own sister. He imagined her sinking deeper and deeper, only this time as he reached out, her fingers rotted away in his hands.

If he'd had a chance, he hoped he'd have done whatever it took to save her. But he *knew* Luis would have. He looked down at the boy underneath him, at the scars and the piercings and the way his braids had started to fray. Luis was *good* in a way that Corny wasn't. He didn't have to force himself to be good. He just was.

Corny pushed himself off Luis, his cursed hand fraying the acrylic of the carpet. He felt cold all over, thinking what he'd almost done. What he'd become. "Go ahead. Take her. Make the trade."

Luis remained wide-eyed, his breathing ragged. He stood hastily. "I'm sorry," he told Corny.

"It's what you have to do," Corny said.

The key caught what little light there was, gleaming like one of the steel rings piercing Luis's skin, as he uncuffed Ethine. She gasped, pushing herself up onto her knees and holding out her arms as if she expected to have to fight.

"Your people came for you," Luis told her.

She rubbed her wrist and said nothing. The shadows made her face look very young, although Corny knew she wasn't.

He bundled up her clothes with his glove-covered hand.

"I really am sorry," Luis whispered.

Corny nodded. He felt a hundred years old, tired and defeated.

They crept down the hallway, to the front door. It opened with a creak to reveal three creatures standing in the dirty snow, their faces grave. The foremost of them had the face of a fox and long fingers that tapered into claws.

"Where's Dave?" Luis asked.

"Give us the Lady Ethine and you shall have him."

"And you'll leave us unharmed once we hand her over?"

Corny asked. "Dave and Luis and me and Kaye and all our families. You'll go away and leave us alone."

"We will." The fox faerie spoke in a monotone.

Luis nodded and let go of Ethine's arm. She darted out in her bare feet and boxers, standing between the other faeries. One removed a cloak and spread it over Ethine's shoulders.

"Now give us Dave," said Luis.

"He is hardly worth your bargaining," one said. "Do you know how we found you? He led us here for a bag of powder."

"Just give him to me!"

"As you desire," said another. He nodded to someone behind the side of the trailer and two more of them stepped out, holding a body between them with a bag over its head.

They set him down on the step. He flopped, head lolling.

Luis took a step forward. "What did you do to him?"

"We killed him," said a fey with scales along his cheekbones.

Luis froze. Corny could hear his own heartbeat thundering in his blood. Everything seemed very loud. The cars on the road roared by and the wind made the leaves crackle.

Corny crouched and pulled off the cloth bag. Dave's ashen face looked as though it were made from wax. Dark circles ringed his sunken eyes, and his clothes were wrinkled and filthy. His shoes were gone and his toes looked pale, as if frostbitten.

"My Queen wishes to inform you that your brother lived so long as you were her servant," said the fox faerie. "That was her promise to you. Consider it kept."

A fierce gust of wind tore the fabric from Corny's hand and whipped at the cloaks. He closed his eyes against the sting of snow and dirt, but when he opened them, the faeries were gone.

Luis screamed, running out to where they had been, turning. His screaming was raw, terrible. His hands were fists, but there was nothing to strike.

Lights flashed on in the windows of two of the trailers. Corny reached out his gloved hand to touch Dave's cold cheek. It seemed impossible that they hadn't saved him. Dead like Janet. Just like Janet.

Corny's mother came to the door. She had the portable phone in her hand. "You woke up half the—" Then she saw the body. "Oh my god."

"It's his brother," Corny said. "Dave." That seemed important. Across the street, Mrs. Henderson came to the door and looked out through the glass.

Corny's stepfather came to the door. "What the hell's going on?" he demanded. Corny's mother started punching numbers into the phone. "I'm calling the first aid squad. Don't move him."

Luis turned. His face looked blank. "He's dead." His voice was hoarse. "We don't need an ambulance. He's *dead*."

Corny stood and stepped toward Luis. He had no idea what to do or say. There were no words that could make things better. He wanted to wrap his arms around Luis, comfort him, remind him he wasn't alone. As his bare hand moved toward Luis's shoulder, he looked at it in horror.

Before he could snatch his hand back, Luis caught him around the wrist. His eyes sparkled with tears. One streaked down his face. "Yes, good," he said. "Touch me. It doesn't fucking matter now, does it?"

"What?" Corny said. He reached up with his other hand, but Luis seized that, too, fingers scrabbling to pull off the rubber glove.

"I want you to touch me."

"Stop it," Corny shouted, struggling to move away, but Luis's grip was unyielding.

Luis pressed Corny's palm to his cheek. His tears wet Corny's fingers. "I really did want you to touch me," he said softly, and the longing in his voice was a surprise. "I couldn't tell you that I wanted you. So now I get what I want and it kills me."

Corny fought him. "Stop it! Don't!"

Luis's fingers were stronger, pinning Corny's hand in place. "I want to," he said. "There's no one to care what I do anymore."

"Stop! I fucking care!" Corny shouted, then abruptly went still. The skin of Luis's face wasn't bruised or wrinkled where his bare hand touched it. Luis let go of Corny's wrists with a sob.

Corny ran his finger reverently over the curve of Luis's cheekbone, painting with his tears. "Running water," Corny said. "Salt."

Their eyes met. Somewhere in the distance a siren wailed closer, but neither of them looked away.

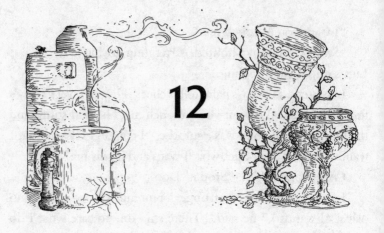

12

Yet each man kills the thing he loves,
By each let this be heard,
Some do it with a bitter look,
Some with a flattering word,
The coward does it with a kiss,
The brave man with a sword!

—OSCAR WILDE, "THE BALLAD OF READING GAOL"

Kaye saw the flashing lights from a block away. She sprinted onto the gravel street of the trailer park just as the ambulance pulled out. Neighbors stood on their patchy snow-covered lawns in robes or coats hastily thrown over nightclothes. The door to Corny's trailer was shut, but the lights were on inside. Lutie hovered above Kaye, darting back and forth, her wings beating as fast as Kaye's heart.

It seemed to Kaye that there were no right decisions anymore, only endless wrong ones.

She pulled open the door to the trailer and stopped, seeing Corny's mother pouring hot water out of a kettle. Her husband sat on one of the armchairs, a cup balanced on his leg.

His eyes were closed and he was snoring faintly.

"Kaye? What are you doing here?" Mrs. Stone asked. "It's the middle of the night."

"I—" Kaye started. A slight breeze signaled Lutie's blowing into the room. The little faerie alighted on top of a Captain Kirk bust, causing one of the cats to take a swipe at it.

"I called her," Corny said. "She knew Dave."

Knew Dave. Knew. Kaye turned to Luis, who was gripping his cup so tightly that his fingers looked pale. Papers rested on the floor beside him, a scattered stack of photocopied forms. She noticed his reddened eyes. "What happened?"

"Luis's brother overdosed on our steps." Mrs. Stone shuddered, looking like she might be sick. "They couldn't pronounce him dead because they're just volunteers, but they took him to the hospital."

Kaye looked toward Corny for an explanation, but he just shook his head. She sank down on the linoleum floor until she was sitting with her back to the wall.

Mrs. Stone put down her mug in the sink. "Corny, can I talk to you for a minute?"

He nodded and followed her down the hall.

"What really happened?" Kaye asked Luis, her voice low. "He didn't overdose, did he? Where's Ethine?"

"I bargained with a faerie to save Dave's life a long time ago. After my dad shot him. I tried to take care of him, like a big brother's supposed to—keep him out of trouble—but I didn't do such a good job. He got into more trouble. That meant more bargains for me."

Dread settled into the marrow of Kaye's bones.

"When I called at that rest stop, he went right to them,"

Luis said. "He traded where I was at for more Never. Even though he's burnt up his insides with it. Even though I'm his brother. And you know what? I'm not even surprised. It's not even the first time. So now he's dead and I should feel something, right?"

"But how did he die—?" Kaye started.

"I'm *relieved*." His words were a lash turned on himself. "Dave's dead and I feel relieved. Now, what does that make me?"

Kaye wondered if everyone felt like there was a monster underneath their skin. It was obvious that the relief wasn't the largest part of what he felt. It was obvious that he was in pain, that he'd been crying. And yet it was what he was dwelling on, an imperfect mourning.

Corny and his mother walked back into the room. He had his arm around her and was speaking softly. Kaye cried out at the sight of his bare hand on her arm, but the cloth under his hand was neither unraveled nor discolored.

"Sorry," she said, realizing how loud she'd been.

Luis looked around as though he'd just woken from a dream. He got awkwardly to his feet.

Corny's mom rubbed her face. "I'm going to wake up Mitch. You three go on and get what sleep you can."

Kaye stopped Corny in the hallway. "Is she okay?"

He shook his head. "We missed Christmas, you know. My mom's been going crazy thinking about Janet and not knowing where I was. I feel like an ass. And now this."

Kaye thought back to the handful of unopened presents sitting under the tree at her grandmother's and realized they must have been for her. "Oh," she said, and caught his warm, dry fingers. He didn't pull away from her. "What about the curse?"

"Later," he said. "War council in my room."

Kaye flopped on top of the tangled sheets of his bed, kicking her feet off one end. Luis sat on the floor and Corny sprawled beside him, close enough that their legs touched.

Lutie flew in, landing on Corny's computer. Luis must not have noticed her before, because he jumped up like a snapped cord.

"It's just Lutie-loo," Kaye said.

Luis looked at the little faerie with suspicion. "Fine, just . . . just keep it—her—away from me right now."

"Kaye, here's the summary-in-ten-seconds version of what you missed," Corny said quickly. "The Seelie Court wanted to trade Luis's brother for Ethine. We traded, but Dave was already dead. They'd killed him."

"And the curse?" Kaye asked.

"It got . . . accidentally removed," said Luis. He looked down at the threads of the carpet, and Kaye could see a worn patch that she didn't remember.

She nodded, since clearly neither of them wanted to talk about it. Lutie was perched on a cell phone cradle.

"It's weird," Corny said, resting his head on his knee. "Silarial was looking for Ethine but not you. She could have sent her people to swoop down out of the sky and grab you, or at least try."

"Maybe Sorrowsap is still watching over Kaye," said Luis.

Corny made a face. "Okay, but if you were the Seelie Queen and your plan was to use Roiben's name, would you waste your time getting one of your courtiers back?"

"He's right," Kaye said. "It doesn't make any sense. Killing Dave . . ." She glanced quickly at Luis. "It's like she'd already gotten everything she wanted. She had time for pettiness."

"So Silarial needs Ethine? What for?" Corny asked.

Luis frowned. "Didn't you say that Ethine would get the throne if Roiben won the duel?"

Kaye nodded. "He said something about how his sister would probably just hand back the crown, since she's so loyal. Maybe Silarial needs her to do that? I mean, it was odd that Silarial agreed to that bargain in the first place."

"I don't know," Corny said. "If there was even a chance I had to forfeit my crown, I'd be pretty happy if the person I had to give it to went missing. Of course, my crown would have lots of rhinestones spelling out 'tyrant' so not everyone would want to steal it either."

Kaye snorted. "Idiocy aside, you're right. You'd think she'd *want* Ethine dead."

"Maybe she does," Luis said.

"So, what, Silarial kills her and puts the blame on us? I don't know. . . ."

They sat in silence as the moments ticked by. Corny yawned while Luis stared at the wall, bright-eyed. Kaye imagined Talathain dueling Roiben, his sister grim-faced on the sidelines, the Queen smiling as though she'd eaten the last tart off the tray, Ruddles and Ellebere watching. There was something she was missing, something that was right in front of her.

She stood up with a gasp. "Wait! Wait! Who is Roiben fighting?"

Luis squinted up at her. "Well, we're not sure. I guess Silarial's knight or whatever courtier she thinks can kick his ass. Whoever's going to wield her secret weapon."

"Remember what we were talking about in the diner—how it seemed like Roiben had a good chance at beating Talathain? How it all seemed too simple?" Kaye shook her head, the thrill of discovery fading to a jittery nausea.

Corny nodded.

"I don't think there is a secret weapon," Kaye said. "No armor, no unbeatable swordsman. Getting his true name out of me—she never needed it."

Luis opened his mouth and then shut it again.

"I don't get what you're saying." Corny said.

"Ethine." Kaye said, feeling like the name was a slap. "Silarial's going to make Roiben fight Ethine."

"But . . . Ethine's not a knight," Luis said. "She couldn't even get away from us. She can't fight."

"That's the point," said Kaye. "There is no contest of skill. If he doesn't murder his own sister, Roiben dies. He has to choose between killing her and killing himself."

She wanted to stay angry with Roiben, to hang on to the feeling of betrayal so that it pushed back all her hurt, but at that moment she couldn't help pitying him for loving Silarial. Maybe more than she pitied herself for still loving him.

"That's . . ." Corny stopped.

"And if he's gone, there'll be no one to stop Silarial from doing whatever she wants to whomever she wants," Luis said.

"And charm an endless army of people," Kaye said. "Scores of frozen sentries."

"You were a distraction," Luis said. "A red herring. Keep Roiben looking at you, wondering if Silarial's going to get his true name, so he doesn't notice what's right in front of him."

"Neither fish nor fowl," Kaye said softly. "Good red herring.

That's right, isn't it? Kind of funny. That's what I was. A good red herring."

"Kaye," Corny said. "It's not your fault."

"We have to warn him," she said, pacing the room. She didn't want to admit that it bothered her that she wasn't going to be carried off for the Tithe, she wasn't the key, she wasn't even important. She'd just made things worse for Roiben, distracted him. Silarial had played them both.

"We don't even know where he is," said Corny. "The hollow hill in the graveyard isn't even hollow anymore."

"But we know where he *will* be," she said. "Hart Island."

"Tomorrow night. At this point, basically later today." Corny walked to his computer and jiggled the mouse, then typed in a few words. "It's an island off of New York, apparently. With a giant graveyard. And a prison—although I don't think it's in use. And—oh, perfect—it's completely illegal to go there."

All three of them slept squished into Corny's bed, with him in the middle, his arm over Kaye's back, and Luis's head pillowed on his shoulder. When he woke, it was late in the afternoon. Kaye was still curled up beside him, but Luis sat on the rug, speaking softly into Corny's cell phone.

Luis said something about "ashes" and "afford," but he shook his head when he saw Corny watching, and then turned to the wall. Padding past, Corny went out to the kitchen and turned on the coffeepot. He should have been worried. They were hours from heading into danger. Still, as he measured out the grounds, a smile spread over his face.

He immediately felt guilty. He shouldn't be so happy when Luis was mourning his brother. But he was.

Luis liked him. Luis. Liked. Him.

"Hey," Kaye said, scrubbing her hand through her tangled hair. She'd stolen one of his T-shirts and it hung on her like a dress. She grabbed a blue cup out of the cabinet. "Here's to the sweet balm of coffee."

"By the grace of which we'll accomplish the task before us."

"Do you think we will?" Kaye asked. "I don't know if Roiben will even listen to me."

The coffeepot gave a death rattle, and Corny poured three cups. "I do. He will. Honest. Drink up."

"So . . . you and Luis?" Her mug almost hid her grin.

He nodded. "I mean, not now with everything happening, but yeah, maybe."

"I'm glad." Her smile faded. "You don't have to go tonight. I'm not trying to be a martyr; it's just that with Luis losing his brother . . . This is my problem. They're my people."

He shrugged and put his arm around her shoulder. "Yeah, well, you're my problem. You're my people."

She leaned her head against him. Even just risen from bed, she smelled like grass and earth. "What about your fear of megalomaniacal fiends? I didn't think our recent trip was the ticket to getting over that."

He felt crazy with confidence. Luis liked him. His curse was gone. Everything seemed possible. "Let's get the fiends before the fiends get us."

Luis came out of the bedroom, closing the phone against his chest. "I saw your mom this morning. She said that she wanted to talk to you when she got home from work. I didn't tell her anything."

Corny nodded, reminding himself to seem calm. Reminding himself not to kiss Luis. He hadn't brushed his teeth and it didn't seem like great timing anyway.

"I'll leave a note. Then we'd better go. Luis, if you have to stay here and sort out stuff—"

"What I need is to stop Silarial from hurting anyone else." He looked Corny dead in the eye, as if daring him to pity him.

"Okay," Kaye said. "We're all in. Now what we need is a map and a boat."

"Hart Island is in Long Island Sound, off of City Island, which is off of the Bronx. Not exactly within paddling distance." Corny held out a mug to Luis. When he took it, their fingers brushed, and he felt the opposite of cursed.

"So we need a boat with a motor," Kaye said. "There's a nautical goods store on Route 35. I could turn a pile of leaves into money. Or we could find a marina up there to filch from."

Luis busied himself adding sugar to his coffee. "I've never steered a boat or read a navigational chart. Have you?"

Kaye shook her head, and Corny had to admit that he hadn't either.

"There's mermaids in the East River," said Luis. "Probably in the Sound, too. I don't know much about them, but if they don't want us to get to Hart Island, they could pitch us into the water. They've got vicious teeth. The good news is that they're part of the Undersea, not any of the courts of the land."

Corny shuddered at the thought. His mind went to Janet, held underneath the waves by a delighted kelpie. "We could trade them something, maybe," he said. "They might take us there for a price."

Kaye looked over at him warily. He figured she was remembering how they'd traded an old carousel horse to that same kelpie for information. Before they knew how dangerous the kelpie was. Before it murdered Janet.

She nodded slowly. "What do mermaids like?"

Luis shrugged. "Jewelry . . . music . . . sailors?"

"They eat people, right?" Corny asked.

"Sure. When they're done with them."

Corny smiled. "Let's bring them a couple of big steaks."

They bought an inflatable green raft and two oars at the boat store. The clerk looked at Kaye strangely when she counted out hundreds of curled and tattered dollars, but her smile charmed him into silence.

They got back into the car.

Luis rode shotgun and Kaye rested in the back with her head on the raft's cardboard box. As Corny changed lanes on the highway, he looked over at Luis, but Luis looked out the window, his eyes not focused on anything. Whatever he saw, it wasn't something Corny could share. Silence filled up the car.

"Who was it?" Corny asked finally. "On the phone?"

Luis looked toward him too quickly. "It was the hospital. They were upset about me not having a credit card or a landline phone and him being under eighteen. And even though they didn't know if I'd be allowed to claim him, they started talking about my options. Basically, I have to come up with the money for cremation."

"Kaye could—"

Luis shook his head.

"We could sell the boat when we're done with it."

Luis smiled, a small lift of his lip. "I want him to have a good burial, you know."

At Janet's funeral there had been a coffin and a service, flowers and a stone. Corny had never asked about the cost, but his mom wasn't rich. He wondered how much she'd gone into debt for his sister to be buried in style.

"My parents—they're out where we're going." Luis's finger turned his lip ring.

"Hart Island?"

He nodded. "That's where potter's field is. Where they bury the 'friendless' dead. Which basically means the dead with no living relatives, who are renters and in credit card debt. My parents. I was underage, so I couldn't claim them. If I'd even tried, they'd probably have hauled Dave and me off to child services."

The possible replies scrolled in front of Corny's eyes. *Wow. Are you okay? I'm so sorry.* All of them inadequate.

"I've never been there," Luis said. "It'll be good to go."

They drove over the drawbridge, to the very edge of City Island, and parked the car behind a restaurant. Then, sitting in the snow, they took turns blowing up the raft, like they were passing around a joint.

"How are we going to attract those mermaids?" Corny asked, while Luis huffed into the little tube.

Kaye picked up a receipt from the floor of his car. "You got something pointy?"

Corny searched through his backpack until he came up with a discarded safety pin.

She poked her finger and, wincing, smeared her blood onto the paper. Walking to the edge of the water, she dropped it in. "I'm Kaye Fierch," she said firmly. "A pixie. A Seelie Court changeling on a quest for the King of the Night Court. I come here and ask for your help. I ask for your help. Three times I ask for your help."

Corny looked at her, standing in front of the water, her green hair pulled back from her glamoured face, her battered purple coat blown by the wind. For the first time, he thought that even in her human guise she had somehow grown formidable.

Heads bobbed in the black water, pale hair floating around them like sea grass.

Kaye went down on her knees. "I ask that you bring us three to Hart Island safely. We have a boat. All you have to do is pull it."

"And what will you give us, pixie?" they answered in their melodious voices. Their teeth were translucent and sharp, like they were made of cartilage.

Kaye walked back to the car and brought out the ShopRite plastic bag full of meat. She held up a raw and dripping shank. "Flesh," she said.

"We accept," said the mermaids.

Kaye, Corny, and Luis dragged the boat onto the water and pushed off. The mermaids swam around them, pushing the boat and singing softly as they went, their voices so beautiful and insistent that Corny found himself dazed. Kaye appeared tense, sitting at the prow like a ship's figurehead.

Looking over the side, Corny saw a mermaid coming up through the water, and for a moment it seemed like she wore his sister's face, blue with cold and death. He looked away.

"I know who you are," one of them said to Luis, her white, webbed hand reaching up onto the side of the boat. "You brought the troll's potion."

He nodded, swallowing.

"I could teach you how to heal better," the mermaid whispered. "If you came with me. Under the water."

Corny put his hand on Luis's arm, and Luis jumped as if he'd been stung.

The mermaid turned her head toward Corny. "What about vengeance? I could give you that. You lost someone to the sea."

Corny choked. "What?"

"You want it," she said. "I know that you do."

The mermaid reached up, her webbed hand settling on the side of the raft, near Corny. Scales skived off, shining on the rubber. "I could give you the power," she told him.

Corny looked down at her gelatinous eyes and her thin, sharp teeth. Envy curled in his gut. She was beautiful and terrible and magical. But the feeling was distant, like being envious of a sunset. "I don't need any more power," he said, and was surprised to find he meant it. And if he wanted vengeance, he'd get it on his own.

Kaye made a soft noise. Corny looked up.

There on the far shore, behind heaps of mussel shells, a great crowd of beings had gathered. And beyond them, abandoned buildings stood near rows and rows of graves.

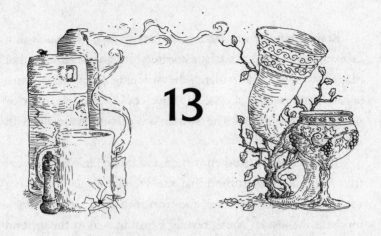

Kaye pushed through the crowd with Corny and Luis, shoving lavender-skinned bodies and batting aside clouds of pin-size sprites. A phooka with a goat head and dead white eyes called to her as she passed, licking its teeth with a cat's tongue. "Licksy tricksy pixie!"

Ducking beneath the arm of an ogre, Kaye leaped onto a grave marker to avoid three spindly hobmen locked in an embrace in the dirt.

From the top of the marker, she surveyed the court. She saw Ruddles drinking from a bowl and passing it to a number of other animal-headed beings. Ellebere stood beside him—hair fading from wine to gold as it fell over his shoulders, his armor a deep and mossy green.

Roiben himself was talking animatedly to a woman as slim as a wand, her long black hair knotted into a jeweled cape that draped over her back to match the twitching tail also hung with jewels. From where she stood, Kaye couldn't tell whether or not they were arguing. The woman was gesturing broadly with her hands.

Then, abruptly, Roiben turned and looked in Kaye's direction. Kaye was so surprised that she fell. She forgot to flap her wings. Her head hit a stone, and tears sprung to her eyes. For a moment she just lay there, resting her head against the ground and listening to the Folk milling around her. It was awful to be so near him, awful how her heart leapt.

"You shouldn't eat the bones if you chew them like that." She heard someone say nearby. "They're too sharp. Cut up your insides."

"Haven't you become a little beetleflower?" said another voice. "Marrow's better than meat, but you've got to go through the bones to get it."

Corny reached out a hand to pull Kaye to her feet. "I don't think he saw you."

"Perhaps not, but I did." A woman, her wings so tattered that only the veins hung from her back, looked down at Kaye. She held a knife that curved like a snake, and her armor gleamed the same shining purple as the carapace of a beetle.

"Dulcamara," Kaye said, standing. "My friends need to talk to Roiben."

"Perhaps after the duel," she said. Her pink eyes regarded Kaye with contempt.

"They have to talk to him *now*," said Kaye. "Please. He can't duel. He has to call it off."

Dulcamara licked the edge of her blade, painting it with her mouth's blood. "I will play messenger. Give me your words and I will carry them to him with my own tongue."

"They have to tell him themselves."

Dulcamara shook her head. "I will allow no more distractions from you than he has already borne."

Corny stepped up. "Just for a moment. It'll only take a moment. He knows me."

"Mortals are liars. They can't help it," said the faerie knight. Kaye could see her teeth were as sharp as the knife in her hand, and unlike the mermaids', hers were bone. She smiled at Corny. "It's your nature."

"Then let me go," Kaye said. "I'm no mortal."

"You can't." Luis put his hand on her shoulder. "Remember? He's not allowed to see you."

Mortals are liars. Liars.

"Indeed," Dulcamara said. "Get close to him and I will run you through. No more of the glamoured games you played in the Seelie Court."

Over and over Kaye heard the words repeat: *Liars. Untruth. Lie. Lying. Dying. Dead.* She thought about Corny's fairy chess. She had to change the rules of the game. She had to solve the quest. She had to be the single variation. But how could she lie without lying?

Kaye looked over at where Roiben stood, his armor being strapped onto his back. His long hair had two plaits braided in the front, each one wrapped with a sharp silver clasp at the end. He looked pale, his face pinched, as though with pain.

"Oh," Kaye said, and then she leaped into the air.

"Stop!" Dulcamara shouted, but Kaye was already flying,

her wings flapping frantically. For a moment, she had a view of the lighthouse on the far shore of City Island, and the glimmering city lights beyond. Then she half landed, half fell at Roiben's feet instead.

"You," he said, and she couldn't parse the tone of his voice.

Ellebere grabbed her wrists and wrenched them behind her back. "This is no place for a Seelie Court pixie."

Ruddles pointed at her with a clawed hand. "To stand before our Lord and King, you must have completed your quest. If not, custom allows us to rend you—"

"I don't care what custom dictates," Roiben pronounced, waving off his chamberlain. When he looked at Kaye, his eyes were empty of any emotion she knew. "Where is my sister?"

"Silarial's got her," Kaye said in a rush. "Ethine's what I came to talk to you about." For the first time since the Tithe, she was afraid of him. She no longer believed that he would not hurt her. He looked as though he might relish it.

Lick the Queen of the Seelie Court's hand, Rath Roiben Riven. Lick it like the dog you are.

"My Lord," said Ruddles, "though I would not choose to contradict you, she may not remain in your presence. She hasn't completed the quest you bestowed on her."

"I said leave her!" Roiben shouted.

"I can lie," Kaye choked out, her heart beating like a drum against her skin. The ground tilted under her feet and everyone around her went silent. She had no idea if she could pull this off. "I can lie. I am the faerie that can lie."

"That's nonsense," said Ruddles. "Prove it."

"Are you saying that I can't?" Kaye asked.

"No faerie can tell an untruth."

"So," Kaye said, letting out her breath in a dizzy rush. "If I say I can lie and you say I can't, then one of us must be telling an untruth, right? So either I am a faerie that can lie, or you are. Either way, I have completed my quest."

"That reeks of a riddle, but I see no fault," the chamberlain said.

Roiben made a sound, but she couldn't tell if it was an objection.

"Clever." Ruddles's grin was full of teeth, but he patted her on the back. "We accept your answer with pleasure."

"I suppose you have succeeded, Kaye," said Roiben. His voice was soft. "From this moment forward your fate is tied to the Unseelie Court. Until the time of my death, you are my consort."

"Tell them to let me go," Kaye said. She'd won, but her victory felt as hollow as a blown egg. After all, he didn't want her.

"Since you're my consort, you may tell them yourself," said Roiben. He did not meet her eyes. "They ought not deny you now."

Ellebere dropped Kaye's arms before she could speak. Stumbling, she turned to glare at him and Ruddles. "Go," she said, trying to sound commanding. Her voice broke.

They looked to Roiben and moved at his nod. It was still hardly privacy, but it was the closest she was likely to get.

"Why have you come here?" he asked.

She wanted to beg him to be the Roiben she knew, the one who said she was the only thing he wanted, the one who hadn't betrayed her and didn't hate her. "Look at me. Why won't you look at me?"

"The sight of you is a torment." His eyes, when he raised them, were full of shadows. "I thought if I kept you out of this war, it would be the same as keeping you safe. But there you were in the middle of the Seelie Court as though to prove me a fool. And here you are again, courting danger. I only wanted to save one thing, just one thing, to prove there was some good in me after all."

"I am not a *thing*," Kaye told him.

He closed his eyes for a moment, covering them with long fingers. "Yes. Of course. I shouldn't have said that."

She caught his hands and he let her draw them from his face. They were as cold as the falling snow. "What are you *doing* to yourself? What's going on?"

"When I became King of the Unseelie Court, I thought we could not win the war. I thought that I would fight and I would die. There is a kind of mad glee in accepting death as an inevitable cost."

"Why?" Kaye asked. "Why bind yourself to such a miserable fate? Why not just say 'screw this, I'm going make birdhouses' or something?"

"To kill Silarial." His eyes glittered like chips of glass. "If she isn't stopped, no one will be safe from her cruelty. It was so hard not to crush her neck when I kissed her. Could you tell it from my face, Kaye? Did you see my hand tremble?"

Kaye heard her own blood pounding at her temples. Could she really have confused loathing with longing? Recalling the blood on Silarial's mouth, she thought of the way his eyes had seemed glazed over with passion. Now it seemed closer to madness. "Then why did you kiss—"

"Because they're my people." Roiben swept his hand over

the field, taking in the graveyard and the prison. "I want to save them. I needed her to believe I was in her power so she might agree to my terms. I know it must have seemed—"

"Stop." Kaye felt a cold finger of dread shiver up her spine. "I came here to tell you something," she said. "Something I figured out about the battle."

He raised a single silvery brow. "What is it?"

"Silarial's going to choose Ethine as her champion."

His laugh was almost a sob, short and terrible.

"Call off the duel," Kaye said. "Find some excuse. Don't fight."

"I wondered what terrible thing she might set against me, what monster, what magic? I forgot how clever she is."

"You don't have to fight Ethine."

He shook his head. "You don't understand. Far too much is at stake tonight."

Coldness spread from her heart to freeze her body. "What are you going to do?" Her voice came out sharper than she'd intended.

"I'm going to win," he said. "And you would do me a great service if you told Silarial that I said so."

"You wouldn't hurt Ethine."

"I think it's time that you went, Kaye." Roiben swung a strap with his scabbard attached over his shoulder. "I won't ask you to forgive me, because I don't deserve it, but I did love you." He looked down as he said the words. "I do love you."

"Then stop doing this. Stop not telling me shit. I don't care if it's for my own good or whatever stupid reason—"

"I *am* telling you shit," Roiben said, and hearing him swear made her laugh. He smiled back, just a little, like he got the joke. In that one moment he seemed heartrendingly familiar.

He reached out, still smiling, as though he were going to touch her face, but he traced the shape of her hair instead. It was not even a real touch, feather-light and never coming to rest, as though he were afraid to dare more. She shivered.

"If you really can lie," he said, "tell me this will end well tonight."

Icy air blew up a thin flurry of snow and tossed back Roiben's hair as he strode past graves to the area marked for the duel. The Night and Bright Courts waited restlessly in a loose circle, whispering and chittering, pulling their cloaks of skin and fur and cloth closer. Kaye hurried behind the edge of the crowd to where the Bright Queen's courtiers stood, their shimmering gowns blown by the wind.

Ellebere and Dulcamara walked beside Roiben, their insect-like armor glittering against the frost-covered landscape and the stone markers. Roiben dressed as gray as the overcast sky. Talathain and another knight flanked Silarial. They wore green-stained leather with gilt studding their shoulders and their arms like the markings on a caterpillar. Roiben bent in so deep a bow that he might have touched his lips to the snow. Silarial made only a shallow bob.

Roiben cleared his throat. "For decades there has been a truce between the Seelie and the Unseelie Courts. I am both proof of and witness to that old bargain, and I would broker it again. Lady Silarial, do you agree that if I defeat your champion, you will concede a concord between our two courts?"

"If you deal my champion a mortal blow, I so swear,"

Silarial said. "If my champion lies dying on this field, you will have your peace."

"And do you have a further wager in this battle?" he asked her.

She smiled. "I will also give over my throne to the Lady Ethine. Gladly I will set the crown of the Seelie Court upon her head, kiss her cheeks, and step down to be her subject should you win."

Kaye could see Roiben's face from where she stood, but she could not read his expression.

"And if I die on the field of battle," Roiben said, "you shall rule over the Unseelie Court in my place, Lady Silarial. To this I agree."

"And now I must name my champion," said Silarial, a smile slitting her face. "Lady Ethine, take up arms for me. You are to be the defender of the Bright Court."

There was a terrible silence among the gathered throng. Ethine shook her head mutely. The wind and the shifting snow came down as the tableau held.

"How you must hate me," Roiben said softly, but the wind seemed to catch those words and blow them out to the audience.

Silarial turned in her frosting-white dress and strode from the field to her bower of ivy. Her people clad Ethine in a thin armor and placed a long sword in her limp grip.

"Go," Roiben told Ellebere and Dulcamara. Reluctantly, they left the field. Kaye could see the doubt in the faces of the Unseelie Court, the tension as Ruddles ground his teeth together and watched Ethine with gleaming black eyes. They had thrown in their lot with Roiben, but his loyalties were uncertain and never more so than at this moment.

Hobmen paced the outside edge of the ring, scattering herbs to mark its boundaries.

At the center of the snowy bank, Roiben made a stiff bow and drew his sword. It curved like a crescent moon and shone like water.

"You don't mean to do this," Ethine said, but in her mouth it was a question.

"Are you ready, Ethine?" Roiben brought his sword up so that the blade seemed to bisect his face, casting half into shadow.

Ethine shook her head. *No.* Kaye could see Roiben's sister shiver convulsively. Tears ran down her pale cheeks. She dropped her sword.

"Pick it up," he said patiently, as if to a child.

Hurrying, Kaye walked to where the Bright Lady of the Seelie Court sat. Talathain raised his bow, but did not stop her. The sound of blades crashing together made her turn back to the fight. Ethine staggered back, the weight of her sword clearly overbalancing her. Kaye felt sick.

Silarial looked down from her perch, coppery hair plaited with deep blue berries knotting a golden circlet atop her head. She smoothed the skirt of her white gown.

"Kaye," she said. "What a surprise. Are you surprised?"

"He knew it was going to be Ethine before he went out there."

Silarial frowned. "Oh?"

"I told him." Kaye sat down on the dais. "After I figured out his stupid quest."

"So you're consort to the King of the Unseelie Court?"

Silarial raised one eyebrow. Her smile was pitying. "I'm surprised you still want him."

That stung. Kaye would have protested, but the words twisted in her mouth.

"But then, you will only be his consort as long as he lives." The Bright Lady turned her gaze to the two figures fighting in the snow.

"Oh, come on," Kaye said. "You act like he's the same kid you sent away. Do you know what he did when I told him about Ethine? He laughed. He laughed and said he'd win."

"No," said Silarial, turning too quickly. "I cannot believe he would play cat and mouse first if he intended to kill her."

Kaye squinted. "Is that what he's doing? Maybe it's just not easy to murder your own sister."

Silarial shook her head. "He craves death, just as he craves me, though perhaps he wishes he didn't want either. He will let her stab him and perhaps tell her some sweet thing with a mouth full of blood. All this taunting is to make her angry, make her swing hard enough for a killing blow. I know him as you do not."

Kaye closed her eyes against that thought, then forced them open. She didn't know. She honestly didn't know if he would kill his sister or not. She didn't even know what to want, both choices were so terrible. "I don't think so," she said carefully. "I don't think he wants to, but he's killed a lot of people he didn't want to kill."

As if on cue, there was a great cry from the audience. Ethine lay in the snow, struggling to sit up, the tip of Roiben's curved blade at her throat. He smiled down at her kindly, as if she had merely fallen and he was about to help her up again.

"Nicnevin forced him to kill," Silarial said quickly.

Kaye let the anger she felt bleed into her voice. "Now you're forcing him."

Roiben's words carried over the field. "Since it seems that the crown of the Bright Court will come to you *after* your death, tell me upon whom you wish to bestow it. Let me do this last thing for you as your brother."

Relief flooded Kaye. There was a plan. He had a plan.

"Hold!" Silarial shouted, leaping up from her makeshift throne and striding out onto the field. "That was not part of the bargain." As she passed through the ring of herbs, they caught with greenish fire.

Wailing rose from the Unseelie Folk while the Bright Court went deathly silent. Roiben stepped back from his sister, taking the blade from her throat. Ethine fell back in the snow, turning her head so that no one might see her face.

"Neither was your interrupting this fight," he said. "You may not reconsider our bargain now that it no longer favors you." His words silenced the Unseelie Court's cries, but Kaye could hear the rest of the crowd murmur in confusion.

Ethine stumbled to her feet. Roiben extended his hand to help her, but she didn't take it. She looked at him with hate, but there was no less hate when she looked upon her mistress. She picked up her sword and held it so tightly her knuckles went white.

"My oath was that the crown would go to Ethine if you killed my champion. I did not promise that she could choose a successor." Silarial's voice sounded shrill.

"That was not yours to promise," Roiben said. "What is hers in death, she may give with her last breath. Perhaps she will even pass it back to you. Unlike the Unseelie crown that is won by blood, the Seelie successor is chosen."

"I will not have my crown bestowed by one of my own handmaidens, nor will I be lessoned by one who once knelt at my feet. You are not one part what Nicnevin was."

"And you are too much like her," said Roiben.

Three Seelie knights strode onto the field, clustering close enough to Roiben that were he to move toward Silarial, they might be faster.

"Let me remind you that my forces overwhelm yours," said Silarial. "Were our people to fight, even now, I would win. I think that gives me leave to dictate terms."

"Will you void our agreement, then?" Roiben asked. "Will you stop this duel?"

"Before I let you have my crown!" Silarial spit.

"Ellebere!" Roiben shouted.

The Unseelie knight drew a little wooden flute from inside the wrist of his armor and brought it to his mouth. He blew three clear notes that traveled over the suddenly quiet crowd.

At the edges of the island, things began to move. Merfolk pulled themselves onto shore. Faeries appeared from the abandoned buildings, stepped from the woods, and rose out of graves. An ogre with a greening beard crossed a pair of bronze sickles over his chest. A thin troll with shaggy black hair. Goblins holding daggers of broken glass. The denizens of the parks and the streets and the shining buildings had come.

The exiled fey.

The crowd's murmuring became shouts. Some of the assemblage scrambled for arms. The solitary fey and the Night Court moved to surround the Seelie Court gentry.

"You planned an ambush?" Silarial demanded.

"I've been making some alliances." Roiben looked as though he were swallowing a smile. "Some—many—of the exiled fey were interested to know that I would accept them into my court. I would guarantee their safety even, for a mere day and night of service. Tonight. Today. You are not the only one with machinations, my Lady."

"I see you have played to some purpose," said Silarial. She looked at him as though he were a stranger. "What is it? For what do you scheme? Ethine's death would weigh on you and the stain of her blood would seep into your skin."

"Do you know what they wish for you when they give you the Unseelie crown?" Roiben's tone was soft, like he was telling a secret. Kaye could barely catch his words. "That you be made of ice. What makes you think it matters what I feel? What makes you think I feel anything at all? Surrender your crown to my sister."

"I will not," said Silarial. "I will never."

"Then there will be a battle," Roiben said. "And when the Unseelie Court is victorious, I will snatch that crown from your head and grant it as I see fit."

"All wars have casualties." Silarial nodded to someone in the crowd.

Talathain's hand came down hard over Kaye's mouth. Fingers dug into the soft pad of her cheek and the flesh of her side as she was dragged onto the field.

"Make one move, make one command," said Silarial, turning to Kaye with a smile, "and she will be the first."

"Ah, Talathain, how you have fallen," Roiben said. "I thought you were her knight, but you have become only her woodsman—taking little girls to the forest to cut out their hearts."

Talathain's grip on Kaye tightened, making her gasp. She tried to tamp down her terror, tried to convince herself that if she stayed very still, she could figure a way out of this. No ideas came.

"Now give up your crown, Roiben," Silarial said. "Give it up to me as you should have when you got it, as fit tribute to your Queen."

"You're not his Queen," Ethine said, her voice numb. "And neither are you mine." Silarial spun toward her, and Ethine plunged her blade into the Bright Queen's chest. Hot blood pocked the snow, melting dozens of tiny craters as though someone had scattered rubies. Silarial stumbled, her face a mask of surprise, and then she dropped.

Talathain shouted, but he was too late, much too late. He pushed Kaye out of his arms. She fell on her hands and knees, near the Bright Queen's body. Stepping over them both, he swung his golden sword at Ethine. She waited for the blow, not moving to defend herself.

Roiben stepped in front of her in time to catch the sword with his back. The edge sliced through his armor, opening a long red line from his shoulder to his hip. Gasping, he fell with Ethine beneath him. She shrieked.

Roiben rolled off of her and into a crouch, but Talathain had knelt beside Silarial, turning her pale face with a gloved hand. Her ancient eyes stared up at the gray sky, but no breath stirred her lips.

Roiben stood stiffly, slowly. Ethine's body shook with shallow sobs.

Talathain looked over at her. "What have you done?" he demanded.

Ethine tore at her dress and her hair until Kaye caught her hands.

"He did not deserve to be used so," she said, her voice thick with tears and mad faerie laughter. Her sharp nails sank into Kaye's flesh, but Kaye didn't let go.

"It's done," Kaye soothed, but she was frightened. She felt as though she were onstage, performing a play, while the hordes of the Unseelie Court and the exiled fey waited uneasily for a signal to crash down upon the Seelie Court they surrounded. "Come on. Stand up, Ethine."

Roiben cut the golden circlet from Silarial's hair. Chunks of braided coppery strands and berries hung from it as he held it aloft.

"That crown is not yours," said Talathain, but his voice lacked conviction. He looked from the Unseelie Court to the exiled fey. Behind him, the champions of the Bright Court had moved to the edge of the dueling grounds, but their expressions were grave.

"I was just getting it for my sister," Roiben said.

Ethine shuddered at the sight of the circlet, caught with hair and ice.

"Here," Roiben said, picking it clean with quick fingers and shining it against the leather of his breastplate. It came away red as rubies. His brows knitted in confusion, and Kaye saw that his armor was wet with blood, that it seeped down his arm to cover his hand in a dripping glove of gore.

"Your . . . ," Kaye said, and stopped. *Your hand,* she'd almost said, but it wasn't his hand that was hurt.

"Put your puppet on the throne," said Talathain. "You may make her Queen, but she won't be Queen for long."

Ethine trembled. Her face was pale as paper. "My brother needs his attendants."

"You brought her flowers," Roiben said. "Don't you remember?"

Talathain shook his head. "That was a very long time ago, before she killed my Queen. No, she won't rule for long. I'll see to that."

Roiben's face went slack, stunned. "Very well," he said slowly, as though he were puzzling out the words as he said them. "If you would not swear loyalty to her, perhaps you will kneel and swear your loyalty to me."

"The Seelie crown must be given—you cannot murder your way to it." Talathain pointed his sword at Roiben.

"Wait," Kaye said, pulling Ethine to her feet. "Who do you want to get the crown?"

Talathain's sword didn't waver. "It doesn't matter what she says."

"It does!" Kaye shouted. "Your Queen made Ethine her heir. Like it or not, she gets to say what happens now."

Ruddles strode out onto the field, giving Kaye a quick smile as he passed her. He cleared his throat. "When one court ambushes and conquers the gentry of another court, their rules of inheritance are not applicable."

"We'll be following Unseelie custom," Dulcamara purred.

"No," Kaye said. "It's Ethine's choice who gets the crown or if she keeps it."

Ruddles started to speak, but Roiben shook his head. "Kaye is correct. Let my sister decide."

"Take it," Ethine told him hollowly. "Take it and be damned."

Roiben's fingers traced over the symbols on the crown with his thumb. He sounded distant and strange. "It seems I will be coming home after all."

Talathain took a step toward Ethine. Kaye dropped her hand, wanting to be ready, although she had no idea what she'd do if he swung.

"How can you give this monster sovereignty over us? He would have paid for his peace with your death."

"He wouldn't have killed her," Kaye said.

Ethine looked away. "You have all turned into monsters."

"Now the price of peace is merely her hatred," said Roiben. "That I am willing to pay."

"I will never accept you as King of the Seelie Court," Talathain spat.

Roiben set the circlet on his brow. Blood smudged his silver hair.

"It is done, whether you accept it or no," said Ruddles.

"Let me finish the duel in your sister's place," said Talathain. "Fight me."

"Coward," Kaye said. "He's already hurt."

"Your Bright Lady broke her compact with us," said Dulcamara. She turned to Roiben. "Let me kill this knight for you, my Lord."

"Fight me!" Talathain demanded.

Roiben nodded. Reaching into the snow, he lifted his own sword. It was cloudy with cold. "Let's give them the duel they came for."

Kaye wanted to scream, but she thought she understood.

Roiben won his crown in blood. If he backed down now, there would be a target on his back in the Court of Termites. By contrast, if he killed Talathain, the rest of the Seelie Court would fall in line.

Talathain and Roiben circled each other slowly, their feet careful, their bodies swaying toward each other like snakes. Both their blades extended so that they nearly touched.

Talathain slammed his blade down. Roiben parried hard, shoving the other knight back. Talathain kept the distance. He stepped in, swung, then retreated quickly, staying just outside Roiben's range as if he were waiting for him to tire. A single rivulet of blood ran like sweat down Roiben's sword arm and onto his blade.

"You're wounded," Talathain reminded him. "How long do you really think you can last?"

"Long enough," Roiben said, but Kaye saw the wetness of his armor and the jerkiness of his movements and wasn't sure. It seemed to her that Roiben was fighting a mirror self, as though he were desperate to cut down what he might have become.

"Silarial was right about you, was she not?" said Talathain. "She said you wanted to die."

"Come find out." Roiben swept the sword in an arc so swiftly that the air sung. Talathain parried, their blades crashing together, edge to flat.

Talathain recovered fast and thrust at Roiben's left side. Twisting away, Roiben grabbed the other knight's pommel, forcing Talathain's sword up and kicking against his leg.

Talathain fell in the snow.

Roiben stood over him, pointing the blade at the knight's throat. Talathain went still. "Come and get the crown if you want it. Come and take it from me."

Kaye wasn't sure if she heard a threat or a plea in those words.

Talathain didn't move.

A faerie with skin like pinecones, rough and cracked, took Talathain's golden sword from his hands. Another spat into the grimy snow.

"You'll never hold both courts," Talathain said, struggling to his knees.

Roiben teetered a little, and Kaye ran out to put her arm under his. He hesitated a moment before leaning his weight against her. She nearly staggered.

"We'll hold the Bright Court just as your mistress would have held us," Dulcamara purred, squatting down beside him, a shining knife touching his cheek, the point pressing against the skin. "Pinned down in the dirt. Now tell your new Lord what a fine little puppy his cleverness has bought him. Tell him you'll bark at his command."

Ethine stood stiff and still. She closed her eyes.

"I will not serve the Unseelie Court," Talathain said to Roiben. "I will not become like you."

"I envy you that choice," said Roiben.

"I'll make him bark," Dulcamara said.

"No," Roiben said. "Let him go."

She looked up, surprised, but Talathain was already on his feet, pushing his way though the crowd as Ruddles called out, "Behold our undoubted Lord Roiben, King of both the Unseelie and the Seelie Courts. Make your obeisances to him."

Roiben swayed slightly, and Kaye tightened her grip. Somehow he remained standing, although his blood slicked her hand. "I'll be better than she was," she heard him say. His voice was all breath.

14

*In a certain faraway land the cold is so intense that
words freeze as soon as they are uttered, and after
some time then thaw and become audible so that
words spoken in winter go unheard until the next
summer.*

—Plutarch, *Moralia*

When Kaye and Corny walked into the small apartment, Kate was lying on an air mattress in the middle of the floor. She was drawing in a magazine. Kaye could see that the little girl had blacked out Angelina Jolie's eyes and was in the process of drawing bat wings over Paris Hilton's shoulder blades.

"Cute kid," said Corny. "Reminds me of you."

"We got lo mein and veggie dumplings." Kaye shifted the bag in her arms. "Grab a plate; it's leaking on my hand."

Kate scrambled to her feet and pushed back a tangle of dirty blond hair. "I don't want it."

"Okay." Kaye set the cartons on the kitchen counter. "What do you want?"

"When's Ellen coming home?" Kate looked up, and Kaye could see her brown eyes were rimmed with red, as though she'd recently been crying.

"When her rehearsal's over." The first time Kaye had met Kate, the girl had hidden under the table. Kaye wasn't sure if this was better. "She said she wouldn't be that late, so don't freak out."

"We don't bite," Corny put in.

Kate picked up her magazine and climbed up on Ellen's bed, scooching over to the far corner. She tore off tiny pieces and rolled them between her fingers.

Kaye sucked in a breath. The air in the apartment tasted like cigarettes and human girl, at once familiar and strange.

Kate scowled ferociously and threw the balled-up paper at Corny. He dodged.

Opening the refrigerator, Kaye took out a slightly withered orange. There was a block of cheddar with mold covering one end. Kaye chopped off the greenish fur and put the remaining lump on a piece of bread. "I'll grill you some cheese. Eat the orange while you wait."

"I don't want it," Kate said.

"Just give her bread and water like the little prisoner she is." Corny leaned back on Ellen's bed, cushioning his head with a pile of laundry. "Man, I hate babysitting."

Kate picked up the orange and threw it against the wall. It bounced like a leather ball, hitting the floor with a dull thud.

Kaye had no idea what to do. She felt paralyzed by guilt. The girl had every reason to hate her.

Corny switched on the tiny television set. The channels were fuzzy, but he finally found one that was clear enough to show Buffy staking three vampires as Giles clocked her with a stopwatch.

"Rerun," Corny said. "Perfect. Kate, this should teach you everything you need to know about being a normal American teenager." He looked up at Kaye. "There's even the sudden addition of a sister in it."

"She's not my sister," the girl said. "She just stole my name."

Kaye stopped, the words like a kick to the gut. "I don't have a name of my own," she said slowly. "Yours is the only one I've got."

Kate nodded, her eyes still on the screen.

"So what was it like?" Corny asked. "Faerieland?"

Kate tore off a larger chunk of the magazine, crushing it in her fist. "There was a pretty lady who braided my hair and fed me apples and sang to me. And there were others—the goat-man and the blackberry boy. Sometimes they would tease me." She frowned. "And sometimes they would forget me."

"Do you miss them?" he asked.

"I don't know. I slept a lot. Sometimes I would wake up and the leaves would have changed without me seeing them."

Kaye felt cold all over. She wondered if she'd ever get used to the casual cruelty of faeries, and hoped she wouldn't. At least here, among humans, Kate would wake up each day until there was no more waking.

Kaye fidgeted with the sleeves of her sweater, worming her thumbs through the weave. "Do you want to be Kaye and I'll be Kate?"

"You're stupid and you don't even act like a faerie."

"How about I make you a deal," Kaye said. "I'll teach you

about being human and you teach me about being a faerie." She winced at how lame that sounded, even to her.

The frown hadn't faded from Kate's face, but she looked like she was thinking things through.

"I'll even help," Corny said. "We can start by teaching you human curse words. Maybe we could skip the faerie curses, though." Corny took a deck of cards out of his backpack. Printed on the back of each was a different cinema robot. "Or we could try poker."

"You shouldn't bargain with me," the girl said, as though by rote. She looked smug. "Mortal promises aren't worth the hair on a rat's tail. That's your first lesson."

"Noted," Kaye said. "And, hey, we could also teach you the joys of human food."

Kate shook her head. "I want to play the cards."

By the time Ellen walked in, Corny had beaten them both out of all the spare change they'd found in their pockets or under Ellen's bed. *Law & Order* was playing on the television, and Kate had agreed to eat a single fortune cookie. Her fortune had read: "Someone will invite you to a karaoke party."

"Hey, one of the guys on the street was selling bootleg movies for two bucks," Ellen said, throwing her coat onto a chair and dumping the rest of her stuff onto the floor. "I got a couple for you kids."

"Bet the back of someone's head blocks the screen," Kaye warned.

Ellen picked at the noodles on the counter. "Anyone eating these?"

Kaye walked over. "Kate didn't want them."

Ellen lowered her voice. "I can't tell if she's just a picky eater

or if it's some *thing*—doesn't like sauces, barely can stand cooked food at all. Not like you. You used to eat like you had a tapeworm."

Kaye busied herself packing up what was left of the food. She wondered if every memory would snag, like wool on a thorn, making her wonder if it was a symptom of her strangeness.

"Everything okay?" Ellen asked her.

"I guess I'm not used to sharing you," Kaye said softly.

Ellen smoothed Kaye's green hair back from her head. "You'll always be my baby, Baby." She looked into Kaye's eyes a long moment, then turned and lit a cigarette off the stove. "But your kid-sitting days are just beginning."

Luis didn't want enchantments or glamours to pay for his brother's funeral, and so he got what he could afford—a box of ashes and no service. Corny drove him to pick them up from an ancient funeral director who handed over what looked like a cookie tin.

Although the sky was overcast, the snow on the ground had turned to slush. Luis had been in New York since the duel, dealing with clients and trying to hunt up enough paperwork to prove that Dave really was his brother.

"What are you going to do with the ashes?" Corny asked, climbing back into the car.

"I guess I should scatter them," said Luis. He leaned against the cracked plastic seat. Someone had tightened up his herringbone braids, and they shone like ropes of dark silk when he tilted his head. "But it freaks me out. I keep thinking of the ashes like powdered milk. You know, if I just add water, they'll reconstitute into my brother."

Corny rested his hands against the steering wheel. "You could keep them. Get an urn. Get a mantel to put it on."

"No." Luis smiled. "I'm going to take his ashes to Hart Island. He was good at finding things, places. He would have loved an entirely abandoned island. And then he'll be resting near my parents."

"That's nice. Nicer than some funeral home with a bunch of relatives who don't know what to say."

"It could be on New Year's. Like a wake."

Corny nodded, but when he moved to put the key in the ignition, Luis's hand stopped him. When he turned, their mouths met.

"I'm sorry . . . that I've been," Luis said, between kisses, "distracted . . . by everything. Is it morbid . . . that I'm talking . . . ?"

Corny murmured something that he hoped sounded like agreement as Luis's fingers dug into his hips, pushing him up so they could crush their bodies closer together.

Three days later they brought another package of meat to the mermaids for a ride to Hart Island. Corny had found a vintage blue tuxedo jacket to put on over a pair of jeans, while Luis slouched in his baggy hoodie and engineer boots. Kaye had borrowed one of her grandmother's black dresses and had pinned her green hair up with tiny rhinestone butterflies. Lutie buzzed around her head. The mermaids insisted on taking three of the hairpins along with the steak.

Corny looked back at the city behind them, shining so brightly that the sky over it looked almost like day. Even this far out, it was too light for stars.

"Do you think the coast guard is going to spot us?" Corny asked.

Luis shook his head. "Roiben said not."

Kaye looked up. "When did you talk to him?"

Touching the scar beside his lip ring, Luis shrugged. "He came to see me. He said that he formally extended his protection. I can go wherever I want and see whatever I see in his lands and no one can put out my eyes. I got to tell you, it's more of a relief than I thought it would be."

Kaye looked down at her hands. "I don't know what I'm going to say to him tonight."

"You're a consort. Shouldn't you be consorting?" Lutie asked. "Or maybe you can send him on a quest of his own. Make him build you a palace of paper plates."

Kaye's mouth quirked at the corner.

"You should definitely ask for a better palace than that. Reinforced cardboard at least." Corny poked her in the side. "How did you solve his quest, anyway?"

She turned and opened her mouth. Someone shouted from the shore.

A girl with a head full of gingery stubble was calling to them as she dragged her canoe up onto the island. Beside her, a golden-eyed troll unpacked bottles of pink champagne and a package of snap-together plastic glasses. Another human girl danced on the sand, her paint-stained trench coat whirling around her like a skirt. She turned to wave when she spotted them.

Even Roiben was already there, leaning against a tree, his long woolen coat wet at the hem.

Kaye jumped out, grabbing the rope and splashing through

the shallow water. She held the raft still enough for Luis and Corny to follow her.

"That's Ravus," Luis said, nodding in the direction of the troll. "And Val and Ruth."

"Hey!" The stubble-headed girl—Val—called.

Luis squeezed Corny's hand. "Be right back."

He walked over to them just as the stubble-haired girl popped a bottle of champagne. The cork shot out into the waves and she yelped. Corny wanted to trail after Luis, but he wasn't sure he was welcome.

Especially when both girls wrapped Luis in their arms.

Kaye tucked a strand of hair behind her ear and looked out at the waves. "You can see the whole city from here. Too bad we can't see the ball drop."

"This reminds me of something in a fantasy novel," Corny told her. "You know, mysterious island. Me, with my trusted elven sidekick."

"I'm your trusted elven sidekick?" Kaye snorted.

"Maybe not trusted," Corny said with a grin. Then he shook his head. "It's dumb, though. The part of me that loves this. That's the part that's going to get me killed. Like Dave. Like Janet."

"Do you still wish you weren't human?"

Corny frowned, glanced toward Luis and his friends. "I thought those were our *secret* wishes."

"You showed me it!"

"Even so." He sighed. "I don't know. Right now, being human is actually working out for me. It's kind of a first. What about you?"

"I just realized that I don't have to do normal things, being a faerie," Kaye said. "No need to get a job, right? I can turn leaves into money if I need it. No need to go to college—what would be the point? See above, no need for a job."

"I guess education isn't its own reward?"

"You ever think about the future? I mean, you remember what you and Luis were talking about in the car?"

"I guess." He remembered that Luis had hoped Dave would go to school with him.

"I was thinking about opening a coffee shop. I thought that maybe we could have it be a front, and in the back there'd be a library—with real information on faeries—and maybe an office for Luis to break curses out of. You could work on the computers, keep the Internet running, make some searchable databases."

"Yeah?" Corny could picture green walls and dark wood trim and copper cappuccino machines hissing in the background.

She shook her head. "You think it's crazy, right? And Luis would never go for it, and I'm probably too irresponsible anyway."

He grinned hugely. "I think it's genius. But what about Roiben? Don't you want to go be the Faerie Queen or whatever?"

Across the field, Corny saw the troll rest a massive, monstrous hand on Luis's shoulder. Luis relaxed against the creature's bulk. The girl with the dark hair—Ruth—said something and Val laughed. Roiben stepped away from the trees and started toward them. Lutie sprung off Kaye's shoulder, launching herself into the air.

"I thought Luis hated faeries," Kaye said.

Corny shrugged. "You know us humans. We talk an enormous amount of shit."

The funeral was simple. They all stood in a semicircle around Luis as he held up the metal tin of ashes. They'd dug a shallow pit near the edge of the numbered grave markers and passed out champagne.

"If you knew my brother," Luis said, his hand visibly shaking, "you probably already have your own opinions about him. And I guess they're all true, but there doesn't have to be only one truth. I'm going to choose to remember David as the kid who found the two of us a place to sleep when I didn't know where to go, and as the brother that I loved."

Luis opened the tin of ashes and dumped them. The wind caught some and lifted them into the air, while the rest filled the hole. Corny wasn't sure what he'd thought they would look like, but the dust was gray as an old newspaper.

"Happy New Year, baby brother," Luis said. "I wish you could drink with us tonight."

Roiben stood by the water, swigging out of a bottle of champagne. He'd loosed his salt white hair and it covered most of his face.

Kaye walked over to him, pulling out a noisemaker from her pocket and sticking it in her mouth. She blew and the long checkered paper tongue unfurled with a squeak.

He smiled.

Kaye groaned. "You really are a terrible boyfriend, you know that?"

He nodded. "A surfeit of ballads makes for odd ideas about romance."

"But things don't work like that," Kaye said, taking the bottle from his hand and drinking from the neck. "Like ballads or songs or epic poems where people do all the wrong things for the right reasons."

"You have completed an impossible quest and saved me from the Queen of the Faeries," he said softly. "That is very like a ballad."

"Look, I just don't want you to keep hiding things from me," Kaye said, handing him back the bottle, "or hurt my feelings because you think it's going to keep me safe, or sacrifice yourself for me. Just tell me. Tell me what's going on with you."

He tipped the champagne so that the liquid fizzed on the snow, staining it pink. "I taught myself to feel nothing. And you make me feel."

"That's why I'm a weakness?" Her breath came out like a cloud in the icy air.

"Yes." He looked out at the black ocean and then back at her. "It hurts. To feel again. But I'm glad of it. I'm glad of the pain." He sighed. "Most of the time I'm glad of it."

Kaye took a step closer to him. The bright sky silvered his face with light and highlighted the way the points of his ears parted his hair. He looked both alien and utterly familiar.

"I know I failed you," Roiben said. "In the stories when you fall in love with a creature—"

"First I'm a thing, now I'm a creature?" Kaye said.

Roiben laughed. "Well, in the stories it is often a creature. Some kind of beast. A snake that becomes a woman at night, or someone cursed to be a bear until they can take off their own skin."

"How about a fox?" Kaye asked, thinking of Silarial's story of the thornbushes.

He frowned. "If you like. You're crafty enough."

"Yeah, let's say a fox."

"In those stories, one is often asked to do something unimaginably terrible to the creature. Cut off its head, say. A test. Not a test of love, a test of trust. Trust lifts the spell."

"So you think that you should have cut off my head?" Kaye grinned.

He rolled his eyes. "I should have accepted your declaration, whether I thought it was wise or no. I loved you too much to trust you. I failed."

"Good thing I'm not really a fox," Kaye said. "Or a snake or a bear. And good thing I'm sneaky enough to figure out a way around your dumb quest."

Roiben sighed. "Once more I mean to save you, and yet you come to my rescue. If you hadn't warned me about Ethine, I would have done just what Silarial expected."

She looked down so he wouldn't see her cheeks go pink with pleasure. She stuck her fingers into the pockets of her coat and was surprised to feel a circle of cold metal.

"I made you something," Kaye said, pulling out the bracelet of green braid wrapped in silver wire.

"This is your hair?" he asked.

"It's a token," Kaye said. "Like from a lady to a knight. For when I'm not around. I was going to give it to you before, but I never quite got around to it."

He ran his fingers over it and looked at Kaye, astonished. "And you made it? For me?"

She nodded, and he held out his hand so she could clasp it on him. His skin felt hot to the brush of her fingers.

Across the water, along the shore, fireworks went off. Streaks of fire ballooned into carnations of light. Golden explosions rained around them. She looked over at him, but he was still looking at his wrist.

"You said it was for when you're not around. Will you not be around?" he asked her when he looked up.

She thought about the owl-eyed faerie in Silarial's court and what he'd told her. *They say that nameless things change constantly—that names fix them in place like pins.* Kaye didn't want to be fixed in place. She didn't want to pretend to be mortal when she wasn't, nor did she want to have to leave the mortal world. She didn't want to belong to one place or be one kind of thing.

"How will you rule both courts?" she asked instead of answering his question.

Roiben shook his head. "I'll try to keep one foot on each side, balance on the knife edge between both courts for as long as I can. There will be peace so long as I can hold them. Provided I don't declare war on myself, that is."

"Is that likely?"

"I must confess to a good deal of self-loathing." He smiled.

"I was thinking of opening a coffee shop," Kaye said quickly. "In Ironside. Maybe help people with faerie problems. Like Luis does. Maybe even help faeries with faerie problems."

"You know I just made a very advantageous bargain predicated on the fact that no faerie wants to live in the city." He sighed and shook his head as if he'd just realized that arguing with her was useless. "What will you call your coffee shop?"

"Moon in a Cup," she said. "Maybe. I'm not sure. I was thinking that maybe I could move out of my grandmother's—spend half my time working in the shop and half my time in Faerie, with you. I mean, if you don't mind me being around."

He smiled at that and it seemed like a real smile, with no shadows at the edges. "Like Persephone?"

"What?" Kaye leaned in and skimmed her hand under his coat, tracing the vertebrae of his back. His breath hitched.

Roiben let his hand fall lightly, hesitantly, across the wings of her shoulders. He sighed like he'd been holding his breath. "It's a Greek story. A human one. The King of the underworld—Hades—fell in love with a girl, Persephone. She was a goddess too, the daughter of Demeter, who controlled the seasons and the harvests.

"Hades stole Persephone away to his palace in the underworld and tempted her with a split-open pomegranate, each seed shining like a ruby. She knew that if she ate or drank anything in that place she would be trapped, but somehow he persuaded her to eat a mere six seeds. Thereafter, she was doomed to spend half of each year in the underworld, one month for one seed."

"Like you're doomed to spend half your time dealing with the Bright Court and half with the Night Court?" Kaye asked.

Roiben laughed. "Very like."

Kaye looked at the far shore, where fireworks still heralded the new year above the jagged teeth of buildings, and then toward where Corny and the others blew noisemakers and drank cheap champagne from plastic goblets.

She slid out of Roiben's arms and whirled on the sand of the beach. The wind blew off the water, numbing her face.

Kaye laughed and spun faster, gulping the cold briny air and smelling the faint firework smoke. Pebbles crunched under her boots.

"You still haven't told me," he said softly.

She stretched her arms out over her head, then came to an abrupt halt in front of him. "Told you what?"

He grinned. "How you managed to complete the quest. How you claimed to be able to lie."

"Oh. It's simple." Kaye lay down on her back on the snowy beach, looking up at him. "This is me," she said, her voice full of mischief as she reached out with one long-fingered hand. "I'm a faerie that can lie. See? This is me lying."

TURN THE PAGE TO READ

THE LAMENT OF LUTIE-LOO

A NEW SHORT STORY SET IN THE REALM OF FAERIE

Lutie was about the height of a large mug of tea. Or a pencil that had been sharpened a few times. Or a paperback book that could be tucked into a purse.

Small enough to hide in Kaye's hair. Small enough to not quite fit in fashion doll clothes unless she altered them with needles the length of her arm. Small enough to be thought of as utterly, completely inconsequential. Because of her size, from the moment she was born, tumbling from a flower and still slightly fuzzy with pollen, Lutie-loo was never given an *important* job. Just one silly errand after another.

When Silarial had sent her to the Unseelie Court with Spike and Gristle and the Thistlewitch, Lutie thought her fortunes were changing. The way the Lady had spoken of the task, it had seemed so important! But watching over Kaye, a child ignorant of her own magic, was barely even babysitting. It certainly wasn't a quest.

And sure, Kaye had turned out to be wild as her pixie blood, twice as clever, and three times as headstrong. She'd wound up responsible for the death of Silarial . . . and the overturning of two courts. But that definitely hadn't been part of the *plan*. And it wasn't because of anything Lutie had done.

Now Lutie was an honored member of Roiben's Court. She wanted for nothing. And nobody wanted her to do anything either. She was just expected to sit on her duff, drink dew from petals, and overlook how no member of the Gentry saw her as anything more than an oversize and slightly more intelligent bug. And, of course, most mortals didn't see her at all.

"I just need to *find* Ethine, and then I can ask her what her problem is," Kaye said. She was sitting on a stool in the back kitchen of her coffee shop, Moon in a Cup, looping glittery green laces through the eyelets of a pair of Doc Martens. "I guess I can understand why she was angry—but it wasn't his fault! She has to have realized that by now."

Lutie buzzed sympathetically, alert to the possibility that maybe finding Ethine was something she'd be good at. After all, Lutie could talk to people. She could ferret out information. And she wasn't likely to get into as many arguments as Kaye would. This would be a good job for her. "Maybe *I* could find her. Maybe."

But Kaye wasn't paying attention. "*Silarial ordered* her to fight Roiben. Even though Ethine had no idea how to use a sword and was going to *die* if Roiben fought back. And if Silarial *had* gotten her way and Roiben decided to sacrifice himself, Ethine would have had to *kill her own brother*. Maybe she would have blamed him for that too." Kaye shoved her foot into the boot, slamming it against the tiled floor with the force of her anger.

Kaye lived in New York, despite the iron and the iron sickness that came with it. The last time she visited Roiben, she'd redecorated his throne room, throwing out a dozen hideous and doubtless treasured Unseelie objects over the protests of his councillors, including many bloodstained textiles and a mouse-skin rug. Kaye didn't understand leaving things well enough alone. She never had. Once, Lutie had watched the Thistlewitch instruct Kaye not to take off a protective glamour. Kaye immediately went and did exactly the thing she'd been forbidden from doing.

Lutie loved her, but Kaye was not a reasonable creature. She certainly couldn't understand someone like Ethine, who seemed like she just wanted all her problems to go away.

"Ethine is proud," Lutie said. "Proud and sad and dull."

Kaye made a face. "If I just explained . . ."

Lutie could picture Kaye running around Faerieland, accidentally overthrowing governments and causing one huge scene after another. Lutie was sure Roiben would not like that, especially if it got his sister even angrier with him. But maybe Lutie could find Ethine herself and arrange the meeting. It was true that a great court lady like Ethine was probably no more interested in what a sprite had to say than a pixie, but all the Gentry loved protocol. And a messenger would make everything more formal. Besides, if Ethine was totally against speaking to Kaye, at least Kaye would go in forearmed. Or be persuaded not to go at all.

Lutie cleared her throat to make her suggestion again. "I could look for her."

Kaye gave her an evaluating look. Lutie flew in place, attempting to look competent. And larger.

"No," Kaye said finally, shaking her head. "It's too much of a bother for you."

"I can do it!" Lutie said, rather more sharply than she'd intended.

Kaye appeared surprised. "I am sure you *could*."

"It will be my mission," said Lutie. "I will do deeds of daring!"

Kaye's green eyebrows rose. "I hope not. But if you really want to go, then fine. I bequeath this annoying quest to you. Find Ethine and bring word to me of her whereabouts, and possibly news of what crawled up her ass to make her such an awful—"

"Yes!" Lutie said, zooming through the air joyfully. "I will find the sister. I will arrange everything!"

Kaye grinned up at her. She said she believed Lutie could do it, and Kaye could no more lie than any of the Folk. Lutie felt a burst of hope. If she could pull this off, not only would it make Kaye happy, but Lord Roiben would be pleased too. Perhaps the gloomy King of the Court of Termites would cheer up and grant her a medal or a hollow tree to call her own. And perhaps he'd send her on an even more important quest.

It took her all day to assemble and pack the things she thought she might need—a long steel pin tucked into a leather sheath, to serve as a sword; doll gowns and a few other items filched from a dollhouse, jammed into a velvet gift bag she was using for a rucksack; and three organic single-origin chocolate-covered coffee beans, for energy.

Then she realized she had no idea how to find Ethine. She was sure she could. But that didn't mean she had the first idea how. So she pondered and she pondered and she ate one of the chocolate-covered coffee beans.

It was very late when she found herself flying above the stump of a tree beneath the Manhattan Bridge. She tried to find something optimistic in the way the roots had cracked up through the pavement before humans had chopped the tree down, but it was hard.

She slid through a window and flew inside, to the waiting room of the potion-maker and alchemist for the solitary fey of New York. Ravus the troll lived here. She knew him because he'd once been part of Silarial's court and because he had a human companion who'd been one of Kaye's roommates. As she recalled that, she also realized she wasn't sure how much time had passed since then. What had happened to the girl? Lutie couldn't remember.

Ravus had been exiled from Silarial's court, she knew that. He'd been at court when she had, although their paths hadn't crossed. He was just so *huge* that being around him scared Lutie. He could crush her easily, absentmindedly, in the swat of one giant hand.

But because he was the maker of a powder that allowed the Folk a resistance to iron, many solitary fey and even Gentry visiting the cities came to see him. Everyone used the powder, even Lutie. It made living near the iron bearable. Maybe Ethine had been one of them. Or maybe he'd heard a rumor.

Lutie was hoping. And she was further hoping he'd be friendly about it. And not ask for too much in exchange for the information.

There was a little bell near the door to Ravus's chambers. She rang it and waited nervously as the tinkling sound echoed through the dark.

A few minutes later, a large wooden door creaked open, a sliver of light spilled out, and there was a heavy tread on the floor. Ravus appeared, his skin a green that looked a bit sickly in the gloom. Lutie's tiny heart sped like the whir of humming-bird wings.

"Welcome," he said in his deep voice. "What is it you seek?"

"A courtier," Lutie told him, darting past and into his workroom. "Lord Roiben's sister." A long wooden table was laden with ingredients—dry snakeskins; tiny pale bones; and stoppered and waxed glass bottles of many different shapes, bearing labels in the troll's looping hand. The first tag read: LAST HOPE OF A HEART.

The room she'd entered was very tall, with a loft suspended above her. She could see a bed with disarranged sheets and one pale leg sticking out, bare to the thigh. Too pale, Lutie thought. Was it a dead body? Lutie rose a little without quite meaning to. Then the person on the bed turned over in sleep. For a moment, Lutie was relieved. The paleness was only moonlight. But a moment later she noticed the distorted shape of the girl, with an abdomen like that of an enormous spider.

What had he done to her? Was it some kind of alchemical experiment?

"I don't have your courtier hidden among my poultices," Ravus said, pitching his voice low. "But come have some tea and I will see what I can recall."

He already had a cup for himself poured, she realized when he freshened it. Then he took down a thimble from one of his shelves and filled it with tea from the same steaming pot. "There are biscuits around here as well, if Val hasn't eaten them all."

Val. Valerie. That was the girl's name. She remembered now. With hair like a copper penny.

Ravus brought a plate over to the table, along with a cup,

which he turned over to make a sprite-size stool. Lutie sat, holding her thimble much as one might hold a pail. The scent that wafted up to her nose was a delicious blend of elderflower and nettle. The cookies piled on the plate appeared to be studded with rosemary. But Lutie couldn't help a nervous glance toward the loft.

"Ethine left," she said, trying to focus on her mission.

Ravus nodded. "Stomped off in a huff, isn't that right?"

"Yes, and Kaye wants her back." Lutie took a sip of the tea. "She thinks Roiben is sad."

Ravus grinned, showing too-long canines. "The fearsome Lord of Termites? I never imagined him anything so ordinary."

Lutie buzzed in understanding. Sometimes it did seem like when Kaye talked about Roiben, she was attributing nuanced emotions to a handsome murder-loving murderer. "But you do know where she is?"

"I do, as a matter of fact," he said. "Ethine came to a friend of mine for a potion to change her hair. She didn't want to glamour it because she was going to the High Court, where they'd be very likely to see through any magic. And the silver is so distinct. After all, it's the same as his."

"The High Court?" Lutie squeaked. She didn't like that, not one bit.

"No one wants to storm off to serve a lesser court," Ravus observed mildly.

Lutie finished her tea disconsolately. The High Court of Elfhame, where High King Eldred ruled, had been collecting lower courts since the time of Queen Mab. It was said that they made you swear not to the royals themselves, but to a crown that never broke. So far, they hadn't marched on Roiben, but she was sure they would very much like for him to pledge his fealty to the High Court and bring a large chunk of the East Coast into their fold. They were scary.

And it meant that Lutie would have to fly over the sea to the isles of Elfhame. She hated flying great distances, especially over water. There was nowhere to land when her wings got tired, and birds and fish often thought she'd make a delicious snack until she showed them otherwise. But that was an obstacle—and all quests had obstacles. She could overcome them, she was sure of it.

There was a creak on the stairs. The girl—no, a woman now, with the same copper penny hair that Lutie remembered—was coming down, in what appeared to be an oversize band shirt stretched over her enormous abdomen and fuzzy slippers. "Is someone there?" Val called.

"I better be off," Lutie squeaked. Kaye wasn't going to like to hear what had become of her friend.

"Did we wake you?" Ravus asked Val, smiling warmly at her. Surely he wouldn't look at her like that if he was the cause of her suffering.

The woman shook her head and yawned. One hand went to her belly. "Heartburn."

And something about the gesture made Lutie finally recognize what was wrong with Valerie. Or not wrong at all. She was *pregnant*.

Faeries didn't reproduce often or easily, not like mortals. And while Lutie had seen pregnant human women before, there was something somewhat shocking about thinking that a mortal was carrying a faerie child. But it was still embarrassing that she'd thought all those things about Ravus.

Lutie fled.

At Fisherman's Wharf, she stared out at the water, reassuring herself. Her quest was going well, she thought. Once she got to Elfhame, it wouldn't be hard to find Ethine in the High Court, and then no matter what she said, Lutie could come right back—job complete! Really, it wasn't even that hard of a job. She could handle much worse. With that happy thought in mind, she snuck into a dollar store, where she filched both a plastic saddle for a toy horse and a ball of yarn. Then she startled a seagull awake. It snapped its beak in her direction immediately. Jumping back, she lifted her hands and spoke in the language of birds. "Do my bidding. Bear me on your back and fly me wheresoever I say."

It stopped attacking, and Lutie threw her makeshift harness onto its back.

She could totally handle this job! Everything was going just fine.

The gull hurtled up toward the stars with a great cry. On its back, the journey was swift and sure, carrying her away from the lights and metal stink of Manhattan, out over the waves. It wasn't long before she spotted the three isles—Insmear, Insmire, and Insweal—shrouded in fog, their hills and valleys an emerald green never to be found in the mortal world. Despite herself, her heart gave a little leap. Here was a place only for the Folk, thick and heavy with enchantment. As the gull flew closer, even the scent of the air made her giddy. It was a feeling she'd only had before at Silarial's court, the feeling of coming home.

The seagull landed on one of the black rocks of near the shore. Lutie climbed down off its back, untied the saddle, and waved the creature off. It looked around in confusion, as though unsure of how it came to be there, and then began grooming its feathers.

"Silly thing," Lutie said, petting its head with some affection. From there, Lutie headed toward the palace, pausing only to alight on the branch of a tree and change into a strapless red-and-gold Barbie ball gown that gave her the shape of a bell.

Guards were stopping those that approached the towering knowe, but as usual, no one bothered with Lutie. As a sprite, she flew right over the guards' heads. They gave her as little notice as a mortal might give a lightning bug.

Inside, the hollow hall was bustling with activity. There appeared to be no revel that night, and instead courtiers sat around the room, a few trailing between groups. Lutie looked for other sprites and found a clump of them among a particularly thick knot of trailing roots. They wore fanciful little gowns of petals and scraps of velvet, lit to fine effect by the glow of their bodies. Lutie was suddenly very conscious of the fact that she was wearing the dress of a doll, even it if was very nice. She wasn't sure if she felt provincial or very modern.

"Um, hello," said Lutie.

One of the other sprites—a boy—stepped away from the others. He looked her over with some disdain, and she gave him an equally haughty look back. "You're not of the High Court," he said. "Where do you hail from?"

"West of here," she told him. "East of elsewhere. I am looking for a courtier." Lutie was not enormously skilled with glamour, but she could draw an image in the air. She swept her hand in the space between them, and a picture of Ethine formed, an Ethine with dark hair. It held a moment and then faded into shimmers.

The boy frowned. "And for what reason should I help you?"

"That's easy." Lutie fished around in her rucksack and came up with a chocolate-covered coffee bean. "I will trade you a rare treat from the mortal world, which will please your tongue and work upon your blood, filling it with joy."

He looked skeptical, but after a moment, reached for the bean. "I will make this trade, strange one. The courtier is known as Ethna, one of the Princess Elowyn's ladies. She belongs to the Circle of Larks, who love music and art above all other things. Look for a woman with golden skin and you will find her close by. I would try that group there." He pointed. "Where Edir is about to embarrass himself with his poor playing."

Lutie squinted. Then she nodded, pleased with herself. Another obstacle overcome! And all because of her good planning.

The sprite boy bit the edge of the chocolate bean. As she flew off, she saw more sprites had gathered around him, taking bites of their own. One looked a little confused, having clearly bit through the chocolate layer and into the bean itself.

She discovered Ethine close to where the boy had pointed, serving herself a goblet of lilac wine near where poetry was being recited. Her dyed-black hair was drawn up into combs. She wore a gown in the pale blue of the morning sky with rose dusting the edges.

"Excuse me," Lutie said, hovering in the air in front of her.

Ethine looked at Lutie in surprise, but not recognition. She was probably unused to being addressed by a sprite. "Yes?" she said, not at all encouragingly.

"I am from the Court of Termites, sent here by your brother's consort. Kaye wishes a meeting with you." Lutie hoped that sounded formal enough. It was certainly a longer sentence than she usually spoke.

"No one knows me here," Ethine's voice dropped to a harsh whisper. "And I do not wish to be known."

"Maybe we could talk alone." Lutie was unwilling to be dismissed. After all, she was on the verge of her first successful mission.

Ethine looked toward the other court ladies and the Princess Elowyn. "I suppose," she said, seeming to realize that arguing with Lutie in the middle of the brugh was going to make the scene she'd been attempting to avoid. "Follow me."

Ethine led her into the hall, then to a room off of it, a parlor thick with the scent of earth and flowers. "So Kaye sent you?"

Lutie nodded. "Yes, she wants to talk. She wants you to reconcile with Lord Roiben."

"Lord Roiben," Ethine scoffed, turning his title into the focus of her contempt. Lutie fluttered in astonishment, wondering if she would be so foolish as to say something like that to his face. Not many would and expect to survive it.

"You're still angry with your brother," Lutie said, then regretted it when Ethine turned her glare upon her.

"If he'd only put his pride aside," Ethine said. "I know he was angry. The Unseelie Court treated him poorly. But he and Silarial could have united the courts without any bloodshed."

Lutie looked at her with bafflement, but then, she didn't understand much about politics. Nor did she understand the point of imagining how things could have been had everything happened differently. "Will you meet with Kaye? Just to talk."

Ethine shook her head. "No. Her coming here will just draw attention—and to no purpose. I do not intend to see my brother again."

"She might come anyway," Lutie warned. "If you pick the time and place—"

"Tell her not to come," Ethine said, her voice rising. "Tell her I won't see her, no matter what she says and no matter to whom she says it."

Lutie sighed. This was not the sort of success that would get her medals and praise and trusted with important tasks in the future. She'd found Ethine and she'd gotten an answer, but it wasn't the answer anyone wanted.

"Yes," said Lutie, wings drooping. "I will."

Ethine left the parlor without looking back. After a moment, Lutie decided to follow her. She had to find another seabird to take her home. But perhaps first she would have a bit of oatcake and a gossip with the sprites she'd met. That would make her feel better and fortify her for the journey. And if it made Ethine a little nervous that she was still around, well, that might be a little bit satisfying.

With those thoughts running through her mind, she flew out of the parlor. She was moving fast enough that she didn't notice the man.

At least not until his gloved hands closed around her. Lutie screamed in her tiny voice. She struggled and bit and kicked, but that only made him grip her more tightly.

"Got you." He wore a crown on his brow and a scowl on his face. "You should be honored. It's not everyone who can be the prisoner of the eldest prince of Elfhame. And you're going to help me get my father's crown."

Those ominous words made Lutie struggle harder. He gave
her an amused look and then tossed her into a sack, drawing it
tightly around her. There was a strange scent on the cloth.

Within minutes, Lutie was asleep.

🐚 🪶 🐚 🐚

She woke in a cage made of woven gold. It had the shape of
a birdcage, but the bars were much narrower and the things
inside were clearly intended for a sprite. She was lying across a
cushion. Beside her sat half of a plum and a miniature blown-
glass goblet of watered wine.

She went to the edge and looked down. The cage hung up
in the corner of a room, the rest of which appeared to be filled
with revelers. Clearly, a party was going on.

Lutie had to get out of the cage. Now was a good time,
while there was so much noise that no one was likely to notice.
There was a clasp on the door, twisted tight with thick wire.
She set to work on that, sticking her arm through the bars,
pushing on it as hard as she could.

"Look," said a girl's voice. "The sprite's awake. What does
your brother want it for?"

Outside of the cage, two of the Folk stood: One, a girl
from the Undersea, with the characteristic webbed ears and
that strange translucence to her teeth. The other was apparently related to the prince who'd captured her. Lutie might
have guessed, even without the girl's words. He had the same
features, with spilled-ink hair and a sneer to rival his brother's.
Another prince, then.

"Debauchery, I'd wager," said the young prince. "He
grows easily bored."

The girl wrinkled her nose fastidiously.

"Let me out," Lutie said, although she had little hope. "Please."

The girl gave a tinkling laugh, but the boy drew closer. His eyes glittered with something Lutie didn't like.

"We're all trapped in cages, little sprite," he told her. "How can I free you when I can't even free myself?"

"Get away from there, Cardan." Lutie raised her eyes to see that the elder prince, the one who captured her, had come into the room. The boy—Prince Cardan, she supposed—and the girl retreated. He swiped a bottle of wine from the table and they headed toward a set of stairs.

Lutie watched them go with regret as her cage was taken off its hook. "Awake at last," he said. "Allow me to introduce myself. You may address me as Prince Balekin, or if you prefer, my lord."

"Yes, my lord," said Lutie, accustomed to the Gentry and their love of pomp and ceremony.

"Now you will give me your name," he said. Without his gloves, his knuckles seemed to have thorns growing from them, thorns that ridged his wrists, disappearing up under his clothes.

"Lutie," she told him.

"A mere scrap of one," he told her, although he could hardly expect her to give him the whole thing.

When she didn't answer, he carried the whole cage out of the room, sending it swinging so that the wine spilled, the goblet shattered, and the plum went hurtling around like a boulder. Lutie clung to the side, looking out at all the rooms they passed through.

It turned out that questing was terrible and that she was terrible at questing.

The party went on with people drinking and singing, in

various states of undress. Eventually, Prince Balekin came to a door and passed through into an office, where he set the cage down heavily on a desk.

"Now admit it, you're from the Court of Termites," he said.

Lutie was startled. "How did you—"

"I have spies," he said. "They overheard that you were looking for a courtier. Ethna? Isn't that right? I never gave her much notice before, but I have now. In particular, I noticed that the roots of her hair are a rather startling silver."

Lutie's heart thudded in her chest. This wasn't how the mission was supposed to go. She'd considered what would happen if she didn't manage to complete the job—if she couldn't find Ethine and had to go home in disgrace. But she'd never considered causing harm.

"What do you want?" Lutie demanded.

"Just confirmation that I was right. And now I have that." He smiled, smug. "She's on her way here. I imagine that the three of us will have a lot to discuss."

Lutie fumed in her cage. She kicked the plum, although it bounced back at her and she had to jump out of its way.

Prince Balekin called for servants to bring a tray with wine and figs. He called for another servant to bring him Ethna, from his sister's circle, who would be arriving any minute.

When she did come, she looked out of sorts. She wore the same gown she'd had on before, but over it was a cloak that she waved off a servant's attempt to take. "My lord," she said, with a curtsy. "Your invitation was very kind. And your messengers were very insistent, but—" She bit off her words as she noticed the cage with Lutie in it. "*You*. What are you doing here?"

"You were once called Ethine of the Court of Flowers, isn't that right?" Prince Balekin asked, ignoring her question to Lutie.

"A long time ago," she said, stiffly.

"So, you're really his sister." Balekin grinned the kind of slow malicious grin that signaled something really bad was going to happen.

"We are estranged," Ethine said. "The last time I saw my brother, we were at swords drawn."

Balekin's gaze went to Lutie. "True," she said. "All true. She hates him."

"Ah," said Balekin. "But she will invite him here, nonetheless. You see, Prince Dain would take my rightful place as my father's heir. He has worked at that goal, to make High King Eldred trust only him. You know that Princess Elowyn has been pushed out of the line of succession in much the same way."

"Princess Elowyn doesn't care to play politics," Ethine said.

"Well I do!" Prince Balekin shouted, and she took a nervous step back. He held up his hands consolingly. "And if the mighty Lord of the Court of Termites agrees to join the High Court, I can show my father that I am worthy of being his heir."

"If you believe that I can make my brother do anything, you are much mistaken." Ethine sighed. "He might come here for me, but he wouldn't bow his head to his own beloved. Not for her sake, not for mine or for the sake of the people who were once those he loved best in the world."

Oh, this was all her fault, Lutie thought. If Roiben came and made a bad bargain for Ethine's sake, it was because of her. Because of her failure. Back in Ravus's workroom, Lutie had worried that Roiben was a handsome murder-loving murderer with no heart. Now she hoped that was true. If he had a heart, he was going to get in a lot of trouble.

"Write and invite him," urged Balekin. He took a piece of paper and set it on his desk, beside an inkwell and a feather, the end cut into a fresh nib.

"Yes, and then I will take the message!" Lutie said. Perhaps if they sent her with it, she could go to Kaye. Kaye would have a plan.

Balekin shook his head. "You will stay in your cage and tell me all you can of the Court of Termites. Once the Lady Ethine composes her correspondence."

Ethine stared at the pen as though it was a snake that might turn upon her at any moment and bite. "I will not write to him. And your sister would not like to see one of her ladies so ill-used."

"I am the eldest prince of Elfhame and I will do what I like with you," Prince Balekin said. "And if Elowyn doesn't like it, more's the pity."

"Let me," Lutie said.

He turned a scowl on her. "You're an eager little thing, aren't you?"

"Yes!" Lutie said. "Very eager. I was on an important mission to arrange a meeting. And now a meeting will be arranged."

At that, Balekin threw back his head and laughed. "I suppose it is no bad thing that you have your own priorities, especially since they don't conflict with my own."

"Do not do this," Ethine cautioned, but Lutie ignored her.

Balekin untwisted the wire on her cage. Lutie considered attempting an escape. He might grab her, but if he missed, she was very hard to catch once she got going. She could be out the window and then away from Elfhame entirely.

But if she left Ethine behind, then Balekin would make her write to Roiben. And he might be able to get the message there faster than Lutie flew. And it wasn't really doing a job well if you made everything worse for all the people you were supposed to be helping. With a sigh, Lutie remained motionless as Balekin took out the plum, mopped up the spilled wine and plum juice, and placed the writing materials on the floor of the cage.

Kaye was clever. Now Lutie just had to be clever too.

She began to write:

> Kaye,
> Wonderful news! Everyone will be happy
> to hear that I found Ethine in the Court
> of Elfhame. All it took was asking around.
> Roiben ought to come and meet with her.
> Ending the enmity between them seems
> possible. Have him come as soon as he is able.
> Obviously, he is very busy. Still, he should
> come. The sooner the better. Alone. Go
> and tell him as soon as you can. Every day is
> another day without them speaking.
>
> > Sincerely,
> > LUTIE

Balekin took the note out of the cage when she was done writing. He snorted, reading it over. "Laying it on a bit thick, no?" he asked.

Lutie gave him her best blank look, and he shook his head.

"It'll do," he said finally. "So long as he comes. If not, it will be you who suffers. Do you understand?"

She nodded, torn between relief and fresh worry.

"You will remain here," Balekin told Ethine. "Hardly the first of the Court of Larks to slip into the Court of Grackles for a little fun. Come, make merry. Drink deep. Drown your sorrows."

Ethine gave him a scandalized look, but she let him escort her out. That left Lutie alone in the cage. She retrieved the wet cushion from the side of the cage and threw herself down on it. She tried to consider this as just another obstacle to the successful completion of a quest, but it didn't work. She was too worried. Would Kaye understand her message? Kaye was clever, but would she remember to be clever just then? It was hard to think of anything else.

Time passed. Enspelled human servants came, first to hang her cage in the hall, and then at strange hours to shove scraps into it from whatever food was being served elsewhere. Bits of fat and gristle. Hard ends of cheese. Shriveled grapes. Lutie ate them and drank the stale, warm water too. Who knew when they might forget her entirely.

She saw the young Prince Cardan argue with the Undersea girl. "Betrayer, do not believe you won't be betrayed in turn," he told her. "And don't think it won't give me pleasure when you are. Maybe more pleasure than your company ever did."

When the girl stalked off, he noticed Lutie looking. "You know what my brother usually does to sprites? He traps them under glass to use as lights until they die. Because that's all they're good for."

Lutie pushed herself against the bars on the opposite side of the cage. "He won't be High King," she said, because that's all she knew Balekin wanted.

Prince Cardan laughed. "You think Dain would be better? Or me, prophesied to be a monster?"

Lutie stayed pressed against the bars until he went away, hating the High Court and everyone in it.

Another time, she saw Ethine staggering, too sick with drink to stand, her body thudding into a wall as she passed. Lutie called down to her, but she didn't seem to hear.

Then one of the servants took Lutie's cage down from the hook and brought her into a parlor, where Lord Roiben was sitting, drinking a cup of tea. He was dressed entirely in black, his shining hair spilling over his shoulders in a cascade, like mercury from a broken thermometer. Balekin stood nearby, with Ethine beside him. She looked tired, dressed in a gown embroidered with lavender stalks. Her hair was silver again, and short.

Lutie's heart sank. Kaye wasn't there. Kaye wasn't coming to save her.

"Lutie," Roiben said, peering into her cage with his wintry gray eyes. "I got your message."

Lutie nodded glumly. He'd come as soon as he could, just like she'd said, but had no idea what he was walking into. Still, she couldn't be sorry when he began unwinding the clasp on her cage. She'd prefer not to be a prisoner a moment more.

"What are you doing?" Balekin asked him, moving closer.

Roiben didn't pause in his unwinding of the wire, though, and a moment later Lutie was loose, flying up as high as she could, clinging to a bit of decorative molding on the ceiling. She didn't want to be in grabbing distance of Balekin or his creepy servants.

Or any of the rest of them, for that matter.

"I freed her," Roiben said mildly. "What else could you possibly imagine I would do, as she is a subject of mine? You ought not have kept her like that."

Balekin stared at him. Perhaps he'd thought a sprite would be beneath Roiben's notice. Perhaps Roiben's bloodthirsty reputation gave the prince some reason to believe the Lord of the Court of Termites would be amused by cruelty.

Roiben went on. "It is a kindness to be able to see my sister again. But I would speak with her alone."

Balekin nodded with a half smile that this was part of his plan. He gave Ethine an encouraging push toward Roiben. "I hope that, whatever the outcome, you will consider swearing fealty to the High Court. I am sure Ethine will speak well of her time here. She's pledged herself already, you see."

Lutie startled. She hadn't considered that, although it was obvious that living at the High Court, as a courtier in a princess's inner circle, Ethine would have been asked to make a vow of loyalty. But it meant that Roiben had no claim on protecting her, even if he'd known she was in danger.

"I do see," said Roiben.

Balekin went out, closing the door behind him. Lutie was sure he was spying somehow, but she had no idea how and didn't want to risk getting grabbed again by investigating.

"You didn't want me to come, did you?" Roiben asked her when Balekin left. "You seem unhappy. I suppose you're doing this for him?"

"In a manner of speaking," Ethine said. Lutie thought that probably meant she had no choice.

"Sit beside me," Roiben said. "Tell me what I can do to fix things between us."

"You destroyed everything I loved," Ethine told him. "There was no Court of Flowers without Silarial. Talathain was lost, and worst of all, you were unrecognizable in your cruelty. I thought I knew you, but I did not. And I am not sure I knew Silarial either."

"You will not want to hear this," Roiben said. "But I felt the same, once. When I realized that she had known what it was she was sending me to endure, that she had not cared enough—"

"But she couldn't have known!" Ethine protested.

"She did." Roiben gave a long sigh. "They were sisters, for one, and more alike than not. I like to believe it stung a little to give me up. But she got Nephamael in the bargain, and he was more loyal to her than either of them pretended. And a better schemer by far. With him by her side, she brought down the Unseelie Court. Had Kaye not poisoned him, I imagine he would have passed it all over to his mistress. She very nearly had both courts."

Ethine pressed her lips together in a thin line. "You could have been the one to pass it over. You could have bowed your head and presented her with the Unseelie Court, like the greatest jewel in her crown. She would have made you her consort. Perhaps you could have even wed and ruled together."

The corners of Roiben's eyes crinkled. "You said as much, once. But it is a difficult thing to be loved for one's dowry alone."

"Don't jest!" Ethine said.

"Then let me be as frank as I can. I loved another. I love another. Do you understand me? It was not merely pride or rage or any of the other things that you accuse me of, although I felt them in the full measure. I would not have been Silarial's consort, not if I gave her the Unseelie Court. Not if I bowed my head and humbled myself. Not if she begged me."

That startled Ethine. She looked at Roiben as though once again he was utterly unknowable. "But you can't mean—"

"I do mean it. I love Kaye with my whole heart. And whether you think well of that or ill, it's the truest truth I have ever spoken. Silarial wasn't the person you thought she was, and you are angry with me that you came to know it. The only good thing bowing my head to her would have done is allow you to keep your eyes shut."

Lutie expected Ethine to protest that, but she didn't.

"I hurt you," he said. "In the duel. But that's not why you're angry, is it? What you cannot forgive me for is Silarial's death."

"You wish to remind me that I am the one who murdered her," Ethine said. "As though I can forget it."

"I wish to remind you of nothing. I am not the one who sought you out. It is Kaye who cannot leave things well enough alone."

Lutie thought that truer words were never spoken.

"Yet you say you love her!" Ethine protested.

"Yes, I love Kaye. And also, I know her." Roiben smiled faintly. "Just as I know and love you."

"Are you angry with me?" Ethine asked in a very small voice. "For taking Silarial away forever?"

He shook his head, closing his eyes, as though he couldn't bear looking at her while he spoke. "I was relieved to be spared the choice you made."

For a moment, they just sat together in silence. After a while, Ethine reached for his hand and he let her take it, then drew their clasped fingers to his heart.

Finally, he said, "So, sister. What is it I must do here? These are your people now."

"I know what you will say to bowing your head," Ethine said. "Even if it is for my sake. Let us not repeat what is past."

"What happens if I don't swear fealty to the High Court?" he asked. "Let me be more specific: What will they do to you?"

"I don't know," Ethine replied, her voice so low that Lutie understood her more from the movement of her lips than anything else.

Roiben let go of her hand and stood. "Prince Balekin," he called. "I had a visit with my sister. Now let's get to the meat of the matter. Come out. I would bargain with you."

It took a moment, but the doors opened and Balekin strode through. He was trying to look confident, but something in his manner showed that he was worried. He ought to be. Lutie had seen Roiben fight. He had come alone, just like she'd said in her stupid note, but she'd seen him cut through more guards than Balekin had in his employ.

Of course, killing the eldest prince of Elfhame would probably mean war.

"So," said Balekin. "What bargain do you propose?"

"Ah, you wish to play out the game. I will say that I wish to take my sister home with me. You will remind me that she belongs here, that you are a prince. Perhaps add a few ominous things that are meant to imply you will not be a good guardian. As though I cannot see you've treated her poorly."

"She was offered every pleasure of my household," Balekin protested.

"And now I am here to unwind the wire of her cage," said Roiben. "Let me guess. You wish the fealty of the Court of Termites."

Ethine stood up from the couch. "Wait. Roiben." She put a cautioning hand on his arm.

Lutie held her breath. What had she done? Not just ruined the mission, but stolen the sovereignty from the Court of Termites. Kaye would never forgive her. Oh, this was very, very bad.

Roiben turned to Ethine. "You think it was pride that kept me from bowing my head, but it was never that." Then he looked at Balekin. "You release all claim on her if I agree that the Court of Termites swears fealty to the High Court?"

Balekin frowned, as though trying to figure out how he'd lost control of the situation. "Yes . . ."

"Done," Roiben said, his voice clipped. He looked up. "Lutie, perhaps you'd prefer to travel in the pocket of my coat? It's velvet lined."

"Wait!" Balekin said. "We must go to my father and tell him the news. You must come and take the oath and tell him of my role. This is my triumph."

"Let us be off, then," said Roiben, offering his sister his arm. She placed her hand on his and they walked through Balekin's estate, past his guards and out through the doors. Balekin called for horses.

Lutie was sorry she'd ever thought of Roiben as a handsome

murder-loving murderer. She darted down, grateful he didn't want to squish her. Even more grateful he didn't want to leave her behind.

"This is all your fault," Ethine said to Lutie.

"I know," Lutie replied mournfully.

"Nonsense," Roiben said. "Lutie-loo sent me a very clever message. Do you know what an acrostic code is? Mortals like them very much. The children use them to write poems at school, using the letters of their names."

"What are you speaking of?" Balekin said. "I read that letter myself."

"Yes, you might well have, since I imagine you forced her to write it. But did you notice the first letter of each of the sentences?" said Roiben. "W-E-A-R-E-H-O-S-T-A-G-E-S. We are hostages. As I said, clever."

"But if you knew—then why did you come alone?" Ethine cried. "Why put yourself in his power?"

Roiben gave her a real smile. A slightly smug one. "I didn't. Dulcamara and Ellebere are both with me. And I won't be going to visit the High King Eldred with you, Prince Balekin. You see, I've already been there. With your brother Dain. I have already given him my fealty—should he become the High King, I have agreed to swear to him and to him alone."

"No," Balekin's eyes went wide. "How?" His fingers reached inside his coat, as though seeking a blade.

But as he did, out of the shadows came Roiben's knights. Dulcamara with her skeletal wings and her ruby-red hair and her fierce smile. Ellebere with his insectile armor. And behind them, knights of Elfhame.

"Brother," said a man who could only be Prince Dain.

Roiben didn't wait to hear what they would say to each other. He and Ethine moved toward Dulcamara, and minutes later they were all in the sky, on steeds made of smoke, racing through the dark. The velvet lining was soft around Lutie, the cloth warmed by the heat of the body that wore it. She looked up from Roiben's pocket and watched the stars turn over her head.

Back in New York, Kaye was putting together a party in miniature for Lutie. She'd covered two bricks to make a banquet table, set it on top of her own dining room table, and piled it with foodstuffs. A cupcake set on a silver-chased compact mirror. A single sticky sesame wing on a chipped child's saucer, as large to Lutie as a whole turkey. Three raspberries and a blueberry, stuffed into a freshly peeled lychee. And then, around that, food for everyone else.

"Congratulations!" said Kaye. "You made it out of the High Court and stopped a coup. Pretty good for a first mission."

Kaye had invited Ravus and Val, whom it turned out Kaye had known was pregnant. Corny and Luis were there too. And Roiben, who looked surprised by his own happiness. No Ethine, but that was fine. She was, apparently, traveling to the part of the Court of Termites that had once been the Court of Flowers. Maybe looking for Talathain. Maybe just going back to doing courtier things. Lutie was glad not to have her there, making things awkward.

"Will you ask a boon from me?" Roiben said.

Lutie drew herself up. She thought about what the awful prince had said to her in the cage, about sprites not being good for anything. And she thought about how hard the job had really been, way harder than she'd thought.

"I want another job," said Lutie.

His eyes crinkled in amusement and she worried he was going to laugh at her. She held her breath.

"I didn't ask you to assign yourself a punishment," said Lord Roiben of the Court of Termites. "But who am I to argue with such a generous request? Consider it done."

#HASHTAGREADS

Bringing the best YA your way

BECKY ALBERTALLI
APRIL TUCHOLKE
NIC STONE MORGAN MATSON
ROBIN BENWAY CASSANDRA CLARE
DARREN SHAN
SCOTT WESTERFELD
T.E. CARTER
SOPHIE MCKENZIE
STEPHEN CHBOSKY
AMY MCCULLOCH
JENN BENNETT
CLARE FURNISS
ADAM SILVERA GAYLE FORMAN
CHELSEA PITCHER ANNALIE GRAINGER
LAURA BATES HOLLY BLACK

Join us at **HashtagReads**,
home to your favourite YA authors

Find us on Facebook
HashtagReads

Follow us on Twitter
@HashtagReads